HIGHLAND WOLF PACT COLLECTION

By Selena Kitt

eXcessica publishing

Excessica LLC
486 S. Ripley #164
Alpena MI 49707

To order additional copies of this book, contact:
books@excessica.com
www.excessica.com

HIGHLAND WOLF PACT

By Selena Kitt

Chapter One

Scotland, Middle March
Year of our Lord 1502

Sibyl Blackthorne wasn't afraid of anything.

That's what her father had told everyone, from the time she was a toddler. It was probably because she was an only child, and a girl, that Robert Blackthorne, her dear, sweet father had encouraged her to do more masculine things than feminine ones. Who could blame the man for wanting a son? If she'd been a boy, she could have carried on the family name, assumed the family title, and run the family estate.

But Sibyl was a girl, and all she was good for was marrying. After all thesword fighting, archery and riding lessons, Sibyl's only real contribution to her family was her pretty face and ability to catch a husband. She found the whole process ridiculous and told her mother so, several times, while her mother instructed the servants to lace her corset tighter, pinch her cheeks for color, and powder the tops of her breasts as if they were dinner rolls and they were dusting them with flour.

Her protests, however, did her no good whatsoever. Her father wasn't even around to protect her anymore—a fact that made her tear up every time she thought about it, so she tried not to—and in the end, her uncle got his way. Godfrey Blackthorne was a man who wouldn't take no for an answer, whether it was from the Archbishop of Canterbury or even the king himself. He wasn't going to let a little slip of a girl like Sibyl thwart him. So Sibyl had been effectively sold—

that's how she saw it, even if it was a perfectly legal marriage pact, drawn up between her uncle and her betrothed and signed by King Henry VII—to a man she not only didn't love, but a man she didn't even know.

She had thought the worst part would be adjusting to living in Scotland, but she was wrong. The worst part, at least so far, had been her betrothed himself. The man she had anticipated meeting during the entire month-long trek across the English countryside, through the Scottish lowlands, to a dank, dark structure the Scots actually called a "castle," had turned out to be far worse than the uncle she had left behind.

"We need to get ye ready fer the hunt, ya ken?" Moira bustled into the room, her arms full of fabric. Sibyl felt like a doll they dressed up several times a day and paraded out for her fiancé's approval. She didn't understand—it wasn't as if the man hadn't already agreed to marry her. But Alistair seemed to delight in each new outfit. She found it rather disconcerting.

"I don't want to go." Sibyl sighed, leaning against the window ledge and peering down at the courtyard below. The men were already tussling in the yard, energy high, anticipating the kill. She'd been excited at the prospect of a hunt at first. Her father had led many on their estate back in York, and she'd ridden alongside the men with her own bow. Her father had even marked her cheeks and forehead with the blood of the first boar she'd ever taken down by herself from horseback. She was an excellent shot—she could hit her mark at fifty yards.

But when her fiancé had informed her, in no uncertain terms, that English ladies didn't carry weapons on a hunt, that they rode side-saddle, like respectable women, Sibyl knew she was, once again, just going to be paraded out in front of everyone for show. She wasn't going to get to hunt at all on this "hunt." And, she had decided, if that was the case, she was just going to stay in her room and read a good book. That was far preferable than riding side-saddle on some old, tame, brood mare while her husband-to-be bragged about his hunting prowess, nudging his men and whispering to them about Sibyl's long, curly red hair and big, sea green eyes.

"Now, come along." Moira clucked and fussed, putting the pile of dark green velvet on the bed. "Yer betrothed bids ye hunt wit'im."

No, her betrothed bid her to ride on a horse beside him like a good little girl.

"More clothes?" Sibyl looked down at the blue silk day dress she had worn to breakfast. "Isn't this sufficient?"

"Aye, more clothes, and be grateful, lass!" Moira's eyes flashed. "This dress could feed a family in my village fer a year."

A year? Surely not! Sibyl had always been a bit spoiled, even at home, although her toys had been things like her own falcon, Peri; a Norwegian longbow; and her stallion, Prince. Her mother had purchased her dresses over the years, but Sibyl had refused to wear them, and her father had indulged her. For years, she had gone around Blackthorne Castle wearing breeches like a boy, much to her mother's embarrassment. Only when company came did her mother put her foot down. Then there was the struggle of fighting Sibyl into a bathtub, brushing the tangles out of her long red hair, and lacing her into a dress.

Of course, that didn't stop her from challenging their guests' sons to foot races or shooting contests, which she usually won, much to her father's delight. It also usually ruined whatever clothing she was wearing. She would end up with dirt smeared all down her front, or mud caking the hem of her gown. Then there was the time when she was twelve and she stripped down to her chemise and had a boy unlace her corset so they could go swimming in the waterhole and try to catch frogs with their hands. Even her father had been angry that time.

Sibyl lifted her arms obediently at Moira's urging, letting the old woman take off her day dress and toss it on the bed. She was used to the process now, had gotten used to it back home, when her uncle—her father's brother, a man so unscrupulous, he had wooed and won Sibyl's mother after her father had died—had insisted on finding her a "match." It had been an endless supply of dresses then too, and a continual parade of men who wanted to hold her hand. Some of them had even dared to kiss her cheek, or even her mouth. Those she had kicked in the shins. The one who had pinned her against a wall in the south garden and grabbed her breast had been kicked somewhere more private. Her father had taught her that too.

Her uncle had soon discovered that Sibyl's value, while it was quite high in looks, decreased considerably once a man had actually met and attempted to court her. Her uncle could order her bathed and groomed and dressed, but he couldn't control her behavior—as much as his threatened, and actual, beatings made the attempt. So her uncle had changed his strategy, and had started looking for men much further away, who might have had heard of her beauty, but who were too far away or too busy to actually travel to meet his young, marriageable stepdaughter.

The best match—in her uncle's estimation—had been Alistair MacFalon, laird of clan MacFalon and warden of the Middle March in Scotland. It wouldn't have been Sibyl's choice, but Sibyl didn't have a choice. The agreement had been made over ale and fish in King Henry's court. The King himself had suggested and approved of the match. Sibyl knew then, with a sinking heart, that she was done for. Before she knew it, her mother had kissed her dryly on the cheek, murmured something about behaving and doing her "wifely duty," and then Sibyl was on the road to Scotland with a pack of armed guards and one ladies' maid.

Rose was a silly girl who liked to talk about fashion and clothes and court and who was doing what with whom and when, until Sibyl was bored to tears. Rose especially liked to talk about men. She talked about royalty, she talked about lords and ladies and earls and duchesses, she talked about men she'd met at court, she even talked about the guards who were escorting them through the English countryside to what would be Sibyl's new homeland. Rose talked so much, Sibyl was grateful when the girl started slipping out at night, because Rose would talk until she finally fell asleep—and then, she snored.

A few nights, Sibyl awoke to the sound of something she thought, at first, was an animal, hurt and crying in the forest. Then, she realized, it was Rose. She'd heard her talking enough to recognize the sound of her voice, even if it was a non-verbal sort of scream. Sibyl listened, ashamed of herself for doing so—but the woman was so loud, the whole camp had to have heard her, she reasoned!—knowing that Rose was having marital relations with one of the guards. Her mother hadn't told her anything about them, but the ladies' maids at her father's estate did so like to gossip, and Sibyl had gleaned most of it from them. That, and from watching the animals in the forest, the dogs in the yard.

But Rose wasn't married. She knew standards were different for ladies' maids than they were for women of Sibyl's station—but the consequences weren't. It had taken them a month to finally reach the Scottish border, and by then, Rose was with child. Sibyl was furious when the captain of the guard, who lined up his men and fired off the question about who had been bedding with their charge's ladies' maid, came back and told her that none of the men would confess.

"Was it an immaculate conception then?" Sibyl had snapped.

She had been tempted to fire them all. She fantasized about riding the rest of the way on her own, showing up at her betrothed's castle alone, on horseback, with no escort. She knew, however, that her uncle would hear of it, and his reach was long. He would punish her somehow for such a transgression.

The captain of the guard had suggested they leave Rose by the side of the road and simply move on. This had angered Sibyl even further, so she had ordered they stop at the next town for longer than the guard wanted, and she had searched out a family that would take Rose in. She would have to work, of course, in trade for her room and board, but at least she and her baby would have a safe place to stay.

That left Sibyl without a ladies' maid at all, which suited her just fine. Although she hadn't quite anticipated the dressing problem she was going to have. Instead of lacing herself up into a corset—which was impossible, she discovered—she went without it altogether. She wore those dresses that laced or buttoned up the front, and once she reached the castle, it was Moira who greeted her, clucking over her appearance, insisting she be bathed and dressed before meeting her husband-to-be, so that she look like a "proper English lady."

It was important to her betrothed, Sibyl quickly discovered, that she look like a "proper English lady" at all times. It became clear that her Scottish husband-to-be had agreed to marry her almost solely on the basis that she was highborn, English, and a lady. This last was debatable, but as long as she looked the part, so far he hadn't seemed to care. He just liked to look at her, and show her off, and brag about his conquest. Alistair MacFalon did a lot of bragging about his conquests.

"There." Moira nodded in satisfaction, curling the last of Sibyl's long, thick auburn tresses around her fat, sausage fingers. "Ye look as pretty as a pitcher."

Sibyl frowned into the mottled looking-glass seated in front of her. She'd been trussed up like a turkey in her corset and dressed in green velvet like a Christmas tree. Moira put a green velvet hat with silver ribbons threaded through it on her head, securing it with pins that Sibyl knew would be useless on a hard ride. But the effect was stunning, she had to admit. As girls went, she was kind of a pretty one, she thought, cocking her head and squinting at the glass. Whenever she had lamented her carrot-colored hair as a child—the village boys had teased her mercilessly about it—her father had told her she would appreciate it, one day, when she was older and men started to take notice of her.

There had been one boy, a gruff, dark-haired chap who worked in her father's stables, who had looked at her in a way that made her skin tingle and flush. He had told her once he thought she had beautiful hair. "Like fire," he said softly, helping her off her horse. At the time, it had been tangled and full of brambles, but he hadn't seemed to notice. Her body had slid all the way down his long, lean frame when he gave her a hand, a sensation that made her gasp and his nostrils flare like her stallion, Prince, when he caught scent of something interesting.

Other girls had said, rather cattily, that she was "too pretty for her own good," whatever that meant. They seemed to think beauty was wasted on a girl like her—one that would rather go hunting for deer than dance and flirt with boys.

Sibyl stood, smoothing the velvet dress over her hips, seeing herself as her fiancé must. She was tall—taller than most girls—and thin. Too thin, really, and quite muscular. It came from years of being so active. Her skin wasn't the type to turn brown from the sun, but it was freckled, much to her mother's chagrin. They dotted her nose, her arms, even her breasts—hence all the white powder. But she had to admit, in spite of all her flaws, once she was dressed up, she made quite an elegant looking young lady. Her mother would have been proud.

Her father, she thought, frowning at her own image in the mirror—what would he have thought of her impending marriage? Her betrothed? She thought she knew. And the answer wasn't a good one.

"Yer as ready as ready can be." Moira gave a satisfied nod, ushering her toward the door. "Hurry up now, he'll be waitin' fer ye."

"I forgot my wrap," Sibyl said, turning back halfway down the dank, damp hallway. Moira sighed, turning to go back for it. "No, no, you go. I know you have other work to do. I'll fetch it myself."

"Ye sure?"

"Of course." Sibyl was already heading back to her room.

She gave a quick peek to make sure Moira was continuing on her way before closing the door. Her wrap was sitting on a chest and she snatched it, but she also knelt to peer under the big canopy bed, reaching to grab a satchel she had packed slowly over the past several weeks since arriving in Scotland. Inside was a canteen—stolen and filled with water—three days' worth of food, if she stretched it, a flint, and a knife, stolen from the kitchen. Thanking God for the current fashion of big skirts, she pulled hers up and pinned the satchel to her chemise.

It bumped against her leg when she walked, but she thought her skirts would hide it well enough. She was willing to take that chance. She'd already decided as much. Pulling her wrap around her shoulders, she headed back out of her chambers, walking slowly down the stairs so as not to call too much attention to what she had hidden under her skirts. Just carrying it made her flesh prickle like a plucked goose when she thought of what might happen if her betrothed found out she was planning an escape from his dank Scottish castle.

"G'day, Lady Blackthorne!"

The sound of her name made Sibyl gasp as she came around the corner to head toward the courtyard.

Alistair's brother, Donal, was heading toward her, a bow slung over his shoulder. She looked at it longingly, knowing if she could get her hands on that, she wouldn't need to worry about stretching her stale bread and dried fruit.

"Good morning, Donal." Her smile for him was genuine.

Donal MacFalon might look a little like his brother with his angular features, but unlike his sibling, he had dark, shoulder-length hair to his brother's dirty-blond curls. And also unlike his brother, Donal's smile always reached his eyes, and those eyes weren't gray, but blue, like a summer sky, and they seemed to twinkle all the time. He had been very kind to her since her arrival at the MacFalon castle and had gone out of his way to make her feel welcome.

"Are ye ready fer yer first Scottish hunt then?" He offered her his arm and she took it, letting him escort her out into the breezeway.

"Yes, very much. I just wish I could ride astride and carry a bow," she lamented.

Donal laughed—he had a wonderfully robust laugh that made everyone around him merry—looking down at her with those glittering eyes.

"If my brother wasn't such a stick in the mud, he'd let ye." He dropped her a wink. "Scots women do'na ride side-saddle. And I know many a woman who could outshoot me brother."

"Well then I'd like to be a Scot, please."

"When ye marry Ali, that's jus' what ye'll be, lassie. King Henry and yer uncle—er, yer stepda—they're counting on this marriage t'help squash the border skirmishes."

"Yes, I'm a very important pawn." Sibyl made a face.

Her uncle, who was now also her stepfather, had used her to gain the king's favor, assuring him an alliance between a highborn English lady from the Blackthorne family with the MacFalons, who controlled a great deal of the land in the Middle March, would help quell the border skirmishes that cost the crown both money and resources.

The feudal lands on either side of the border were valuable. Lachlan MacFalon, Alistair and Donal's father, had done his best to keep the continued fighting between the English and Scottish to a minimum, but after his death, things had degenerated quickly. Alistair, Laird Lachlan MacFalon's firstborn son, was not the man his father had been, and Sibyl had seen for herself how little respect he elicited in his own men. Alistair could never inspire the respect of the English, whether they were peasants or royalty, like his father had.

But Alistair was laird of clan MacFalon now and something had to be done about the thieving, poaching, and bloodshed on the border. This was King Henry's solution—and Sibyl's uncle had been instrumental in putting it all together.

"So ye ken what this is all about then?" Donal inquired, eyebrows raised.

"Oh, I ken." She nodded, meeting his knowing eyes. "I mostly definitely ken."

She understood it quite well. She had just decided that she wasn't going to be a party to it. She was tired of being played like a pawn in their little chess game. This was the first opportunity she would have to escape and she intended to take it, the moment a chance presented itself. It was at least a week of travel on horseback to the village where they had left Rose, but she knew the family would take her in. She just hoped Alistair wouldn't put out a reward for her return because anyone in a poor village would turn her in without a second thought if they believed they would be paid for doing so.

"I'm sorry, lass," Donal said softly as they walked into the courtyard where the men were waiting with their horses and their hunting gear. She felt their eyes all turn to her, an affect she knew delighted her betrothed. He seemed to like the way men's eyes followed her around his keep.

"It's not your fault." She smiled up at the man holding her arm, wondering if things would have been different if it had been Donal who was the first son instead of the second, if it was Donal to whom she had been engaged. He wasn't a bad looking man, and his kind heart and sense of humor seemed to soften his sharp features. "But thank you."

One of the men—his name was Gregor, he had made it a point to introduce himself to her on several occasions—nudged his companion with an elbow and leaned over to say something she couldn't hear. It was something snide and nasty, she was sure, about the Englishwoman who had come to live in their land. She hated being so different—and those differences being so obvious—but there was nothing to be done about it.

Sibyl pasted on a smile as they made their way across the courtyard toward her betrothed. He was smiling too, although something always felt forced about this expression on his face. Whenever she looked away from him it would fade, and his thin, red lips would sink into a frown. Then, if she looked at him again, the smile would reappear—but, unlike his brother's, it never, ever reached his eyes.

"I've delivered yer bride t'ye safely, brother." Donal gave a decidedly English bow as they approached the spot where Alistair was waiting for her out in the yard. Winnifred, the tame, old gray mare she'd been riding since she arrived, stood beside his big, black steed, Fian. Old Winnie was fitted with a side-saddle.

"Ye look like a summer day, Lady Blackthorne." Alistair greeted her with a slight bow, one arm folded across his middle, one behind his back. She had been called Lady Blackthorne all her life—her father had been an earl, which made her a viscountess—but it felt like an insult here in this land, among these people.

She was on eye-level with her betrothed's bare knee, a sight she still had a hard time getting used to. The Scots wore the strangest outfits, and the plaid blanket they wore strapped and pinned around them most of the time was the strangest. Donal said it was a Scotsman's best tool, but she doubted the veracity of his claim. She wasn't one to insist on everything being prim and proper—she was, after all, the girl who had spent most of her childhood wearing pants—but seeing a man's bare legs hanging out all the time was unnerving.

"Thank you, m'lord." She acknowledged his compliment as the groomsmen came over to help her up into her saddle, but Gregor got there first. She couldn't do anything but smile as he manhandled her up onto her mount, his hands in places no man's hands should ever go in polite company. She gritted her teeth and bore it, as her fiancé seemed to either not care, or wasn't paying attention. The horse didn't stop grazing on the early spring shoots of clover.

"Alistair." Her betrothed tightened his grip on Winnie's reins, forcing the horse closer to his own, as he reminded Sibyl that he wanted to be called by his Christian name. "Ye ken?"

This made Sibyl's knees, hidden under mounds of green velvet, brush up against his bare ones. It also shifted the makeshift satchel she had hidden under her skirts and she stiffened, trying not to let on. She looked up at him—his was a war horse, far taller than her own—as he leaned over to murmur something close to her ear. "That's the name ye'll be callin' on yer wedding night, lass."

"Yes… Alistair." She gave a short nod, heart thudding hard in her chest, wondering if the man even remembered her own Christian name, and doubted it. She just wanted him to let her horse go, so she could steer Winnie away from him. Sibyl didn't like to think about wedding this man, let alone bedding him. But all he seemed to think about was the latter.

"I like the way ye say it." He didn't let Winnie's reins go. In fact, he pulled the nag closer. The horse whinnied in protest, but she side-stepped, her flank brushing his big steed's. Alistair's mouth was now right against Sibyl's ear. His breath reeked of alcohol. "And from such a pretty mouth."

She was relieved when he pulled away slightly, but only far enough for him to look into her eyes. His were as gray as a storm cloud, his features sharp, angular. His hair was a dusty, dirty blond and a lock of it constantly fell over one eye. His gaze moved over her mouth, tracing the line of her lips, and Sibyl thought for a moment he was going to do something very unknightly with everyone's eyes on them.

"Jus' a week away now," he murmured, those gray eyes lifting to meet her own. "Are ye lookin' forward t'yer weddin', Lady Blackthorne?"

She'd been fitted for her wedding dress before she left—it was part of the not inconsiderable dowry she had carried with her from England. The gown was waiting on a dress dummy in a room all its own down the hall. The train was long enough to fill it.

"Every girl dreams about her wedding day," she answered properly, and quite loudly.

Other girls might have dreamed about and planned their wedding day, but Sibyl Blackthorne wasn't every girl. She reached out to take the reins of her horse from his hands. He was surprised, and this gave her the advantage. She had her horse five steps away from his before he could even respond. "So I hear we're not hunting for boar?"

She said this last to change the subject and mitigate the sting of her actions. Alistair straightened on his horse, looking coolly down at her. He didn't like what she'd done, that much was clear. She was going to have to do more to make up for it.

"I heard the men talking about wulvers," she said innocently, actually batting her eyelashes at him. She'd seen Rose do this with one of her guardsmen and had practiced it herself in a looking glass when no one was around. She felt ridiculous doing it, but she'd had a feeling it would come in handy. She was right. "We don't have those in England. Are they like badgers?"

The men, who had been watching the whole encounter, couldn't help their laughter. Even Alistair reluctantly smiled, that same smile that never reached his cool, gray eyes, and gave a little chuckle at her ladylike misunderstanding.

"Wolves," Alistair corrected her with that same condescending smile.

"Wulvers are wolves?" She blinked at him in surprise. "So wulver—that's Scottish, er, Gaelic, for wolves?"

She was surprised to hear it, as she'd never been on a hunt for wolves. Her father had told her, when he was a boy, wolves were one of the five "royal beasts of the chase," but their numbers had dwindled over the years until they were almost nonexistent in England.

"Nuh, m'lady." Alistair's brother, Donal, pulled his horse up beside hers. She was now sandwiched between the two MacFalon brothers. "Not jus' any ol' wolves. Wulvers is a whole other animal."

"What do you mean?" She cocked her head at Donal, frowning. "What kind of wolves are they?"

"They's not really wolves at all, ya ken?" Donal's blue eyes glittered, a smile twitching at the corners of his mouth.

"No." She shook her head, knowing he was somehow putting her on, but not quite understanding how. "I most definitely do not 'ken.'"

"They's wolves that turn into men." Donal leaned forward on his saddle to whisper this loudly. The rest of his men were watching her reaction, all of them smiling. "And men that turn into wolves. Wulvers—ya ken?"

"Do'na scare the poor girl t'death." Alistair chastised his brother when Sibyl didn't respond to his stage-whispers. "She'll run back t'her room and hide on ye."

"I will not." Sibyl's spine straightened instantly, which wasn't easy to do in a side-saddle. For some reason, side-saddles always made her want to slump, an offense her mother often chastised her for. "I'm not afraid of wolves. Or… wulvers."

"Aye, she's a brave lass." Donal straightened in his saddle, laughing. "Might wanna give'er a bow, brother."

"She hasn't seen a wulver yet," Alistair countered, steering his horse closer to Sibyl's. "I'll keep ye safe, lass. No need for ye t'worry."

"Thank you." Sibyl nodded, giving him an obligatory smile. "But I really would like to have a bow. Would that be possible?"

She looked between the two men and saw Donal trying to hide a smile. He clearly understood his brother's desire to have a dainty, feminine English companion, and just how far Sibyl actually fell from that mark.

"Your brother tells me that Scots women ride astride and carry bows in a hunt," she said, hoping she wasn't getting Donal into too much trouble by repeating his words. Alistair gave his brother a long, cold look.

"But ye're English, m'lady," her betrothed reminded her in his Scottish brogue. "Mayhaps—"

"But shouldn't I learn your ways?" She decided to try batting her eyelashes again. It seemed to have an effect on Alistair's mood. "I would like to learn all of your ways. Can't you teach me how to use a bow?"

This last seemed to decide her fiancé and Sibyl could almost see him fantasizing about holding her close while he instructed her on the proper way to hold the weapon. Alistair motioned to one of the groomsmen and told him to bring over a longbow and a quiver of arrows. She slung both over her shoulder, feeling much better about her plan. Poor Donal had no idea what he'd just given her, and surely wouldn't have encouraged it if he'd known.

"Thank you," she mouthed to Donal when she was turned away from Alistair so he couldn't see. The younger MacFalon just winked and turned his horse toward his men.

"Let's ride!" Donal yelled and all the horses' ears pricked up.

"Stay wit' me," Alistair urged as the rest of the men took off, riding across the field of heather toward the line of trees in the distance. "Stay close."

She did as she was told—she was starting to get used to that, a fact which disturbed her—riding at half the clip the other men were, keeping up only with Alistair.

"Are ye really not afeared, Lady Blackthorne?" Alistair asked as they neared the trees. The other men were already into the woods, heading down a well-worn path on their horses. "Of the wulvers?"

"I… don't know." It was a lie.

She knew they were all fooling, just putting her on, trying to get her to react in typical feminine fashion at some Scottish folk tale about men that turned into wolves or the other way around. And if they weren't—if Alistair really believed in these strange, fantastical creatures—she had even less respect for him than she'd managed to muster already.

"I wanna show ye somethin', if ye can be a brave lass." He smiled at her, a secret smile that, this time, almost reached those cold gray eyes.

“Of course.” She gave him a nod as they entered the woods, the temperature dropping a good ten degrees just from the cover of trees. “I can be brave.”

Her father had taught her to be a brave girl, after all. She followed Alistair deeper and deeper into the woods, their horses side by side on a path they seemed familiar with. She heard the men whooping and hollering ahead of her and longed to be with them, riding astride instead of side-saddle, wearing a pair of breeches instead of this heavy velvet dress. Her father had taught her a lot of things, she realized, and most of them would be useless to her here, living with this man who wanted her to be something she wasn’t.

She had to smile at the thought of Alistair and Donal and his men believing she would be scared of an old wives’ tale. There were far more frightening things in the world, she was coming to realize, than what old women and men told youngsters around the fire to scare them into being good. She’d heard those tales herself as a child, stories of dragons and unicorns and griffins. Maybe they had scared her once, when she was what Moira would call a “wee bairn,” but not anymore.

She rode fearlessly into the forest, realizing she was far less afraid of wolves—or wulvers, whatever they were—than she was of marrying Alistair MacFalon.

Chapter Two

Sibyl would have enjoyed the ride through the woods, if it hadn't been for Alistair's constant yammering. The man loved to hear himself talk and she had no idea how they were going to find anything to hunt with his constant chatter scaring away all the game. She listened with half an ear to his words—he was going on about some tournament he had won in England, a feat probably meant to impress her, since he was Scottish and she English—but she was paying far more attention to the woods around her.

Her father had taught her to track. Not just to hunt, which often involved tracking an injured, bleeding animal through the forest, if you were unskilled enough not to make the first shot a kill shot, but to actually track. He had taught her the difference between animal prints. She could even differentiate between a chipmunk and a squirrel print. Her father and his men had taught her the names of all the plants, their medicinal uses and their dangers. He had taught her how to care for herself out in the woods—how to build a shelter, make a fire.

She was thinking these things, and how they would come in handy when she escaped, paying attention to the sounds of the men in the distance—she could tell they were still on the hunt and hadn't found any wolves, or wulvers, or anything else for that matter—the sound of a stream off to her right, the crackle of branches to the left, a small animal, a fox or perhaps a rabbit, when she heard something that made her pause and rein in her horse. It was a familiar sound, one she'd heard a hundred times—the sound of an injured animal.

"Lady Blackthorne?" Alistair reined in his horse, glancing back at her inert form with a frown.

Her ears were as attuned as the horse's. She had heard something to their right, off in the direction of the stream, but the sound was gone now. Alistair spoke up again and she waved at him to be quiet. It wasn't a gesture he was used to heeding and he bristled and blustered at her boldness, making it impossible to really listen.

"Please," she insisted, holding up her hand for him to stop. "I thought I heard something."

"Twas nothin', surely." Alistair winked. "Not a wulver, a'course. Wanna hop up 'ere wit'me, lass?"

He patted his bare thigh with a wink.

"No, thank you." Sibyl shook her head, averting her eyes and frowning, still listening for the sound. She might be willing to bat her eyelashes to get her hands on a longbow, but she wasn't willing to indulge this man's fantasies that she was afraid of imaginary animals.

"Ye sure?" he offered again, leaning forward in his saddle so he was eye-to-eye with her. "I promise ye a good ride."

Sibyl's hand itched to smack him across the face and thanked God she was out of arm's reach. Just seeing the smug, self-satisfied look on his face made her realize, even if she was chased, caught and killed by whatever roamed these woods at night—even the fantastical "wulvers"—she couldn't marry this man. She preferred being eaten by wolves.

A long, baying howl rose up around them and Sibyl sat up straight in her saddle, eyes wide, not from fear, but in surprise. That wasn't just a wounded animal, it was a dangerous one. A wild dog—or perhaps a wolf. She knew the sound of a pack call well enough. Her father had taught her about the way canine packs hunted. Often one would lure a victim down a path where the pack waited, and then an ambush would ensue. He'd warned her never to follow a lone canine anywhere, even if it pretended to be hurt.

"Surely you hear that!" she exclaimed hotly, meeting Alistair's amused gaze.

Sibyl urged her mare onward, but Winnie didn't move. She might have been old and slow, but she wasn't stupid. The horse knew what she'd heard and so did Sibyl.

"Aye, I did," he agreed. "Ye think it was a wulver, then?"

"No." She scowled at his persistent attempt to try to scare her into his lap. "But it was a pack call. There's an animal in trouble."

"And how'd ye be knowin' that, lass?" His fair eyebrows went up in surprise and Sibyl could have kicked herself for saying it. He liked his women beautiful and dumb, and so far she'd been perceptive enough to attempt both in his presence.

"I…" She swallowed, and was once again saved by another long, keening howl.

This one was closer, and the sound of it actually made goose flesh rise on her arms.

"Come." Alistair smiled again, eyes narrowing as he guided his horse to the right.

Sibyl urged her horse forward and the mare reluctantly followed Alistair's big, black steed through the trees. There was no worn path here, but horses had been through this way before nonetheless. The foliage was denser, the ground covered in bluebells. It was a lovely ride, to tell the truth, and Sibyl would have enjoyed it immensely if it hadn't been for her companion, her damnable saddle and dress, and, alarmingly, the sound of that wounded animal.

"There it is again." Sibyl stopped her horse, straining to hear. The men were off to the north, so it wasn't a result of an arrow finding its mark. At least, not from any of MacFalon's men. Mayhaps there were other hunters in these woods, she mused, or mayhaps trappers. Although, this was MacFalon land, and anyone setting traps would be seen as a poacher. It was a crime punishable by death in the Middle March, but Donal said you had to catch them first. The border was thick with thieves—reavers, they called them—always poised to steal from a laird.

"Come." Alistair jerked his head forward, urging his horse on, and Sibyl sighed and obediently followed.

They were headed in the direction of the sound of the wounded animal. As the horses made their way through the trees, the cry grew louder. This wasn't the wolf call she'd heard. This was the sound of an animal trapped, perhaps injured. Might be it was the wolf's kill she was hearing? Surely Alistair had to hear it now? But she didn't stop again, didn't ask him. He seemed to know exactly where he was going. The path narrowed, the horses parading through the trees single file, dappled sunlight falling on the carpet of bluebells that scattered the forest floor.

"Are ye ready t'be brave, Lady Blackthorne?" he called over his shoulder, grinning back at her.

She'd never seen him smile so wide or look so delighted doing so. It gave her a chill and she slowed her already sluggish horse, letting Alistair pull even further ahead.

"Look 'ere." Alistair stopped his horse, the big steed dancing sideways, perhaps surprised by the sudden maneuver.

Sibyl's mare halted without her doing anything and the horse's ears twitched. The old nag shook its head, shuddering Sibyl on its back, and she wondered at the motion. A fly in its ear mayhaps? But Winnie seemed jumpy all of a sudden, and for this horse, that was a miracle. Even Fian, Alistair's war horse, was stomping and pawing at the dirt.

And then she saw it.

The animal was enormous, but the cage even bigger. Sibyl sat rooted in her saddle, staring at the white wolf pacing back and forth, round and round. It saw them and its hackles rose, teeth bared in a snarl. Its eyes were a bright, luminous blue, a color she didn't even know existed in nature.

"A wolf!" she whispered, incredulous, sliding down from her horse—side-saddles did make for an easier dismount. She'd never seen one before. Coyotes, dogs, yes. Drawings and paintings of wolves, even a horribly, smelly wolf hide her father's huntsman liked to wear, but never a real wolf.

Winnie nickered and tossed her head as Sibyl passed. The horse, divested of its rider, decided to back a safe distance away from the giant, iron cage. She wondered at the construction of the thing as she neared it, barely hearing Alistair's cry of caution. Someone had dragged this monstrosity—the cage, not the wolf—down the path to this small clearing, had perhaps even created the spot itself, scattering underbrush to make way for it.

"Is it a trap?" she wondered aloud, glancing up as Alistair quickly dismounted and tethered his stallion to a nearby tree, urging her to stay back.

Even the seasoned war horse backed away from the pacing, snarling wolf, but Sibyl was too entranced to keep her distance. The wolf was snow white with silver streaks, the most beautiful thing she'd ever seen in her life. She wanted to reach out and touch it, but she wasn't that foolish. Its canines were long and impossibly sharp, still bared at them as Alistair grabbed Sibyl by the elbow and pulled her safely back against him.

"Are ye scared, lass?" He had trapped her in his arms. She struggled against his hold, but he had her held quite fast, and his grip only grew tighter as she squirmed to get free. The truth was, she wasn't afraid of it—she was in awe. "Ye know, wolves're ferocious animals. Man-eaters."

She stopped wriggling in his arms, listening to him speak, her gaze locked with the wolf. It was such a beautiful creature and, looking into its eyes, she saw a sadness there that was quite human. It knew it was trapped, doomed to die, and was desperate to escape. The animal had stopped pacing. It stood facing them, head lowered, eyes fixed on them, black lips lifted to reveal two rows of sharp incisors and pink gums. A thick, low growl came from its throat.

"How did it get here?" she asked softly, although she had a feeling she already knew.

"Our huntsman baits 'em." His hands moved over her dress, no longer holding her arms clasped against her middle. They moved slowly down her hips as he talked. "Makes 'em groggy enough t'move 'em. If he finds a wolf afore the hunt, he pens it up 'ere fer 'is laird."

"Do you release it then?" She stiffened, breath caught, as she felt him slowly hiking up her dress in front. The satchel, heavy against her thigh, was still pinned there. "For the hunt?"

"Nuh, lass. Did ye forget, I'm laird?" He chuckled. She'd never heard him quite so smug. There was something gleeful and almost sinister in his voice. "Tis *my* kill. *My* conquest."

"Your… conquest?" She swallowed as she felt the cool forest air against her shins, her garters and hose little protection. He had lifted her skirt to her knees now. Her heart hammered hard in her chest. She was far more afraid of Alistair finding her satchel than she was of the enormous wolf baring its teeth at them. "You mean to kill it now, like this? In a cage?"

"Aye." He hiked her skirt up a little higher, making Sibyl gasp aloud. The wolf snarled, snapping at the air, shaking its big white head from side to side, spraying her legs with froth. "And drag it out behind me horse."

"But… she's with pup," Sibyl whispered with dawning horror. The animal's belly was swollen and distended. It wasn't just horrifying that his men would lock up an animal, let him shoot it in a cage, and then pretend their laird had done something courageous by "hunting" it—but that they would do so while it was breeding? That was beyond the pale.

"Aye, she is." Alistair chuckled. "We'll rid the woods of more than one wolf today."

Sibyl felt her cheeks flush hot with rage. Her heart had previously been filled to the brim with disdain for this man, but now it overflowed completely. She couldn't hide her derision and was glad he couldn't see the contemptuous look burning in her eyes. The wolf, who had been growling and pawing at the bottom of the cage as if it could manipulate the latch, suddenly stopped, cocking its head to the side like it was listening for something.

Alistair, of course, hadn't noticed. He was too interested in getting under Sibyl's dress to pay any attention to the animal he had imprisoned, and Sibyl trembled, terrified he might actually discover what was beneath the cover of her skirts. He mistook her quivering for excitement, exhaling hot against her neck with breath that reeked of alcohol and tobacco, slobbering against her ear and panting harder than the dog he held captive.

"I'll teach ye," he said, his voice low and thick with lust. Sibyl felt her heart flutter like a wild bird looking to escape her ribcage. She wasn't only afraid of being discovered now. Alistair's intentions were becoming clearer every moment. "Would ye like t'learn how t'pull the bow, m'lady?"

She'd almost forgotten it, still slung over her shoulder. His hand moved, his rough palm stroking her right thigh over her silk chemise. He was inches from the satchel. Moments away from discovering her secret. Sibyl shuddered to think what he might do, if he found she planned to escape. A low moan escaped her throat at the thought, and she saw the wolf looking at her, head still cocked, blue eyes bright with such a profoundly sad, almost human-like understanding, it was almost painful.

Sibyl recognized the desperation in the animal's eyes. They were both trapped in a cage with no way out. The animal had paced and pawed and sniffed in every corner, frantically looking for escape, but it was futile. They were both railing against a force neither of them could overcome, throwing themselves against bars that would never break.

"My arrow aims true, lass," Alistair growled into her ear, fingers digging deep into the flesh of her thigh, pulling her back against him so hard it jarred her teeth and nearly made her bite her tongue. There was something like steel against her backside, another bar of her cage, and she couldn't bear it, not for another moment.

"Noooo!" she wailed, the cry coming from her throat unbidden as she twisted in his arms. Her protest was joined by another, keening wail, this one came from the wolf in the cage, who lifted its big, snowy head and howled, its nose touching the top bar. They were both crying in unison, she and this white wolf, eyes turned skyward, begging for their freedom.

"Ye'll not deny me!" Alistair snarled, gripping her thigh so hard she knew he must be leaving marks. Her eyes never left the wolf. Its hackles were up, a low rumble coming from its throat. "Ye're mine! Ya ken?"

"No!" Sibyl roared, yanking herself forward, out of his arms, and stumbled toward the cage. Her motion forced Alistair backward and she heard him trip and fall and she had a brief, fleeting hope he would hit his head on a rock and bloody himself to death.

The wolf gave a short, sharp bark, so near her ear it made her head ring with the sound, but she was already reaching for the latch, had already decided that dying here in this forest in the jaws of this beautiful animal was far preferable than being pawed by the creature behind her who called himself a man.

The bolt stuck. It had been in this place a long time, this cage, the latch rained on and rusted, and for a moment, she thought it wasn't going to come open, and she would be the one undone here on the forest floor in a crush of bluebells, devastated under her betrothed's rutting, animal lust.

She panted with the effort, the wolf pawing at the bottom of the cage, turning in circles in excitement, whining softly, and she heard Alistair swearing in Gaelic behind her, picking himself up from the forest floor and dusting himself off.

"This isn't hunting!" She scowled as she pushed and pulled, and with one, final crack, the bolt shot back. "This is murder!"

Sibyl knew it was the end. She dropped to the forest floor and covered her head with her arms, knowing what was coming, preparing herself for it as best she could. She thought of her father, saw his face, the way he had beamed at her the first time she'd hit her mark with a longbow, the pride and delight there. He would have been proud of her today, defying her uncle's plan for her, standing up to Alistair, setting the wolf free, even if it meant it would cost her everything. Even her life. An honorable death was preferable to being attached to the shameful excuse of a man she had been sold to.

But none of that meant she wasn't terrified.

Sibyl's whole body shook as she asked God for a quick death, whispering the words of a prayer over and over into the dirt, as if it could protect her from the bone-crunching, agonizing pain that was coming. The snarl of the wolf grew louder and she heard Alistair yell behind her, no words, just a short, sharp sound, as the wolf leaped out of its prison, clearing Sibyl's huddled form in one bound. She felt the thud of its paws behind her and knew it was free.

"Get back!" Alistair warned and Sibyl heard the fear in his voice. It was trembling.

She forced herself to look, to glance behind her at the wolf, standing tall outside its cage now. If she had been standing, the top of the wolf's head would have easily cleared her shoulder, maybe even higher. Alistair looked tiny in comparison as he crouched back against a tree. He had drawn a knife from his boot and was brandishing it at the wolf.

"Stay back!" he insisted in a strangled voice, looking over at Sibyl with wide eyes. "Yer bow! Throw me the bow!"

Sibyl had forgotten it again. The bow and quiver had slipped from her shoulder and rested on the forest floor. She snatched up the longbow, quickly pulling an arrow from the quiver, cocking it, drawing the string, and taking aim.

"Shoot it!" Alistair howled, still waving his dirk at the animal.

The wolf's shoulders were hunched, head down, teeth bared, but it didn't attack. Nor did it run. Sibyl wondered at this as the animal turned its head to look back at her. Those blue eyes shifted from hers to the bow she held in her hands, as if it understood she was holding a weapon, and what that meant.

"Sibyl! Shoot it!" Alistair insisted, lashing out at the wolf with his knife, slicing the animal's hide across its chest. Blood bloomed in stark contrast to its white fur.

The wolf howled, reacting instantly, its teeth sinking into Alistair's forearm and shaking the dagger loose. It sailed some distance away, landing at the feet of Fian. The big, black steed had backed as far away as was possible on his tether and Sibyl noted that Winnie was gone altogether, back down the forest path, presumably headed toward home. That meant she had no horse upon which to escape and cursed herself for her thoughtlessness in not tying the animal up. She would just have to take Alistair's, she decided.

Sibyl stood, bow still drawn taut, taking careful aim. This was her one chance and she wasn't going to waste it.

A shout to her right, coming from the direction of the stream, startled her, making her heart leap up high into her throat, but it didn't sway her aim. She knew it was likely one of Alistair's men but she didn't care. She would be on Fian and away before they caught her.

Sibyl's arrow found its mark.

The wolf howled, bounding off, and Alistair screamed, a high-pitched sound that echoed in the quiet woods, making the horse behind her whinny and yank at his tether.

Sibyl lowered her bow, staring into her betrothed's wide, pained eyes.

"Ye shot me," Alistair croaked, staring at her in disbelief and then looking over to see his forearm pinned to the tree on his right, an arrow sunk clean through his flesh and deep into the tree's bark.

"My arrow aims true, too, ya ken?" Sibyl kept the tremble from her voice, eyes blazing. She didn't take her gaze off him as she picked up the quiver and slung it and the bow across her shoulder. "I could have killed you. Remember that."

She turned to grab Fian's reins and ran into the bare chest of a man with thick, dark hair almost as long as her own. Sibyl barely reached his shoulder and she looked up, up, into the man's face, into his bright blue eyes, her breath catching in her throat. He was a Scot, but he was not one of Alistair's men, of that she was sure. He wore only a Scot's tartan plaid, wrapped and belted at his waist, part of it pulled like a sash across his broad, bare chest.

"I… I must…" Sibyl struggled to find her voice, wrestled her mind for words that would make sense when strung together all in a row. The man's presence was disarming enough, but the look in those bright blue eyes made her knees feel wobbly under her skirts. "Be… be away."

The man didn't speak, but his look pinned her to the spot. She was mindful of her surroundings—of Alistair's cries for help, of the big, black horse that had pulled free from his tether and had turned to gallop back up the forest path, of the sound of men and dogs and horses in the distance—but she was far more aware of her own body than she'd ever been before in her life. Her blood rushed through her veins, her heart its hot, thudding pump, lungs pulling in breath in fast, cooling gulps, limbs tingling, torso a burning inferno, as if the man's look alone had caused her body to catch fire.

"Ye'll pay for this!" Alistair roared, writhing in pain on the ground. He was trying to work the arrow out of the tree with his other hand, but it was buried halfway in. The trees in these woods were yielding, their trunks soft with the dampness that permeated this land, and Sibyl knew just from looking at it, the arrow would have to be clipped.

"I must be away," she whispered, hearing the sounds of the men, dogs and horses growing nearer, knowing the repercussions for what she had done would be severe if she was caught here in these woods still wielding the longbow that had impaled her future husband through his forearm.

But her means of escape had, well, escaped. Both Winnie and Fian had disappeared down the path and she had no choice but to attempt her flight on foot. She turned to run, knowing she didn't have long, but she was waylaid once again by the stranger's bare chest. He had somehow sidestepped and appeared in front of her, even though she was now facing the opposite direction, heading deeper into the woods.

"Tiugainn!" The man spoke Gaelic, a dialect she only remotely understood, but his meaning was clear enough in the way he took her by the elbow and steered her down the path. At least, Sibyl thought as she struggled to keep up with his long strides, they were headed in the right direction.

"Let me go!" she cried, trying to shake out of his grip, but it was no use.

The man's enormous hand easily encircled her upper arm and the strength in it was surprising. He pulled her along and she stumbled after him, unable to yank herself free. The dark-haired stranger didn't follow the path. He steered them to the right, through the trees, where the underbrush was thick and the hem of Sibyl's dress caught on branches and made her falter. The sound of the stream grew louder as they traveled deeper into the forest.

Sibyl felt a rage growing in her belly, now that the wolf was gone and she knew she wasn't going to die—and least, not imminently—and they had vanished far enough down the path that Alistair's voice had grown dim. She could no longer hear his men approaching on horseback, and the sound of the dogs was faint.

Beside her, the half-naked Scotsman finally stopped, cocking his head and listening. His hair fell like a black waterfall over his broad, brown shoulders, eyes narrowing, shifting from side to side, a gesture she knew from years of being taught how to stay aware of her surroundings by her father. He was scanning, looking for movement, listening, perhaps, for anyone pursuing them, but Sibyl wasn't going to stay around long enough to find out. She'd had enough of being pawed by one man or the other.

"Let me go!" she insisted, taking advantage of his hesitation to finally wrench herself free.

She began to stalk away from him, the satchel under her skirts heavy, weighing her down. Once she was away from this stranger, she would stop to unpin it. The longbow and quiver were still slung over her shoulder, and for that she was grateful. Once she had found a place to cross the stream and she'd left any trace of her scent behind, a certain dead end for the dogs Alistair would surely send after her, she would start looking for game.

"Ow!" Sibyl complained when the stranger grabbed her again, and this time not just by the arm. He had her from behind, the way Alistair had held her against him in front of the wolf's cage, but her reaction was far different on this occasion. The stranger's body was big, muscular, his arms easily enveloping her small frame. "You big, dumb oaf! Let me go!"

She had no idea if he understood her, but she thought she sensed his demeanor change at her words. Still, he didn't loosen his hold and no matter how much she struggled, there was no way to break free.

"If you don't let me go, I'm going to scream!" Sibyl cried, wriggling in his arms. This only made the man tighten his grip, which left her gasping for breath.

"Bidh sàmhach!" he growled in her ear. She didn't know what that meant either but she could guess.

The stream was visible ahead, rushing over crags and rocks, the current strong and steady. She couldn't hear anything over the sound of the rushing water, but the man stood completely still. Something had drawn his attention, but she wasn't sure what.

"Could you… just… let me go…" Sibyl managed, drawing short, painful breaths, her ribcage aching from the way he held her so tightly. "I—"

"Bidh sàmhach!" he insisted again, this time shaking her. She felt like a rag doll in his arms. Closing her eyes, she listened too, straining to hear what had captured his attention, but there was nothing but the water surging over the rocks.

"Thank the Lord," she muttered when the man's arms loosened and she could breathe again. She rubbed her aching sides, scowling back at the giant brute. "I don't know who you are, but I am perfectly capable of—"

He frowned down at her, gaze sweeping over her muddied and torn dress. While it once would have fed a family in Moira's village for a year, it was now suitable as little more than rags. She had lost her hat ages ago, somewhere back near the wolf cage, where she had left her betrothed pinned to a tree with an arrow.

"What are you doing?" Sibyl protested, but barely had time to get the words out before the big man had divested her of her weapon and had thrown her over his shoulder and began carrying her downstream. "Stop! Let me go!"

Her words were lost in the rush of the water and he didn't seem to hear her at all as he moved quickly—much faster and more nimbly than she expected of a man of his size—down the shoreline. She beat at his back with her fists, but he didn't seem to notice that either, and before long, her hands ached. It was like hitting a slab of rock. When he stopped, she lifted her head to look around, noting their position, away from the protection of the tree line now.

And then she heard it. Could he really have detected the sound, so far away? The dogs were barking again. On the hunt. She imagined Alistair telling the story to his men, making up something so he, of course, looked like the wounded hero. Perhaps he would tell them she had been kidnapped by the massive brute who now had her thrown over his shoulder—and really, was that far from the truth? She knew he wouldn't tell them she had put an arrow through him. That much he would leave out, she was sure. She hoped.

"They're coming!" she hissed, beating at the human rock's back again. She hit him in the side, eliciting a satisfying grunt from the man, and did it again, pleased when she heard his sharp intake of breath. "Let me go! They're coming for me!"

"Bidh modhail!" he snapped, his hand coming down hard on her behind. Sibyl hadn't been spanked since she was a child and, while it really didn't hurt, given how much padding she had on under her skirts, the humiliation of it reddened her cheeks and made her instantly quiet.

And then they were flying.

It wasn't really flying, but it felt that way. He was so agile, so quick and light on his feet, it felt as if he had simply taken flight as they crossed the stream. Behind them, the dogs grew closer. They were onto a scent—likely her own and she cursed herself for not grabbing her hat, which would allow the dogs to pick up her trail—and pursued it with fervor. Sibyl bounced on the big man's shoulder, squealing at one point, thinking surely he would fall and she would go tumbling head-first to her death onto the slippery, moss-covered rocks, but then they were across, heading into the cover of the woods on the other side.

Once they were a sight distance from the tree line, the man upended her with a grunt, putting her back onto her feet. Sibyl pushed an already tangled mass of auburn hair away from her face and glared up at him. He didn't smile, but his eyes danced, clearly amused at her stance—hands on her hips, face upturned—and the words that came tumbling out of her mouth.

"You bumbling idiot! You could have killed us both!" she snapped. "I didn't ask for your help. Do you understand me? I don't want your help! No! Go! Away with you!"

She shooed him away like an annoying fly but the man didn't move. He just looked down at her with those devilish blue eyes.

"Goodbye! Mar sin leibh!" She didn't know many phrases in Scottish Gaelic, but she had learned a few from Moira. Hello, goodbye, please and thank you. So she said the words, hoping he would understand, and from the look on his face, it was clear he got her meaning. "I'm going! Mar sin leibh! Goodbye!"

She turned and stalked off, getting as far as the nearest tree before he grabbed her again.

"Will you stop that?" she cried, pushing at his arms as they encircled her and turned her to him. "No! Chan eil! Chan eil!"

She repeated the Gaelic word for no, seeing the frown on his face at her protest.

"Shh." He touched a finger to her lips, shaking his head.

"Chan eil," she objected again, but this time, the word came out in a mere whisper. "No… please…"

"Tha." His thumb traced her jawline as he looked down at her, the sunlight dappled across his face and chest. She knew the word—*tha.* Yes. It meant "yes." Sibyl felt her breath quicken as the stranger traced her lips with one finger, his gaze falling to her mouth, then to her throat, then further down, to the way her breasts nearly overflowed the top of her disheveled dress.

"Tha," he said again, lifting his gaze to meet her eyes. So blue. His eyes were so blue. "Yes."

"You… you speak English?" she whispered, cocking her head at him in wonder. "Who are you?"

A howl from deeper in the forest startled them both and the hair on the back of Sibyl's neck stood up. Perhaps the animal's howl was in response to the dogs, because they were barking across the river, sniffing up and down the shoreline, searching for their scent. The men weren't far behind. They were closing in.

"The wolf," she gasped, stepping instinctively closer to the stranger, and he encircled her with one arm, pulling her close against his big frame. She lifted frightened eyes to his, knowing the animal was wounded, that it might attack them, even now. And Alistair's men were close—too close. "It's the wolf!"

"Nuh." He said the word in English, but his brogue was thick as he met her eyes. "A wulver."

"A… wulver." She swallowed, trembling in his arms, and before she knew it, the stranger once again had her thrown over his shoulder, carrying her deep into the forest, but this time, Sibyl didn't speak a word of protest.

Chapter Three

She bounced around on his shoulder as he made his way deeper into the woods but Sibyl was far less concerned about the bruises she was going to have all over her body than she was about the sound of dogs at their back and the howl of the wolf that grew louder with every step. He was taking her away from one threat, but they were heading straight into another. The stranger, however, didn't seem very concerned about that.

Sibyl was starting to get nauseous, traveling upside down, with only a view of the forest floor and her captor's tartan plaid. She clutched that garment for dear life, amazed at how fast the man could travel, with little sign of exhaustion or even slowing. And then, he stopped. It was so sudden, she clutched at him, afraid of what might have immobilized him so quickly. She couldn't see around him.

"Laina." He said the word, but Sibyl didn't know what it meant. She looked up at him, puzzled, when he set her on her feet. The upending made her dizzy and she clung to him again, just to keep from collapsing, and he wrapped an arm around her waist, holding her up easily, without a second thought.

The sudden howl that filled the forest sent goose flesh up and down her arms and Sibyl turned her head slowly, eyes wide, following the big man's gaze. The white wolf stood a stone's throw away, staring at them through the trees. Her fur was matted with blood, like a red bib down her front, where Alistair had cut her. She was still just as beautiful—and just as dangerous—as the last time Sibyl had seen her.

"Wait!" Sibyl cried, but it was too late.

The man approached the animal without even a modicum of caution and Sibyl, still dizzy from her upside-down ride through the forest, hung onto a tree, cheek against the rough bark. Her captor didn't appear at all afraid and neither did the wolf. Sibyl watched in disbelief as the wolf sank down until her belly rested in the dirt, head bowed as the man advanced.

"No!" Sibyl protested when the man unslung the bow and quiver. "Chan eil!"

He didn't heed her, but he didn't pull the bow as she thought he would. Instead, he set it aside as he knelt before the wounded wolf. She'd never seen a man so fearless. Even her father's huntsman, who had taught her bird calls, who had shown her how to silently, patiently trap small game, had advocated caution with even the smallest of forest creatures. Animals were notoriously unpredictable.

"Laina," he said again, reaching his hand out, and Sibyl cringed, expecting the wolf to bite him as she had Alistair.

But the wolf accepted the man's attention, whining softly as he inspected her wound. It was almost as if the animal understood that he meant her no harm. Sibyl watched in disbelief as the man's hand moved through the wolf's fur, one hand scratching lightly behind her ear as he examined the wound with the other. Sibyl's curiosity got the better of her and she approached cautiously, fascinated by the animal.

"She's hurt," Sibyl said softly, nearing the two of them. "Alistair, he… he cut her with his dirk, after I got her free."

"She will'na die." The man looked up to meet Sibyl's eyes. She noticed, for the first time, that they weren't just blue—they were the same, incredibly bright blue as the wolf's. It was startling. "But she thanks ye fer yer kindness."

"You *do* speak English." She stared at him, incredulous, still not quite comprehending his words, even though they were in her native language. "Who are you?"

"Aye, though I haven't spoken yer tongue in some time." He gave a small nod, a brief smile flashing across his face. His voice was deep and rich, his brogue was thick. "I'm called Raife."

"My name is Sibyl." She looked from him to the wolf, who whined and panted, her side heaving with effort. The poor thing must be badly hurt, she thought.

Sibyl sank to the ground next to the man called Raife, reaching out tentatively to touch the wolf's fur. The animal acknowledged her touch, glancing at Sibyl as she ran a hand over the wolf's thick coat, but didn't seem to mind. Sibyl glanced at the stranger, wondering if he was some sort of animal trainer. A man had come to her father's castle once with a big bear who had sat at his feet. He had fed it scraps and led it around on a leash.

"She was caught and put into a cage," Sibyl went on, amazed at how the wolf let them touch her, with not even a growl of warning. She must be tame, like the old man's bear, she thought. "My… that man… he…"

"Aye, lass, I ken." Raife wiped at the wolf's blood with the end of his plaid. He had unwrapped the part that went over his shoulder to do so, and was now kneeling completely bare-chested on the ground. "I was sent for 'er."

"Sent… for her…?" Sibyl repeated the words, but they still made no sense at all, no matter what language they were in. "Does she belong to you?"

"Chan eil… er, nuh." He shook his head, using his plaid to stem any further flow of blood. "Mo bràithair… ah… me brother."

"Ohhh," she breathed, nodding. "He's an animal trainer, your brother? He tames wild animals?"

Raife stared at her for a moment, those blue eyes dancing again. Then he let out a laugh, loud and long, shaking his dark head. The wolf shook its white head too, whining softly, and then began to pant again. Raife turned his attention back to the animal, his big hand moving along her side, petting her gently.

"Easy, easy," he murmured, frowning, eyes troubled. "She canna change like this, when she's so close to pup."

"Change?" Sibyl's head came up, hearing something else. It wasn't just the wolf she heard whining. Through the woods came the sound of dogs barking. They were still on the hunt, although this time, they weren't hunting for wolves—or some imaginary half-man, half-dog the Scots called wulvers—they were hunting for her.

"Do you mean… is she giving birth?" She stared at him with wide eyes.

"I have t'get 'er back." He cocked his head, frowning, and Sibyl knew he heard the same thing she did. The sound of men, shouting to one another. It was Alistair's men. They had crossed the stream and had picked the scent back up again. "Laina, can ye move? Can ye get up?"

"Laina..." Sibyl said the word and the wolf glanced at her, whining but struggling slowly to her feet. "Her name is Laina? The wolf?"

"Wulver," Raife corrected, taking the wolf's giant head in his big hands. The animal looked into his eyes, whimpering, and he nodded sympathetically, petting her behind the ears. "Tha mi duilich."

Raife stood and the wolf looked up at him expectantly. Sibyl did too. She had no idea what came next. Without this man and his strange pet, she was alone in these woods with no horse and a posse of men at her heels. She knew she had to run, if she had any chance of escape, as far and as fast as she could. She'd already lost too much time.

"The men're close." Raife seemed to read her mind. "They'll find ye."

She nodded, heart thudding in her chest as she heard a clear shout, "This way!" and could have sworn it was Donal's voice. Perhaps it was too late after all. Alistair's men would find her and then what? She tried to imagine the consequences he would mete out for her actions and shuddered at the thought. But when she looked at the wolf and thought of her pups, she couldn't for a moment regret her decision.

"Ye choose." Raife's eyes lifted, scanning the woods and Sibyl knew what he'd seen before she even turned her head. She saw it in the momentary flash of anger in his eyes. Alistair's men were in sight now. "Stay 'ere or come wit' me."

She nodded, glancing through the trees, seeing the dogs running ahead. Was there a choice, really? The decision was a simple one. Raife, whoever he was, had been protective and, if a bit rough, kindhearted. His caring for the wolf had shown her that much. Alistair, on the other hand…

"Ye must hold on tight," Raife said over his shoulder, loosening the plaid around his waist and pulling the fabric free.

"Sir, you mustn't!" Sibyl gasped, covering her face with her hands, glimpsing far too much of his backside before she could turn away from him as he disrobed.

"Climb on and hold tight!" He told her and she gasped when she felt him behind her, his mouth right next to her ear. "I do'na wanna leave ye here."

"Please," she whispered as he stepped away from her, not daring to open her eyes. "Cover yourself. I don't—"

A howl rose up behind her, covering her whole body with goose flesh. Sibyl sank to her knees, giving up, hearing the men shouting, dogs barking. There was no escape now, unless the strange, naked man who called himself Raife and his pet wolf behind her could somehow magically spirit her away. It was too late. Tears, hot and salty, fell through her fingers. She sobbed, knowing she would never be free.

A soft whine made her look up. The white wolf stood in front of her, the Scotsman's plaid secured around her neck, completely covering her wound. Then, another wolf, this one even bigger, its black fur as dark as night, eyes as blue as the sky, appeared beside the other. Sibyl stared at it in disbelief, her breath held as its big head cocked to contemplate her. The white wolf had been tamed, but this wolf was as wild as they came. She knew it, just looking in its eyes, those bright, clear blue eyes. Was this the white wolf's mate? She wondered this, even as she heard the hunting party's approach, the low growl emitting from the dark wolf's throat, and thought, not for the first time since she'd woken up that morning, that this would be the last day she drew breath.

Then the animal nosed her hands away from her face and gently licked the tears from her cheeks. His tongue was warm but she couldn't help her instinct to move away from those big, sharp teeth.

"Is this wolf tame as well?" she managed to whisper, too afraid to look away from the pair to glance over her shoulder at Raife. "Is it… your pet?"

No answer. The black wolf gave a short, sharp bark and the white wolf howled, glancing through the trees at the horses. The horses had a much harder time negotiating the woods, the underbrush thick, the big stallions unsure in their footing. The hounds, however, had an easier time. They were drawing close. Too close.

"Raife?" Sibyl swallowed, daring to look over her shoulder, forgetting for a moment that the man was fully naked, but there was no one there.

No one at all.

"Raife?" She frowned, whipping her head around, looking for the man. Her bow and quiver were on the ground. His plaid was around the white wolf's wounded neck. But the Scot was nowhere to be found. "Raife!"

She dared to call his name, even though it might draw the attention of Alistair's men to her, jumping to her feet. Behind her, the black wolf barked again, a short, piercing sound. Sibyl grabbed her bow and quiver, slinging it over her shoulder as she scanned the woods. He couldn't have disappeared into thin air!

She gasped when she felt a cold nose against her palm, a warm tongue. The black wolf moved in alongside her, forcing her hand through its thick fur as it rubbed up against her, almost like a cat might, emitting a low growl, then a plaintive whine. The animal was enormous, making the big, white wolf look small in comparison.

"They're coming for me." She whispered the words to the wolves—there was no one else there. Raife had disappeared, had left her alone with these animals. She knew she was alone. But if Alistair was going to catch her, she didn't want him to kill the wolves. At the very least, she could save them. "You have to go! Run!"

She pushed hard against the black wolf, its muscular body budging only slightly. The animal growled, turning its head to look at her.

"That's right!" she insisted, feeling tears burning her eyes. "Go! Shoo! Go away!"

Beside her, the other wolf barked. The white wolf flanked her now, standing between Sibyl and the dogs. They were coming. They were all coming. The black wolf issued a returning bark, moving in closer, until she was pressed between the two of them, almost as if they could hide her.

"Go!" she cried, trying to push at them, but they were too big, too strong. "Please! Go!"

It happened so fast she couldn't even react. The white wolf shoved her hard, knocking the wind out of her, and she stumbled against the black wolf. Sibyl was falling and, instinctively, she reached out for something to grab onto, and the only thing at hand was the neck of the great black wolf. Then they were running. Flying through the forest. Sibyl couldn't scream, although she wanted to. She could barely breathe.

At first, the wolves ran side by side, keeping Sibyl from falling off the black wolf's back. She tried hard to stay on, struggling with her heavy dress, the satchel pinned under her skirt, until she managed to get a leg securely over the wolf's back so she was sitting astride him, like he was a horse. A horse with no saddle. A very slippery horse with no saddle.

"Dear God, help me," she whispered, feeling something graze her temple. When she lifted a hand to her head, it came back bloody, and she saw an arrow quivering in a nearby tree. "Please help me."

They were running so fast the forest was a blur whenever she opened her eyes, so she kept them closed, burying her face against the larger wolf's neck. The animals ran hard, panting, and she felt the wolf's muscles straining between her thighs with every leap over a stray log, every dodge around a tree. Beside them, the white wolf whimpered, but she managed to keep pace.

Sibyl listened for the thunder of the horses, the bark of the dogs, but miraculously, the sounds disappeared. She clung to the wolf, trembling on its back, too afraid to look up and see where they were going, too frightened to look back, wondering what had happened to the man, Raife. A sudden, horrible thought occurred to her while the wolves spirited her away as she felt blood from her temple running down her cheek.

Raife had been killed.

She was suddenly sure of it. The man had been felled by an arrow, shot by one of Alistair's men. It was the only explanation. The thought brought such an overwhelming sadness she couldn't help her tears. She'd known the man for all of half an hour, and yet she was sobbing, thinking of him bleeding to death in the middle of the woods. Maybe it was because, in spite of his short, gruff nature, he'd tried to protect her, and had been so gentle with the white wolf.

Sibyl sensed the temperature change around her, the cool sunlight of the woods giving way to something else. She opened her eyes to darkness, clinging to the wolf, arms tight around its neck, thighs squeezing its flanks so hard they ached. She couldn't see her arms wrapped around the animal's neck. Even the white wolf had disappeared from view, although she heard it panting and whimpering next to them.

"Oh Raife." She whispered a prayer for the poor, dead man, burying her face once again against the wolf's fur. She shivered, suddenly cold, even in all her velvet, even with the wolf's body, flushed from its run, between her thighs. The animal slowed and she dared to open her eyes. She glimpsed a faint light as she peered around the wolf's big head.

"Stad!" A voice echoed all around them.

She couldn't tell where it was coming from and Sibyl gasped, grabbing the wolf's fur in her fists. They were underground—she knew that much. It was cold and no sun reached this place. Maybe they were in a cave? The thought of entering a wolf den with these two animals gave her a chill that went bone-deep, far worse than the chilly temperature making goose flesh rise on her skin.

But the voice that had spoken was most definitely human.

And as soon as the wolves heard it, they stopped.

The white wolf gave a quick bark and Sibyl felt the wolf beneath her growl. It rumbled through her body and the sound made her shiver. She held on tighter, even if she was afraid of the animal that carried her on its back. So far, it hadn't done anything to hurt her—it had, in fact, carried her away from grave danger. The disembodied voice, while human, was far more unknown.

"Please," she whispered, cheek pressed to the wolf's soft pelt. "Don't hurt me. Please."

"A bheil a' Ghàidhlig agad?" the voice asked, closer now.

"I don't understand," she pleaded in the darkness, the figure of a man drawing nearer. "I'm an Englishwoman. I don't—"

Beneath her, the wolf moved.

It didn't so much move as *change.* The animal's fur, thick and soft, grew sparse and then seemed to disappear altogether. One moment she was leaning forward over the wolf's neck, nearly horizontal, and the next minute she was hanging on for dear life, her body almost completely vertical. She screamed, her cry echoing back at her, and let go, falling to a hard, rocky floor.

"Are ye hurt, lass?" The voice beside her spoke English. She understood it perfectly well. In fact, she could have sworn she recognized it. But that was impossible.

"Raife?" she whispered, feeling the man's warmth as he knelt beside her. "Is it you? Can it be you? How…?"

"Come." He lifted her in his arms and Sibyl put hers around him and sobbed against his neck in the darkness.

It was too much. The whole day had been too much, from her daring escape attempt to this very surreal moment as this strange man carried her past the sentry. She heard the guard say, "Siuthad!" the voice definitely male. "Càite bheil Darrow?" and the man who held her responded in Gaelic, but she was already slipping further into darkness.

She had a moment to chastise herself, knowing her father would have been appalled at such a feminine display of weakness, but her body had simply given up. She found herself disappearing down another deep, dark hole, cheek resting against the bare chest and beating heart of a man who, she could have sworn, was a giant, black wolf only moments before.

Surely she was dreaming.

Sibyl woke on a mattress, looking around in the flickering light of an oil lamp, blinking up at the shadows and a man whose face was becoming increasingly familiar. She remembered the hunt first—her ride with Alistair into the woods, the revelation that the animal they were pursuing was a pregnant female locked in a convenient cage, her subsequent emancipation of that animal, her shooting of her fiancé, and her eventual escape—and then her capture.

Well, she didn't exactly remember her capture, but she could only infer that it had happened. She remembered the dogs barking, the horses, the shouts of the men. She remembered huddling, trembling and sobbing like a child, on the forest floor. And then—

And then her mind had taken flight.

Surely she had been captured, taken down here into a cold, dank place with sheetrock walls that could only be in the dungeons of Alistair's keep, and her imagination had done the rest. She couldn't trust her memory—the wolves, the ones that had carried her to dubious safety, had been a dream. She was sure of it.

She had been sick with a very high fever once when she was a child and had dreamed all sorts of things. Her father's huntsman had been twisted by her imagination into a bear, her mother into a vulture, her dear father into a barking dog. She knew the mind could play tricks that way.

This man, Raife—was he her jailer then? He sat beside her on a log-stump stool, still wearing only that wrapped tartan plaid, bare-chested in the dim orange glow as he pressed a cool, wet cloth to her head. She didn't recognize him as one of Alistair's men, but perhaps the master of the dungeon was little more than a prisoner himself, locked away down here taking care of Alistair's mistakes, keeping her betrothed's secrets.

"Where am I?" Her voice cracked. How long had she been asleep?

"'Ere lass." He spoke English, but in her dream, he'd spoken Gaelic. So that must mean she really had been dreaming. Of course she had, because in her dream this man had changed from a giant, black wolf back into this human form.

"Yer wit' me," Raife reassured her. That cool cloth felt so good, and it made his hand feel even warmer as he brushed hair away from her face. "Yer safe."

Maybe she was still dreaming, but somehow she knew this was true.

A low whine reached her ears and Sibyl frowned, trying to sit up. Raife frowned his own objection but he helped her, grabbing onto her elbow and steadying her when her intention was clear.

"Easy," he urged as she swung her feet to the floor. "Yer wounded."

"Wounded?" She touched her head, an ache throbbing there, vaguely remembering something. Then it came back. The arrow stuck quivering in the tree. The blood trickling down her cheek. She touched her temple and felt a bandage there. It was real. That sudden realization brought a chill and she shuddered, meeting Raife's eyes.

It was real.

It was all real.

"Wulvers?" she whispered, her lower lip trembling.

Raife gave a slow nod.

But it couldn't be real. Her mind balked.

"Laina!" The shout echoed in the distance and Sibyl's spine straightened.

The white wolf. Raife had called her Laina. Who was calling for her?

"Darrow." Raife stood, glancing down at Sibyl, frowning.

Sibyl remembered that too. The sentry who had stopped them, he had asked about someone named Darrow. She didn't know any of the other words in Gaelic, but she knew that was a name.

"Mo bràithair." Raife took a step toward the door, that shout growing louder, calling the white wolf's name.

"Your brother." Sibyl stood, steadying herself against him. He was as solid and still as a tree rooted in place. "He owns the wolf?"

Her mind wouldn't let her believe anything else.

"Darrow!" Raife called his brother's name, opening the door. "Trobhad an seo!"

The shouting stopped but Sibyl heard footfalls heading toward them. And that low whine intensified. She located the source of the sound across the room and realized it was the wolf. She was still laboring, panting softly, and beside her was an older woman dressed in tartan plaid tending to her and a much younger woman by her side.

"Laina?" Sibyl whispered the wolf's name and her white head came up briefly. Those blue eyes locked with hers. And then she was laboring again, her side rising and falling quickly, the sound of her panting filling the room.

"Laina!" Darrow bellowed, bursting into the room. He was as tall as his brother, but lankier, not quite as broad. He had the same thick, dark hair, those piercing blue eyes that desperately searched the room for the sight of the wolf laboring on a mattress on the floor across the room.

The wolf howled and Darrow went straight to her side.

"Tiugainn!" the midwife muttered to herself, doing something Sibyl couldn't see, but there was blood, plenty of it, on both women's hands. The wolf actually snapped at the old woman, but she didn't actually bite her.

"Tha e cunnartach!" The midwife shook her head, removing a hand covered in blood from the behind of the wolf. Sibyl had seen enough calves and horses born to know what was happening, but she leaned in to ask Raife for sure.

"What is it?"

"The pup is facin' wrong ways," he murmured, his eyes on the scene before them. "She's tryin' ta turn the bairn."

"The pup…" Sibyl frowned. "But… shouldn't there be… more?"

Horses and cows usually carried only one offspring to term, but wolves were like dogs—they had litters. She had played with lots of puppies in the warmth of her father's castle kitchen where the bitch would give birth in a large crate, and then the puppies would crawl all over each other in it until they were big enough to let roam.

"Wulvers birth one."

Wulvers. Not wolves, wulvers. Raife had corrected her again and again, but Sibyl had dismissed his insistence as a language barrier. In Scotland, wolves and wulvers seemed interchangeable. At least, that's what she had initially believed. Now, watching the white wolf, Laina, give birth, she wasn't so sure.

"Bidh curramach!" Darrow growled at the midwife as she did something that made Laina howl in pain.

"Wulvers birth as wolves," Raife explained as Sibyl watched, feeling weak-kneed and weak-stomached. "She can'na change while she's laborin'. Tis why she could'na free herself."

"From the cage?" Sibyl watched as Raife's brother bent to press his head against Laina's furry one. She licked his cheek, whimpering softly, and the man whispered something in Gaelic that she couldn't quite hear and wouldn't have understood regardless.

"It's their first bairn." Raife put an arm around Sibyl's waist, perhaps sensing her uneasy footing. "Nature knows its own way. Wolves birth young far easier than humans."

Raife had caught her just in time, too, because Sibyl felt her knees buckle as the wolf pup was born. The midwife exclaimed in triumph as the slick, dark-furred creature emerged covered in a bloody sac, head-first, as it should be. And then for the second time that day, Sibyl felt the world begin to go dark as, right before her very eyes, the white wolf Laina changed.

Sibyl told herself she was dreaming. That the naked, blonde woman and the crying babe between her open thighs had always been there. Or perhaps, the wolf was still there, and Sibyl was in the grip of a horrible fever, imagining the wolf taking human form. Her vision went dark around the edges, but she saw it all anyway.

The wolf's body arched and moved, its snout shrinking, mouth open in what appeared to be a wide yawn that swallowed up its whole face. The animal's limbs stiffened, muscles moving underneath, as if something were alive beneath its flesh. Then its fur slowly vanished, as if it was being pulled into its skin from the inside. The skin was as pale as a baby's beneath, pale as any human. Everything changed, everything about her, except for the color of her bright blue eyes. Those were the same, from beginning to end. Sibyl focused her attention there, her own eyes wide with disbelief and fear.

Her eyes were telling her truths her mind didn't want to see.

Maybe the arrow that had grazed her scalp had taken her sanity with it?

"Balach!" the old midwife announced. The younger woman cleaned the child up with a cloth and handed it to the mother.

"Balach." The young mother's voice was soft, her blue eyes full of tears as she met Darrow's in the light of the lamp. "Garaith."

"Tis a boy." Raife smiled, his arm tightening around Sibyl's waist as he explained this to her in hushed tones. "The next in our line. They'll name him Garaith, after me father."

The woman—she was a woman now, full figured and lovely with the longest blonde hair Sibyl had ever seen—brought the baby up to her breast, and Sibyl saw the slash there beneath the woman's collarbone as the midwife covered her with a sheet, a little late to protect her modesty. The wound had been tended, but she would have a scar there for the rest of her life.

A bloody souvenir from Alistair's dirk.

Sibyl remembered the way he'd slashed at the white wolf, the one she had freed from the cage. The one who couldn't free herself, because she was carrying young and couldn't transform from wolf to human in order to undo the latch. The one who had run through the forest beside the black wolf, the wolf that had carried Sibyl to safety, down here into its den.

The black wolf who had changed in the darkness from animal to human right under Sibyl's very own hands—that was the man, Raife, who stood beside her. And now this animal, Laina, had turned from she-wolf to human woman before Sibyl's very own eyes. The young she had birthed had transformed from a whining pup to a wailing human child with thick, black hair like his father.

Like his uncle.

Raife hadn't been mistaken when he corrected her use of the word "wolf" to "wulver."

"What magic is this?" Sibyl's voice barely escaped her throat in a whisper. "What devilment? Who are you?"

She looked up to meet Raife's impossibly blue eyes, saw the man, Darrow, glance back at her and frown, the woman, Laina, looking between them, concerned.

"What are you?"

For the second time that day—only the second time in her entire life—Sibyl fainted.

Chapter Four

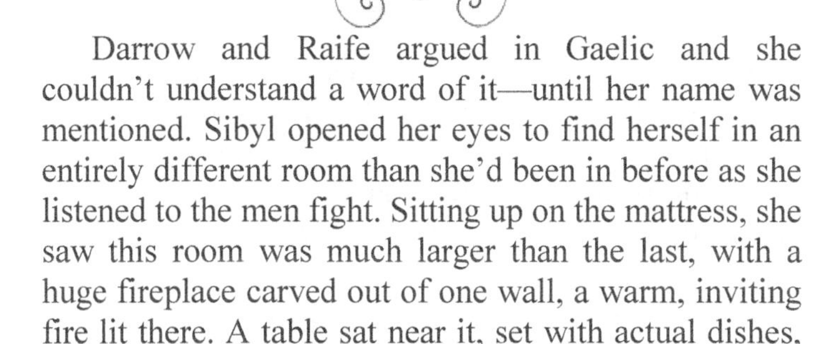

Darrow and Raife argued in Gaelic and she couldn't understand a word of it—until her name was mentioned. Sibyl opened her eyes to find herself in an entirely different room than she'd been in before as she listened to the men fight. Sitting up on the mattress, she saw this room was much larger than the last, with a huge fireplace carved out of one wall, a warm, inviting fire lit there. A table sat near it, set with actual dishes, silverware and napkins, something she hadn't expected in this strange place.

Just the sight of the set table made her stomach growl. She tried to remember the last time she'd eaten and then she recalled the food she had hidden under her dress. Listening to the two men yell at each other in Gaelic and glancing occasionally toward the door to make sure no one was coming, she lifted up her skirt and unpinned her satchel. It had come partially open and she frowned, digging through, hoping she hadn't lost anything.

The bread she'd stolen was hard but she ate it anyway. The dried fruit and jerky was tough, but tasty. Sibyl's stomach thanked her and asked for more, but she only ate a handful of her rations, not knowing when she might need them. She knew she would have to slip out of this place the first chance she got and head south, back to the village where they had left her ladies' maid, Rose. It had been her original plan, and while she had been waylaid by these…

Wulvers.

Sibyl shuddered, instinctively shrinking back against the stone wall as she repacked her satchel. Glancing at the table, she suddenly had a horrible thought. What if she was the one on the menu? These half-men, half-wolves certainly had to eat, didn't they? Why wouldn't they eat her? The one called Raife had brought her here, but it was clear his brother, Darrow, didn't think that had been such a good idea, if the sound of them yelling and throwing things at each other was any indication.

She knew they were somewhere deep underground. Maybe inside a cave. Somewhere hidden in the mountains she had seen from her window perch at Alistair's castle, the mountains that lay beyond the forest where they'd been hunting. They wouldn't want anyone to know where they were hiding, would they? No, of course not. They certainly couldn't let Sibyl go, after she'd been in their den. Could they?

Her blood turned to ice water in her veins as she glanced from the set table to the doorway. There was a door, thick and heavy, but sound drifted in. The sound of the two brothers, arguing over her fate. She was sure of it. Not only had she heard the one called Raife say her name—the other one kept saying the word "shasennach." She'd picked that up quickly, because many of Alistair's men called her that. It meant Englishwoman, although the way the Scots said it, she might as well have heard them calling her "pig."

Darrow said the word with the same scorn she'd heard from many of Alistair's men.

She had been a stranger in a strange land at the MacFalon castle, but now she was in a whole other world. These creatures might look like men, but they were not. Whatever witchcraft or devilry they possessed to make them look human, they were still animals, and animals, even tame ones, could be dangerous when provoked. Even her father's hounds would bite you if you disturbed them during a feeding. And she'd heard the animal trainer, the one who had come through with his "tame" bear, had later been mauled and killed by that same animal after he'd spent years with it.

Was Raife fighting in her favor, she wondered hopefully, ears tuned, listening for him to say her name again. She had freed the white she-wolf, after all. Maybe that would work in her favor? Or maybe… Sibyl looked again at the set table, shivering in spite of the warmth of the room.

Maybe she was going to be their dinner.

She dug into her satchel, finding the kitchen knife she had stolen wrapped in a cloth napkin. She unwrapped it and looked around for a place to hide it. Surely these creatures, even if they were something wicked and unnatural, could be killed? She would have to be ready, in any case. She stowed the satchel under the bed and had just climbed back onto the bed, looking for a place to hide the knife, when Raife opened the door and stalked into the room.

She sat and blinked at him, not saying a word, as he looked at her with her skirts hiked up past her knees, something that once would have made her blush with modesty, but the past day's events had changed her. The only flush that crept into her cheeks came because she realized she'd been caught with the knife she'd been planning to hide sitting right next to her on the bed.

"Ye plannin' t'knife me in me sleep, lass?" Raife glanced from Sibyl to the knife, his gaze lingering curiously on her slim calves in their short stockings and garters before she flipped the torn, muddy fabric of her gown back over them.

"Of course not." But her hand moved to touch the knife at her side, her eyes never leaving his.

"It mus' all seem verra strange to ye," he said softly, taking a step closer to crouch down to eye-level next to the bed.

"A bit." She swallowed, her hand involuntarily clenching the knife, wondering if she could stab him before he changed into a wolf and snapped her neck in his big jaws. Not that the man had to change into any fantastical creature to kill her. He could easily snap her neck in his big hands, too.

"I will'na hurt ye." He held his hand out for the knife, his eyes soft, kind, as light as a blue summer sky. Sibyl hesitated, glancing down at the weapon in her hand, knowing it was useless against him if he was lying, but still unable to let it go.

"A'right, lass, 'ave it yer way. Keep the knife." He sighed and stood, looking down at her in the firelight. "Are ye hungry? Stale bread and jerky isn't much, even for a skinny lass like yerself."

"I'm not skinny!" she protested, moving to stand too, knife in hand. She barely came to his shoulder and had to look way up to meet those startling blue eyes of his. How had he known what she'd eaten? She wondered, frowning up at the raised eyebrows on his smirking face.

"Ye can keep yer pack, too," he told her. "The one under the bed."

"How—?"

"Wulvers have a keen sense a smell." He tapped his decidedly human nose, but Sibyl was remembering the wolf's snout, the way he'd licked the tears from her face in the woods. Was it really possible, to transform from human to wolf and back again? She had seen it with her own eyes when the she-wolf changed and still, her mind didn't want to accept.

"I had 'em set a table for ye in 'ere," he explained, nodding at the dishes. "Thought ye might like some stew."

"No, thank you." Her stomach growled audibly and he arched his eyebrows again, a gesture that Sibyl found infuriating. Almost as infuriating as being called "skinny." And "lass."

"Tis jus' rabbit." He smiled like he could read her mind, going over to the fire and using a long, thick pole with a hooked end to lift a black iron pot. "We don't eat humans, Sibyl."

"Ever?" She licked her lips when he plucked the lid from the pot and the smell of stew wafted through the room. Her body clamored for real food, making her knees feel weak.

"Nuh, not fer twenty years," he assured her, picking up a ladle from the table and dishing out a bowl of the heavenly-scented stuff. "I've never tasted a human."

"That's comforting," she said wryly, watching him dish up a second bowl before he put them both on the table and hung the pot back over the fire. She couldn't help staring at the fireplace, wondering at its sheer size, the way it was literally carved right out of the mountain's surface.

"Where does the smoke go?" she wondered aloud, edging closer to the fireplace, unable to help her curiosity.

"Yer a keen one, ain't ye?" He grinned, sitting at the table and leaning back to look at her, that amused smile still on his face. “Have ye ever gone swimmin’ in a hot spring?”

“No.” She shook her head. She’d heard of them—warm pools that heated all by themselves. They had them in Bath. “But I’ve heard tell of them. I didn’t know there were any in Scotland?”

“Aye, jus’ but a few, up’ere in the mountains,” he explained, sticking a spoon into his bowl of stew and stirring it around. The scent of rabbit meat and gravy and vegetables drew Sibyl even nearer. Raife nodded toward his steaming bowl. “They give off steam, ya ken? So we made our chimneys so the smoke, it looks jus’ like steam risin’ up from the pools. No one’s the wiser.”

“Ingenious.” She slid into the seat across from him, glancing down at the bowl of stew he’d ladled for her. The dishes were made of metal, pewter perhaps, she thought. The spoons were wooden. She put her knife on the table.

“Rabbit?” she asked, putting her nose closer to the delicious smelling concoction.

“Aye, jus’rabbit.” He lifted the spoon to his lips. “Ye’ve tasted rabbit afore?”

“Of course,” she scoffed, putting a spoon into the bowl and stirring it around. It certainly smelled like rabbit. She took a taste and moaned softly, closing her eyes in bliss. Food! Her stomach clenched, asking for more.

“G’head, lass,” he said, taking another spoonful himself. “Twill’na bite ye.”

“What about you?”

“I will’na bite ye either.” He smiled softly, cocking his head at her in the soft, orange glow of the fire. “If we were goin' t'kill ye, don'tcha think we would've done it a'ready?"

"Mayhaps." She continued to spoon stew in, warming her clamoring belly, hoping that logic was sound. In truth, this man had been far better to her in the space of just a day than her betrothed had been to her in the entire month she'd known him. Raife had saved her from Alistair's wrath—and his pursuing men. This man had carried her to safety, had bandaged her wounds, had taken her in, knowing his brother, and likely his whole pack, would object. He had given her food and shelter and had asked for naught in return.

The only problem was, this man could change into an animal at any moment.

Of course, apparently, so could her betrothed. They were just different sorts of animals, she mused. And she was beginning to think that these creatures—wolves, wulvers, whatever they were called—might be preferable.

"Thank you for the food." She glanced up at the man eating across from her. His chest was bare and strangely hairless in the firelight, his plaid secured around his waist with a thick leather belt. She would have expected far more fur on a man who was a wolf half of the time, but all his hair appeared to be on his dark head. "It is far better than jerky and dried fruit."

"How much did ye have packed in that bag under ye skirts?" he asked, looking pointedly at her torn, tattered clothing. She'd been grateful for the fabric when she'd had to hide her satchel underneath.

"A few days, maybe a weeks' worth," she replied, scraping her bowl with her spoon, sad the stew had disappeared so quickly. "But I'm skinny, I don't need much."

“A’course.” He chuckled, taking her bowl back over to the fire and spooning more stew into it. “And where were ye runnin’ off ta?”

“Back…” She almost said ‘home,’ but she didn’t have one of those anymore. And she couldn’t for the life of her remember the name of the village where they’d left Rose. “Toward York.”

“York is home then?” He placed another full bowl of stew in front of her and she grabbed her spoon, digging in greedily.

“It was.” She nodded, talking through mouthfuls of stew. “My mother and uncle… he’s really my stepfather now, I suppose… they live in York.”

“And ye were promised t’Alistair?” The man took his seat again, leaning back and crossing his arms as he studied her. “Laird of clan MacFalon?”

“Yes, but…” She swallowed a bite of stew, meeting those blue eyes across the table. He missed nothing, this man. “I didn’t want to marry him.”

“That explains why ye put an arrow in ’im?” Raife’s eyes pinned her to her seat.

“I suppose.” She lifted her chin defiantly. “But he deserved it.”

“Ye’ll nuh get an argument from me about that.” He shook his head, the dark look in his eyes clear enough. Her betrothed’s reputation preceded him. “I should’na brought ye here, lass. My brother’s naught right about much, but was right about that.”

“I can be on my way tonight,” she assured him, although she wasn’t as sure as she sounded. She didn’t like the idea of staying here in this wolf den—but the thought of being out there on her own in the forest at night, not knowing if Alistair’s men were still searching for her, also made her hesitate. “Is it… night?”

“Ye’ll stay the night ’ere,” he told her firmly. “I’ll take ye back in the mornin’.”

“Take me back…?” She couldn’t go back, not to Alistair and Castle MacFalon, not ever.

“I’ll escort ye wherever ye like, Sibyl.” He spoke her name softly. It was tender in his mouth, even sweet. She’d never had anyone say her name like that in all her years and didn’t understand her own reaction. It made her feel soft inside, as soft as his tartan plaid, as soft as the fur at the nape of the black wolf's neck where she’d clung to him as they rode through the woods. “All the way back t’York, if that is yer wish, lass. Ye saved Laina’s life. Tis the least we can do for ye.”

Sibyl hadn’t forgotten about the white she-wolf, about the way she had transformed before her very eyes. The image was burned into her memory. And while it was true that she’d saved the wolf from her cage, it had felt, to Sibyl, that she had been somehow saving herself.

“Is she… are they…?”

“They’re well, she and the bairn.” He smiled, eyes softening at her concern. “I’m sorry if'n our argument scared ye. Darrow’s worried about his new bride. They should’na’ve left ’ere, wit’ her so close t’pup.”

“She was captured by the MacFalon huntsman.”

“Aye,” he agreed. “And she could’na change form, not in ’er state.”

“So you… how do you…do what you do?” Sibyl cocked her head, wondering at it. “Does everyone here change? Are you all… wulvers?”

She couldn't believe her own questions, given how impossible, how incredible it all seemed. Thinking about it still made her a little woozy, but she couldn't continue to deny what she'd seen with her very own eyes nor could she just continue to faint at the thought of something so unnatural. The facts were the facts. The she-wolf Laina had transformed, and so had this man.

"Yer a curious lil thing." He smiled. "We are what we are. And have always been."

So he didn't want to talk about it. She sat back, still feeling woozy, but for a whole different reason.

"I'm stuffed." She gave a satisfied sigh.

"Would ye like a bath?" he asked. "Ye can soak in one of the hot springs. Kirstin'll show ye…"

"No." She shook her head, eyes widening at the thought of being so vulnerable in such a strange place. She'd let her guard down enough to stuff herself full of food.

"We will'na harm ye, lass," he assured her for the umpteenth time. "I saved ye from being captured by the laird's men, a'member? I promise no harm'll come t'ye here."

"I don't doubt you…" She met his eyes, knowing it was true. In spite of the strangeness of her predicament, in spite of the apparent reality of this new world, where men turned to wolves and back again, she believed him. "But your brother, Darrow? He sounded like he might have been considering having *shasennach* for dinner."

Raife laughed at her use of the Gaelic word.

"He's angry I brought ye here." The man shrugged his big, heavily muscled shoulders. "But ye freed

Laina. I could'na let ye stay out there alone. Not wit' MacFalon's men searchin' for ye."

"I don't know..." Sibyl glanced toward the doorway, considering her options. "Maybe I should just go now..."

If they were really going to let her go, she thought, she needed to do so as soon as possible, before they changed their minds. If Darrow was angry about her being there, he would only grow angrier over time.

"Tis dark and there's no moon. Ye would'na get far." Raife shook his head, eyes narrowing. "Tis not safe out there."

"I'm not sure it's safe in here," she murmured, remembering Darrow's anger, the way he spat the word *shasennach.*

"Trust me, we can'na kill a human. It'd bring King Henry and all of yer kind down on our heads, because of the pact," Raife informed her. "Not that yer betrothed wasn't already breakin' it."

"The pact?" She cocked her head, puzzled, as someone knocked on the door.

"Come in," Raife called.

"Are ye finished then?" A pretty, young girl with long, curly, dark hair peeked around the door, dimples showing as she smiled at Raife. She wore plaid too, as a skirt, belted at the waist, but underneath it was a long-sleeved, saffron tunic. Her legs were bare though, and so were her feet. It was still strange to Sibyl that Scots women went around with their hair uncovered and so much of their skin bared.

"Thank ye, Kirstin." He smiled at the girl, waving her into the room. "Will ye take Lady Sibyl to me private spring for a hot bath and get 'er somethin' else t'wear?"

"A'course!" Kirstin agreed, smiling at Sibyl, and she suddenly recognized her. This was the young woman who had tended the birth with the old midwife. "I'll take these ta the kitchen and bring somethin' back fer ye."

"No, you don't have to." Sibyl shook her head, glancing down at her dress. It was torn and dirty, but it would be quite warm. She'd lost her hat—not that it had been much protection—and her wrap too, but this dress would serve her well out there in the woods, she thought. "I'll be fine in this."

"Ye can'na wear that." Kirstin wrinkled her brown little nose. She was a brown girl, all over, her arms and legs, even the tops of her feet. She spent time in the sun, Sibyl thought, watching the girl clear their bowls and spoons, putting them onto a wooden tray she'd carried in with her. "I'll get ye a proper plaid. And ye must have somethin' t'sleep in. I'll be righ'back."

Something to sleep in. That, of course, begged the question—where was she to sleep? Here, in this room? With… him? Sibyl glanced up, meeting his dancing blue eyes, and she could have sworn he was reading her very thoughts. She felt her cheeks redden, her body warming all the way to her toes. There was only one bed in this room, and while it was plenty big enough for two, that was hardly the point. Still, she couldn't force the man out of his own room. That didn't seem right either.

"This room is yers, while yer here." Raife stood, nodding at the mattress Sibyl had woken up on. "I'll be outside if ye need me."

"But… isn't this your room?" She frowned, glancing around at the walls decorated with claymores and crossed swords. She had a feeling they weren't all for show, like they appeared to be in Alistair's castle. "I can't take your room. Please, I don't need—"

"I will'na hear of it." Raife held up his hand, shaking his head and smiling as he looked down into her eyes. She felt like she could get lost in them, the way she did on warm, lazy days, watching clouds drift by. "Ye take yerself a bath, Lady Sibyl. Get a good night's rest. We'll talk more in the mornin'."

He turned to go, but she couldn't let him. Not without saying it. She reached out and touched his wrist, thick and heavily veined under her palm as she clasped it in her hand. Raife glanced down at where she touched him, then his gaze skipped to meet hers. Those eyes turned dark, from blue skies to the deepest part of the ocean.

"Thank you." She swallowed, sliding her hand down into his, squeezing gently. His hand was so big, it swallowed hers. "I… don't know how to thank you."

He didn't say anything for a moment. He looked down at their hands, locked together, then back into her eyes. She thought she just might lose herself in them, truly. Was she under some sort of spell? Bewitched? Is that how it worked? Her heart hammered. Her breath quickened. Her skin felt too tight, all over, as if she couldn't quite contain herself.

"Ye were brave, lass." His voice was low, eyes soft, as he lifted his other hand to touch her cheek. His fingers were rough, calloused, tracing the line of her jaw. "So verra brave… yer father woulda been proud."

His words brought tears to her eyes. Her lower lip quivered and she swallowed, trying to hold them in, but they wouldn't stay back. They spilled over, down her cheeks, and Raife moved to cup her face in his hands, gently wiping them away with his thumbs.

“G’nite.” He took a step back, turning toward the door as Kirstin came in, carrying clothes.

“Good night,” Sibyl called. She saw him hesitate, give a brief nod, and then he was gone, closing the door behind him.

She stared after him, remembering what he’d said that had brought her to tears. She had been thinking about her father just before she had freed the she-wolf, saying that very same thing to herself. *He would have been proud.* And while she believed it was true, the thing she couldn’t quite understand was—how had Raife known that?

How had he known?

Chapter Five

Sibyl gave all her clothes to Kirstin and, after a long soak in the hot spring—where she nearly fell asleep and might have drowned if the Scotswoman hadn't come in—she let the girl wash and dress her for bed like a child and tuck her in, too. Sibyl's eyes closed all on their own. She couldn't keep them open. The girl moved around the room, straightening and singing to herself, but Sibyl was only peripherally aware. The day had been long and she was exhausted. Before she fell asleep, she caught the scent of Raife on her pillow. It was the last thing she remembered, smiling to herself, until she woke up in the middle of the night to the sound of a baby crying.

She woke with a start, the room cool—the fire had burned low—not knowing where she was. Then it came back to her in an instant. She remembered everything. Everything. And the chill wasn't all that made her shudder. She was in a wolves' den and, if any of them wanted to kill her, that door wouldn't keep them out. Sibyl put her head back down on the pillow—it still smelled like Raife—and tried to sleep again.

But the baby continued to cry.

She tried to judge how close it was. Things seemed to echo down here. Sound was strange. But it sounded very close. Right next door mayhaps. Laina's baby? Was it ill? The sound went on and on. The baby was frantic now.

Sibyl got up, glancing around for something to put on, but her dress was gone. She was wearing her underwear and a long shirt that came to mid-thigh. There was a plaid on the chair and a leather belt. Sibyl did her best, cinching the belt around her waist over her nightshirt, so the plaid hung just past her bare knees, and then pulled the extra plaid fabric over her shoulder, tucking it into her belt. She considered going out into the hallway barefoot—she couldn't find her stockings or garters—but the mountain floor was cold, so she tied her soft-soled shoes on before opening the big door to her room.

The sound of the baby crying was louder here. It was a lusty, wailing cry. The poor thing sounded hungry. Sibyl crept down the dark hall, heart thudding hard in her chest, hoping she wouldn't run into any wolves. She didn't exactly relish coming face-to-face with an animal in the darkness, even if Raife had assured her that none of them meant her any harm.

"Laina?" Sibyl called the woman's name outside the next door. The baby's cry was definitely coming from there and, as far as she knew, this was the room she had woken up in. This was where the white she-wolf had birthed her baby. She knocked, waiting for an answer. "Laina? Are you in there?"

She told herself she should just go back to her room, close the door, and ignore it. This wasn't her place, it wasn't her child. She told herself, while she was at it, she should probably just go back to her room, grab her satchel, and slip out of this place in the middle of the night. But she did neither. Instead, she put her hand on the latch and pushed. The door swung open.

"Laina?" Sibyl saw the woman on the mattress near the fire, her back bare, the sheet pulled up. The baby was beside her on the mattress, waving his fists in the air, his face red from crying. Hungry, she thought. She had been an only child but she had spent enough time with her father's healer, tending birthing and nursing women, to know that cry.

The midwife was gone. She wondered where Darrow was, but mayhaps, like many animals, male wolves were a danger to their own young? She couldn't remember enough about wolves and their behavior, cursing the fact they'd been outhunted in England by mid-century. Was Laina so exhausted from the birth she slept right through the babe's cries?

"Are you all right?" Sibyl crept closer, suddenly imagining this woman turning back into the great, white wolf she had been, imagined the wolf seeing a human approaching her baby, seeing her as a threat and tearing Sibyl's throat out.

In spite of that image, in spite of her fear, Sibyl crept forward. She touched the woman's shoulder and Laina moaned softly, but didn't wake, even when Sibyl shook her.

"Laina?" Sibyl reached down, scooping the baby up in her arms in hopes of comforting and quieting it, at least for the moment, turning the woman toward her with her other hand.

That's when she saw the blood on the sheet and all over the mattress. Laina was bleeding, and badly. Sibyl felt the oppressive cold of the mountain overtake her. She'd watched women bleed to death in childbirth. Every woman she'd ever known who had become heavy with child was terrified of dying during the process.

"Laina! Wake up!"

Sibyl shook the woman, hard. If she could keep her awake, it would help mitigate the blood loss. How much could one person lose before they died? Sibyl wondered. She'd watched her father's men bleed from injuries before and had helped the healer on more than one occasion. One man had lost a leg to the tusk of a boar and she had watched the healer tie it off with his belt and save the man. But how could you ebb this flow of blood? She couldn't cinch the poor woman in the middle! She tried to remember the births she'd attended with the healer, looking to jog her memory. She'd tended births with the healer on more than one occasion before her mother found out and put a stop to the whole thing.

"Shh, shhhhh." Sibyl hefted the baby up on her shoulder, pulling the sheet back, seeing blood pooling between the woman's bare legs. "It's all right, little one. Let's take care of your mama so you can eat, hungry baby."

She talked to herself, pressing the woman's abdomen, watching more blood seep out between her thighs. This was bad. Very bad.

"What're ye doin'?" Raife's voice startled her and Sibyl gasped, whirling to see him standing in the doorway. "I saw ye leave yer room."

Saw her? Where had he been, she wondered, that he saw her leave? She hadn't seen him in the darkness. Of course, she couldn't see in the dark and had simply followed the sound of the baby crying. Could wulvers see in the dark? She wondered, meeting those bright blue eyes.

"I heard the baby," she explained. "It wouldn't stop crying. I thought… I wondered… I think… I think she needs help. She's bleeding and I can't wake her."

"Laina?" Raife frowned, stepping into the room, unmindful of the woman's nude body or any modicum of modesty. Sibyl noticed, for the first time, the woman had an intricate marking, covering her thigh and hip. It looked as if someone had drawn on the woman in ink. "Where's Darrow?"

"I do not—"

"Laina, I brought the—" Darrow stopped in the doorway, seeing his brother standing over his wife's bleeding form, Sibyl holding his child. The tall man snarled at her and Sibyl shrank back. "Get outta here!"

"She's hurt, brother." Raife took a step between Sibyl and Darrow, one hand on his brother's chest, keeping the man away from Sibyl's trembling form.

"I fetched Kirstin." Darrow frowned, looking down in concern at Laina's inert form. "I woke and she was bleedin'. I—"

"I need more t'stop this!" Kirstin was already on her knees, using the bloody sheet between the woman's legs. "Darrow! More cloth, or she'll die!"

"Tis so much blood." Raife's eyes were wide with fear and Sibyl didn't blame him. Birthing was bloody, dangerous business.

"It happens, sometimes," Sibyl said softly, hoping Darrow didn't hear her.

"I've never seen a wolf bleed like this after a birth!" Kirstin protested, grabbing the cloth Darrow brought, trying to stem the blood flow, but it was useless.

"Women do," Sibyl countered. "Women die in childbirth all the time."

"But *wulvers* do'na, ya ken?" Kirstin snapped. She was afraid too—terrified. Sibyl was surprised by their reaction. In her world, everyone knew this could happen. "I've never seen this. Get Beitris, Darrow! Quick now!"

Darrow ran. The old midwife might know what to do, but Sibyl wasn't sure she would, if it was true that wulvers did not bleed out this way after birth. There wasn't time for consulting texts. Sibyl knew what to do for this kind of bleed, had learned on the knee of her father's healer, and remembered as much as she was going to.

"Do you have dried goldenrod?" Sibyl asked Kirstin. The girl was up to her elbows in blood over Laina's inert form. "Shepherd's purse?"

"Nuh." Kirstin shook her head helplessly, meeting Sibyl's eyes. She saw tears in them. Laina would certainly die without intervention and the girl knew it.

"I saw some on the way in," Sibyl murmured. She had, although how she remembered it, given the circumstances, she couldn't quite explain, except that, like her father had taught her, she had an awareness of her surroundings most people did not. "But it is the middle of the night. I would not be able to find it. And she does not have until morning."

Raife touched Sibyl's arm, alarm in his eyes. There was no time for panic.

"Do you have cayenne?" Sibyl asked Kirstin. "To add heat, for cooking?"

"We do 'ave some!" Kirstin brightened. "Inna kitchen!"

"Good!" Sibyl nodded, "Get it. Stir a teaspoon into boiling water. Make her to drink it scalding hot. She will not want to. Force her."

Darrow showed up with Beitris, the old midwife, whose eyes grew even wider than Kirstin's at the amount of blood on the bed.

"Take the babe," Sibyl instructed the old midwife as Kirstin ran out, hands still covered in blood, to look for the cayenne. “And put him at her breast. Make him suckle.”

The baby was still mewling with hunger, his face turning back and forth, rooting.

“Should’na be a problem, he’s starvin’.” Beitris knelt with the child, tucking it in against Laina’s pale body. “But won’t it cause ’er t’lose more fluid?”

Beside them, Darrow howled. It was an inhuman sound that rose the hackles on the back of Sibyl’s neck. There was so much pain in the sound, it would have brought Sibyl to her own knees if Raife hadn’t been beside her, holding tight to her elbow.

“No, it will help,” Sibyl assured the old woman. The baby had latched on already, suckling, greedy. She looked up, meeting Raife’s concerned gaze. “I hope it will help enough before we can get back.”

“We?” He stared at her, aghast.

“Take me back into the woods.” Sibyl looked up at him, remembering the breakneck speed the wolves had run on the way in. “We will find what we need.”

Raife met his brother’s eyes, a low communication passing between them.

“We’ll be righ’back, brother. She’ll live. Sibyl knows what t’do.” Raife looked down at Sibyl, taking her small hand in his giant one as he led her into the dark hallway, and she hoped against hope that the words he spoke were true. She stopped for a moment in her room to empty her packed satchel out onto the bed.

“Hang on tight,” he instructed, his eyes grim in the tunnel’s torchlight.

“I will.”

She couldn’t watch. Instead, she closed her eyes and wrapped her arms around his neck and she *felt* him shift. Firm, hard, hairless flesh transformed into softness and fur, the muscle and bone changing underneath. She didn't understand this magic, but she didn't have time to think about it, because Raife was running, and she was riding.

They passed the sentry without stopping and he did not stop them, likely recognizing Raife needed no challenge or permission. Raife had been right—there was no moon and it was so dark she could see nothing. She would have to rely on Raife's sense of smell and sight.

"You'll know the goldenrod," Sibyl told him. "It smells like old, wet socks."

He found it right away. The wolf shook his big head and sneezed as she gathered it in by the armfuls, shoving it into the satchel she'd emptied for this purpose.

"Shepherd's purse smells like..." Sibyl frowned, trying to think how to describe it. But the wolf howled. He'd found it a ways down the path and came back to lead her to it in the darkness. She tripped over rocks and had to steady herself against his thickly muscled hide.

"Pungent, isn't it?" Sibyl made a face, yanking the shepherd's purse up by the roots. "But it will do the job. I hope. Hurry, Raife. Get us back."

He howled, a sound that shook her to her bones as she grabbed onto his neck and he ran like the wind. The entrance to the cave, hidden even during the daytime, was a black hole. Sibyl clung to him, hoping what was in her satchel might save a woman's life tonight.

"Boil this!" Sibyl slid off Raife as he skidded just past the doorway where she knew Laina lay near death. She didn't wait for him before bursting into the room, already pulling the pungent herbs from the satchel and handing them over to a stunned, worried-looking Kirstin. "You're going to make a tea for her to drink."

"Laina?" Sibyl sat beside the woman. She was more lucid, the baby at her breast being held there by Darrow. "Can you hear me?"

The blonde woman shook her head, moaning, but it was a good sign.

"Her belly is still distended." Sibyl pressed down hard on it and Laina howled. Good. More blood seeped from between her legs into the absorbent cloth. The sac where the baby had been housed in Laina's belly needed to firm up, contract, and grow smaller. The same contractions that had pushed the baby out would make that happen.

"What are ye doin'?" Beitris frowned. "Ye're makin'er bleed more!"

"Leave 'er be," Raife snapped. He was human again—Sibyl didn't need to look around to know that, she heard it in his voice. "She knows what t'do."

He had more faith in her than Sibyl actually possessed but she was grateful for the vote of confidence. Kirstin already had the goldenrod and shepherd's purse in a pot of boiling water over the fire.

"Massage her like this." Sibyl showed the old woman, who frowned but did as she was told. Raife stood over them, watching, as Kirstin poured the hot herb water into a tin cup.

"Somethin's firmin' in 'er," Beitris observed, glancing between Laina's legs. "I think the blood is ebbin'."

"Yes." Sibyl blew on the surface of the cup, smelling the goldenrod and shepherd's purse. It was enough to make her want to gag. "Kirstin, help sit her up a little."

Darrow did it instead, taking the baby off its mother's breast to do so. Kirstin took the baby, who wailed at being taken away from his mother, but Sibyl had to get the concoction down the woman's throat. Laina moaned but swallowed, her eyes half-opening, focused for a moment on Sibyl, then on her husband. There was a recognition in those eyes that gave Sibyl hope. Laina knew where she was, who she was, who this man was to her. She was still here on this side of the veil then.

"Thank ye." Darrow choked out the words as they put Laina back down on the mattress. It was ruined, soaked in blood, and Sibyl wondered how someone could lose so much and still be breathing. It was a miracle. "Tis the second time ye've saved 'er life."

"I'm glad I could help." Sibyl looked up at Kirstin who was holding the crying child in her arms. "Keep that baby nursing as much as possible."

"He seems to have a great appetite," Raife observed as Kirstin knelt to put him back at Laina's breast. "He's yer son, wit'out a doubt, brother."

Raife's hand fell to Darrow's shoulder and Sibyl saw tears brimming in the younger brother's eyes as his own hand covered Raife's larger one.

"And keep her drinking this," Sibyl instructed, pointing to the pot of boiling herbs. "All night long."

"I'll stay awake wit'er," Darrow assured her as Sibyl stood. "Thank ye again."

"I'm right next door if you need me." Sibyl didn't want to go, but the immediate danger had passed, and Raife insisted. He barked orders, telling the old midwife and Kirstin to clean Laina up, Darrow to get men to dispose of the old mattress and retrieve a new one.

Then Raife walked her to the room next door where he turned her to him, his big hands on her shoulders. He made her feel so small in stature in his presence, but she never felt small within. That was likely what made him a leader, she realized—man, wolf or wulver.

"I've never seen anythin' like that afore," Raife said softly, glancing down the hall where men carried out the bloody mattress. "I'm so glad ye were here. We would'na've known what t'do."

Sibyl just nodded. She didn't know what to say to that.

"Tis why wulvers change when they birth." Raife's eyes hardened. "Females can'na change back while puppin'. Wulvers do'na experience the same dangers as humans durin' birth. Tis a blessin' and a curse."

"I don't understand." Sibyl frowned, opening the door to her room as two men moved in behind them, carrying a clean mattress for Laina, making more room for them in the tunnel hallway.

"Lilith's curse." Raife stood in the doorway, filling it with his big frame, not coming in, although she moved into the room to sit on the edge of the bed. She thought she had been exhausted before. Now she was dead-tired. "The first wulver was the daughter of Lilith."

"Adam's first wife?" She cocked her head at him. "From the Bible?"

"The same," he agreed. "Humans descended from Eve. Wulvers descended from Lilith."

Sibyl considered this new information, trying to absorb it.

"Lilith was a'cursed by God t'give birth t'demons," Raife explained softly, reminding Sibyl of the old Biblical story. She was far more familiar with the story of Adam and Eve, of course—that was the story of her own ancestors, of an evil, wanton woman who tempted her mate into wickedness—but occasionally Lilith was mentioned in church as God's first, failed attempt at creating woman. It seemed her gender was difficult to get just right.

"We're those demon descendants," Raife told her. "Half-human, half-wolf. We live in the borderland between worlds. Sibyl? Are ye a'right?"

She felt faint again at his words, although she told herself she was not, under any circumstances, going to faint. Not again. But her eyes closed and the world spun anyway.

"Sibyl?" Raife was close to her now, squatting next to the bed, holding her up.

"It's been a long day." She opened her eyes and half-smiled at him. "It's a lot to take in all at once. Wulvers… half-human, half-wolf. The… descendants of Lilith, you say?"

"Aye." He brushed hair away from her face, smiling softly. "Ye should sleep, lass. Ye worked hard dis day."

"So did you." She cocked her head at him. "And Laina. Poor thing. She worked hardest of all."

"Wulver females ain't like human women." Raife spoke the obvious, but his face was pale, his eyes betraying him, showing fear he clearly had never experienced in the same way before. "They're cursed, but different."

"Eve and her descendants were cursed with the pain of childbirth." Sibyl sighed, lamenting her own women's curse, remembering the women she'd seen die birthing their young. "Always afraid of pain and death."

"Aye." Raife's eyes clouded. "But Lilith was a'cursed as the bearer of demon seed. "

"Demons… are you demons then?" she murmured, frowning at the thought. She'd seen drawn depictions of demons with horns and red skin. These wulvers, whatever they were, did not appear evil, or even unnatural. Although, in their human form, the way Raife appeared in front of her now, they seemed extra-human, as if they'd been taken directly from the pages of some ancient text.

"We are what we are." Raife sighed. "Some of us accept that better'n others."

"Darrow…?" She met his eyes, questioning. There was something in Raife's tone that made her think of his brother and Raife nodded sadly.

"Darrow and Laina, too." He glanced toward the door, as if his brother might be standing there, listening to what he had to say. "They believe they can change the way we are. But we've always been this way and always will be."

"Change…?" Sibyl frowned. "How?"

"Tis a silly legend." Raife waved the idea away. "Chasin' rainbows. There's supposed to be a plant that can keep wulvers from changin' into wolves. The huluppa tree."

"The… that's… a type of willow, isn't it?" Sibyl remembered it from her teachings with the healer and her father. They had taught her to read and identify all the names of the plants.

"They've gone out, searchin' the woods fer it," Raife said, his eyes hardening at the thought. "That's where they were when she was caught. I told 'im she should'na be out, so close t'pup."

"It is supposed to keep you from changing?" Sibyl tried to remember everything she knew about the huluppa. It was just another variation of willow, although it wasn't anywhere near as abundant as some of the others. "Willow… willow is a pain reliever. But it keeps the blood from clotting!"

Sibyl sat straight up, eyes wide.

"Was she eating the willow?" Sibyl gasped. "That explains why she was bleeding so much!"

"And it did'na even work." Raife scoffed, shaking his dark head. "She still changed."

"I wonder…" Sibyl considered the possibilities. Could a plant really stop a wulver's transformation, like barley stopped burns or buckbean killed intestinal worms?

"I know Laina thinks tis unfair. And she's reason to fear the change. Males can change at will," Raife explained. "Females… they have no choice. They change when they pup. They change when they go into heat."

"Heat?" Sibyl cocked her head, trying to work out what he was saying, and then she understood, feeling her own cheeks filling with heat.

"Moon blood…?" he explained, smiling at the way her cheeks pinked up.

"Menses." Sibyl blushed even brighter, saying the word in a man's presence. Even she knew you didn't talk about such things in front of menfolk. But she couldn't help thinking about Laina—poor Laina. She was tied more to her body and its cycles than Sibyl had ever thought about being. And here she'd believed *she* was limited by her gender!

"I will look for this willow before I am on my way," Sibyl decided with sudden determination. She would help Laina and her kind, if she could. It would be good to liberate the wulver woman from her gender's prison, even if she couldn't change her own.

"Ye'll go t'sleep and we'll talk more on th'morrow." Raife was giving orders again. He stood, an imposing figure in his plaid, thick arms crossed over his broad chest.

"I will find it." Sibyl's chin stuck out in defiance, more determined than ever.

"I b'lieve ye." He chuckled, turning to go. "Thank ye for what ye did fer her. She's as much like a sister to me as Darrow's brother."

"And Kirstin?" Sibyl's cheeks reddened when Raife hesitated at the doorway to turn and look at her. She didn't know why she'd asked, but the words had escaped her mouth before she could stop them.

"Kirstin?" Raife smiled, looking amused. "What about 'er, lass?"

"I just… noticed the way she looked at you." Sibyl squirmed on the bed, feeling his gaze pinned on her. She couldn't help but notice the way Kirstin looked at him, like he was some sort of a god, or God himself. Not that she blamed the girl, not in the least.

"And what way's that?"

"The way a woman… looks at a man… who…" she stammered.

Oh damn him, she thought, unable to get the rest of the words out.

"I've no mate, Sibyl," he told her, his words soft but clear, those blue, blue eyes trained right on her, seeing into her, into parts and places she had yet to even explore herself. "There's no woman or wulver who's been marked by me."

Marked. She wanted to know what that meant, but she was afraid to ask.

"G'nite, lass." He moved to close the door but Sibyl stopped him once again with her words.

"Where are you going?" she called.

"I'll be right outside," he assured her, smiling around the door's edge.

"In that drafty tunnel hallway?" She frowned, glancing around the big room, noting a thick lamb's wool rug by the fire. It would do nicely. Besides, even if she was a little afraid of him, she was more afraid of what was out there, beyond the closed door. She thought she might actually feel safer with him here, in the room. "No. Sleep here. I insist."

"Here?" His eyebrows went up when he looked at her and Sibyl swallowed at the heat in his gaze. "Wit' ye?"

"Oh, I mean…" She blinked, biting her lip. "You can sleep by the fire. Or have another mattress brought in…"

"Yer reputation will'na survive 'til mornin', lass," Raife said softly. The look in his eyes warmed her from head to toe and she tried to ignore her body's response.

"My reputation?" Sibyl gave a short, strangled laugh. The memory of Alistair and her uncle and their concern for her reputation seemed very far away in this strange place. "I don't care about my reputation any longer."

"Ye'll," he assured her with a short nod. "If ye want to return to yer world."

If. Not when, if. As if it was a question. And was it? She wondered. She wouldn't have thought twice about it a few hours ago, would have jumped on the first horse she could find and rode hell-bent on getting away from this place, away from Scotland, away. Away.

But she had been so focused on running away, she hadn't considered where she might be running to.

"I'll be right outside," he told her again, once more pulling at the door.

And Sibyl interrupted him yet again.

"This is silly!" she exclaimed, throwing her hands up in helpless desperation. "This room is big, there's a fire. You can't sleep in the hallway. You'll catch your death!"

"No." His gaze didn't move from her face, his eyes saying so much, his mouth so little. "I can'na sleep in 'ere."

"Why not?" she protested.

"Because…" He hesitated just a moment before finishing his sentence. "I can'na trust myself around ye."

"Trust yourself…" She laughed again, she couldn't help it. "To do what? Not eat me?"

He smiled back at her, but there was no humor in it. In fact, the look in his eyes told her he was far from joking. Everything about him bespoke of the seriousness of his words, even though they might have been spoken in jest.

"That's na'what I'm hungry fer when I look at ye, lass."

Sibyl couldn't answer that. There weren't words. She felt the heat of his gaze on her body as if he had touched her with his admission, as if he'd undressed her in an instant and had his way with her. She couldn't move, she couldn't breathe. She couldn't even think.

He seemed to understand her sudden silence. That understanding was in his gaze as he dropped it to the floor and murmured, “G’nite,” for one final time before he pulled the door closed.

Chapter Six

It felt as if no time had passed at all when Kirstin knocked and entered her room in the morning. Maybe it was because it was still dark—there were no windows here, no sunlight streamed in to tickle her nose. Sibyl was still bone-tired but she got up, knowing she had a long way to walk today. And the next. And the day after that. She had no idea how long it was going to take to get back to Rose's village, but however long it took her, she was going to have to stay off the roads, avoid Alistair's men, and somehow stay dry, warm and fed.

Had Raife meant it when he said he would escort her wherever she wanted to go? There were no horses here, but if she could travel on a wolf, or even with one, she would feel far safer. The thought of traveling with him made her feel warm, even in spite of the room's early morning chill.

"G'mornin!" Kirstin called out, smiling as she put a tray onto the table.

"Good morning." Sibyl stretched and yawned and ventured out, stomach clenching in hunger the moment she smelled the food.

There was a bowl full of something like porridge, a few slices of bread, some soft cheese, and a tin cup of milk. She sat at the table, spooning in delicious mouthfuls of porridge—there was dried fruit, seeds and nuts in it—as Kirstin stoked the fire. It had died down to embers overnight.

"Ye can wear these while yer here." Kirstin held up the plaid and leather belt Sibyl had taken off the night before, the same one she'd worn to tend Laina. "We're doin' our best t'wash and mend yer dress."

"Thank you." Sibyl made a face just thinking about that green velvet dress. "How is Laina this morning?"

"Better, thanks t'ye." Kirstin smiled her gratitude.

Sibyl let the girl dress her. She would have insisted on doing it herself, but she wasn't familiar with how it all worked. The plaid had loops the belt went through, and then the belt cinched at her waist, over the shirt she'd worn to bed. It was all very convenient, she thought, as Kirstin arranged the plaid fabric over her shoulder, tucking it back into the belt.

"I feel naked," Sibyl murmured, glancing down at her bare legs and feet. She touched her long, uncovered hair. She wasn't used to going around without some sort of head covering. It was common in Scotland, she'd noticed, but English ladies didn't go out without a hat. Kirstin had taken her corset along with her dress, and Sibyl discovered she could take a full breath for the first time in months. She hadn't felt this free in a long time.

"Ye look lovely." Kirstin combed Sibyl's hair as she finished eating her porridge and drank her milk. It was goat's milk, rich and delicious. "Are ye sure ye don'na have Scots blood in ye? Yer hair's as red as a rooster's crown!"

"Mayhaps, somewhere back in my family tree." Sibyl smiled. "Although my mother would faint if she heard me say it."

She didn't like thinking about her mother. Or her home. She didn't have a home anymore, not really. Whatever connection she might have maintained between herself and the place she'd grown up had disappeared the moment she'd decided to run away. Whatever her life had been before, it would never be again.

"My dress will be ready soon?" Sibyl looked at her hopefully. Even if she didn't wear it, she realized she could sell it for the cloth alone and pay for food for her trip, if she could find a buyer. She tried to remember the places they had passed on their journey over the border, if there had been anywhere promising she might sell a velvet gown.

"I had 'em take it out into the sun t'dry." Kirstin put more wood on the fire. The room had grown cool overnight and she wondered if they had to keep a fire going all day, even in the summer. The mountain retained the cold and Sibyl wasn't used to being bare-legged. She was actually shivering.

"Sun?" Sibyl cocked her head as she tied her soft-soled shoes, wishing she had a pair of riding boots instead. "Outside?"

"A'course outside." Kirstin laughed, taking Sibyl's tray and heading toward the door. "Raife was askin' after ye. Would ye like me t'take ye t'im?"

Sibyl nodded, standing and following Kirstin out of the room. It was time to go, she decided, with or without an escort. She didn't know if Raife had been serious about taking her wherever she wanted, but she wouldn't turn down his offer, if he made it again.

They made their way through the tunnels and Sibyl kept as close to Kirstin as she could. They passed people, men and women all dressed in plaid, and a few wolves too, which made her shrink instinctively toward the cool tunnel walls.

"They will'na hurt ye," Kirstin assured her as they traveled deeper into the mountain. "Raife has guaranteed yer safety."

"I'm not so sure Darrow is going to listen to him," Sibyl muttered, remembering how Raife's brother had glared at her and argued with him, even if she had helped his wife the night before. Darrow didn't like her presence, didn't want her there.

"Raife leads our pack," Kirstin informed her. "Even if Darrow does'na like it, he'll follow. He must."

It didn't surprise Sibyl in the least that Raife was their leader.

"So you…" Sibyl cleared her throat, thinking of how to phrase the question as they went through the busy dining hall. There were people still sitting at long tables, talking in Gaelic, laughing together, eating breakfast. "Raife mentioned that you don't… eat… people?"

"Not for a verra long time. Tis against the pact," Kirstin said as they passed through the kitchen. "We jus' wanna live peaceful here."

"And all the swords?" Sibyl eyed a rack of them, literally hundreds of blades, as they passed into a tunnel. If these men were peaceful, their weaponry told a different story.

"Our men are trained as warriors, tis true." Kirstin shrugged as they neared the end of the tunnel. There was sunlight there, at the end of the darkness. "But they do'na fight unless they have ta."

The sun was welcome and Sibyl turned her face up to it, breathing in the cool mountain air. There were women washing clothes to the right, standing barefoot in a stream. The valley they entered was covered in green, spotted with the purple of heather, and in the middle of it all was a sight that made Sibyl gasp aloud.

"Have ye not seen the warriors?" Kirstin glanced back in surprise at Sibyl as she shrank toward the opening in the side of the mountain, but she couldn't have been any more surprised than Sibyl was herself.

I'm not going to faint again, Sibyl told herself, leaning against the solid rock, the world tilting sideways as she watched the half-men, half-wolves wielding their swords against each other in the early morning sunlight, the sound of steel against steel ringing over the mountain. As strange a sight as it was, Sibyl spotted Raife instantly, his long, dark hair trailing behind him in waves as he half growled, half roared and leapt completely over his opponent.

She didn't know how she recognized him, because his face wasn't his own—his snout was long, his canine teeth sharp as he snarled and swung his sword behind him to catch and stop the other half-wolf's blow. But she did. She knew him instantly.

Her heart stopped, her knees wobbled, hands trembling as she brought them to her quivering mouth. The big half-wolf—he seemed twice his human size to Sibyl from here—sniffed the air, eyes flashing and ears twitching as those blue eyes turned their way.

He was a wolf from the neck up, but his body was the same—broad, tanned chest, ridged abdomen, the muscles in his back taut as he kept his opponent's sword at bay. Raife's heavily muscled thighs bulged as he twisted and avoided the swing of the other wolf-man's weapon. The sound of steel striking rock rang through the valley and Sibyl gasped as Raife gave a low, keening howl, shaking his head quickly from side to side.

One moment he was a wolf—half a wolf, at any rate—and the next he was changed back to a man, tossing his heavy sword aside with a scowl as he approached. The other wolf-man did the same, and she saw that Raife had been fighting with his brother, Darrow.

"I told ye to come get me when she woke," Raife snapped at Kirstin.

"Did ye?" She blinked at him and Sibyl sensed something pass between them. Clearly Kirstin had defied his wishes. "She wanted to come outside. Didn't ye, Lady Sibyl?"

"I did ask," Sibyl admitted, blinking at him in surprise. "I thought, mayhaps, I should go soon…?"

"I must speak wit ye." Raife gave a slow nod, glancing at Kirstin, eyes narrowing briefly.

He held out his hand to Sibyl and she hesitated only a moment before taking it. She tried to ignore the heat in her cheeks as she did so, letting him help her over the rocks, trying to ignore the eyes on them as Raife led her away from the mountain. The women doing wash watched them, whispering behind their hands. Kirstin had gone over to join them and Sibyl knew the girl must be telling them all about their strange human interloper and her odd ways.

She'd expected to be a stranger in a strange land when her uncle had informed her she would be a Scotsman's English bride, but she had never expected anything like this.

They walked down the sloping hill and up another. There were no more rocks to clamber over, but Raife didn't let go of his steadying hand as they made their way over the crest. When Sibyl looked back, she noticed they were out of the line of sight of the rest of the pack, although she could hear the women singing and the ring of steel as swords began clashing again.

"Did we scare ye?" Raife asked, glancing down at her.

"No." She was lying, but just a little. She had started to get used to this world, as strange as it was. "I don't scare easily."

"Tis true." He smiled, stopping as they neared a tree, leaning against the trunk to look down at her. He still held her hand in his, thumb rubbing over the top of her knuckles. "Ye're a brave lil lass."

"Was there something you wanted to speak to me about?" She swallowed, looking up, way up, into his observant blue eyes.

"I've some bad news for ye." He glanced back the way they'd come, brow knitted, jaw working. "I sent scouts out early, before dawn. I'm afraid…"

"He's looking for me." She knew it was true. Of course it was. Alistair wasn't going to give up that easy.

"I can'na let ye go." Raife's hand swallowed hers. "Til I'm sure tis safe."

"Raife…" She blinked up at him, feeling strange in her Scot's plaid, especially the way he looked at her in it. This was not her home, these were not her people. "I cannot stay here. I must be away."

"Where'll ye go?" He reached out to brush a stray strand of auburn hair away from her cheek, looking concerned. "Is there someone waitin' for ye, lass?"

Their eyes met and she knew he was thinking about Alistair. So was she. Her betrothed would certainly be looking for her, although he wouldn't want to marry her, not anymore. Or mayhaps he would, still—only to make her life a living hell. That would be more

Alistair's predilection and if the thought of being married to him had repelled her before, it terrified her now. She could never allow herself to be brought before him again, in any capacity.

"I'd keep ye safe." Raife's eyes were so expressive and his heart was in them. "If… if there's no one who already has claim on ye."

She hesitated, considering his words. She knew what he was asking and was afraid to answer him, to tell him the truth. He knew she'd been promised to Alistair—but he also knew she didn't want that marriage. She had run away from it, straight into this man's world, but in her rush to escape, she hadn't thought past her immediate future. She couldn't go home to England, not to her mother and her uncle. She knew she would never see them again, after what she had done.

She wasn't just an interloper, an Englishwoman in Scotland, she was now a human in a world full of strange creatures, forever a stranger in a strange land, unwelcome. She had no home, not anymore, and never would again, she realized with a slow, dawning horror. She would spend the rest of her life hiding—what did it matter, then, where she did so?

"No," Sibyl said softly, swallowing hard. "There is no one."

"Then stay." He took her other hand in his, so he was holding them both.

She glanced down at them, and then up into those impossibly blue eyes. She was thinking about Laina and her baby and the change that came over the she-wolf, unbidden, putting her into sudden, grave danger in a world that didn't understand her kind. She thought of God's curses and didn't doubt for a moment that he was a man like Alistair, someone who craved power but never did anything to earn it. She'd been raised a good Christian, a good girl, and where had that gotten her?

Sold into matrimonial slavery to a stranger, that's where.

Sibyl felt the rough callouses on Raife's hands, looked up at the kindness in his eyes, and thought she could stay here. She could, at least for a while. Mayhaps she could be of some use in this place. She might even stumble across the plant that could change all of their lives, relieve them of the curse of living this way, hidden in the side of a mountain.

Maybe they could help each other, Sibyl thought, meeting Raife's kind, searching eyes.

And maybe, she realized, they weren't that different after all.

"Ye're welcome 'ere, ye ken?" Raife rubbed his thumbs over Sibyl's knuckles, looking down at her hands in his.

"Thank you." She couldn't express her gratitude to him, not really.

How strange it was, to be grateful to be welcomed in a place no human even knew existed.

How strange it was, to be so suddenly alone, so estranged from the world, she no longer belonged anywhere at all.

How strange it was to hold a man's hand who had, just a few moments earlier, been wielding a sword as some fantastical creature, the stuff of legend come to life.

How strange it was, to look up at this half-man, half-wolf, and feel things she never had before, things that scared her more deeply than wolves or even the threat of capture or death.

How strange it all was.

How strange indeed.

It didn't take as long as she expected to adjust to living with a pack of wolves. Or, wulvers, as Raife often reminded her. Sibyl was surprised how kind and welcoming they all were. She'd never been one to spend her time idly, even back home, and so it was easy to ingratiate herself to the wulver women by offering to help cook, do laundry, and take care of the pups. She thought it was funny how they called them pups, even though they were really all human babies, once they were born.

It took her only a day to insist Kirstin stop bringing her meals on trays, treating her like—and calling her—"Lady Sibyl." She was tired of titles, tired of pretending to be a "proper highborn lady." She'd had enough of that with the MacFalons. With the wulvers, she could be more fully herself than she'd ever been in her life. Here, they didn't think twice about her ability to shoot a longbow or ride a horse astride—they had those too. The wulver warriors trained on them, riding through the valley, their hooves tearing up the heather.

She was free to come and go as she pleased, either in the valley or within the mountain, but the sentry on duty had warned her, and so had Raife, that she wouldn't be allowed to depart the tunnel. It was for her own safety, Raife said, and she believed him. Alistair's men were out looking for her and had come as far south as the mountains. But even if Alistair and his men found the entrance to their mountain, the sentries could hold them off until the warriors arrived to defend the den. Besides, the entrance was hidden, deep down, and there was an enormous rock that could block it, if need be. Raife had assured her they were safe here.

Sibyl took one look at the wolfen warriors swinging their swords and claymores and believed him without a doubt. She'd been a little afraid of them at first, even after they'd changed back into men and put away their swords, but once they all gathered for a meal in the dining hall at the center of the mountain, laughing and joking and talking—in Gaelic of course—Sibyl found herself relaxing.

The only one she was still wary of was Darrow. She didn't see him much for the first week or so. Kirstin took meals in to Laina and he stayed with her much of the time, eating meals in their room. She only saw him out on the training field while she helped the women herd the sheep, feed the pigs and goats, or do the laundry, standing barefoot in the cold stream, beating shirts and plaids against the rocks. She tried avoiding Darrow's gaze as much as possible, but it was funny, every time she looked up, it was Raife she saw, keeping a close eye on her.

Every night, she would ask Raife, when he knocked on her door to check on her, to say goodnight, if Alistair's men had given up, and every night, he would shake his head, a sad look coming into his eyes. At first she thought it was because he didn't like disappointing her, but as time wore on, she wondered if, perhaps, it was because she was asking at all. Asking meant she wanted to leave, didn't it? And the truth was, the more time she spent with the wulvers, the exact opposite was true.

So she stopped asking Raife, but she still desired to know, so she gathered up her courage and started asking Darrow. Whenever she saw him, she felt his dark gaze, an unspoken hostility emanating from him. Raife said he'd accepted her, that he wouldn't challenge his pack leader's decision to allow her to stay, but she wasn't so sure about that. Darrow led the men every day out of the mountain to look for any signs of the Scots and clan MacFalon. He was the one who would know.

It was on her first visit to see Laina after the birth she dared to ask him. She thought she would visit during the morning hours, when the men trained out in the valley and she knew Darrow would be out there. Laina was happy to see her, sitting up on her mattress, nursing the baby. She was still too pale, but the cut beneath her collarbone was healing and she smiled and beckoned when Sibyl knocked.

"Such a beautiful baby," Sibyl exclaimed, smiling as she looked down at the child's sleeping face. He looked so much like Darrow and Raife, with that slight indent in his chin and those full red lips. And that hair. All that thick, dark hair. "I've never seen a child with so much hair!"

"All wulvers have thick hair on their heads," Laina smiled, brushing the baby's locks away from his face.

"But nowhere else, I noticed," Sibyl replied, flushing at her own observation.

"Noticed, did ye?" Laina grinned, showing a row of straight, brightly white teeth. Sibyl noted their canines were just slightly longer than most humans. She blushed even more when Laina's fair brows went up and she cocked her head to look at Sibyl knowingly at her comment. "Aye, tis true. Jus' t'hair on our heads—til we change."

Sibyl hid her shudder. She was used to living with the wulvers now, but the transformation from wolf to human and back again still disturbed her.

"An' I wish we did'na." Laina sighed, leaning over to kiss the babe in her arms as he fell completely asleep at the breast, his lips sticky with milk.

Laina didn't seem to care that she was uncovered. Modesty was the last thing the wulvers seemed to care about, Sibyl had noticed. Maybe if she'd grown up the way they had, changing from human to wolf, she wouldn't care about clothes either. Kilts seemed the perfect solution, as they could tie them around their necks or waists and cover what they needed. There weren't any bothersome buttons or laces.

"Change, you mean? You wish you didn't change?" Sibyl frowned, pushing Laina back onto the mattress when she went to rise to put the baby in his cradle. It was wooden, small, and close to the floor, where the mattress was. The only raised bed in the mountain was in Raife's room—the one Sibyl had been sleeping in every night. The rest of the wulvers slept on the floor on mattresses or rugs, rolled up in their plaids.

Sibyl took the baby, careful not to wake him, and put him in his cradle next to his mother. He stirred just slightly, settling on his stomach, sucking his fist in his sleep. He was a big boy already, growing fast, she noted.

"Ye do'na know." Laina shook her head sadly, stroking the baby's damp head. There was a fire going and the room was quite warm. "I'm so glad he's a boy and not a girl."

"Why?" Sibyl rankled at her words. How often had her own father wished she was a different gender? She couldn't count how many times she'd heard it. It seemed, to her, having a gender preference one way or the other just made life more difficult between parent and child.

"Boys, they can choose, ye ken?" Laina lifted those incredibly blue eyes—all the wulvers had those same eyes—to meet her own. "Girls, we can'na."

Sibyl remembered what Raife had told her about the wulvers, about Lilith's curse, although she wasn't really sure what to believe. It was like listening to the bible stories about Noah and the flood, or Jonah and the whale. Even as a child, Sibyl had questioned such tales. How could all of God's creatures fit in one boat, even an enormous one? How could a man survive for three days in the belly of a whale? Even the story of the Garden of Eden seemed, to her, just another way the church made everything appear a woman's fault.

"And boy wulvers, they can turn into those... halflings? Half-wolf, half-man?" Sibyl remembered seeing Darrow and Raife wielding their swords, growling and snapping at once another. "But women can't?"

"Aye," Laina agreed, leaning back against the mountain wall behind her. She was tiring, Sibyl noted, and told herself she'd take her leave soon and let the new mother rest. "If only I could find the huluppa."

"It's dangerous for you to take willow," Sibyl reminded her, shaking her head vehemently. "It's the reason you nearly bled to death. Please don't take any more."

"It'll be safe, now he's birthed." Laina's shoulders straightened, eyes narrowing, face determined. "I'll find it. Tis out there. I know tis."

Chasing rainbows. That's what Raife had said, Sibyl remembered. But Laina seemed very determined to find the plant that might keep her from changing from human to wolf and back again.

"But it's *not* safe," Sibyl insisted. "You can't go out there anymore. You have a child to care for."

"Not when I've turned," Laina said bitterly. "Once me moon-blood returns, I'm at the mercy of me cycles again. I will'na even be able t'care for 'im when I'm changed."

It was a horrible predicament, Sibyl thought. So very unfair.

"What do wulver women do, then?" Sibyl wondered aloud.

"We care fer each other's bairns," Laina replied with a sigh. "But we're all a'the mercy of t'moon and our cycles. If'n we could choose…"

Oh what a great freedom it would be, Sibyl thought, if *any* woman could choose. Wulvers and humans weren't so different after all, she realized.

That's when Darrow came into the room, opening the big door. Sibyl still wondered at the strength and craftsmanship it had taken, to carve out rooms in the caverns, to create doors and fireplaces. Sibyl froze in place, still sitting beside the baby's cradle, her gaze meeting Darrow's. His expression changed when he saw Sibyl, smile fading, eyes hardening to glittering points, sharp, blue jewels.

"I… should go." She got to her feet, moving toward the door, toward escape. Of course, that meant moving toward Darrow, which required a great deal of courage on her part.

"Ye do'na'ave t'go, Sibyl," Laina protested, holding a hand out to her husband. He went to her, moving past Sibyl, and she breathed a sigh of relief when he sat beside his wife on the mattress, when he was no longer between Sibyl and the door. "We're jus' talkin'bout findin' the huluppa, Darrow. He's been helpin' me look fer it."

Laina reached out to touch her husband's cheek, a look of love passing between them that made something buzz like bees in Sibyl's lower belly. She'd seen men and women look at each other with love before—even lust, she thought, remembering Rose—but this was different. There was a connection between the two of them that made human lust, and even love, seem infinitesimal in comparison.

"I can help you find it." The words come out of her mouth without a second thought. She'd told Raife she would help Laina find it, and if she had to be there, why not? "I know plants and herbs very well. I was taught by a healer and an apothecary. That's how I knew what would help stop your bleeding."

"Aye?" Laina's fair, arched brows went up in surprise. "Oh, Sibyl, you do'na know wha't'would mean t'me!"

"Laina, mayhaps, now t'bairn's birthed…" Darrow hesitated, glancing at the baby asleep in his cradle. Sibyl knew, from the look on Darrow's face, what he was thinking, the words he didn't say. He wanted her to stop looking for the plant, that much was clear, but he was torn. He could see how much it meant to her. So could Sibyl. "I do'na wanna leave ye."

"But she'll help ye, Darrow!" Laina turned shining eyes to her husband, ignoring his unspoken message. "I know ye'll find it!"

"Mayhaps." Darrow frowned, turning his gaze back to Sibyl again, still standing in the doorway.

"With Alistair's men still looking for me, though…" Sibyl bit her lip, meeting Darrow's eyes.

They were as blue as the rest of the wulvers, but they could darken, like his brother's, like the sky when it was ready to storm. They were dark now.

"Aye, he's lookin' fer ye." Darrow frowned. "But I'll keep ye safe, if'n ye're really willin' t'go out and look wit' me, lass."

"I'd be happy to, while I'm here," Sibyl agreed, smiling at Laina. If it would keep the woman from roaming the woods in search of the elusive plant, Sibyl really would be happy to do it. Although she didn't relish riding out into the woods with Darrow. But he wouldn't hurt her—not with Sibyl under his brother's protection. Would he?

"Thank ye, lass." Darrow gave her a nod. "I'll come fer ye on t'morrow. After trainin', ya ken?"

"That would be fine." Sibyl nodded, shutting the door behind her.

She walked back toward her room, thinking about Darrow's obvious distaste of her. Even after she'd saved Laina's life—twice—the man didn't seem to like her. She wondered at it. Most of the wulvers had gone out of their way to make her feel as at home as possible. They didn't tease her about her English accent, like the Scotsmen at Alistair's castle had. They didn't make fun of her penchant for baths like the Scottish, or her insistence on things like her own silverware and tin drinking cup. Of course, Raife had a lot to do with that, she knew. He, too, had gone out of his way to make her feel as at-home as possible.

Sibyl opened the door to her room, thinking mayhaps, if she went out into the woods with Darrow, looking for the elusive huluppa, he might eventually warm to her. She couldn't figure out if it was because she was English, or human, or what. She was so lost in thought, she didn't notice the door to the hot spring cavern was open, the orange glow of a torch lighting the way. She didn't notice until Raife stepped into the room, his long, dark hair wet, his body beaded with water in the low light of the fire.

He was stark naked, his plaid just thrown over his shoulder, hiding nothing. They stared at each other, unblinking. Sibyl felt her cheeks redden and knew she should look away, but she didn't. The man's body was as hard as rock, chiseled like granite, shoulders wide, chest hairless but thick, his waist narrowing, abdomen so ridged it was like a mountain range in its own right. Sibyl followed the terrain of his body with her gaze, the water running down his tawny skin in little rivers, seeing that Laina had been wrong about the wulvers being completely hairless except for the locks on their head. Raife had a thick, dark patch of hair between his legs, the snake there slowly rising to point in her direction.

"Sibyl." He said her name, sounding hoarse, and cleared his throat as he slowly pulled his plaid down to wrap the length of tartan fabric around his waist. "Kirstin said ye were visitin' wit' Laina. I jus' wanted t'soak in the spring…"

"Of course, it's your room." She cleared her own throat, finally averting her gaze, but of course it was far too late. She'd seen everything—again. Just like when he'd taken off his plaid in the middle of the woods before he changed from man to wolf. Except this time she'd seen him from the front. She'd seen far more than any woman should see of a man—unless she happened to be married to him, Sibyl supposed. "I should… go… I…"

"Tis me who should be leavin'." Raife shook his wet head, giving her a sheepish smile. "I should'na've come in wit'out askin' ye. I'm sorry, lass."

"No, it's your room," she said again, keeping her gaze focused on his face, although that wasn't much better, because those strikingly blue eyes said everything he was thinking. Everything she was thinking. Everything she knew she shouldn't want—that no good, Christian girl should want from anyone besides her husband. And she didn't have a husband. She had narrowly escaped that fate.

But looking at Raife made her think of all the things Rose had whispered to her about men, about their hands on her, about the way they growled and thrust and took what they wanted. Being around Raife made her feel wanton, sinful, depraved. It was a wholly unfamiliar feeling, but not completely unpleasant.

"Tis yers, while ye're here," he reminded her again as he strode toward the door. He kept saying that, had given up his room for her, but slept every night somewhere outside that door, keeping watch. It was both comforting and disconcerting.

"Raife..." She touched his arm, still wet from his bath, but his skin was warm. Her eyes lifted to meet his, almost forgetting what she wanted to ask the man. His presence was always disarming to her, but now, with him wet and half-naked and looking at her like he could literally eat her alive—and she had no doubt he could do it—he made her forget everything.

"Why does Darrow hate me?" she asked softly, finally regaining her speech.

"He does'na hate ye." Raife's brow knitted in concern. His gaze fell to his arm where she touched him, the heat between them palpable. "But he... he does'na like the English. And t'one thing he hates more'n the English is a MacFalon."

"I'm not a MacFalon," Sibyl reminded him.

"Nuh." Raife smiled. She loved his smile. It made her feel warm from head to toe. "I tol' me brother 'bout the arrow ye put through the man's arm."

"It should have been through his heart," Sibyl said darkly. Every time she thought of Alistair, she felt murderous.

"Nuh, lass." He shook his head, covering her hand with his own, making hers disappear. "T'would've started a war. Ye did the right thin'. The clan'll stop huntin' fer ye soon enough."

"And then I can go…" She hesitated, the word "home" on her lips but not uttered. There was no home. Not anymore.

"Aye." He had that sad look in his eyes again. Did he really not want her to go? "When tis safe. But not til then."

She nodded, taking a step back as he reached to open the door. He stopped, glancing back at her, and she thought she might faint at the look in his eyes, there was so much fire in them.

"Darrow'll come 'round," he said softly before he closed the door behind him.

She didn't say anything. She couldn't. She suddenly understood the way his gaze followed her, what it meant. He looked at her, Sibyl suddenly realized, like she'd seen Darrow look at Laina.

Like a wulver looked at his mate.

Chapter Seven

The wulvers were the best family she'd ever had. Sibyl often thought this as she drifted off to sleep, going over the events of the day, which were always interesting. It had taken some getting used to seeing a wolf's head on a man's body, hearing a man speak through a wolf's mouth, but she could enter the valley without a second thought now as the wolfen warriors trained. It took her a little longer to get used to seeing the flash of a wolf's eyes in the darkness of a mountain tunnel, but she'd spent long enough with them to know none of them meant her harm.

She didn't know when it had happened, but at some point, the wulvers' mountain and valley had started to feel like home. And everywhere she went, every which way she looked, Raife was there, watching her. Watching over her. He seemed to think of himself as her personal protector, and that's why, when Sibyl started going out into the forest with Darrow, Raife had completely lost it.

Darrow had come for her as he said he would, and while Sibyl knew what Raife's response would be, she had gone anyway. She hadn't asked him—and she'd known, in her heart, that the pack leader wouldn't have allowed it if she had. So she had simply agreed, putting her arms around Darrow's neck, letting him carry her into the woods where she had left her past behind.

She spent the ride with her face buried against his fur, not knowing what she was more afraid of, Alistair's men finding them, the thought Darrow might be taking her into the woods to do away with her, or the knowledge she was going to have to return and face Raife's wrath. Of course, so would Darrow, she knew. He must really love his wife, she thought, as the big gray wolf slowed and then stopped near a small stream. It was hardly a trickle compared to the rushing one she and Raife had crossed to escape their pursuers, but it was the place Laina said they'd found the other willow.

"That's not huluppa," Sibyl said, knowing it right away. She was already off the wolf's back, inspecting the leaves. They were too wide and broad, a deeper green. Of course, she'd only seen huluppa in the apothecary's books and was going from memory alone.

"Tis the stuff Laina took back wit' us last time," Darrow said, coming up behind her as Sibyl inspected the tall tree. She glanced back, seeing he'd changed—from wolf to man, and into his plaid, which had been secured around his neck as they rode through the woods. His face darkened at the thought. "The stuff that nearly killed 'er."

"It was the willow. I'm sure of it," Sibyl agreed, frowning, fingering the leaves. "It will make anyone bleed more heavily, even though it takes away pain. It worries me."

"Aye." Darrow followed her as Sibyl made her way down the little stream. "And me."

"But you still brought me out here to look for it?" She puzzled over this as she unslung her satchel, gathering agrimony. It wasn't huluppa, but it was good for stopping a bleed and always good to have on hand. She'd already started teaching Kirstin and the old midwife, Beitris, about herbs.

"She's me mate." Darrow shrugged one bare shoulder. The marking there matched the one on

Laina's thigh and hip. It was intricate symbolism, a sign they were mates.

"You love her." Sibyl couldn't help the smile that came over her face as she gathered feverfew, putting that in her satchel too. It was good for indigestion.

"Aye." The look in Darrow's eyes said everything.

They walked up and down the stream, Sibyl inspecting the plants, warning Darrow against the touching the henbane. It was poisonous.

"Aye, wulvers have a keen nose." Darrow made a face, stepping around the poisonous plant. "Tis why I thought we'd've found it by now."

"It is curious." Sibyl frowned, cocking her head—she thought she heard something—but Darrow was already near, reaching for the dirk tucked away in his plaid as he put a protective arm around her from behind.

"Alistair…?" she whispered, glad for his embrace because she felt dizzy. There were men moving through the woods. It was far off, distant, but she knew the sound.

"Ye've good ears, lass." Darrow grinned, cocking his head as he looked down at her. "Those're reavers."

"Thieves?" She shivered, remembering Alistair and Donal constantly complaining about the reavers, the thieves who raided their cattle and poached game on their lands at the border.

"Ye're safe wit' me," Darrow assured her, sheathing his dirk again. "They steal from the MacFalons. They hate the English. And the MacFalons are more English than Scots now."

"You hate the English, too," she replied softly as Darrow let her go again and they resumed their hunt for the elusive huluppa, heading downstream together. "And the MacFalons."

"Aye," Darrow agreed and she saw the hard look on his face. It made her sad and a little afraid. She was English, after all.

"Why?" she asked, kneeling down to pluck soapwort from the roots. It was perfect for washing clothes. "I thought there was some sort of a pact…?"

She'd heard tell of this pact, but didn't know any real details. She just knew there seemed to be some sort of peace pact between the wulvers and the MacFalons.

"Aye, me father brokered the deal." Darrow stopped, waiting for her. "Twas a mistake I'd sorely like t'undo."

"But… wouldn't that mean war between the wulvers and the MacFalons?" She shaded her eyes against the sun, looking up at him.

"I'd rather fight a war," he snarled. "We train e'eryday fer war but ne'er fight."

"King Henry seems to want peace." She stood, slinging her satchel over her shoulder and picking her way along the stream. "That's why I was promised to Alistair MacFalon."

"King Henry wants lands an'titles, like all the English."

"What do Scots want?" she asked, glancing over her shoulder. Darrow was far more sure footed than she was.

"A good woman, a warm bed, and food in their bellies." He grinned at her and she couldn't help but laugh.

"And wulvers?"

"The same, I s'pose." He shrugged, still smiling. He had a nice smile, like his brother's, just a little more lopsided.

"Not lands and titles like the horrible English?" she teased.

"We're not interested in titles." Darrow scoffed at the idea. "We have our land."

They had a whole kingdom inside a mountain. Sibyl was still in awe of their tunnels, their rich valley. And their family. The pack. They were closer than anyone she'd ever known. They were laid back and laughed out loud and long like the Scots she'd experienced when she was staying with the MacFalons, but there was a loyalty and close-knitted connection in the wulvers' den she'd never seen anywhere else.

"I do'na think all the English are horrible, lass." Darrow's words stopped her.

"Just me then?" She wasn't laughing and neither was he.

"Ye saved Laina's life," he said, reminding them both. "I'm grateful to ye."

"So you've said." She gave a little nod. "But still, you look at me like I was a chamber pot and you'd like to toss me out a window."

He threw back his head and laughed. She couldn't help laughing too. It seemed to break something up between them, something that had been in the way, like a mountain crumbling to the ground under a force of nature.

"Not so bad as that," Darrow told her.

"No?" Sibyl was still smiling, but she doubted his veracity. She'd seen the way he looked at her.

"Ye bein' wit' us, lass, livin' wit' us, in our den?" He stopped, leaning his bare shoulder against the bark of a tree. Sibyl stopped too, turning back to him. "Tis dangerous."

"Dangerous?" She wrinkled her nose, thinking. "Why?"

"Alistair MacFalon's a'ready violatin' t'pact, if'n he's trappin' wulvers."

"Yes." She nodded slowly, remembering how proud he was of the fact he had a wolf trapped in a cage. A pregnant female he intended to kill and parade back to the castle as if it had been some great feat. "I believe he is."

"He's a cruel man, lass." Darrow's eyes narrowed, his head cocked. She knew he was listening to the reavers, although she could no longer hear them. They were too far off.

"I know," Sibyl agreed. "Believe me, I know. I couldn't stay with him, Darrow. I couldn't marry that man, no matter what my family wanted me to do."

"Raife said ye're brave one." Darrow gave a short nod. "Ye saved Laina, and I said I'm grateful to ye, and I am. But when I heard what he'd done… I wanted…"

"War," she whispered, knowing it before he even said it. "Of course you did. She's your wife. You love her."

"Aye." The look in his eyes was like steel. It was clear he would do anything for his mate, and that he'd had nothing but vengeance on his mind when Laina had returned, wounded, in labor, and then nearly died birthing their son.

Not that Sibyl could blame him. She felt murderous when she thought of Alistair, and the man had done nothing more than paw at her. She couldn't imagine what Darrow had felt, seeing his mate that way and finding out it was Alistair MacFalon who was responsible.

"So why didn't you go after him?" she asked. "The pact?"

"Aye." That steel flashed in his eyes. "Me brother has other ideas, 'bout keepin' t'peace. Said she was'na kidnapped or killed, so we could'na retaliate."

"So Raife stopped you."

She didn't fully understand this pact between the wulvers and the MacFalons, but she was beginning to see it more clearly. She remembered Raife saying he'd been sent to find Laina, but she wondered at that now. Mayhaps Raife had gone looking for her on his own—in hopes of finding her, yes, of course. But also in hopes of avoiding Darrow's rage, his need for vengeance.

"Aye, he stopped me." Darrow shook his head at her. "But he's agreed t'keep ye wit' us, let ye live in our den. Sibyl, if MacFalon knew we had ye…"

Just like Darrow had wanted vengeance, she knew how Alistair would react if he discovered her held "captive" by the wulvers.

"It would surely mean war," she whispered. And that was why Darrow said it was dangerous for Sibyl to be living amongst them. She was putting everyone at risk. Darrow. His wife, Laina. Their new baby. And Raife. She was putting Raife in danger, just by being with him. And he was putting his entire pack at risk by letting her stay.

"Aye," Darrow agreed softly.

"So why don't you tell the MacFalons?" she asked. She had fleetingly thought, mayhaps, Darrow wanted to take her into the woods to be rid of her. But she'd risked it, because of the way he looked at Laina. Any man who loved his wife that much couldn't be bad, not truly. But it hadn't crossed her mind until then that mayhaps he had another solution on his mind. Mayhaps those men in the woods were Alistair's men after all? "Why don't you take me to him right now?"

The thought made her physically ill. She had to clutch at the tree beside her to keep from collapsing. But she realized it wasn't so much the thought of having to face Alistair again that made her feel dizzy and sick.

It was the thought of never seeing Raife again.

Sibyl met Darrow's eyes and saw how torn he felt. Maybe it wasn't personal after all.

"Because I fear a war a'tween wulver brothers more'n I want one wit' clan MacFalon," Darrow replied finally, his gaze never leaving her.

Sibyl nodded, understanding. So she was safe with Darrow after all. Raife had been right. Darrow wouldn't defy his brother. He wouldn't kill her or take her to the MacFalons. He would respect Raife's wishes. And mayhaps, she thought, as they started walking through the woods again, he now had another, more ulterior motive.

And then he came right out and said what she'd been thinking.

"And I hope ye really can find the tree me Laina's been searchin' fer."

"I hope so, too." Sibyl couldn't help laughing.

They spent hours looking for the huluppa tree. Darrow changed several times, in order to carry her further, faster, than the two of them could travel on foot. But their search ended before Sibyl found what they were looking for. Darrow glanced at the sun, telling her they must head home, although she'd wanted to continue on.

When they returned, Sibyl and Darrow were both surprised to find that Raife had taken the place of the sentry, pacing back and forth at the entrance of the mountain, waiting for them both. Darrow faced his brother defiantly. Sibyl tried to slink by like a dog with its tail between its legs, but Raife caught her around the waist, pulling her to him and growling, "Wait fer me in yer room," before sending her on her way.

She heard them snarling at each other as she hurried back to her room. Raife came to her a short time later, his back and side scratched and bleeding, face smeared dark red, and she was terrified to ask what had happened. She instantly wanted to apologize, to beg his forgiveness, but she did neither.

Instead, she went to the fire to heat water to treat his wounds. He let her, watching as she washed the blood away with a warm cloth, seeing the wonder in her eyes as the gouges in his flesh healed all by themselves in no time at all. More wulver magic, she learned. Their strength made them great warriors, but their healing capacity made them near unbeatable.

"Me brother says ye were out helpin' him find huluppa?" Those were the first words he said.

"Yes," Sibyl replied honestly, still stunned at the way his skin pulled itself together right in front of her eyes without even leaving a scar. "For Laina."

Raife gave a slow, curt nod, those disarming blue eyes studying her face.

She stopped and looked up at him, puzzled.

"What did you think I was doing out there with him?" she finally asked and hid a smile when he scowled and wouldn't answer her.

Sibyl had been ready to call Kirstin for bandages, a needle and thread, but there were now no wounds to stitch up. Raife's skin was as clear and smooth as it had been before his altercation with Darrow. She knew it was some sort of magic and knew, too, she should have been afraid, but she wasn't. She'd spent her life being trained by men and women who lived in fear of being hunted down and hung for practicing witchcraft. But the knowledge of herbs and other healing techniques weren't devilry, she knew. And this—the way this man changed from animal to human and back, the way his skin healed, this wasn't the devil either.

We are what we are. That's what Raife said and it was true. They simply were. Animals were animals, humans were humans and wulvers were… wulvers. They were all God's creatures.

Sibyl's fingers moved over Raife's skin where the wound had been, feeling the muscle tighten underneath. Her hand smoothed the hot, corded terrain of the man's neck, brushing his hair aside to inspect the place where blood had been spilled. She had wiped it all away. He was completely healed.

"Sibyl…" He spoke her name and she lifted her eyes to meet his. They sat close on the bed, her bare leg grazing his, their plaids pulled to mid-thigh, his face swimming in her vision. "Do'na defy me, lass."

"I didn't ask your permission." She felt her spine straighten as she glared at him.

"Aye, ye did'na." He clasped her hands in his, bringing them down to his lap. "But ye're me charge and if'n I'm t'keep ye safe…"

"Your brother kept me safe." She stuck out her chin, defiant. "Were you worried he might turn me over to the MacFalons? Or mayhaps just kill me himself?"

"Were *ye* worried 'bout it?" Raife chuckled. He lifted Sibyl's hands, turning them both over and placing a kiss in each palm. His mouth was so soft, lips warm, and the feel of his breath made her chest tighten. "Darrow would'na hurt a hair on ye head. He knows how I feel 'bout ye."

"How do you… feel?" Sibyl swallowed, her words broken. She'd asked, but did she really want to know?

"I've said too much." He dropped her hands, moving to stand, but Sibyl couldn't let him.

So she did the only thing she could think of to stop him.

She climbed into the man's lap and pressed her lips to his.

Raife's big arms encircled her, enfolded her, completely enveloped her. Sibyl disappeared against him and she liked it. Being with him always made her feel safe but this was different. Something stirred in her, something deep, dark, primal. Raife groaned like a man being tortured when she turned her head and gasped for breath, opening her mouth to his, and he took it, tongue probing, hands roaming through the thick, red mass of her hair.

"Oh Raife," she whispered against his lips, her own hands roaming all on their own, down the hard, muscled planes of his chest, feeling the ridges of his abdomen under her fingers. "Please tell me… please… how *do* you feel?"

"I can'na." His voice was hoarse, pained. "Sibyl, do'na ask this of me."

"Because it's too dangerous?" she frowned, remembering Darrow's words. "Because you're protecting the pack?"

Raife nodded, slowly, that tortured look in his eyes like a knife in her heart.

"Your brother wants a war," she mused, touching a finger to that sweet dent in his chin. "But *you* want peace."

"We've sacrificed e'erythin' for peace." He sighed. "I can'na risk it all fer me own…"

"Your own what?" she whispered. She'd seen the way he looked at her, the way his gaze followed her wherever she went. She'd heard the way the wulver women whispered about it. That look. The same look Darrow gave his wife. The look a wulver gave his mate. "What am I, Raife? Am I anything at all?"

"Ye're e'erythin', Sibyl," he said honestly, his big heart in his eyes. "Ye're more'n I e'er dreamed of, mor'n I e'er hoped t'have. And still… I can'na…"

Sibyl nodded, feeling a lump in her throat, her lips trembling as she rose from his lap.

"Then I'll go," she said. Darrow had convinced her of the danger, and Raife had confirmed it. Just her presence here was putting them all at risk. "It's better if I go."

Of course it was better. She would find her way back to the village where they'd left Rose. The woman would be big with child by now. Sibyl could help. She could make her own way in the world, somehow. And if she carried a weight in her heart for the rest of this life, the heaviness of loss, the possibility of what might have been between her and this man, she could bear it. She would have to.

"Nuh, lass." Raife stood too, looking down at her in the firelight. "Ye're safe 'ere. I said I'd keep ye safe, and I will."

"You'll *keep* me…" She turned her brimming eyes up to him, everything inside her aching. "But you won't… *take* me?"

"I can'na." He caught her tear with his lips, kissing her cheek before leaving her, closing the door behind him.

She didn't ask Raife's permission when Darrow asked her to go again, and Raife never gave it. But he was always there, waiting, when they returned with a good supply of useful herbs and sometimes wild berries or some other treat. Every time they came back, she thought Raife would rail at them, tell her she couldn't go off gallivanting in the woods with his brother, but he didn't.

He would glare at Darrow as the wolf changed back into his human form. The brothers wouldn't say a word to each other as Darrow started into the tunnel to go see his bride, and Raife pulled Sibyl close, his arms tight around her, hands checking to see if she was whole and unbroken, as if he believed just stepping out of his sight would instantly cause her harm.

"I'm fine, Raife!" She would laugh and take his hand as they walked through the tunnels toward the smell of dinner cooking. And then she would tell him all about their trip, and show him what she found, and he would listen as if it was the most interesting thing he'd ever heard tell about.

Then, one day, she found it.

He had known instantly, just by the look on her face, that their trip had finally been a success. Raife had swept her into his arms, his embrace much tighter than usual, his face buried against her neck, his whispered words, "Thank God. Ye do'na hafta go back out again," sending a shiver through her.

But now…

The willow Sibyl had found and transplanted was dying.

She'd found the plant Laina could not, much to Darrow's relief, and she had transplanted it here near the stream. There was plenty of light, plenty of water, and yet the plant did not thrive. There was no reason for it and she could not figure it out.

"Tis the curse," Laina told her simply when Sibyl went to visit her and the baby, bringing her broth to sip.

Sibyl once would have said she didn't believe in curses, but she had seen things now most human beings would never witness. The sight of a half-man, half-wolf carrying a sword and riding a horse was something you would never forget as long as you lived. It made you doubt and believe everything at once, including all the fairy stories and legends she had heard tell over the years.

"Mayhaps," Sibyl would say, whenever Laina blamed the willow's slow death on the curse. But if it was the curse, and the willow was actually the cure for the change, as Laina and Darrow believed, then why would it not live here, in the place the wulvers called home?

Laina had an explanation for that too.

"It only grows in the borderland," Laina told her, when Sibyl explained where she had found the plant. It had been too close to Alistair's lands for comfort, and Raife had protested, but Darrow had been the one who agreed to take her out that far, to protect her if need be. "T'will not live on one side or th'other."

This seemed ridiculous to Sibyl, and she was determined to prove Laina wrong, but so far, the frustrating plant had done just the opposite. She wanted one of the wulver women to try eating the leaves before the plant died, but Laina was insistent she be the one to try it first.

"I'll pay the consequences, whatever they may be," Laina told her. "I do'na want anyone else t'suffer any ill effects. I'll try it first."

Laina had been doing so herself all along, harvesting and drying various species of willow, from roots to leaves to bark, and taking them to test their effects. That was how she ended up nearly bleeding to death during the birth of her son. She had lived through the ordeal, but just barely. It had taken her weeks to recover from something Kirstin said wulver women usually bounced back from right away.

And in the time Sibyl had spent with them, she'd seen this for herself. Wulver women changed when it was time to give birth. They had one pup, two at the most, and their births were short and painless. They changed back immediately, as did the male pups. The girls took a little longer to change into human form, but babies, regardless of gender, stayed human until they came of age. Girls changed when they began to bleed, and they would continue to do so for the rest of their lives, until their moon time was done. Boys could not only control when they changed, they could also transform into halflings, half-man, half-wolf. Female wulvers were either human or wolf. There was no in between.

It was Laina's desire to stop the change, so that female wulvers weren't slaves to their own bodies. Wulver traditions were oral, passed down from generation to generation, but there was one text they considered their "bible" of sorts, and Sibyl had spent time going over it herself since she'd come to live with them. It was told in pictures with only some words—human wulvers were incredibly deft with their hands and could draw anything, their mountain walls were covered with beautiful drawings—but Sibyl's father had taught her to read.

While most wulvers did not read, Sibyl understood the words in the book. Laina had been excited to learn this, and wanted Sibyl to pour over the text, to find the things Laina could not. Sibyl understood the woman's urgency, at least to some degree. She, herself, felt trapped by her own gender. All of the things her father had taught her—to ride, to hunt, to shoot, to track—were useless to her sex. She understood Laina's anger at feeling trapped in her body, unable to change what nature had made her.

But she didn't fully understand until, one early morning while she helped wash clothes in the stream with Kirstin, she was told the story of Laina's mother and how she had died. It was so eerily similar to how Laina had been caught, Sibyl found herself getting goose flesh at the telling of the tale.

The women took turns telling it, each of them bringing something new to the story as they went on. They told of a time when wulvers and wolves were trapped, hunted and killed. It had been just twenty years ago when "the MacFalon" and his bloodlust for wolves drove the wulvers underground. He would capture them in cages, torture and kill them. There was even a mandate from the Scottish king that wolves must be hunted at certain times of the year.

Sibyl wondered if this man they called "the MacFalon" was Alistair's grandfather, a man whose reputation had been far worse than his son's. Alistair's father, according to Donal and everyone who spoke of him, hadn't been the type of man who would shoot an animal for sport. She couldn't imagine he had done what these women described "the MacFalon" doing.

The tale took another turn when the women told of two young female wulvers becoming trapped in a MacFalon cage. One was in estrus, they said—in heat. The other was heavy with pup and the trauma of the cage had forced her into labor. Neither female could change back to free themselves, and they had been separated from their men folk.

In the morning, the MacFalon himself had come to see what he had trapped in his cage. He found both of the wolves, the one in heat snarling at him, the other just birthing her pup. The young wolf pup, eyes hardly open, slipped out of the bars of its cage and ran.

"I thought wolf pups change when they're born?" Sibyl had asked, pounding cloth against the rocks.

"Boys do, right away," Kirstin explained. "Girls, they take longer. It can be up to a day afore they turn human."

So it had been a girl who had escaped that day. A young wolf girl who would later be called Laina, a name her own mother, the wolf the MacFalon had shot through with an arrow while still in the cage, had chosen before she was born. He would have shot the other wolf as well, if she hadn't changed. Her heat was nearly over, so mayhaps it was time, the women said. Or mayhaps it was the shock of seeing her friend murdered.

But the MacFalon, suddenly faced with a dead wolf and a very alive, nude woman, decided to drag his wolf kill behind his horse and throw the other woman across his saddle—after he restrained her, of course.

"T'would've been war then," Beitris, the old wulver midwife, had told her with a nod. "Once the wolfen warriors heard wha'happened, they took to their horses and went ridin' after the MacFalon armed wit' claymores."

"What happened?" Sibyl had asked, glancing down into the valley where the wulver men practiced the art of warfare every day, keeping their bodies in condition, just in case.

"King Henry."

Sibyl had stared at them in disbelief, but they weren't jesting. Not even a little.

"He was'na the king then," the wulver women explained. "Nuh yet."

"He came ta Scotland seekin' warriors t'win the crown."

She knew King Henry VII had been in Brittany, recruiting the French troops, when this incident was supposed to have happened. Had he really come to Scotland in hopes of finding more?

"And got 'em, he did!" One of the other older wulver women cackled, her rheumy blue eyes flashing.

"He came lookin' for the wulver warriors," Kirstin explained. "King Henry wanted 'em t'fight for 'im. Dis was all before I's born, a'course."

"King Henry fell in love wit' Avril," the wulver women told her. Sibyl listened to this tall tale with big eyes. She knew the name Avril belonged to Raife's mother. "She was wit' child when he rode back t'England."

"And the warriors promised t'fight for the future King of England, if the MacFalon would agree t'keep the peace. So they brokered a deal."

"The wolf pact."

That's what the wulver women had called it.

"King Henry VII?" Sibyl had wondered aloud, utterly enthralled with the tale, even while she doubted its veracity.

"He could'na take her back wit' him, ya ken?" the old woman said, shaking her head. "So she came back t'us."

"Birthed her child 'ere wit' us," the old midwife, Beitris, said. "And Garaith raised him like 'is own."

"Garaith?" Sibyl knew this name too. "Raife's… father?"

"Darrow's father," Beitris countered. "Raife is descended from King Henry VII 'imself."

Sibyl had smiled then, thinking it had to be more stuff of legend.

"So King Henry negotiated a peace pact between the wulvers and the Scots," Sibyl had mused. This tale was so fantastical, it was hard to believe. "And the MacFalon honored that pact?"

That seemed unlikely, given the man's penchant for violence and hatred of the wulvers.

"The MacFalon was killed in battle," the old midwife told her.

"His son had become laird by then," one of the wulver women explained.

"And there's been peace for nigh on twenty years."

"Until now," Sibyl whispered to herself, thinking of Alistair's wolf hunt.

If there had been such a pact, Alistair had to be aware—so why was he breaking it?

She didn't understand, but she knew it wasn't good for the wulvers.

It wasn't until she heard this story that Sibyl finally understood Laina's passion for breaking the wulvers' curse. Sibyl had never been close with her own mother, but she couldn't imagine losing her in such a traumatic way. The wolf-child—Laina—had been found by the wulvers in the woods and taken back to the den, adopted by another female who had just had a pup. Kirstin and her adopted sibling, Laina, had been raised together as sisters, although everyone knew what had happened to Laina's real mother.

Sibyl had done her best to help the young wulver woman and her cause, and she redoubled her efforts after hearing the wolf pact story, if for no other reason than she didn't want the girl to take any more chances with her life and her health. Sibyl had poured over the wulver text, had read and re-read the legends, had listened to story after story told around the fire, at the dinner table, at the stream while they washed or in the kitchen where they prepared meals.

Sibyl had seen pictures of the huluppa tree, and had recognized it as a willow, just as Laina had. But it was Sibyl who had found it growing in the forest at the side of the very stream she had crossed to escape Alistair's men. Now, as Sibyl stared at her little transplant, she knew it would likely be dead by the time Laina was ready to venture out of the den.

And what then?

Would Laina go out on her own to find it growing on MacFalon land?

Sibyl knew she couldn't let that happen.

Chapter Eight

"Tis time t'sup."

Sibyl shaded her eyes and looked up at Raife. The wulver men fought bare-chested and bare-legged, like any Scot, but they were far bigger and more muscular than most men, even when they weren't transformed into half-wolf form. Raife's body glistened with sweat, his dark hair damp with effort as he squatted beside her near the stream. They spent the morning training but their afternoons in various other pursuits. Today they had sheared sheep and he had bits of fluff stuck in his dark hair.

"Tis dyin'," Raife observed, pinching another brown leaf off the plant—Sibyl could have sworn it turned brown just in the time she'd been watching. "Laina will'na be pleased."

"I know." Sibyl sighed, reaching out to pluck a bit of white from Raife's hair. "We will have to keep her busy here until I can go out and find another."

"N'more woods fer ye." He scowled at the little smile that came over her face.

"Darrow will protect me," she said. Darrow would have done anything for Laina. If that meant going out into the woods with Sibyl, well, he would even venture to do that.

"I can'na let ye go again." Raife shook his head, frowning at the dying plant as if it was all the fault of the willow. "Tis far too dangerous, lass."

"No more dangerous than a human living in a wolf's den." She teased, laughing, standing and holding her hand out to him.

"Ye're safe 'ere, Sibyl." That scowl on his face deepened as he stood, ignoring the hand she had held out to help him. "Have we not proved it t'ye?"

"Of course. You know I jest." She blinked at him in surprise. "You have proven to be a perfect gentleman. Far less of an animal than my…"

She didn't finish the sentence, both of them knowing just who she meant.

"Aye." Raife grimaced, turning his back on her and heading toward the mountain. "The perfect gentleman."

"Where are you going?" she called after him.

"Dinner!" he yelled back, not turning. "I best eat somethin' afore I decide t'devour ye instead!"

"Raife!"

But there was no way to catch up to those big, long, heavily muscled legs of his.

She stood there for a moment, fuming, watching him walk away. What right did he have to be angry at her? She'd offered herself to him, had made herself vulnerable, and had been rejected. Everything he said and did told her that he wanted her, and yet he refused to claim her.

Claim me.

Everything in her begged him, but while they talked and laughed and flirted, while he looked at her like he could, indeed, devour her, he did not act. She was confused by her own feelings for him, how powerful and intense they were. The truth was, she wanted to be claimed by Raife, wanted it more than anything she'd ever wanted in her life, but it just wasn't meant to be. She was a human, he was a wulver. He was leader of his pack, and his choice of mate mattered greatly.

But she wanted him. She ached for him. To be claimed, marked, made his.

That's how the wulvers talked about marriage—which involved a "marking," according to Laina. Each wulver pair had an intricate, matching tattoo engraved on their skin, men on their upper arms and women on their hip and thigh. These tattoos disappeared, of course, covered by fur when they changed into wolves, but in human form, the wulvers had an outward, fixed mark, proof they were matched and mated. It was far more permanent than a wedding ring.

But they hadn't talked about it since that day in her room, the day she'd climbed into his lap like a fool and kissed him. She felt she couldn't say anything without hurting them both, so they just didn't speak of it. But it was always there between them. Always.

And while they didn't talk about it, Raife would bristle at things, like he just had, and walk angrily away from her. She didn't know if he was angry at her or with himself. All she knew was, when Raife walked away from her, it was like her own heart being ripped out of her chest. His anger made her angry. He made her want to hit him—not that it would do any good. He made her want to pound on his chest and scream and cry, but that wouldn't do any good either.

It seemed, no matter what she did, he remained resolute, distant. He would allow her to draw close, intimately so, looking at her with such affection, such deep emotion, it made her throat close and her heart ache. But then, he would do something like this. He would push her away again, keeping her at arm's length.

She saw the men corralling the horses. Raife had stopped to talk to his brother. The horses ran free in the valley during the day, but they kept them penned at night, just like the sheep and the goats. The wulvers would not harm them—unless it was during one of the female changes. The females were unpredictable, and while they wouldn't harm a human, they might take down an animal. It was just safer, Raife had told her, to pen them up at night.

Otherwise, they could have roamed the valley to their heart's content. There was no way out of it, unless you took a horse up a winding, treacherous mountain path and down the other side. Or went through the mountain den itself. She knew they had taken horses out through the den before—when the wolfen warriors were ready for warfare—but not very often.

Raife had taken her riding on more than one occasion. He'd been impressed with her horsemanship, a fact that made her smile. Here, with the wulvers, all those things she'd been taught actually had some practical use.

Sibyl found herself in the midst of the horses without even thinking. Her body just propelled her forward. She grabbed the reins of one of the big war horses—Angus was the horse Raife let her ride, a black beauty with a white patch around one eye. He liked her and nuzzled her shoulder as she approached. He accepted her weight without protest as she mounted him, pulling her plaid up slightly so she could sit astride. She loved riding this way.

"Sibyl!" Raife snapped when he saw her nudge the horse and squeeze him with her thighs, urging him forward. "Come back, lass!"

But she ignored him, ignored the calls of the other wulver men as she leaned forward over the neck of the horse as Angus crested the first hill. There was nowhere to go in the valley, of course. It was a large area, but completely contained, surrounded by the mountains. She could have ridden the horse through the tunnels—they were wide and tall enough—but by the time she reached the entrance, they would have stopped her.

There was only one other way out. She had asked Raife about the trail that went up the side of the mountain and he'd told her it was an alternate route out of the valley, in case something happened to the tunnel. It was treacherous and dangerously high, but she pointed her horse in that direction and rode hard. Both she and the Angus were out of breath by the time they reached the base of the mountain.

When she arrived at it, she reined in the horse, looking at the path. It started out innocently enough, a wide, grassy plane that narrowed into a mountain trail, but it wound up and up, so high just looking at it made her dizzy. It had looked different at a distance. Safer. Now it seemed impossible to traverse, although the horse seemed willing enough to go. He'd been trained to travel it by the wulvers.

Was she really going to do this?

She closed her eyes, swallowing hard, and of course, her mind filled immediately with Raife. She saw his lop-sided smile, those bright, dancing eyes, that long, thick, dark hair of his, the way he towered over her, the way his hand swallowed hers.

"Sibyl!"

She startled at the sound of her name, glancing over her shoulder to see Raife thundering up to her on his horse. His face was dark with anger as he grabbed the reins of her horse just as she dug her heels into Angus's side in an attempt to get him to move forward.

"Dè tha thu a' dèanamh?" he snapped. "Where do ye think you're going?"

"Away." Her lower lip trembled as he pulled her horse toward his so they were standing side by side. "Away from you."

"Away from me?" His brow knitted, mouth turned down in a frown.

"I can't stand it anymore, Raife." She felt tears stinging her eyes and tried to blink them back, turning her face away so he wouldn't see them. "I'm leaving."

"Yer nuh goin' nowhere."

One moment she was sitting in the saddle, looking up at the dizzying zenith of the mountain, and the next she was in Raife's arms, sitting in front of him, side-saddle on his horse. His arms surrounded her, face close, eyes searching hers.

"I can'na let ye leave."

"Because I'm safer here?" Sibyl let out a wail of a laugh. "Yes, Raife, I'm safe. I'm so very safe. You keep me locked up here, your prisoner, to keep me safe. I'm safe from Alistair and his men. I'm safe from everything out there. But do you know what I'm *most* safe from?"

"Sibyl—"

"You!" She put her hands against his chest and pushed at him, but of course, he didn't move. The man was like a rock. "I'm safe from *you* most of all!"

"Is that what ye think?" He gave a strangled laugh. "Ye think yer safe from me, then?"

"I know I am." She stuck her chin out, defiant, meeting his burning eyes.

And then he kissed her. He seized her mouth with a hot, angled kiss that took her breath away. This was no cautious, gentle peck. This was hunger and desperation and a longing so deep it went straight to her core. Sibyl moaned uncontrollably, arms going around his neck just to hang on and keep the world from spinning her into oblivion. Raife's hands wandered over her body into places no man had ever touched, squeezing her breasts, pulling her hips against his, even daring to move between her thighs, cupping her throbbing sex over the cover of her plaid.

"D'ye feel safe now?" he growled as he grabbed a handful of her hair, pulling her head back so he could get to her throat. His mouth was doing things she didn't understand, her body responding so completely it was like it wasn't even her own. She was melting in the saddle in front of him.

"I feel *you*," she whispered, wiggling against him, something hard and hot, insistent, throbbing against her hip. "Oh Raife, please. Let me feel you."

"Och, Sibyl," Raife groaned, grasping her wrists when her hands moved down his chest, his belly, reaching for him. "Ye're testin' me beyon' me bounds, lass. I can'na. I…"

She turned her face from him and slid out of the saddle without another word. He could have held onto her, but she would have been left dangling from the horse, feet not touching the ground, so he let her go so as not to hurt her, as she knew he would.

"Sibyl!" he called, voice hoarse, but she didn't answer him.

She just kept walking deeper into the valley, toward the entrance in the side of the mountain that led to the wulvers' den. Raife didn't follow her and she didn't expect him to. He would distance himself again. That was the pattern and it was killing her, bit by little bit, as if she was being picked apart, flesh stripped from her body until she was nothing but bone, laid bare.

It hurt that much.

“Sibyl!” Laina called her name as Sibyl’s eyes adjusted to the darkness. Coming into the den was always such a surprise to her system, even though the wulvers adjusted easily. Of course, they could see almost as well in the dark as they could in the light. “How’s our lil plant?”

Sibyl smiled, putting on a happy face, but she didn’t want to tell Laina the truth. Instead she distracted them both by fussing over the baby. He was a handsome fellow with big blue eyes and a thick, thatch of dark hair. He looked so much like Raife—and Darrow—it hurt her heart.

“You are looking so much better, Laina.” Sibyl smiled, chucking the baby under his chin. “Your color is coming back.”

“Tis not all that’s comin’ back.” Laina frowned at the way the baby turned his head, looking for something to chew on and found his fist. “He’s started solid food. The elders say me moon cycles’ll start up again soon.”

“The plant… it’s…” Sibyl swallowed as they entered the center of the mountain. All the tunnels led to and through here. It was the heart of all things, this place where they cooked and ate together.

“Tis dyin’ isn’t it?” Laina sighed, switching the baby to her other shoulder. “It can’na live anywhere but the borderlands. I knew it. I’m gonna hafta look fer it meself.”

“Laina, no.” Sibyl frowned, catching Raife’s eye across the room. He had obviously penned the horses before coming into the den. He stopped to tease Kirstin about something—she flushed pink and laughed, hitting him on the arm.

Everyone loved Raife, especially all the wulver women. Sibyl had noticed it from the very beginning, but once she found that he had not chosen a mate, she also discovered that most of the wulver girls dreamed of being that one. Not that she could blame any of them, of course. He was quite a catch, as far as wulver men went. There was no one bigger or stronger in the pack, which was likely why he had assumed the role of leader, but she didn't think that was all of the reason. There was something different about Raife. Something calmer, more reserved than the rest of the wulver men. They liked to wrestle and tussle like little boys. Raife was far more serious than that.

Which made times like this, when he smiled and teased one of the girls, even more unusual. Sibyl found herself bristling at it and she tried to ignore it, turning her attention back to Laina and her tiny baby.

"You need to stay here for this little man," Sibyl reminded Laina.

Sibyl saw Darrow enter the kitchen, carrying a thick, heavy sword. He hung it in a notch on the side of the mountain wall. There were hundreds of others there. The men forged new swords all the time. She was fascinated with the process and Raife had laughed at her when she once tried to lift one off the ground—she'd wielded a small sword of her own back at her father's castle—finding it far too heavy. She couldn't believe how the wulver men swung them around, over their heads, the strength it must take.

"How can I care for 'im when I'm a wolf?" Laina's lower lip trembled.

"But... isn't that what your wulver sisters are for?" Sibyl asked.

She knew the other wulver women cared for the babies when the moon time of a mother returned. Wulvers wouldn't hurt their young, but a human baby required things a wulver pup did not. Sibyl thought it was ironic, because a human woman could care for a wulver pup or a human child, but a wulver, with no hands or thumbs or even voice, had a much harder time caring for a human child.

"But he's *my* bairn," Laina protested.

"I know." Sibyl smiled at the infant who sucked greedily at his fist. "He has your long fingers."

"Ye *do'na* know, though." Laina kissed the top of the baby's head, her eyes sad as she looked at Sibyl. "Even if ye mated wit' Rai—a... wulver... ye would never hafta worry about changin'."

Raife.

That's what Laina had almost said.

Even if you mated with Raife.

Sibyl glanced over at him. He was talking to his brother, their heads bent, expressions serious. Did everyone in the pack think she was in love with him? She wondered. Did everyone think what Laina had almost said aloud?

She had thought about what it would mean, to be a wulver's mate.

To be Raife's mate.

She would have denied it aloud—and had, on several occasions, when the women had teased her about it. They soon learned not to mention it, because if they did, Sibyl would bristle. And Raife—no one ever said anything about Sibyl in front of Raife. The last man who had said something suggestive about

Sibyl had spent the afternoon in the pigpen, shoveling it out.

But as much as she denied it, she thought about it. She felt the way his eyes followed her, wherever she went. He always knew where she was, at all times. He spent nights sleeping in the cold hallway somewhere outside her door, wrapped in his plaid. She couldn't count the times she'd stood on the other side of that door, her ear pressed tight, imagining she could hear him breathing, feel the pound of his wulver heart. Of course, it was really only the sound of her own quickened breath, the thud of her aching human heart.

Because, if nothing else, her heart beat for him.

She knew it wasn't unheard of, a wulver choosing a human mate. It had happened before. Raife's own father had been a human man, after all. But Raife was the leader of his pack. He had a responsibility, not just to himself, but to all of them. He hadn't yet taken a mate, but they expected him to, and soon. They expected him to choose a wulver woman, someone who matched him in spirit and strength, a woman who wouldn't put herself at risk every time she gave birth to a new heir.

And Sibyl knew any issue from a human and wulver would be a changeling. No human-wulver pairing ever resulted in a child who was fully human.

She had been sold to a man who was as different from her as night from day, or so she once thought. The Scots ways were odd to her, so often opposite her own, but the more time she'd spent in their presence, she'd grown used to the soft brogue, their jokes and forward behavior. Donal and his men had endeared themselves to her, over time. Well, most of them had.

It was mostly Alistair, her intended, who had still rankled her.

Now that she'd lived with these wulvers, she knew what real "difference" was. They couldn't have been further apart, she and these creatures. They were wild, untamed, a close-knit pack of warriors, the men strong and protective, the women nearly as strong and just as territorial. Sibyl had watched them argue, tussle, fight and make up, had listened to the women tell stories and watched them take care of their young.

And yet, in their hearts, she had found they were the same as she was. Their needs and wants were no different. They hungered. They fed. They laughed. They wondered. They loved. And in that last, in her estimation, they were perhaps superior to her own breed. They loved with a passion and devotion she had never seen before. The connection between wulver mates went far beyond contracts. In her world, men of power and pieces of paper served to join two factions.

She had been little more than a pawn on her uncle's chessboard. King Henry had sought to unite the English and Scots, to ease the tension between them by uniting families along the border, so everyone was invested in the future generations that issued from each union. She was but one bride who had been sold for that purpose, she knew. And ultimately, if her uncle was to be believed, James IV of Scotland would marry a Tudor and the union of Scots and English would wind its way all the way to the top of the hierarchy.

"Sibyl?" Laina's voice brought Sibyl out of her reverie. Sibyl tore her eyes from Raife, focusing on the woman and her baby.

"I'm sorry?" Sibyl apologized. She hadn't heard a word, didn't even know if Laina had been speaking at all.

"He'll claim ye." Laina was the only one who dared speak of it aloud, although even she was cautious and spoke in hushed tones, so no one overheard them. "If'n ye let 'im."

"Who am I to let him?" Sibyl laughed, trying her best to sound as if it mattered not at all. Besides, what did Laina know? Sibyl had climbed into the man's lap and humiliated herself—and he'd refused her. "I am just a woman. I get no say in such matters."

"From what I hear, ye had a great deal t'say 'bout such matters wit' an arrow." Laina leveled a knowing look in her direction. "Ye're more wulver than English at heart, I think."

Sibyl had escaped her captor, had defied her uncle, had shamed her mother. That was not a ladylike, English thing to do. There was nothing to return to for her anymore, and if there was, she wasn't sure she would want to go back. Her world had died the moment she fled. Now she belonged nowhere. She lived in this fantastical place, with these strange creatures, but she didn't belong with them either. That's what it came down to, in the end. She wasn't just a stranger in a strange land, she was forever an outsider, a foreigner who could never fit in.

An Englishwoman could act like a Scot, could someday become Scottish in language and mannerisms, but a human woman could never become a wulver. That was a transformation no person could ever perform, no matter how much they wished it were true. Just as Laina, who longed to change her wulver nature, could never prevent her own change.

We are what we are. That's what Raife often said, and it was true. More true than Sibyl wanted to admit, even to herself.

"Hello, Darrow." Sibyl glanced up as Laina's husband joined them, kissing the top of his son's dark head, looking upon him with great affection. Sibyl didn't stay long between them. She was too afraid they might start asking her about the huluppa tree again and she didn't want to have to tell them the truth.

She told herself she'd go the next day and pull off a shoot and try to get it to root, and replant it. Mayhaps she could get it to grow somewhere else further downstream. Maybe it needed partial shade instead of full sun. She was still puzzling over this when she took her seat across from Laina and Darrow at the long table. Raife had insisted she sit by him from the very beginning. At first, she thought it was so he could translate for her from Gaelic, but then he had insisted everyone start speaking English. Of course, they still didn't pay much attention to the rule, especially at dinner, when everyone talked at once, hundreds of people sitting at four long tables.

Sibyl didn't care much, not really. She was too hungry most of the time to pay attention to the jokes and laughter, the talk of training and babies. Besides, it allowed her to keep Raife's attention. They sat and talked together every night at dinner like they were in their own little world. She liked it that way and she thought he did too. She'd learned a lot about the wolf pack—and its leader—this way. And she had revealed a great deal about herself and her life before this, far more than she would have otherwise, if she'd been focused on making small talk with the other wulvers, whether it was in English or her poor attempt at Gaelic.

But tonight, Raife was quiet. He ate his bacon and sopped up gravy with biscuits and just grunted yes and no answers to her questions. In spite of her halting attempts at conversations, he stayed quiet, thoughtful. It was only when Darrow made a joke across the table in Gaelic that made everyone laugh that Raife took notice and snapped at his brother.

"Beurla!" Raife insisted. "English!"

He taught Sibyl that way, saying the word in Gaelic, then repeating it in English.

"You mustn't force them for my sake." Sibyl nudged Raife with her right elbow, trying not to make it too obvious she was doing so, as he told his brother to speak English at the dinner table.

The pack gathered for dinner in this one large, central room, a fire always burning cozily in the kitchen's giant hearth. This was the heart of the mountain and the foundation of the pack. This was where they met, where they ate, and at night, where many of them slept. It was during her first week in the mountain, unable to sleep, when she'd wandered into the kitchen, her stomach looking for biscuits, that she'd found them all huddled together like the pups in the kitchen back home.

The bed she slept on, she discovered, was Raife's, but while she'd protested to Kirstin about taking his room, she assured Sibyl that he rarely occupied it. He wrapped himself in his plaid, like the rest of his pack, and slept on the kitchen floor with a hundred other canines. Aside from Raife's, rooms with doors inside the mountain were usually reserved for mating couples and birthing females. Darrow and Laina were in a much smaller room next to Raife's. It was the room

Sibyl had first woken up in, where Laina had given birth.

Raife had not taken a mate to fill his room, much to his pack's frustration. So far, he had, according to Kirstin, been far more interested in training, not only himself but his pack mates, for a war he never wanted to fight. It was strange to Sibyl, given it was Darrow who seemed far more interested in starting a war, even if he wasn't quite as diligent about training and preparing for such.

"I told 'em t'speak English." Raife frowned down at her, his expressive blue eyes showing concern over her confusion at Darrow's Gaelic words. Raife had made it a new pack-wide rule that, in Sibyl's presence, English should be spoken at all times. All of them could speak and understand English, although they spoke it with a thick, Scottish brogue, but most of them forgot and needed reminding when she was around.

"I am learning Gaelic," she protested, sticking her tongue out at him when he raised those dark, arched brows at her. She picked up a biscuit and waved it at him. "Aran. See?"

"Seo?" Raife lifted his glass of wine, tipping it toward her, asking what it was.

"Uhhhh." Sibyl frowned. She was drinking goat's milk—the goats were kept in the valley behind tall fences, or else they would get eaten instead of milked—and she knew the word for "milk" was "bainne." Laina, still nursing her baby balach, Garaith, said the word "bainne" enough for Sibyl to remember it.

She noticed that many of the pack were watching her. Kirstin, who had been a patient, excellent Gaelic teacher so far, was particularly interested in Sibyl's struggle.

"F-f-f..." She knew it started with that sound. She remembered that much. "Fiodh! Now give me!"

Sibyl reached for his wine to take a drink, triumphant. It hit her belly with a mellow burn and immediately made her light-headed. She hardly ever drank spirits.

"No, lass." Raife couldn't help grinning, watching her drink the rest of the wine in his cup. "*Fion* is wine."

"What did I ask for then?"

"*Fiodh* is wood." Raife chuckled.

"Methinks ye give me brother plenty a'dat."

Sibyl's cheeks reddened at Darrow's words and the laughter that ensued.

"Darrow." Raife scowled a warning at his brother.

"The scouts say Alistair's men 'ave finally given up searchin' f'her." Darrow met his brother's eyes across the table.

How long had it been? She wondered. She hadn't been counting the days, but it was still summer. So Alistair had given up on her. It was a relief to her, and it must be to them too, she thought.

But then Darrow said, "Tis time fer her t'go back t'her own kind."

"Darrow, enough," Raife snarled. His words brought silence to the whole pack. They all stopped talking, putting down their food, looking uneasily between the two men.

"Yer gonna start a war," Darrow said, standing and staring pointedly at Sibyl.

She shrank against Raife's side, afraid of the anger in Darrow's eyes. This was a man who had taken her on his back deep into the woods, who had been willing to risk his own life—and hers—in hopes of finding some sort of relief for a wulvers' plight. They had talked together on those trips, had jested and laughed, had found they had more in common than not. Sibyl had come to believe that Darrow had not only accepted her among them, but that he even liked her. Now, looking at the anger on his face, she wondered if she'd been mistaken.

"Ye *wanna* war!" Raife threw up his hands and stood too, a head taller than his brother.

"Not like this, I do'na." Darrow pointed a finger at Sibyl so that everyone around the table turned their heads to look at her. "She puts all of us at risk. Ye wan'me t'speak English? I'll say't in plain English then! Are ye doin' what's right fer the pack? Or are ye doing what's right fer yerself?"

Sibyl couldn't breathe. She knew it was true, that her mere presence here put them all in danger. She'd tried to leave, but Raife wouldn't let her, said it was safer here for all of them. She'd never felt so welcome anywhere before, but she also had never had a family like the wulvers. She didn't want any of them harmed.

But if Alistair's men had finally given up…

"What about ye, Darrow?" Raife glanced down at Sibyl and then back to his brother, eyes flashing. "Ye wan'me t'say't plainly? Ye risked yer woman's life and the life of yer bairn, and if it weren't for this woman ye want ta toss out into the woods on her own, *ye'd've lost 'em both!"*

"Raife…" Sibyl's wide eyes met Laina's across the table, seeing the pained look on the woman's face.

The two men stood, face to face, eyes locked, unmoving.

"Raife, please." She tugged his hand as she stood beside him. "Don't."

He wasn't listening. A low growl came from his throat, from both of them. She imagined them leaping across the table at one another, brother against brother, tearing each other to pieces, and couldn't stand it.

"D'ye wanna tell 'er the truth, or should I?" Raife asked his brother. Darrow reddened but did not speak, so Raife continued, his voice thundering through the cavern. "They stopped lookin' fer her over a month ago, but ye kept yer mouth shut til now, didn'ye? Now that ye got what ye wanted outta 'er, that is. Now yer fine tossin'er out on 'er own!"

His words sunk in, deep. She felt faint.

Sibyl put her hand in Raife's, squeezing hard.

"Tiugainn," she whispered, pleading with him in his native tongue, begging him. She couldn't stand another moment of this. "Tiugainn!"

He looked down, seeing her eyes brimming with tears, and the word registered in his eyes.

Come. Come on.

He turned away from his brother, away from his pack, and followed her into the tunnels.

Chapter Nine

There was nothing but silence as they made their way through the tunnel. Slowly, she heard the sound of the pack beginning to talk again, but it was far away now. She saw the light of a torch in the distance and knew there was a sentry on duty, as always, near the front of the cave.

Raife stopped outside her room, hand on the latch, looking down at her.

"I'm sorry 'bout that, lass," he apologized softly. "Me brother overstepped 'is bounds."

"Is it true?" Sibyl asked. "Did the MacFalons stop looking for me over a month ago?"

"Aye," Raife admitted, frowning. "Darrow did'na tell ye because he wanted ye to find the plant."

"And you did not tell me either." She blinked at him. "Why?"

"Ah lass…" He sighed, shaking his head. "T'isn't safe for ye out there, even if the MacFalons stopped lookin'. The MacFalons and the wulvers, we've a history…"

"I know." Sibyl knew, more than she let on. Raife didn't know what the wulver women had told her by the stream that day.

"Ye know?"

"The wolf pact." She rolled her eyes when his brows went up in surprise. "I am not an idiot. I know the story. But I don't care about that. What I want to know is…"

"Sibyl, I can'na…"

"Tiugainn," she said softly in Gaelic. "Come."

Raife reluctantly followed her into the room—his room, a place he hadn't slept in over a month—shutting the door behind him. Sibyl went to the fire and fed it. The flames were low and she used a poker to stoke it, glancing over her shoulder to see Raife still standing in front of the door like a sentry.

"Tiugainn." She said it again, holding her hand out to him. "Sit with me by the fire."

The rug in front of it was made from lamb's wool, soft and white and inviting. She had fallen asleep in front of the fire a few times on that rug, wrapped up in her plaid, just like a real Scot.

"Yer startin' t'look like one of us." Raife approached slowly, looking down at her in her shirt and plaid as she pulled her knees up, resting her chin on them. She'd gotten used to this way of living quite quickly. No more corsets. She liked going around with bare legs, even running through the valley in bare feet. It was like reliving her childhood again. "Yer even gettin' some color."

"Just my freckles." She rolled her eyes, patting the floor beside her. "Sit."

Raife did as she asked, sitting next to her on the rug in the firelight. She searched his face and that faraway look in his eyes as he stared into the flames, and wondered what he was thinking.

"D'ye like it 'ere?" he asked softly. He didn't look at her when he asked. She knew he was thinking about her mounting that horse, riding hell-bent on escape. She'd told him she felt like a prisoner, but it wasn't true, and she felt guilty now for saying it.

"Yes," she confessed. "It's beautiful."

Sometimes she was afraid to admit how much she'd grown to love it in the den. As strange and frightening as it had once been, it was now just as familiar, like home. Even her childhood home had never felt like this. Traveling through the mountain and its tunnels had become routine, and their valley, with its sheep and goats and pigs, its running stream and fields of heather, was one of her favorite places in the world.

"Bóidheach." Raife turned his head to look at her, reaching out to touch her face. His fingers were rough against her flushed cheek. "Tha thu bóidheach."

"No." Sibyl felt her cheeks redden at his words, biting her lip and shaking her head. "Not me."

"Yes, ye know those words." He tilted her chin up when she tried to avoid his eyes. "Yer beautiful. Me bonnie lass."

Hearing him say it made her feel dizzy and flushed, but she told herself it was the warmth of the fire that made her feel that way, not the heat of his gaze.

"Darrow was right. He's always been right." Her voice trembled. "I'm putting all of you in danger just by being here."

Raife shook his head but he didn't deny it.

"I can't continue to risk your lives," she said, the thought of Alistair and his men attacking the wulvers in their mountain too horrific to contemplate. She had the image in her mind of four hundred wulvers being slaughtered, blood splattered everywhere like red paint against the mountain walls, turning the stream that ran through it red. She couldn't be responsible for that. She wouldn't.

"Raife, will you tell me the truth?" she whispered.

"Sibyl, do'na ask this of me." His voice was hoarse, pained.

"Please," she begged him. "You knew Alistair and his men had stopped looking for me. A month—over a month ago! *You knew.* Why didn't you tell me?"

"I'm weak." Raife sighed, closing his eyes and hanging his dark head. His hair spilled across his cheek, a black waterfall, obscuring her view of his face.

"You're the strongest man I've ever known," Sibyl countered, reaching out to touch his arm.

"I can'na let ye go, lass." He lifted his head to meet her eyes, the look in them so filled with longing it took her breath away.

"And I don't want to go," she confessed, swallowing, feeling tears brimming at the thought. She couldn't leave them. Couldn't leave *him.* "But I *should* go, Raife."

"Nuh." His jaw tightened, eyes flashing. "Ye will'na leave me."

His words thrilled and terrified her at the same time.

"There is a woman in a village not too far from here. She was my ladies' maid, but she..." Sibyl swallowed, remembering. How long ago it seemed now. "She found herself in the family way while we were traveling."

"Wit'out a family?" he guessed.

"Aye."

"Listen t'ye." His smile was infectious. "*Aye.*"

How much of his Scottish brogue had she picked up? Sibyl wondered, smiling at her own choice of words.

"They wanted to leave her on the side of the road." Her face hardened when she remembered the men denying relations with Rose, as if she had been the one solely responsible for her chastity. "I found a family to take her in. I know they would take me in, too."

"Nuh." His brow knitted as he looked at her in the firelight. "I can'na allow it."

"Allow it?" Her shoulders straightened and squared as she faced him. "No. You do not allow anything. You do not get a say, Raife. You are not my father. You are not my…"

He didn't say anything as she struggled to finish the sentence and found she couldn't.

"But I am." Those incredible blue eyes, so bright in the firelight, sought hers. "I'm yers. I've been yers since the moment I first saw ye, Sibyl."

And hadn't she been his, from that very moment when he broke out of the underbrush, throwing her over his shoulder and carrying her out of her intended's reach? Hadn't she been his, ever since?

"Raife…" She whispered his name, so dear to her, a name she spoke in her mind a thousand times a day. "You've been right to deny me. You're protecting your pack, your family. No matter what I feel… I can't be yours."

"But y'are, lass." He traced the outline of her hand, still gripping his arm, with his index finger. "I'm yers and ye're mine. Nothin' can change that. N'matter wha'happens."

"Things are so different here." She felt a tear tremble on her lashes and she let it fall. "Wulvers get to choose who you love. But I never had a choice. I was used as a political pawn, sold by my uncle to a man who… who…"

“I’ll not let ’im hurt ye.” Raife cupped her face in his hands, turning her chin up so she was forced to look at him through the blur of tears.

“I was born a girl and not a boy,” she whispered, remembering her father’s constant lament. “Do you know what that means?”

“Aye.” He smiled, those blue eyes dancing devilishly. “I do.”

“No, you don’t,” she choked, jerking her head away from him. “You don’t understand. You’re a man—you can do what you like. I’m a woman. I only ever had one thing of value in the world to offer.”

“And what’s that?” Raife asked softly.

“My virginity.” The words hung between them, much to Sibyl’s horrible shame. Even after all of the training her father had bestowed upon her, she had, in the end, still been sold to the highest bidder as his ornament, his brood mare.

“It’s hardly yer only valuable feature,” Raife teased. She sniffed and tried not to smile at his words. “Although I would’na dismiss it outta hand.”

“But it is all that makes me valuable to *them.* To *him.*” She sneered, remembering Alistair’s snide comments, the way he’d treated her like property.

“But ye’re here now,” Raife reminded her. “And here, ye get to choose.”

“Then I choose you.” She met his eyes, knowing if she did this, there would be no going back, not ever. And she didn’t want to go back. Not anymore. She wanted this man, more than she’d ever wanted anything. He made her want to give up everything for him, to him.

“Will you take me now?” she urged, kneeling up in front of him so they were eye to eye in the firelight.

She leaned in to him, her mouth quivering as she touched her lips to his. She felt his spine stiffen, heard his gasp at the daring press of her mouth.

"Please," she pleaded, her lips burning where they touched his. "Raife, please..."

"Believe me, lass, I want nothin' more." He captured her face in his hands again, searching her eyes. "But Sibyl... what ye're askin'... wulvers mate for life. This is'na simple matter of a man takin' yer virginity. I'd be claimin' ye. Makin' ye me own."

"If you really don't want me...." She swallowed, blinking in surprise at his words.

A simple matter? Did he think she took it so lightly?

"Och!" He closed his eyes, pressing his forehead to hers, a pained expression on his face. "Tis not that, lass. *Tha gaol agam ort.*"

"I... I don't know..." She didn't understand his Gaelic words.

"I love ye." He opened his eyes and met hers. "I love ye, Sibyl."

His mouth took hers and all the feeling between them was caught in that kiss. Sibyl whimpered, putting her arms around his neck, spilling into his lap, unable to contain herself. Raife moaned like he was in pain when she tumbled into his arms, so eager for him she scrambled to get closer, desperate for more of the hard press of his chest against the soft give of her breasts, the way his hands roamed through her thick, red hair.

"And I want ye," he confessed, breathless, when they parted. "But I do'na jus' want yer maidenhood. I want *all* of ye. Yer brave heart, yer quick mind, yer very soul, lass. I would claim ye and mark ye and ye would belong to me alone. And if I can'na have that—"

"Don't you know how much I want you?" she choked. "How much I want to be yours? Really and truly yours?"

"Ye realize what yer askin'?" His eyes were bright with the knowledge, and the fire in his gaze matched her own.

"Yes," she whispered, knowing only that she wanted him, needed him, that more than anything, she loved him. She had never experienced anything like it before, and knew she never would again.

"On th'morrow I'll declare ye as me mate in front of our family, our pack." His words thrilled her to her very foundation and she trembled with anticipation in his arms. "Tonight, I claim ye as mine own."

Finally.

Her body screamed it, her mind too, as she wrapped herself around him, giving into the feelings that had been building between them for overlong. Raife held her in his arms a long time in the firelight, kissing her lips until they were raw and swollen and she was desperate for more, something more, but she didn't know what. She felt as if she wanted to climb inside his skin and wear him like a coat.

"Hungry lil thing," he murmured against her mouth as she pulled at her clothes, too hot to keep wearing them. "Easy now. Lemme."

She watched, reclining on the rug, swallowing hard as he unbuckled her leather belt, pulling it through the loops on her plaid. This caused it all to fall apart in his hands, the yards and yards of material coming away in an instant. Her Scots clothes gave no resistance. There was no corset, nor a hundred tiny buttons to grapple with. She surrendered the last bit of her clothing herself, pulling her shirt off over her head, leaving her completely nude on the rug.

"Bóidheach." Raife's gaze moved over her form and his hands followed, tracing the curve of her waist, the swell of her hips, the gentle slope of her thighs.

"Mine," she whispered, reaching for his thick, leather belt, unbuckling it.

"Aye," he whispered again as he pulled off his plaid in the dimness.

She'd never been so afraid in her life, even watching him change into a wolf, as she was when he disrobed in front of her. Looking at him, rising up stiff and erect, her breath caught in her throat. She didn't know what to expect now that they were both naked together, whether it was from man, wolf or wulver. The stories she'd heard her ladies' maids tell had contained a lot of innuendo but not a lot of details.

"I'm afraid," she confessed, clinging to him as he leaned in to kiss her.

"I do'na wanna harm ye," he whispered, feathering kisses over her bare shoulders. "Och, lass, ye're so beautiful. It hurts me heart. "

She smiled, fingers playing in his long, dark hair as he lowered his mouth to her breast.

"Oh!" Sibyl cried out when his tongue flickered back and forth against her nipple, staring at him, aghast at the sensation. Was it supposed to feel like this? She remembered watching babes suckling at their mother's teats but she had never in her wildest dreams imagined it would be like this.

Raife chuckled, rolling one nipple between thumb and forefinger, continuing to assault her other breast with the hot lash of his tongue. She couldn't help the low moan that escaped her throat, the way her hands groped him in the dimness, finding all the lean, hard slopes of his body, so different from her own softness, beyond exciting.

He kissed and suckled at her breasts for a long time, so long it made her squirm and cry out, begging him for more, although more of what, she still wasn't sure. It was endless, exquisite torture, his titillating exploration of the open, yielding terrain of her body. She gave herself over to the sensation, gave herself over to him, to the flickering quiver of his tongue, to the rough press of his hands against the small of her back, pulling her into the saddle of his hips.

"Oh Raife," she whispered, her thighs trembling as she wrapped her legs around his waist. She couldn't stand this torture, not for another moment. "Please, oh please, I want you."

He let out a low groan when she rocked her hips against him.

"Nuh-yet." He kissed his way down her belly, flicking his tongue into her navel, tracing an invisible line straight down to the triangle of fiery red hair between her legs.

All of the sensation seemed focused there, between her thighs, where she felt soft, moist, swollen with heat. She twisted in his arms, his big hands on her hips as he settled himself between her legs. Always curious, Sibyl went up to her elbows to stare down at him, incredulous, as he nuzzled her sex, parting it with his tongue. His tongue!

"Raife! No!" she gasped in shock, but her protest didn't last long.

Not once he'd drawn her into his mouth, his tongue probing like a hummingbird looking for nectar. He moaned against her sex and Sibyl moaned too, writhing on the lamb's wool rug, hips rising against the flicker of his tongue. His mouth covered her, sweeping up and down and back again, his big hands cupping her behind, pulling her in to him.

"Oh Raife, Raife!" She called his name over and over, hands lost in the silk of his dark hair, the gentle throb between her legs mounting, building up and up, her heart thudding hard in her chest, matching the rising rhythm

Something was happening. Something strange and wonderful and beyond her understanding. Sibyl gave into it. She had no choice. The man between her legs was doing things to her body no one had ever taught her or even told her about. Her breath came fast, hands reaching for him, as if Raife could give her some relief from the delicious torture he was inflicting. The pleasure shook her body, making her thighs tremble, and then, then…

Raife didn't stop when she cried out, when her nails raked his back and scalp at the final, sweet culmination of her pleasure, an ultimate, carnal satisfaction shuddering through her, something completely out of her control. Sibyl stared at him in wonder and awe as he lifted his head to look at her in the firelight, his face glistening as if he'd been eating honey straight from the hive.

"Raife?" she whispered, still trembling as he leaned up to kiss her. The taste on his tongue was strong, musky, his face still wet with her.

"Mine," he whispered against her neck, his body covering hers. She felt the rake of his teeth against her flesh, as if he might truly eat her alive, and she thought she would let him, didn't care if he ate all of her up. It might even ease this horrible ache she had for him.

Even after the powerful, heady climax he'd brought her to, she wanted him. Still wanted him.

"Yes," she urged, wrapping arms and legs around him, hanging on tight. "Yours. Make me yours."

"It may hurt ye." He sounded regretful as he lowered his forehead to her breasts, nuzzling her still, sending shockwaves through her body. "I'll go slow."

She nodded, whimpering when she felt him press between her open thighs, so hot and throbbing, insistent. There was no resistance on her part. She received him with every breath. Even the cry that escaped her throat when he finally pushed into her was an affirmation, welcoming him home. Raife stopped, poised above her when Sibyl's nails dug into his neck, her heels into his lower back, meeting her gaze in the firelight.

The tears that trembled in her eyes weren't from pain or fear. How could she tell him they were tears of joy at being his, finally, completely and utterly his? Raife leaned in and kissed her eyes closed, kissed the tears from them, no words between them. There was no need for them.

He moved in her and it was like flying. Her arms slipped around his neck, face buried there as they rode toward release together. Her body was taut, wound up like a lute string, a hunger burning in her like she'd never experienced before. She knew what it was like to crave this man, to spend her days longing for him, but this was entirely new. How was it possible to have him in her arms and still want him just as much?

"Oh Raife, please!" she begged him over and over, yearning for more, her body twisting and thrusting up against him all on its own, as if she might attain some sort of relief from the fever burning between her thighs. So much heat. So much delicious friction.

"Och, me love!" he cried, his motions matching her own fervor, impaling her again and again with steel heat, forged between her legs. Sibyl clung to him just as she did when he took her for a ride as a wolf, squeezing him between her thighs, feeling the hard, muscled planes of his body working as she grasped for something just out of reach.

Almost there, she thought. *Almost there.*

"Oh!" Sibyl's eyes flew open, meeting his dark, midnight blue gaze. His eyes were dark in the firelight, focused solely on hers, their bodies slick and slippery as they came together. "Oh, Raife!"

She called his name, her whole body quivering with feeling as he gave one, final shuddering thrust of his hips, a cry escaping his lips as they both took one final, flying leap toward freedom, coming crashing down to earth together as one quaking mass of flesh.

She cried.

She couldn't help the overwhelming emotion that overtook her body and she sobbed in his arms.

"I hurt ye, lass, och! I'm so sorry," he whispered, kissing her wet cheeks again and again, and then she was laughing, because he had so misunderstood her feeling. They were tears of pure joy, not pain. She had never been in any less pain—at least, in her heart—as she was at that moment.

"No! No!" she protested, holding him fast.

"Ye're a dervish, woman," Raife complained when he went to move from her but she clung to him, desperate to keep him with her, in her, forever. If they could just stay this way and lock the world out, life would be perfection, she reasoned.

"I am *your* dervish," she whispered back, and he kissed her, claiming her mouth as his own, just as he had claimed the rest of her from the inside out.

"I did hurt ye." Raife frowned when she finally let him climb off of her, looking down at the blood staining the lamb's wool in the firelight.

"Nay, ye claimed me." She touched his cheek. "Sometimes claimin' what's yers involves a lil bloodshed. Twas worth it."

"Listen t'ye." He grinned and stretched, his body like carved bronze in the firelight. "Yer soundin' more like a Scot e'ry day."

"I can be a Scot," she mused, thoughtful now. "But I can never be a wulver."

"Nuh." He touched her cheek, eyes searching hers. "But ye're mine, anyway. I've claimed ye and I will'na let ye go."

"But what about…" She frowned, cocking her head at him. "What about the pack? Darrow? Will they accept me as your mate?"

"Aye." His eyes hardened. "They'll accept ye if'n I tell 'em to."

She wasn't so sure.

"Did you inherit your place? Or did someone name you leader of your pack?" She puzzled over this. She hadn't fully come to understand how it worked, the hierarchy in the wulver pack.

"Tis a process." He smiled at her curiosity. "We do'na inherit titles the way the English do. The leader chooses his successor, but the leader has t'meet all challenges and win in order t'keep 'is place."

"So… your father chose you?" She wondered at this. She would have thought Garaith would have chosen Darrow, given he knew Raife's true parentage.

"Aye." He nodded slowly.

"Were there any challenges?"

"Aye."

"Darrow?"

He nodded again. Of course his brother had challenged him, Sibyl thought. Darrow would have felt slighted by his father's choice. Hurt. Angry. It explained so much of Darrow's character to her now, she was almost relieved at learning this.

"Why did your fathcr choose you?"

"Why d'ye think?" Raife raised his brows, eyes bright.

"Because…" She hesitated, considering her options, realizing all at once why Garaith had chosen Raife over Darrow, a son fathered by another man over his own flesh and blood. "Because you were willing to keep the peace. To honor the pact."

"Aye." He laughed. "Ye're a smart lass."

"Darrow is angry." She frowned, remembering the hardness in his eyes when he spoke of the English—and the MacFalons. "He hates the English. I think he might even hate the MacFalons even more."

"The MacFalons are more *shasennach* than Scot," Raife scoffed. "The Middle March has gone the way of the English. The MacFalons're hated on both sides of the border."

"But your brother, he wants war?" she murmured. "He wants to defy the wolf pact?"

"Aye." Raife sighed, shaking his head. "I love me brother, but he has a bad temper. He does'na have the level head t'lead. He would've gone t'war over Laina."

"What if it had been me in that cage?" she mused, seeing his face darken at the thought. "Wouldn't you have felt the same?"

"Mayhaps." Raife frowned, brows drawn together in thought. "I did'na have a mate when I told Darrow we would'na ride against the MacFalons. But I did what I thought was best for the pack, the best fer all."

"That's why your father chose you," Sibyl whispered, feeling a wave of pride for this man wash over her. "Because you can see the whole and know what is best."

"Mos' times." He blinked at her, looking surprised. "I may've been more clear-headed before I met ye."

"They say love makes you mad." She laughed.

"It surely does." His gaze dropped to her nude body, still sheened with sweat, her thighs moist with a mix of her juices, his seed, and her virgin's blood. She was a mess, but he looked at her as if he might just swallow her whole.

"I'm mad fer ye, Sibyl," he whispered hoarsely, pressing his palm to her belly, petting her gently, lightly, making her shiver. "I've been pantin' after ye fer so long, like a damned dog…"

"A wulver," she countered with a smirk.

He laughed, leaning in to kiss her.

"Does it bother you, that I'm not…?" she asked softly when they parted.

"Not what?" He nuzzled her throat, his mouth doing things to her body, making her tingle all over.

"Not a wulver."

"Yer Sibyl." He raised his head to meet her eyes. "Yer mine. Tis all that matters."

She wasn't so sure of that. Raife hadn't denied her—and himself—for so long for no reason. He knew his pack wouldn't like the fact he'd chosen a human mate instead of a wulver woman. He knew his brother would object, loudly and vehemently, especially given her connection to the MacFalons. And she knew it, too. What would happen, when she was marked, his? Not just here, but out in the open?

"Will I birth a pup?"

She had asked the wulver women about it. Kirstin had told her, as had Laina. Human women who mated with wulver men still birthed wulvers. Their child would be able to change, just like all the wulvers could. But would the child appear first as a baby? Or as a wolf pup?

"Nuh." Raife laughed. "He'll be like ye til tis time to change. When he becomes a man."

"He?" She raised her eyebrows at him. "Already a boy? What if he's a she?"

"I do'na care, lass." He laughed again at her look of consternation. "Boy, girl, human, wulver. It does'na matter t'me. All that matters is that ye're mine."

"Now that you've *finally* claimed me," she teased, sliding a thigh over his and moving her body closer. "I thought I might have to lock you in this room, strip myself naked and…"

"Ye might as well've just run me through wit' a sword. T'would've been less painful!" Raife groaned, lowering his head to her breasts in surrender. "E'ery minute I had t'resist ye was torture…"

"But you don't have to resist any longer." She turned her face up to his to be kissed.

"No." He grinned, obliging her, nibbling at her lower lip with his teeth, licking the corner of her mouth, pressing his big thigh between hers.

"When can we do it again?" she whispered into his ear, nipping at his earlobe, making him let out a low groan. "That… that thing you did with your mouth… I really liked that…"

"I have so much more t'teach ye." He chuckled, kissing her fully on the mouth, holding her little body in his arms.

"More?" Her eyes lit up.

"Aye, much, much more," he agreed, eyes alight. "Come wit' me, lass. Let's get cleaned up so we can get dirty again."

Chapter Ten

The hot spring was the purest of luxuries. She thought everyone in England would live in a mountain if they knew about hot springs. The water was warm without the need of a fire, like magic. Raife lit a torch on the wall as they went through a door in their room, further into the mountain, deep into a cavern.

The warm water was a wonder, steam rising all around them. They soaked in the pool together, drifting. Sibyl closed her eyes and leaned back, floating, letting Raife run soapy hands over her body, a delicious tease. She whimpered when his hand cupped her sex, washing gently. She saw him inspecting her there, parting her so he could peer at the pink, soft flesh inside.

With a satisfied look, he sank low in the water, kissing her there. Sibyl moaned and rose to meet him, her knees over his shoulders, amazed at how the sensation was resurrected in her instantly. She didn't understand how it could be, something so forceful and compelling that could overtake you again like that. But she didn't need to comprehend it, not with Raife's mouth between her thighs, driving her to heights she didn't know possible.

She just needed to feel it.

Her lover, her mate, was skilled, his fingers sliding into her flesh, in and out, a rhythm that reminded her of the way they rocked together when he was pressed deep into her womb. The motion made her long for it, for him, and she whimpered and clutched at him, her nails raking his shoulders and scalp as he floated her across the spring, his mouth fastened tight to her mound.

"Oh, Raife, Raife!" she cried, body arching, bucking in the water, the feeling overcoming her, a mighty surge, making her nipples harden and her hips roll under his lashing tongue.

Then she truly was floating, flying free, soaring above it all.

Raife held her in his arms, whispering her name, and the word "mine," again and again. She loved being his. Finally, fully and completely, she belonged to this man. She felt his love for her—and his lust. There was something about the way he took her, claimed her, that filled her more completely than she knew any human man would have been capable. It wasn't about the physical act. They were connected—deeply, inexorably connected.

"I want you." She opened her eyes to meet his, her hand reaching down under the water to find him, thick and hard and ready to enter her again.

"Aye." He looked at her through eyes half-lidded with lust, his face flushed, skin hot against hers. "And I want ye…"

He lifted her, seizing her nipple gently between his teeth, making her gasp before he began to suckle. Sibyl cried out, wrapping her legs around him, trapping his hardness between them. She felt it throb and moaned at the sensation. Raife leaned back against the side of the pool, burying his face against her breasts, tongue skipping from one nipple to the other as she squirmed in his arms.

"It's so hot," she cried as the steam rose around them, her skin flushed red.

"Aye," he agreed, sliding a hand behind her neck and bringing her head down to kiss her. She gave into his kiss, the press of his mouth, his tongue exploring. He smiled down at her when they parted, looking at her with such love, such desire, she was glad for the buoyancy of the water.

"Come." He put his palms up on the edge of the pool, sliding onto the ledge, water sheeting off his body, a cloud of steam surrounding him. He held his hand out for her, but she was transfixed by the sight of him. She'd watched him undress, had seen him, had felt him inside of her, but now she was face-to-face with the length of him, rising up, throbbing with every beat of his heart.

"Sibyl…" he murmured as she came closer, ever curious, cocking her head to look at him as she reached out to take him in her fist.

She looked up and met his gaze with questioning eyes, watching his face as her fingers caressed him. Could she make him feel like he made her feel? She wondered, remembering the hot, wet rhythm of him thrusting into her, mimicking it with her hand. Raife moaned in response, his hips moving with her motion.

"Och! Sibyl!" he gasped when she dared to lean forward and cover the head with her mouth. It was a sudden, inspired action on her part. She couldn't help remembering how good it felt to have him licking and sucking at her flesh, and her curiosity and natural experimental nature just took over from there.

"Do you like it?" she murmured, looking up at him, inquiring with her eyes.

He just moaned and grabbed her hair, bringing her mouth back to his length, sliding her head down until she thought she might gag on it. But she didn't care.

The pleasure in his voice made her bob her head faster, taking more and more of him, as much as she could manage—which wasn't easy.

"Ahhh lass, wait, wait," he cried, but she wasn't listening. She heard that catch in his voice, the strangled cry that meant he was reaching his peak, and she wanted to take him there, the way he had for her.

And then he moaned and drove deep into her throat, hand cupping the back of her neck as he filled her mouth with his seed. It was white hot, bitter, and Sibyl couldn't do anything but swallow. She sucked and swallowed automatically, the taste burning her throat, making her eyes tear up. It was the most delicious thing in the world, looking up and seeing Raife completely lose control, giving in to her, giving her everything, flooding her mouth with his very essence.

"Och, lass, I'm sorry," he gasped an apology, slipping into the water so he could take her in his arms. "I could'na stop…"

"Don't apologize," she protested, wrapping her legs around his waist, her arms around his neck, eyes bright as she met his. "Oh, let's do it again…"

She rubbed against him, hips grinding under the water, but he was soft now, spent.

"Soon." He chuckled, still panting in her ear as he held her close. "Give a man time to rest between."

"How long?" she cocked her head at him, completely earnest, and he laughed.

"Hungry kitten." He smiled, closing his eyes and leaning back against the rocky side of the spring. "Soon, I promise."

She sighed, tucking her head under his chin, letting herself float with him. She wanted him inside of her.

All the time. She would stay joined with him, forever, if she had her wish.

"Are ye ready t'be a wulver's mate?" he asked, opening one eye to peer at her.

"Isn't that what we just did?" she teased.

"I'm pack leader," he reminded her, kissing the freckles on her shoulders. "There'll be other responsibilities."

"My mother tried to make me a good girl and learn all about how to run a household, but alas," Sibyl lamented. "I was better at shooting and riding."

"Yer strengths are suited t'our life 'ere, lass." Raife slid his hands over her under the water, following her curves. "It's like ye were born t'be 'ere."

"Maybe I was." She cocked her head and looked at him. "Maybe it was God's hand who guided me here after all. If God could curse us, mayhaps he could save us too."

"Mayhaps." He kissed her softly, the steam rising all around them. "Ye're a wonder, Sibyl Blackthorne."

"What will be my new name?" she wondered aloud.

"Yer new name?"

"Don't I take your name, when we are married?"

"We do'na hold to that here." He smiled. "We'll 'ave a declaration and a markin'. Followed by a giant feast. And then three days alone so I can ravish ye in e'ery possible position..."

"I like the sound of that…" She sighed happily, tilting her head so he could kiss her throat.

"But ye'll still be called Sibyl Blackthorne," he said, meeting her eyes in the dim light. "I do'na need a change of names t'know ye're mine. Ye'll forever be mine no matter what ye're called."

She had cringed at the thought of becoming Sibyl MacFalon, but she rather liked the idea of becoming Sibyl…Wulver? Did the wulvers even have surnames? Blackthorne was her family name, associated with her father, whom she loved, but a mother who had given her to her uncle to do with as he wished. The name had been a mixed blessing her whole life.

Sibyl's head came up and she looked at her new mate and future husband through the rising steam, frowning, a thought suddenly occurring to her.

I never told him my full name.

Had she? She could have sworn she had not.

"Raife…?"

"Yes, lass?" He didn't open his eyes. He looked so relaxed and content, floating with her in the water.

"How… how did you know my family name?"

The question hung between them. Raife slowly opened his eyes, meeting hers. She saw something flicker there before he answered, something that told her he wasn't going to tell her the truth. Or maybe, not all of it.

"Tis common knowledge the MacFalon was marrying a Blackthorne," he said.

Mayhaps that was true. But she frowned and traced the lines between his brows with her fingers, realizing she'd come to know him far more than she had let on. She knew this man's expressions, when he was being honest, and when he was not. Especially since the latter was so uncommon between them.

"You heard that, all the way up here, in the mountain?" She kissed his cheek, water beading there.

"Tis me job t'know these things." He raised his brows at her. "I can'na protect me pack wit'out that knowledge. We've avoided war wit' the MacFalons fer twenty years. That was me father's legacy and I want it t'live on."

"The wolf pact." She sighed, snuggling her head under his chin. "Everything is politics."

"Not e'rythin'." Raife's hand moved to cup her breast and she smiled. But she wasn't willing to let him distract her so easily. Not now. Like the wulvers, she had scented something, and she was going to follow it. She just wasn't exactly sure where she was headed.

"Your father…?" she asked softly. "You mean… King Henry?"

She felt his spine straighten at her words.

"Who told ye'bout that?"

"Just… gossip…" She shrugged. "You're not the only one who pays attention, you know."

"Tis true." Raife sighed. "Although I'd like t'forget it more of'en than not."

"But he created the wolf pact, didn't he?"

"Aye, he did," Raife agreed. "But twas for his own personal gain, ye ken? He wanted the MacFalons and the wulvers united against a common enemy."

"King Edward IV."

"Aye." Raife's mouth pursed into a thin line before he went on. "So the Tudors could sit on the throne again. He came here jus'after the Anglo-Saxon wars. We did'na care for the English and neither did the MacFalons, but fightin' for Henry meant me father could gain some measure of peace in our pack. We could stop fightin' the Scots and mayhaps go into the woods without fear of our women being hunted and killed… or raped."

"Raped…" She shuddered, something suddenly occurring to her that hadn't before. The wulver women had spoken of it as a romance, the relationship between

King Henry VII and Raife's mother. But now that she understood the bond between a wulver and his mate, she wasn't so sure. "Your mother? And King Henry?"

"She did'na love the man," he replied flatly. "She did'na have much of a choice in the matter."

That thought made Sibyl shiver in spite of the heat of the water.

"And she became pregnant with you?" she murmured, thinking out loud. "But I thought wulvers shift when they're in heat? Don't they change into wolf form?"

"Aye, lass, they do."

Sibyl stared at him while he let that sink in.

Laina lamented not being able to be with Darrow in human form when she was in heat, at her most fervent. She would change with little warning, and be unable to change back until her moon blood cycle had passed. It happened to all the wulver females. If Raife's mother, Avril, had become pregnant with him, that meant she had turned. And while she was in her wolf form, King Henry had…

"No…" Sibyl's eyes widened in shock. "He took her when she was… as a wolf?"

"Aye." His jaw hardened, eyes dark in the light of the torch. "Some men see wulver women as a challenge."

"Oh no." She closed her eyes against it. That poor woman, Sibyl thought. She couldn't imagine what Avril had been through. She'd watched her friend give birth in a cage and then be murdered by the MacFalon, was taken prisoner herself, and then what? She'd been kept in a cage as a freak show, something to be shown off by the MacFalon when guests arrived? Guests like Henry Tudor, the possible future King of England?

"Did your father know? I mean... Darrow's father...?"

"Garaith's me father," Raife told her. "He treated me as his son."

"But he knew you weren't *really* his son?"

"Eventually, aye." Raife's face was pained. "But not when Henry made the pact. Not when he got the MacFalons and the wulvers t'agree t'fight fer him."

"Your mother didn't tell him," she whispered, knowing it was true. Of course Avril wouldn't tell her husband, her wulver mate, what had happened to her while she'd been captured. And Sibyl's womanly heart knew instantly why Raife's mother had kept it a secret.

"Not afirst," Raife said, confirming Sibyl's suspicions. "If me father'd known, he would've..."

"It would have been war," she murmured.

"Aye. She was tryin' t'save us from that," Raife said, his voice hoarse. "And I think she did."

"But she was pregnant," Sibyl mused aloud. "She couldn't hide that for long."

"Me father took the pack huntin' for Henry's crown," he reminded her. "He was'na 'ere for me birth."

"And when he returned?"

"I was raised by Beitris until me mother pupped Darrow. Then she finally told me father the truth."

"But he didn't go after Henry?" Sibyl wondered aloud.

"By then, Henry'd been crowned King of England. And me father'd seen the result of living peacefully 'ere in the mountain, wit'out constant threats from the MacFalon," Raife explained. "Alistair's father, Lachlan MacFalon, was a different sort of a man. He was enjoyin' the new peace as much as me father and our pack."

"Your poor mother…"

"She was a strong woman. And brave." Raife lifted Sibyl's chin, smiling into her eyes. "Like ye."

"She obviously loved you and your father very much." She kissed him softly, her lips wet not just from the hot springs water, but also from the tears slipping down her cheeks. The sacrifice Raife's mother had made for her pack, for her mate, made her own look small in comparison. But she knew, she would do anything for Raife, even what Avril, his mother, had done.

"Me father would've done anythin' for peace after Laina's mother was killed and his own wife taken," Raife said, speaking Sibyl's thoughts aloud. "Sondra—Laina's mother—was his brother's own wife."

"The MacFalons..." She said the name with such bitterness. "I wish I'd never heard of them."

"The names matter naught, in th'end."

"What do you mean?" She lifted her head to look at him.

"MacFalons, Blackthornes, Tudors… wulvers, Scots, English. Men should be ready to fight when they 'ave to—but far too many men wanna go t'war when there's no real reason. Peace is possible. I think, when he made the wolf pact, Henry finally discovered a way to unite warrin' factions that worked."

"A piece of paper?" she scoffed. "The wolf pact?"

"Nuh, lass—the promise of a woman."

"I don't understand." Sibyl wrinkled her nose, puzzled.

"The English and the Scots had a'ready been fightin' for East March in the Anglo-Saxon wars. We

Scots're a hearty lot. They can'na beat us down fer long. Fightin' the Scots was'na goin' t'work and Henry knew it."

"So he made you all sign a piece of paper?"

The wolf pact. As if a piece of paper could keep men from fighting, she thought. It had worked for a short time, but Alistair had broken it by caging and killing wulvers again. There was no piece of paper that could bind a man so completely…

And then, Sibyl realized—mayhaps there was.

A pact could be broken. Peace treaties were signed all the time, and men still went to war.

But a marriage contract? That was something altogether different. That was a holy covenant, sanctioned by God and the pope himself. It was undissolvable, or nearly so.

"What did Henry promise to give them, if the MacFalons and the wulvers fought for and won him the crown?" Sibyl swallowed, afraid of the answer.

"He promise ye to the MacFalons." Raife said it, sounding so sad, and it hit her in the heart like an arrow. "A Blackthorne woman was the prize, the MacFalon's spoils of war."

"But I wasn't even born!"

"Not quite," he agreed. "T'would've been yer cousin promised then, by yer uncle. Yer family have long been Tudor supporters. Yer father and 'is brother?"

"Yes. Of course," she agreed, her voice faint, even to her own ears. "The Blackthornes have always been favorites of the Tudors."

"Yer uncle once had a young wife and a daughter, did he na?"

"Yes." It had been before she was born, but she'd been told about it by both her mother and her father. Her uncle had never remarried. "But they both died of fever..."

"Aye. But that girl was promised ta the MacFalon," Raife informed her, a fact Sibyl's parents had both failed to mention. "Godfrey Blackthorne was 'ere with Henry in 1483 as one of the first members of the Yeomen of the Guard. He swore himself liege to the Tudors and promised his own daughter in marriage to a Scot in exchange for lands and a better title. He was the second son, ya ken?"

"And then she died…" Sibyl remembered the way her uncle had treated her after her father's death, how he had treated her mother too. They were little more than property to him. A means to an end. Would he have treated his own daughter the same way? She had often wondered that, but now she knew the answer.

"Aye. Twas lucky fer yer uncle that ye're a girl and could be promised ta the MacFalon's son." Raife shook his dark head, kissing the top of hers.

"Lucky I was a girl…" she whispered.

She'd never expected to hear that phrase in her whole life.

All that time her father had spent lamenting she wasn't a boy! She had heard the arguments about who she would and would not marry her whole life. In the end, while her mother capitulated and often agreed with Sibyl's uncle, her father had put his foot down.

Until her father had died and her uncle had married her mother and suddenly had final say in who she married…

"King Henry promised the MacFalons an English bride, a highborn lady, and everythin' that came wit'it," Raife told her. "All the riches, the land, the titles. Henry had no daughters at the time, but he promised the MacFalon his son would marry a Blackthorne, the daughter of his verra own right hand man."

"Godfrey Blackthorne." She couldn't believe it. Sibyl's uncle had planned it all along. "You knew this story? About the Blackthornes and the MacFalons?"

"Aye." Raife sighed. "I knew who ye were, Sibyl Blackthorne—and why ye were bein' traded t'Alistair MacFalon."

"I guess everyone knew but me." Sibyl frowned, thinking of her uncle and his long-ago agreement. He'd promised his own daughter in marriage, and when he couldn't manage that, he'd promised Sibyl instead. But she wasn't his to give! Not until…

"I knew then, ye belonged t'me." He sighed, shaking his head. "I heard ye yellin' at one of the MacFalon men, something about pig offal and a pot to piss in?"

"What?" Sibyl turned to him, blinking in surprise.

She vaguely remembered the altercation. Gregor, the worst of Alistair's men, had confronted her while she was taking out a horse to ride early one morning. Only a week or so after her arrival, it had been long before the castle was awake, the sun not even quite cresting the horizon, and she was sure she could sneak out for a short time just to ride through the woods on the path. That was all she had in mind then—although a plan of escape was just starting to form, the more time she spent with her betrothed—but Gregor had foiled even that. She'd been furious, she remembered, and had cursed at him as he caught the reins of her horse to take her back to the castle.

"I'd heard ye'd come t'da MacFalon keep." Raife shrugged, looking sheepish. "Darrow said he'd seen ye. Said ye had hair like fire and a temper to match."

"So you were watching me?" She stared at him. "From the woods?"

"Aye." He nodded. "That's when I knew."

"Just by looking at me?" She snorted, rolling her eyes.

"Well, I did watch ye handle the horse." He grinned. "And I saw ye kick Alistair's man in the shin when he tried to pull ye onto 'is mount."

She flushed, remembering that, too.

"I knew ye were plannin' t'escape." He smiled. "So I waited."

"You… waited?" She gaped at him. How could he have known? She hadn't even known, then, that she was going to run away.

"I had ta have ye, Sibyl." He crushed her to him, so hard it hurt her ribs. "Ye did'na belong ta the MacFalons. Ye belong wit' me. Ye chose me. And I chose ye."

She remembered him asking her, giving her a choice in the woods. To go with him or to stay. She had chosen him. And he, in turn, had chosen her. It was an act far more powerful than contracts. She would have rankled at the idea of belonging to a man, once upon a time, she realized. She would have railed about men and their belief that women were nothing but property to be owned. Now it just made her feel warm, and safe, and very, very loved. Maybe it was because she'd finally found the man she really did belong with. Maybe it wasn't such a bad thing, belonging to a man, if it was the right one.

"My uncle didn't care about me." Sibyl said this out loud to someone for the first time. She'd thought it, even believed it, but she'd never spoken of it. "He didn't care who I loved, if I loved… if I was loved."

"Aye." Raife's eyes darkened. "All yer uncle cared 'bout was workin' out a way t'keep his favor wit' the king."

It was true.

Growing up, Sibyl had been so close to her father, it seemed strange to her not to have a champion around when he was gone. Her life had turned completely upside down after his sudden death, and in her grief, while she had questioned her uncle's precipitous marriage to her mother and his control over their fortune, she hadn't paid enough attention. Not nearly enough.

She had been sheltered by her father, protected more than she knew. Once her uncle was involved in deciding her future, her world had crumbled around her. Her father had often said, "Sibyl will marry for love, not fortune," when her mother pressed the point that Sibyl was growing older, into her marriageable years.

It was her uncle who had been there all along, working behind the scenes, orchestrating a match that would benefit himself, as well as king and country. Sibyl would be given in marriage to Alistair MacFalon as their reward, the spoils of war. A contract that couldn't be broken, once it was made, one that solidified the bond between the English and Scottish far greater than any peace treaty.

But he never could have done so if Sibyl's father had been around to protest it.

That realization made her stomach turn over.

She remembered her father in his last days. He had taken suddenly ill after dinner one night, and no amount of medicine would make him better. She had, with their local apothecary, tried everything, but he could hold nothing down. It all ran through him, until there was nothing left. It was days from the onset of the illness until his death, just days, and she had barely had time to grieve his loss before her uncle had begun petitioning the king to marry his brother's wife.

It was an arrangement that required not only the king's blessing, but the pope's as well, because while not blood related, marrying your brother's widow was frowned upon. Of course, Godfrey Blackthorne had the king's ear and could get what he liked. Her uncle always seemed to manage to get what he wanted, no matter the cost.

Sibyl let Raife pull her close, his arms around her comforting, as she closed her eyes and remembered who had just happened to be visiting the night her father had taken ill. Would his own brother have done something so horrible, so heinous? She couldn't imagine it, didn't want to, but her uncle's motivations had suddenly become clear.

Had her uncle killed her father—poisoned him, mayhaps? With Sibyl's father gone, he could not only honor the king's wishes and provide the MacFalons with a highborn daughter to marry, he could also inherit all of his brother's lands, his title—even his wife. Because a marriage contract, that was a covenant that could not be broken. Once her uncle was married to his brother's widow, he would inherit everything. And once Sibyl was married to Alistair MacFalon…

"Marriage." She spoke the word softly, feeling it tighten around her neck like a hand. How close she had been to marrying a man she not only didn't love, but one that would have spent a lifetime treating her like his property. She wondered, now, what her father's motivation had been, treating his girl like a boy. Mayhaps he had hoped to protect her from his brother's plan, and in the end, he had—even though his trust in his family had cost him his life.

It was the strength he had instilled in her that had given her the courage to escape.

Without that, she never would have met Raife.

"Are ye proposin', lass?" Raife grinned, running a wet hand over her hip.

"I'm already yours," she reminded him with a smile. "I just realized… what you said. It's marriage. That's how the king seeks to end the border wars."

"Aye," Raife agreed. "He's now promised 'is own daughter, Lady Margaret, ta James IV. Henry finally found what works t'keep the peace. Join two warrin' factions by marriage. Men are hotheaded, tis true. Look at Darrow. But wives and mothers'll not stand by and watch their sons slaughtered, their daughters widowed."

"Yes, *Darrow* is the hot-headed one," she teased, remembering Raife's reaction when his brother had taken her out into the woods alone.

"I'm not hot-headed," he protested. "I've worked hard t'keep the peace. D'ye know how long I waited t'claim ye? I wanted ye, lass, but I had t'do what was right fer e'eryone."

"Is this right?" She tilted her face up to him, really questioning. "For everyone?"

"I do'na care anymore," he confessed, burying his face against her neck, holding her close with trembling arms. “I love ye. I need ye. I will’na give ye up, not ever.”

“You’re risking everything for me.” She swallowed, knowing it was true. “To mate with me.”

“Ye’re mine, Sibyl Blackthorne.” Those blue eyes of his darkened, her body fitted to his like hand in glove. “Ye’re me chosen. Me mate. I will’na let ’im ’ave ye.”

“But at what cost?” she murmured, closing her eyes in pleasure as he kissed her neck. “Will there be war again?”

“The border skirmishes grow less factious e’ery year,” Raife replied, his breath hot against her collarbone, his mouth a wonderful distraction. “The MacFalons’ll get over their injury. Alistair’ll lick his wounds and King Henry’ll find another highborn English lady for ’im t’bed. He can’na ’ave mine.”

“No, he cannot,” Sibyl agreed happily enough, moaning softly when Raife’s mouth found her breast.

She didn’t want to think about Alistair, or her uncle, or any other man besides this one.

But Raife’s words stayed with her.

Would Alistair back down? In his heart, Alistair was a coward. But it was his pride that was injured, and she didn’t know if he would recover from that. Raife was so honorable, she knew he didn’t understand men like Alistair, but Sibyl had lived with her uncle, and they were two peas in a pod. Alistair was the type of man who would stab another man in the back. Or murder a wolf in a cage and drag it out as if he had made a real kill.

It wasn’t so much what was true, as what things looked like on the outside, to the rest of the world, that mattered to men like Alistair MacFalon and Godfrey Blackthorne.

"What's the matter, lass?" Raife lifted his head to look at her when she didn't fully respond to his caresses.

"So much pain and sacrifice," she murmured, so grateful to be here with him she could barely breathe. Everything that had happened in the past—Sondra's death, Avril's capture, even Raife's unplanned conception—it all seemed to culminate here, for her and Raife, for their future offspring and the generations that had yet to come. "Your poor mother, your father…"

"Our children will'na have t'sacrifice so much fer peace." Raife's eyes grew serious as he looked at her. There was so much pain and heartache there, she wouldn't add any more to it, to speak about her uncle, her father, her sudden realization that the former had likely killed the latter. They'd both experienced pain, regret. What was the sense in talking about it anymore? He'd been through enough. His pack, and his kind, had sacrificed more than enough.

"We do not have children," she reminded him with a soft, devious smile, sliding her hand down to capture him, firm and at the ready.

He grinned. "We'd better get t'makin' some then."

Chapter Eleven

Raife had said he would declare her his mate to the pack the next day, but they didn't leave their room the next day. Or the day after that. Kirstin brought them food and drink, and they needed the sustenance, that was certain! And whenever Raife or Sibyl would answer the door, Kirstin's eyes would sparkle and she would flash a knowing smile, but she never said a word.

It wasn't until the third day, when Sibyl was so sore she could hardly walk, that Kirstin finally spoke up. But she didn't say the words Sibyl expected to hear—no teasing or jest about her pack leader's newly chosen mate—but rather gave her a message that would change her life forever.

Raife was sleeping by the fire when the knock came. Sibyl heard it, a small, tentative thing. Too early for breakfast, she thought, getting up and pulling on her shirt to go investigate. Kirstin was standing out there in the tunnel and beckoned Sibyl to come with her.

"What is it?" Raife was awake, calling for her, as she put on her plaid and tied her shoes.

"Go to sleep. I'll be right back," Sibyl whispered. "Someone is in need of a healer."

It was a white lie, and perhaps not a lie at all. Kirstin had been quite urgent and was, still, as Sibyl joined her in the tunnel. They walked together, heading toward the kitchen, as Kirstin finally told her.

"The MacFalons have Laina." Her words were whispered, choked. She sounded so very afraid and there were tears in her eyes.

"What?" Sibyl slowed, stopped, staring at the woman in disbelief. It couldn't be true. It simply couldn't.

"The scouts jus' came back wit' the news," she whispered, glancing up and down the tunnels, as if someone might overhear. "They're gonna tell Raife and Darrow."

"No," Sibyl breathed, grabbing Kirstin's shoulders and shaking her. "No! They will go after her and then…"

Kirstin's eyes grew even bigger, and Sibyl didn't even know it was possible. They were already as big as saucers in her pale face. Sibyl cursed Laina under her breath.

"Was she out looking for huluppa?"

"What else?"

"Is she… alive?" Sibyl didn't even want to think about the alternative. Although, after what Raife had told her about his mother, she knew there were things that could happen to a woman that had further-reaching consequences than a quick death.

"They took her ta the MacFalons," Kirstin whispered as they approached the kitchen. It was early and most of the pack was still asleep, wrapped up in their plaids in front of the big fireplace. "The scouts say they painted a message inside the cage. In blood."

"In Laina's blood?" All the color drained out of Sibyl's face.

"The MacFalon's out to start a war," Kirstin whispered as they tiptoed through the kitchen. "He's defyin' the pact."

"He wants me." Sibyl said this as they stepped out into the cool morning air. The sun was just coming up over the horizon. "This is about me."

"I think so." Kirstin nodded, standing there in the cold, shivering, her eyes wild with fear.

"I can't... I can't let this happen." Sibyl looked around the valley, at this place she had come to call home. A place that felt more like home than any other ever had, even her father's own estate. Then she met Kirstin's eyes and knew why the woman had come to her, why she had pulled her aside to tell her quietly, without yet involving Raife or Darrow. Why she had led her out here in the morning light.

Kirstin was a wulver woman. She knew sometimes sacrifices had to be made, that there were some things the heart of a man just couldn't handle. And Sibyl was a part of them now. This was her pack—this was her family. Her worst fear had come to pass. Alistair was going to start a war. He was willing to risk it all simply to retain his property. She was nothing but a possession to him, something that had been stolen. Something he wanted returned.

And, like a demented, twisted child, he was going to get his toy back, no matter the cost.

If that meant war—well, that was a game to him too, wasn't it?

But Sibyl knew the costs, the real costs in human and wulver blood. Laina's had already been spilled. She prayed her friend was still alive. The image of little Garaith filled her mind, and she couldn't imagine him growing up without his mother. How many more wulver lives would be lost because of Alistair's selfishness? She imagined Alistair's men coming into the tunnels, the stream running with wulver blood, and her heart broke into a thousand pieces.

This was her family, now more than ever. Raife's face came into her mind and she heard his objections in her head, even though he didn't yet know this news. He would choose another, far more dangerous solution than the one she was about to undertake. But war was no solution. She had to keep the peace—the peace his mother had sacrificed for, the peace his father had fought for, the peace they all had come to accept and expect.

She would have to make this sacrifice to save them all.

She put her arms around Kirstin and the two women hugged, hanging onto each other tightly, knowing it would be the last time they embraced.

Kirstin already had a pack for her and Sibyl teared up when she saw her little satchel, the one she had pinned under her skirts when she had escaped Alistair MacFalon. Was she really going to do this? But when she met her friend's eyes, she knew there was no other way. The wulvers would ride out if Laina wasn't returned, and she couldn't risk Raife's life, the lives of everyone in the pack, when all Alistair wanted, in this end, was his own way.

He wanted his property back. Sibyl would simply return it to him.

"There is water, some food," Kirstin told her. "Ye must hurry."

But there was no time.

There was always a sentry at the entrance of the cave. She couldn't go that way, and besides, she needed something faster than her own feet. She was no wulver. She couldn't cross the rocky terrain on foot like they could, faster than any human. Kirstin hugged her one more time before heading back into the mountain, letting Sibyl do what she must.

The horses were penned, and she found Angus, the horse Raife often let her ride, in the dimness, calling to him with a special whistle. She didn't give herself time to think. She saddled the horse and climbed on, knowing if she was going to do this, she had to do it fast, before Raife awoke and found her gone. Before the scouts had a chance to tell him and Darrow how Laina had been captured by Alistair and used as bait to lure them all into a bloody trap.

The horse didn't want to go. It nickered and pawed at the ground when Sibyl climbed up onto its back. She urged it on, squeezing its flanks between her bare thighs and steering the horse upward, through the mountain path. She had never been on it, but she knew where it went. Raife had told her about the treacherous way up and then down the mountain, a pathway no human had ever travailed. Only wulver warriors had the skill to traverse this path.

And she was neither.

Thankfully, the horse knew the way, had traveled it more than once in its lifetime, had been taken up and down the mountain during training exercises that were, finally, serving some purpose. Sibyl leaned over the horse's neck, holding onto the bridle, and let it take her where it would. There was nothing else to do, except hold on and pray. The path was little more than the rocky edge of a cliff, the shear drop-off so steep she couldn't see the side of the mountain if she dared to look down to her left.

The path wound up, up, taking her higher into the mountains until she gasped for breath and clung to Angus's mane, her eyesight blurring and her mind bolting. She wanted nothing more than to escape. The early morning cold made her bones ache and her teeth chatter. What had she been thinking, stealing a horse and riding away into the mountains? What did she think she was going to accomplish?

But she knew, and kept it out in front of her as she managed to stay on the horse as it neared the top of the mountain and started down the other side. She was going to sacrifice herself for the man she loved. A war between the MacFalons—and their local border allies in the Middle March—and the wulvers would bring King Henry's wrath down on all of them. So what if he had once negotiated a peaceful pact between them? It had been in his best interest to do so. He needed the wulver warriors and the Scots to unite and fight for his right to wear the crown.

Now that crown—and all the power than came with it—belonged to him alone.

No matter how strong the wulvers, no matter if one of their warriors was worth ten of Henry's, eventually the numbers would win out. Raife would be killed, Darrow too. They would all be slaughtered, the females widowed, the babies orphaned, left alone to fend for themselves in the mountain. Sibyl thought of Kirstin, of Laina's baby, and clung more tightly to her horse.

She could stop this. If she simply returned and offered herself to Alistair, to do with as he wished, she could get him to let Laina go. His pride had been wounded, and mayhaps he would take her back and marry her after all. Or mayhaps he would set her aside, return her as damaged goods to her uncle, who would likely attempt to beat sense into her until she was senseless.

Not that any of that mattered.

They could do anything they wanted—Alistair, his men, her uncle. It wouldn't matter, as long as they freed Laina and honored the pact.

The horse, so used to following the path, wanted to turn around and go back. She had to steer it onward, thankful she had spent so much time with Darrow searching for the huluppa tree. She knew how to get back to Alistair's lands, the border between Scotland and England—the borderland between worlds, between humans and wulvers.

She found the path where she had found the huluppa tree, found it growing, healthy and strong, on the other side of the stream. It was mid-morning when she found the cage, the horrible word, written in blood, goading Raife and Darrow and the rest of the wulvers to war.

"Tiugainn."

Come.

In Laina's blood.

Oh Laina, Laina, please hang on, Sibyl thought, tasting her own blood in her mouth where she'd worried the inside of her cheek raw. She glimpsed the tree where she had pinned Alistair with an arrow and wished she had a longbow now. But it wouldn't do her any good. One woman and one bow were nothing. She couldn't stand up to Alistair and the MacFalons.

She couldn't do anything but surrender.

The day was warm, the bluebells so thick on the forest floor she could hardly see green. The mountain's chill faded as she rode closer to the MacFalon castle. Something in the distance, behind her, gave her pause as she stopped her horse just shy of the edge of the woods.

The long, keening howl of a wolf.

A wulver.

It was Raife. She knew her mate's call, would know it anywhere, and he was and would forever be her mate, she realized. It wouldn't matter if Alistair accepted her back, married her, and she spent her life with the MacFalons, raising his children as Scots. Raife would forever have her heart.

She knew Raife's mother had felt the same about Darrow's father, even if she had sacrificed herself to a king. Avril had already been mated to and in love with Garaith, was being held prisoner when King Henry had taken a fancy to her. A woman's heart knew the truth—and while Sibyl would be forever grateful that Raife had been the result of her sacrifice—she understood now what it was to really love someone.

To love them so much you would give your own life to save theirs.

And what else could Avril have believed, except that Henry, who would someday sit on the throne of England, already had the power to wipe out her entire pack? Henry had been a kind captor, but a captor nonetheless. And in the end, he had let her go, had given her back in exchange for an army of wulver warriors who had fought for his right to wear the crown.

All in the name of peace.

"Raife." Sibyl whispered his name, feeling him still, tasting him on her lips, her body filled with him. It always would be, now. She wore the shape of his heart within her breast, and nothing else would ever fill it again. She was his and always would be, no matter what happened now.

She hadn't stopped to think, had just stolen this horse and rode out with the hope she could avert a disaster, but she stopped now. She stopped and remembered him, every look, every touch. How much time they'd wasted, how many couplings she had missed out on, too afraid to say yes to him, to life, to love. But how sweet those few joinings had been, how perfect, how complete. They would last her forever.

They would have to.

"Tha gaol agam ort," she whispered in Gaelic. *I love you, Raife. I never said the words, but I do. I love you more than life itself.*

She rode out into the clearing alone, head held high.

Alistair's men met her halfway to the castle. She had hoped Donal would be among them, that he would listen to reason, but he wasn't. The same Scots who had made derogatory comments about her behind her back were no longer afraid to make them to her face. They called her a harlot, a strumpet, a whore. The one called Gregor grabbed the horse's bridle and spit in her face. He yanked her by the arm, pulling her off her horse and throwing her face first across his saddle.

And Sibyl just hung her head and let them, thinking the whole while, *I love you, Raife.*

That was all she knew and all that mattered.

She hadn't expected kindness from anyone, but Moira clucked and fussed over her as much as she ever had. Sibyl didn't realize it would be so hard to give up her plaid, how dependent she had become on its warmth, its safety, its freedom. Moira threw it in the fire and burned it and Sibyl had never been more bereft. It was as if her heart had been thrown into that fire. The tears came, relentless. She couldn't stop them and she stopped trying after a while.

"Ye have gone and done it now," Moira whispered as she cinched Sibyl into a corset that crushed her ribs and forced her breath up high in her chest. "I'm surprised the MacFalon will still have ye."

So was Sibyl. She had yet to see Alistair, but she was being groomed and dressed for him. They had started calling him "the MacFalon" in her absence. She wondered at that—his men hadn't the respect for him they had for his father, at least that had been the case when she left. But things had changed and she couldn't quite understand why or how.

"Yer t'be married t'im today." Moira nodded as the women brought in Sibyl's wedding dress, the train so long it took four of them to bring it all in.

"Today?" Sibyl felt her knees go weak at the thought, at the sight of that wedding dress she couldn't imagine wearing. "But I must speak with him!"

"Ye'll have plenty of time after yer married fer that."

"You don't understand," Sibyl whispered. She had been on MacFalon land already for over an hour. If he didn't let Laina go—and soon—the wulvers would come looking for her, armed and ready to do battle. "He must let her go."

"Her?" Moira raised her bushy white eyebrows. "The she-wolf?"

"I hear she threw herself on a spike when one of the men tried to... be with her…" One of the other girls whispered. Sibyl recognized her as one of the kitchen maids. Moira had enlisted extra help today, since Sibyl was to be sewn into her wedding dress.

"No," Sibyl whispered, looking between the two younger women with wide eyes as they snugged Sibyl's gown down over her hips.

“Why would ye?” The dark-haired scullery maid gasped in shock at this news. “It’d be like lyin’ wit’a dog!”

“Well I would’na mind bein’ wit’ one,” the blonde remarked with a grin that showed a considerable gap in her teeth. “If he was hung like a dog…”

All the women cackled at that and Sibyl couldn’t stand it another minute.

“Where is Donal?” she asked. There was no one else who would listen to reason. Maybe she could talk to him, if they weren’t going to let her see Alistair before the wedding.

“Alistair has had him locked up down the hall,” the gap-toothed blonde told her, arranging Sibyl’s long train behind her.

“He came ta the defense of the she-wolf,” the dark-haired one snorted. “He did’na want ’er harmed. He said if they broke the wolf pact, the wulvers would come for ’er…”

“Of course they will come for her.” Sibyl rolled her eyes, glancing at the open door. Half her train was still stuck in the hallway.

“Come back ’ere!” Moira called as Sibyl grabbed a knife off the table, where the maids had put a tray of bread, meat and cheese, and stalked out of the room.

Sibyl ignored the maids and Moira, wading through the fabric of her wedding dress toward the man standing at the end of the hallway. It was the one called Gregor—the same one who had thrown her over his saddle, who had pulled up her plaid to spank her in front of the men, and who likely would have done more, if another man hadn’t ordered him to take her inside.

"Where is Laina?" She held the dagger up, snarling at the guard. "The wolf—the wulver. The she-wolf. Where is she?"

"I… I do'na know," he stammered, glancing down the hall at the maids, who gathered up the length of Sibyl's train as they made their way toward them.

"Who do you guard behind this door?" she demanded to know, still brandishing the knife.

"Sibyl?" came a muffled voice. "Lady Blackthorne?"

"Donal!" She brightened at the sound of him, pounding on the door. He pounded back, definitely behind it.

"Me brother wants war wit' the wulvers!" he called. "Let me out of 'ere!"

"Let him out," Sibyl told the guard. "Do it. Now."

"I can'na." The man mopped his greasy brow with the back of his hand, frowning at her. "I've me orders."

"Come back now, ye hear me?" Moira tugged at Sibyl's train—the women had caught up. "Come get ready fer yer weddin."

"You will open this door," Sibyl insisted, hand wrapped around the hilt of the knife, pointing it straight at the man's chest. "Or I will stab you straight through the heart with this before you can even draw your sword."

The women behind her gasped, but Sibyl ignored them.

"Do not test me," she snapped, eyes flashing.

The guard took one look at Sibyl's face and then fumbled for his keys. He undid the big padlock and Donal rushed out of the room, knocking the man flat on his back, the wind escaping his throat in a hiss.

"Stay down," Donal instructed, drawing the man's sword before he could even think about getting up.

"Donal, you have to help me," Sibyl begged. She knew he would listen to her—especially now that she'd discovered Alistair had him locked up. "Your brother has broken the wolf pact. Do you know where Laina is?"

Just the mention of the woman's name brought tears to Sibyl's eyes.

"Lady Blackthorne, ye must come wit' me." Moira wasn't just pulling on Sibyl's train now, she was yanking on it. "I must get ye ready fer yer weddin'!"

"I will worry about my wedding later!" Sibyl cried, grabbing a yard of the fabric attached at her waist and yanking it back, making the older woman stumble. "Right now I have more important things to concern myself with!"

"How d'ye know of the wolf pact?" Donal asked, frowning at the guard still on the ground as he inched his way past Sibyl, the fabric of her dress making it difficult to move along the floor.

"I have been living with the wulvers this whole while," she explained, hearing the maids gasp again. That little piece of gossip would keep them going for years, she thought. "Do you know where she is? If he will just let her go, war can be avoided."

"I do'na know." Donal shook his head. "I came t'her defense, and I ended up locked in 'ere."

"What?" Sibyl gasped as she felt her train being tugged again, but this time it wasn't Moira or the maids. This time it was the guard. He had tunneled beneath the fabric and was now caught in it near the door Sibyl had stormed out of.

"Get back 'ere!" Donal yelled, but the man had freed himself from his white satin prison and practically fell down the stairs at the end of the hall. "He'll tell me brother I'm free."

"It will be war," Sibyl whispered. "The wulver's mate is coming for her. We must find her and let her go. If we can just free her…"

Had she sacrificed herself for nothing? Sibyl wondered, looking back at Donal's face. The color had drained from it. Was Laina already dead, as the maids had intimated? She couldn't bear the thought. Tears came to her eyes, spilling down her cheeks.

"Ye cry fer a dog?" The dark-haired maid rolled her eyes.

"Shut up!" Sibyl snapped. "Donal! Where are you going?"

But he was already halfway down the hall, sword in hand, going after the guard.

Sibyl quickly followed, shoving by Moira and the maids, but she found herself stuck halfway down the stairs, her train too heavy to move on her own. Donal had the guard by the throat, but it was too late, he had already sounded the alarm. Alistair's men were gathered at the foot of the stone steps, looking up at Donal holding one of their men at sword point and Sibyl standing at the top of them in her wedding gown.

"Please!" She pleaded with them all, hoping she could reason with someone, anyone. "Let the she-wolf go! If you let her go, then the wulvers will not come after you!"

"Let 'em come!" Alistair's voice echoed through the great hall as he stalked into it, his men parting as he approached the stairway.

"It will be war!" she cried. The sight of her betrothed made her dizzy with disgust and she clutched the stair's railing.

"King Henry will'na stand fer it," Donal insisted. He still had the guard at sword point. "He does'na want war wit' the wulvers."

"Yer wrong, brother." Alistair called up the stairs, smiling that cold smile that never reached his eyes. "King Henry wants his demon seed dead. He wants no challenge t'is throne."

His words carried through the hall. The maids gasped, of course—Sibyl didn't expect anything less. But everyone seemed to understand his meaning. They all knew the legends, the stories that had been told about the wulvers and the wolf pact. Perhaps some of them had even been alive, Sibyl realized, looking back at Moira's pale face and the way she crossed herself at the mention of the wulvers, when a young man named Henry had come looking for soldiers to help him win a crown. When that same man, who would one day be king, had taken what he wanted from the wulver woman, as men were wont to do, and had abandoned her with child, as men were also wont to do.

The consequences for those actions were far-reaching, and likely riding toward them right now, half-man, half-wolf, fully armed and ready for battle.

"Raife doesn't want the crown!" Sibyl's voice shook when she spoke the words. It was true, but would anyone believe it? She didn't know.

"Raife is it?" Alistair sneered at her. The hatred in his eyes, the hatred that had always been there, just barely veiled, filled her with dread as he came up the stairs, two at a time, passing his brother to get to Sibyl. "And has he taken what's mine?"

"I am not yours." She felt her lower lip tremble but she couldn't stop the truth from spilling out of her mouth. "I will never be yours."

"Ye're wrong about that." Alistair grabbed her to him, crushing his mouth against hers in a painful, bruising kiss. His tongue forced its way past her teeth as he gripped her behind in one hand, her breast in the other, right in front of everyone like he didn't care who saw. And of course, he didn't. He wanted them all to see that he owned her. She was surprised he didn't strip her naked and take her right there on the stairs.

If it weren't for the presence of the priest down there, ready to perform the marriage ceremony, she knew he really might have.

"King Henry promised me a proper English bride and the rule of all of Middle March if I would kill those flea-ridden dogs," Alistair growled, spittle spraying her ear. "There is no more wolf pact."

"No," she whispered, closing her eyes to it.

It couldn't be. Was King Henry so afraid of losing his title, his throne, to a bastard son who didn't want to have anything to do with the crown? No one knew about Raife—and his claim to the throne was tenuous, at best. He wasn't just Scottish—he wasn't even fully human! Henry had a son in line for the throne. The Tudors had regained the title after much maneuvering and fighting, but it was theirs. And the wulvers had helped them win it.

"I've a thousand men ready to kill 'em all as soon as those dogs ride up to the gates!" Alistair announced, his arm still around Sibyl's waist as he grinned down at his men. There were only a hundred or so gathered in the hall, but that didn't mean a thing. She was certain there were more where that came from—these were just the ones who had heard the commotion and had come running.

"Isn't that so?" Alistair called out. The men rallied, crying back with a rousing, "Aye!"

They were riding into a trap, just as Sibyl had feared. The wulvers would come down the mountain on horses, armed and ready for battle, transformed as half-man, half-wolf, a few hundred strong. In a battle, they were almost invincible, their healing capacities and super-strength making them fierce warriors, which is what had made them such a force to be reckoned with when Henry recruited them.

But a few hundred wulvers against a thousand men, all set on killing them? It would be an ambush. A slaughter. Sibyl saw Raife falling, saw Alistair—or more likely one of Alistair's men, because the man himself was too coward to face a wulver—running a sword through her mate's heart. They might be able to quickly heal from wounds, but they could still be killed. Their hearts could still stop beating.

And if Raife's heart stopped beating, hers would too.

"Have you ever seen a wulver?" she snarled at Alistair, raising her voice so they could all hear her words. "Have you ever faced a beast who is half-man, half-wolf? They are warriors. I have seen them. They have held me captive for over a month! *They do nothing else but train for war.* They are far more ready for it than any of your farmers or even your best-trained men! I have seen them rip an animal's throat out with their bare hands!"

"We can'na fight magic," the men whispered. Sibyl's heart soared when she heard the mutterings down below. They crossed themselves and kissed the crosses around their necks. She was sowing the seeds, but she needed more help. "Tis witchcraft. Tis against nature."

"She's trying t'scare ye!" Alistair pushed Sibyl away from him and she tumbled, losing her footing, as he went back down the stairs. "They'll be as easy t'put down as dogs, you'll see!"

"Donal… please…" Sibyl cried, thankful the man was still standing there. He caught her fall. "You must do something."

"Me brother's laird of clan MacFalon." Donal helped her stand, shaking his head sadly. "He's the MacFalon now. That was me father's doin', nuh mine. These men do'na follow me."

"But they will!" she insisted, glancing down at the lot of them. More were coming into the hall all the time, having been drawn by the shouting. "The Scots do not have a hierarchy like we do in England. They will follow the strongest leader. Alistair is not that man!"

"Ye bitch!" Alistair sneered up at her, hand on the hilt of his sword. She didn't care if he came after her. He could run her through with it—death would be a merciful blessing now—as long as she could save Raife and her wulver family. "Ye lying, whoring lil cunt!"

"You must lead these men to do the right thing!" Sibyl spoke only to Donal, seeing a light in his eyes, the same light she'd seen in Darrow's. It was the passion of the second son, one not born into distinction but who desperately craved it, who went after it like a moth to flame.

"Many of these men are too young to a'member the wulver warriors," Donal said, his voice carrying through the hall. "I was jus' a chile when King Henry came ta the MacFalons, askin' fer our allegiance. But some of these men do a'member. Don't ye?"

Sibyl glanced down, finding some gray-haired men among the group who pursed their lips and nodded in agreement, much to her relief.

"But some of these men followed me father when King Henry created the wolf pact. Some of these men followed King Henry into battle to fight for his right to wear a crown in a foreign land. Their fathers fought alongside mine, and they fought alongside the wolf warriors for God and country, to secure a peaceful future for their families."

Sibyl watched Donal's face change as he talked, as the men, even the younger ones, started really paying attention to his words. Alistair's face grew red with anger.

"How much bloodshed d'ya wanna see?" Donal cried, throwing his arms wide. "D'ya want yer homes burned, yer women raped? Hav'ya seen what warfare does? Me father saw what the border wars did 'tween the Scots and the English. Me father, yer laird, told King Henry he wanted t'live in peace, and King Henry agreed. Scots, English, wulvers—we all bleed. If we fight—we'll die."

The crowd murmured its assent. Many of Alistair's men were too young to remember that kind of bloodshed, but they grew afraid, not only of what the reality of war might mean, but of taking up arms against an army rumored to be more than human. Sibyl smiled triumphantly as she realized Donal had swayed them. Even if Alistair ordered them out to kill the wulvers now—would they do so? She didn't think they would.

"Do'na listen t'im!" Alistair cried. "I've heard from King Henry himself! He—"

A commotion erupted through the crowd. Something was going on outside. Sibyl cocked her head, hearing the sound of a horn, some sort of call. She didn't understand it but she was glad it had distracted everyone from Alistair's words. The thought that King Henry himself had made some sort of agreement with Alistair to eliminate the wulvers made her blood turn cold.

"What's that noise?" Alistair huffed, crossing his arms like a petulant child at the interruption. He clearly didn't like his brother getting all the attention. "Stop it at once!"

"Tis the wolf pact, brother. The one ye do'na have the honor t'honor." Donal walked slowly down the stairs, coming to stand face-to-face with his older brother. Alistair's eyes grew wide with fear. "They're invokin' single combat rite."

"No." Alistair's voice barely got above a whisper. She could hardly hear him. "I will'na."

"According to the wolf pact, ye must," Donal insisted. "Yer father signed that agreement in blood, and yer honor bound t'it!"

"I'm nah!" Alistair stamped his foot, arms still crossed over his chest. "I will'na!"

"Men!" Donal called, eyes bright as he saw them turned toward him, listening, paying close attention. "Take yer laird t'face the wulvers."

Alistair howled like a child, but there were too many of them. They grabbed him and hauled him out of the hall, out the open door. She watched the men do as Donal ordered with great relief, knowing they would follow him. Alistair could talk until he was blue in the face, it didn't matter anymore. Donal was a man who inspired these men, whose integrity showed in everything he did.

"What is single combat rite?" she wondered aloud.

Donal heard her, turning to glance back as he started following his men.

"T'will be leader against leader," he called back.

"Raife," Sibyl whispered.

She didn't think twice. She used the dagger still in her hand to cut away the train of her wedding dress, freeing herself, and ran down the stairs.

Chapter Twelve

"Blood rite!" The words were whispered from one person to another in the crowd as they gathered out in front of the MacFalon castle.

Sibyl looked around at all the people and wondered at the number. Why were they all here? Alistair had claimed he had a thousand men at the ready and he was not speaking in jest. But the rest of the people, where had they come from? The villages around the MacFalon lands weren't this densely populated. Could word have spread so quickly?

Sibyl pushed her way through the crowd, searching for the source of the horn that sounded loudly above her head. People stopped and looked at her bare legs in her ruined wedding dress, whispering behind their hands, and suddenly she realized—these were her wedding guests. They had come to see their laird marry an Englishwoman and had ended up attending something akin to a joust. That was all she could imagine as this, "single combat," or "blood rite" everyone was talking about.

Either way, it would be a good show, Sibyl thought grimly, as she made her way to the front of the growing crowd. Alistair had been so sure she would come, that there was going to be a wedding. He had trapped all of them, she realized in horror. He would kill the wulvers, marry his Englishwoman, inherit her lands and titles, and gain the favor of the king. In the end, he would get his way, just as he wanted.

She saw Raife sitting on his horse just across the field. They had come through the woods, just as she had, riding hard. But they were fully armed, their horses geared up for war, the wulvers too. She saw the men she had watched train, men who had teased and funned with her, men she had supped with, men she had watched sleep in a pile at night, half on top of one another, snoring like dogs.

She didn't want to see any of them harmed, not one of them, and she had the same feeling about Donal as she watched him approach Raife on horseback. Alistair was still howling his objections, his men holding onto him as Donal approached the wulver leader. Raife leaned forward in his saddle, listening to Donal speak, nodding slowly.

Sibyl's heart shattered into a thousand pieces, just seeing Raife alive and well, his bare chest under his plaid wet with perspiration. They had rode hard to get there so quickly, Sibyl realized, glancing up at the sun in the sky. It had only been a few hours since she'd arrived at Alistair's. They were armed as men, and had not yet transformed.

Mayhaps bloodshed and panic could still be avoided, she thought.

"One of our pack's blood has been spilled! Ye, Alistair MacFalon, are in violation of the wolf pact!" Raife raised his sword high, speaking to the gathered crowd, but he was looking straight at Alistair. "We're invokin' single combat blood rite!"

"There is no wolf pact!" Alistair spat, shaking loose of the men who held him. "We hold t'no such thing."

"Will it be war then?" Raife stared the man down.

The crowd murmured its disapproval and Sibyl glanced at many of them, who were dressed in finery for attending a wedding but hadn't at all planned on being slaughtered in the midst of a battle between man and wulver.

"Ye have t'honor the pact!" A cry rose up from the crowd. Sibyl didn't know from where, but she was grateful when the rest of them began to take up the chant.

"Honor the pact! Honor the pact!"

Alistair reddened, his face twisted in a sneer at the sudden turn of the crowd's allegiance from their laird.

"I'll honor it!" Alistair announced loudly, bowing in Raife's direction with much show. "The wolf pact allows for blood rite if either party feels the pact has been violated."

He was explaining to the crowd, Sibyl realized, her heart hammering in her chest at his words. He had that smile on his face, that cold, calculating smile. What was he up to? Whatever it was, she didn't like it.

"But as laird, I've a right t'call for a stand-in!" Alistair raised his voice, looking at his men, his eyes a cloudy, glittering gray. "Which of ye brave men will stand in me place?"

Sibyl held her breath, waiting. Of course Alistair would take this way out—and it looked, to the crowd, as if he were being magnanimous by calling on one of his "brave men" to take his place. Of course their laird couldn't fight—he was laird. He had a clan to run, after all. Sibyl hated the way he made it look, as if the men who stood by, considering his offer, were the ones who were cowards for staying silent.

"*He* broke the pact!" someone murmured.

Sibyl's head came up, eyes widening as those phrases peppered the crowd.

"*He* took the wolf-woman!"

"Fight yer own battles!" This last was spoken so clearly it echoed against the castle's gray walls.

"Donal?" Alistair turned to his brother, looking up and smiling at him on horseback. "As second son, tis yer place to stand in for yer laird."

"Tis true. The pact allows for a stand-in." Donal reined his horse away from his brother, glancing over his shoulder as he clearly replied, "But all have the right of refusal, brother. Even the second son. And I'm sorry, but I refuse. Do as the man said—fight yer own battles."

A cheer—an actual cheer—went up from the crowd.

"Ye wanna see a fight?" Alistair called, his face twisted in a scowl as he called for his sword and a man brought it to him. The crowd cheered again. Of course they wanted to see a fight. They'd come for a wedding, but a fight was even better, she judged from the reactions.

Sibyl had seen all manner of jousts back home in England but she didn't understand how this was going to work. Alistair swung his sword through the air, showing off for the crowd. He looked back over his shoulder at Raife, goading the man.

"Ye ready, dog?"

Raife shook his head and a slow smile spread across Alistair's face.

"Afraid, are ye?" Alistair called loudly—for the benefit of the show, of course. "Get down here and face me like a man."

"Tis my brother who's callin' for blood rite." Raife's voice rose over the crowd, sure and clear. Just the sound of it made Sibyl want to run to him. "Tis Darrow ye'll be facin'."

"Dog-boy, is that what ye said?" Alistair swung his sword, stabbing at thin air. "What was yer name again? Ruff? Ruff?"

Alistair barked and howled and the crowd laughed.

Sibyl had been so focused on Raife, she had missed Darrow in the crowd of wulvers. He reined his horse up next to his brother and Sibyl saw the horn he'd blown still in his hand. His eyes were dark, so dark, glittering as he slid off his horse. He handed the horn to his brother and drew his sword as he approached Alistair in the middle of the field.

Sibyl thought of Laina. She thought of their little blue-eyed boy back in the mountain, a baby Sibyl had seen birthed, had put to his mother's breast so he could help keep her from bleeding to death. Sweet, gentle Laina, whose mother had been captured by the MacFalons, who had birthed Laina in a cage, and had been killed before she even had a chance to hold her daughter.

Smart, determined Laina, so insistent, so sure she could find a "cure" for their wulver affliction. Where was Laina now? Sibyl scanned the crowd, hoping against hope to see her face. Had the maid told her the truth when she said Laina had thrown herself upon a spike? Could it possibly be true? She didn't want to believe it.

"Come on, dog." Alistair turned toward Darrow as the big man approached. The crowd gasped at the size difference between the competitors. Darrow towered over the Scot—and Darrow was small compared to his brother, Raife, who sat still in his saddle, watching. Donal had reined his horse in on Sibyl's side of the field and she moved closer.

“Let’s get this over wit’!” Alistair said loudly. “I do’na wanna get fleas.”

More laughter from the crowd, but it was nervous laughter. They had seen Darrow now and had judged Alistair’s chances accordingly. So had Sibyl. Darrow had bloodlust in his eyes and she couldn’t blame him. If they didn’t stop this, he would be likely to kill Alistair, and then what? Would it simply mean more war?

“Donal,” Sibyl called when she was beside the man. He glanced down, frowning at her, reining his horse away. She was standing quite close and put her hand on the horse’s flank. “This blood rite? They fight until blood is drawn then? How does it work?”

Donal shook his head but the answer came from an old man to her right.

“Blood rite’s ta the death, lass.” The old man gave a single nod, his gaze on the men approaching each other across the field. “A life for a life.”

“Oh no.” She looked up at Alistair’s brother, panicked. “Donal, no!”

“Tis the pact,” he informed her, his head whirling around as the first sound of steel striking steel rang out. “Let it work, as it should. One of ’em’ll die today.”

“T’will be an honorable death,” the old man beside her agreed.

An honorable death? What did that mean, if Darrow was dead? She saw the look in Raife’s brother’s eyes and knew, without Laina, he believed he had nothing to live for. She wanted to run to him, to plead with him to live, for his child’s sake. *Don’t orphan your son,* Sibyl thought, her heart breaking as the men crossed swords again. She couldn’t look. She couldn’t bear to watch.

"Is it over?" she whispered, covering her face. "Please let it be over."

Steel against steel. The grunt of men hefting heavy swords. The rising cry of the crowd as one or the other man landed a blow. Had it been a death blow?

"Please tell me it's over," she whispered, saying a prayer in her head for Darrow. She had no love for Alistair, but it was Darrow she didn't want to perish in this "blood rite."

Darrow howled. It was a long, keening howl, a wulver wail, and Sibyl's head came up, sure she would see the man split in two on the field.

But it was Alistair who was down, Darrow's foot on the man's chest, sword at his throat. Darrow's head was thrown back, his dark hair spilling down his shoulders as he howled, not at the moon, but at the sun.

"Wait!" Alistair waved his arms, gasping for air. "Call it off! I did'na kill'er!"

Sibyl could see, even from her vantage point, the abject terror in Alistair's eyes.

"Yer bitch is alive! She's—" Alistair croaked, gasping for breath as Darrow took a step back, frowning at the man.

"Show me!" Darrow didn't take his sword from Alistair's throat.

"Bring'er!" Alistair choked, his voice strangled. "Fer God's sake, get the bitch!"

Sibyl watched, breath held, as one of the men—Gregor, the same one who had manhandled her, the one who had escaped them on the stairs—led a stumbling woman onto the field. Could it be? Her heart soared in her chest as the Scot shoved the woman forward. Sibyl couldn't see her face—it was obscured by cloth. She had a grain sack pulled over her head, hands bound behind her with rope.

Was this some trick?

"Laina?" Darrow called but didn't look over his shoulder as they approached from behind. He didn't take his eyes off the man under his blade.

"Darrow!" Laina responded, voice muffled under the bag. Her voice was full of pain, horror, unspeakable things Sibyl didn't want to think about, but it was also filled with longing and the sound of hope.

Darrow sheathed his sword, giving one last, low growl in his throat at the man on the ground, before turning to his wife. Gregor pushed Laina forward and she fell into her husband's arms as he pulled the sack from her head. Her face was filthy, tear-streaked, as she turned her eyes up to him and he embraced her, a look of relief on his face that was palpable. He yanked at her restraints, pulling her free so Laina could put her arms around her husband's neck.

Sibyl sobbed, her own relief taking flight in her chest as she saw Laina was alive. Alive! She could hardly believe it. She looked across the field and saw Raife watching them. He was a blur to her—they were all a blur through her tears. She wouldn't have heard anything, expected anything at all, if she hadn't heard the collective gasp from the crowd.

She saw it a moment too late. Alistair was up, stalking toward the reuniting couple, his sword drawn. Sibyl heard a scream. She thought it might be her own as she sank to her knees in the grass, watching Alistair grab Darrow's shoulder for leverage and shove his sword straight through. Laina screamed, wiping blood from Darrow's mouth as it flooded their kiss, the tip of the sword narrowly missing her.

It happened so quickly Sibyl thought she was dreaming. She screamed again, but the crowd drowned out the sound as Alistair pulled his blade and lifted it high in the air, aiming to take Darrow's head clean off his shoulders. Raife was riding toward them, and so was Donal, but it was over before either horse had reached the bloody scene.

Darrow pushed Laina to her knees, turning and unsheathing his sword just in time to catch the steel of Alistair's sword in mid-air. The swords clashed and tangled for just a moment, and then Darrow pushed forward hard, moving Alistair off-balance, and then he swung. Sibyl screamed again—she heard it in her own head—as she watched Alistair's head topple from his shoulders. Donal's horse had to sidestep it as it rolled in the grass, Alistair's dead eyes staring up at a cloudless blue sky.

Darrow went to his knees, his shirt and plaid blooming bright red, and Laina helped lie him down in the grass. Raife was off his horse, kneeling before his brother's body, and Sibyl ran to them without another thought.

"Is it fatal?" she gasped, hands already moving on Darrow's belly, searching for the wound. So much blood. So very much blood.

"What d'ye care?" Raife looked at her, his blue eyes clouded, dark. His gaze raked her and Sibyl looked down, seeing the ruin of her wedding dress, now soaking up Darrow's blood.

"Bring 'im inside," Donal ordered his men. "And take yer laird's body to the tombs. We'll be planning a funeral."

Laina sobbed over Darrow's body. She refused to let him go when the men brought a carrying litter to take him inside.

"Where're ye going?" Raife grabbed Sibyl's arm when she went to follow, yanking her back to face him.

"To help!" she cried, trying to shake him loose, but he was too strong. "Raife! Let me go!"

Beside them, the men were putting Alistair's body on another litter. His head was still at their feet, a sight that turned Sibyl's stomach. She avoided looking down, meeting Raife's eyes. She had never seen that look in them before, so dark, so…

"He's the man ye want." Raife glanced down, letting go of her arm long enough to grab Alistair's head by the hair. She found herself face to face with her betrothed, his face still retaining that same wide-eyed look he'd worn when Darrow lopped off his head. "Here's yer prize. Take it. It's yers. Ye earned it."

The crowd around her gasped as Raife tossed the man's head at Sibyl.

And she caught it.

It was a reflex action from years of playing ball with the boys in the yard, and Sibyl watched, aghast, as the man she loved left her there, sinking to her knees in the middle of the empty field wearing a bloody wedding dress and holding the head of a man she had once promised to marry in her lap. Raife left her. He left her. The pain that seared through her middle was far worse than any sword he could have used to run her through.

Sibyl threw her head back and howled.

"He still will'na see ye." Laina shook her head sadly as Sibyl asked, for the hundredth time, if Raife had asked about her. "But he'll come 'round. He's jus'... well. Wulvers are stubborn."

"Some of us more'n others!" Darrow called from across the room, attempting to sit up.

"Oh no you don't!" Sibyl rushed over, pushing him back into bed, checking his bandage, seeing blood blooming there. "Speaking of stubborn. Stay in bed, will you, please?"

"Even wulvers need t'heal, Darrow." Laina agreed, climbing into bed with her husband and pushing him back onto the mattress. "What'm I gonna hafta do t'keep ye in bed, hm?"

"Lemme think on that..." Darrow grinned, wrapping an arm around Laina's waist and pulling her in for a kiss. It was a sight that both delighted Sibyl and hurt her heart.

"Keep him in bed," Sibyl warned, taking Darrow's tray and carrying it toward the door.

"Oh, aye." Laina giggled as she kissed her husband down onto the mattress.

"No strenuous movements!" Sibyl warned, backing out of the door, still carrying the tray.

"Tell me stupid, stubborn brother I wanna see him!" Darrow called.

"Lemme take that, banrighinn." Kirstin frowned, stopping Sibyl in the hallway to relieve her of the tray. "Ye should'na be carrying a tray like a servant."

Banrighinn—that was the Gaelic word for "queen." Kirstin—who had come without being asked to help nurse Darrow back to health—had taken to calling Sibyl banrighinn, even though Raife had never marked her, hadn't claimed her in front of the pact. Kirstin was as sure as Laina that the man would come around. Sibyl wasn't so sure. But being called any variation of "queen," no matter the language, was taking some getting used to.

"It keeps me busy," Sibyl argued as she handed over the tray. Darrow had eaten stew and half a loaf of bread—his appetite was definitely back.

She was still surprised that Darrow had survived his wound, but somehow Alistair had managed to miss most of his major organs. And the ones he had hit had healed themselves miraculously fast, in true wulver fashion. Alistair, however, had not managed to survive his wounds, and wouldn't have, even if he'd been a wulver. Sibyl had been sure Alistair's death would start a war between the wulvers and the clan, but so many people had seen the despicable thing their laird had done, word quickly spread.

Donal had been declared laird before Alistair's body was laid to rest.

"Donal was askin after ye," Kirstin told her, unable to hide the small smile on her lips. Kirstin had taken a bit of a shine to the man. Even Sibyl, lost in her old world, had noticed.

Kirstin looked at Sibyl with sympathetic eyes. Everyone knew she was in love with Raife—and everyone knew the man refused to speak to her. She had tried, several times, to reason with him, but he simply looked at her with those sad, blue eyes, and walked away. He managed to escape her and whatever she had to say, even if it meant mounting his horse and riding away.

There was nothing more she could do, Sibyl had decided. So she tried to keep herself busy. She did her best to help heal Darrow, who couldn't travel for at least another few days. The other wulvers had returned to the mountain—Raife had sent them home to let the women wulvers know what had happened—but Darrow, Raife and Laina had stayed behind.

Donal welcomed them graciously into his home and offered them all a room and food for as long as they required. He had been very kind, as always, a marked difference from his brother, and the way he conducted himself as laird had been the exact opposite as well. When Sibyl had begun to sob at Alistair's funeral—she caught Raife's eye during the proceedings and couldn't get the image of him throwing Alistair's head at her—Donal had offered his shoulder.

"Thank you, Kirstin." Sibyl smiled at the young woman, making her way down the hall, heading to the stairs. "Is he in the chancery?"

"Aye." Kirstin carried the tray down beside her and they parted ways at the bottom of the stairs, Kirstin going left toward the kitchen, Sibyl right, toward Donal's chancery.

The place had been Alistair's chancery just a short time ago. It was the place she had first met her betrothed, she remembered, as she knocked on the door.

"Come in!" Donal called.

Sibyl opened the door, peeking inside to see him sitting at a wide, oak desk, studying a piece of paper in his hand.

"Lady Blackthorne!" He smiled as she came in, leaving the door open as she approached the desk. "I was jus' askin' Kirstin t'find ye."

"She found me." She smiled, sitting down in a chair opposite him, the fabric cool on the backs of her legs. She had borrowed a plaid from one of the kitchen maids, even though Donal had given her back her dowry, which consisted of an entire English wardrobe fit for a viscountess. She couldn't go back to wearing velvet and satin, she decided, no matter how much the ladies' maids Donal had hired to tend her encouraged her to do so.

"I've had word." Donal glanced down at the paper in his hand, squinting at it.

"Goodness, that was fast." Sibyl's heart thudded hard in her chest. She had asked him to send a letter as soon as humanly possible, and Donal had agreed.

"I sent a wulver messenger."

"Ah." Sibyl nodded. So, faster than humanly possible, then. "And what word?"

"Tis good news." Donal handed the letter over and she saw that it was written in English. "King Henry will continue to honor the wolf pact."

"And Alistair's plan?" Sibyl glanced over the letter and saw the king's seal, making it official.

"Twas all 'is own." Donal shook his head sadly. "King Henry knew naught of it."

"I'm sorry, Donal." She reached out and touched his hand across the desk, squeezing gently. "If I could have saved him too…"

"He brought it on himself, lass." Donal sighed, leaning back in his chair and rubbing a hand over his tired eyes. "Me brother was always… a problem."

"At least the wulvers are safe." She gave her own sigh of relief, sitting back in her chair. "And clan MacFalon is safe."

"Aye, although King Henry writes that, as new laird of clan MacFalon, I need t'find meself an English bride," Donal said, cocking his head at her. "Or he'll find one for me."

"Is that so?" Sibyl swallowed, meeting his eyes over the big desk.

"I wondered, lass…" He cleared his throat, cheeks turning slightly pink, and Sibyl knew what he was going to ask. She thought of what she might say to perhaps avert the direction he was headed, but could think of nothing.

Instead, she sat, struck dumb, just staring at him.

"I wondered if ye might consider havin' me?" Donal got the question out, going on, continuing to talk, as if by talking he might stave off her inevitable rejection. "I know ye do'na love me. But that could come, with time. We have everythin' in place already, I jus' thought…"

"A marriage of convenience?"

"Aye." He shrugged helplessly. "It does seem logical and convenient."

"I wish my heart would listen to logic." She looked down at her hands, her lower lip trembling as she thought of Raife. It was hard to get him out of her mind, even when she was trying to keep herself busy. "I keep trying to tell it… to stop loving him…"

Her tears overflowed. There was something about this man's presence that made her feel safe, letting her emotions surface. She looked at him, wondering what life would be like here, if she were to take him up on his offer. What else did she have to do, after all? Raife would not have her, and she had been ruined for anything or anyone else. What did it matter where she lived, how she spent the rest of her days, if she couldn't be with the man she loved?

But she couldn't do that to this kind-hearted man. He deserved to be loved, really loved, the way she loved Raife. She remembered the way Kirstin had smiled when she mentioned the man's name and wondered at it. Did Donal not know or see the girl's affection? She thought of telling him but held her tongue. She was in no mood to be matchmaker.

"I'm sorry." Sibyl swallowed, trying to swallow her tears, but they stuck in her throat. She sobbed into her hands, shaking her head, and she felt his hand on her shoulder.

"Och, lass… I'm sorry… I did'na mean…"

"No, it's not your fault!" She accepted a handkerchief, wiping at her face. "You have been so kind, so generous. I wish I could say yes, but my heart belongs to one man. One… stubborn… awful… horrible… wolf… man…"

She wailed, wishing she could disappear altogether. It was so horribly humiliating, to love someone so much, and have them completely ignore your existence.

"Aye, he's broken yer heart, hasn't he, lass?" Donal lifted her chin, forcing her to look at him.

"Into so many pieces I will never put them together again," she whispered. "I wish he would just talk to me. Or at least listen…"

He nodded, glancing over her shoulder, then back into her eyes.

"What would ye say ta the man?" Donal asked softly.

"That I love him." She twisted the handkerchief in her hands. "That I only did what I did because I love him. Because I wanted to keep him safe."

"I understand." Donal gave a long, deep sigh.

"I wish he did." Sibyl half-stood, ready to go. She wanted to go hide in her room, bury her face in a pillow and sob the rest of the day away. But there were potatoes to peel in the kitchen. And linens to change on the beds. Anything to keep her hands, and her mind, busy.

"Ask 'im." Donal nudged her gently.

"I cannot!" She handed him his handkerchief. "He will not give me the time of day."

"Mayhaps he has a few minutes now?" He glanced over her shoulder again and Sibyl frowned, turning her head in that direction.

The sight of Raife standing in the doorway made her heart drop to her knees. His face was a mask, unreadable, but his eyes were as blue and expressive as ever. He had heard her, that much was clear. But had he listened? Did he care?

"Raife?" she whispered, using the chair to hold herself up, because her knees turned wobbly.

"Ye asked t'see me?" Raife turned his gaze to Donal, ignoring Sibyl.

"Aye, I did." Donal waved him in with a sigh. "Come in."

"I was just leaving." Sibyl lowered her head and moved to sidestep him as Raife came into the room. She had just decided that running up to her room and burying her face in a pillow to sob for the rest of the day was exactly what she was going to do.

"Och!" Donal rolled his eyes, throwing up his hands. "Nay, *I* was jus' leavin'!"

It happened so fast. One minute, Donal was standing there, the next, he was on the other side of the door, and a key was turning in the lock.

Raife frowned, reaching for the door handle, turning it. But it wouldn't budge.

"Unless ye plan on breakin' down me door, ye'll be workin' this out between ye!" Donal called through the thick, solid wood door. "I'm tired of havin' t'comfort that poor girl's tears on me shoulder."

Raife scowled at Sibyl, as if her tears were her own fault, and Donal's comfort was too.

"I jus' have one more thing ta say afore I go," Donal called, clearing his throat. "Son, if'n ye do'na want her—"

"Go!" Raife snapped at the closed, locked door. "Leave us!"

They both heard Donal chuckle and then there was silence.

"So ye did it for me, eh?" Raife crossed his big arms over that giant, bare chest of his—the MacFalons had all tried to get him to wear a shirt under his plaid, but he refused—scowling at her. "Ye ran back here into yer lover's arms for me benefit?"

"Yes, you big, dumb oaf!" Sibyl snapped. "As a matter of fact, I did! Did it ever occur to you that coming back here and marrying Alistair was something I didn't actually want to do?"

Raife's brow knitted, his frown deepening. Sibyl had held her tongue long enough. She had chased him all around the grounds trying to get him to listen to her, and now that he was a captive audience—until he broke the door down—she wasn't going to let the chance pass her by. She had practiced everything she was going to say in her head, in a cool, even tone, and all of that went completely out the window when she was faced with him.

"Did it ever enter your thick skull that maybe, just maybe, I was doing it to keep King Henry and the entire English army from attacking the wulvers?" she cried, her hand itching to reach out and smack him upside his big, dumb head.

"We're wulvers, Sibyl!" he roared right back at her. She didn't even shrink from his anger—at least he was responding. "We can take care of ourselves!"

"Your brother was run through with a MacFalon sword. He could have died!" She reminded him. "Now multiply that by a hundred. A thousand. How many wulvers would I have had my hands inside, trying to stop the bleeding, if war had broken out?"

Raife shook his head, ready to deny it, to argue with her, but she couldn't keep any of it at bay anymore. She had let some of it out on Donal's wide, generous, kind-hearted shoulder, but it wasn't Donal she was mad it, and it wasn't Donal she had been so afraid she was going to lose. It was Raife. It was her big, giant, stubborn, bull-headed, sweet, kind, protective, loveable man of a wolf she had been so scared she was going to lose. It was this man who she had been willing to sacrifice everything for, who she would rather have known was living safely up in the mountain, while she suffered at Alistair's sadistic hands, than lying dead somewhere on MacFalon land.

"What if… what if it had been you…" she whispered, eyes brimming with tears. She saw a look of concern pass over his face, the way he reached for her but stopped himself. "What if it had been your severed head… in my lap…?"

She couldn't get the words out, couldn't stop picturing it in her mind. She sobbed into her hands, turning away from him, and then heard him say something she couldn't quite believe.

"Would ye have cared if it had been?"

Sibyl lifted her head, gaping at him.

"Oh you bastard!" she whispered, a sudden wave of anger overtaking her. She launched herself at him, pounding her fists against his chest. "How can you say that? How can you even ask that question?"

Raife caught her wrists, half-smiling, an expression she hadn't seen on his face since they'd been there. It made her want to smack him.

"Ye never told me, lass," he said softly, meeting her clouded gaze.

"What?"

"Ye never said the words," he said again. "How was I supposed t'know?"

"Are you mad?" she murmured. "Am I… dreaming?"

"D'ye or don'ye?" He pushed his chin out, defiant, glaring down at her.

Sibyl looked at her wrists, encircled by his big, giant paws, and then up at his face.

"You want me to say the words?" She shook her head, incredulous. "Because giving myself to you, that wasn't enough? Because risking my life to save your thick hide wasn't enough? You need me to say the words?"

He shrugged. "T'would be nice."

"Raife…" She burst out laughing. She couldn't help it. "My God, you idiotic, ridiculous man. I love you! Is that what you wanted to hear? *Tha gaol agam ort!"*

His eyes searched her face for the truth. She prayed he found it.

"Do you understand that?" she asked softly. "In your own language? *Tha gaol agam ort."*

"Are ye done insultin' me now?" he asked, letting her wrists go.

"No!" She hit him again, this time square in the chest with both fists. "You lumbering lout!"

He caught both wrists again and pulled her close, trapping her arms between them. Then he kissed her. Everything they hadn't said to each other went into that kiss, everything they both wanted, everything they hoped for, all their desperate fears, all their dreams of a future together. Sibyl tasted salt on their lips.

"I love you," she whispered when they parted. He kissed the tears from her cheeks. "Tha gaol agam ort, you boorish fool."

"And I love ye," he said hoarsely. "Ye strange, irrational woman."

She rolled her eyes at him and he kissed her again, this time capturing her mouth in a desperate slant, as if he could put every moment they had missed into it.

"And if ye ever…" His mouth dipped to her neck, nipping and biting her there, making her cry out. "Do anythin'…" His tongue moved down to her collarbone, making her moan as his hands moved under her plaid, seeking the heat of her skin. "So idiotic again…"

"You'll what?" she challenged, sliding a thigh between his, feeling the steel heat of him, satisfied when she heard him groan.

"Wulvers mate for life, lass, I told ye," he breathed against the tops of her breasts. "I guess I'll have to kill us both."

"Oh but what a way to go," she whispered as her man, her mate, her wulver, cleared Donal's desk with one fell swoop, knocking everything to the floor so he could sit her up on it.

Sibyl wrapped her arms and legs around him, hungry, desperate for him, unable to quench the fire he'd started burning inside her without him.

"Ye'll'na leave me again, lass." Raife said the words as he entered her, making her cry out and cling to him. "Ne'er again."

"I promise," she whispered into his neck, trembling at the thought of losing him again. "I am yours."

"Say it again," he growled, thrusting deep.

"I'm yours!" she cried, biting her lip.

"Again!"

"Yours!"

"Mine!" he groaned, driving in deep, filling her completely. "Mine!"

Sibyl wouldn't let him go. Even when they came and knocked on the door, asking if everything was all right—someone had obviously heard all the clatter—she refused to let him go. She wasn't going to ever let him go again.

Her father used to tell everyone that Sibyl Blackthorne wasn't afraid of anything, and that had been true. But she had been stupid, and reckless, in her fearlessness.

That was back when she didn't have anything to lose.

Now she knew what it was to love a man—a wulver—and how it felt to lose him.

She wasn't fearless anymore.

But she was wonderfully, desperately, humanly in love.

And Sibyl would take that over being brave, any day of the week, any month of the year, for the rest of her life—and his.

Epilogue

Scotland
Year of our Lord 1504

"An'wha'if she births a son?"

Sibyl heard Darrow's question, spoken in a harsh whisper outside the big wooden door, and turned her face into Laina's soft, white fur. The woman was in her wolf state—it was her moon time and she could not change into her human one—but her eyes said everything her mouth couldn't. Laina heard her husband's protests and knew they pained Sibyl, far more than the labor she was enduring.

Sibyl wanted Raife by her side, wanted his hand in hers. Instead he was pacing back and forth outside her door, growling at every passerby, while Sibyl labored in front of a warm fire, Beitris, the old midwife, tending her. Laina had come, in spite of her wolf form, knowing her presence alone would give Sibyl comfort, and it did.

"Do'na pay'tention t'em, lass," Beitris soothed, putting a soft, wrinkled hand on Sibyl's damp brow.

But how could she ignore them? She knew they were worried. They were worried that this baby would be a boy, who might threaten King Henry VII's claim to the throne. The king's first son, Arthur, had died of the English sweating sickness. Rumors ran rampant that King Henry had become paranoid, fearfully keeping a hold of his crown. Advisors of and protectors to the king, of which Sibyl's uncle, Godfrey Blackthorne, was one, were telling Henry he must purge all illegitimate pretenders to the throne and raise up the only legitimate son had had left—Henry VIII—to take his place.

There was also talk of King Henry keeping his alliances with Spain by marrying off Arthur Tudor's widow, Catherine of Aragon, to Henry VIII. The younger Henry was just a boy, though, still unable to enter a marriage contract. Sibyl had received a letter from her mother—all her correspondence went through Castle MacFalon, since they had maintained the wolf pact and their amiable ties with Donal, the new laird and warden of Middle March—stating that King Henry VII had lost not only his son, Arthur, but that Queen Elizabeth had died as well, and the old king had set his own sights on Catherine of Aragon as a way to possibly hedge his bets and secure the Tudors on the throne.

Sibyl didn't care who the king married, as long as he didn't remember his other, illegitimate son, Raife, and change his mind about leaving the wulvers in peace. Raife was her husband, her mate, and now, he was about to be the father of her child. His brother, Darrow, was worried, she knew—if the baby were a boy, King Henry VII might get word and feel his crown was being threatened. Of course, the rest of the pack was worried this baby would be a girl. They wanted a male, to lead the wulvers.

It didn't seem to matter what gender child she gave birth to, Sibyl was stuck between a rock and a hard place. And at that moment, she felt as if she was pushing that rock uphill!

"King Henry's got another son," Beitris reminded her. "I'm sure he'll have sons as well and the Tudors'll reign long."

"""I don't care if the Tudors have boys or girls or wulvers—as long as *my* mate and *my* children stay with *me* and don't lay claim to any English or Scottish thrones," Sibyl panted, trying to will the pain away.

"Women can'na lead!" Beitris laughed at the thought and Sibyl rolled her eyes. Even wulver women, who were so strong and capable, believed women couldn't lead, whether it was a pack or a country.

"Maybe the Tudors will be ruled by a red-haired woman!" Sibyl snapped, feeling another pain coming on.

"Tis yer time," Beitris soothed. "Do'na worry. This bairn'll be leader'o'his pack."

Sibyl didn't care if this baby would lead the wulvers or follow another, she just wanted to hold it to her breast and see it open its eyes. Her first baby had been born too soon, a tiny wisp of a thing Raife could hold in one palm. She had insisted, then, he be at the birth, and he'd held her hand through the whole ordeal. But when she'd looked up at his face, when she'd seen the way his eyes clouded over at the sight of his tiny, dying son, Sibyl knew she couldn't again put him through something so traumatic.

Men might deal every day in matters of life and death, but a woman's heart was stronger than a man's when it came to birth. So this time, Sibyl insisted he wait outside. Bad luck, she told him, for a man to be at the birth of his child. It was certainly true in her world, amongst humans, that men weren't invited into the birthing chamber. This was women's work. Her work. And she knew she had to do it alone.

"I wish Kirstin was here!" Sibyl moaned as the pain came again and she bit down hard on the leather strap

Beitris gave her. Sibyl was trying to be as quiet as she could so as not to alarm her already anxious husband.

Laina licked the back of Sibyl's hand, her tongue warm and soothing, as if to say, "I understand."

But Kirstin was gone. Sibyl didn't like to think about losing her friend, about the sacrifices Kirstin had made to be with the man she loved. Laina's own sacrifice, the wolf's sad eyes and soft whine, said enough. Too much. It broke Sibyl's heart that she had failed them, that she'd been unable to really help the plight of the wulver women—even if she had, in the end, found a way to "cure" the curse.

"Oh no, not again," she whispered, her fingers digging into Laina's soft, white fur.

Sibyl thought she just might die from the pain alone. She'd thought, when she birthed Robert—named after her father—that it had been bad, but he'd been so small. This baby was full term, his head like a boulder she was trying to push uphill. She grunted and strained and tried not to cry out, but the pain was too intense. She couldn't hold out any longer. The man she loved, the only man who had ever claimed her—mind, body and soul—was standing on the other side of that door, and she wanted him.

She needed him.

"Raife!" Sibyl screamed his name, feeling as if she was being split in two. This was pain beyond pain. She couldn't even see straight. Her body had taken over. Everything was out of control.

"Sibyl!" The door burst open and Raife barged in. He was at her side in an instant, holding her in his big arms, the circle of his embrace safer than any she'd ever known in her life. "Are ye hurt?"

She couldn't help her short, strangled laugh. She wasn't hurt, no, but she was hurting. Beyond hurting. But with him there, it was instantly better. He made everything better.

"Tis almos'time," Beitris told him calmly, pressing a warm cloth between Sibyl's open legs. "Yer son'll be'ere soon."

"It could be a daughter!" Sibyl panted, clinging to her mate, cheek pressed against the broad expanse of his chest.

"Aye." Raife chuckled, kissing the top of her head. "A bonnie red-haired lass like 'er mother."

"Tis ginger, that's fer sure," Beitris gave a nod between Sibyl's thighs.

Sibyl blinked in surprise as Raife bent his dark head to look but then another pain hit and she was sinking. There was nothing but a red, thrashing haze of pain and an overwhelming urge to bear down.

"Noooo! Please! Raife!" Sibyl screamed, abandoning the leather strap and giving into the agony. She turned her face against his upper arm—the marked one. She carried a matching mark, intricate Celtic swirls, down her hip and thigh. Her marking had been painful, she remembered, but it had been nothing like this.

"Yer safe, lass," he whispered, stroking her damp hair, her shaking body, as she strained and thrashed in his arms. "I've got ye. Let'im come. He's strong. He wants t'meet ye."

"Tis time!" Beitris was doing something between Sibyl's legs but she didn't know what. She had her eyes closed, face buried against Raife. "One more good push!"

Sibyl screamed, digging her nails into Raife, doing as the old midwife asked. The world was on fire. Everything burned.

"Balach!" Beitris announced proudly, as if she had been the one who had done all the work.

"A boy," Sibyl whispered, opening her eyes to see the little red-haired, wailing child between her legs. "Raife, it's a son!"

"Aye." Raife's voice caught in his throat as she lifted the child, still attached to his mother by the pulsing cord, and brought him to his wife's breast.

"He's perfect," Sibyl whispered, glancing up to see Darrow standing in the doorway, watching. How long had he been there? She wondered.

Her usual modest nature had abandoned her. Now she just wanted everyone to see her child. Sibyl motioned for Darrow as Laina licked the baby with her pink, wulver tongue, making him startle. Robert, her little black-haired bairn, had been less than half this boy's size. No wonder she had felt as if she'd been pushing a rock!

"Balach," Darrow murmured, taking a step into the room, and sinking to his knee before his brother's new son. "What'll ye call'im?

"Griffith." Raife traced a cross over the newborn's forehead with his index finger.

"Griff." Sibyl pressed her lips to the baby's forehead. The Gaelic name meant red-haired and was more than fitting. "Will he be a red wolf?"

"Aye." Raife smiled fondly at her, running a hand through her red tresses as Beitris covered up mother and child with a sheet, tucking them in for warmth now that the hard work was done. "He'll fulfill the prophecy a'last."

"What prophecy?" Sibyl frowned at her mate, looking at Darrow and Laina as they both admired the little red-faced, red-haired child in her arms.

"The red wulver." Beitrus, the old midwife, crossed herself, her wide, rheumy blue eyes meeting those of her pack leader's. Raife gave a slow nod and met his brother's eyes. Darrow looked like he couldn't quite believe his own.

Laina threw back her shaggy, white head and howled. The sound never failed to send a shiver down Sibyl's spine and this time was no exception. But Laina wasn't alone. Out in the den, where the rest of the pack had been waiting to hear word of their pack leader's new bairn, the call was returned. Answering howls echoed through the tunnel's deep walls. Sibyl heard the word *banrighinn* being repeated in Gaelic out in the tunnel. Banrighinn meant queen. They were speaking of her, of the birth of their new leader.

"I told ye, lass." Raife's arm tightened around her. "I knew ye were meant to be me mate the moment I laid eyes on ye."

Sibyl smiled at his words. She couldn't imagine belonging to anyone else—man, wolf, or wulver. But what was this talk of some wulver prophecy? She had poured over the wulver text—what amounted to the wulver's "bible"—and had never read anything about a "red wulver."

"What is this prophecy?" Sibyl demanded as the baby in her arms squirmed. Laina whimpered, nuzzling her husband's hand, and she knew if the woman had been in human form, she would have been forthcoming. "Beitris?"

Clearly the men didn't want to tell her.

"The red devil's savior." Beitris whispered the words, crossing herself again.

"He's jus'a bairn." Raife scoffed, leaning over to look at his son. Sibyl noted he had Raife's strong jaw and dimpled chin. But he definitely had her thick, red hair. "No need puttin' too much on'him t'start."

"His eyes." Darrow's voice broke as he looked down at the child in Sibyl's arms. "He *is* the red wulver."

Sibyl saw Raife's expression change. She saw the face of a new father change from pride and wonder to something akin to awe and maybe even a little fear. She'd never seen her mate afraid of anything in her life and seeing that expression, even fleetingly, on Raife's face, gave her pause.

Then Sibyl looked down at her newborn son.

He had opened his eyes, but instead of the deep, wulver blue she expected, they were red.

Redder than his hair.

As red as blood.

"Raife?" She turned her own, frightened face up to her husband's. She was so surprised by her son's features, she might have actually dropped the baby in her arms if he hadn't turned his head and latched onto her breast, suckling deeply.

"Tis a'right, lass," Raife soothed, smiling down at the bairn. He didn't look frightened anymore. Now he looked resigned. "He's perfect, jus'like ye."

Sibyl glanced down again at the baby, whose eyes were still open, staring up his parents in his own kind of wonder. The red she'd seen in his eyes was gone. They weren't wulver-blue, but instead green, like her own.

Had she seen it at all? Had it been a trick of the light?

Then the baby gave his mother a milky smile, as if he knew just what she was thinking.

Sibyl saw another, brief flash of red in her son's eyes before he closed them and knew it had been no trick of the light. She wasn't dreaming.

She'd given birth to the red wulver who would fulfill some sort of prophecy. The howls and wails that echoed off the walls of the wulvers' den told her that every single member of the pack knew and understood what that meant.

Everyone except her.

Once again, she was an outsider, a human in a wolf's den. She might have been their queen, mated to their king, but she had no idea what she was in for. As usual. She knew Raife would explain, as would Laina, and even Darrow. Whatever this prophecy was, she had a feeling she wasn't going to like it.

For the moment, she decided, she was going to pretend it didn't exist. Mayhaps there was a God who pulled the strings and provided them with books like road maps, full of things like curses and prophecies and commandments.

Mayhaps the future was the future, and she couldn't change it. Or mayhaps she could, and her son would lead the way toward a different one for all of them.

And mayhaps the Queen of England would someday be a red-haired woman, she thought, smiling to herself at that ludicrous idea.

All Sibyl knew was that this red-haired, red-eyed baby was her son, and she was going to hold onto him and keep him close as long as she could manage.

The End

HIGHLAND WOLF PACT
Compromising Positions

By Selena Kitt

Chapter One

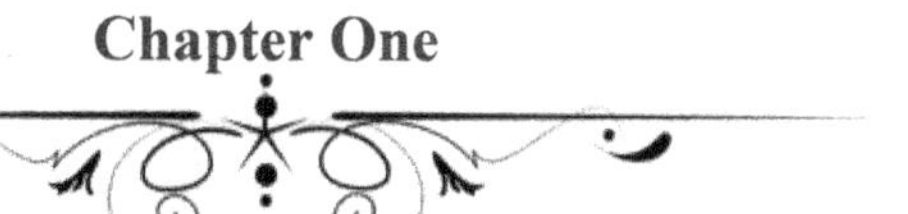

Scotland
Middle March – near Castle MacFalon
Year of our Lord 1502

If she hadn't caught scent of the man, she never would have ended up in the trap.

Kirstin cursed the stranger as she struggled, strung halfway up the side of a huge oak tree, the limb holding her weight moving only slightly as she snapped and pawed at the net. She had caught his scent and had followed her nose to the edge of the wood, where it ended in a clearing. In the middle of the clearing was an enormous burial cairn. This was where the man knelt, one bare knee on the ground, his elbow up on the other, forehead pressed to his closed fist.

She had believed him to be praying, too distracted to notice her, so she had crept forward, curious. That had been her mistake. The movement had caught the attention of the man's horse. The big, black animal had thrown its head and yanked at the reins, tied to a stake on the ground, pawing the grass as it caught her scent. Kirstin's fur had prickled, standing on end, as the man turned his head to look at her.

He was a Scotsman—his plaid gave that much away. He didn't call out or move for a weapon when he saw her, as she expected a man might, when faced with a wolf in the early morning light. The man easily could have drawn the bow he had slung over his back, although if he moved, she would have been gone faster than he could cock an arrow. But he stayed still, his gaze meeting hers across the dewy grass.

And there was something about those eyes...

The moment their gaze locked, Kirstin felt it. Something crackled, like lightning flashing through storm clouds. The horse continued to whinny and paw his big hoof at the ground, but the human and the wolf didn't move. They just looked at each other, sizing each other up. If she had been a regular wolf, she probably would have instantly turned tail and run. But if she had been a regular wolf, she never would have followed thc scent of a human this close in the first place.

Her tail twitched and her nose wrinkled when she caught his scent again as the wind shifted. He wasn't afraid. She would have smelled that—it was a tinny, copper scent, similar to blood, a mixture of sweat and adrenaline. The man whose eyes searched hers across the clearing wasn't afraid—although he should have been. She wondered at it, cocking her shaggy head and whining softly at her own confusion.

That's when he spoke.

"Are ye a wulver, then?" he called in a thick, Scottish brogue. He didn't make a move, didn't reach for a bow or a sword, but his words frightened her far more than any weapon would have. If this man knew the difference between a wolf and a wulver, and even suspected she was the latter, she was in far more danger than she thought. But then she remembered, she'd tied her own plaid around her neck before she left the den, and it was tied there still.

She had turned tail and run, even though he'd stood, calling after her, "Halt! Come back!"

If only she hadn't followed his scent. If only the horse hadn't noticed her and alerted his master. If only she hadn't taken off running. Or mayhaps if she had run the other direction, through the clearing instead of back into the woods. If she had only stayed home, snug in her den, taking care of her pack the way she always had...

But she couldn't lament this last.

Because while most of her pack was safe back in the den, their pack leader was at Castle MacFalon, sitting by his brother's bedside, waiting to see if he'd recover from wounds that would've instantly killed any mortal man. The warriors had returned to their den, exhausted, hungry, with a tale so horrifying, Kirstin didn't even want to imagine it. But it was all she could think of as she took off running through the woods, following their scent on the trail. It would take her to the borderlands, back to Castle MacFalon, where one of her pack lay dying...

Not dying. She twisted in the net, glimpsing the ground below. It was going to be quite a hard drop to the forest floor. *He's not going to die. Not if I have anything to say about it.*

But she wasn't going to be able to do anything if she didn't get out of this damnable net. Kirstin twisted her big, furry head to see if any hunter was around. Had the man kneeling in the clearing been the one who laid this trap? She wondered. If so, he had seen her. He had watched her turn and run back into the woods. Straight toward the hidden net.

Kirstin felt a howl rising in her throat, nearly uncontrollable, at her sudden lack of freedom. Adrenaline coursed through her and she turned the howl into a low growl, forcing herself to be still, to stay calm. She couldn't let her animal side take control, even if she was in wulver form. She had to stop, to think, to get herself out of this. She would have to change into human form, find the dirk she had sown into her plaid, and cut herself free.

Before the hunter found her.

"Easy, lass."

The voice came from below and she froze, hackles rising, bladder tensing in her belly. He must have come from downwind, quietly tracking her, to appear so suddenly without her knowledge. She couldn't see him, but she knew the man had a bow. She'd seen it slung across his back. He had a dirk hidden under his plaid, like any good Scotsman would. He could, right now, have an arrow aimed at her side.

"I'm not gonna hurt ye." He spoke softly, from right beneath her.

She twisted in the net, trying to see him, and couldn't, but she could sense him. Smell him. It was the same scent that had caught her attention as she followed her pack's trail, the one that had intrigued her enough to leave the path and head toward the clearing.

"I hafta come up t'free ye," he explained. He'd come into the woods quietly, on foot. She didn't scent his horse at all. "I'm afeared somethin's caught. The trap will'na let go from 'ere."

His voice moved below her and she caught a glimpse of him out of the corner of her eye. She gave a low growl, baring her teeth. It was pure instinct. The man came up the trunk on her left side, climbing fast and efficiently. Kirstin twisted in the net, snapping at him as he got nearer.

"Easy, lass, I mean ye n'harm," he soothed.

He was already above her, standing on the branch the net was strung from. Then he sat, edging his way slowly toward her, leaning over so he could reach the place where the rope that held the net stretched taut over the branch.

"Ye mus' be from t'wulver den?" He talked softly as he worked.

His hands were big, untangling the rope, which was tensed with Kirstin's full wulver weight—almost double her human one. He had dark, shoulder-length hair that swept across his cheek, and he used his other hand to push it out of his eyes.

"Did ye come t'help Laina and Sibyl, then?" He stopped when he heard Kirstin whine softly at that. He cocked his head and looked at her. Up close like this, the steel in his eyes had softened, like storm clouds parting to reveal a deepening, blue sky underneath. He seemed to understand her response, almost like he'd read her thoughts. "Darrow's healin' more e'ery day. Sibyl says she thinks he's comin' outta t'worst of it."

Just hearing those familiar, beloved names made Kirstin's heart beat faster. Could it be true? Was this man a friend of the wulvers? If he knew Sibyl, Laina and Darrow, should she trust his words? But it wasn't his words, it was his actions that swayed her. The man was up in a tree, trying to free her. What really convinced her, though, was his lack of alarm. She didn't sense or scent any fear in him at all.

"We'll get ye down from 'ere and I'll take ye back t'Castle MacFalon." The man's brow creased as he tried to solve some problem with the trap she couldn't see from her vantage point. He glanced at her and half-smiled, a dimple appearing in his cheek. "I'm Donal MacFalon, by t'by. Laird of the MacFalon Clan. 'Though I'm t'first t'admit, I'm still gettin' used to the title."

Donal MacFalon. The wulvers had come home talking about him. She had listened to their tales in the dining hall, where the wulver women fed their travel-weary warriors a hot meal, and remembered the way they'd spoken of Donal MacFalon. Unlike his brother, this was a man of integrity, they said. And like his father before him, he would honor the peaceful pact made between man and wulver.

She really could trust him, then. At least, as much as she was likely to trust any man.

Kirstin whined softly, reaching out toward him with a paw. She could just reach the soft leather of his boot and she tapped it gently. Donal looked down at her and smiled when he met her eyes again. There were no storm clouds in those eyes at all now. Just a deep, sparkling blue, as reflective as the lake in the wulver valley.

"Yer safe, lass," he assured her with a slow nod. "I apologize fer the trap. Alistair—me brother—was set on catchin' all t'wulvers and killin 'em..."

She growled at this—although she knew the man's brother, Alistair, was dead. He'd been the one responsible for Darrow's wounds.

"Aye, 'tis jus' how I feel 'bout it." Donal made a face. "It'll likely take us months t'find all the traps an' take 'em down."

Kirstin yipped in surprise, a high pitched sound, when the rope holding the net lengthened, but just for a moment. Then it went taut again.

"Oh fer the love'a—" He struggled with the rope, his body swaying on the limb, and Kirstin prayed he wouldn't fall to his death.

Then she heard it. It wasn't far off, coming from deeper in the woods—the sound of men. It wasn't just one, but several. She glanced at Donal, but he was busy trying to finagle the trap and hadn't heard anything. Of course, he was human—his sense of hearing and smell were seriously impaired compared to hers.

She whined softly, looking at the man, Donal, wondering how to tell him. Mayhaps they were his men, heading this way? She hoped so. The might be able to help him get her out of this damnable trap, because she wasn't sure he was going to be able to do it on his own.

"Easy, lass," he said again, softly, as he maneuvered the rope. "Almost there."

She whined louder, reaching out with her paw to touch his calf. He glanced down, frowning, lifting his gaze to meet hers.

"What is it?"

Kirstin turned her head in the direction of the men. She could hear them clearly now. Couldn't he?

Donal held his hand up, cocking his head. He'd heard them. Good! He moved quickly and almost silently, easing his way up higher in the tree. Using the leaves as cover, he nearly faded into the tree itself in the greens and blues of his plaid.

Kirstin panicked. She was caught in a trap with men heading her way. The howl rising in her throat was irrepressible. Twisting in the net, she pawed and snapped at it, determined to free herself, even if it meant falling to the forest floor below.

"Easy, lass, easy!" Donal soothed, his voice low and soft. "I'll not let 'em hurt ye. I promise ye!"

She whined, turning her head to look at him. She could see him through a thick, Y-shaped branch, his head appearing above it. Did she dare trust this man?

Her instinct to escape was strong, almost overpowering.

"I promise ye," he said again, giving her a slow, firm nod. "No harm'll come to ye on m'watch."

Kirstin heard them coming closer, along the path. Not his men, then, or he wouldn't be hiding. So who was it heading through the forest in the early morning light? Hunters?

She whined again, thrashing in the net.

"Shh!" Donal put his finger to his lips, shaking his head as he stood behind the thick tree limb.

Kirstin tried. She stilled, smelling them now—five men, heading their way. She made herself go limp in the net, turning her head so she could see Donal, see his eyes. He wasn't afraid—but he had a concerned knit to his brow. He didn't expect anyone coming through the woods on his land then. She saw he had his bow in his hand and he stood there, frozen, waiting.

Kirstin heard an arrow being knocked—and it wasn't Donal's. She wanted to warn him, to give him a chance to defend himself, but there was no need. He spoke before the other bow was drawn.

"If ye draw that arrow, I hope ye're a better archer than ye're a hunter." Donal's own bow was aimed in the direction of the interloper. "If I have t'drop from this tree a'fore I finish what I came up 'ere t'do, one of us'll be dead a'fore supper—and I do'na plan to miss the crispy skin of the swine I dragged in from t'woods t'mornin' a'fore last."

Kirstin heard another bow draw, this one from a different spot on the forest floor behind her, and she knew then that Donal was in trouble. She glanced up at the laird, seeing him preparing to launch himself from the tree, when a voice stopped him.

"Laird MacFalon, feel free to finish your task, free your quarry, and exit your perch."

Kirstin growled, feeling the hackles on the back of her neck rising. The voice was smooth, confident, even slightly amused—but she didn't trust the man it came from. She didn't know why—it was just instinct, but she trusted her instincts. Maybe it was just because the accent was so different from their own Scottish brogue. This man was English and spoke in the clipped way she was used to hearing from the Englishwoman, Sibyl, who had recently been living with them in the wulver den.

"I promise, this pair of mongrel poachers will hinder you no further," the Englishman assured them from below. "And, at your word, they'll hinder this world no longer either."

Don't trust him. Kirstin wanted to tell Donal, but she had no voice. Instead, she gave a low whine that turned into a growl in the back of her throat.

"Aye, thank ye, stranger." Donal frowned at Kirstin, hearing her animal warning.

The Scotsman was at a disadvantage, and he clearly knew it. He had to trust the Englishman, given that he had not only one, but two, arrows pointed in his direction, likely at very vital parts of his anatomy. Kirstin had a feeling that, whoever was below—especially if they were the poachers who had set the trap in which she was now ensnared—would rather have Donal dead before he left the tree than face him on level ground.

"Spare the curs, Lord Eldred," Donal called down. So he knew the man, then? But he'd called him "stranger?" Kirstin wrinkled her nose in confusion. "If they're honest poachers, they're hungry, and their wives and bairns will be as well. An empty belly's an ailment that spread quickly under m'late brother's watch—and t'will be cured under mine. As England's good King Henry's shown, there's none more loyal than those given mercy and a full belly—when warranted."

"You already have the makings of The MacFalon." The Englishman chuckled. "And your instincts are correct—I am Lord Eldred Lothienne, at your service."

So thc laird had been guessing at the man's identity then, Kirstin realized, looking up at the Scot.

"Easy." Donal squatted, speaking low to Kirstin, keeping his balance as he unhitched the rope and secured it, dropping a long end, presumably so he could lower Kirstin down once he was on the ground. At least, she hoped. "I know ye've got n'reason t'trust me, but I'll not harm ye—I'll free ye, I promise."

She gave a conciliatory whine as Donal began climbing down the trunk of the tree. Twisting in the net, she glimpsed the Englishman standing at its base out of the corner of her eye. He spoke like an English lord, but he was dressed in travelling clothes, a pack secured to his back. He gave Donal a gloved hand down and the Scotsman gave a low whistle when an arrow thunked into the tree trunk beside his head.

Lord Eldred shouldered Donal aside as two more loosed arrows hit the tree across the way, answering the first, these from the man's captains, still hidden somewhere in the wood.

"It appears the mongrels have given a parting shot before running off into the forest." Lord Eldred frowned into the woods, where the poachers had retreated. "Shall my captains and I pursue?"

"Nay, if they're local, they'll know these woods well—and they'll be as invisible as the fey folk a'fore ye run 'em down." Donal looked at the other man, head tilted, eyes narrowing slightly. "Ye marked 'em a'fore they were even in position. And ye weren't due t'visit 'til the morrow, but ye're in the MacFalon woods. Scouting, mayhaps? The tales of yer skill in the wild haven't been overtold, Lord Eldred Lothienne."

"Nor have the tales of your courage and generosity been overtold, Donal MacFalon," the Englishman replied with a smile, clapping the other man on the back. "It would appear that King Henry was correct in his assessment. You are as forthright as your brother was treacherous. It'll be a burden lifted to carry that message back to the King. I'd wager my finest bow that you won't be threatening the peace agreed upon with the wulvers."

"Ye can wager yer *life* on that." Donal glanced up at Kirstin, still stuck in the net. She was panting lightly, waiting patiently for the men to free her, trusting Donal at his word. Not that she had much choice, given the circumstances. The Scotsman grabbed the end of the rope he'd left dangling, unhitching it with a sharp tug, and Kirstin felt the net begin to move.

Her heart raced, and the closer she got to the ground, the more the fur on the back of her neck stood up. Her instinct told her to run. Or fight. And she had to force herself to stay still in the net.

"All of these wulver traps shoulda been disarmed." Donal frowned as he slowly lowered Kirstin toward the forest floor. She tensed, seeing the Englishman fully for the first time. He was an older man—a good ten, maybe fifteen, years older than Donal, at least—with a thick, dark beard shot with streaks of gray and salt and pepper hair. His dark eyes missed nothing, and his gaze settled on her and stayed there, making her hackles rise further. "I do'na know if they missed this one, or mayhaps someone's re-arming them. 'T'will be quite a job for ye and yer captains t'undertake, I'm afeared."

"King Henry has entrusted it to me, and it will be done." Lord Eldred squatted near the net, not touching her, but his gaze moved over her in wolf form as if cataloging her. Kirstin shuddered, feeling a growl building in her throat.

"What's free is what's good, and what's good is what's free." Donal unsheathed his dirk and began cutting the net apart.

"You plan to just let her go?" Lord Eldred asked, craggy eyebrows rising in surprise. "In that form?"

"She'll change and come back," Donal assured him, working more of the net free. "Won't ye, lass?"

Kirstin just looked at him, feeling his hands moving in her fur, soft, tender, as he worked to free her.

"You trust a wulver?" Eldred Lothienne stood, taking a step back as Kirstin lifted her head to look at him.

"Aye. She's not a wulver warrior." Donal snorted, shaking his head, unwrapping part of the net from her hind leg. "She's a female, here to see to her wounded kin."

Kirstin blinked at him in surprise, at how much the man had deduced when she hadn't yet said a word to him.

"Ye go make yerself decent, lass," Donal told her softly, freeing her from the last of the net. Her body shook with the effort it took her to stay still. "And I'll take ye back wit' me to Castle MacFalon t'see yer kin. Ye ken?"

She gave a low whine, but her gaze was on the Englishman, not the Scot. It was the former she didn't trust, although she had no idea why not.

"I'll take ye to Darrow," Donal said softly, his hand moving through her fur, scratching her affectionately behind the ear. She was still stunned by his lack of fear.

Kirsten glanced down at the dirk in his other hand, the one he'd used to open the net, shredding hours of someone's handiwork. He hadn't thought twice about destroying it. Kirstin let out a growl, head low, getting quickly to her feet. She heard them before she glimpsed them, two men appearing out of the woods on foot.

"Just my captains," Lord Eldred announced, waving them over, but Kirsten had already escaped deeper into the woods, in the opposite direction.

"Come back, ye ken?" Donal called after her as she disappeared into the brush.

Kirstin crouched there for a moment, panting lightly, feeling the adrenaline course through her body as she listened to the men talking, trying to decide what to do. If it had just been the man, Donal, she wouldn't have hesitated, but the other three men gave her pause. The two that had gotten away—where were they? She was sure they had been traveling together, but the man, Lord Eldred, had called them poachers.

Mayhaps she'd been mistaken, her senses changed from hanging so high up in the tree…

She glimpsed Donal pulling an arrow from that same tree she'd been hanging in—the arrow that had nearly hit him.

"Well-made. A local arrow?" Lord Eldred asked, looking at it over Donal's shoulder.

“Aye, ’tis an honest hunter’s arrow, not unmarked, fer a poacher’s purpose.” Donal frowned at it, turning it over in his hands. Then he slid it into his own quiver, looking at the Englishman. “Thank ye fer yer assistance wit’ the marksman. I did’na wanna make two more widows t’curse t’MacFalon name if I did’na hafta.”

“I understand.” Lord Eldred nodded, glancing toward the woods in her direction, and Donal did, too. They would be wondering about her, if she would return—a question she was pondering herself. She had options.

She could turn tail and run home. That was one option. But had she come all this way, just to turn around again? It had taken her nearly a week to convince the wulver warriors of her need to tend to Darrow. Her need to see him, to make sure he was all right—to help heal him and make her pack whole—overwhelmed her. It had been the force that had compelled her on this journey in the first place, and she was determined to see it through.

The man, Donal, could take her to Darrow. She sensed he was honorable, and knew from the wulver warriors who had returned, that he could be trusted. She didn’t know about the other men, but something in her said that Donal would protect her, if need be. Besides, she thought with a smile as she crouched fully behind a tall, thick oak tree, she could change into wulver form and snap all their necks before the first one could draw his blade, if she so chose.

She walked, barefoot, out of the brush, into the clearing where they stood talking. They didn’t sense or see her until she was almost on top of them, even though she was in human form now.

"Ah, there she is." Lord Eldred spotted her first, his dark, glittering gaze sweeping her up and down.

Kirsten had changed back, pulling her plaid around her to cover as much as she could. It was a versatile garment, yards of fabric that could cover her from head to toe if needed, now gathered into the semblance of a skirt, crossing in front and pinned in place to cover her breasts. Although, if the Englishmen's gazes were any indication, she was showing far more skin than they were used to seeing.

Donal turned toward her, smiling as she approached, his words fading away mid-sentence. She had smoothed her long, dark hair out over her shoulders, picking out the leaves and twigs as best she could, making herself as presentable as possible without the benefit of a looking glass or even a stream or pond.

She saw the apple in Donal's throat move up and down as he swallowed, his gaze sweeping over her, too, from her bare feet and knees peeking out from under her make-shift skirt, to the V her plaid made between her breasts, then up to her face, their eyes meeting and locking. She had that same sense again, the one she'd experienced when she stopped in the clearing where he'd knelt, head bent in prayer. She didn't understand it, but it gave her a sudden rush of feeling, and her cheeks flushed with it.

Kirstin didn't even register the other three men—they were staring, too, although she only sensed this peripherally. It was as if the whole forest had narrowed suddenly into one, shining, sun-dappled path, and it led straight to Donal MacFalon. Kirstin's knees felt wobbly as she continued her careful approach, running a nervous hand through her hair again, seeing Donal's gaze distracted by the motion. He traced the dark waterfall her hair made over her creamy, bare shoulders, skipping to her cleavage, then up again, to her eyes—and then, finally, settling on her mouth.

She opened it to say something, but she couldn't find the words. She could only stand there, a few feet from the man, trembling like she had been while trapped in the net. Her heart galloped in her chest, and something pumped through her veins that was hotter than her own blood, something foreign and uncontrollable.

A low whistle came from one of the Englishmen, who leaned in to say to the other, "Imagine her in an English gown."

The second man shifted against the tree where he was leaning and remarked, "I'm imagining her out of one."

That statement made Donal's eyes flash and he turned his attention to the two young men. Lord Eldred caught the look and got between them, raising a gloved hand.

"Gentlemen, remember yourselves," the bearded Englishman snapped. He turned to her then, bowing slightly, and asked, "What's your name, m'lady?"

M'lady? She smiled and wrinkled her nose at that, looking back at Donal. He stared at her still, bemused.

"Kirstin," she said simply, her eyes locking again with the man standing transfixed beside her. She was glad there was a tree nearby—still stuck with two arrows—for her to lean back against. "And you're Donal MacFalon? Laird of Clan MacFalon?"

"Aye." He gave a slow nod. "That I am, lass—and I'm vera glad t'meet ye, now that yer not stuck yonder in a tree."

She laughed at that, glancing up at the branch where she'd been dangling not too long ago.

"Thank ye fer savin' me, kind sir." She held out a hand to him, and he took it, bending slightly at the waist as any gentleman would. She expected him to kiss the back of her hand like she'd heard from Sibyl was the English custom—since they were in the presence of an English lord—but instead, he turned her hand over, palm up, and pressed his lips to the inside of her wrist.

Kirstin's breath caught in her throat, and she melted. His mouth was soft and he had two days' stubble on his cheeks that prickled the sensitive skin of her wrist. Somehow, that one, small kiss, sent a thousand pulses of light through her body, bringing senses alive she'd never known before, even as a wulver. She looked at him in wonder, staring into those slate-blue eyes. They were focused solely on her like she was the only thing left in the world to look at.

"Pleasure to meet you, m'lady." Lord Eldred interrupted their interlude, holding his gloved hand out for hers, but Kirstin held the edged of her wrapped plaid and dropped into a brief curtsy instead. Sibyl had taught it to her and some of the other wulvers, and she used it to keep from having to touch him. For some reason, the thought was anathema to her. The older man nodded, lips pursing for a moment before he smiled and turned to introduce his men. "I'm Lord Eldred Lothienne, and these are my captains—William and Geoffrey Blackmoore of Blythe."

"Sirs." She curtsied for them, too, seeing Donal still watching her out of the corner of her eye. She wasn't looking at him anymore, but she was very aware of his presence. It seemed to fill the whole forest.

Lord Eldred chuckled at that. "As lord of the royal hunt, neither I, nor my men, are knights. The royal huntsmen are required to get their hands dirty doing work knights would likely feel unfit for them."

Kirstin gave a nod, acknowledging that, wondering just what kind of dirty work the man in front of her and his captains had been up to in the forest before they came along, but she didn't say anything.

"I am quite accustomed to living in the wild," Lord Eldred assured her, his dark eyes glittering, even in the dim light of the forest. "As I know you are, m'dear."

"She's a wild one, I'll give him that," one of the captains—Geoffrey—said softly to the other. She didn't think Donal heard it, but she did—and so did Eldred Lothienne. He gave them both a warning look, but his eyes raked over her when he turned back again.

"Would you like to come back to our camp for the night, m'lady?" The other captain, William, dared to ask. "Mayhaps the outdoors, sleeping out under the stars, would be more to your liking than the creature comforts of Castle MacFalon?"

She opened her mouth to say something, but Donal beat her to it.

"Nay, the lass's coming wit' me." Donal took a step nearer to her, frowning at the men on horseback. "She's anxious t'meet up wit' the rest of 'er pack."

"You have wulvers at the castle still, then?" Lord Eldred asked.

"Aye." Donal gave a short nod. "One of 'em was wounded."

"Darrow." Kirstin spoke his name, feeling her heart breaking at the thought of one of her pack—the brother of their pack leader, no less—helpless and in need of tending.

“We’ve four wulvers stayin’ at Castle MacFalon,” Donal informed the Englishman. “Raife’s their pack leader. Darrow, the wounded wulver, is his brother. The other two are their mates.”

“Mates.” Geoffrey snickered at that, but the look Lord Eldred gave him made him cover his mouth with a hand and straighten his posture.

“They’ve all been given welcome refuge wit’ us ’til Darrow’s healed,” Donal said, glancing at Kirstin as he spoke. Then he turned to Lord Eldred. “I’m sure you’ll be interested t’meet them at t’castle tomorrow—when ye officially ‘arrive’?”

“Indeed.” The Englishman nodded, reaching out and shaking Donal’s outstretched hand. “We’ll continue with our reconnaissance until then, and see you after sunrise tomorrow. If we find any more traps, we’ll disarm them.”

“Thank ye. I’ll make official welcome t’ye tomorrow as laird of Clan MacFalon,” Donal replied, squeezing the man’s gloved hand with his big, bare ones. Kirsten couldn’t help noticing how rough and calloused they were. Donal MacFalon was clearly not afraid of hard work. “But I hafta say, I’m grateful we’ve had a chance t’meet informally, man t’man.”

“Indeed.”

“I jus’ find all that infernal pageantry hides more than it reveals ’bout men, d’ye ken?”

“I do ‘ken’. We shall see you in the morning, MacFalon.” The older man dropped him a wink, grinning, and turned to go. They had no horses and she wondered where they were.

That made Kirsten wonder where Donal’s horse was—and how they were going to get back to Castle

MacFalon without it. When she turned back to look, Eldred and his men had already melted into the woods.

"Something's amiss wit' that man..." she whispered to herself, rubbing her bare arms. She'd broken out in gooseflesh.

"Lord Eldred?" Donal asked, looking in the direction the men had ridden off in.

"Aye..." She nodded, meeting his concerned gaze.

"He acted honorably." Donal frowned, tilting his head at her. "Less stuffy than I expected of a king's lord."

"Mayhaps." She swallowed, knowing she couldn't tell him about the warning signals that had gone off inside her upon meeting Lord Eldred Lothienne—Donal wasn't a wulver, he couldn't understand.

"He's 'ere t'make sure we keep t'wolf pact," Donal explained, kicking at the shredded net still lying on the ground that had ensnared her. "To see that all such traps are dismantled and disposed of. 'Tis a noble purpose, ye ken?"

"Mayhaps," she said again and sighed. "I hafta say, I'm glad I never had t'play politics. It seems dishonest."

"I s'pose it might seem that way," Donal mused. "But it's really nuh different than posturing a'fore a battle or sword fight. Each side wants t'win the day wit'out the death or loss of self, friends or countrymen, ye ken?"

"Ye make a good politician." She smiled up at him with both mouth and eyes, and he smiled back, just as brightly. She felt a little foolish, standing there in the middle of the woods, smiling at a strange man, but there was no helping it. Just looking at the man made her face break into a smile.

“S’tell me, how’s me kin?” She took a step toward him, pressing a hand to his forearm. He glanced down at where she touched him—his forearms alone were thick as tree branches, she noted. Strong, solid. “How’s Darrow?”

“He’s not getting’ any worse, and likely getting’ better,” he soothed, putting a big, calloused hand over hers. A slow heat filled her at his touch, the way his voice dipped, seeming to caress her with sound alone. “But I’m sure yer healin’ hands’ll be of great use t’him—and a glad reprieve fer Sibyl and Laina. They’ve been splittin’ nursin’ duties and are sorely taxed.”

“How did ye know?” she asked him, his fingertips moving over hers, not letting go.

“That ye’re a healer?” he guessed.

“Aye.”

“Who else’d c’mon t’MacFalon land, seekin’ their injured kin?” He smiled. “Besides, ye’ve a kindness in yer eyes that belies ye—e’en when yer a wulver.”

“Aye?” She blinked up at him in surprise.

She didn’t think, in her entire existence, that anyone had ever said anything like that to her before. She’d been a healer since she could remember, a midwife, taking care of the wulver children when the other wulver women went into estrus and changed, but it was something that went unacknowledged, for the most part. They all had their individual skills and talents, and everyone understood that they would use them for the good of the pack.

She’d never realized how much the pack took each other for granted, until that moment.

And, looking up into Donal’s eyes, she didn’t think she’d ever been quite so fully *seen* before that moment.

It made her feel far more naked and vulnerable than she'd ever experienced, even after she'd changed from wulver to woman with no plaid at the ready.

"There's such love and loyalty among ye wulvers." He patted her hand, looking down at her fondly. "It's been a rare gift t'bear witness to it. I do'na understand why men would make enemies of ye. 'Tis absurd."

"Thankfully, t'English king agrees wit' ye. 'Tis why t'wolf pact exists," she reminded him, throwing in a bit of honesty for good measure. "Although King Henry created it t'use t'wulver warriors fer 'is own benefit."

"I've seen t'wulver warriors," Donal said, shaking his head. "I would'na wanna fight on t'opposite side."

"Yer a wise man." She smiled at him, glancing around, wondering again where his horse was. Still in the clearing? She wanted to get to Castle MacFalon, to see Darrow for herself, to talk to Laina and Sibyl, to see her pack leader, Raife. That alone would quell her jittery insides.

"And a devoted one," Kirstin noted, remembering how she'd seen him, head bent, at the burial cairn. "I did'na mean t'interrupt yer prayer vigil. Is that ancestral land? Yer burial ground?"

"Aye." He nodded. "I admit, I was surprised t'see ye. But truth be told, y'have e'ery right t'be on that spot, as well, lass—mayhaps e'en more'n I do."

"Me?" She gave him a puzzled smile. "Why?"

"My family's burial ground's built on t'ancient den of yer kin—da wulvers," he explained.

"I did'na know that." Her eyes widened in surprise. "It's our sire and his warriors who share and pass down wulver history. As a healer, I know it's important t'learn and pass on ancestral knowledge of t'healing arts. I imagine the same's true of leaders—whether they be wulvers or men."

"Aye, 'tis true of t'good ones," he agreed. His fingers brushed hers again, this time turning her hand over. She watched, transfixed, as he brought it to his mouth, his lips caressing the inside of her wrist once more, making her knees feel like jelly underneath her plaid. "Yer pack's blessed t'have such a devoted healer in their midst."

"Thank ye." She swallowed, trying to find her voice. It was caught in her throat, breathy. "I'm truly anxious to see my kin, if—"

Donal dropped her hand, turning to give a whistle that startled her. Thankfully, the tree was still there behind her, giving her legs more strength than she felt they actually had in the moment.

"That's t'call of a kestrel," she observed, admiring his ability to mimic the bird.

"Aye, 'tis," he agreed, turning toward her again.

In the distance, Kirstin heard a horse's hooves.

She swallowed as Donal leaned toward her, hand above her head, against the tree. He was a big tree of a man himself, his body thick and muscled. She swore she could feel every one of them tensing in front of her, every last sinew stretch and bulge of his veins. He was only inches from her and she wondered, briefly, if he might be about to more than just chastely kiss the inside of her pulsing wrist.

Then she glanced up and saw he had hold of the two arrows in the tree above her head. He was slowly working them out of the trunk, his breath coming a little faster with the effort, his bare knee grazing hers.

"The kestrel's a sound heard both in city and forest," he explained, giving the whistle again, even though she could hear his horse coming to the call.

She couldn't help noticing the way his dark hair brushed the plaid over his shoulders. He likely kept it long, like most Scots, to remind them of their wildness—their closeness to nature, and the animals that lived there. Animals that, perhaps, man himself had once been.

"So it won't alert t'enemy?" she guessed, thinking of his bird call as she heard the horse whinny nearby, pawing at the forest floor, announcing his presence.

"Aye, wise woman." Donal showed straight, white teeth as he smiled down at her, yanking the arrows finally free with a sudden jerk. She gasped at the motion and bit her lip as the big man turned to his horse. "Here's Kestrel now."

"Yer horse is named Kestrel?" She laughed, looking at the big, spirited, fearless black beauty as Donal grabbed the reins and tugged the war horse nearer to her.

"Ye were naughty, Kestrel, givin' away me position," she scolded as the animal drew near.

It wasn't too afraid of her, now that she was human again, but all animals could sense the difference between wulver and human. It took Donal's comfort to get the big, black nose lowered in surrender, nuzzling her shoulder.

"I forgive ye." She smiled, petting the soft velvet of his snout. "He did'na like me much when I was a wulver."

"He did'na know ye." Donal smiled, watching her rub her cheek against the horse's nose.

"He's beautiful," she confessed, smiling up at Donal.

"Kestrel thinks t'same of ye, lass." Donal put his boot in the stirrup and pulled himself into the saddle. Mounted, he seemed like a giant, his smile brighter than the sun that shone through the trees behind his head as he held a hand out for her.

She didn't hesitate. She grabbed the arm he offered and slid onto the horse, settling into the saddle behind him. She sat astride, like any good Scotswoman would, although she wore nothing under her plaid.

"Do ye ride?" he asked over his shoulder.

"Aye." She nodded against his broad back, her arms going naturally around his waist. Her fingers could feel the hard muscle of his abdomen, even through his plaid.

"Good." He smiled—she couldn't see it, but she could hear it in his voice. "Then I won't hafta tell ye t'hold on."

Kestrel took off like a shot and Kirsten gasped, holding tight to Donal MacFalon while clenching horse flesh between her quivering thighs. She pressed her cheek against his back, clinging to him, feeling the steady rhythm of the animal beneath them both as they headed back toward the castle.

But that was nothing compared to the animal Kirsten felt coming alive within her since she'd seen this man and caught his scent across the clearing.

She felt Donal's thighs flexing against her own as he guided the horse on a path through the woods, and the scent of the man, even though she was currently a woman and not a wulver, made her salivate. Her whole body seemed to want to melt against his on the saddle, as if the motion of the horse could drive them together and make them one.

He didn't have to tell her to hang on—but she did. She hung onto him as if he was her second skin, as if she could crawl inside him. She clung to him, trembling, not understanding her own feelings at this closeness, at the way they moved together on the saddle.

Kirstin thought she felt him chuckle at the way her fingers locked feverishly around his waist, at the way she clutched him between her legs, and wondered if he knew she was bare and exposed beneath her plaid.

Because Donal MacFalon seemed determined to give her the ride of her life.

Chapter Two

"Kirstin!" Sibyl's eyes widened, at first in shock, then in happy surprise.

Kirstin slipped into Darrow's room, afraid of what she might find. Donal came in behind her—he'd shown her to Darrow's room himself—and stood just inside the half-open door, watching as Kirsten crossed over to a bed so big it made the giant, wulver man in the center of it appear small.

"Sibyl." Kirstin cupped the Englishwoman's sweet, freckled face, brushing her auburn hair away and kissing her cheek, so very glad to see her whole and unharmed, after her sacrificial ride from the wulver's den to Castle MacFalon. Donal had assured her Sibyl was fine, but it was good to see it for herself. "How is he?"

"He'll live." Sibyl sat back down in the chair beside the man's bed, continuing to tear sheets to make dressings. Sibyl frowned at the wulver tossing and turning on the mattress. He gave a low growl in his sleep, shaking his head, and for a brief moment he hovered between human and wulver form—a sight Kirstin was used to, but one that gave both Sibyl and Donal pause. Sibyl met Kirstin's gaze and she saw tears in the redhead's eyes. "No thanks to the cowardice of Alistair MacFalon."

Kirstin swallowed hard at the name, seeing a dark cloud pass over the Englishwoman's face. Sibyl had been promised to Alistair—Donal's older brother, who had been laird of Clan MacFalon until his recent demise—and had been willing to sacrifice herself in marriage to a cruel man she didn't love in order to save the wulver pack.

Sibyl couldn't have known—and Kirstin certainly hadn't realized, when she put the Englishwoman on a horse and sent her away from the wulver den, heading back toward Castle MacFalon—that Alistair was setting a trap for the wulver warriors, using his betrothed as bait. He'd also kidnapped Darrow's mate, Laina, just in case the wulvers decided not to pursue the Englishwoman who had been living in their midst.

But it had been Alistair's intention all along to lure the wulver army out of their mountain den and destroy them. Kirstin had heard the story, told by the wulver warriors, of Alistair's cowardice and treachery. She'd heard them talk of the way Darrow had demanded single combat blood rite—a fight to the death between two men. It was a codicil in the wolf pact intended to avoid all-out war between the Scots and the wulvers.

Alistair had refused to fight or to honor the wolf pact, which his own father had signed in blood, until the crowd shamed him into it. Kirstin knew the coward had called for a stand-in, but not even his own brother, Donal, would step up for him. The wulver warriors told the story of Alistair MacFalon's cowardice, how he'd cried like a little girl when Darrow began to best him, begging for the fight to be called off, because Laina was, in fact, not dead after all, as the Scotsman had boasted.

And when Alistair had her brought out as proof, bound and bloody but very much alive, he'd used the distraction when Darrow's back was turned to run the wulver through. What Alistair hadn't counted on was a wulver's strength, determination, and incredible resilience. Darrow had managed to turn and lop off the coward's head before collapsing at his mate's feet.

Kirstin had heard the story told a dozen times before she left the den, but she didn't really understand its reality until she saw it in Sibyl's red-rimmed eyes. She couldn't imagine what the poor woman had been through and she put her arms around her in comfort before turning her attention to the wulver recovering from his wounds in bed.

"I'd like t'take the opportunity once again to apologize fer me brother's heinous actions." Donal spoke from the doorway, looking between the two women. "I can'na say't enough. And I hope, in some way, I can make up fer—"

"You can stop with the apologies, Laird MacFalon." Sibyl looked at him fondly, her eyes softening as she saw him standing guard near the door. Kirstin saw the way the woman looked at Donal, with such great affection, and instantly, her body reacted in a way that had never happened before. Kirstin's spine stiffened, her hands clenching into fists, and deep in her chest, she felt a growl rising, even though she was in human, not wulver, form. She swallowed it down, confused by her own response, hearing Sibyl's voice praising the laird of the MacFalon Clan. "You've been more than generous with your time and your resources, Donal."

Donal. Sibyl called the laird by his Christian name? Kirstin met Sibyl's eyes and saw the tears there—real tears. The woman had been through hell and back, that much was clear. Donal MacFalon was a man with a big heart and a strong sense of integrity—she'd kenned that much already. Of course, he would offer Sibyl a kind hand, a big, strong shoulder to cry on.

Why should that bother her? Kirstin wondered. And yet, the tiny hairs on the back of her neck were standing up, and her blood felt as if it was boiling in her veins when Sibyl spoke of the laird.

"He's been such a comfort to me," Sibyl told her, reaching out a hand for Kirstin's. She allowed Sibyl to take it, to press it to her damp cheek, even though her hand trembled slightly in anger. What in the world did she have to be angry about? She reasoned with herself, trying to shake off the feeling. If she could control her wulver side, she could certainly control this—whatever this sudden feeling was.

Except, she couldn't. She didn't understand it, but she couldn't control the feeling at all.

"I can't thank him enough for everything he's done," Sibyl went on. Each word grated on Kirstin's ears, raked like a wulver's claws on slate. She gritted her teeth, listening to Sibyl's praise of the man, wondering why she had a sudden urge to throw the redhead from the nearest high window.

She had come to love Sibyl like a sister! What in the world was wrong with her?

Kirstin's eyes fled Sibyl's, returning to the doorway, where Donal stood, hand on the hilt of his sword, at the ready. His cheeks reddened slightly while Sibyl sung the man's praises as if he were the second coming of the human's worshipful Christ, and Kirstin tried to fight her desire to separate the woman's yapping head from her little body.

"It's been me pleasure, Sibyl," Donal muttered, clearing in his throat. "The least I could do fer ye..."

"Well, he rescued me from a trap." Kirstin's voice was much more strident than she meant it to be, and she stood there, crossing her arms over her chest, feeling her face growing red. "I mean, he... I..."

"Oh, Kirstin, no..." Sibyl gasped at the thought. "The same one Laina was trapped in?"

"Nay, t'was a net." Donal frowned. Kirstin knew Laina had been trapped in a cage, a message left in her blood for the wulvers to find after she'd been taken to Castle MacFalon. "Should've been disarmed. But we'll have help with that in the morning. King Henry's sent his royal huntsman to ensure all the wulver traps are taken out of the MacFalon woods."

"Oh, that's wonderful news." Sibyl perked up at that, eyes bright. "Does that mean... King Henry intends to honor the wolf pact then?"

"Aye." Donal gave a satisfied nod. "I expect the wulver messenger Raife dispatched will return with similar news. But Kirstin and I—we met Lord Eldred Lothienne and his captains in the woods. They were already working on disarming the traps."

"I ran into an armed one," Kirstin said wryly.

"Are you all right?" Sibyl asked.

"Donal saved me," Kirstin reminded her, taking far too much pleasure in saying it, and enjoying the way Donal smiled in response. Kirstin approached the bed, putting the back of her hand to Darrow's forehead. No fever—that was a good sign. "Where's Laina? I would've thought she wouldn't leave 'is side."

"I sent her to fetch some bread and soup for our wounded warrior." Sibyl sighed. "Every time he sees her, he wants to get up, and he's going to pull out all the stitching I did."

"So ye did stitch 'im up then?" Kirstin lifted the dressing to look. Sibyl was a fine healer, for a human, and had done a good job with needle and thread. The wulver in him had done a great deal of healing already, Kirstin noted—although she was shocked by how bloody the wound still was. It must have been very serious, quite deep. Wulvers healed from the inside out. Superficial wounds could heal within hours, sometimes minutes.

"Yes, I think we have him well in hand," Sibyl agreed, watching Kirstin's hands moving over Darrow's body, checking him for other injuries. She didn't feel anything broken or out of place. "It's just keeping his pain controlled—and keeping him in bed—that we have to deal with until he's well enough to come home."

"Home..." Kirstin smiled at Sibyl's choice of words.

The Englishwoman had run away from this castle, away from the cruel Alistair MacFalon, her betrothed, and had ended up in the wulver's den. Sibyl had spent months falling deeply, madly in love with Raife, the wulver pack leader. Kirstin had watched it happen, had been heart-glad of it. Raife sorely needed a mate, and while many of the wulver women had hoped to be marked by him, he'd never taken to any of them.

Until Sibyl came along. Not a wulver—not even a Scot! An Englishwoman. A *shasennach.* But Raife loved her, and she loved him. Sibyl had been so changed. She no longer wore English gowns—even her English accent had begun to fade. And she now thought of a wulver den as her home!

"It'll be good t'have t'pack together again." Kirstin agreed, seeing Donal's brow knit at her words. It was a phrase that should have instantly filled her with peace and calm, but she, too, felt a strange new tug at her heart she didn't quite understand at her own words.

"Kirstin... you should know..." Sibyl glanced at Donal, biting her lip, and Kirstin felt that strange zing of feeling again, like a lightning strike. Then it was as if someone had suddenly dropped a weight on her chest. It was hard to breathe. What was it that Sibyl wanted her to know, and what did it have to do with Donal MacFalon?

And why in the world did it matter to her, all of a sudden?

"Raife is... angry with me," Sibyl confessed. Donal snorted from the doorway at that, and Sibyl's cheeks filled with color to match her hair. "To put it mildly. And he's likely to be angry with you, too."

"Is that all?" Kirstin asked, filled with relief. Sibyl blinked at her, looking so hurt Kirstin couldn't help but go and put her arms around her. "I ju't mean—a'course he is. He's a wulver. I knew he would be. Ye had t'know he'd be angry..."

"Well... yes." Sibyl sighed, wringing the cloth in her hands as Kirstin knelt by her chair. "Of course, I expected he'd be angry with me for leaving. But I did it to save him, Kirstin!"

"Aye." She patted the Englishwoman's worried hands. "Ye should've seen him when I told 'im ye'd gone."

Kirstin paled at the memory alone. She'd never seen Raife in such a state. Sibyl searched her eyes, and Kirstin knew what she was looking for. She wanted proof that Raife loved her, that he wanted her, that he had truly meant it when he said that Sibyl was his one true mate.

"I thought he was goin' to take me head right offa me shoulders," Kirstin confessed, swallowing hard. "He was crazed. He could'na b'lieve ye'd gone."

"I couldn't believe it either." Sibyl lowered her head at the memory. "I really thought, if I came back here, and told Alistair I'd marry him, that the wulvers would be safe..."

"Aye." Kirstin nodded. "I know Raife'll be angry when he discovers I've come 'ere. But Sibyl, I could'na stay 'way. Not when I knew Darrow was hurt—and 'tis all my fault. If I hadna put ye on that horse..."

"But we couldn't have known," Sibyl whispered. "We both thought we were doing the right thing."

"Och, what a fine mess this is," Donal said softly from the doorway, and when Kirstin met his eyes, she saw the sympathy in them.

Kirstin opened her mouth to speak, to explain, but a voice interrupted her.

"Kirstin! What in the da world're ye doin 'ere?" Laina exclaimed from the doorway, carrying a tray. She was so startled, she nearly dropped it—Donal's quick reaction kept that from happening. He carried the tray over to the bedside table while the women gathered together.

"I came t'bring all'ye home, safe'n'sound." Kirstin put her arms around her. Laina's thick, white-blonde hair was pulled into a long plait down her back. She was dressed in her plaid, just like Sibyl. "How's Darrow?"

"Cranky." Laina smiled at him and Darrow moaned in his sleep, like he'd heard her. "But I s'pose that's understandable, given he was run-through with a broad sword."

"And how're *ye*?" Kirstin asked, touching the other woman's bruised and battered face. Laina was a stunning beauty, and Kirstin could tell the marks had already begun to heal. Wulver women didn't mend quite as quickly as the warriors, but they still had a significant ability to mend themselves. "They hurt you?"

"Alistair's men—a few of them." Laina shook her head, glancing over at Donal, who looked like he wanted to make yet another apology for his brother's conduct. "But I'm no worse fer t'wear."

"How's me bairn?" Laina grasped her shoulders, searching Kirstin's face with the hungry eyes of a mother who had been without her babe overlong. "Garaith's well?"

"Aye, he misses ye," Kirstin replied, smiling at the memory of Laina and Darrow's dark-haired little boy. "But Beitris is taking good care of him in your absence."

"I miss 'im so." Laina sighed. "I need t'return soon a'fore me milk disappears altogether."

"He'll be well enough t'travel soon." Kirstin assured her, glancing at Darrow, thrashing on the bed now. He was clearly waking up.

"I'm well enough now," Darrow muttered. Kirstin smiled. It was good to hear his voice. "If ye'd stop givin' me that witch's brew, I'd be on me horse and... Laina?"

Darrow went up on an elbow, the sheet falling down his chest to his waist, revealing the bandage that wrapped around his middle. He rubbed his eyes, blinking.

"Where's Laina?"

"She's here," Sibyl assured him, pressing Laina closer to the bed so he could peer at his mate. "You're feeling no pain because of that witches brew, Darrow.

But if you keep pushing yourself, you're going to pull those stitches and bleed out."

"He's a wulver, not a man." Laina pushed him back on the bed in spite of her words, covering him again with the sheet as she pressed a gentle kiss to the top of his head. "He'll heal much faster than ye're used to."

"I understand that, but he's a very lucky wulver, given his wounds," Sibyl reminded her softly.

"Raife." Darrow blinked up at the ceiling. "We need t'go. Where's Raife? And what's that MacFalon doin' in m'room?"

He tried to get up again, but Laina succeeded in keeping him down with another kiss, this one pressed to his lips.

"The tonic I give him for pain makes him wake confused," Sibyl explained softly to Kirstin. Then she spoke loudly to Darrow. "Donal is the laird of Clan MacFalon now, Darrow. He is honoring the wolf pact. We're safe here. I don't want you riding a horse just yet."

"Where's Raife?" Darrow asked the ceiling, then looked at his mate, frowning. "Where's m'brother? Raife! Raife!"

He yelled Raife's name so loudly Kirstin thought he might tear his stitches just from the force of the word. It seemed to echo throughout the whole castle.

"Donal, do you know where Raife is?" Sibyl asked, standing and pressing a hand to Darrow's chest, helping Laina keep him in bed.

Donal gave her a pained look. "He will'na come, if'n yer in 'ere, Sibyl..."

"Why?" Darrow pushed Laina aside, glaring at Donal.

"He won't be in the same room with me," Sibyl confessed, tears coming to her eyes.

"He b'lieves ye left 'im fer Alistair." Darrow's gaze narrowed at her. "Did ye? Why did ye come 'ere, Sibyl?"

"She was tryin' t'save yer hide," Kirstin snapped, wagging her finger at him. Then she looked around the room, putting a hand on Sibyl's quivering shoulder. "All of ye. She was goin' t'exchange herself for Laina, t'keep t'wulver pack safe."

"Alistair would never've let t'wulver woman go," Donal said softly. He was speaking to Kirstin—she had the feeling that the rest of the people in the room had heard this already. "His intention was t'kill all t'wulvers."

"Why?" Kirstin asked, giving him a long, puzzled look. "The MacFalons've honored t'wolf pact fer years."

"He claimed t'was an order from King Henry, but given that Henry's sent 'is huntsman t'help us dismantle the wulver traps, I do'na b'lieve it." Donal glanced around the room, from person to person, and Kirstin felt the weight of his words as he spoke. "I think m'brother felt threatened by t'wulvers. Especially after they kidnapped 'is bride."

"I wasn't kidnapped," Sibyl protested with a snarl that any wulver would have been proud of. "I ran away."

"Aye," Donal agreed. "But Alistair did'na wanna b'lieve that, ye ken?"

"But why defy t'English King's wishes and break t'wolf pact?" Kirstin asked him. "I do'na understand..."

"He was m'kin, but I will'na make excuses fer 'im." Donal told her with a sad shake of his head. "He was a cruel and duplicitous man."

"It's been awful." Sibyl's voice shook and she cleared her throat, blinking back her tears. "But Darrow's healing nicely and the wulvers are safe. That's the important thing."

"Aye," Donal agreed. "Thanks to ye, Lady Sibyl."

"And if we can keep Darrow in bed," Sibyl said, giving him a long, quelling look. "Mayhaps he'll be ready to travel within the month."

"The month?" Darrow exploded, struggling against Laina's hold—she was a woman, but she was a wulver, after all. "I'll be ready t'go in two days! Less, if ye stop makin' me drink that godawful—"

"Laina, keep your mate in bed, please." Sibyl crossed her arms and glared at him.

"Mayhaps I should show Kirstin to a room?" Donal suggested, smiling as Kirstin glanced over at him. "I thought I'd have Moira find 'er a more suitable wardrobe?"

"She's a wulver and a Scot, MacFalon." Darrow glared at him, eyes narrowed. "D'ye expect 'er t'wear more'n 'er plaid?"

"I notice yer wearin' a plaid, Lady Sibyl," Donal noted with a smile, ignoring Darrow's obvious hostility. "In spite of the closet full of English clothes me brother had made fer ye."

"Sibyl might have been born English, but she's been chosen by our pack leader as his mate," Kirstin reminded him—reminded all of them. "She is *banrighinn* now."

"*Banrighinn*?" Sibyl stumbled over the Gaelic word.

"Queen." Donal translated quietly, looking at Sibyl with soft eyes.

"Aye," Laina agreed. "*Banrighinn*."

"I'm no one's *b-banrighinn*," Sibyl muttered, flushing. "Besides, Raife won't even talk to me, let alone mark me."

Kirstin saw Sibyl look longingly at the intricate tattoo that decorated Darrow's shoulder. A matching one was inked on Laina's hip and thigh, marking them as one another's.

"Raife's a stubborn fool," Kirstin snapped, putting an arm around Sibyl's shoulders.

"Kirstin!" Raife's voice boomed as he appeared in the doorway, his big frame filling it completely. His face was a thundercloud, his brow low and drawn. There were new worry lines on his face, and his eyes were as dark as a night sky. "What're ye doin'ere?"

"I came t'tend the wounded," Kirstin said simply, feeling Sibyl shrink against her side at the sight of Raife.

"There's only one wounded, and from t'sound of 'im yellin' fer me, he's jus' fine," Raife snapped, pointing at his half-naked brother. "I want m'pack back in the den. Darrow, are ye well enough t'travel?"

"Aye, brother." Darrow's voice sounded strong as he pushed the covers back, sitting up and swinging his bare legs over the side obediently. He clearly thought he was ready to follow his leader, but bright red blood bloomed on the sheet Sibyl had tied as a bandage and he winced.

"No, Darrow," Laina soothed softly, trying to press him back onto the bed.

"Raife, he's not well enough to travel!" Sibyl cried, fleeing to Darrow's side in order to look at his wound.

Kirstin could see, when she slid the bandage aside, that some of the stitches had been pulled by his motion. "Please, don't move him! I beg you."

"He's a wulver," Raife growled, glowering at his brother. He wouldn't even look at Sibyl, even if he was speaking counter to her words. "If he's awake, he can travel now."

"He was run-through with a sword, you man-beast!" Sibyl hissed with anger.

Kirstin saw rage flicker in Raife's eyes. The whole room sizzled with the heat of their argument—and it was clearly not the first time they'd had it. Donal was already stepping in, trying to make peace.

"Ye can all stay as long as ye need." Donal put a hand on Raife's arm. "We've plenty of room."

"I'm grateful fer yer honorable treatment and hospitality." Raife straightened, frowning, glancing down at Donal—Raife was a head taller, and Donal was a big man. "But we need t'get home."

"Don't be in such a hurry ye lose one of yer own," Donal said softly, watching as Laina and Sibyl worked to re-bandage Darrow's now openly-bleeding wound.

"In other words, don't be a bull-headed fool," Kirstin translated, glaring at Raife, arms crossed over her chest.

"Kirstin..." Raife snarled in her direction, eyes narrowing, a warning. Then he spoke to Donal. "Can ye make room for one more of m'charges, Donal? I hate t'ask, but she's clearly taken it upon herself t'impose."

"'Tis no imposition at all," Donal soothed. Kirstin caught his eye and saw something in his that made her smile. He was amused by this whole scene—Darrow's stubborn posturing, Raife's even more stubborn resolve. Then his words, the warmth in them, made her melt. "She's more'n welcome. Ye'll are."

"Good. Then it's settled." Laina brushed her mate's hair away from his face, looking concerned again. "Darrow stays put until he's ready t'travel."

"You're not going any farther than your chamber pot," Sibyl insisted, shaking a finger at the wulver in her care. "Not until I'm convinced your outsides are ready to keep your insides *in*."

"If yer goin' t'be 'ere, then ye can keep me posted on Darrow's progress." Raife pulled Kirstin aside, speaking quietly. His gaze softened as he glanced at his brother, growling at the two women who fussed over his wound. "I'm sure Laina can use t'help."

"I imagine, so can Sibyl," she said pointedly, waiting for his response. There was one, but it was deep, buried in the bright blue, gold-flecked recessed of his eyes. It was so brief, a human might not have even noticed, but Kirstin did. Raife was in pain. A lot of pain. And none of it was physical.

"Donal, may I speak wit' ye?" Raife turned away from Kirstin to talk to the MacFalon.

"Aye," Donal agreed amiably.

"Darrow, mayhaps ye could come wit' us?" Raife asked, and Darrow actually started to get out of bed again.

"No!" All three women shouted at once.

"Raife, are you deaf?" Sibyl cried. "I've told you over and over—I am not letting him out of this room."

Raife folded his arms over his chest and glared at her, but he didn't say a word.

"I think she knows what she's speakin' of," Kirstin reminded her pack leader, poking his shoulder. "She's been carin' for him since he almost got himself killed."

"T'was her doin'," Raife snarled, speaking lowly, for Kirstin's ears, not Sibyl's.

Sibyl had gone back to tending to Darrow, urging Laina to try to get him to eat something, although she did glance up at them, a look of such hurt in her eyes it broke Kirstin's heart to see it.

"No, Raife, t'was mine," Kirstin confessed. She swallowed hard, seeing the way Raife's gaze turned to her, his eyes blazing. "I was t'one told her that Laina'd been taken. I was t'one who put 'er on a horse. If ye want t'blame someone, blame me."

Kirstin waited, breath held. She waited for him to rage at her, to accuse her. She saw Donal's eyes flash, saw his hand move to the hilt of the sword at his side, but that was all. He was waiting, too, watching Raife for a reaction.

Raife's jaw worked, and his gaze skipped over Kirstin to focus on Sibyl. She stood beside the bed, facing him, cheeks pale, pleading at him with her eyes. Kirstin saw the love Sibyl had for him—she felt it. There was a deep, unspoken apology in the way she looked at him that moved Kirstin, and she expected it to move Raife, too. Even Donal was affected by it—there was a great deal of sympathy in him for Sibyl.

Then Raife's eyes hardened and he turned back to Kirstin, directing his words at her, although his intended target was the petite redhead across the room, and he verbally hit his mark—hard.

"I'm sure ye did'na 'ave t'do much convincin' t'get 'er t'run back t'marry 'er betrothed."

Sibyl gasped as if someone had just punched her in the gut. Laina's arm went around her shoulders, and she drew the redhead close to her, steering her around the bed.

"Why don't the three of us go down t'get somethin' t'eat," Laina suggested softly, guiding a trembling, stricken Sibyl around Raife, toward the door. "Kirsten, let's go."

"Ye—" Kirstin pointed at Darrow. "Stay in bed.

"Aye, jus' hand me t'food then." Darrow nodded at the tray beside him.

Kirstin slid the tray onto the bed, watching him move to his elbow to tear bread and dunk it into the stew. He was getting his appetite back. That was good.

"And ye." Kirstin turned back to Raife, who pulled a chair up beside his brother's bedside and straddled it. Her voice shook as she addressed their pack leader. He was a formidable man on a good day, and a downright frightening one when he was angry and glowering, like he was now. "Did ye get knocked on t'head out there on the battlefield? Do ye need me t'examine ye?'

"Nuh." Raife grunted, waving her away. "Leave us."

"Are ye sure?" Kirstin leaned in and opened one of his eyes wider with her fingers, peering in. "Given t'way yer actin', I'm not so sure. Might you've left most of yer mind out there somewhere on t'field? Should I go look fer it?"

Darrow snorted a laugh from the bed and Raife gave him a cool look.

"Kirstin..." Raife shifted his attention to her, catching on to her not-so-gentle hints at his behavior.

"That woman's t'best thing that's e'er happened t'ye." Kirstin pointed to the door where Sibyl had been led out, so hurt by Raife's words she could hardly walk. "Yer mad t'let 'er go."

"She made 'er choice." Raife's lip curled in disgust when he spoke. "Leave us, Kirstin."

"How can ye say that?" Kirstin wasn't ready to give up—not yet. She imagined Laina had been too distracted by Darrow and his wounds to really take Raife to task, and he wasn't going to hear it from Sibyl. He clearly wasn't listening to her at all. Maybe Kirstin could get through that thick skull of his. "How can ye sit here and not understand why she came? What she sacrificed fer ye?"

Raife's brow lowered as he scowled. "I did'na ask her to."

"Nuh, you did'na. And she did it anyway," Kirstin reminded him. "Because she loves ye. God only knows why, ye stubborn, foolish, pig-headed—"

Raife stood, his hand going to the hilt of his sword. Darrow continued to shove stew-soaked bread into his mouth, glancing between the two of them, chuckling to himself.

"A'righ', a'righ'!" Donal stepped between the two of them, Kirstin barely coming up to Donal's shoulder, and Raife a head taller than that. She just glared between the two men. "Mayhaps it's time fer ye t'join t'women in t'kitchen and let us menfolk—"

"Oh, don't ye start, Donal MacFalon!" Kirstin turned on him, eyes blazing. "The menfolk're t'ones who made this mess in t'firs' place! We weren't t'ones goin'round forcin' people into marriage or kidnappin'em and holdin'em against their will! Last time I looked, we women were jus' tryin' t'clean up after ye 'menfolk'!"

She poked her finger into the middle of Donal's chest, punctuating her words, hearing Darrow sputter a laugh behind her, which just made her madder.

"How did I get in t'middle o'this?" Donal held his hands up in surrender. "'Twas Alistair who trapped

Laina, not I. And Sibyl's marriage t'Alistair was arranged by King Henry, not I. I've gone outta me way t'honor t'wolf pact, I've taken in wulvers into me castle, which, I might add, has most of me men and all of t'women afeared, in spite of my assurance of their safety. I fail t'see how anythin' I've done could possibly be construed as... "

"Oh,what could ye possibly know about it?" Kirstin snapped, crossing her arms over her chest and uttering an exasperated sigh. "D'ye know what it's like to be afeared the one ye love's gonna die, and ye might be t'cause? Because that's the weight that woman carried on 'er lil shoulders, and *that's* the reason she came 'ere to *yer* castle. T'satisfy *yer* brother's demands."

Donal's spine stiffened and he frowned down at her. "I fail t'see how me brother's actions have anythin' to—"

"Give it up, man," Darrow called, his mouth half-full with stew-soaked bread. "No use arguin' wit' a woman—especially not a *wulver* woman."

"What would ye like me t'say?" Donal asked, giving Kirstin a truly puzzled look. "That yer right?"

"That would do well, fer a start," she agreed, realizing she'd been directing her anger at the wrong man—Donal wasn't even a wulver, or part of her pack. He was their host, and had clearly been generous and kind. She'd overreacted, and she knew it, but she wasn't quite sure how to fix that, especially with Darrow snickering and Raife growling.

"If King Henry's gonna send ye another English bride, ye might as well get used to sayin' that phrase," Darrow remarked, licking his fingers clean and grinning over at them.

Even Raife had to chuckle at that.

"What're ye babblin' about?" It was Kirstin's turn to scowl, raising a quizzical eyebrow at Donal.

"Well, Sibyl was s'posed t'marry t'eldest son, Alistair," Darrow explained, his eyes glittering with amusement. "Now he's dead and Donal's The MacFalon. I imagine King Henry'll jus' decide t'give 'er to *this* brother instead..."

"Enough, Darrow." Raife snarled at his brother, moving to draw the sword at his side. "Unless ye want another hole in yer belly."

"What would ye care?" Kirstin snapped. "Ye don't want Sibyl anymore—do ye?"

"Kirstin..." Raife said her name through gritted teeth, looking at the chuckling Darrow, not at her. "Do'na make me cut off that sharp tongue of yers."

"Enough." Donal spoke, his voice clear and definitive. He turned to Kirstin, taking her by the elbow, putting his hand at the small of her back, and steering her toward the door. "Come wit' me."

As soon as they were in the hallway and Donal had closed the door behind them, Kirstin hissed at him, "That man's insufferable! How can ye sit by and watch 'im treat 'er that way? He's actin' like—"

"Aye, he is." Donal put a finger to her lips to keep them from moving anymore, and the motion startled Kirstin. Her breath stopped, and for a moment, so did her heart. Those slate-blue eyes of his pinned her in place and she stilled, listening to him. "But he's in pain. He feels betrayed, and e'en if he realizes she did'na love m'brother—and I can attest to the fact that she mos' definitely did'na—his pride's hurt. Give 'im time. He'll come 'round."

She nodded, not saying anything, feeling the press of his finger against her mouth, suddenly aware of how close they were standing in the hallway with no one around. There were distant sounds of people, and the low rumble of Darrow and Raife talking behind the closed door, but she swore the beating of her own heart was much louder than any of that.

Donal didn't say anything either, but his gaze moved down from her eyes to focus on her lips, where his finger was tracing their outline, so lightly she felt as if a butterfly was kissing her. She shivered, feeling something thick and hot pumping through her veins, forcing blood into places that throbbed in sweet, swollen torture.

She heard him draw a sharp breath in when her tongue peeked nervously between her lips for a moment, and then Donal took a step back, his hand moving to the door knob.

"I'm sorry," she murmured, and she was, but not because of what she'd said. She was sorry that he'd moved away, instead of toward her. She was sorry she hadn't bridged the distance herself.

He cleared his throat. "Ye mus' be hungry."

You have no idea.

"Aye." She nodded, agreeing, although it wasn't her stomach that was growling.

"The kitchens're downstairs, through t'great hall," he told her, pointing to the staircase he'd brought her up. "Moira'll be feedin' Sibyl and Laina. She'll be happy t'feed ye, too."

"Smooth as silk," Kirstin murmured, giving him a bemused smile. "Ye're a true politician, aren't ye?"

Donal chuckled, shaking his head.

"Open yer mouth," he directed, putting a thumb against her chin to try to get her to comply.

"What?" She smiled, waving him away. "Why?"

"I jus' wanted t'see fer m'self if that tongue's as sharp as it feels."

"Oh fer heaven's sake..." She couldn't help laughing, but she also couldn't help feeling a little bad about what she'd said. "I did'na mean—"

"Och, lass, I understand." He smiled, too, and that good-natured warmth had returned to his eyes "Ye show a great deal of love fer yer pack, and e'en more spirit in defendin' it. Tis a fine and lovely thing. As are ye."

"Smooth as silk..." she said again, feeling the warmth of his words filling her all the way to her toes.

"Trust me when I tell ye, I've been doin' e'erythin' I can t'help pave t'way fer a reunion a'tween Sibyl and Raife." He rolled his eyes at the closed door. "I intend t'see't happen a'fore the wulvers leave."

"Ye mean—ye don't wanna marry 'er yerself?" The words escaped her mouth before she could even think and she felt her cheeks redden when he looked at her, nonplussed.

"Marry Sibyl?" He blinked in surprise at the thought, then he chuckled. "And risk me head being divided from me shoulders by that half-beast in there?"

"Oh, so that's all that's stopping ye?" Kirstin asked, arms crossed, eyes narrowing, as she turned to go.

"Och! No, lass." Donal caught her around the waist, whirling her toward him, and she found herself pressed fully against his big, solid frame. The hilt of his sword dug into the soft flesh of her belly and his hands pressed against her lower back, keeping her close. "Mayhaps, yesterday, if King Henry'd offered the woman t'me, and she hadn't already been claimed by the insufferable wulver in there, I would've accepted..."

"Would ye?" she challenged, feeling a slow fire heating her chest at the thought. For some reason, thinking about any other woman with this man filled her with such a rage it made her tremble. She didn't understand it, and she wondered if her own confusion showed on her face, because Donal looked at her with such warmth and sympathy, it made her legs weak.

"Mayhaps yesterday," Donal said softly. "But not today."

Kirstin swallowed. "What changed between yesterday and today?"

"I met a beautiful wulver woman wit' a big heart an'a sharp tongue."

"Oh..." Kirstin felt like she couldn't breathe.

"I want ye t'get some food in yer belly," he told her. "And I'll have Moira find ye s'more clothes—a good pair'a boots fer walkin' and ridin'."

"I'll be fine," she assured him, but his arms tightened around her in protest.

"I'd like t'take ye ridin' on the morrow, Kirstin," he said. "I'd like to show ye somethin', if'n ye let me."

"Oh..." She hesitated. She barely knew him—and this was a man, not a wulver. She knew well enough from Sibyl that it wasn't proper for a Scotswoman or Englishwoman to be alone with any man—but she remembered the ride in from the forest on the back of his horse, and couldn't resist.

"I'll understand if ye wanna stay 'ere and nurse the ailin' Darrow, but..." His gaze moved to the closed door, then back to her.

"Nuh." She shook her head, seeing the disappointment in his eyes, feeling it in her gut, and she was quick to dispel it. “I mean, aye. Aye, I’ll go wit’ ye.”

“Good.” A smile lit up his features. “And we’ll talk more about what we can do, t’bring those two together. Because somethin’ needs doin’.”

“Aye, that it does,” she agreed, scowling at Raife as if she could see him through the door.

“I’m glad ye came.” Donal turned her chin back to look at him, and the look in his eyes, so full of emotion, turned her knees to jelly. But he had her, held against him. She wasn’t going anywhere. His gaze moved down to her mouth, and his head inclined, and for one breathless moment, she thought for sure he was going to press his lips to hers.

“Sir, I came fer the dishes.” Behind them, the voice was small and unsure and Donal let Kirstin go, whirling around. “Moira sent me.”

Kirstin looked at the little kitchen maid who had somehow snuck up behind Donal. She was a small blonde with big, round blue eyes and a gap between her teeth. She stood, looking between the two of them, curious.

“Go ’head.” Donal waved her into the room so she could retrieve Darrow’s supper dishes.

“Ye were sayin’?” Kirstin prompted him, but the moment was gone. Kirstin could still feel the steel heat of his body against hers, even though they now stood a doorway apart. “Somethin’ about bein’ glad I was ’ere...?”

“Aye.” He cleared his throat as the maid hurried out with the dishes on a tray. “I know ye’ll be a great help t’Sibyl and Laina.”

"Gayle." He smiled down at the maid as she scuttled by him. "Will ye take Lady Kirstin down to the kitchens so she may join 'er kin?"

"I'm not a lady," Kirstin protested before Gayle's eyes even fell to study Kirstin's plaid—and lack of footwear. Or any other adornment.

"Her kin?" Gayle's eyes widened then and she took a step back. "She's a wulver, then?"

"Aye, but I promise, she will'na bite ye," Donal assured the maid, giving Kirstin a pointed look.

The blonde, Gayle, didn't look so confident.

"I'll see ye on the morrow," Donal called after her and Kirstin smiled back at him as she followed the maid down the hall. He watched them head down the stairs before going back into Darrow's room.

As Donal had promised, Sibyl and Laina were in the kitchen, being fussed over by a stout old woman who kept bringing more food to the table. Gayle deposited the dishes and was quickly off again, giving them all a long, fearful, sidelong glance as she slipped through the door.

"Ye look pale," Kirstin observed, putting a cool hand against Sibyl's cheek. "How long's it been since she's eaten anything?"

The question was directed at Laina, who shook her head.

"I'm not hungry." Sibyl pushed the bowl of stew away from her. Kirstin caught the delicious scent and her stomach growled.

"Ye still need t'eat, *banrighinn*." Kirstin pushed the bowl closer,

"Don't call me that." Sibyl's eyes filled with tears.

"But ye're, *banrighinn*," Laina agreed, smiling as Moira put a newly baked loaf of bread on the table. It was warm and Kirstin couldn't resist tearing off the end, dipping it into the bowl.

"Here, you eat it." Sibyl pushed it toward her. "You must be starving."

"I ate a rabbit on the way," Kirstin confessed, her mouth full of warm bread. "But this is delicious."

"There's more where that came from, lass," Moira assured her with a pat of her hand on Kirstin's. "I'll get ye a bowl. Ye see if ye can get this one t'eat."

"Thank ye." Kirstin washed the bread down with a swallow of mead from the cup Moira set in front of her.

"Moira, this is Kirstin," Laina said, making the introductions. "She's a midwife in our den—and a healer. She came t'help wit' Darrow."

"Och, well he's a handful," Moira agreed with a laugh, putting a bowl of stew down in front of Kirstin, who dug in, her stomach making grateful, growling sounds. "We can certainly always use an extra set of hands 'round 'ere."

She glanced at the door where the maid had disappeared.

"They're afeared of us," Laina explained to Kirstin, speaking of the maid who'd left soon after bringing Darrow's dishes down. "Wulvers. *Demons.*"

"They're young and foolish." Moira brought out a knife and began slicing the bread. "Do'na pay attention to 'em. Lady Sibyl, please will ye eat some bread? I'll butter it fer ye. Mayhaps some jam?"

Moira brightened at this, rushing off to get some.

"Och, I need me bairn." Laina gave a little groan, sitting back in her seat and pressing her breasts with both hands, her face pained. "He's not ready t'wean."

"Ye can express yer milk," Moira suggested. "Since yer bairn's away and yer husband's not yet up to the task."

The old woman chuckled at the way Kirstin gasped, looking at the younger woman's shocked face.

"She's not married, this one?" Moira observed with a toothy grin.

Kirstin flushed, eating stew faster.

"Kirstin?" Laina laughed. "Nay, she's not found 'er mate, nor had 'er first estrus."

"Isn't she a little old?" Moira blinked in surprise.

"Oh, she's had 'er first moonblood," Laina told her, explaining to the confused Scotswoman. "Wulver woman have their first moonblood sometime during our thirteenth summer. That's when we can start changin'. Into wulvers, ye ken?"

"Hm." Moira's face didn't smooth out—she still looked puzzled.

"After our first moonblood, we're ready to be mated," Laina explained.

Laina's words even had Sibyl interested, Kirstin noticed. Sibyl was listening, spreading the brambleberry jam Moira had brought over onto a piece of buttered bread.

"But we do'na have our first estrus—when we go into heat—until we find our mate."

"So ye only bleed once?" Moira asked in awe. "And then not again until you mate?"

"Aye." Kirstin agreed, dunking her bread into her stew. It was venison, thick, fatty and rich. And utterly delicious.

"Och, I wish I was a wulver then!" Moira exclaimed with a laugh, taking a seat at the low table with them. "I'd stay a maiden forever."

“Well, there’s something to that.” Laina smiled, glancing over at Kirstin. “A wulver woman who’s never mated always has control over her change.”

Kirstin nodded in agreement. She still had full control over when she changed from woman to wulver and back again. There were very few wulver women who went their whole lives without finding their true mate, although Kirstin often thought she might end up like the old midwife, Beitrus, who had trained her and taught her all her healing skills. Mayhaps that was her calling after all, she mused, taking another swig of mead.

“But it isn’t matin’ that brings on estrus,” Kirstin interjected. “It’s *findin’* yer mate.”

Moira gave them a puzzled shake of her head, looking between the two wulver women as if trying to figure something out. Then, slowly, realization dawned on her, even before Kirstin explained.

“A wulver woman doesn’t hafta remain chaste,” she told Moira, knowing how shocking that sounded to the Scotswoman. It had been even more shocking to the Englishwoman who was now their *banrighinn*—their queen. Maidenhood was highly prized in the human world, she’d discovered. “After our thirteenth year, we reach maturity. We can be wit’ whomever we choose after that. But we can’na become wit’ child ’til we meet our true mate.”

“Yer true mate?” Moira mused, mulling this over.

“Aye. Wulvers have one true mate.” Laina smiled, glancing toward the ceiling. Darrow was upstairs, recovering—her one true mate, the father of her bairn. “Fer life.”

“How d’ye know ye’ve found ’im?” Moira asked. “Yer one true mate?”

"Oh, believe me, ye know." Laina's smile widened, her eyes dancing. "Besides, a month later, ye change into a wulver during yer estrus, and ye can'na change back 'til it's through."

"Ye can'na control it?" Moira asked, eyes growing big. "And I thought bein' a Scotswoman was bad!"

Sibyl snorted, saying through a mouthful of bread and jam, "Try being an Englishwoman."

"Sibyl's been workin' on our cure." Laina put her arm around the redhead's shoulder. Sibyl almost smiled, which made Kirstin's heart feel a little bit lighter.

"A cure for the curse?" Moira laughed. "Oh what a happy day that would be!"

"Well, the *wulver's* curse," Laina countered. "It wasn't broken soon enough for my mother, but maybe it can be for our daughters."

"Raife and Darrow think it's a fool's errand." Sibyl picked the crust off her bread. "They keep telling me I'm wasting my time. But too many wulver women have paid the price for not having control over their cycles."

"Men, they never understand the woman's plight." Moira sighed. "No matter their species, do they?"

"They're stubborn animals, regardless." Laina squeezed her arm around Sibyl, who rested her head on the blonde's shoulder.

"Especially wulvers." Sibyl wrinkled her freckled nose and sighed.

"He loves ye," Kirstin assured her. She knew it was true—she'd seen it in his eyes. Sibyl was his one true mate, and always would be. "He'll come 'round. He's jus'..."

"Raife." Sibyl said his name with such longing it made Kirstin's heart break for her.

"Aye." Laina rolled her bright, blue eyes—all wulvers had blue eyes—and groaned.

"I want to give Darrow time to heal," Sibyl said. "But the truth is—he's probably already well enough to travel. I'm still shocked that wound didn't kill him instantly."

"I told ye, wulvers heal vera fast."

"That's an understatement." Sibyl laughed, and Kirstin thought how good it was to hear her laugh again.

"D'ye want more t'eat, Lady Kirstin?" Moira asked, nodding at Kirstin's empty stew bowl.

"It's jus' Kirstin—and yes, actually, I'll take another bowl." Her appetite was incredible all of a sudden. Moira got up to get her more food and Kirstin noticed Sibyl was finally eating a little of her own stew.

"The truth is," Sibyl said. "I'm afraid, if I tell Raife that Darrow could travel now—he'll go... and leave me behind."

"Nuh, he would'na do that," Moira exclaimed, putting a new, steaming bowl of stew in front of Kirstin, who dug right in. "Would he?"

"He's stubborn." Kirstin made a face. Talk about understatements.

"Well, then we'll have to keep Darrow recoverin' in bed." Laina's eyes brightened. "Ye ken?"

"Aye." Kirstin's smile widened as she caught on to Laina's plan. "Until Raife starts comin' round."

"Oh, aye!" Even Moira brightened "And there are plenty'o'ways ye can bring a man back to ye, lass. They're simple creatures, in t'end."

“How?” Sibyl looked around the table, frowning. “He won’t talk to me, he won’t even *look* at me! He leaves a room if I come into it.”

“Trust us.” Kirstin’s heart felt a lot lighter, knowing that both Laina and Moira were in on this new plan to get Sibyl and Raife together again.

“Ye leave it to us, lassie.” Moira chuckled, patting Sibyl’s hand. “He won’t know what hit ’im.”

Chapter Three

"That man is more stubborn than a corpse." Sibyl slid off her horse, tying it to a tree.

"Aye," Kirstin agreed, doing the same, tethering her horse as well.

Moira had made them all a delicious breakfast. The women had gathered around the kitchen table, laughing at Donal's jokes—the man's eyes lit up from the inside every time he made Kirstin laugh—when Raife came in. He saw Sibyl and froze.

"Come in, eat!" Moira called, waving him into the room. She even bravely put herself between Raife and the exit, but it was no use.

"I'll meet ye at the catacombs," Raife said stiffly to Donal, giving him a nod and turning to go. He actually had to dance his way around Moira, who moved from side to side, insisting he stay and have something to eat, but in the end, he'd escaped.

The men—Raife and Donal—were already there. Their horses were tethered across the field. Kirstin couldn't help remembering seeing Donal across the clearing, head bent, praying at this burial cairn and the memory filled her with a warmth she was coming to both understand and expect.

They'd tried to talk Laina into coming with them to explore the first den catacombs, but she didn't want to leave Darrow, even if Moira said she'd look after him. Not that Darrow really needed that much looking after—his wound was healing nicely and it had taken all three women finally telling him their plan to keep him in bed, at least until Raife came around, to finally subdue him and keep him from jumping on a horse and heading to the catacombs himself to take part in the wolf pact reaffirmation.

Laina confessed privately to Sibyl and Kirstin that she was going to take Moira's suggestion and see if Darrow could alleviate some of the pressure she was experiencing because she was without her nursling. Before they left the castle, Sibyl had warned the pair not to do anything too strenuous, but Kirstin had heard the moans coming from their room before the two women had even reached the end of the hallway.

"Raife migh' be stubborn, *banrighinn*, but he's our leader fer a reason," Kirstin reminded her. "He's both smart and wise. I've never known a man wit' a heart any greater, and he's as far from a coward as a wulver gets. If he knows the righ'thing t'do, he'll do it."

"I just miss him." Sibyl stood at the entrance to the catacombs, taking Kirstin's hand in hers with a sigh. "The stupid oaf."

"Well—he *is* still a man." Kirstin squeezed her hand. "Which means, he needs to be pushed—or dragged—in the righ' direction sometimes."

They looked at each other, grinning.

"Let's hope this herbal silvermoon does what Moira claims." Sibyl looked doubtful as the women linked hands. Sibyl's head came up at the sound of a distant gun shot. "What was that?"

"Poachers?" Kirstin wondered aloud.

They were on MacFalon land, but reavers—thieves that preyed along the borderlands, always poised to steal a laird's cattle—were prevalent. Middle March was like a lost world of misfits, where everything rode along a knife edge. The English and Scots clashed constantly up and down the border of their two countries. It was one of the reasons Sibyl was in their midst in the first place. It had been the English king's idea to "marry the border"—giving English brides to Scottish lairds all throughout Middle March.

"So near the castle?" Sibyl shivered, stepping a little closer to Kirstin. It wasn't easy being a human woman, Kirstin thought to herself. They were fairly defenseless. Wulver women, on the other hand, could take care of themselves if need be, whether they were human or wulver.

"Could be. We ran into some yesterday." Kirstin frowned at the memory and her eyes narrowed in the direction of those woods and the trap where she had been ensnared. Had poachers re-armed the trap? It was possible, she supposed—but for some reason, Sibyl's remark stayed with her. *So close to the castle?* They weren't that far from the keep. They likely could have walked their way back within half an hour. It was hardly any time crossed on a horse. Poaching on a laird's land was punishable by death. Would a poacher risk his life so close to Castle MacFalon? She didn't know. Maybe a hungry one, as Donal had said.

"Did I tell ye, t'was the king's own huntsman who came along and chased off t'poachers?" Kirstin asked, scanning the edge of the woods for movement. Her wulver's eyes would be better, but even in human form, she saw more than any person could, even in the dark.

"King Henry's huntsman?" Sibyl perked up at that. She was English, after all. Sometimes Kirstin forgot. "Mayhaps he has news about the wolf pact?"

"Donal says he'll defend t'wolf pact, e'en if King Henry does'na," Kirstin reminded her. She didn't see or smell anything—her sense of smell as a human was seriously impaired, compared to her wulver one—and decided there was no immediate danger.

"But that would mean war." Sibyl shivered again, although Kirstin couldn't tell if it was at the thought or because they were stepping down into the depths of the catacombs. "Between the Scots and the English. Between the wulvers and... everyone. No one wants that."

"Nuh." Kirstin's blood ran cold at the thought of the wulver warriors going to war. They'd armed themselves and had ridden out of the mountain den to save Sibyl and Laina. The memory of hundreds of horses thundering though the mountain, their usually barred, secret entrance thrown wide, still gave her gooseflesh.

She really had believed, if Sibyl went back and offered herself to Alistair MacFalon, that the man would return Laina unharmed and war could be avoided. She hadn't imagined the depth of Raife's rage at Sibyl's self-sacrifice or how he might interpret the act. Jealousy was a strange emotion, she decided, as they reached the bottom of the catacombs.

It had been a very long descent. They were deep underground and it was dark, dank, and cold.

"Did the huntsman bring any word from the king?" Sibyl asked, reaching up to take an oil-soaked torch down off the wall.

"Lord Eldred said he was disarming traps." Kirstin slipped a flint out of her pocket and used it to light the torch. "Although t'tell the truth—I do'na trust 'im any further than I could toss 'im."

"When you're a wulver, I think you could toss him a fair distance." Sibyl grinned in the sudden, orange-glowing light of the torch.

Kirstin laughed at that.

"Moira said the MacFalon tombs were to the left, that way." Sibyl pointed and, with her keen ears, Kirstin though she heard the sound of Donal's voice. He and Raife were supposed to be performing the yearly wolf pact reaffirmation. It was a quiet ceremony, done once every year between the laird of Clan MacFalon and the leader of the wulver pack. Scotsmen were a superstitious lot, and while there was peace between them and the wulvers, it was a wary one. It wasn't easy for humans to trust things they didn't understand, and they didn't understand the wulvers.

"So t'old den mus' be down that way?" Kirstin pointed to the right. It was hard to believe that she hadn't known this part of her own pack's history until Moira had told them the night before, while Kirstin finished the rest of what was left of the woman's delicious stew—much to Moira's delight.

"Yes, she said the silvermoon was supposed to grow by a spring. Are there springs down here?" Sibyl frowned at the high, wide, rock walls. To Kirstin, they were like coming home. Familiar markings and drawings painted the way. She would have liked to spend hours looking at them, transferring them onto paper, but there was no time. They were on a mission to find the silvermoon.

"There're springs in our mountain den," Kirstin reminded her.

"Oh, yes..." Sibyl looked sad at that and Kirstin knew she was thinking about the hotspring in Raife's mountain room. The pack leader had access to that spring to bathe and relax in. "So your ancestors once lived down here? I wonder how long ago?"

"Generations." Kirstin followed Sibyl down passageway. The ceilings were vaulted, high. She wondered at the construction of the place. It was a marvel. Had they carved these out of rock under the ground, or had they built them up? "Me mother's mother lived in our mountain den. I did'na e'en know this place existed 'til Moira mentioned it."

Well, that wasn't completely true. Donal had said something about it yesterday, hadn't he? When she'd mentioning stopping and seeing him praying. But he hadn't told her its history, not like Moira had.

"It reminds me of home." Sibyl gave a little half-smile and she peeked into one of the rooms. "Your home, I mean."

"'Tis yer home, as well, *banrighinn*." Kirstin squeezed her hand, peering into the room and seeing it had once been a woman's room. Dried herbs, old, hung on lines. There was an old table in the center of the room with a few old, cracked mortars and pestles. But the room smelled of healing, a familiar, welcome scent.

"This was a healer's room," Sibyl remarked, sniffing the air. Even she could smell it. "I wonder if there is any dried silvermoon in here?"

"Whatever they left here will'na be of any use anymore." Kirstin looked around. "'Tis all cleared out. They planned their move."

"It's not as big as the mountain," Sibyl observed

"Not as safe, either." Kirstin imagined the possibilities.

The entire pack could get trapped in a den like this. In their mountain, they were safe within, and they had a valley where they had a running stream and sunlight and they could raise their sheep for wool and meat. In a den like this, they'd have to go up top to hunt. No wonder the MacFalons were wary of the wulvers, she thought. They'd once been much closer neighbors—and she imagined her ancestors had made a meal of a few of Donal's. The wulvers hadn't hunted and killed humans for meat in generations, but they had, once.

"You always have such giant kitchens," Sibyl exclaimed as they reached the end of the passageway that opened into a wide space. A large fireplace took up almost all of one wall, and a long table where all the wulvers had once sat to sup together spanned the big room.

"Wulvers like t'gather in one place." Kirstin smiled and could almost picture her wulver ancestors tussling and laughing and playing and eating here. Many of the wulvers slept in the kitchens together in a big wolf pile by the fire at night, especially before they were paired off. Kirstin had spent many a night in a big, warm, fuzzy pile of wulvers. There was nothing else like it.

"Moira said the spring was near the kitchen."

"Aye, 'tis likely," Kirstin started across the open space. "Water's life. There's always a spring in a wulver den."

"Through here, do you think?" Sibyl edged around the corner of a rock wall and they both heard the sound of running water. The passageway got lighter as they went through it, making the torch unnecessary.

"Beautiful!" Sibyl put the torch into a notch on the wall as they entered the grotto, looking around in wonder. "I wondered how anything could possibly grow down here."

"Someone carved that into t'rock t'let the light in." Kirstin looked at the running body of water where a slant of sunlight lit its clear surface. It came from high above, an opening in the deep rock. She wondered at the construction of it. Where did it come out, she wondered, on MacFalon land? Had anyone accidentally discovered it before? But there was a grate—metal bars—over the opening.

"Moira gave me a picture of silvermoon." Sibyl dug into a pocket in her plaid, searching for it, but there was no need.

"It's righ' there." Kirstin pointed to the plant growing up between the rocky crags at the edge of the spring.

"Why do they call it silvermoon?" Sibyl wondered, squatting to gather it.

"'Tis silver in t'moonlight." Kirstin glanced up at the skylight above. "The leaves're reflective. You can see't clearly at night if the moon's full."

"Really?" Sibyl rubbed the leaf of one of the plants between her fingers. "I've never seen it before."

"'Tis an ancient wulver plant," Kirstin told her "I've only e'er seen pictures of it. Like the huluppa ye found growing on the borderlands."

The huluppa was the other plant, mentioned in what was considered the "wulver bible," that Sibyl was using to try to develop some sort of cure for the wulver woman's curse.

"It wouldn't surprise me if it only grew here." Sibyl frowned at the plant. "I can't get that damnable huluppa to grow anywhere else. I tried growing it in the wulver valley, but it will not take root. And I can't find the cure for a wulver curse without it. Your wulver plants behave oddly."

"Like wulvers." Kirstin laughed.

"They use this in the wolf pact reaffirmation ceremony then?" Sibyl asked.

"Moira says so." She nodded. "But the men do'na know where t'harvest it. Beitrus is our oldest healer and t'wulver who always came wit' Raife to t'wolf pact reaffirmation e'ery year, and wit' his father, Garaith, a'fore him, t'bring the silvermoon to the ceremony."

"What does it do?" Sibyl brought it to her nose, smelling its sweetness.

"Our book describes it as a mender." Kirsten took some too, feeling its slippery surface. She could smell it already, light and almost minty sweet. "'Tis what Moira said t'was for. It's largely symbolic in t'ceremony, a'course. As a binder, it brings things together. Helps hold them in place."

"It would be useful for Darrow's wound, then." Sibyl brightened. Then her face fell. "Although, the faster I heal him..."

"Well, mayhaps it'll bind more than just physical wounds this day."

Sibyl looked up. "What do you mean?"

"We'll take it to the men, like me ancestors a'fore us," Kirstin explained. "They'll use it t'help bind t'wolf pact. But mayhaps it'll also work t'help mend things a'tween ye and Raife. Heals broken bones—and broken oaths."

"Mayhaps." Sibyl looked so hopeful, and Kirstin truly was.

A binder like this was a powerful herb, especially in raw form. Besides, she reasoned, Raife couldn't possibly hold out much longer. His resolve was already weakening. She'd seen it in his eyes the night before, and again this morning, when he'd come into the kitchen, seeing Sibyl laughing.

It was when he realized it was one of Donal's remarks she was laughing at, that he'd turned around and stalked away. She was learning a great deal about that emotion, jealousy, from these two. It was a powerful thing. Made it hard to keep your wits about you. It made you see things that weren't there, that a rational person would just shrug off. Raife couldn't, for a moment, think Sibyl and Donal were a match, could he?

Of course, thinking of it herself, put her own feelings in a jumble. Donal was free to marry whomever he liked—or, at least, whomever the king liked, and since he'd already sent Sibyl to the MacFalons, she was obviously a good choice. And technically, Sibyl was free to marry whomever she liked as well. She hadn't been marked, even if she and Raife had consummated their love.

But thinking of a match between Sibyl and Donal was ridiculous, because... well, just because. Besides, Sibyl loved Raife. And Raife loved her too, if he would just stop seeing through green, jealous eyes instead of his clear, bright blue ones. Kirstin hoped the silvermoon truly would do what they all hoped. If it did not, they were going to have to resort to more drastic measures.

"Shall we take this to Donal and Raife?" Sibyl suggested, a small smile playing on her lips.

"Aye." Kirstin picked her way over the rocks in her soft boots, careful not to fall into the spring. The water would be cold, not like the hot springs back at the mountain den.

Sibyl took the torch from the wall and led the way. She was in a hurry now, no longer looking into rooms and exploring. Kirstin would have liked to spend more time down here—and mayhaps she would in the next week or so, if they stayed long enough—but Sibyl was a woman on a mission.

They passed the entrance to the catacombs, the light practically a pinpoint far above the long stairway, but they didn't stop. Sibyl pushed on, heading in the other direction, where the MacFalon ancestors were entombed. It seemed fitting that the wolf pact reaffirmation took place where so much history had taken place between the two—the wulvers and the MacFalons.

Kirstin heard the men talking, just their voices, a low rumble, not the words. They rounded a corner in the passage and the cavern opened up into a wide space. An altar stood at one end, unadorned, a slab of rock. That's where Donal and Raife were talking. Surrounding them were the catacombs, hundreds of slotted tombs, sealed off with the remains of the MacFalon's ancestors.

"Raife." Sibyl put her torch on the wall—the men had lit several around the room, making it far brighter than the passageway they'd traversed. "I brought you something you need."

Kirstin hung back, letting Sibyl move forward toward the men. She saw Donal glance over at her, his face breaking into a smile, those grey-blue eyes lighting up in delight. She knew the feeling—it felt as if a bird had just taken flight in her chest, soaring, leaving her breathless at the sight of him.

She remembered the way he'd pulled her aside that morning, telling her about his meeting with Raife at the catacombs, the planned reaffirmation of the wolf pact.

"I'd like ye to come t'me there after the ceremony," he told her softly. She was very aware of everyone's eyes on them. "There's somethin' I'd like t'show ye."

She'd agreed. It was when she told Moira, Laina and Sibyl about her intention to go out to the catacombs to meet Donal that Moira had expressed her concern about the lack of silvermoon at the ceremony. That's when this plan had been hatched. Sibyl and Kirstin had quickly made preparations to follow the men to the catacombs, while Laina stayed behind to tend to her husband's needs—and he, to hers, Kirstin thought with a smile.

Now that they were here, silvermoon in hand. Kirstin wondered if it had been such a good plan. Raife scowled at the interruption, which wasn't an unusual expression for him lately, but it was a dark scowl. His mood had shifted suddenly from somber to wary as Sibyl approached. Kirstin felt as if she was watching some priceless vase toppling back and forth, waiting to see if it would fall or right itself again, unable to do anything but observe.

"You, too, Donal." Sibyl smiled at the laird, remembering him only when he greeted her warmly, and Kirstin saw instantly that this was a mistake. Raife's scowl deepened as he glanced between the two of them, and she saw the green of jealousy move into his eyes.

Sibyl went on, not realizing, holding out the plant leaves as a peace offering.

"It's silvermoon," Sibyl announced happily. "Moira said it's always been used at the wolf pact ceremony, to bind things, and I thought—"

"Ye thought what?" Raife's lip curled in anger. "Ye'd come down 'ere on sacred ground and violate t'wulver's ancient first den t'bring me some leaves?"

"Well, I..." Sibyl hesitated, glancing back at Kirstin. "I was told... a wulver woman usually brings them..."

"Ye're nuh a wulver," Raife reminded her coldly, straightening and crossing his big arms over his chest. "And ye do'na have business 'ere."

"Raife," Kirstin protested, seeing the crestfallen look on Sibyl's face.

"'Twas a kind thought, Sibyl." Donal reached out and touched the Englishwoman's arm. "Thank ye. Leave it on t'altar."

"I brought the new spring mead instead," Raife told Sibyl as she brushed by him to put the leaves on the altar next to two cups and an uncorked bottle. "We do'na need the silvermoon."

Sibyl didn't answer him. She walked by, head held high, moving toward Kirstin, who was the only one who saw the tears she was blinking back. She also saw the look of pain flash over Raife's face as he looked at his mate's retreating form. Kirstin thought, for a moment, that he might say something to bridge the gap between them.

He did call out, but it wasn't what Kirstin expected.

"Why don't ye put the silvermoon on Alistair's tomb?" Raife reached out and grabbed the leaves in his big fist that Sibyl had so carefully pulled, stalking over to where Sibyl stood next to Kirsten. "Or mayhaps ye'd like t'give't to the other MacFalon brother?"

Raife whirled to glare at Donal. Kirstin had heard them talking, even chuckling together, before the two women had come in. Now Raife looked at him like he wanted to tear his limbs off.

"Here, Donal, mayhaps this'll bind 'er to ye better than I could cleave 'er to'me." Raife tossed the leaves up in the air toward Donal and they floated down toward the dirt.

"Raife!" Sibyl called as he brushed past her, staring, aghast, as he stalked around the corner, headed toward the exit. She turned to Donal, her cheeks almost as red as her hair. "I'm so sorry. He's... just..."

"Raife." Kirstin sighed, shaking her head and looking after him.

"Do'na concern yerself, Sibyl." Donal shook his head too, sighing. "The man's more stubborn than most. And most men're stubborn."

"Should ye go after 'im?" Kirstin wondered aloud.

"I've tried." Sibyl shook her head. "He won't talk to me."

"*Banrighinn*, I'm so sorry." Kirstin put a soothing hand on her shoulder.

"I should go back and tend Darrow." Sibyl stooped to carefully retrieve the silvermoon Raife had cast aside, her head bent. Kirstin's gaze met Donal's and they exchanged a knowing, sympathetic look. Sibyl stood, putting the leaves into a pocket in her plaid, turning to look at them with a sniff, blinking quickly to clear her eyes. "Mayhaps Moira will have some idea how the silvermoon might help his wound."

"Mayhaps," Kirstin agreed as Sibyl went by her.

Donal was still looking at Kirstin, and his gaze made her feel warm all over.

"Are you coming, Kirstin?" Sibyl called, reaching for the torch she'd brought in.

"Oh... aye." Kirstin sighed, turning to follow her, but Donal's hand on her arm stopped her.

"I beg yer pardon, *banrighinn,*" Donal called to Sibyl, his gaze never leaving Kirstin's face.

"Why do people keep calling me that?" Sibyl sighed, rolling her eyes as she turned back toward them. "Can't you see that he doesn't want me to be his... whatever it is..."

Sibyl looked at them, her gaze moving from Kirstin's face to Donal's and back again, then flitting down to see the way Donal was holding onto Kirstin's arm.

"I'd asked Lady Kirstin t'come to the catacombs so that I might show 'er somethin'..." Donal's hand tightened on Kirstin's arm, a slow, steady squeeze. She felt the blood rushing through her, suddenly hotter than she remembered. "Might ye find yer way back t'Castle MacFalon on yer own?"

"Unaccompanied?" Kirstin shook her head in protest. "But—"

"Absolutely!" A slow, secret smile started at the corners of the redhead's mouth. The way she looked at them made Kirstin blush. "Don't you even think of coming with me, Kirstin. I'm heading straight back to the castle with this silvermoon. I know the way—and so does the horse. You two don't worry about me."

"Thank ye." Donal winked. "We'll be back to the castle in time fer dinner."

"Oh, you both take your time!" Sibyl backed toward the passageway. Her smile was almost a grin, now, her eyes sparkling with a life Kirstin hadn't seen in them since she'd arrived at the castle. "All the time in the world! I'll tell them not to expect you any time soon."

"Sibyl!" Kirstin protested, her cheeks flaming now, and she was glad for the darkness of the environment. "Please."

"I won't say a word." Sibyl mimicked locking her lips with a key. "I'm good at making excuses. You two... just... enjoy yourselves!"

"Oh fer heaven's sake," Kirstin muttered as Sibyl gave them a wave and ducked down the passage where Raife had recently disappeared. She glanced up at Donal, seeing the laughter in his eyes, and couldn't help breaking into a smile. "What did she think we were goin' t'do, make a fire and strip naked t'dance 'round it?"

"I would'na be averse to either of those things." Donal laughed when she punched him in the upper arm. He rubbed it like she'd actually hurt him. "What man would say no to a pretty woman offerin' t'strip and dance naked in front of the fire fer 'im?"

"'Twasn't an offer." She nudged him with her shoulder.

"Och, that's a shame." He grinned.

She felt the heat in her face and decided to change the subject. "So—what is it ye wanted t'show me?"

"This." He waved his hand around at the MacFalon tomb. "And the ruins of t'first den, a'course—but it seems Sibyl beat me to it?"

"Aye, we went to the spring to get the silvermoon," Kirstin admitted. "But we had to be quick. I'd love to really explore."

"Good." He smiled, hands behind his back, rocking onto his heels. "I thought ye might."

"So this is where ye buried yer brother?" she mused, moving forward toward the newest tomb.

"Aye." Donal sighed.

"I'm so sorry." Kirstin put her hand against the cool stone. "'Tis not easy t'lose a sibling, e'en if—"

She couldn't finish, wouldn't hurt him with the words.

"Ye can say it, lass." Donal moved in behind her, his voice close to her ear. "I hold no delusions 'bout me brother."

"I'm sure ye had a lot of good times, when ye were young." She gently stroked the stone, wondering what Donal had been like, when he was a wee lad. She could imagine him, bright-eyed, mischievous, always laughing. Not so different from now, mayhaps.

"Aye, some. He changed when I was... vera young." Donal pressed his hand to the front of the tomb, his fingers overlapping hers. "But after our mother passed—she died of a fever, soon after she weaned me, and the healers could'na cure her—Alistair became an angry child. Bitter. Cruel."

Kirstin sighed. "It's so hard t'lose a mother."

"Me father said Alistair was born with a black streak in his heart only our mother could lessen. Alistair was her shinin' star. They loved each other overmuch." Donal gave another sigh, dropping his hand from the tomb's cold surface. "Me father said Alistair was always proud to show off t'her—whether t'was his skill wit' sword or bow, or jus' a boast about 'is ridin' and wrestlin'. She indulged 'im."

"She sounds like a lovely woman," Kirstin murmured, turning to face him.

They were very close in the dimness. She saw the way his gaze moved over her face in the light of a torch.

"All I remember of her is golden hair fallin' into me face, a rosy-cheeked smile, and the warmth of fallin' asleep against her breast." Donal's gaze moved over these parts of Kirstin as he spoke, from the cascade of dark hair over her shoulders to her definitely flushed cheeks, and then down, to her bosom, exposed at the V of the white shirt Moira had brought her to wear under her plaid.

"Alistair had far more of me mother than I ever did," Donal confessed. "And when she died, me father said... Alistair's heart caved in."

"Nothin' can e'er replace a mother's love," Kirstin agreed softly.

"So what about yer parents, Kirstin?" he inquired as they turned together and started walking slowly through the catacombs.

"Oh, me mother was a healer and a midwife," she told him. "Me father—he was the warmaster fer Raife's father, Garaith."

"But I thought Raife's father... was...?" Donal hesitated, looking at her, as if wondering, but she put his mind at ease.

"King Henry?" Kirstin smiled, nodding. "'Tis not a secret in the pack. In fact, 'tis the stuff of legend. But Raife never even met King Henry. Garaith raised him, and Raife always thought of him as his father. And Garaith treated him as such, passin' on leadership of the pack to him, even though Darrow was his blood, not Raife."

Donal sighed. "I wish me father'd been s'wise."

"Ye mean, by makin' ye laird instead of Alistair?"

"Aye. He could've," Donal told her. "Scots do'na hold to the 'first-born' standards of t'English. But I think he felt he owed m'mother. And he hoped it'd change Alistair, givin' him that kind of responsibility."

"But it did'na."

“Nuh. It only made things worse,” he said sadly. Then he brightened, looking sidelong at her. “So yer father was Alaric, the Gray Ghost, then?”

“Aye.” Kirstin laughed, surprised he knew her pack’s history. “But t’me, he was jus’ me father. Not grim at all. He loved t’tell stories and laugh—at least, he did, until me mother didn’t return from her fall medicinal gathering one year.”

“Och.” Donal’s face fell. “Wha’happened, lass?”

“He rode out t’find me mother,” she said, frowning at the memory. “T’was t’last night I saw ’im.”

“They searched?”

“A’course.” she nodded. “But they found no sign of either of ’em.”

“I’m sorry.”

“Well, I was a mature wulver by then, not a child, like ye were when ye lost yer mother,” she said. “I think t’was e’en harder for me adopted sister, Laina.”

“Laina’s yer sister?” He looked at her in surprise.

“Not by birth,” she explained. “But when ’er mother was killed by The MacFalon, me mother had just pupped me, and she adopted Laina and suckled ’er as ’er own. T’was hard on Laina t’lose not jus’ one but two mothers.”

“The MacFalon killed Laina’s mother?” Donal’s voice shook with anger. He stopped walking, leaning against the stone of the tombs to look at her.

“Yer grandfather.” Kirstin nodded, facing him. “Before t’wolf pact.”

“*She* was the one...” Donal breathed, realization dawning.

So he did know the history then.

“Aye. She-wulvers can’na change when they’re in estrus or givin’ birth,” she explained. “Both Laina’s mother and Raife's were caught in one of The MacFalon's traps. Laina's mother gave birth to Laina in that cage. The pup was small enough and escaped. But The MacFalon shot an arrow through Laina's mother's heart."

Donal closed his eyes as if in pain, whispering hoarsely, "I'm so sorry."

"Raife's mother..." Kirstin went on. "Her estrus'd jus' ended, and she changed back t'human form. I hear tell that The MacFalon put the naked woman over his saddle and brought 'er home as a gift to t'visiting King Henry, and dragged t'body of t'wolf behind 'is horse..."

"I've heard t'same," he replied, opening his eyes and shaking his head in disgust. "So that's how Raife was conceived then?"

"Aye." She nodded in agreement. "And how t'wolf pact came into bein'. King Henry told t'wulvers he'd deliver the kidnapped Avril—that was Raife's mother's name—and swear eternal peace between the MacFalons and the wulvers, if only the wulver warriors would fight for 'im t'gain the throne."

"Because he was'na King Henry yet, then, was he?"

"Not yet," she told him. "He gained the throne because he had the full force of the wulver warriors behind 'im."

"'Tis a horrible tragedy, Kirstin." He reached out and took her hand, pressing it between both of his. "So many wulver lives lost. Ye know, there was a time when yer number was very great."

"Aye," Kirstin agreed with a little shiver. "'Tis the reason the Scottish king started demanding hunters kill the wolves twice a year."

"Yer pack outgrew this den."

"Our new den's far more secret than this one and I'm glad of it, even though we have the protection of t'wolf pact," she confessed. "Still, wulvers've gone missin'. Like me parents. Not as many as a'fore, though. A'fore..."

She gave another shiver, remembering the stories she'd been told about the days before the wolf pact.

"I've heard 'em, too." Donal nodded. "Men would, as you say, drag their corpses behind 'em on their horses."

"Must've been a surprise when they got back t'the castle and discovered they were draggin' a man or woman instead." Kirstin gave a little, strangled laugh at that. "That's when they knew they'd killed a wulver, not a wolf. The ol' timers say we lost more'n half our wulver population a'fore t'wolf pact was signed."

"I'm glad there's no longer a feud a'tween us." Donal squeezed her hand in his. "I meant it when I said I'd defend t'wolf pact wit' me life, Kirstin."

She met his eyes, seeing the hardness there, behind the softness, knowing he meant it.

"Thank ye."

"Ye know, I saw yer father trainin' in the yard at t'castle when t'wulvers came. I was jus' a boy," he told her, not letting go of her hand as they started walking again.

"Did ye?" She smiled up at him as they headed toward the passageway leading between the MacFalon tombs and the first den.

"He bested e'ery wulver or man that faced him in trainin'," Donal remembered. "All the boys gathered whisperin' how like a ghost he really was. I've ne'er seen a man or wulver move like that. No one laid a blade on him."

"He was a fine warrior," she agreed as they moved into the tunnel.

Donal held Kirstin's hand tight in his own. "I'm glad the Gray Ghost's daughter isn't so evasive—I would'na wanna lose 'er in the dark."

"If ye think me father was fast, ye shoulda seen me mother." Kirstin laughed, swinging his hand as they walked. "If she had'na been faster than the Gray Ghost, I would've had two dozen brothers and sisters!"

Donal chuckled at that.

"Besides, don't ye know that wulvers can see in the dark?" she asked, glancing over at him.

"Yes, I did know." Donal squeezed her hand, smiling.

"C'mon." Kirstin was excited to explore as she pulled Donal deeper into the tunnels, following the recent prints she and Sibyl had left in the long accumulated dust.

Chapter Four

They made their way down the passage, side by side. Donal carried the torch to light the way. If the den had been inhabited, there would be torches lit along the walls, she knew, both for light and warmth. She didn't mind the damp or the cold—Scots were a hardy people, and wulvers even moreso.

Besides, with Donal beside her, she couldn't possibly be cold. Her body radiated like a furnace when he was around. They'd known each other barely a day, but already she responded whenever he entered a room, or even when she heard his voice. Laina had spoken his name that morning, as they went down to breakfast, and Kirstin's whole body had flushed with heat as if a flame had been ignited inside her belly.

And Laina had noticed.

Mayhaps Kirstin had been successful at keeping it from everyone else, even at breakfast when her gaze kept skipping over to Donal—every time she looked at him, he was looking at her, too—but Laina was her sister. They'd nursed together, hunted together, had their first moonblood within weeks of one another. Laina knew her like no one else.

Stopping and pulling Kirstin into an alcove, Laina had cupped her face in her soft hands, searching her eyes. Then Laina had broken into a grin, laughing at the way Kirstin blushed and pushed her away, but she knew. Kirstin's protests had fallen on deaf ears, her insistence that it was nothing met with peals of delighted laughter.

"He's yer one true mate," Laina exclaimed, grabbing both of Kirstin's hands in hers when she whirled to go. "Do'na spend another minute denyin' it or runnin' from it. There's no sense. He's t'one, Kirstin. Yer body knows it. I can see't jus' by lookin' at ye."

"Ye can'na..." Kirstin swallowed, afraid she really could. She'd spent the night on a bed so soft it was like sleeping tucked under the wing of a goose. After the forest floor or the kitchen of the wulver den, it should have been like heaven, but she'd tossed and turned, fitful and restless. Laina was right. Her body had responded almost instantly to Donal, from the moment she'd met him in the forest, and it was only getting worse.

"Aye,'tis true." Laina's blue eyes danced.

"But he's..." Kirstin had struggled with it all night long, vacillating back and forth, unable to come to terms with it. "He's a human!"

"Aye." Laina agreed, shrugging. "But at least he's a Scot. Our own *banrighinn* is a *shasennach.* What difference does it make? Look how long Raife tried to fight against it, and fer what? She belongs t'him, and he t'her. Donal's yers, Kirstin. Oh, I'm so happy fer ye!"

Laina had thrown her arms around Kirstin and pulled her into a giant wulver hug that, if the sisters had been transformed, would have ended up in a tussle on the floor. And might have, still, if they hadn't been in the hallway of the MacFalon castle.

So Laina knew. And in spite of the arguments she kept making to herself, Kirstin knew, too. And now, Sibyl knew, or at least, suspected. The question was—did Donal know?

And if he did—if he felt the same as she—what in the name of all that was holy were they going to do about it?

"Ye've been down 'ere a'fore?" Kirstin asked as they walked together. Donal kept hold of her hand under the pretense of making sure she didn't stumble in the darkness. Even if he knew wulvers could see in the dark.

"Aye. We liked t'play 'cloak'n'find' down 'ere," he told her. "If our da knew, he would've tanned our hides, but what boy could resist such a find?"

"There're certainly plenty'o'places t'hide," Kirstin agreed, smiling at the thought of them running through the tunnels. She stopped at one of the rooms and pushed open the door, letting go of his hand to enter. "I think this was t'healin' room."

"I always liked t'way this room smelled," Donal observed, sniffing, as he followed her inside. "I liked hidin' under this table."

Kirstin examined the abandoned mortar and pestles. "My grandmother's mother probably stood right 'ere, mixin' herbs."

The thought was both strange and comforting to her.

"Ye come from a long line of healers and midwives," he said admiringly. "Wise women."

"Aye." She ran a finger through the dust on the table, wondering how long it had been since one of her ancestors had stood here, preparing poultices or mixing remedies. "Longer than I e'en realized. S'much history 'ere—fer both our families."

"This place's been a part'o'me since I was wee," he told her, glancing around the room, his eyes filled with memory. "I used t'wonder what it was like, when t'wulvers lived 'ere, when it was full'o'life..."

"A wulver den's always busy." Kirstin smiled as they stepped out into the hallway. She took time to peer into more of the rooms, most of them small individual dens for wulver families. "These tunnels would've been full'o'wulvers, comin'n'goin'. I wonder where they kept their livestock?"

"Up top." Donal pointed at the high ceilings. "There's an old barn not too far from 'ere—I think they kept horses and sheep there. It's on MacFalon land, but I wonder if it might've been wulver land long before it belonged to me family..."

"Mayhaps." Kirstin smiled in the darkness when his hand found hers again, keeping her close when she wanted to wander ahead. She didn't mind.

"I'm still amazed that a horse doesn't spook when a wulver rider gets on," he remarked.

"Ye can break a horse to a wulver rider, jus' like ye can a human one," she scoffed. "They get used to it. I imagine horses don't much like human riders either, to begin wit'."

"Aye." Donal chuckled. "I've near broken me tailbone enough t'know that's t'truth."

"This would've been t'pack leader's quarters." Kirstin opened a door larger than the rest, revealing a room three times the size of the others. There was a large bed in the center of it, raised high, its base built of stone. It had clearly been built inside the room and was too large for anyone to move. Kirstin stopped, frowning as she looked at the mattress and coverlet still on the bed. "'Tis strange..."

"Hm?" Donal inquired, stepping closer.

“E’erythin’s covered in dust... but this beddin’ looks freshly laundered.” In fact, the whole room looked cleaner than the rest of the den. There was an animal skin in front of the big fireplace that looked quite new.

“Oh... aye.” Donal cleared his throat, rocking back on the heels of his boots when she looked at him. “I confess, we did’na jus’ play down ’ere as children. When we were older, we found other uses fer this place...”

“Did ye bring lasses down ’ere, then?” She crossed her arms at the thought, staring at the bed.

She could picture a younger Donal, fumbling under the plaid of some kitchen wench he’d invited down here.

I want t’show ye somethin’...

I just bet he had!

“A few.” He cleared his throat. “T’was away from t’pryin’ eyes of m’father—and Moira. That woman misses nothin’. Eyes like a hawk. One time...”

But Kirstin was striding across the room, away from him.

“Where ye goin’, lass?” Donal puzzled, seeing her moving along the back of the room near the big fireplace, her hands tracing over the stone.

“I’d wager ye did’na show yer lassies this secret...” Sure enough, her guess was correct. There was a section of the wall that, when pressed, revealed a narrow stone passage. She could hear the running water of the spring.

“What’s this?” Donal asked, following Kirstin through the dark passage, toward the light at the end. The sun was higher now and the room glowed as if lit from the inside, the slant of light coming in from above, making the water of the spring look cool and inviting.

"There's a way in from the kitchen," Kirstin pointed to the other exit, where she and Sibyl had come in.

"That's how Alistair did it!" Donal's eyes widened, and then he chuckled, shaking his head as he notched his torch into the wall. "He'd disappear down the tunnel, and I'd go lookin' fer him—and he'd end up in the kitchen somehow."

"Now ye know how." She laughed.

"He always was a sneaky little buggar," Donal mused. "But how did ye know about it?"

"'Tis the same in our den," she explained, picking her way over the wet rocks in her boots. "The pack leader's room has access to the spring. Did ye not know it was 'ere?"

"Oh, aye," Donal agreed, catching her arm before she could slip. She smiled back at him gratefully. "I jus; did'na know about t'secret entrance. This is one of m'favorite places in the world. So calm and peaceful. Ye've a spring in yer den now?"

"Aye, there's always a spring in e'ery den," she told him as they reached flatter ground. The rock here was dry, warmed by the slant of the sun, and Kirstin drew up her plaid to sit down, pulling off her soft boots. "Water's life. 'Tis said t'very first wulver was born in a spring like this one, to his wulver mother, Ardis."

"Born in the water?" Donal marveled, sitting beside her on the rock as Kirstin scooted forward to slide her feet into the cool water.

"Aye," she told him as Donal tossed his boots aside, too, dangling his feet in next to hers. "I've seen it done."

"Doesn't the bairn drown?"

"Nuh, the bairn's a'ready livin' in water." She wrinkled her nose at the question, which seemed so silly to a midwife.

"How do they breathe?"

"No need 'til they're birthed."

He splashed her bare calves with his foot, making her laugh and nudge him with her hip. They sat very close, thigh to thigh, separated only by their plaids. Kirstin felt the press of his belt against her waist.

"Tell me more 'bout t'first wulver," he said, moving more comfortably against her, his arm sliding behind her. His palm was flat against the stone, but he still framed her with his body, making a little niche for her to settle into.

"Well, some say we're descendants of Lilith," she told him, wondering just how many lasses Donal had brought down here. Did he do this with all the women he fancied? She didn't like thinking about that, but she couldn't help it. "In yer bible, she was the first woman, but she was cast out of Eden, doomed to give birth to demons."

Donal grunted, disapproving. "And wulvers're the demons?"

"Aye." Kirstin glanced up at him, but he was looking down into the water. It was a deep spring, fresh water, crystal clear. He didn't seem to mind how close they were, so Kirstin fit her head against his shoulder. "Men's history is so oft different from a woman's, ye ken?"

"Aye, lass." He nodded. "But what'd Lilith hafta do wit' t'first wulver?"

"Likely naught." She snorted a little laugh. "Seems the masculine view of the feminine has twisted all women into demons these days. Mythology becomes history becomes reality. But the older legends... they ring truer to me. Me mother told me this, and her mother a'fore her. 'Tis the story of Ardis and Asher."

"Who were they?" Donal's hand moved from the stone to her hip. Kirstin didn't shy from his touch. Instead, she snuggled closer. Her heart was racing as fast as if she was on a hunt.

"Ardis was a wolf who could change into a woman, but only durin' t'full moon. She fell in love with a huntsman named Asher, who saved her from a trap near the spring."

"Hmm." Donal mused. His fingers traced lightly up her arm toward her shoulder. "Why does this sound familiar?"

Kirstin smiled at that. He had saved her from a trap, just like Asher had saved Ardis. The similarities didn't end there, though. She looked up to see his gaze on her now. His eyes were clear blue today, no clouds, his brow smooth. A smile hovered on his lips, which were full and slightly parted and she had an incredible urge to press hers there.

"He took one look into her eyes and knew she was meant to be his," she whispered, feeling his hand moving over her shoulder.

"Mm hmm..." He nodded, as if he understood this, too.

"And Ardis took one look at him..." She bit her lip, knowing this was her confession, not just the story of

Ardis and her found one. "And knew he was her true mate."

"Her true mate?"

She nodded. "Wulvers only have one, their whole lives."

"Good." His meaning was clear and she felt her body tremble slightly as his hand moved through her hair.

"They would meet at night at the spring to make love in the moonlight e'ery full moon," she said, swallowing as she felt his fingertips brush the back of her neck, the tiny hairs there already raised and sensitive. "Me mother told me that the moonspring shone a silver light for them so they could see each other, but no one else could see them or their secret meetin' place."

"And this is where the silvermoon grows," he said. "I've ne'er seen it anywhere else."

"It only grows at a wulver spring," she replied. "They say it's because Asher wept into their secret spring when Ardis was murdered by the witch, Morag."

"Ardis was murdered?" Donal blinked at that, but his fingers didn't stop moving, stroking, petting her.

"Aye, but their child was t'first wulver," she told him. It wasn't easy to continue with the story, considering how distracted she was by his body—and her own. "A lil boy with red hair and red eyes. He's our first descendent. Asher raised 'im alone but they say Asher visited the spring e'ery full moon, and wept fer 'is lost love."

She was glad the story was over, because she couldn't possibly think anymore. Something inside her was growing, taking control. It felt a little like the tension she experienced just before she changed from human to wulver form. Except this was more intense. Every nerve ending felt alive, her senses keen. The smell of the man beside her, even to her human nose, was intoxicating. She wanted to devour him.

"'Tis a sad story." Donal's whole hand, not just his fingers this time, slipped behind her head, cradling it against his shoulder.

"Aye," she whispered, but she wasn't thinking about the story, or Asher and his lost Ardis, even if the feelings coursing through her were so similar, bred into her, generations of matings just like the first.

"I ken Asher's tears," Donal said softly, the briefest of creases appearing on his brow. "You can'na find fault wit' a man who weeps when all he loves is taken from 'im."

"'Tis always a risk t'love."

Oh, what a risk it was. Kirstin had heard it said her whole life, had listened to wulver women lament their inescapable love for their mate, had seen Sibyl's pain at the thought of losing Raife, and still, she had never fully understood, not until this moment.

To love this man would mean risking losing him. And that would mean losing everything.

"Aye, 'tis a risk." Donal nodded slowly, "But when a man finds what he wants more than anything; else, there's nothin' can quiet the fire inside him."

Kirstin saw that fire in his eyes, felt it in her own loins, in the heat of his body as he leaned in toward her, so close she was dizzy with him.

"Not e'en the spring water of Asher and Ardis," he murmured, before pressing his lips to hers.

His kiss was everything she had dreamed it would be.

Her mouth opened under his, letting him guide her head, slanting his so he could press his tongue deeper, probing the soft recesses of her mouth. She let out a soft moan when his hand moved to the small of her back and he pressed himself fully to her, the hard, ridged planes of his torso against the yielding softness of her breasts.

Her body responded instantly to his touch, as if a fire had been lit inside of her. Kirstin wasn't inexperienced—her kind didn't have any qualms about doing what came naturally. But the act, to her, had always been one of comfort and warmth, nothing more than a closeness that felt, well, pleasant. And that was all. The male wulvers she'd been with—just two, in her pack, who she had a particular affection for—had seemed to enjoy it far more than she ever had.

"Kirstin, yer so beautiful," Donal whispered as they parted, his gaze moving from her eyes down to her mouth, as if he wanted to capture it again. "So vera sweet. I'm afeared we should'na be 'ere, doin' this... but I can'na help meself when I'm 'round ye."

"Aye." She touched his cheek, feeling a day's stubble there, the roughness of it thrilling her. "I feel the same."

"I've been dreamin' of kissing ye since I met ye in the woods yesterday." He slowly traced the outline of her lips with one finger. "I'm surprised I held meself back this long."

"Is that all ye wanna do?" The disappointment in her voice was obvious, maybe too obvious. "Jus' kiss me?"

"Nuh." He chuckled, moving his hand down to her shoulder, running one finger over her collarbone, spreading gooseflesh over her skin. "But I'm afeared I can'na do everything I want. Not unless ye wanna come wit' me now to the vicar t'say yer vows. And I thought, mayhaps, you'd like a lil longer courtship than one day."

"Why?" Kirstin shook her head, smiling, bemused. "I'm a wulver, Donal. I know me own nature better than most men e'er will. I know who ye're t'me. I knew it the moment we met."

His eyebrows went up, a smile playing on those full, oh-so-kissable lips. "Who'm I?"

"Yer Donal MacFalon," she said simply, as if it explained everything. And to her, it did. He had eclipsed everyone and everything until she could see naught else. "Yer the man I've been waitin' a lifetime fer. Yer me one true mate."

"Aye," he breathed, kissing her again, this time with a soft assurance that spread through her like warmed honey, filling all the cracks and crevices in her soul. It was like coming home, like breathing after coming up from being underwater, lungs bursting, and finally breathing the air your body craved.

"I've ne'er experienced anythin' like this a'fore," he confessed, kissing the corner of her mouth, then licking it. "I do'na understand it."

"Ye do'na need t'understand it," she murmured, tilting her head back for the press of his lips on her long, slender throat. "Ye jus' need t'feel it."

"I feel as if I'm fallin' in a dream, and I'm afeared to wake up. Kirstin, I want ye," he growled into the hollow of her throat, his teeth raking her flesh, sending needlepoint pricks of sensation all the way to her fingertips. "I *need* ye."

"I'm yers," she admitted fully, to him and to herself. She didn't care if he was a man and she was a wulver, if it was unconventional, or even impossible. Laina had said it would come like a lightning strike, that you couldn't mistake the feeling for naught else, and she had been correct, even if Kirstin hadn't really believed it. Until now. "I've been yers since the day I was born."

"Och, lass, the things I wanna do t'ye..." he groaned, wrapping his arms around her, encircling her completely so she was lost in them.

"Stop talkin' and do 'em," she moaned, turning toward him fully and sliding a thigh over his, hooking her wet foot around his ankle.

He let out a low growl as he claimed her mouth again, He wasn't gentle anymore. There was no holding back. Kirstin encouraged him, wrapping her arms around his neck, opening her mouth to his deep, probing kiss, feeling his hands moving over the soft curves of her body through her plaid. But it wasn't enough for her. Not nearly enough.

Donal let out a strangled groan when Kirstin's hand moved under his plaid. The MacFalon was a true Scot, so there was no barrier between her fingers and the heat of his erection. She wrapped him in her fist, claiming the MacFalon sword as her own in one easy stroke, making the man's arms tighten around her until she thought he might break her spine.

"I can'na hold sway wit' what ye do t'me, lass," he panted in her ear as she pumped him slowly in her hand. "I can'na stop where this is goin'."

"I'll die if ye stop." She nibbled his lower lip. The man's honor was too ingrained. He was far too used to maidens who teased and tempted, who withdrew to protect their precious virginity. "I do'na want ye to e'er stop. Make love to me. Make me yers."

Her eyes met his in the slant of sunshine coming from the window high above and she saw the lust in them, knowing it was reflected in her own. There was no holding back from this for either of them. It was a force out of their control, compelling them forward, drawing their bodies together. She could no more ignore the urge to mate with this man than any woman could deny the force that brought wee bairns into the world from their full-moon bellies.

"Och, lass, please." Donal's voice was hoarse as she rubbed her thumb over the mushroom-head of his cock, feeling sticky wetness. And still, he tried to do the honorable thing. "I can'na..."

"Aye, ye can." Kirstin took his hand and guided it between her legs, to the center of the universe. He cupped her, moist and swollen, just one thin piece of cloth separating him from the Promised Land. "'Tis yers. Now and always. Fer the takin'."

His mouth moved against hers as he moved her body underneath his on the rock. He was careful not to put too much of his weight on her, but Kirstin wanted it. She wanted all of him. They rolled together on the flat rock, Kirstin caught between the earth's unforgiving stone and Donal's hardness. Their plaids were easy garments to remove and made a buffer between their skin and the rock beneath them when Donal spread the material out.

"Come t'me, lass." Donal stretched out in his shirtsleeves, holding his arms out to her.

Kirstin pulled her shirt, its long tail hanging down to mid-thigh, over her head, and Donal groaned when he saw her bared to him. Then she did as he bid her, stretching out beside him on their plaids, letting him touch her everywhere, the sensation so sweet, so beyond words, it was sublime.

Kirstin expected him to mount her, take her, claim her. This was the wulver way, and she rolled to her belly in anticipation, but Donal was not eager to force himself on her, not right away. Instead, he kissed the wings of her shoulder blades, the dimples at the small of her back, his tongue moving down the split of her behind, making her flush with heat. He drove her mad, with his tongue, his hands, his words.

By the time he flipped her over and pushed her knees back, she was so ready for him, she was sopping. And still, he didn't take her. His big, calloused hands moved over the soft velvet of her thighs, parting them so he could get his broad shoulders between them. She moaned when she felt his breath, hot against her throbbing sex, and cried out when he began to feather kisses on her mound.

Nothing had ever felt so good.

His tongue was magic, and he seemed determined to devour her from the inside out, to drink her up completely as if he wanted to drown in her juices. Her hands moved through the mass of his hair, trying to pull him to her, but he wouldn't be budged. The sweet torture went on and on until she thought she couldn't stand it another minute.

That's when he finally—*finally*—knelt between her trembling thighs, his cock rising up like a sword between his. The man still had his shirt on and she tugged at it, wanting all of him. Donal peeled it off over his head and she gasped at the sight of him, broad chest and ridged abdomen from years of training. His arms were heavily muscled from wrist to shoulder and she grasped his upper arms in both hands as he propped himself over her, gazing into her eyes.

"Are ye ready, lass?"

"Aye," she agreed, too breathless to say much else. "Please, do'na make me wait another moment."

He didn't. He parted her flesh easily, with perfect aim, sinking in swiftly, all the way to the hilt. Kirstin howled, digging her nails into his upper arms, arching beneath him at the sensation of being filled, being taken. She'd never been face-to-face with a man this way, at this moment. Donal claimed her, not just with his body, but with his eyes, pinning her beneath him.

He waited, watching her face, arms tense, thighs bulging against the supple softness of hers, his cock throbbing inside of her, so big it almost hurt. It felt as if he had penetrated her all the way to her womb, piercing her insides and making them spill forth more of her wetness. Kirstin licked her lips and then bit down on her bottom one as he began to move.

"Och, lass, ye feel s'good," he murmured, his eyes fluttering closed for just a moment as he withdrew almost all the way and sank back in again. She whimpered, arching up, wanting more. He opened his eyes to look at her, eyes searching. "Are ye'll right?"

"Please, do'na tease me," she pleaded, using every muscle she owned between her legs to clamp down on him. Donal let out a low moan, hissing air between his teeth on his next intake of breath. "I'm n'delicate. I will'na break, I promise ye."

His eyes lit up at her words and he leaned in to claim her mouth once more. Kirstin let him have that, too. She let him take it all. She was his, meant for this man—for this moment. Her body writhed under his as he began to thrust, his tongue and cock making the same, delicious motion, a hot, velvet friction that built up and up. Any experience she'd had before of quick, awkward fumblings in the dark and a fast, rough hump that left her aching and somehow wanting more, were completely taken over by this singular experience.

This man knew exactly what he was doing, every movement, every whispered word, every touch. He knew just where to touch her, and when, and how. Donal drew her bottom lip between his teeth and sucked it, his thrusts coming deeper, harder. When she thought she couldn't take another moment of sensation, of that breathless, aching need, his mouth moved lower to her swaying breasts, capturing a dark-tipped nipple between his lips and sucking that instead.

"Och, Donal!" she cried, looking at him in awe, wondering if there was some pleasure-string connected between her breast and her sex, because it felt as if his mouth was on them both at once.

"That's it, lass," he panted, hips grinding into hers, making little moon-like circles, his steel heat buried so far up inside her she could have sworn she tasted him in the back of her throat. "I want ye. I want ye t'give yourself t'me. All of yerself."

"Oh aye, aye," she gasped, but she didn't understand him, because she was. This was everything she had to give him, her whole body, her mind, her soul, it was all of her, splayed for him. All for him.

"Look a'me, lass," he whispered, his blue eyes gone grey with lust. "Look a'me. I want ye t'give it to me. All of it. I want all of ye."

"Oh Donal," she cried, feeling something blooming low in her belly, opening like a flower, as he moved faster, grinding his pelvis into hers. "Oh what... what... I... ohhhhh!"

"Do'na close yer eyes," he insisted, his voice low, throaty, commanding her. "Look a'me when ye give yerself t'me. Ohhh Kirstin, yer so beautiful, so..."

She shuddered underneath him like an earthquake, her body taking over in a way she'd only ever experienced during her change. And this was something else altogether, something uncontrollable. She'd never been more in or out of her body at the same time, even when she was transforming from human to wolf. Delicious waves of pleasure rocked her body, her sex pulsing around his shaft, sluicing juice all down the length.

Donal watched her, his face lost in an expression of awe and wonder, and then he grabbed her shoulders, driving himself into her with three good, long, hard thrusts, burying his cock into her depths and his face into her neck. His seed spilled, hot as a geyser and just as forceful, deep into her womb.

This was the moment they'd both been searching for, and they found heaven and home all at once in each other's embrace. As he began to withdraw, Kirstin caught him between her thighs, crying out at the loss.

"Do'na leave me," she begged hoarsely, clinging to him, even as she still quivered with her climax.

"Nuh, lass," he whispered. "I'll ne'er leave ye. Not as long as m'body draws breath. Yer mine, Kirstin MacFalon, and ye'll be mine e'ermore."

"What did ye call me?" she whispered, lifting the curtain of hair away from his stubbly face as he leaned in to kiss hers, brushing his lips over her forehead and cheeks and chin, soft presses of love.

"Kirstin MacFalon," he said again, going up to his elbow to look down at her. "Me wife. If ye'll 'ave me. I know 'tis fast, but ye said ye felt the same way I did..."

"Oh, aye," she breathed, arms snaking around his neck, her face moving to the soft, damp skin of his throat. "I'd settle for nothin' less, Donal MacFalon."

"Do I need t'ask Raife fer yer hand?" He cocked his head, quizzical. "What do wulvers do?"

"Ye do'na e'en need t'ask me, Donal." She traced the strong, square line of his jaw with her fingertip. "Wit' wulvers, there is naught any askin'—only claimin', and ye've a'ready done that."

"Isn't there some sort of markin'?" he asked.

"Aye," she agreed, nodding. "But if I'm t'be t'wife of The MacFalon, I should hold t'yer traditions."

"We should do both." He caught her hand and turned it, face up, so he could kiss her palm. "King Henry wanted me t'mend the rift at t'border by marryin' an Englishwoman, but instead I'll marry t'border b'tween t'wulvers and t'Scots."

"Seal t'wolf pact wit' a kiss?" she teased, sliding a thigh over his. Their feet were still wet from the water, but the slant of sun was warming and drying them.

"I'll seal it wit' more'n that." He kissed her, mouth open, tongue meshing with hers, tracing slowly over her teeth, exploring every inch of her.

"Oh Donal," she whispered when they parted, dizzy with wanting him. "I want ye so much... when can we do't again?"

"Och, I'm a man, not a wulver," he groaned as she reached her hand down to squeeze his length. To her surprise—and apparently to his as well, given the way his eyebrows went up—he began to stiffen in her fist. "Ye bring out the beast in me, lass."

"Good."

She pushed the man to his back, tracing her tongue over around the mounds of hard muscle on his chest, pausing to flick each nipple, making the cock in her hand swell. The hair on his chest curled around her fingers as she explored every glorious plane and angle, a hand raking over his belly, a delicious, ridged mountain range of flesh. Her tongue traced the dark line of hair that traveled from navel to nest, his snake now rising up, staring at her with its one good eye.

"Och, lass, yer mouth—"

She sucked the head between her lips, tasting his musk, her juices, taking as much of him inside her as she possibly could, all the way to the back of her throat, and still she couldn't take him all. The man was more claymore than broad sword, a giant mass of swinging steel meant to take what was rightfully his. And she wanted to be taken.

Her fingernails raked the soft seed sacks hanging underneath his cock, and Donal hissed, shifting his hips, pushing himself deeper into her throat so she gagged a little on his length. But she didn't mind. His hand moved through her hair, guiding her, a hot, steady rhythm they both lost themselves in. She could have gone on forever, worshipping his staff, kneeling at the altar between her mate's thighs, but he pulled her off, looking down at her with half-closed eyes.

"Yer mine," he whispered hoarsely, his eyes filled with it, both the longing and the knowledge at once. "I will'na let ye go, Kirstin, not e'er."

"Ye talk overmuch," she teased, rubbing the head of him against her swollen, red lips. "How 'bout ye show me instead of tellin' me, Donal MacFalon?"

"Oh, aye." His eyes darkened at her words. "I'll show ye."

"If ye can catch me." She grinned and was off like a shot before he could move, laughing as she heard him swear behind her, struggling to catch up.

She made it into the pack leader's chambers, almost all the way to the bed before he caught her from behind, grabbing her around the waist and pulling her into his big arms. She giggled and squirmed, loving the way he roughly turned her to face him, hands moving down to squeeze her bottom.

"Caught ye," he growled in her ear, his erection rising up to nudge her belly, trapped between them. "Now I get t'claim ye."

"Aye." She nodded, wrapping her arms around his neck as he lifted her easily in his arms. Kirstin's legs went around him, heels digging into the small of his back as he lifted and aimed her, sliding his thick length in, deep and hard, as if he were running her through. Kirstin cried out at the sensation, thinking she would never, ever stop wanting this, craving him, needing him.

Donal moved toward the bed but Kirstin shook her head.

"Like this," she whispered hoarsely, beginning to move her hips in little circles. "Standin', jus' like this."

He moaned and turned toward the fireplace. The room was full dark, the only light coming from the torch at the end of the passageway. They could barely see each other, but it didn't matter. Kirstin felt every big, beautiful inch of him as he pressed her to the rock wall beside the big fireplace, driving up inside her with fierce, harsh thrusts that threatened to break her spine against the stone.

Not that she cared.

She was crazed with heat, her nails raking his back like claws, her teeth sinking into the hard, muscled skin of his shoulder. Donal grunted at that, but he didn't stop pounding into her, the slap of their flesh a hot, rhythmic beat. Kirstin's sex squeezed and massaged him, and she rocked in his arms, meeting him thrust for thrust.

"Yer lil cunny is so tight, lass," he panted in her ear. Words during mating were new to Kirstin, but she liked them. She liked the way he panted them, hot breath against her ear. "I could ride ye from dusk 'til dawn and still want more."

"Aye," she gasped, her walls quivering at his words, the dam threatening to flood. "Oh Donal, do'na stop. Do'na e'er stop."

"Nuh," he agreed, but he did stop, just for a moment.

To slide out of her, whirl her around, and bend her almost in half as he took her again, fingers probing between her legs, finding her crevice, and sliding back into the hot cavern of her sex. Kirstin's hands raked the stone, looking for something to hold onto, bracing herself against the rough thrust of his hips, the sweet torture of his cock up against her womb like a battering ram seeking entrance to something deeper inside her.

"Och, lass, I can'na hold out much longer," he cried, fingers gripping the curve of her hips, hard enough to leave bruises.

"Give it t'me," she urged, remembering his words to her. "I want all of ye. Please. Fill me wit' yer seed. Please, please, please, pl—"

Her sex was already spasming around his shaft, that unbelievable, quivering wave of pleasure pulsing through her, milking him. Kirstin howled, reaching back as he thrust forward, feeling the hard muscles of his behind working as he buried himself in to the base, shoving her flat against the wall, legs spread, feet completely off the ground, crushing her with his shuddering weight.

He didn't say anything then. He just picked her up in his arms like a bit of fluff and carried her to the bed. He pulled her on top of him, wrapping them up in the coverlet. It was soft and freshly laundered and they floated on a cloud together in the darkness. She might have slept—must have, because when she woke, there was a fire lit in the fireplace and her mate was no longer in bed.

"Donal?" She lifted her dark head from the pillow, hand searching the mattress for his big frame, but finding only empty space.

"Here, m'love," he called.

She saw him sitting on a deerskin by the fire, something in his hands.

Kirstin wrapped the coverlet around her and went to him, putting her arms around him from behind, kissing the broad, hard planes of his back, resting her cheek there as she knelt on the deerskin. She had woken, afraid she'd been dreaming, only to find him still here. Questions loomed in her mind, threatening the flood of happiness rushing through her veins, and she pushed them away.

They'd deal with reality later. This, here, now—was all that mattered, all that ever would.

"I found somethin'." Donal put a hand over hers at his middle, caressing. "Come see."

"Is it food?" she asked, crawling around to sit beside him. "Because I'm starvin'."

"I'll rustle us up some game." He chuckled, meeting her gaze in the firelight. "Och, Kirstin, yer so beautiful ye make me chest hurt."

She smiled at him, bemused. This man said the most extraordinary things.

"Is that a book?" She blinked in surprise at the leather-bound tome in his hands.

"Aye." He nodded, flipping through the pages. "I got up t'build a fire, and one of the stones at the bottom had come loose from our... uh... acrobatics. When I went to seat it, I found this..."

"Mmmm." She snuggled closer at the memory, her sex pulsing already, wanting him. How was it possible to want someone so much? "Is that... that's a wulver!"

The drawing was unmistakable. She recognized the half-wolf, half-human form, and more than that, the drawing itself had been done by a wulver hand. Wulvers were all amazing artists and could draw nearly anything. Their style was definitive.

"Aye." He flipped to another page and Kirstin squinted at it in the firelight, seeing a drawing of a birthing wulver and her pup.

"'Tis a midwife's text!" she exclaimed, taking it from his hands and pulling it into her lap. "Look, there are drawings of plants—it's full of them!"

"Yer pleased?" He smiled as she turned more pages, wishing she could read the text.

"Oh, aye," she breathed, looking up at him with bright eyes. "Sibyl and Laina'll be pleased, too."

"I do'na care 'bout pleasin' Sibyl and Laina." He pulled her into his lap, settling her there, and she felt his erection begin anew against her bottom. "I care 'bout pleasin' ye, Kirstin MacFalon."

"Ye do please me." She turned her face to his to be kissed. She would never get enough of this man's kisses, until the day she died. "Ye please me greatly, Donal MacFalon. I can'na wait to call ye husband as well as mate."

"And I can'na wait to mate wit' ye as yer husband." He used her hair to pull her head back, exposing her throat to his hot, hungry mouth.

"Aye," she agreed happily, lost in the fantasy of being his, even if the reality of being The MacFalon's wife meant something else altogether.

"No, I meant it, I can'na wait," he breathed, taking the book out of her hands and pushing her back onto the deerskin. "I want ye now."

She opened her arms and surrendered herself to him.

Chapter Five

Kirstin's hackles rose before she even knew the man was in the room. She turned to see Lord Eldred standing near the back of the gathering hall. He was dressed as an English lord today, not like the huntsman she'd met him as, but there was no mistaking those keen eyes. They surveyed the room quickly and she straightened when she saw his gaze hesitate as he came to her. A small smile flitted over his features and he gave her a brief nod before turning to someone at his side who wanted his attention.

"Kirstin?" Laina slid into the chair beside her, breathless from her race down the stairs and into the gathering room. "Did ye hear?"

"Hear what?" Kirstin's attention moved from Lord Eldred—she still didn't understand why he raised her hackles the way he did—to Laina, although her gaze stopped at Donal, sitting like a king in full dress plaid at the front of the room. The ceremonies were getting close to starting—the hall was filling up with people—and while Donal smiled and nodded to the man who was bending his ear, Kirstin could tell he was impatient.

"Lorien's back." Laina told her.

"Aye, I saw 'im." Kirstin smiled at the memory of the big wulver she'd greeted when he came into the castle. Donal had frowned at the way Kirstin hugged him, the way he swung her up in his arms and kissed her cheek in greeting. "He brought word from t'king."

"Aye, so y'know 'tis good news?" Laina asked.

Kirstin nodded. Lorien had been happy to give her the news, even before he told Donal, which had irritated Donal even more. But Lorien had been like a brother to her since she was small. They'd grown up together, played together, and yes, so they'd been together, when they were adolescents. For a while, Kirstin thought Lorien might be her true mate, but once she'd seen Laina with Darrow, and now Sibyl with Raife, she knew it wasn't meant to be. He was a friend, sometimes lover, but not her one true mate. She'd never gone into estrus around Lorien. Her body knew what it wanted.

And it wanted Donal

Lorien had returned safe and well, though, and that made her happy. And he had confirmed what Lord Eldred had told them in the forest. King Henry was honoring the wolf pact. It should have been a relief, but for some reason, Kirstin's hackles remained raised.

"Does Raife know? What 'bout Sibyl?" Kirstin looked around for both of them.

"I think they know. I'm jus' so relieved." Laina gave a happy sigh. "Our bairns'll be safe from war and strife."

Kirstin nodded in agreement, the mention of bairns sending a sharp stab of pain through her heart. She shook it off, glancing back to where Lord Eldred was shaking hands. Her mistrust of him had been based on her fear that he was lying about the wolf pact, that King Henry had actually been behind Alistair's plan all along. But mayhaps she was being too cautious. If Lorien had returned with word—she still marveled at his travel time, but wulvers could travel very fast, over long distances, without wearying—then she had to trust it.

Didn't she?

"How did ye hear?" Kirstin asked her pack-sister, frowning. "Did Donal tell ye?"

"No, I saw Lorien jus' a few moments ago," she replied. "He came up t'see Darrow. I had to practically tie that man to his bedposts to keep 'im in it, in spite of t'sleep-stuff Sibyl had 'im drink."

"And how's Darrow healin'?" Kirstin asked. She'd come to nurse her fellow pack mate and she'd spent all her time so far with Donal. She felt a little guilty about that—but when her gaze found Donal's and he pinned her with those glittering, steel-blue eyes, she didn't feel too horribly bad about the way she was spending her time at Castle MacFalon.

"He's well." Laina smiled. "Truth told, he's ready to travel, and itchin' to get home. We hafta get Raife and Sibyl reunited, and soon, or Darrow's goin' t'ruin everythin'."

"Tell 'im he has to keep up the ruse," she insisted. Donal's gaze hadn't left her, although someone had bent to tell him something. The way he looked at her made her feel as if he was stripping her bare with his eyes alone.

"I promise, I'm doin' m'best t'distract 'im." Laina sighed, tossing her long white-blonde hair over her shoulder, turning more to face Kirstin. "And *ye've* been distracted yerself these past few days."

"Aye." Kirstin flushed, when Donal dropped her a wink and she felt her blush deepen, hearing Laina laugh beside her. Were they so obvious? She wondered.

They'd met for the past three nights at the spring. Donal told her they could spend the night in his room and no one would care—he was the laird, after all—but

Kirstin didn't want everyone in the castle talking, any more than they already were. Besides, their reenactment of Ardis and Asher beside the spring in the wulver den felt right to her. She was at home in the first den—and in Donal's arms.

"Yer so in love wit' him." Laina nudged her with her hip, laughing softly, delighted.

"Aye, I am." Kirstin admitted. If she couldn't admit it to her sister, who could she admit it to? She was completely besot. There was no getting around it, no more denying it. She had fallen like all wulvers do—hard, fast and without warning. It was like waking up finding you'd fallen asleep on a charging horse with no saddle and no reins, and you could do nothing but hold on for dear life and enjoy the wild, albeit slightly terrifying, ride.

"Have ye told 'im?" Laina lowered her voice, so the people filling the chairs around them wouldn't hear. Kirstin was saving the seat beside her for Sibyl. "About... how't works, for wulvers? Or does he know?"

"I... I do'na know what he knows. We haven't really talked overmuch..."

Laina chuckled knowingly at that.

The truth was, she was afraid to tell him. More than that—she was afraid of the truth herself. Her body was changing. She could feel it, in every cell. It wouldn't be long—another week, maybe two—and she would change. And she wouldn't be able to do anything about it.

If Donal had been a wulver warrior, they would run off under the full light of the moon when her estrus-time came and mate like the animals they were. But Donal wasn't a wulver, he was a man.

A very powerful, handsome, and virile man, to be sure. Their lovemaking had been wild, raw and abandoned. Kirstin had surrendered herself to him completely, and he had claimed her as his own. She couldn't have wanted any more from a wulver lover. In fact, the words he spoke into her ear while he was inside her, the things his hands did to her woman's body, far surpassed the animal act wulvers performed under a full moon. To Kirstin, their lovemaking left nothing to be desired—just thinking about it made her feel warm all the way to her toes—except for one thing.

Unless they made love while Kirstin was in wulver form, she could never bear his children. She-wulvers only experienced estrus as wulvers. The weight of this fact was like a thousand stones pressing on her heart. The MacFalons were Scots, so they weren't quite as particular about producing heirs as the English, but Donal was a man, and men wanted sons to carry on their lineage. They wanted daughters they could marry off to their neighbors to create alliances. And she wanted to give him sons and daughters.

She was a midwife—she'd been bringing pups into the world since she was a child herself, attending Beitrus—and the thought of not being able to bear children of her own left her feeling cold and alone. Looking at Laina, she thought of her wee bairn, the sweet, big-eyed, dark-haired Garaith, holding his chubby fists out to be picked up. She remembered the way Darrow had looked when his son was born, how proud he'd been. If she couldn't give that to Donal, she didn't know how she could possibly stand it.

And how could she tell him? How could she look him in those beautiful, kind, blue eyes and tell him that, loving her meant he would never have an heir? She wondered, sometimes, after their lovemaking, when he was stroking her hair or just watching her in the light of the fire, if he had put all the pieces together and figured it out for himself. Mayhaps he already knew the wulver ways, as Laina had intimated? But somehow, she didn't think so.

Because if he knew, she had a feeling he would end things between them as quickly as they'd begun.

And that's what she was really afraid of. Now that she had given in to herself—mind, body and soul—given into him, she couldn't imagine losing him.

So she had managed, every time he hinted about moving forward with marriage plans, to distract him, to keep things secret, just a little longer. She had been using Sibyl and Raife as a good excuse—not until things were settled between her pack leader and his mate, she said. Then they could share the news with everyone.

"Ye haven't talked 'bout it at all?" Laina asked, frowning, bringing Kirstin out of her reverie. "What'll ye do? Where'll ye live? How'll ye—?"

"Shh, 'ere comes Sibyl." Kirstin stood, welcoming Sibyl into their row of chairs with a hug.

Kirstin noted that Raife was watching his mate closely, although only from the corner of his eye, trying to appear as if he wasn't. Their latest plan to throw the two together had involved going riding under the pretense of looking for wulver traps—Lord Eldred had been keen to show them the various places where he and his men had begun disarming them—with Sibyl and Kirstin riding behind Donal and Raife.

Donal and Kirsten had planned to ride off and leave the two together alone in the woods, but Kirsten's horse had spooked at something—Laina claimed it was because she was so close to her estrus, but she didn't know for sure—and had taken off at a gallop. Donal and Raife gave chase, and by the time they caught her, Raife was so angry he threatened to pull Kirstin over his saddle and wallop her like a pup. Was it her fault the horse had spooked? Then, to top it off, it had begun to rain, and Lord Eldred begged off to go somewhere with his men, while the four of them rode back to Castle MacFalon in silence.

So much for plan B.

They'd moved on to plan C, which they would implement some time later in the week. It had to be soon, though, because while they were still bandaging Darrow's wound, he had nearly healed, and if Raife came out of the glowering mood he was in and started paying closer attention, he would know they were trying to deceive him. The only thing that kept Darrow in bed was the prospect of helping to alleviate his wife's discomfort because of her lacking nursling. He was clearly enjoying that part of the ruse.

Sibyl sat beside Kirstin with a smile, but there was no time for small talk. The room was full to capacity with all of the MacFalon armsmen as well as local villagers and several of the guests who had stayed on, after being invited to the wedding of Sibyl Blackthorne and Alistair MacFalon—which had never taken place.

The castle was still full of them, and Moira was busier than ever trying to feed everyone. Kirstin imagined the woman would be glad when they were all gone, which would likely be soon. Right about the time the wulvers left for home. Raife said the guests were staying on only to see if they'd turned themselves into wolves—like they were a curiosity or a freak show—and Donal had reluctantly confirmed as much.

Now, though, they were all crammed into the common room to watch the pomp and circumstance of their new laird being affirmed. He would also name his new guard captain and hunt master this day. After the ceremony would be a great party—poor Moira had been cooking for days and had brought in several extra sets of hands from the village to help her—and Kirstin was looking forward to it.

Beside her, Sibyl fidgeted, pulling at a stray thread at the edge of her plaid. Her nails were ragged, as if she'd been biting them, and she looked even more pale than usual. Her gaze kept skipping to Raife, who sat on the other side of the hall, as far away from her as he could get, while still being able to keep an eye on her.

Kirstin tried to listen and pay attention, but she kept getting distracted by Donal in his dress plaid. Her mind kept wandering to what he looked like out of it, and that made her feel as fidgety as Sibyl. It wasn't until Donal introduced Lord Eldred Lothienne to his clan that she really started listening. Up until then, the master of ceremonies had droned on about MacFalon lands and tracts and sections, as if he had to tell them every bit of dirt and rock the new laird of Clan MacFalon owned. Kirstin didn't know—mayhaps, according to some law, that's exactly what he had to do, but why subject them all to it?

Lord Eldred shook hands with the laird and Kirstin heard whispers around her about who he was and speculation about what he might be doing there, but no one had to wait long. The man was happy to steal the spotlight, stepping in front of Donal, literally upstaging him as he spoke to the crowd.

"I've come to deliver a message from King Henry VII of England," he proclaimed. His voice boomed through the hall, carrying all the way to the back, bouncing off the wall. "In my hand, I hold a royal decree, sealed by the king himself. This is a proclamation written in his own hand, reaffirming the crown's support of and enforcement for the original wolf pact decree as it was written."

This news was met with sighs of relief and general applause.

The people who lived on the MacFalon lands had long known about the wulvers, even if those from far-away did not quite believe the tales of the half-men, half-wolf warriors who lived in the borderlands.

And they had all heard the stories of what life was like before the wolf pact, when wulvers ran free and hunted men. No one wanted those days to return.

Many of the MacFalons strained their necks to look over at Raife, and Kirstin felt dozens of eyes turn her way as well. Laina clapped along with the rest of the crowd, nudging Kirstin to do the same. Kirstin nudged Sibyl, urging her applause, and she complied, although not with much enthusiasm.

This worried Kirstin, because Sibyl had been quite concerned about King Henry's response. They'd all hoped Alistair's claims that King Henry was behind his plan to eliminate the wulvers were just lies, and now they had proof, from the England's high royal huntsman himself. She would have thought Sibyl would be thrilled.

Lord Eldred handed the sealed proclamation to Donal. He actually had to turn around to do it, and Donal accepted it graciously. Lord Eldred handed him another piece of paper, also sealed, leaning in to say something to the laird no one else could hear. Donal gave a nod, his brow knitting for a moment, before setting both scrolls aside.

"King Henry VII of England will condemn any act against the wolf pact," Lord Eldred went on, bragging about his position as royal huntsman, and how the king had put him in charge of enforcing his wishes. Lord Eldred also made the announcement that, due to the recent death of King Henry's eldest son, Arthur, the crown was in mourning, otherwise King Henry himself would have made the trip.

Lord Eldred strutted like a peacock, completely commanding the room, and just watching him made Kirstin's blood boil. This was Donal's day, his affirmation of laird, and this pontificating fool was literally standing in front of him in order to address the crowd. No one seemed to care much, though. They were all taken in by his swagger, which made Kirstin's lip curl in a sneer she actually had to cover with her hand.

"Oh no." Laina whispered, craning her neck to look behind them. "Oh no, no, no."

"What is it?" Sibyl asked, turning to look.

Kirstin whirled in her chair and saw him.

Darrow was up, dressed, and making his way into the hall.

"Oh nooooo!" Kirstin echoed Laina's sentiment with a howling whisper. "Go! Fetch 'im a'fore Raife sees!"

But Sibyl was already up, heading toward the back of the room to corral her charge.

Laina followed and Kirstin sat there for a moment, watching as the master of ceremonies attempted to take control again—it was time for Donal to name Aiden and Angus MacFalon as his guard captain and hunt master, respectively. They were Donal's cousins, a lively pair of brothers with long, dark hair and bushy brown beards who liked nothing more than to drink and eat, as far as Kirstin could tell, but they were amiable enough. And, she supposed, it was good that they were big men, thick and barrel chested. People moved out of the way when they came into a room. Even Lord Eldred stepped aside as the brothers approached their laird to take the knee and pledge their fealty. She watched this happen out of the corner of her eye, but her attention was focused on Laina and Sibyl, who were now trying, as quietly as they possibly could, to drag Darrow back to bed before Raife saw him.

When Darrow opened his mouth to speak—likely to tell his wife to leave him the bloody hell alone, and not quietly either—Laina put a hand over his mouth. That's when Kirstin got up and made her way through the crowd standing in the aisles—there weren't nearly enough chairs for them all—to see if she could help get Darrow sorted before Raife caught wind. She saw Donal look her direction and she smiled at him, hoping he'd understand. He would, of course, once she'd told him why she'd slipped away.

Kirstin found Laina and Sibyl pushing a frustrated Darrow back through the crowd, but given the number of people, and Darrow's resistance, they weren't getting far.

"Darrow, please," Laina pleaded. "Don't do this. If Raife sees ye..."

"I need t'be'ere," Darrow insisted, ignoring the looks people were giving him. "Lemme go, woman!"

"If he sees ye up, he'll insist on leavin'," Kirstin hissed, getting in front of Darrow—at least the three of them made some sort of barrier. It wasn't much, but it was something. "Please, Darrow, think of Sibyl. Think of yer *banrighinn*."

That did stop him, for a moment.

He frowned down at Sibyl, head tilted, considering. Kirstin could almost see his thoughts flitting over his face. He'd gone along with their plan thus far. What was a little longer? Laina said he'd been angry about not coming to the ceremony, but she said she would placate him. In the end, though, Sibyl had given him something to make him sleep, because nothing else would calm him. It appeared he'd either only pretended to take it, or he'd woken up sooner than they'd expected.

"Darrow." Sibyl looked up at him, and Kirstin saw the tears in her eyes. Sibyl took a step back, shaking her head. "Go. Go to him. He's your brother, and you're right, you should be here."

With that, Sibyl ran. Laina looked at Kirstin with wide eyes, then at her husband—who was already pushing his way through the crowd, now that he had Sibyl's blessing. Kirstin could hear Donal announcing that the time for mourning his brother, Alistair, had come to an end.

"Go to'im!" Kirstin pointed after Darrow. "I'll take care of Sibyl."

She found her just outside the doors of the great hall, the ones that opened to the outside. Sibyl was crouching at the side of the stairs and Kirstin flew down them. When she reached her, Kirstin went to her knees beside Sibyl's small, trembling form, pulling a curtain of red hair away from her damp face.

"I'm sorry," Sibyl whispered. Then her body jerked violently and she leaned forward to vomit onto the dirt.

"Oh *banrighinn,*" Kirstin whispered, holding her hair back as Sibyl emptied her stomach of what little she'd had for breakfast onto the ground. When she was done, Kirstin pulled her into her arms, rocking her and stroking her hot, flushed face with cool hands. "How long've ye known?"

"Known... what?" Sibyl frowned at her, blinking in surprise.

"Ye do'na know?" Kirstin's smile widened and she hugged her closer. "Oh m'sweet, lovely *banrighinn*, ye're wit' child. Ye're carryin' Raife's bairn. Ye'll bear t'wulver heir. Don't ye know what this means? He can'na deny ye now!"

The doors of the hall flew open and Kirstin heard Donal's voice from a distance, carrying to them, thanking everyone for coming and telling them that the kegs were being tapped outside—hence the avalanche of Scotsmen and women pouring forth from the gathering place.

"I'm pregnant?" Sibyl whispered, disbelieving.

"Aye. I'm almos' certain of it." Kirstin nodded, cupping her face in her hands.

"No." Sibyl's chin quivered and she pulled away, standing up and wiping her mouth with the back of her hand. "If I tell him... that will be the only reason he takes me back. I can't. I won't..."

And with that, she turned and ran. Kirstin went to follow her, but there was such a crowd rushing down the stairs, it was impossible. Even with her bright red hair, Sibyl was soon swallowed up.

"Kirstin?" Someone grabbed her arm and she looked up to see a man with a very bushy brown beard holding onto her. She recognized him as one of the recently pledged MacFalon brothers, either Aiden or Angus, but she couldn't remember which.

"Aye." She tried to shake him loose, but he held her, not rough, but firm.

"The MacFalon requests yer presence in 'is chambers."

Kirstin followed Angus—it was Angus, not Aiden, who came to fetch her, she remembered when she saw the jagged scar on his calf and the story he'd told about the axe that had caused it—around the side of the castle, through the crowd. There was no sense going back up the stairs against the herd coming down it. Even with Angus's bulk leading the way, it would be too much of a fight. Instead, he took her through the breezeway and into the castle, down another long hallway.

Her heart was beating too fast, wondering why Donal had requested her so formally, why he hadn't come to get her himself. Mayhaps it was just another part of the ceremony, but she had a feeling it had to do with Darrow coming into the hall, and Raife realizing that his brother was now fit to travel. She wished she'd managed to catch Sibyl before she ran, but she would deal with that later—as soon as she could talk to Laina, alone.

Angus paused to knock on the big, solid, oak door.

"Aye, enter," Donal called out. He sounded weary. Mayhaps all the pomp and circumstance had been as exhausting for him as it had for her. She smiled, thinking of the night they would spend together in the first den, just the two of them alone. She would do her best to make him forget all of it, the responsibilities of being laird, the thousand small and large things weighing him down.

Angus pushed the door open with a grunt and Kirstin marveled at how heavy the thing was. It was thicker than her wrist. She didn't think a full grown wulver warrior could break it down without quite an effort.

"Kirstin." Donal's smile only reached his mouth, which was very unusual. She glanced around, expecting to see Darrow and Raife, perhaps even Laina, ready for the fight that surely was about to ensue, but there was only Donal, sitting behind a wide, dark desk scattered with papers and maps and other documents, including two scrolls, their seals broken.

The King's seal, she realized, as Donal asked Angus to leave them and close the door behind him.

"Is somethin' t'matter?"

He held his arms out to her, now that they were alone, and she went to him. Donal pulled her into his lap, kissing her hungrily, hands moving greedily under her plaid, seeking the velvet of her skin. His tongue made soft, swirling patterns with hers and she melted against him, moaning softly when he cupped her sex, parting her thighs to give him more access.

Had he called her here for this, then? She wondered.

But doing this here was dangerous, and they both knew it.

"Donal," she whispered, burying her face against his neck as they parted, feeling the hardness of his body against hers, the steel of his erection through his plaid. "We should'na do this—not 'ere, not now. There're hundreds of people waitin' t'see their laird..."

"Damn them all t'hell n'back," he swore, grabbing a handful of her hair and pulling her head back so he could take her throat, leaving hot, wet trails with his swirling tongue. "Yer mine, Kirstin. D'ye hear me? And I want e'eryone t'know't."

He shifted in his chair, and she gasped when his cock pressed against her behind and his hand moved to cup the fullness of her breast. She couldn't deny him—wouldn't. She was his, truly. They were destined—she was sure of that. Her body knew it far better than her mind. It wept for him, opened to him, ached for him.

"Tonight," she whispered, crying out when his hand moved once again under her plaid, cupping and rubbing her through the thin silk barrier. "At our spring. We'll be together then... but now..."

"Kirstin." Donal wrapped his arms around her waist, surrendering to her words, bending his head to her breasts and resting it there. She stroked his hair, long, silky, soft under her fingers, a lion's mane. She sensed a sadness in him, a desperation that had never been there before.

"What is it?" she murmured, cradling his head against her breasts. "Tell me..."

He lifted his face to look at her, searching her eyes, looking for something.

"Let's run away." A small smile played on his lips at the shocked look that must have appeared on her face. "I'll ask Raife t'take me into yer pack. I know it's been done before. I'll live among t'wulvers, be one of ye. We can be together, as we're meant to be. I can'na be wit'out ye. Not as long as I draw breath."

She stared at him, heart hammering in her chest. All of the scenarios she'd seen playing out in her mind, and yet, this had never been one of them. She had never dreamed that the laird of Clan MacFalon would give up everything to follow her into the wulver den.

"I can'na ask that of ye..."

"Ye do'na need t'ask, m'love." He stroked her cheek with his fingertips. "I will'na lose ye. I can'na."

"We can talk 'bout it later." She swallowed, nodding, hearing the sound of the crowd, both inside and outside the castle walls. There were hundreds of guests roaming the halls, and they would expect to see their laird sooner rather than later. "But righ' now, ye have responsibilities. People are waitin' on ye, Donal MacFalon, and I—"

She was thinking of Sibyl, of Darrow and Raife and Laina. There were more immediate fires to put out, that Donal likely did not yet even know about.

"I do'na want them." His voice was urgent, hoarse, as he turned his face up to look into her eyes. "I want ye."

"And I want ye," she assured him, wiggling in his lap to prove it. He groaned and she smiled. "But ye can 'ave both."

"No, I can'na."

Her brow wrinkled at his words. "What d'ye mean?"

The look on his face struck fear—real fear—into her heart. They'd been playing at being together, pretending they could, at some point, announce their betrothal to the world. That Donal could present her to his people as The MacFalon's new wife. It begged so many questions it made her head hurt to think of them. Her mind told her one thing, her body, heart and soul another.

She'd been ignoring her head in favor of the latter.

"This." Donal angrily grabbed one of the scrolls off the desk, depositing it into her lap. "This is what I mean."

"What?" She puzzled as she unrolled the paper. It was finely inked and signed, adorned with the English king's seal, now broken.

"Can ye not read?" he thundered, standing and practically spilling her onto the floor. Kirstin caught herself against the desk, watching Donal begin to pace the room like a caged animal, hands behind his back.

"Nuh," she confessed in a small voice, sinking into the chair he'd vacated. "I can'na... only my name, a few words..."

He gaped at her for a moment, truly shocked.

"Wulvers do'na need t'know how t'read!" she exclaimed, rolling her eyes. "What does it say?"

Donal hung his head for a moment, eyes closed. Then he lifted his gaze to meet hers.

"It says King Henry's sendin' me an English bride," he told her softly. "And he expects me t'marry her wit'in the month."

"What?" She breathed, glad she was seated, because her legs wouldn't have held her if she hadn't been.

"Aye." He started his pacing again, back and forth. "Lady Cecilia Witcombe, the Earl of Witcombe's only daughter. She's on her way t'Castle MacFalon righ' now. Will probably arrive wit'in a fortnight."

"This is..." She raised the scroll in her trembling hands. "From King Henry? Himself?"

"Aye." Donal whirled, stalking toward the tall bookcases at the other end of the room. "King Henry says I'm t'marry this stranger or forfeit m'claim to the MacFalon lands."

"How can he do that?" she cried, seeing him turn on his heel and pace back in her direction, his face nothing but scowl. "He isn't Scotland's king—he isn't yer king *or* mine."

"Alistair made an agreement wit' him as The MacFalon," Donal reminded her darkly. "And I'm duty-bound t'honor it."

Agreements. Duty-bound. Honor. Words her heart did not recognize or care about in the least. Her heart knew this man was hers, no matter what claim the English king thought he had on him. Kirstin hung her head, looking at the scroll in her hands, knowing it had all been too good to be true. They'd been dreaming of being together, when all along, they'd both known it was impossible.

"Mayhaps 'tis for the best," she whispered. Big, fat tears fell onto the parchment, blurring the words.

"What? How can ye say that?" Donal exploded, stalking over and grabbing the scroll. He crumpled it in his big fist with a sneer, tossing it aside. Then he took a knee in front of her, grasping both of her hands in his. His tone was pleading, desperate. "Kirstin, I love ye. D'hear me? I love ye more than any man has e'er loved a woman. I've naught interest in any other."

The thought of him bedding another woman, let alone marrying her, made her stomach clench in pain. She met his eyes, tears trickling down her cheeks, seeing the pained look on his face and knowing it was mirrored on her own.

"Donal... if ye refuse..." She swallowed, not liking to think of it. "You do'na know what yer sayin'. Yer not thinkin' clearly. Ye can'na give up yer lands, yer position as laird of Clan MacFalon, not for me, not for any woman."

"So I should keep it t'marry a woman a do'na love?"

"Mayhaps." Her own words pierced her heart and she saw them run him through, more painful than any sword. And she was going to have to break him further, now that they were facing these harsh realities. "Donal... there's somethin' else I hafta tell ye..."

"What is it?" He looked as if he was waiting for something to fall out of the sky and land on top of his head.

"I did'na wanna talk 'bout this 'ere, now, but..." She lowered her head, shaking it, the weight of it breaking her heart in two. "I do'na know how t'say't."

"Tell me." He lifted her chin, forcing her to look into his eyes. "Ye can tell me anythin', lass."

"Donal, e'en if we run away, as ye suggest..." She swallowed, trying to gather enough courage to say the words, to face the reality out loud. "E'en if Raife would agree t'such a thing, and we go live among me pack..."

"He damned well will agree," Donal snapped, his face a thundercloud.

"Listen t'me." Kirstin took his face in her hands, clean-shaven today, smooth. "Yer a man, and I'm a wulver. We'll ne'er be t'same."

"I do'na care 'bout that," he said with a shake of his head. "It does'na matter, Kirstin, we—"

"I'll never be able t'have yer children," she blurted out.

The words hung there between them and she saw his confusion, his bewilderment. So he didn't know, then. Didn't understand how it worked for the wulvers, the basic mechanics. It was impossible—it would always be impossible.

"What?" He shook his head again, as if to clear it.

"A she-wulver can only accept her mate's seed when she's a wolf," she confessed. "I can'na have yer bairn, because we can'na mate when I'm changed. D'ye ken?"

"Aye." He looked thoughtful, the realization slowly dawning. "But Raife... how was he conceived, then?"

She swallowed, telling him the awful truth. "King Henry took Avril when she was in heat. When she'd changed to a wulver."

"What?" he breathed.

"Some men see't as a challenge, a badge'a honor, t'take a wulver woman when she's in animal form..."

He gaped at her, clearly unaware of this part of the history between their families.

"Men like yer brother, I imagine," she murmured, hammering the point home. "Or yer grandfather."

"Och, Kirstin..." He held his arms out to her and she went to him, let him cradle and rock her. They huddled together on the floor behind his desk like children hiding from their parents. He stroked her hair, kissed her temple, whispered how much he loved and wanted her until she thought her heart would overflow with feeling for him.

"Listen t'me," he urged. "'Tis ye I want. Children would be a wonderful expression of our love together, if they were possible, but they're not necessary. Ye're the one I want."

"'Tis easy t'say that now." She sniffed, fitting her head under his chin. "Mayhaps 'tis time t'face some hard truths. We've been livin' the dream of Ardis and Asher, but mayhaps that dream's over now... and it's time t'wake up to the reality of who we really are."

"I know who I am." Donal's arms tightened around her. "I'm The MacFalon, and ye're mine. I will'na let ye go. That's the truth."

"The truth..." She gave a long, shuddering sigh. "The truth is, ye would'na be happy wit' the wulvers. And I..."

"Oh Kirstin, ye've been happy 'ere," he countered, whispering against her hair. "I know ye have."

"Aye," she confessed, holding back a sob. "I love ye, and Moira, and yer family, and the castle... I do. But..."

"Then stay," he urged, wrapping her up completely in his arms as if that alone could keep her. "I'll send word t'the king that I will'na marry this Englishwoman, and—"

"And start a war?" she cried. "Bring King Henry and 'is army down on yer head, so soon after reaffirming t'wolf pact? Put me pack and yer family in danger? At the vera least, lose everythin' ye own?"

"I do'na care 'bout that..." he told her hoarsely.

"But I do," she replied softly. "And we both know, e'en if... e'en if Lady Cecilia Witcombe wasn't on 'er way t'marry ye... no one would accept the laird of Clan MacFalon marryin' a wulver."

"'Tis not true..." He denied it, but she heard the hesitation in his voice.

"Aye, 'tis," she insisted. "I've heard what they say 'bout us. They all talk, when ye're not 'round to silence 'em. They say things like 'I'd love to lie wit'er, but I'd be afeared t'get fleas'."

"Who said it?" he growled. "I'll 'ave their heads."

"You can'na quell hundreds of years of prejudice and superstition with yer sword, m'love." She smiled. She didn't want to tell him about the Alistair loyalists, the ones who continued to hate the wulvers. There was one man in particular, Gregor, who had said very rude, crude things, but she'd done her best to ignore him. "Ye'd hafta chop off e'ery head in the land t'were that yer solution."

"There's a way..." he insisted. "There mus' be."

"If'n there is, I do'na know't." She sighed, closing her eyes against the truth, not wanting to face it.

"Leave't t'me." He lifted her chin and kissed her lips, soft and sweet. "I should'na've burdened ye wit'this. But I wanted ye t'hear't from me, a'fore..."

"A'fore?" She raised her eyebrows.

He sighed, a pained look crossing his face. "A'fore ye heard it from someone else. Like Lord Eldred."

She shuddered at the mention of that man's name. Of course he would make it a point to make that sort of announcement at his leisure. He liked to take the spotlight, and he would likely see it as a good opportunity to do so.

"What're we gonna do, m'love?" she lamented, searching his eyes for an answer.

"Right now?" He brushed hair away from her face. "We're goin't'go out there, put on smiles, an'dance."

"I can'na dance wit' ye," she protested with a shake of her head. "Not now..."

"I can'na dance *wit'out* ye." He pressed his mouth full to hers and she tasted the salt of her tears slipping between their lips.

She would do as he asked, although, the thought of joining the gathering after this news made her stomach turn. And then she remembered Sibyl's morning sickness.

"Oh, Donal, there's somethin' else," she said.

He sighed. "I do'na think I can stand another thing..."

"It's Sibyl... she's wit' child."

He blinked in surprise. "Well, this is good news, isn't it? It solves our problem of tryin' t'get those two together, doesn't it?"

"No." Kirstin laughed, shaking her head. "Sibyl refuses t'tell him. She says she will'na use it t'get him back."

"Och." He smacked his forehead with his hand, rolling his eyes. "Women!"

"We're the bain of man's existence, aren't we?" She giggled.

"Aye," he agreed, grinning. "And the boon."

"I love ye, Donal MacFalon," she said suddenly. "No matter wha'appens, I'll always love ye."

"And I love ye, Kirstin MacFalon." He pressed his forehead to hers, looking deeply into her eyes.

"I do like the sound of that." She sighed.

"Good, because I'm goin' t'marry ye. Some way, somehow, I'll make ye mine. I promise ye that."

Kirstin nodded, kissing him back when he touched his lips to hers again, not protesting in the least—because she wanted so very much to believe him.

Chapter Six

"Raife, I can'na go back wit' ye." Kirstin wrung her hands, meeting her pack leader's concerned gaze with her own pleading one. "He's me one true mate."

Raife scowled at her over the breakfast table, although she wasn't surprised. He wore a scowl most of the time now. They were leaving on the morrow, and still, his face hadn't cracked a smile. She couldn't believe he was still holding out, keeping his mate at arm's length. This was their last-ditch effort to bring the two of them together, and it had better work, because they'd run out of other options.

Unless they locked them in a room together that neither could escape, she couldn't fathom any other plan but this one.

"He's not a wulver," Raife protested, glancing over at his brother, Darrow, who snorted at this from behind his mug of mead. Laina just looked into her bowl of meal, scraping the bottom brown bits, ignoring Raife's cool look in their direction.

Kirstin had to point out the obvious. "Neither's Sibyl"

"We're talkin' about ye, nuh me." Raife's scowl deepened. And here she thought that wasn't even possible.

"I love 'im." Kirstin confessed, glancing up as Moira brought a bowl of hard-boiled eggs to the table. It was dangerous, telling Raife this in front of Moira and the servant girls who hurried around bringing food out to the gathering hall and the people there. The wulvers ate in the kitchen with the servants, not because they were forced to, but to avoid the stares and whispers of most of the MacFalons.

Raife frowned, but for the first time, he looked like he was taking her seriously. "You've given yerself t'him?"

She nodded, glancing at her sister. "Laina says I'll go into estrus soon."

"But ye can'na 'ave bairns wit' this man," Raife reminded her, his voice soft, more concerned than angry now.

"Aye." She swallowed, nodding again.

"And he knows that?"

"Aye."

"Kirstin, he's the laird of Clan MacFalon." Raife reached across the table to take her hand in his. "How well d'ye think those people out there're goin' to accept ye? They do'na e'en like havin' us eatin' at t'same table beside 'em."

What he said was true and made her eyes fill with tears. Raife frowned at that and sighed, watching her tears fall into her lap as she lowered her head, letting a dark curtain of hair hide her face.

"Kirstin, I'm not sayin' it t'be cruel," he murmured. She knew he wasn't, and his kindness and sympathy hurt more than anything else. Raife had been chosen their pack leader for a reason. He was both intelligent and shrewd, and he almost always knew the right thing to do—unless it involved his own love life, apparently. "Besides, I do'na b'lieve King Henry'll e'er allow the match."

"But he upheld t'wolf pact." She lifted her tear-filled gaze to meet his.

"There's a difference a'tween livin' peacefully alongside wulvers and marryin' them, ye ken?" He squeezed her small hands in his giant ones. "But if it's what ye really want, I'll n'stop ye."

"Thank ye." Kirstin's lower lip trembled. She wasn't even acting—she didn't have to. "I'm afeared ye may be right 'bout King Henry. He's... he's sent a royal decree."

"What decree?" Raife glanced up at Darrow and Laina to see if they knew about such a decree but they both kept quiet, busying themselves with their breakfast.

"King Henry's promised Donal another bride. An English one." She wasn't lying. She comforted herself with that as Raife's eyebrows went up in surprise.

"I was afeared of that." He shook his dark head, frowning.

"He sent a sealed scroll wit' his royal huntsman. King Henry's ordered 'im t'marry S—" She stopped herself mid-sentence, biting her lip. Mayhaps now she was putting on a bit of an act for his benefit. But it worked. His eyes widened when she wouldn't finish the sibilant word and simply said, "An Englishwoman."

"An Englishwoman," Raife murmured. He was an intelligent wulver and could put a puzzle together. She was counting on it. His gaze skipped to Laina and Darrow, who avoided it. Even Moira rushed off to busy herself with something at the other end of the kitchen. "What Englishwoman?"

Kirsten lowered her head, feeling his hands tightening over hers in a vise-like grip. She nearly yelped, but used it to elicit a sob of pain from her throat.

"Kirstin!" he growled, letting go of her hands—he'd realized he was hurting her—and grabbed her little shoulders, shaking her. His eyes were wild. She saw the fear in them—and knew his pain. It wasn't Raife who would have to fight to keep his mate from marrying someone else. Sibyl was no longer promised to anyone but him. And mayhaps, after this little ruse, he'd finally realize that it was only Raife she'd ever loved.

"What Englishwoman?" Raife thundered, standing and knocking the chair out from under him.

She shook her head, remaining mute, pretending she couldn't talk because she was sobbing so hard—and it wasn't hard to do. Because the tears were real. There was an Englishwoman who would soon be at the MacFalon doorstep who expected to marry Donal and bear his children on orders from her king. It brought up pain so great for Kirstin, she could barely breathe, let alone talk, and she just sobbed into her hands, unable to answer Raife's questions.

"Sibyl...?" Raife's big fingers dug into her shoulders. *"Is it Sibyl?"*

"Enough, Raife!" Darrow snapped, glaring at his brother.

"Look at 'er!" Laina clucked, shaking her head. "She's so upset, she can'na e'en speak..."

"D'ye know?" Raife pointed a finger at Darrow, then Laina. "Who's this Englishwoman?"

"I—" Laina looked at Darrow, blinking innocently. "I... uh..."

"Well..." Darrow cleared his throat, leaning back in his seat. "Uh..."

"Ne'ermind!" Raife kicked the toppled chair out of his way as he stormed toward the exit. He nearly knocked over the little blonde maid, the one with the gap between her teeth called Gayle, as she came in. She shrank away from him, pressing herself flat against the wall, clearly afraid of the wulver warrior.

"I'll speak to The MacFalon meself and wring it out of his scrawny neck..." Raife growled, sweeping past the maid without even seeing her.

"He's in the chancery!" Moira called helpfully after him, chuckling when the door swung closed.

"Did it work?" Kirstin lifted her tear-filled cheeks, lowering her hands completely. She'd been peeking out of them between her fingers until that moment.

"Aye. That was quite a performance." Darrow scowled, tearing roast chicken off the carcass in front of him. His appetite had come back threefold, his body requiring more protein to heal faster, and Moira had been happy to roast a chicken or two a day for him. "I hope so. Now it's up to The MacFalon."

Kirstin wasn't about to tell them how little she'd had to pretend.

"The MacFalon plans t'keep Sibyl in the chancery 'til Raife arrives?" Moira asked, pouring more mead into Darrow's empty glass.

"Aye." Kirstin sniffed, cooling her red cheeks with the wave of her hands. "Angus'll signal 'im when Raife's almost there, so Donal knows just when he should propose to Sibyl."

That thought brought more tears to Kirstin's eyes, even though she knew it was all a ruse. She didn't like the thought of Donal proposing to anyone—except her. And he'd done that, several times already, in the past couple weeks. If only she could accept him...

"Nothin' like jealousy and possessiveness t'motivate a wulver t'action." Laina smiled coyly, nudging her husband with her elbow.

"Since t'dawn of man, when Eve took that first bite of apple." Darrow sighed, reaching to the middle of the table to grab one out of a bowl of fruit, taking a large chunk of apple flesh out with his teeth and chewing noisily. "Ye women've been so vera cruel."

Kirstin wiped her face with the edge of her plaid, and both Darrow's words and the bulge beneath it reminded her.

"Speakin' of the dawn of time..." Kirstin produced the book from where she'd hidden it in the folds of her Scots garment. "I've somethin' I wanna show ye."

"What's this?" Laina frowned at the leather-bound tome as Kirstin put it up on the table.

"I found it in t'first den," she confessed, flushing when Laina gave her a knowing smile. Did everyone know that she and Donal had been sneaking off to meet there? "Hidden in t'pack leader's room."

"Is that what I think 'tis?" Moira saw the book, her craggy gray eyebrows going up in surprise.

"Is it a witches book?" Gayle, the blonde maid, peered over Moira's shoulder at it, her eyes wide. "It looks like witchcraft t'me."

"It's the Book of the Moon Wives." Moira scoffed at the girl's assumption, retrieving the chair Raife had kicked and sitting upon it so she could look through the book in question. "I thought t'was jus' the stuff of legend..."

"I've ne'er heard of such a thing." Laina stood to go look over Moira's shoulder as well, watching the woman turn pages.

"I'd heard such a book existed," Moira told her. "But I thought t'was jus' a tale, or mayhaps that it'd once existed but it'd been lost long ago."

"T'was well concealed," Kirstin said, blushing at the memory of how they'd discovered the book, but no one noticed. They were all too interested in its contents—everyone except Darrow, who continued to pick meat off the chicken carcass with his fingers.

"What kinda book is't?" Gayle inquired, curious but at the same time looking as if she might bolt at any moment should the book do something untoward.

"It's said t'be a history of wulvers'n'men," Moira informed them. Then she chuckled. "Well, mayhaps a history of wulvers'n'women might be a better description. It's a sort of midwives'n'healer's guide."

Laina perked up at that. "Not many words..."

It was true, the guide was mostly pictures, although there were some words. Those words they saw were written mostly in Gaelic, and sometimes another, ancient language. The handwriting was mixed, making the assumption that the book had been written by more than one hand a good one.

"At the time, neither human women nor wulver women were allowed t'learn t'read or write," Moira said.

"Only ladies need to learn t'read." Gayle wrinkled her nose. "I can'na waste m'time learnin' nonsense."

"If we start teachin' women t'read, mankind is doomed," Darrow joked, ducking when Laina reached out to smack his head.

"I wish I'd learned." She stuck her tongue out at him.

"I can'na read the words..." Kirstin lamented with a sigh.

"Nor I..." Gayle shrugged.

"I can," Moira said, surprising them all. "But I do'na know all of the plants. Some, but n'all...

Laina and Kirstin looked at each other and they both said, “Sibyl.”

“Aye,” Laina nodded, her eyes shining. “She can read—*and* she knows all t’plants. Likely more than all of us combined.”

“Mayhaps the cure lies within these pages...” Kirstin smiled at her sister.

“’Tis my greatest hope,” Laina confessed. “For yer sake, and mine... and the sake of our daughters.”

“Gayle, more mead!” Another servant girl stuck her head into the kitchen and the little blonde sighed, moving to get back to work.

Moira abandoned the book to fetch a pitcher for Gayle to take out to the guests.

Laina came over, standing beside Kirstin’s chair, gently stroking her long, unbraided hair. Kirstin put her arms around her, resting her cheek against Laina’s belly.

“I do’na like th’ idea of ye stayin ’ere, sister.” Laina sighed. “What’ll we do fer a midwife? Who’ll deliver the wulver heir?”

Darrow’s head came up at that, distracted from his mission of debriding the chicken of all its meat. She had told Laina and Darrow, but had sworn them to secrecy.

“Shhh!” Kirstin urged her sister to be quiet, glancing around at the servants. They were all busy, but still, you never knew who was listening. “Do’na give ’way that secret a’fore our *banrighinn*’s ready t’reveal it.”

“’T’would bring Raife ’round in a heartbeat,” Darrow said again, for the hundredth time. He’d been quick to suggest they just outright tell their pack leader about Sibyl’s condition, but the women had talked him out of the idea. He kept pushing it though, saying it was the one sure thing that would be certain to endear Sibyl to him again.

"Aye, but I ken Sibyl's hesitation," Laina told her husband. "She'd ne'er know if Raife wanted 'er—or the bairn..."

"No man'd walk away from a woman carryin' his heir." Darrow licked his fingers noisily. "That woman's more precious than gold."

She knew he wasn't talking about her, but Kirstin couldn't help the tears that welled up at his words. She saw Gayle looking at her curiously as she carried a tray toward the door and Kirstin averted her eyes, not wanting her to see. She didn't want anyone to see.

So she bolted. She heard Laina calling after her, alternately berating Darrow for his thoughtlessness, but Kirstin didn't stick around to hear the rest. She pushed past Gayle, who nearly spilled her tray, and ran down the hallway blindly, her chest tight with Darrow's words.

More precious than gold.

Would she be worth nothing, then, if she could not bear Donal an heir? Even Raife had been doubtful about that aspect of their relationship. He and Sibyl had no such restrictions, as her budding pregnancy proved.

Kirstin heard men's laughter at the end of the hall and slowed, seeing Angus and Aiden slapping each other on the back. Donal stood to the side, head cocked, listening. She wiped her tears, considering turning around and running the other way, when she heard it.

Shouting. Banging. Someone was pounding on Donal's chancery door—from the inside. Too curious to resist, Kirstin approached. Donal smiled when he saw her, slipping an arm around her waist and bending his head to her ear.

"I locked 'em in."

"What?" She startled, hearing Raife demanding to be let out. "Ye did what?"

"That stubborn fool was still gonna walk out, e'en after he'd heard me propose—and her refuse, a'course. I fully expected him t'barge in and go after me like a bat outta hell. I had Aiden and Angus waitin' to come to me aid if need be, jus' to restrain 'im. But e'en after all that, he was not gonna back down. So—I locked 'em in there together."

Kirstin heard Sibyl shouting—screaming at Raife. Weeks of pent-up anger and hurt and frustration that she was finally allowing herself to feel and say. It didn't help that she was with child. The bairn made her far more emotional than usual.

"We should start makin' wagers on how long they'll be in there," Aiden said with a chuckle, nudging his brother.

"I jus' hope he does'na bust up m'grandfather's desk and bookshelves." Donal winced.

"Wait..." Kirstin cocked her head, eyes widening in surprise. "It's quiet..."

"He did'na kill 'er, did he?" Donal whispered.

"Mayhaps *she* killed *'im*," she countered, listening for any sound.

She heard Sibyl give a cry and for a moment thought she might be hurt. Kirstin took a step toward the door, and then another sound followed the first. This one much clearer in origin.

"That's not t'sound of someone bein' murdered." Donal grinned.

"Mayhaps we should give 'em some privacy?" Kirstin waved the two big men away who had leaned in closer to the door. Angus actually had his ear pressed right up to it. "Shoo! Both of ye, go! Moira has roast chicken in t'kitchen. Go do what ye do best! Go eat!"

Aiden and Angus grumbled about it, both of them grinning ear to ear at the sound of Sibyl's moans of pleasure, but they went, as instructed.

That left Kirstin and Donal standing in the hallway, grinning at each other like fools.

"That gives me an idea." Donal jerked his thumb toward the closed, locked door, behind which Sibyl and Raife were making unholy noises, pulling Kirstin to him with his other arm around her waist.

"Tonight..." she whispered, putting her hands against his chest and pushing, but he wrapped both arms around her, not budging.

"Now," he growled in her ear, his big, muscled thigh sliding between hers as he pressed her against the tall, oak door. "I wanna make love t'ye in a bed, in a room wit' windows. I wanna see yer beautiful body in the daylight."

She couldn't resist him. Not with the clear sounds of Sibyl and Raife mating on the other side of the door and Donal's rising erection pressed hard against her hip. She wanted him like she always wanted him. Desperately, hungrily, without question or reserve.

"Aye," she whispered, tilting her head so he could have better access to her throat. His kisses were hot and greedy, his hands roaming over her even though anyone could come down the hall at any moment.

"Come wit' me," he demanded, grabbing her hand and leading her down the hall. They went upstairs, passing maidservants on the way, as well as both Aiden and Angus, who had been waylaid by two pretty girls before they reached Moira's kitchen. Angus's brows went up as Donal dragged Kirstin through the castle. She stumbled after him, blushing from the roots of her hair to the tips of her toes, realizing every single person who saw them must know where they were going, and why...

But when Donal got her into his room, slamming the door behind him and locking it, she didn't care anymore who heard them. They were on each other like animals, tearing at each other's clothing like they couldn't get skin to skin fast enough. Donal's bed was one befitting the laird of Clan MacFalon, a huge four-poster affair, so high there was a stool beside it. The thought of him sleeping there alone at night made her crazy. The thought of him sleeping there with someone else?

That was unfathomable.

"Kirstin, m'love," he whispered against her lips, pulling off the last vestige of her clothing, her shirt over her head, leaving her bare before him.

Donal went to his knees, looking at her in the bright light spilling in from the tall windows, his gaze sweeping her from head to toe and back again. Then his eyes settled between her legs, at the soft patch of fur there.

"Lemme see ye," he murmured, using his big hands to part her thighs. "Open yer cunny fer me."

She slid a hand down to do as he asked, using her fingers to spread her swollen sex, showing him everything he wanted to see. The look of lust in his eyes went from white hot to molten in an instant. Donal growled, wrapping his thickly muscled arms around her and burying his face between her thighs. Kirstin cried out, his tongue lapping at her like a dog, up and down and back again, a fast, frenzied motion that made her thrash, head going back, hips thrust forward. She grabbed a handful of his hair, grinding against his face, against the fierce, hot lash of his tongue.

The man's mouth was absolute magic.

"Donal, nuh, nuh, please," she begged him, knees beginning to buckle, unable to hold her weight under such an onslaught.

He pushed her back against the side of the bed, pulling her legs up over his powerful shoulders, and in one swift motion, he stood, vaulting her up onto the mattress. Kirstin squealed, laughing as she flew through the air, landing breathless in the middle of his bed. It was like landing on a cloud.

Donal crawled up after her, pulling his shirt off, leaving him naked and stalking her, his erection bobbing between his legs as he knelt up between hers. Kirstin thought he would slide inside her, but instead, he pushed her knees back, all the way to her ears, bending her body near in half before leaning in to fasten his mouth over her mound.

"Ohhhhhh my God!" she cried, getting a very clear view of him parting her swollen lips with his tongue, teasing the little button at the top of her cleft, then sliding down to dip into the pink hole of her sex. He drank her up, eyes locked on hers, watching the pleasure rise with the flush on her cheeks.

"Donal! Oh please! Donal!" She called for him, begging, pleading, wanting nothing more than this sweet torture to come to its final conclusion—or, mayhaps, never to end at all. But it couldn't go on forever, and she finally surrendered to him, her body giving in, as it always did, to his demands.

“Och! Ohhhhh yes, yes!” She moaned and writhed, her sex clenching and releasing with her climax, toes curling, feet braced against his shoulders. Her body twisted and vaulted on the bed, but Donal had her hips grasped in his hands, refusing to allow her to go too far.

“Aye, aye, lass, that’s so good,” he murmured, kissing her juicy thighs—she’d already made his covers wet. “A vera good start.”

“Start?” she panted, taking a deep breath as he let her loose, allowing her legs to slide back down, past his shoulders, settling around his waist as he leaned over to kiss her.

“Taste yerself.” He pushed his tongue deep into her mouth. “How good ye taste. I could eat ye fer breakfast, lunch and supper and still have ye fer dessert.”

She blushed at his words, feeling her body sing with them. Nothing affected her like this man, the words he spoke to her when they were alone together. No one knew her like he did, had ever known her this way. It had happened so fast, this falling, it almost felt like flying.

“I wanna taste *ye*,” she urged, reaching down to grasp his shaft.

Donal gave a little grunt of pleasure, letting her yank him closer with each stroke, until he was in her mouth, straddling her. Kirstin swallowed his length, greedy to taste him deep in her throat. She loved the way he moved, the way he gathered her hair in his hands and simply used her mouth for his pleasure. It readied her for him more quickly than anything else, feeling the soft, velvety head of his cock slipping between her lips again and again. Her hands roamed over the glorious terrain of his body, his powerful thighs tense as he stroked himself in and out of her wet, swollen mouth, his sack swaying below, caressing her throat with each thrust.

"Och, wait, wait," he cried, pulling back, sliding himself out of her mouth with a soft popping sound. His erection swayed above her head, just out of reach, a thick strand of white hot liquid dripping from the tip to fall onto her waiting tongue. She swallowed it, eager for more, but Donal rolled off, reaching for and taking her with him.

"Ride me," he commanded, stretching out on his back and grabbing his cock in his fist. "C'mon, lass. Climb on n'go fer a ride."

She gave the head of his cock one last kiss before she straddled him, knees on either side of his hips as she eased herself down onto his length. Donal looked at her with half-closed eyes, watching her slide down slowly until they were joined completely, as one. Kirstin felt him buried deep in her womb, the crown of his cock so far inside her she ached. It was a delicious sort of pain and she moved her hips, grinding, feeling him rock back and forth inside her.

"That's it, lass," he urged, his hands moving to try to span her waist as she undulated on top of him. "Ride me. Mmm, faster."

Her hips rocked, finding their own rhythm, her body in control. Donal reached up to cup her breasts, heavy and swaying, her nipples hard, the flesh around them pursed as if they were asking to be touched. She moaned when he pinched them, that delicious pleasure-string between her breasts and sex zinging like a plucked lute strung, making her ride him faster, harder.

Donal wrapped his arms around her, pulling her in for a kiss, the velvet tip of his tongue stroking the roof of her mouth, sending hot tingling sensations through her limbs, all the way to her fingers and toes. He began to thrust from underneath, faster and harder than she was able, making her moan into their kiss, carried away by the sensation.

"Sit up," he urged, pushing her back, hands on her hips. Kirstin sank down fully on him again with a low moan, her head going back, hair grazing his thighs as they rocked together.

"Look," he urged, grasping her hips, pushing and pulling her, back and forth, rocking himself deep inside her. "Look at yerself, m'love. See how beautiful ye're."

Kirstin caught a glimpse of herself in a looking glass on the bureau across the room and stopped for a moment, blinking in surprise. She saw herself, full-breasts and hips, hair falling over her shoulders like a midnight waterfall.

"D'ye see what I see?" His hands moved up over her curves, cupping the full weight of her breasts.

"Aye," she whispered, looking from her reflection back down to him again.

"She's mine," he reminded her, tracing a finger down the center of her body, between her breasts, dipping briefly into her navel before traveling further south. "Yer mine, Kirstin. I'll ne'er let another man look at ye, let alone touch ye. No other man or wulver'll e'er claim what's mine. D'ye ken?"

"Aye," she whispered, nodding, feeling tears pricking her eyes. She wanted to drown out all the voices in her head—Raife and Sibyl, Laina and Darrow—everyone who had said it was impossible, that her being with this man couldn't be.

But it was.

She had seen it for herself in the mirror, the two of them joined, connected in a way she'd never been with any other man before. He was changing her, day by day. Her body was transforming, becoming fuller and rounder, her breasts heavier, her sex fuller, always moist and ready for him. She was nearer her estrus with every passing moment.

"C'mere." He pulled her down to him, cupping her face in his hands and kissing the tears that had spilled down her cheeks. "Do'na cry. N'matter what happens, I'll let nothin' come b'tween us, m'love. I promise ye."

She nodded, swallowing past the lump in her throat, wanting to believe him.

"Shhh." He slid her off him, rolling and spooning her from behind, wrapping his big arms around her completely, drawing her body against his. His erection slipped between her thighs, riding up and down the seam of her sex.

"I love ye, Donal," she whispered, leaning her head back against his shoulder, seeing their vision in the looking glass, her expression of pleasure crossed with pained surprise when he impaled her on his length, settling her deep in the saddle of his hips.

"And I love ye," he murmured, kissing her lips as he began to move. He rocked into her from behind, keeping her caught against him, completely contained, her arms crossed over her breasts, his hands cupping them, restraining her from any movement.

She could thrash and writhe and squirm, but to no avail. She was his.

"Donal," she cried, feeling him throbbing inside of her, filling every available bit of space. "Oh Donal, m'love, aye, aye..."

"Tell me," he whispered, his lips against her ear, hips moving, their bodies slapping together. "Tell me yer mine."

"Aye," she panted, surrendering, knowing it was truer than he might ever know. Even if she had to be parted from him, she would belong to him, always. "Aye, Donal, aye, I'm yers, always, always..."

Her words made him drive in deeper, the wet sound of their bodies moving together filling the room. Donal kneaded the flesh of her breasts in his big hands, pinching her nipples, making them pucker and ache.

"Please," she pleaded with him, the sensation between her legs almost unbearable, something coiled tight in her belly, waiting to snap. She couldn't stand much more. "Oh Donal, I beg ye, please, please..."

"What do ye want, m'love?" he asked softly, his teeth capturing her earlobe, biting down gently, making her cry out. "Tell me what ye want."

"I want ye," she cried, writhing in his arms on the bed, undulating her hips, trying to take more of him, all of him, swallow every bit of him up. "Och, please, I want ye, I want to feel ye fill me. I want yer seed. I need it, please, give it t'me!"

She felt his body tense, both of his hands sliding down from her breasts, over her belly, reaching between her legs to cup her mound. Kirstin gasped when he rolled to his back, taking her with him, parting her legs as he thrust up from underneath. She saw the four posters of the bed, the high ceiling above, as he drove her upwards toward it, his fingers playing between the wet, swollen lips of her sex.

"Ahhhh! God!" She shuddered as he made fast, furious circles against the sensitive button at the top of her crevice, sending shooting stars through her body.

"Give it t'me," he growled, bucking his hips up fast and hard, pounding into her, an impossible rhythm. "It's mine, Kirstin. Yer mine. Give it t'me."

"Aye!" She howled and shuddered, arching on top of him as her climax overtook her. Her body shook on top of his, both of them slick and slippery with sweat, her sex clamping down hard around his throbbing shaft.

"Och, lass, yer cunny!" he gasped, and she cried out again when he rolled her once more, this time all the way over to her belly, crushing her with his weight as he spread her velvety thighs with the hard, muscled press of his own, opening her completely to the incessant, aching pound of his cock.

"Donal!" she gasped, breathless, unable to say anything else as he grabbed her shoulders, giving two last, hard thrusts and then collapsed on her completely with the force of his trembling weight. His seed burst deep and hot in her belly, white, pulsing rivers of the stuff, so much it spilled out of her. She could feel it sliding down her slit, soaking the bedding beneath them. The maids would know what had happened there, she knew.

And she didn't care.

"Yer mine." Donal wrapped himself around her, still stroking his half-hard member in and out of her slick slit, as if he couldn't stop the primal motion. "I will'na let ye go. I will'na e'er accept another woman in m'life, as m'wife. I can'na."

She nodded, closing her eyes, feeling tears slip down her cheeks onto the mattress coverlet. He eased himself slowly off, a moment she lamented, every time, before pulling her close against him again, spooning her. She saw their reflection in the mirror, Donal's leg over both of hers, thick arms cradling her, making her seem small in them, as if he might be able to hide her, keep her from the world.

But it was out there, just past the locked door. They couldn't deny it forever.

That made her remember Sibyl and Raife and she chuckled to herself at Donal's simple solution. Why had they not done it before?

"Do ye think they're still locked in yer chancery?" Kirstin asked, knowing he'd understand who she meant.

"Probably." Donal grinned, brushing her hair away from her face and kissing her flushed cheek. "Not that they'll care. I'll likely have t'send in Aiden and Angus t'drag 'em out in the mornin'."

"They're leavin' in the morning." Kirstin's heart ached at the thought. Her family was going home, back to the den. Her pack would be complete again. Except she wouldn't be with them. It felt as if she were being split in two.

"Aye." His hand played in her hair, taking a strand between his fingers and twirling it idly around her nipple. "Are ye sad yer not goin' wit'em?"

"No." It wasn't quite true—she was sad, but not regretful, and the latter was what he was really asking about. She didn't regret her decision to stay, even not knowing what would happen.

"I'm expectin' a dispensation from King Henry wit'in a fortnight." He kissed her shoulder, rubbing his stubble there, making her shiver.

"Yer also expectin' yer bride t'arrive wit'in a fortnight," she reminded him softly. "Will't be a race t'see which gets 'ere first?"

"She's n'bride o'mine," he growled, brow knitted. "I did'na choose 'er. I chose ye."

"She did'na get t'choose either," she murmured, thinking of Sibyl, who had come to Scotland to find herself betrothed to a cruel tyrant. "Remember, she's an Englishwoman, comin' into a strange land, to marry a man she does'na know."

"You've an awful lotta sympathy fer a woman who wants t'take yer place?"

Kirstin shrugged. "We do'na know what she wants."

"Well I know what I want." He moved a hand down to cup her mound and she let out a soft sigh of pleasure, turning her face to his and snaking an arm behind his head to pull his mouth to her.

This man was hers. She didn't know if it would be forever, or just for now, but however long it lasted, she intended to make the most of every single moment.

Chapter Seven

“She’s goin’t’need a shave!” Giggles ensued, the high-pitched sort of laughter shared by women whose intentions were both wicked and cruel. “Wanna bring ’er a blade?”

“Hush!” Moira waved the young maidservants out of the room, closing the door behind them after ushering them through. Gayle give Kirstin a wicked, gap-tooth grin before the door slammed shut.

Kirstin didn’t move from her place by the fire, still rolled in her plaid, staring into the flames. The room was warm, but she shivered, as if from fever. She knew the signs. Her time was coming, and soon. She would change then. She had no choice. The giggling maidservants who had laughed and poked fun weren’t wrong, after all. She was abhorrent, a monster, something sick and twisted and wrong.

She couldn’t blame the girls for being disgusted by her.

She wouldn’t blame Donal for not wanting her.

What man would?

“Pay’em n’mind, lass.” Moira picked up a poker to stoke the fire. “D’ye need anythin’?”

“Nuh.” Kirstin sat, pulling the ends of her plaid up around her shoulders and glancing out the window at the setting sun. The moon would rise soon, full and beautiful—and she would be trapped. Trapped by her body, by her own nature. Trapped into her life as a wulver woman.

She should just return home, as Sibyl had begged her to before she left, and find a wulver warrior to settle with, to love and raise pups with—even if no other man besides Donal could ever be her one true mate.

But she knew, there was no wulver warrior who could make her feel the way Donal did. She didn't understand it, nor did she question it. Her nature might have been at odds with her heart's desire, but she trusted her instincts, and every fiber of her being told her that Donal was the man she was meant to be with. It was the only reason she had stayed here in this castle with the MacFalons, willing to withstand all the whispers and jibes.

To be with Donal, her one true mate, her only true love.

She'd said a tearful goodbye not too long ago once Darrow was ready to travel. Sibyl hadn't yet told Raife her secret, even though he'd stopped being a stubborn fool and had finally forgiven her. Too many things could go wrong before she started to show, Sibyl insisted. She'd wait until Raife noticed the physical changes in her body before telling him she was expecting his bairn.

"You'll come to me, when it's my time?" Sibyl had whispered to Kirstin as they hugged goodbye.

"A'course, *banrighinn*," Kirstin assured her, not knowing if she would be able to make it to the den to attend the birth of the wulver heir or not. She didn't know anything for sure—except that she was going to change, and there was nothing she could do about it.

"I have the book." Sibyl kept her voice low. "Laina's excited about something Moira told us about the silvermoon. I have some of it transplanted in a pot, and a gathered a great deal of it to take home and dry. Mayhaps the book will give us the key to the change..."

"Mayhaps," Kirstin had agreed, hugging Laina too, who was anxious to get back to her bairn. She truly hoped Sibyl would be able to translate the book they'd found in the first den well enough to find something useful, something that would allow wulver women to gain some modicum of control over their bodies during estrus and birthing, but she couldn't count on it.

Her own change was coming, and she would have to deal with it.

"'Tis almos'time." Moira said, sounding reluctant to mention it, and Kirstin knew she was. This wasn't the first time they'd had an unpredictable wulver woman in their midst.

"Aye." Kirstin sighed and stood, tucking her plaid into her belt as a knock came on the door.

"I'm 'ere fer t'she-wolf." Gregor stood in the doorway, sneering at Kirstin as she straightened her shoulders and tried to put on a brave, public face, prepared to face this horrible humiliation. He took a leery step back as Kirstin approached and she almost laughed. It was true, she could have torn the man's throat out in an instant, the moment she turned.

"Nuh, I'll take 'er down." Moira insisted, linking her arm with Kirstin's and leading her out of the room. "T'isn't fer t'likes'o'ye."

"Lock 'er up good!" Gregor called after the women as they made their way down the hallway. "We a'ready lost one laird—not gonna lose another!"

As if Kirstin ever would have hurt Donal, in any form, human or wolf. But she didn't say anything as she and Moira made their way down the stairs. She expected to be led to the dungeon—where else would she be locked up? But Moira turned and led her down the hall, stopping outside the door of Donal's chancery.

"He wanted t'see ye... a'fore t'change..." Moira knocked softly on the door and Kirstin's heart broke when Donal opened it.

"Nuh, I can'na..." Kirstin took a step back, but Donal already had her in his arms, pulling her into the room and locking the door, shutting Moira out.

"Aye, lass, ye can and ye will..." Donal buried his face and hands in Kirstin's long, dark hair. "I want ye, I *need* ye..."

"Aye," she whispered, knowing just how he felt, unable to hide her own feelings, not here, in his arms. "Time's almos'up, ye ken?"

"Aye." He lifted his face to look into her eyes, searching there for some answer, some solution to their strange dilemma. "Lemme look at ye."

"I'm sorry," she whispered, feeling tears stinging her eyes, swallowing around a lump in her throat. "I wish I was someone else fer ye, some*thin'* else..."

"Nuh, lass. Do'na say't." Donal groaned, wrapping thick, strong arms around her waist, pulling her body in tight to his. "Ye're e'rythin' I've e'er wanted."

Kirstin shook her head, but her throat was closed with pain and heartache—and her impending change. She couldn't speak. She would lose the ability entirely soon.

"You're m'only love, and if I can'na'ave ye..."

"Shhh." Kirstin couldn't stand any more words and she was grateful when Donal's mouth found hers. This was a language she understood. Her arms went around his neck, fingers playing in the hair curling at the nape, his big hands moving over her tunic and plaid as if he could memorize her with his palms.

She wanted him, was desperate for him. If only he would take her and make her his own, mark her—

marry her. She was a wulver, and wanted his claim, more than anything, but she knew it was the one thing she might never have.

Kirstin knew she should have listened to Sibyl's sensible advice. If anyone knew what it was like to be caught between two worlds, it was Sibyl. Donal was laird of his clan, and now he was promised to another—Cecilia Witcombe, a highborn, English lady, a woman who would arrive this week, a "gift" from King Henry VII.

The contract, arranged by the English king so he could secure the border, was binding. Even if Donal had not signed it, his brother had already agreed to give part of his lands to the English king in exchange for an English bride. So it was an English bride Donal would have.

The king's logic was sound—if the Scots married the English, it seemed reasonable they'd stop killing each other in the borderlands. It was a plan that had been set in motion when Sibyl had come to Scotland to marry Alistair, and one King Henry seemed determined to carry through with. The woman he chose seemed to matter not as all, as long as she was an English lady. It was a perfectly rational solution—but the heart didn't always follow the logical plans set forth by the mind, even the mind of a king.

It had surprised her that King Henry had simply chosen another Englishwoman to take Sibyl's place, rather than forcing her to marry Donal instead of his brother, Alistair. But mayhaps he knew it would bring the wrath of the wulvers down on the crown, because Sibyl was Raife's, and their pack leader wasn't about to let anyone separate them, whether he was the King of England or the Pope.

Now that he'd finally stopped being angry with her for risking life and limb, at any rate.

While Clan MacFalon had welcomed Alistair's younger brother, Donal, as their new laird, and King Henry had made him warden of the Middle March—that responsibility came with more than just a title, she knew. Sibyl's heart had led her astray, from the life of a lady to living in a wolf's den, and her advice to Kirstin before they'd departed had been sensible, even if they both knew it was useless to argue with what the heart wanted.

"Come back with us," Sibyl had pleaded. "Find a wulver to love. They are all good, strong men. Any of them would make a good mate for you. Lorien has eyes for you."

Kirstin had nodded her agreement. In her head, she knew it was true. She should find a nice, wulver warrior and settle down, like the rest of the wulver women. Lorien was a fine wulver, and they'd been together a few times, before she'd left the den, before she'd met The MacFalon. She could return to the den and make a family with him. Every wulver had a true mate—but not all wulvers found them. Sometimes, Sibyl had told her, you had to settle for something else. That "something else" would be a mate that wasn't true.

She knew wulver women who had done just that. They lived comfortable, if a bit bland, lives. Other women, like Beitrus, had refused to settle. She had never found her true mate. An old woman now, she was unlikely to ever find him. So Kirstin knew she had choices. She could leave Castle MacFalon, try to find happiness with a wulver like Lorien, or some other wulver warrior.

There was just one problem with that.

None of them were Donal.

None of them were her one, true mate.

The man had found his way into her heart and she couldn't stop her feelings, no matter how hard she tried. And she had tried. She'd thrown herself into caring after Darrow—the reason she'd come to the MacFalon castle in the first place—until they'd gone back to the den. Then, she'd thrown herself into helping Moira and the rest of the servants, learning the daily workings of the castle. This is what she'd done at home, after all, and came naturally to her.

But none of it had distracted her from Donal.

He was everywhere she went, everywhere she looked, that devilish smile and those dancing eyes. She told herself—often—that the man was, well, just a man. He wasn't a wulver. He wasn't her kind. He would never be able to understand, let alone tolerate, her ways. Kirstin didn't have a choice, not like the wulver men. They could change at will, could even transform into half-man, half-wolf, but wulver women didn't have that luxury.

Wulver women's bodies were tied inextricably to their moon cycles. When they went into heat, they changed into their full wolf form, and when they did, they were unpredictable. Kirstin's life had always been ruled by the moon. Unlike Laina, who had hated that fact and tried her best to find a way to change it, Kirstin had always accepted her lot in life as a wulver.

Until now.

"We are what we are," that's what Raife always said, and it was true. You couldn't spend your life wishing you were someone, or something, else. It was a recipe for heartache.

But that was just what she'd done, Kirstin realized, clinging to Donal, wishing she could stop what was coming. She wanted to blame him, for being so kind, so generous, so damned handsome and irresistible, but she knew better. It wasn't Donal's fault. The man hadn't done anything untoward, hadn't made any advances. He had been honorable—until she practically attacked him at the spring in the first den.

It was, shamefully, all on her. It was her own wild heart that had betrayed her.

Now she was tied to him, utterly in love with him, and she knew it was hopeless. Kirstin knew Sibyl's logical advice would have been easier to follow a month ago, before she'd let herself fall for this man. Kirstin should have returned to the wulvers' den with her family. She should have ignored the calling of her heart to his, should have denied her feelings, should have turned and walked away.

Kirstin remembered her home fondly, with some measure of homesickness, but she knew, in her heart, she would miss this man more. But when Donal had taken his brother's place as laird of clan MacFalon, he had, in turn, assumed his brother's responsibility to "marry the border." To join the English and the Scots, as King Henry VII had instructed him to.

Even if Donal was in love with another woman.

Or, another wulver.

That clearly didn't matter to the heads of state.

What the heart wanted had to be second to what the crown wanted.

"I should go." Kirstin tried to disengage herself from him, but he held her fast in the circle of his arms. To be fair, she didn't try too hard to get away. She spent too little time in the man's arms, and could have spent an eternity there. Since that first morning at the spring when she had fallen into his arms like some lovesick teen and confessed her affection for him, she had found herself taking every opportunity she could to be with him.

"I do'na want ye t'go, lass," he murmured, hands lost in the thick mass of her hair. "I'm n'afraid of ye. Stay wit' me."

She wanted to, more than anything, but there was more than just his betrothal to an English bride standing in their way.

Every time she thought of Lady Cecilia Witcombe, the Earl of Witcombe's only daughter, on her way to marry the laird of clan MacFalon, it made her physically ill. Not that it mattered, Kirstin knew. The king would never approve a marriage between a man and a wulver woman, even if the king himself had once bedded one. There was a big difference between bedding a wulver and marrying one, Raife had said, and he was right.

She and Donal had talked in circles about it, and they kept coming around to the same point.

"Ye know I can'na stay." Kirstin lifted her face to look at him, at those stormy eyes, his brow knitted with worry. "Y'er t'marry another."

"Do'na remin'me." He groaned, his expression pained, as if her words had stabbed him in the gut.

Because King Henry had denied the dispensation Donal had requested.

Donal sent another, but Kirstin didn't hold much hope that it would be granted after the first had been turned down. They had to accept what was, as Raife always said.

She was a wulver. He was a man. A man set to marry another woman, upon order of the English king.

"She'll arrive soon," Kirstin reminded him, reminded herself. "In another day, mayhaps two."

Donal nodded miserably. They both knew it was true, even if they didn't want to think about it.

"Ye lead yer clan, Donal," Kirstin reminded him of this, too. "Ye mus' do what's right fer the greatest good."

"Ye're m'greatest good, lass." He cupped her face in his hands, searching her eyes. "Ye're m'vera heart."

His words broke her. How could she do this? How could she feel this way, knowing she couldn't be with him, and still stand? She didn't know.

"I can'na stay wit' ye," she whispered, her lower lip trembling, in spite of her self-admonition to stay strong. "I can'na stay."

"Then I'll come wit ye."

And there it was again. They went around and around, in circles. It was impossible. He couldn't live in the wulver den with her, and she couldn't live in the MacFalon castle with him.

"Yer family's 'ere," she urged. "Yer obligation's 'ere. Yer wife..."

They both winced at the word "wife." Kirstin didn't like to think about another woman coming anywhere near this man. Even in her human form, Kirstin's instincts turned animal at the thought.

"But me *mate* is *'ere."* He kissed her cheek, the tear that slipped down it caught on his lips. "I want ye, Kirstin. I *claim* ye. D'y'hear me? Yer *mine.* Ye'll *always* be mine."

"I wish t'were true," she whispered as he kissed her other cheek, another tear.

“’Tis true! We can make a life together, lass.”

“How?” she pleaded, wishing she could see a way around it. “If ye marry me, King Henry’ll come down on all our heads. ’T’will be the end of t’wolf pact and the end of the possibility of peace in t’borderlands. I can’na be responsible fer that.”

“Let me worry ’bout that,” he insisted.

“And then what?” she cried. “Ye live wit’ a woman ye hafta lock up once a month because she changes into a wolf?”

“’T’wouldn’t be the firs’ time a man had to deal with a she-devil once a month,” he replied with a grin.

“Donal!” Kirstin laughed. She couldn’t help it. He always made her laugh, took her outside herself. It was the first thing that had attracted her to him. That and those big, dancing, mischievous, blue-grey eyes.

“But m’love...” She turned her wet eyes up to him, hating herself for saying it out loud, but it was true, and it was the one thing she knew they couldn’t change. “I told ye. There’d be n’children. I can’na give ye heirs. We could’na mate while I was... while...”

She flushed, feeling the heat in her face, in her limbs, at the thought of mating with this man, as woman or wulver. The look in his eyes told her he was thinking about it, too. Lately it was all she ever thought about. Her body was so close to estrus, she was aroused almost constantly.

“Nothin’ would keep me from ye, lass.” That dark, determined look had come into his eyes. The man could be stubborn. “Nothin’.”

“Och, Donal.” Kirstin sighed, shaking her dark head. “Ye can’na come wit me, and I can’na stay. ’Tis impossible.”

“’T’isn’t impossible,” he insisted.

“When I change, then ye’ll see.” She lowered her head, not wanting to look at him, to see the expression on his face. She hated herself, hated her very nature. If she could have swallowed some magic potion in that moment that would have given her the ability not to change into a wolf, she would have done it in an instant. “Ye do’na really want me, Donal. Ye will’na, once ye see...”

“I *do* want ye.” His grip tightened, rocking her in his arms. “I’ll always want ye, whether ye’re a woman or a wolf or a... mouse!”

That made her laugh through her tears, but it didn’t erase the reality of what was.

The fact remained, Kirstin couldn’t be this man’s wife, no matter how much they both might want it. And she was sure that Lady Cecilia Witcombe was a beautiful woman who would make Donal the perfect wife. And most importantly, she wouldn’t turn into a beast once a month on a whim. But if the woman had been in front of her, Kirstin would have torn her throat out without a second thought.

That made her an animal.

In fact, she was an animal.

And that was the problem.

“Nuh!” Kirstin choked, voice muffled against his chest, but she hardly had any breath left, and there were no more words, no more arguments to be made. She felt it happening, her strength leaving her limbs.

“Aye, lass,” Donal insisted, his mouth finding hers, sparking a fire in her that was undeniable and unquenchable. They went to the floor, slowly sinking together, and Kirstin knew there was no stopping it. Donal would see for himself, and it would be soon. Far too soon.

"Open up!" Gregor pounded on the door from the outside.

Kirstin barely heard him. Donal's mouth crushed hers and she welcomed the weight of him as they tore at each other's clothes. He was shirtless, and then so was she, her plaid slipping easily off her body, leaving her naked beneath him, more than ready.

The pounding came again.

"G'way, boy!" Donal growled, nuzzling the soft hollow of Kirstin's throat before moving down to her breasts, making her moan when he grabbed handfuls of her hair, pulling her head back so he could get better access.

She wanted him, but she couldn't have him.

Her body burned for him, but it was impossible.

She longed to speak his name, but all that would come out of her throat was a plaintive, keening wail.

"Kirstin, m'love," Donal whispered, and she felt him, eager to enter her, almost as hungry as she was.

She howled when he slid inside her, nails digging into his back as he rutted deep and hard, speaking words into her ear that turned her blood to fire. He pounded into her with such force she could barely breathe, but she didn't care. There were no bodily functions more important than this one in the moment, nothing more compelling than the ache between her thighs.

"Och, Kirstin, yer *mine*," he said throatily, slamming into her again and again. She whimpered her agreement as he grabbed her leg, flipping it over in front of him, twisting her hips to the side, her torso still facing front. She gasped at the new position, how big he felt inside her like this.

"Ahhhh yer cunny is so tight!" he grunted, pumping faster, hips moving at lightning speed. Kirstin felt it happening. Her climax was rising as fast as the moon. Through the window, she saw the sun had sunk below the horizon, and the pale face of the moon was coming up in the sky.

She met his eyes in the dimness, the light from the window fading, no lamp lit. She wondered what he could see, but she didn't have to ask. She saw it in his eyes, the dawning realization, the slow shift from desire to horror. She was changing. There was nothing she could do to stop it.

Kirstin tried to run, but Donal held her fast in his hands, grabbing her hips as she rolled to her belly. He was on top of her, so close, rutting from behind, unwilling to stop. And so was she. Her body shuddered with both pleasure and her change as her sex spasmed around his length. Donal gave a low roar of surprise as her muscles milked his seed, drawing it up from his sack in thick, pulsing waves.

She trembled and howled, the sound filling the room, so loud it felt as if it could shake the whole castle. The steady pounding on the door outside went on and on. It sounded as if they were taking a battering ram to the door out there.

Donal collapsed on her, hand moving in her hair, and then, in fur. Her ears pricked, her hearing keener now, her vision, too. She saw everything her human eyes could not, the shadows fading, the edges of things growing sharp. She heard the sound of Gregor panting outside the door as they struggled to ram it open. She felt the heat of Donal's breath on her fur, the weight of the man who had previously been crushing her, now like nothing.

The pounding had stopped but now the whole castle seemed to shake with the blows as Gregor applied something to the door again and again.

"Kirstin," Donal whispered, his hands cupping her face, finding fur and jowls and soft, twitching ears.

She whined, rolling to her side, their eyes locked. Donal pet her gently, stroking her muzzle, her neck, his expression pained. She'd tried to tell him, but he hadn't believed her, not really. Who would believe it, unless they'd seen it with their very own eyes? He'd seen her as a wolf only once before—and never like this. He'd never actually watched her change.

Kirstin put a dark, grey paw up on the man's chest, seeing her own limbs gone, replaced with that of a wolf. No more hands to grasp with. It was as it ever was, as it had always been. There was nothing she could do to stop or change it, and she knew he would finally understand this now. He would turn away from her in horror and disgust, and she wouldn't blame him.

She braced herself for it. Her emotions were even more powerful now, as a wolf. Everything intensified. Even her love for him. Her desire, too. It broke her and she howled again, a sound full of pain and longing. The pounding against the door stopped for a moment. So did everything else. Donal stared at her like he was seeing her for the first time.

"Shhh," he urged, his fingers lost in her fur, trailing over her ribs. "Yer safe wit' me."

Safe? Kirstin showed him a canine version of a smile, dark lips drawn back from her teeth. He seemed to understand, a smile reaching both his lips and his eyes as he bent his dark head to touch hers.

"Och, yer so beautiful," he whispered. "Yer t'most beautiful creature I've e'er seen."

A great cracking sound shattered the moment, and Gregor spilled into the room, dragging a set of chains behind him.

"He's wit' t'wolf!" Gregor called over his shoulder.

"Do'na touch 'er!" Donal roared, protecting Kirstin's body with his own as Gregor grabbed the wolf by the scruff of its neck.

The man's hand sank into her flesh and Kirstin howled and snapped at him.

"Let 'er go!" Gregor insisted, pulling the chains behind him.

Kirstin heard the sound of them and winced. She couldn't bear it. Even the thought of being locked up now made her growl and buck. When she was human, she would have gone docilely, but now that she was wolf, there would be none of that. Her freedom was paramount.

"Kirstin, listen t'me," Donal insisted, trying to control her scrambling limbs and snapping jaws. "We'll nuh hurt ye!"

But she knew better. Every fiber in her being knew she had to escape the man with the chains and the locks, even if another part of her understood Donal's pleas. Donal loved her—she felt it emanating from him in waves. There was no escaping the feeling, no misinterpreting it. That was the one thing about turning wolf—there was no more room for error when it came to things like that. The world became far more black and white, easy to negotiate.

For weeks, Kirstin had waffled, torn, not knowing what to do. For weeks, she had cursed herself for loving this man, wishing things could be different. Now, as she looked into his beautiful blue-grey eyes, things became suddenly, incredibly clear.

"Hold 'er so I can get this collar on!" Gregor insisted, dragging the chains close. "We've gotta cage t'bitch!"

Donal hit the man. It happened fast. One moment, Donal's arms were around her, his hands in her fur, and the next, he'd stood and brought his fist hard across the man's face. Gregor howled and fought back, and the men tussled, wrestling each other to the floor.

It was the only opening Kirstin needed and she took it.

There were more men in the hallway, but she was faster than they were, by far. One of them nearly clipped her tail with his sword, but she sidestepped, escaping through the breezeway. She used the bench in the garden to launch herself over the wall. It was an eight foot drop and she took that too, whimpering as she landed, feeling the whistle of an arrow beside her ear as she ran for the forest.

It was full dark now but she saw everything. The world was hers at night, full of scent and possibility. She stopped at the edge of the woods, seeing the castle being lit up, room by room. The alarm had been sounded. They would be looking for her.

Donal would be looking for her.

Kirstin threw her head back and howled, hoping he could hear her, hoping some small part of him understood if he did. She couldn't tell him, not like this. It was all she could do.

She turned and ran through the forest, heading toward home. Toward hope.

Her heart pounded, and she howled again, thinking only of Donal. There was no way to convey her message except through the plaintive, keening wail of a wolf.

A wolf, she prayed, she would no longer be, when she returned to him.

If only he would wait for her.

Chapter Eight

"Bloody wulvers," Lord Eldred swore. "This she-wolf is the most evasive one I've ever run across."

Kirstin took some pride in his words as she padded silently behind the trees. She could see the light of their fire from this distance and smell the roasting rabbit. They'd burnt it, which wasn't too pleasant. Her ears picked up their words floating downwind to her.

"How're we supposed to know if it's a wulver or a wolf again?" One of Lord Eldred's captains asked. It was the one called William, she remembered. She'd met him that first day. The day she'd met Donal. Thinking of Donal made her ache and she tried to shake it away, venturing closer to them, careful to avoid making any sudden movements or noise.

"All wulvers have blue eyes," Lord Eldred replied. "Real wolves are born with blue eyes, but adult wolves don't ever have blue eyes."

"How do you know so much about them?" the other captain asked, gnawing on a burnt bit of rabbit. Kirstin's stomach growled but she ignored it. That one was named Geoffrey, she remembered. Seeing them all together made her remember that first day, when she'd been trapped up in the tree and Donal had come to her rescue. It hurt to think of Donal, all the way to her bones. She was still in heat, and her whole body felt swollen, aching for him.

"I've been hunting wulvers since before you were born," Lord Eldred snorted, poking the fire with a long stick. Sparks flew up into the night.

"There are wulvers in England?" Geoffrey asked, chewing thoughtfully. "I've never seen one."

"To my knowledge, this is the last pack of wulvers in existence," Lord Eldred told him.

"So this female we're looking for—she can't turn into one of those half-wolf things?" William mused, stretching his boots toward the fire.

"No, females cannot turn into halflings." Lord Eldred sighed. "Have you not paid attention to anything I've said? You two are woefully unprepared to hunt these animals. You could learn a thing or two from Salt and Sedgewick."

Kirstin wondered about the two Lord Eldred spoke of, the men with the funny, unlikely names. Were these two also wulver hunters?

"So what do we do with her when we find her?" Goeffrey threw a bone into the fire, picking up another piece of meat to gnaw on.

"Sometimes I could swear you're deaf, young captain." Lord Eldred sighed, running a hand through his salt and pepper hair. "I already told you. After she leads us to the wolf den, we kill her. Then we send word to King Henry to call up his waiting army from the borderlands so we can kill them all."

Kirstin froze, staring at the man poking a stick at the fire, her hackles up out of her control. She felt a growl rising in her throat and swallowed it down. The urge to attack—to protect her pack—was overwhelming. She sat back on her haunches, teeth bared, but no sound come out of her. She made sure of that. She wouldn't dare let them find her, not now.

She'd always had a bad feeling about Lord Eldred Lothienne, and now, she finally knew why.

"What about the wolf pact? The MacFalon thinks it's still in effect." Geoffrey spit a piece of gristle into the fire. "If he hears we've killed a wulver..."

"Especially *his* she-wulver..." William's face clouded at the thought.

"Who's going to tell him?" Lord Eldred sneered, looking between the two young captains. "You?"

"No, m'lord..." William held up his hands in a warding off gesture, looking genuinely scared and Geoffrey affirmed his sentiments, assuring his Lord that he wouldn't tell anyone either.

"Besides, even if word did get back to him," Lord Eldred said with a shrug. "By the time he found us, it would be too late. The wulvers would be dead."

Kirstin's body went cold. Her paws felt numb. She could barely feel the forest floor. King Henry planned to kill the wulvers? She had to warn her pack. She had to tell Donal that he'd been deceived.

"So this she-wolf, she'll turn back into a woman?" Geoffrey mused. "A real woman? With woman parts?"

"Once her estrus has ended." Lord Eldred glanced up at the sky, cloudless, the moon high above. "Another day perhaps. You've seen her for yourself, Geoffrey. She's exceptional."

"Yes. I was just wondering..." He cleared his throat, glancing over at William across the fire. "Maybe we could force her to change into human form? Chain her up and uh, have a little fun—before we get rid of her?"

"After she leads us to the wolf den, of course." William interjected.

Kirstin's breath caught, her eyes flashing at the two English captains. She could have bounded into their camp and ripped them to pieces—and she wanted to.

The two young men she wasn't worried about. She would have both of their throats torn out before they knew what was happening. It was Lord Eldred she had to concern herself with. She didn't dare attack while he had two free hands and was able to face her.

"You like to live dangerously, my young friends." Lord Eldred chuckled. "And if she turned back into a wolf in the middle of your 'fun?' As a wolf, she outweighs you by a hundred pounds and could tear your throat out with her teeth in less than a second."

Bloody well right, Kirstin thought with a low snarl. She caught herself, hoping no one had heard it. She often forgot how little humans paid attention to the things their senses told them.

"So, no fun then?" William sighed. "I'd like to say I bed a wulver."

"You'd be in good company. King Henry himself has indulged." Lord Eldred grinned. "Unfortunately, you can't rape a wulver woman in human form. She can turn back into a wolf at will. So if it was a woman's hot cunt you were looking to fill, you'd be out of luck."

"So King Henry bed a wulver... when she was... uh..." Geoffrey looked at William and the realization dawned on both of them at once.

"In wolf form?" Lord Eldred's grin widened. "Yes, indeed he did. The issue from that union runs the wolf den she'll lead us to. If we can find the bitch. I hope Salt and Sedgewick are having better luck than we."

Lord Eldred scowled into the woods. For a moment, Kirstin thought he was looking directly at her and she shrank back behind a tree.

"Do you think we've really lost her?" William mused.

"Mayhaps she's back at the den already," Geoffrey speculated.

"No. I believe she's still actively evading us," Lord Eldred's gaze scanned the woods—Kirstin looked at him from behind her tree. He hadn't seen her then. But he sensed something. "I think she knows we're on her trail."

"Mayhaps Salt and Sedgewick have found her," Geoffrey said with a shrug. "They may already know where the den is."

"It could very well be, but they haven't sent my hawk." Lord Eldred's brow lowered as he looked between his young captains. "You did remind them to send my hawk, if they found the bitch or the den, didn't you?"

"We told them," both Geoffrey and William exclaimed at once, like lads reassuring their father their chores were already done.

Kirstin didn't remember Lord Eldred bringing more than his two captains to the MacFalon castle. He had more men working for him, then, she mused. This Salt and Sedgewick. In secret. Behind Donal's back, working all along for King Henry, who *did* want the wulvers dead, it turned out. Just like Alistair had claimed.

She remembered Lorien bringing word back that the king was upholding the wolf pact. He had been lied to, she realized. They'd all been lied to.

"They're amazing creatures, if entirely unholy," Lord Eldred's gaze still scanned the tree line, making Kirstin sink even further back into the darkness. "Both more than men and more than wolves."

"But the women!" William gave a little grunt, shifting in front of the fire. "Hotter than the blazes."

"I'd still like to get my cock in that one's mouth." Geoffrey sighed, tossing the last bone into the fire and taking out a flask.

Lord Eldred laughed. "She'd snap it off and eat it as a treat."

That was true enough. Kirstin would have been happy to oblige. It took all her energy to resist it, even now.

"Get some sleep, lads." Lord Eldred tossed his stick into the fire. "Tomorrow we meet with Moraga."

"Again?" William frowned.

"I'd like to get my cock in *that* one's mouth, too." Geoffrey took a long swig from his flask.

"She's a witch." William shuddered. "I'd be afraid she'd turn it to stone."

"Could do worse." Geoffrey chuckled. "At least you'd always be hard and ready to please, eh?"

"She wouldn't touch either of you with a Maypole," Lord Eldred scoffed, shaking his head.

"Do we have to meet up with her?" William asked, hurrying on to explain when Lord Eldred gave him a speculative look. "I mean, can't you go alone? We're supposed to meet up with Sedgewick and Salt the day after tomorrow at the old well."

"Scared, young William?" Lord Eldred's eyes flashed, the corners of his mouth curving into a sly smile. "You know, lads, we wouldn't even have to be out here tonight if you hadn't lost the wulver party when they left with that book."

He knows about the book? Kirstin's heart raced in her chest, faster than when she was chasing rabbits. *How?* But of course, he'd been spying. She'd been so busy falling in love with Donal, she hadn't paid any attention to her instincts about Lord Eldred Lothienne.

She'd done nothing except avoid Lord Eldred, when she should have acted on her feelings. She realized, now far too late, that she should have insisted Donal be wary of the man. At the very least, have him watched.

"I have to get my hands on it," Eldred muttered, glowering into the fire.

"What's in it?" Goeffrey asked. "More witches magic?"

"I don't know. That's why I need to get my hands on it, you dolt," Lord Eldred snapped. "But mayhaps Moraga knows of it. At the very least, I can warn her they have it. Mayhaps she can counter whatever they learn from it, if it hinders our plans."

"Your plans, you mean."

"My plans are your plans, Captain." Lord Eldred gave Geoffrey a cool smile, standing and stretching. "Sleep well, lads. We'll see if we can find the she-bitch's trail in the morning. Then we'll meet up with Moraga."

"G'nite, m'lord," called Geoffrey and Lord Eldred slipped into his tent.

Kirstin watched the two captains until the fire burned low. They talked late into the night, about nothing important. She wanted to know more of how they planned to destroy the wulvers, needed to know as much as possible to relay it to Raife when she went back to the wulver den.

It was a dangerous gamble, but she decided she would have to follow them. At least until they met up with the other two men. She needed to know if the wulver den had been discovered. Once she knew that, she would return home and tell her pack they were in danger.

Kirstin shouldn't have expected Moraga to be an old woman, given how the young captains had talked about her, but for some reason, the sight of the shapely blonde shocked her. Moraga welcomed Lord Eldred alone—he'd sent the captains out to wait for Salt and Sedgewick. They weren't due until the morrow, but Eldred had set camp quite a ways from Moraga's cave, near the old MacFalon well. It wasn't until Kirstin saw the woman that she realized why.

The witch wrapped her arms around Lord Eldred's neck and the two of them kissed deeply. The man's hands roamed her English gown. He shoved one of them roughly down the front of it, but the woman didn't protest. Instead, she gave a loud moan, her hips bumping up against his.

Kirstin considered going back to Lord Eldred's camp to wait for Sedgewick and Salt. She had to know if they'd discovered her pack's den. If she was going to be subjected to nothing but the sexual escapades of Lord Eldred and his concubine by staying here, she would rather listen to the bragging and bravado of the two captains while they waited for their comrades to return.

"I take it ye missed me?" Moraga gave a low, throaty laugh when they parted. Her brogue was thick—she was clearly a Scotswoman, and not English, in spite of her dress. Eldred's hand was still stuck down in her cleavage, massaging her breast. Her eyes narrowed as she leaned back slightly in his arms, giving him better access down the front of her dress. "Ye weren't beddin' any wulvers, were ye?"

"Do I look like I have fleas?" Lord Eldred bent his head to kiss the tops of her breasts.

"Good." She gasped when he yanked the front of her dress down, exposing her to him. His mouth fell to suckling her nipple and she moaned. "Ye know I do'na mind ye sleepin' wit' other wenches—as long as ye bring me the good ones so we can share."

Lord Eldred chuckled, moving his mouth to her other nipple, his fingers working the first one. Kirstin's lip curled in disgust. She didn't want to see this. Her gaze skipped around the encampment, looking anywhere but at the kissing, petting couple. There was a pack horse and a riding horse tied nearby. Kirstin had been careful to stay downwind of them both. The woman's camp was surprisingly sumptuous and comfortable. She had a tent up outside the cave, along with a fire pit in front with an iron tripod, a cooking cauldron and table.

"Did ye find the wulver den, then?" Moraga asked. "Are we celebratin'?"

"Not yet." Eldred made a face. "We lost the first party over the creek. And that damned she-wolf has given me the slip all three times I've found and followed her trail."

"I thought ye were a famed wulver hunter?" She gave a throaty laugh when he bit her nipple.

"Mayhaps Sedgewick and Salt have had more luck," he said morosely. "There are no men alive who can track a wulver better than they can—except mayhaps myself. Most men don't even know the wulvers exist, let alone know how to follow them. And if a wulver doesn't want to be tracked, likely the Lord of the Great Hunt himself couldn't track them."

"So ye say." Moraga pulled away from him, covering herself.

"I do have something that will please you, mayhaps, even if I didn't get my hands on that book." Lord Eldred reached into the pack over his shoulder, pulling out a handful of silvermoon. Kirsten could smell it, even from where she stood at the edge of the wood.

"Silvermoon!" Moraga's eyes lit up with delight and she took the bunch from him. "I've ne'er seen it grow anywhere! And what book?"

The witch missed nothing. Kirstin watched the woman expertly bundle the silvermoon for hanging and drying on the little table.

"There was a book." Lord Eldred sighed. "The she-wolf found it snooping down in the first den."

"What first den?" Moraga's blonde head lifted as she looked up from her work.

"There is an ancient wulver den under the MacFalon tombs," Eldred informed her.

"The grotto of Asher and Ardis?" Moraga frowned, her hands slowing in their work. "Ye found the grotto? Where the silvermoon grows?"

"That's where this came from." He nodded at the leaves and branches in her hands. To Kirstin, it looked like he'd pulled a whole plant up by the roots! "That's where she found the book. Some ancient wulver text?"

"Not the Book of the Moon Wives?"

"Yes, that's it."

The witch hissed something under her breath. From a distance, even with her incredible hearing, Kirstin could only make out the word "prophecy," and something about a king with the blood of dragons in his eyes. Was she talking about the red wulver? It was an old prophecy, one that had been passed on to her from her mother, but Kirstin didn't know all of it.

Beitrus called him "the devil's savior," but she didn't know what that meant either. Who would want to save a devil?

"They have the book," Lord Eldred said. "But I don't think they know what it really is—or what to do with it."

The witch frowned. "Ye better hope they do'na find out."

"Why?" he asked. "What's in it?"

"The cure fer their cursc," she said simply. "Or so I'm told."

If Kirstin had been in human form, she would have gasped out loud, giving away her position. Instead, she just whined, a low, pained sound, even to her ears. She waited to be discovered, but Lord Eldred had his arms around the woman, massaging her breasts again through her gown, and the witch was too busy with the silvermoon to be paying attention to anything else.

The book held the cure to the curse? Kirstin could barely breathe. Was it really true?

She'd almost forgotten why she'd run away from her lover's arms in the first place, given everything she'd discovered in the past day or so. She'd escaped with the bleak hope that Laina and Sibyl had found the cure. Something that could give her control over her change once a month.

"Something that will turn wulvers to men?" Lord Eldred asked. "Permanently?"

"Aye." The witch agreed, working with the silvermoon again. "If'n ye b'lieve the legends. I did'na e'en think the book actually existed."

"Oh, it exists," he assured her.

"Did ye see't fer yerself?" the blonde asked, looking over her shoulder at him.

"No." He shook his head. "But my little bird did."

"Oh, was she a pretty lil bird?" The blonde inquired throatily, abandoning her work and turning in the man's arms to put hers around his neck.

"She sang very sweetly," he agreed with a grin. "Buxom little blonde. Reminded me a bit of you, but she was only about this tall, and had a fetching little gap between her teeth."

Gayle.

So that was who had been spying for him. Kirstin tried to remember what she'd said around the woman. She had definitely been there when Kirstin showed Laina the book. And she'd run straight to Lord Eldred Lothienne to tell him about it, the spying little wench. If Gayle had been in front of her, Kirstin would have torn her throat out without a second thought.

"And ye did not bring 'er to me?" Moraga pouted, disengaging herself from his embrace and turning back to her work on the table. "Ye know I hate't when ye do'na share yer toys."

"Mayhaps when this is done." He watched as she took out a curved-bladed dagger. Kirstin cocked her wolf's head, looking at its new-moon shape, the silver glinting. "And I'm sitting on the English throne, with you beside me. We can have any woman we want between us then."

"Aye." Her eyes glittered in the firelight. "And ye still 'ave t'king's trust?"

"I have them all eating out of the palm of my hand." Eldred chuckled, sounding quite pleased with himself. "King Henry's so distraught over Arthur's death, he's afraid of any threat to his throne. He even considered marrying Catherine of Aragon himself."

"She's jus' a child!" Moraga complained. "And she was a'ready married t'his son."

"He may still be considering the match. I don't know," Eldred replied. "But it was easy to convince him that the king of the wulvers was a threat to his line. Raife is his bastard, after all. He does have a claim."

"And The MacFalon?" The woman sharpened the blade on a whetstone. "He still trusts ye?"

"King Henry told him what I advised," Lord Eldred said. "The MacFalon believes England will honor the wolf pact. He has no idea how many wulver traps I've armed, hidden in his woods. I'm surprised the wulver party didn't run into one. Or that damned she-wolf I've been tracking..."

"And t'English king?" she asked, testing the sharpness of the blade on the side of her thumb. Bright red blood bloomed there. Kirstin could smell it. "He still b'lieves ye wanna kill t'wulvers?"

"Why would he think otherwise? That's what I told him," Lord Eldred scoffed. "Besides, no one hates the wulvers more than I do."

"I wish I could be there t'see't." She chuckled. "T'English king's goin' t'get quite a surprise when an army of wulvers kills 'is men and ye take 'is throne. "

"All of England will rejoice when the rightful heir to the throne sits upon it again." The man's spine straightened, making him even taller in the moonlight.

"Aye, the Tudors used the wulvers and stole the throne," the witch agreed, sucking on her thumb, licking off the blood. "Seems fittin' it'll be taken back t'same way."

"They're all conniving thieves, from the first Arthur on—first king of England, pulls a sword from a stone!" Eldred scoffed. "He had no right to it. Why do you think Henry's so afraid someone's going to take it from him? He knows it isn't his. It's mine."

"Aye," she agreed softly. "Ye fight fire wit' fire, enchantment wit' enchantment."

"I thank my ancestors for the day I met you, my devilish little witch." Lord Eldred put his arms around her waist from behind, pushing her long, corn-colored hair out of the way to kiss her neck.

"Ye've done good wit' the silvermoon, I mus' say. It'll do well to bind the spell," she said, tilting her head to accept his kisses. "As soon as I have t'wulver king's blood, we'll be able t'enchant the wulver army fer yer purposes. Then, they'll follow ye anywhere."

"Good." Lord Eldred slid his hands up to cup the woman's breasts again.

"The she-wolves will'na let them go so easily, ye know," she warned. "They're not warriors, but when they're changed, they're formidable. And I can'na compel t'females."

"I have no need for the women or the pups," he sneered. "My first order will be to have the warriors slaughter them all."

"Ye'll wanna keep one," she suggested. "T'continue t'line?"

"No." He frowned. "Once I have the throne, I'll have no need for the wulver army. We'll dispose of them."

"Ye do not wanna keep them locked up somewhere at t'ready?" she asked. "T'defend yer right to the crown?"

"Mayhaps," he mused, thoughtful. Then he chuckled, dipping his head to gnaw at her neck. "You are an evil wench. I love the way your mind works."

Kirstin watched the woman waving her blade over the silvermoon, incanting something softly in Gaelic. Then she turned in his arms, arching her back, knife still in hand.

"Bare m'breasts, Lord Eldred."

He grinned. "As you wish."

He yanked her already low-cut gown down, letting her large breasts spill free. His mouth went to them immediately, but the witch was impatient.

"Now ye," she insisted. "Take off yer shirt."

Lord Eldred complied, pulling his shirt over his head and tossing it aside. The man was still heavily muscled and the blonde eyed him greedily. Kirstin cringed, knowing she was going to have to witness their lovemaking. But what happened next surprised her.

The witch expertly used the curved blade, tracing the edge over her skin, a line of blood swelling between her breasts, over her heart. She did the same to Lord Eldred. The man didn't even wince.

Kirstin watched as Moraga tipped the blade with their mingled blood, letting it drip onto the bundle of silvermoon that shone, luminescent, in the moonlight. Then she hung it over the fire, the blood falling in fat droplets, sizzling into the flames.

Eldred grabbed Moraga to him, the red liquid on their chests mingling as they kissed in the firelight. Kirstin could smell their blood, coppery and bright. It made her hungry and she considered making a meal of them both. Who would know? She could end Eldred and his line right here, prevent any magic, if there was such a thing, that might compel the wulvers. But it was possible the other two, Sedgewick and Salt, already knew the way to her den.

And Moraga's knife was still close, on the table. Even distracted, Lord Eldred was a formidable foe. What if he managed to slip the blade between Kirstin's ribs before her teeth grazed his neck? If she was dead in the forest, she couldn't warn Raife and her pack of Eldred's arrival. No, she couldn't risk it. She would have to wait for Sedgewick and Salt to arrive on the morrow to find out if they'd discovered the wulver den.

Then, and only then, could she go home.

Kirstin curled her lip in a snarl, although no sound came from her throat, as she watched Lord Eldred put the naked woman up on the table. She had a beautiful body, lush curves and big breasts. Moraga reclined, wrapping her full thighs around him as he stood between them to enter her. Even this sick, twisted display made her think of and miss Donal and their lovemaking. Her estrus was fading, like the waning moon above their heads, but she still wanted him.

Moraga cried out, arching as Lord Eldred began to move, thrusting hard and fast. He leaned over to kiss her, his chest wound, just a scratch, rubbing against hers. Again, Kirstin smelled their blood, still dripping into the fire from the luminescent silvermoon, and from the open gashes on their torsos.

"Taste me." Moraga brought the man's face down to her breast and Eldred gave a low moan as she rubbed his cheeks over her wound, spreading blood like war paint. Their fingers played in the sticky liquid, and they left bloody fingerprints on one another, wherever they touched or grabbed.

Moraga's fingernails raked over the man's chest, making him hiss and cry out. She opened the wound, which had begun to coagulate, watching rivulets of blood run down his ridged abdomen.

"You witch," he growled, quickly withdrawing. He grabbed her hips and rolled her onto her belly on the table, entering her again, this time from behind. He began to rut into her, deep and hard, grunting with every thrust.

Kirstin cringed, watching the woman licking the curved blade still sitting on the table, cleaning it of their blood. She could plainly see the witch's face, her eyes glittering in the firelight.

"M'Lord," Moraga murmured, putting the knife down and gripping the sides of the table. Her voice came in a staccato, broken by Eldred's pounding thrusts. "We're bein' watched."

Kirstin froze. She was right across from them, at the edge of the woods, but surely, she was in the shadows. The witch couldn't possibly see her!

"I don't care," he sneered, but his gaze moved up from his lover's body to scan the tree line. "You should be used to it by now. Besides, my men have their hands to keep them company, if they want to watch—or they can buggar each other for all I care."

Moraga moved so quickly Kirstin barely saw it happen. One moment she was splayed on the table, helpless on her belly, being plundered by Lord Eldred, and the next she was up. Her nude body was sheened with sweat in the firelight as she stood beside the bewildered man who had been so recently inside of her.

"Look," Moraga hissed, turning Eldred's face in Kirstin's direction. *"See."*

She can't see me. Kirstin was sure of it. Neither of them could. But the witch sensed something.

And then, so did Kirstin. She caught their scent. Two men—not Geoffrey and William, she knew their smells by now. It had to be Salt and Sedgewick. She didn't know, not for sure, but she wasn't going to stick around to find out.

Lord Eldred made some bird call, signaling with his hands, and she felt them moving in on her, one from each direction, on either side. It scared her that she hadn't heard their approach. She should have been able to track them.

Kirstin froze, paralyzed, hearing a branch crack to her left, the barest rustle of underbrush on her right. She didn't know if they had arrows pointed at her.

She heard an arrow being knocked. Her heart hammered in her chest and she crouched, low to the ground. That's when she saw the silver glint in the moonlight. Her mind didn't want to see it, didn't want to accept that she was watching the curved, silver blade, still stained with blood, spinning in the light of the fire, two feet above the table it had been sitting on.

The witch was whispering something. Incantations. Kirstin couldn't hear the words, but it was clear, Moraga was controlling the blade. Before she knew what was happening, the knife was sailing through the air, all on its own, heading for Kirstin in the woods.

Lord Eldred made that sound again, more signals to his men, but the blade was faster. She knew she couldn't avoid it, although she'd already turned sideways to run along the tree line, thinking she'd take her chances with whatever archer was trying to shoot an arrow at her in the dark.

The blade was enchanted, and it was headed straight for her.

Kirstin went low, as low as she possibly could, nearly flattening herself against the dirt, limbs splayed. The blade was traveling so fast it whistled past her ears. The curved half-moon grazed her fur, and she felt it zing across her back, piercing her flesh. She could smell her own blood, but she didn't have any idea how bad the wound was.

The knife hit a tree somewhere behind her with a sick thunking sound, quivering like a tuning fork. That sound didn't stop, though—in fact, it got worse—and that's when Kirstin realized... *the blade was trying to pull itself free.* And once it did, the enchanted knife would come for her again. Follow her until it found its mark.

Terrified, Kirstin heard the archer's arrow whistle past her, just as she rolled deeper into the woods, shaking herself to her feet. But it didn't pierce her flesh.

The knife was singing in the tree, its hilt wiggling back and forth like the back end of a fish. Kirstin heard the archer cock another arrow, but she was gone, running faster than she ever had in her life, before he could draw his bow.

Chapter Nine

Lorien was one of the scouts on duty, and Kirstin was relieved to see his big, hulking black form as she neared the edges of the familiar forest. She was exhausted from running. Her sides ached with it. But still, she followed him in with a new burst of speed. Two more scouts caught their scent—must have smelled her urgency—and followed them to the hidden entrance of their mountain den. Lorien growled at the sentry, but the half-wolf, half-man standing guard knew her well. She'd been at the birth of two of his mate's pups.

Once they were free in the tunnels, Kirstin ran again, Lorien loping along beside her, giving her concerned, sidelong glances. She knew he could smell her fear. She could smell it herself. She'd never been so scared in all her life. She meant to head straight for Raife—it was early morning, and he was likely already out in the valley, starting the day's training exercises—but when she heard Sibyl's voice, she stopped.

"Laina, I will not allow it. No! Do not ask me again!" Sibyl cried. The voice came, not from the rooms her *banrighinn* shared with Raife, but from the one Laina shared with Darrow.

Kirstin stopped at the doorway, nosing the door all the way open, and saw Laina sitting by the fire, nursing her bairn. Garaith waved his chubby fist in the air, kicking his bare feet, suckling happily. Sibyl sat opposite them in a chair of her own, and she glanced up as Kirstin appeared at the entrance.

"Yes, Lorien?" Sibyl asked, glancing down at Kirstin, and for a moment, she saw her *banrighinn* didn't recognize her. But Laina did.

"Kirstin!" Laina cried, jumping up, her nipple popping out of a very unhappy Garaith's mouth. She quickly gave the protesting baby to Sibyl, covering herself as she rushed toward her sister-wolf. Laina grabbed a blanket off the bed, wrapping Kirstin in it as she began to change. She hadn't tried, not since her estrus, but it wasn't any more difficult than ever before.

"Thank you, Lorien." Sibyl smiled at the dark wolf who stood behind them. "We'll take it from here."

He gave a short bark and a whine, but then turned, and headed back toward the tunnel entrance. Back to sentry duty, no doubt, Kirstin thought. She'd have to thank him later, for bringing her in. If she got the opportunity. She shivered at that thought, putting her newly formed arms around Laina and letting her help her stand.

"You're a mess." Sibyl bounced the hungry Garaith on her hip, trying to quiet him. "Are you hurt? Is that dried blood?"

Kirstin glanced behind her, where the blanket had dropped low on her back, and saw where the blade had streaked across her skin.

"Aye." She had her voice back. What a relief that was! "Sibyl, ye hafta t'take me t'Raife. They're coming. They're goin' t'kill us all."

"Who? What?" Sibyl put the baby up over her shoulder, patting his back.

"Lord Eldred's a traitor to the king," Kirstin accepted the long shirt Laina put over her head. "He plans t'use some sorta witchcraft t'compel t'wulver army t'take t'English throne. I heard 'im. And I saw 'er. The witch."

She shuddered at the memory.

"You're not making any sense." Sibyl handed Laina the baby, who was happy to be back with his mother. "Witchcraft? Kirstin, why are you here? I thought, you and Donal—"

The mention of his name made Kirstin burst into tears. She was exhausted, panicked, grief-stricken, and so afraid, she wasn't sure anymore which way was up. For all she knew, she'd been tracked to the wulver den. She didn't think so—and the scouts were always watching—but she'd been in such a hurry to get home. She couldn't be sure. And, mayhaps, Sedgewick and Salt had already found the den. Mayhaps they were following, even now.

"Ye've t'listen t'me," Kirstin sobbed, pulling the blanket Laina had given her more fully around her. She was cold, hungry, tired, but those things could wait. "Please. Take me t'Raife. Take me t'Darrow. I'll tell 'em everythin'. But I do'na wanna t'have t'say it twice."

"A'righ', we'll take ye to 'em," Laina soothed. "But firs' let's get ye cleaned up and dressed, mayhaps feed ye, and we can talk—"

"There's no time!" Kirstin howled, tears streaked down her face. "They're goin' t'kill ye all. The women, the children—they're goin' t'kill them first. Yer baby, Laina. They're goin' t'kill yer baby. Yer son, Sibyl, the one ye carry in yer belly. They'll cut it out and gut ye like a fish."

She made her language as horrible and her images as vivid as she possibly could. It worked. Sibyl went pale, her hand moving to her still flat belly.

"Kirstin, you're scaring me," Sibyl whispered, meeting Laina's big eyes and they both looked back to Kirstin. Garaith was wailing now, as if he'd picked up on the energy in the room.

"Ye should be scared. I'm terrified. And the wors' part is—I do'na know if we can stop them," Kirstin confessed hoarsely. The weight of her words felt like an avalanche of rock falling over her head, burying her. "Where's yer mate? Where's Raife? Where's my *righ*?"

Righ—her king. If anyone knew what to do, how to keep them safe, it would be Raife.

"He's in the kitchen," Sibyl said. Her lips barely moved. It was like she was frozen. "They're restringing the bows today..."

With that, Kirstin was off, tearing down the tunnels barefoot, wearing just a shirt, the blanket wrapped around her shoulders trailing behind her like a plaid cape. She didn't even stop to see if they were following her.

Raife was far easier to convince than Sibyl and Laina had been.

He and Darrow listened to it all without comment, her whole story, from the time she'd run away from the castle, to the time Lorien had scouted her and brought her into the den. Sibyl sat beside Laina on one of the long kitchen benches, the two women grasping hands. Sibyl was so pale by the time Kirstin was done with her story, her freckles stood out on her cheeks like constellations. She sat with her hand over her belly, and Kirstin knew she was thinking about the bairn she carried. Kirstin was thinking about all of them—all of the bairns, and their mothers.

Her pack. Her family. The last of their kind.

They all stood, gathered around, to hear Kirstin's story, and they all looked to Raife to see what to do. Their leader was quiet, thoughtful, and it was Darrow who spoke first.

"We hafta barricade ourselves in," Darrow urged. "Seal off both exits."

"If we do that, we're sealin' our own tomb." Raife shook his head.

"Donal will protect us," Kirstin insisted. It was the only thing she could think of—and not just because she wanted to go back to the MacFalon castle. "If we go t'him, he'll protect the wulvers. I know he will."

"The wolf pact doesn't exist," Darrow scoffed. "We can'na trust The MacFalon."

"He loves me," Kirstin assured him. Even though she'd left him, she knew this was true. "And he'll honor t'wolf pact wit' his life, no matter what t'English king says."

"Ye said his bride is on t'way," Raife reminded her, frowning. "And King Henry did'na grant the dispensation."

"It will'na matter;" Kirstin assured him. "He'll do it, because he loves me. He'll do it because he cares about all t'wulvers. He will'na wanna see anythin' bad happen t'any of us."

Raife considered this.

"There's plenty of room at the castle... or..." She bit her lip, the idea just coming to her. "Raife, we could go down into t'first den. Our numbers aren't as great as they once were. We don't take up half this mountain anymore. There's enough room in t'first den t'house e'eryone..."

"If we can'na barricade ourselves in, we can face 'em," Darrow countered. "Whoever comes—no man can stand against a wulver warrior."

"Can a wulver warrior stand in the face of magic?" Kirstin asked softly, glancing between Raife and Darrow.

"Nuh magic spell can compel me," Darrow sneered, rolling his eyes. "D'ye really think we'd follow anyone, simply because a witch said some silly words over some silvermoon? She threw a knife at ye and scared ye, 'tis all…"

Kirstin swallowed, looking at Sibyl and Laina, seeing a knowing in their eyes. Men were always doubtful of witchcraft, either afraid of it because they didn't understand or like its power, or distrustful and doubtful. Darrow had always been the latter, even though Laina's belief they could break the wulver-woman's curse was dependent on the idea of magic.

Raife looked at his brother, frowning, then at Kirstin, who stood as tall as she could in her plaid blanket, speaking up so everyone could hear her.

"I assure ye, there *is* a witch," she insisted. "She did'na throw a knife at me, Darrow. She ne'er touched it. It wasn't in 'er hand. It jus'… flew."

Raife was listening—and that was good.

"It grazed me, *Righ*. Look." Kirsten turned, dropping the blanket, pulling her shirt down in back to reveal her wound. "But it did'na stop there. The knife wobbled back and forth in the bark, like this."

She showed them with her hand, mimicking a fish's movement through the water.

"If it had'na hit the tree with such force, I think it would've pulled instantly free and found me heart." She swallowed at the memory. "I'm tellin' ye,

Darrow—that blade was tryin' t'pull itself out so it could finish the job…"

"It was enchanted, *Righ.*" She turned her pleas back to Raife's receptive ears. Darrow just scoffed and rolled his eyes. He was a man who could turn into a half-wolf, and yet he doubted the existence of magic? The strangeness of it almost made her want to laugh.

"It would take days to gather everyone, to pack them all, and at least that long to reach the MacFalon castle," Sibyl said, putting a hand on her husband's arm. "We'd be giving Donal no warning and—"

"We do'na have time." Kirstin interrupted her with a shake of her dark head. "We need t'go. *Now.* We can'na wait. We can'na stay. We hafta go, and we hafta go *now.*"

"Raife, we can't just leave everything..." Sibyl glanced nervously at Kirstin, and then back at her husband. "Aren't we safe here, in the mountain?"

Kirstin saw doubt pass over Raife's face, and he looked at Sibyl. He wanted to tell her they were safe, that they could stay. Kirstin saw that much in his eyes. He wanted to give his mate what she wanted, and Sibyl didn't want to leave. This was the place she called home now, and the fact that she was with child made her all the more protective of her territory.

"Aye." Raife nodded slowly, touching Sibyl's cheek.

"No!" Kirstin cried, ignoring the dark look in Raife's eyes at her protest. "D'you know what yer sayin'? What yer riskin'?"

She'd thought of nothing else, on her run through the woods. She'd seen images in her mind of slaughter and death, the wulver warriors slaying their own mates, their own children, the tunnels in the mountain running with rivers of blood. She couldn't let that happen.

"Kirstin, we're glad ye told us," Darrow said, sighing. "Now we can be prepared if they try t'get in. But y'know nothin' of—"

"Raife, please," she pleaded, ignoring Darrow's words, ignoring the way the wulver warriors agreed with him, nodding their heads. Had the witch's magic already started to work, then? Were they already being compelled? That thought made her blood turn to ice in her veins. "She's powerful, this Moraga. I do'na think her name's any accident. It was Morag who killed Ardis, the first she-wulver. Do ye n'remember the legend?"

"More legends, more magic!" Darrow threw up his hands.

"She's goin' t'compel ye." Kirstin knew it was hard to believe. She wouldn't have believed it herself if she hadn't seen the witch's blade fly through the air all on its own, if she hadn't seen it struggling to free itself from the tree. What could she do to convince them? "Jus' like she did the blade. Lord Eldred's goin' t'use e'ery one of ye to his own ends. But first, he's goin' t'have ye kill yer women, yer children."

"Yer goin' t'draw yer sword on yer mate, Darrow." Kirstin couldn't keep the tears from falling down her cheeks as she looked at her sister-wolf, Laina, and little Garaith, happily suckling at her breast once more. "Yer gonna slit yer own bairn's throat. Is that what ye want?"

"Enough!" Raife said roughly as a small sob escaped Sibyl's throat, her hands low on her belly. "Kirstin, enough! I know y're afeared, but—"

“The wulver mountain’ll run wit’ blood,” she choked. “Ye think ye can’na be compelled, ye think y’re invincible, that ye’d ne’er hurt the ones ye love—but I swear t’ye, if’n we do’na act now, e’ery woman and bairn here’ll fall under yer own swords.”

“Kirstin, please.” Laina’s voice shook as she looked down at the baby in her arms and then at her sister. “Ye’ve been traveling long, ye’re wounded, mayhaps feverish—”

“No.” She shook her head, realizing her arguments were falling on deaf ears. They couldn’t believe it, couldn’t imagine it. Darrow’s doubt was feeding all of them, she could feel it, and they were all going to perish because they thought their mountain den was safe harbor.

The problem was, the danger would come from within, not without. Every wulver warrior would take up a sword and hack his family to bits before mounting a war horse and riding out of the mountain to fulfil Lord Eldred’s demands.

Then, she realized—there was only one wulver she had to convince.

She turned to Raife, her mouth trembling. It was hard to talk through her own, choked sobs. Kirstin sank to her knees before him, taking his big hand in both of her small ones.

“*Righ*,” she whispered, kissing the brown, scarred knuckles, tasting the salt of her own tears. “Please. Think of yer mate. Think of Sibyl.”

She turned her tear-streaked face up to his, seeing the love in his eyes, not just for his mate, but for all of them. His pack. His family. She said the only other thing she could think of that might motivate him to action.

"Think of yer unborn child," she pleaded. "Do'ye nuh wanna see 'im grow into a man?"

Raife stared at her, unblinking, but she saw the confusion pass over his face, saw the realization dawn slowly in his eyes as he shifted his gaze to his wife. Murmurs went through the wulver crowd gathered around them, and Kirstin understood what she'd just done.

"Me... what?" Raife asked, his lips barely moving.

"Ye didn't tell 'im yet?" Kirstin bit her lip, glancing at her *banrighinn*.

Sibyl sighed, giving Kirstin a dark look and shaking her red head.

"Yer wit child?" Raife grabbed his mate's shoulders, turning her fully to him.

"Aye," Sibyl admitted with a small smile.

The wulvers around them cheered. It was a brief moment of celebration in what had been a dark morning.

"How long've ye known?" Raife murmured into her hair, pulling her into his arms.

Kirstin stood, smiling through her tears as she watched them together. She would never have this moment with the man she loved, and that cut through her, sharper than the half-moon blade could have ever pierced her heart.

"Since before we left MacFalon land. But I didn't want to tell you then, you were so mad at me," Sibyl confessed, laughing when Raife pulled her into his arms, right off her feet.

"If ye'd told me, I would'na been mad anymore!" he exclaimed.

"But I wouldn't have known that it was me you really wanted, then, would I?"

"Och." Raife rolled his eyes. "I should spank ye right here and now."

"Can we postpone the spankings until we get to Castle MacFalon?" Kirstin asked, looking between her *righ* and *banrighinn.*

"Aye." Raife had Sibyl pulled so close to him, he was nearly crushing her. Not that she seemed to mind. "Ye win, Kirstin. We'll go."

Murmurs went through the crowd, some doubt. Darrow groaned and smacked his forehead. But he relented. Raife had made a decision, and they would follow him.

"I'm sure Donal would be happy t'schedule a public floggin' fer me and another fer Sibyl if ye wanted one," Kirstin said happily, grinning at him. "I do'na really care, as long as we're all away from 'ere when that witch and 'er consort show up."

"Aye," Raife agreed, speaking now to the whole pack. "Take only what ye can carry. We'll go on horseback. We'll take the horses through the mountain—it's faster—women paired up wit' men. Strap your bairns and wee ones to yer back or yer belly. We leave in one hour."

They were the last to leave the den.

Raife had to make sure every wulver was on a horse or had a traveling companion, every last bairn strapped in. The younglings rode in front of or behind their parents. They strapped what they could to the horses and left the sheep in the valley. The last time they'd brought the horses through the mountain, the wulver warriors had been riding them in full armor. They'd thundered down the high, wide mountain tunnels, the sound of the horses' hooves echoing off the walls, trembling the earth, leaving their mates and young behind. That's when the wulver army had gone to confront the MacFalons, to rescue Laina and save Sibyl.

This time, the war horses whinnied and pawed the ground as they plodded along, impatient to be off, weighed down not by armor but blankets and women and children, as well as their wulver warriors. Once out of the mountain, they rode slowly into the woods, single file. There were too many of them to travel too fast, although Kirstin's heart raced with urgency, her body trembling. She wanted them to be off, to ride fast and furious to the MacFalon castle, to be safe, already.

"The den's empty." Darrow rode toward them—Raife and Sibyl, Lorien and Kirstin—where they waited at the den entrance, Laina on his saddle in front of him, little Garaith strapped across her front. "'Tis time t'go."

Raife stood by his steed, holding the reins. Sibyl was already seated in the saddle. Raife gave Darrow a nod and mounted his horse, sliding in behind Sibyl, who had tears streaking down her freckled cheeks. Raife tenderly kissed the top of her head, slipping an arm around her waist, his big hand covering her belly, rubbing gently. "We'll make a new home, lass. T'will be a'righ'."

Kirstin was the only one left on the ground. She mounted Lorien's steed, allowing him to give her a hand up, settling in front of him. Laina had loaned her a plaid and a pair of boots to go along with her shirt. She felt Lorien's steadying arm go around her. The top of her head only came to the bottom of the big man's chin.

They rode slowly, silently, out of the den for the last time. Kirstin leaned back against Lorien, feeling sad, deflated. What if she was wrong? What if Lord Eldred's men hadn't found the location of the den after all? What if Darrow was right, and they were safer staying, instead of running? She doubted herself, but she also trusted her instincts. Something had told her she had to get home, she had to warn them. They had to go—now. Before something horrible happened.

The tail end of the wulver riders were out ahead of them by a ways. Kirsten glimpsed a toddler strapped to his father's big back. The little towhead was smiling, waving at them, and Kirstin waved back, her heart lightening. Even if she was wrong, it was better to be safe than sorry. All of the wulver women she'd tended, all the bairns that had been born, would be safe at Castle MacFalon before nightfall. They would all be under Donal's protection, and she knew he would defend them, no matter what the English king had in mind. She had no idea how many men Donal could call in from the surrounding clans, but if it meant war... would he go that far? She thought he would.

For her, he would.

The thought of seeing Donal again made her heart race even faster. He would be furious with her for leaving, of course, but he'd forgive her. Raife had forgiven Sibyl, in the end, hadn't he? She wondered if Lady Cecilia Witcombe had arrived at Castle MacFalon yet. That thought made her hackles rise. She'd almost forgotten the reason she'd left the castle in the first place.

The book...

Sibyl had it, strapped to her, across her breasts, like a baby. It was that precious, Kirstin supposed. It contained the cure to their curse, somewhere inside of it. Mayhaps, when they were at the castle, Sibyl could work more on a solution. Kirstin hadn't had the time to ask her about it, in the hurry to get everyone ready to ride.

Kirstin straightened as three riders came barreling toward them, doubling back.

"'Tis jus' the scouts," Lorien assured her softly when she stiffened in the saddle. "Comin' in t'report t'Raife."

She nodded, seeing them pull up next to his horse, turning and riding alongside him, one on either side, another slipping in behind. Raife consulted with both wulvers, nodding at their report. Kirstin could only see him in profile as he turned to talk to them and she tried to judge if he looked worried, but his face was impassive.

Raife said something to the three scouts and they dropped back, letting him ride into the lead. Kirstin relaxed. Nothing to worry about then. She was so exhausted, she thought she might collapse and fall off the horse, if Lorien didn't have an arm around her waist. But she couldn't sleep. She was too tense, too wired.

They weren't fifteen minutes out from the den when it happened.

The only warning she had was that Kirstin felt Lorien straighten in his saddle.

"E'erythin' a'righ'?" she asked, but it happened so fast, the wulver didn't have time to answer her.

Someone dropped from a tree above, right onto Raife's horse. He wasn't a big man, but he had the advantage of surprise. And he had a knife. The man jabbed it into expertly into Raife's side, between his ribs, unseating the big wulver. The horse bucked and nearly threw Sibyl and the stranger, but the man was able to hang on, grabbing the reins and urging the animal forward.

Kirstin screamed. She heard Sibyl screaming, calling for Raife, but the war horse was already tearing through the woods. Kirstin was shocked by the horse's behavior—but then she realized the man was wearing something on his boots, something sharp he dug into the horse's flanks.

Raife had already transformed to wulver warrior, and behind her, so had Lorien. They barked orders, snapped at each other, the scouting warriors already racing after the runaway horse, with Sibyl and the stranger atop.

Darrow barked something to Lorien about keeping the women safe, leaving Laina and his bairn with him. Kirstin climbed down from the horse, putting her arms around Laina and Garaith, still not understanding what was happening.

Darrow and Raife wasted time fighting, snarling at one another, and Lorien threw Kirstin the reins of his horse, stepping in to help Darrow restrain their wulver pack leader. It took the two of them, snapping and circling, to keep the big wulver from going after Sibyl straightaway.

Raife howled, a sound so full of anguish and pain it echoed through the woods, and Kirstin knew it had nothing to do with the wound in his side.

The rest of the pack had heard and were doubling back toward them.

Kirstin realized, far too late, screaming at Raife, "No! Ye can'na go after 'er! Yer what they want! They need yer blood!"

But they already had it, didn't they?

The man had slipped a knife between Raife's ribs and had run off with Sibyl.

It wasn't Sibyl they wanted, though, Kirstin realized.

It was the book strapped to her chest.

This is my fault, she thought, watching in horror as Raife got free and pulled his sword, threatening his own brother with it if Darrow kept him from pursuing their attackers.

This is all my fault.

They'd been waiting for them, she realized. Mayhaps they knew Kirstin would run straight back to the den with her escape plan, leading Raife out into the open where they could get what they needed to take back to the witch. But Darrow was right after all. They would have been safer staying in the den.

Raife took off—Darrow and Lorien couldn't hold him—running after Sibyl. Lorien stayed, on Darrow's orders, but Darrow went after his brother. Kirstin looked at Laina, tears streaked down her face, and felt her own tears wetting her cheeks. Little Garaith howled between them.

"'Tis all m'fault," Kirstin sobbed against her sister's shoulder as the wulver pack began to gather around them on horseback. "They've got 'is blood, Laina. 'Tis all they needed."

"Shhhh." Laina stroked her hair, comforting both Kirstin and her bairn at once.

Kirstin couldn't bear it. She'd led them straight to the wulver den, had put everyone in danger in the hopes of trying to save them. She sobbed in Laina's arms, wishing the earth would open up and swallow her whole. If anything happened to Sibyl, or Raife, or any of her family, because of what she'd done, she knew she could never forgive herself.

"Kirstin," Laina whispered, shaking her gently. "Look!"

Kirstin lifted her head, blinking through her tears, seeing Raife carrying Sibyl in his arms. Darrow followed on foot, and Laina broke away from Kirstin to meet her husband, putting her arms around him. Both wulvers were men again.

"Is she hurt?" Kirstin barely got the words out as Raife approached. Sibyl was, at the very least, unconscious, her body limp.

"He took the book." Raife blinked down at the woman in his arms. "Then he pushed 'er off m'horse."

"No," Kirstin whispered, her hands already moving over Sibyl's inert form, looking for broken bones. "She's alive, Raife. She'll be a'righ', here, put 'er on the ground, I'll—"

And that's when Kirstin saw the blood. Sibyl's plaid was all greens and blues, but there was a dark spot on it that was growing by the moment. She didn't say anything about it to Raife as he knelt, gently depositing Sibyl's body on the forest floor.

"Where's t'attacker?" Lorien growled as Darrow approached. Raife and Darrow were transformed into men again, but Lorien was still half-man, half-wolf, prepared for battle.

"They went after 'im." Darrow jerked his head toward the woods, Laina and his bairn drawn into one arm, his sword drawn in the other.

Lorien, now freed up from having to protect Kirstin and Laina, took off on his horse, barking to three more scouts to join him, so there were now seven out pursuing the man.

"She was thrown from the horse," Kirstin told Laina as the two women bent over Sibyl. Kirstin was sure there were no broken bones, at least any she could feel. Raife watched them work over her, his eyes full of fire.

"I think she may be losin' the bairn," Laina whispered to Kirstin. They both saw the blood on her thighs, the way her plaid was twisted, high up on her legs.

Raife heard them and closed his eyes, his head going back with a long, sustained howl. It made gooseflesh rise all over Kirstin's body as Laina ran to Darrow's horse, unpacking blankets and what medicine she could find.

"I've got black haw and cramp bark." Beitrus made her way to the front of the crowd. The old woman, who had taught Kirstin everything she knew, held out two vials. "It may save the pup."

"Thank ye." Kirstin uncapped one and poured it past Sibyl's lips. The woman coughed at the sudden introduction of liquid into her mouth and Raife grabbed her to him, ignoring their protests.

"Sibyl," he whispered, holding her close. "Can ye hear me? Are ye a'righ'?"

"I'll be fine," she gasped, her eyes opening wide. "If you quit crushing me, you beast!"

Raife chuckled at that, rocking her against his chest, bringing her face to his so he could kiss her.

Sibyl sobbed when she realized she was bleeding. Laina, Kirstin and Beitrus all worked to reassure her that the bairn was likely fine, that bleeding happened sometimes, and they'd done everything they could to help them both.

Kirstin hoped their reassurances turned out to be true. The bleeding did seem to be ebbing, and Sibyl was awake, and coherent. Laina tended Raife's wound—it was superficial, not deep at all. Whoever had slipped the knife in had known exactly what he was doing, and hadn't been aiming for anything vital.

Of course, not—they want him to be able to fight.

They only wanted his blood...

Sibyl finally calmed, but didn't want to get on Raife's horse, when Lorien returned with him. But without the attacker. Or the book.

"What if it hurts the baby?" Sibyl sobbed. "What if I start bleeding again?"

They spent time reassuring her, giving her sips of water, waiting for the tonics to work. It helped stop the blood, and that was a good sign, Kirstin assured her.

Darrow and Raife talked together, low and out of earshot, with Lorien.

"Can't we stay here now?" Sibyl suggested, as Raife came over to get her, lifting her easily off the ground. "In the den? Isn't it the safest place? We can block the exits, like Darrow said, we can—"

"No, lass." Raife pressed his lips to her forehead. "'Tis no longer safe, if they know where the den is. We have to ride to the MacFalon castle."

"I'm scared," Sibyl told him, burying her face against his neck.

"Aye." Raife mounted his horse, pulling Sibyl with him, settling her side saddle. Lorien had tended the animal's wounds, from whatever the stranger had been digging into its sides, with a balm Kirstin gave him.

"I haven't ridden side-saddle in years," she told him, pressing her cheek to his chest.

“Aye, but Kirstin says ’tis safest for t’bairn.” He kissed the top of her head. “We’ll go slow.”

Raife sent the rest of the pack on ahead, toward the castle. They would bring up the rear.

“D’ye want me t’stay ’ere and wait fer t’scouts?” Lorien asked them.

“Ye should ride wit’ us,” Darrow told him, getting on his horse behind Laina and the baby. “We may need ye if they return fer Raife again.”

“They won’t,” Kirstin said miserably as Lorien gave her a hand up onto his mount. ”They a’ready ’ave e’erythin’ they need.”

She scanned the woods as they began to ride, taking it slow, as Raife had promised, hoping, praying, the scouts would catch up to the thief before he could make it back to his camp to give the book and the knife to the waiting witch and her wicked consort.

Chapter Ten

"Where is she?"

Kirstin heard his voice before she saw him. She was leaning back against Lorien, his arm the only thing keeping her from falling face first out of the saddle, drifting in and out of nightmares that would occasionally jolt her awake with a start. It was full dark by the time their little party reached the castle—they'd had to travel much slower than the others—but a large bonfire had been lit out front to guide them in.

Donal's voice came to her out of a dream. She thought she must be dreaming when he lifted her down from the saddle, scowling at the wulver who held her close, and kissed her so long and deeply she could barely catch her breath.

"I do'na wanna wake up," she whispered against his shoulder as he put an arm under her knees and carried her into the castle.

"Shh." Donal's arms tightened as he took the stairs with her in his arms, two at a time.

Moira followed them, clucking over Kirstin as Donal put her on the bed. Now she was sure she was dreaming, because nothing had ever been so soft. She must be in heaven, in the clouds, warm under the sun.

"Sibyl!" Kirstin came awake, sitting bolt upright in the bed. "Raife! Where is e'eryone? Donal, ye hafta keep 'em safe! You hafta—!"

"Easy, lass." Donal undressed her like a child. "E'eryone's safe as they can be."

"Sibyl's bleedin'." Kirstin tried to clear the fuzz from her head. She was so tired. She must still be dreaming, she reasoned. "Someone attacked Raife... they stabbed him. Donal, oh, 'tis all m'fault."

"Shhh." He eased her shirt over her head. Someone was knocking hard on the locked door. "'Tisn't yer fault. None of it."

He picked her up, completely nude now, and carried her over to a bath in front of the big fireplace, placing her into the warm water. He looked at her for a moment, dark hair floating, and she stared at him as if in a dream. Surcly, it was. He couldn't be here, touching her, undressing her, leaning in to cup her face and kiss her like he thought he might never see her again.

"MacFalon!" It was Raife, pounding on the door.

"Keep her 'ere," Donal told Moira, who knelt beside the tub with a washing cloth. "Do'na let 'er outta yer sight. I'll be righ 'back."

Donal unlocked the door and slipped out into the hallway, closing it behind him.

"Moira, 'tis all m'fault," Kirstin lamented, as the old woman began to wash her hair. "I led them straight to t'den. I was such a fool. Are t'wulvers all 'ere?"

"Oh, aye, lass," Moira assured, rinsing her hair with a bucket of warm water. "Most of 'em have camped out on m'kitchen floor in front of the fireplace."

Kirstin smiled at that, but it faded as soon as she remembered.

"He got away. He stabbed Raife, and took t'book, and he got away..." She covered her face with her hands.

"The wulver scouts brought 'em in an hour ago," Donal told her as he came back into the room. "We've got t'book."

"And the knife?" Kirstin gripped the edge of the tub, looking up at him with big eyes. She'd been able to think of nothing else since, memories of the witch flitting through her mind. "With Raife's blood?"

"Aye, m'love." He stroked her hair away from her face. "The wulver scouts brought back four men. Geoffrey, William, and two others."

"Salt and Sedgewick." She shuddered, remembering the way they'd tracked her in the woods, how they'd come up on her out of nowhere. She was sure, now, that they'd been the 'poachers' who they'd come upon in the forest that very first day. They'd been Lord Eldred's men all along, hiding and doing his bidding. "What about Lord Eldred and the witch, Moraga?"

"Moira, lemme finish up 'ere," Donal said, taking the soap and washing cloth from the old woman. "Can ye bring us up some food?"

"Aye," she agreed happily, getting up from the floor and heading to the door.

"Did they catch 'em?" Kirstin asked again, desperate for an answer.

"N'yet." Donal shook his head, rubbing soap over the washing cloth and pushing up his sleeves as he knelt near the tub. "I've got me men out lookin'—and the wulvers are lookin' too."

"It's Raife they want." She met his eyes—oh how she'd missed looking into those blue-grey eyes—pleading with him. "Donal, ye hafta keep 'im safe. He's t'one they want. If they capture 'im, if they get a drop of 'is blood…"

"Shh." He turned her chin to him and kissed her quiet. His first kiss had been like something out of a dream, not possibly real. This kiss was like coming home. She wrapped her soapy, wet arms around his neck, feeling grateful tears slipping down her cheeks.

"They've told me e'erythin'," Donal assured her when they parted. "I should've listened t'ye from the beginnin' about Lord Eldred, lass. If I had..."

"Ye couldn't've known."

His face darkened in a scowl. "We'll find 'em. We'll find 'em both and we'll bring 'em t'justice."

Kirstin searched his face, seeing new lines there, dark circles under his eyes. He smelled of whiskey, and there was a good four days' stubble on his face.

"I missed ye," she confessed. "Did ye miss me?"

"Did I miss ye?" he repeated, blinking at her as Moira carried in a tray weighed down with food. She put it on the little table in the corner. "I had e'ery available man at m'service out lookin' for ye. I've been in me cups for days. I can'na sleep. I can'na eat. I can'na breathe wit'out ye, lass. Did I miss ye? What d'ye say. Moira, did I miss 'er?"

"He put a huge reward out fer yer capture," Moira informed her. "Alive, a'course."

"Ye did?" Kirstin raised her eyebrows in surprise.

"He also had Gregor flogged," Moira told her, pouring cups of mead. "An'banished. If any man dares ever harm a wulver on MacFalon land again, they'll be put t'death. Publically."

"Painfully," Donal agreed, glowering.

"D'ye need anythin' else?" Moira asked, looking at both of them, a small smile playing on her face.

"Jus' tell 'em not t'disturb me," Donal replied, his gaze raking Kirstin's nude form. "Unless it's urgent."

"Aye." Moira grinned, opening the door. "Ye better lock in behin' me, though, jus' in case."

"I will," Donal said, nodding as she went out.

He paused in his bathing of her to go lock the door and Kirstin smiled at that. They were good at locking out the world. She remembered the time they'd spent in the first den, laughing, eating, making love, swimming in the cold spring and drying themselves in front of the fire. She'd known, even then, that their time was limited.

"Is she 'ere yet?" Kirstin asked softly as Donal came back to tend to her.

"Who?" His hands moved over her under the water, big, rough, calloused, they scrubbed her far better than any washing cloth.

"Yer bride," she reminded him.

"I'll not be marryin' anyone else but ye, lass." He leveled her with a cool look. "Not now, not e'er."

"Ye didn't answer me."

"Nuh." He sighed." She's not 'ere yet."

"But she will be..."

And what then? Kirstin wondered.

"I can'na stop 'er from comin'—her party will be welcomed 'ere." Donal scowled. "But I will'na be marryin' her. I intend t'be married t'ye by then."

She looked at him in the firelight, the shadows playing on his handsome face. What woman wouldn't want this man? Lady Cecilia Witcombe would take one look at him and fall instantly in love. Why not? Kirstin had.

And she wouldn't blame her.

"Donal, ye can'na start a war," Kirstin told him. "We were all deceived. King Henry wants t'wulvers dead. All of us. Includin' me. He'll ne'er let ye marry a wulver. We hafta go into hidin' somewhere..."

"If t'English king wants t'go t'war wit' Scotland, then let 'im see if he can take t'border against the Scots *and* t'wulvers." Donal's eyes flashed and she gasped when he roughly scrubbed the cloth over her back.

"I do'na want any more war," Kirstin whispered, feeling tears stinging her eyes. "N'more bloodshed."

"Och." Donal sighed, tossing aside the cloth and reaching for her. His front was soaked from bathing her, his white shirt see-through, clinging to his thickly muscled chest and abdomen. "I'm sorry, lass. I jus'…I will'na let ye go again. I'll fight fer ye. I'll die fer ye."

"No fightin'," she said, frowning. "And mos' definitely, no dyin!"

"Jus' do'na e'er leave me again." He pulled her close, burying his face in the wet skin of her neck, his stubble hard and prickly, making her squirm, but she didn't let him go.

"I'm so tired." She sighed, trying to keep her eyes open, but it wasn't easy in the warm water, in the heat of the fire.

"Let's get some food in yer belly."

He had her stand, shivering, while he rinsed her with a warm bucket of water.

"I'm sorry," she said when he had her step out and wrapped her in a cloth that had been warming by the fire. "For leavin' ye..."

Donal chuckled. "When I saw ye, I didn't know whether to kiss ye or spank ye."

"Ye could do both..." She bit her lip when his gaze swept over her as he patted her dry.

"Do'na tempt me," he growled, wrapping her with a dry cloth and leading her over to the table.

"It must've been a shock, the wulvers ridin' up to the gates…" She sat across from him at the table, the smell of the food hitting her, and suddenly, she was ravenous.

"The scouts on t'walls said the entire wulver army was headin' our way." Donal chuckled, watching as she started eating, not bothering with utensils. "I'd been in me cups for days. No one could find ye... and I was… well, let's jus' say, I missed ye."

She smiled, chewing on a bit of buttered roll.

"But when ye have an entire den full of wulvers ride up t'yer gates, it tends t'sober ye'up," he told her, handing her a napkin to catch the drip of gravy on her chin.

She giggled at that, trying to picture it, her whole pack riding up to Castle MacFalon and begging entry.

"But ye took 'em in?"

"They're yer kin," he said simply, which made her heart swell. Then he said something that made tears come to her eyes. "And mine. A'course I took 'em in."

She was so hungry, she felt faint. Donal watched her eat the salt pork Moira had brought up with her fingers, tearing off thick pieces of dark bread in between bites. He hadn't taken his eyes off her since she arrived, like he thought she might disappear, just an apparition. When Kirstin's belly was full, she sat back with a satisfied sigh. She was still exhausted, and could have fallen asleep right there in the chair, but she didn't want to close her eyes.

She didn't want to stop looking at the man across from her.

"What're we gonna do?" she wondered aloud.

"I'm goin' t'take ye to bed." Donal stood, pulling her up, into his arms. The cloth he had wrapped around her dropped to the floor, leaving her nude. "And I'm ne'er lettin' ye outta m'sight again, lass."

"Ye know what I mean," she whispered, and he nodded, but he didn't answer her with anything but a kiss.

❧

Kirstin woke sometime in the middle of the night, not sure where she was. Then she heard Donal's soft, even breathing beside her, felt the weight of his arm over her, and knew. She was home. Sighing happily, she snuggled back against him under the covers. There was no place on earth she wanted to be more than in this man's arms.

Her mind drifted as she started to fall asleep again. Her body was exhausted, but her mind was on overdrive. Every time she woke, it was with a panicked thought or new fear. Donal helped dispel those, although even now, she had a sinking feeling, like there was something she was forgetting, some little bit of information she'd forgotten to relay that would be the downfall of everything.

She knew it was ridiculous. There were MacFalon and wulver sentries on the castle walls. There were more out looking for Eldred and Moraga. In fact, they'd probably captured them already and put them down in the dungeons with Eldred's four trackers, she told herself. The castle was quiet, asleep. The windows were dark, so it was still night. Kirstin closed her eyes and drifted again, comforted by the sound of the man sleeping behind her.

She'd almost drifted off, finally content, when her eyes opened wide, staring into the fading embers of the fire.

Gayle.

That was what she'd forgotten. Eldred's little spy.

Her heart felt like it was beating in her throat. Could the little maid let him in? Get him a message? Or… worse?

She didn't want to think about worse.

She considered waking Donal and telling him about the maid, but she knew he'd get up and wake the whole damned castle looking for her. Besides, she wasn't sure she was still here. Moira had brought up the food, and she hadn't seen anyone else, but maybe… maybe the maid had left, afraid she was going to be discovered? She didn't want to worry Donal for nothing.

Kirsten was used to moving around at night without waking anyone. She'd extracted herself from a wulver pile often enough to be able to move silently when she wanted to. Donal slept through her slipping out of bed and getting dressed in a clean shirt, plaid and boots. She left him still sleeping as she unlocked the door and slipped into the hallway.

The maid's quarters were off the kitchen, and that's where Kirstin headed. She crept silently down the stairs, heading across the hall. No one was awake yet, she was sure of it, although looking at the windows, they were lighter than they had been a few moments ago. Perhaps it was nearing dawn, after all. She was so exhausted and had missed so much sleep, her internal body clock was off.

Kirstin heard voices at the other end of the hall. She cocked her head. Her hearing was keen and she recognized them both. It was Moira and Sibyl talking. Kirstin's heart leaped in her chest. Was everything all right? The memory of her *banrighinn* bleeding filled her mind and she padded down the hall, heading toward the light coming from a room at the end of it.

"Thank you, Moira," Sibyl said. Her voice was soft, low. "I didn't know who else to ask…"

"Ye can ask me fer anything, lass," Moira assured her. "Where's yer husband?"

"Raife insisted on going to check on the sentries." Sibyl sighed. "Darrow went with him."

Kirstin stopped outside the door, listening. She should have knocked, but she didn't.

"I'm sorry to bother you," Sibyl said again. "You're so busy, with all the wulvers to feed, in addition to the MacFalons."

"Aye, 'tis a handful." Moira agreed with a sigh. "And I'm short maids. Gayle and Shona ran off and I haven't had time t'go into t'village t'hire anyone new."

Kirstin blinked in surprise. So Gayle wasn't at the castle anymore. That was a relief. She almost turned around and went back upstairs. Bed was calling, and she was admonishing herself for eavesdropping, when Sibyl said something that stopped her cold.

"Moira, do you have a good hiding place here in the castle?"

"Fer what, lass?" Moira chuckled. "T'family jewels?"

"No, for this."

Kirstin couldn't see her, even through the crack in the door. She leaned in closer, wondering what in the world Sibyl could want to hide.

"What's this?" Moira asked.

What, indeed. Kirstin held her breath, waiting.

"It's the cure."

She thought her heart would stop beating entirely. The cure? *The* cure? Could it be?

"Fer t'wulver curse?" Moira asked. She sounded as shocked as Kirstin felt. "Ye did it?"

"Yes, thanks to the silvermoon, and the book, and you." Sibyl sighed. "Laina wants to take it and I… I'm afraid she'll find it, if I keep it anywhere near me. She knows I have it. And she knows it works. The problem is, it works too well."

"What d'ye mean?" Moira asked. "How d'ye know it works?"

"Because I tested it," Sibyl told her. Kirstin gaped at the door, blinking in surprise. *Who*? But Sibyl went on to say. "The old midwife, Beitrus. She volunteered. Said she'd lived a long life, so if it killed her, she was ready to go—and if it turned out to be permanent, well, she didn't need to change anymore…"

"Ye let her take it?"

"No, of course not," Sibyl scoffed. "I told her no. I wanted to come up with a safer way to test it. But… she did it anyway."

"Wha' happened?" Moira asked. Kirstin leaned even closer, eager to know herself.

"Well, she's still alive," Sibyl said. "And… it worked. She can't change anymore, even at will."

"Oh no…" Moira clucked at that and Kirstin's heart sank.

"Laina keeps trying to take it," Sibyl explained. "And I can't do that. I can't possibly let her."

"Let me hide it fer ye," Moira said. "I'll keep it safe while yer here, at least."

"Thank you so much."

So Sibyl had done it. She'd found the cure for the wulver curse—but it had turned out to be permanent. Kirstin could hardly believe it. There was a substance that existed that could keep her from changing when she went into estrus. But it would keep her from ever turning into a wulver again…

She couldn't think of anything but Donal, sleeping upstairs, and the woman who would arrive any day, expecting to marry him.

What would it mean, to take such a remedy?

Kirstin wouldn't ever have to worry about changing. There would be no need to lock her up once a month. She could live in the MacFalon castle, side by side with the MacFalons, not as an outsider, but as one of them.

As The MacFalon's woman. His wife.

And… she could have his children.

So what if it was permanent? She wanted to be with Donal. Now and forever.

Permanently.

She'd already decided that. Sibyl's cure would make that possible.

She had to get her hands on it.

"Try t'get some sleep, Lady Sibyl," Moira said softly. "G'nite."

"Thank you," Sibyl called. "Good night."

Kirstin panicked, looking for somewhere to hide. She slipped under the legs of a table that held a vase filled with flowers, crouching in the darkness as Moira came out of the door, closing it behind her.

Did she have the cure? And if she did, what was she going to do with it?

Kirstin watched the old woman carrying her lantern through the hallway. She was heading toward the kitchen. When she saw Moira push open the kitchen door, she slipped out from under the table and followed. The door opened silently and she saw Moira standing with her lantern near the shelves where they kept all the flour and oils she used to cook.

The old woman took down a canister from a high shelf, putting something inside it. Then she put it back up there, standing on her tiptoes and pushing it all the way to the back. Kirstin held her breath, waiting for Moira to turn and discover her. She would say she'd come down for something to eat, she decided, getting her explanation ready, but Moira didn't turn her way. Instead, she headed toward the back of the kitchen.

Kirstin breathed a silent sigh of relief, seeing Moira lift the lantern, looking down at the floor. Kirstin saw many of her pack mates sleeping in a pile on the kitchen floor in front of the low fire burning there, and smiled. It would be the place that most felt like home, she realized, as Moira looked at them, shaking her grey head.

"Wulvers," Moira said with an exasperated sigh, and then she chuckled, heading past the wulver pile, toward the servant's quarters.

Once she was gone, Kirstin made her way over to the shelves, reaching up and finding the canister. Inside, was a tiny vial of dark liquid. She stood there holding it in the palm of her hand, looking at it in the dim light of the fire. Was she really going to do this?

She looked at the wulvers sleeping by the fire, realizing if she did take it, she'd never be part of them again. She would live wholly in the human world.

But she would have Donal. And he would have her.

That convinced her.

She had to find a place to take it, a place away from everyone, because she didn't want anyone to interfere.

Kirstin slipped the vial into the pocket of her plaid to keep it safe.

It was her future.

Hope in a bottle.

She fell asleep in the first den, rolled up completely in her plaid by the spring, the empty vial beside her. The potion had been sweet, tangy, not bitter, as she'd expected. Her last run as a wulver had been through the MacFalon lands, down into the tombs, and had ended in the grotto of Ardis and Asher. She thought of them as she drifted off, not sure if she was sleepy because of the cure, or because she was just plain exhausted.

Donal shook her awake, swearing in Gaelic when her eyes opened to meet his in the early morning sunlight. It came in through the grate above, making the spring look dappled and inviting. Kirstin smiled, remembering the night, putting her arms around his neck.

"I tell ye not t'leave me," he snapped, pushing her away so he could frown at her. "And what d'ye do? Ye run away again?"

"I did'na run away," she protested, stretching and yawning. She felt rested for the first time in days.

"Ye left t'castle! I had n'idea where ye were!" Donal exploded, grabbing her to him and shaking her again. Her plaid fell away and he looked down at her nude body. "I swear, lass, if ye e'er do anythin' like that again, I'll take ye over m'knee and—"

"Spank me?" A smile played on her lips. "Aye, I think, mayhaps, I deserve t'be spanked…"

"Och, yer gonna be t'death'o'me," he groaned, pulling her to him and kissing her. It was a hard, punishing kiss and she whimpered, but she clung to him as they parted, feeling his body against hers, the cool air on her skin. She'd never felt so alive.

But was she different? She couldn't tell.

"Do I look different?" she asked, cocking her head at him.

"Ye look delicious." His hands moved down to cup her breasts. They had made slow, easy, sleepy love the night before. The memory of it made her feel warm all over. But she was rested now, and ready for more of him.

"I took the cure." There was no sense keeping it from him, she decided. Besides, if it worked, it meant they could be together. At least, that was her best hope.

"What cure?" Donal blinked at her, distracted from her breasts by her words.

"This." Kirstin picked up the vial, shaking it. There was a tiny bit of liquid left in the bottom. "Sibyl did it. She made the cure. It works—Beitrus took it, and she can'na change anymore."

"What're ye talkin' about?" Donal looked from her to the vial and back again, as if trying to make sense of her words. "What cure? A cure for…?"

"A cure fer t'curse." She laughed at his dumbfounded expression. "Donal, this means I'll ne'er change again. It means I can marry ye. It means I can have yer bairn…"

Her eyes filled with tears at this last.

"How d'ye know it worked?" He took the vial from her, holding it up in the light. "How d'ye know what else it might do t'ye?"

"I do'na know." She frowned, looking down at her body, then back at him. "I guess I should try t'change and see—"

Donal frowned, looking up at the grating above.

"What?" Kirstin asked, frowning.

He cocked his head, shushing her. "Ye do'na hear that?"

"Hear what?" She blinked at him in surprise. Her wulver ears were far better than his human ones at picking up sound. If there was something to hear, surely…

But I'm not a wulver anymore.

The realization dawned on her as Donal stood, pointing an angry finger in her direction.

"They're soundin' t'alarm." Donal glowered at her. "Ye do'na follow me. Stay put, ye ken?"

"Aye." She nodded, pulling her plaid around her. "What is it?"

"I'm gonna find out." He made his way over the rocks, glancing back at her before he slipped out the exit. "I mean it, Kirstin. Ye'll be safe 'ere. *Stay put.*"

"Aye," she agreed again, nodding. "I'll wait fer ye."

She intended to do as he asked. She really did. She knew she'd scared him, taking off to the first den. She hadn't meant to fall asleep. She just wanted to make sure the cure had worked before she went back to the castle to surprise him with her news.

But the more she sat there, shivering on the rock, the more worried she became. Why had they sounded the alarm? Had Eldred and Moraga somehow managed to complete their spell after all? The thought of Donal riding back to the castle to face an army of enchanted wulver warriors left her choked with fear.

She washed her face and hands in the spring, trying to keep the latter from trembling. She got dressed, sitting back down in the slant of light from above, to wait. Mayhaps it was good news, she told herself. Mayhaps Eldred and the witch had been found. Donal would come back and tell her, and they would celebrate. They would make love in the grotto. Mayhaps they would even make a baby.

That thought made her smile.

That's when she heard it.

She didn't have wulver's ears anymore, but her human ones couldn't mistake the sound.

It was the high, panicked scream of a terrified horse.

Kestrel? Donal's big, black war horse? Could it be?

Fear clawed her throat, but she willed herself to wait, to be still. Donal had told her stay put. But what if he was hurt? What if he was up there, right now? Hurt? What if he needed help?

Kirstin couldn't stay put.

She ran across the rocks and out through the kitchen. Once she reached the tunnels, she changed to wolf form, just because it was faster. But instead of paws and claws clicking on the rock, she looked down at the soft leather of her boots.

Because while she expected to change, while she did what had always come naturally to transform her into a wulver, she didn't change at all.

She *couldn't* change.

Her lungs hurt by the time she got to the stairs and she groaned as she started up them. Her thighs burned when she reached the top. Donal's horse wasn't tethered anywhere. And she didn't have a horse at all.

It was the first time in her life she cursed not being able to turn into a wulver when she wanted to.

She heard it again, the high scream of a horse in pain. Kirstin ran for the woods. Nowhere near fast enough on human legs. She tired far too quickly. She reached the edge of the forest and stopped, listening.

Her ears were faulty, she was sure of it. It was almost like going a little deaf.

In the distance, through the trees, she saw Donal's big, black charger.

She made her way through the brush, approaching the animal carefully from the side. It wasn't until she was almost on top of it that she saw the other, now dead, horse on the ground. Its neck was broken. Had this been the horse screaming?

"Easy, boy." Kirstin soothed, taking Kestrel's reins. The horse's head bobbed, but he didn't seem afraid of her. She saw that he had two arrows in his hindquarters and winced at the sight of the animal's blood. "Where's yer master, hm?"

She blinked as she looked around the forest, wishing for her wulver's eyes to see with. It wasn't light enough to see much with human ones. The sun was just casting its first, early morning orange glow over the land, but here in the forest it was still like dusk.

Kirstin squatted, touching the flank of the dead horse. Whose? She wondered. No identifying marks on the saddle. But she had a strange feeling that she'd seen this horse before. If only her sense of smell were working—she'd know it in an instant.

Kestrel pawed the ground nervously, shaking his big head. Kirstin stood, patting his neck. She'd have to take him back to the castle to tend him. But first, she had to find Donal. Kestrel whinnied and nudged her. Kirstin stumbled, grabbing onto the horses reins, but the big horse had knocked her hard enough to make her fall to the ground.

She sat there for a moment, the wind knocked out of her, and that's when she saw him.

Donal was swinging from a wulver net, trapped high up in the tree.

"Donal!" she called, but he didn't answer.

Kirsten checked her boot for her dirk, making sure it was there, before she began to climb. It didn't take her long to reach him—or to find that, while unconscious, he was, thank the Lord, still breathing. She didn't want to cut him free—the drop to the ground was too far. She'd have to pull the rope and lower him, she realized, although she wasn't sure if she had enough upper body strength to do it.

"Donal?" she whispered, nudging him in the net with her foot as she inched out onto the branch. She realized, from this vantage point, that this was the very same tree, the very same trap, she had been entangled in when she met him. Kestrel had moved closer to the edge of the forest, as if the big animal knew her plan to lower Donal to the ground and had gotten out of the way.

Donal gave a little groan and she leaned over to look more closely at him.

"It's a'righ'," she assured him softly. "I'm gonna get ye down."

"Kirstin." Donal's eyes came open, wide. "No, lass!"

"Make a move to lower that trap, she-bitch, and I'll shoot an arrow through your heart."

Kirstin froze at the sound of Eldred's voice from below.

"Do'na touch 'er!" Donal growled, twisting in the net, trying to see the man who had an arrow aimed in their direction. Kirstin couldn't see him. He was somewhere in the trees. But she could hear him. "I'll kill ye!"

"You're not exactly in any position to be making threats, MacFalon." Eldred chuckled. "I think I'm going to have a little 'fun,' as my captains liked to say, with your wulver-bitch, before I kill 'er."

"I'll kill ye," Donal said again through clenched teeth. "If ye lay one hand on 'er, I'll kill ye!"

"Blah blah blah." Eldred sighed, then he snapped, "MacFalon, you touch that knife in your boot, I'll put an arrow right through her eye."

Kirstin saw Donal's hand stop moving downward and he winced.

"Sad, what's happened to your family," Eldred called. "You're all dirty wulver-lovers now, aren't you? Your father would be appalled to know you had wulvers sleeping in your castle. And your grandfather must be rolling over in his tomb."

Kirstin met Donal's eyes, seeing the anger and fire in his. She could only feel fear, knowing Eldred had his bow aimed at them. She couldn't think of what to do. The animal instinct she'd come to count on had seemed to dry up and disappear overnight. Her limbs felt paralyzed.

"But don't worry, the MacFalon name will die with you this day, Donal." Eldred chuckled. Kirstin felt tears coming to her eyes, panic clawing up her throat. She leaned over, edging just a little closer to Donal, hugging the big branch with her limbs. "There won't be much of your family left to carry on the name after the wulvers are done with them anyway. And you let them walk right into your castle. Foolish."

Donal swore, twisting and turning in the net, going mad, tearing at it with his bare hands, making them bloody. Eldred just laughed. The motion caught Kirstin's eye and she glimpsed him through the trees.

She knew where he was then, at least for the moment. Donal looked at her, his gaze moving from her to the rope, and she knew what he wanted her to do.

But could she?

She wasn't sure she had the strength. Or the courage.

Donal gave a slight nod, urging her, and Kirstin grabbed the rope. She pulled it, hard, and then let go. The length of rope ran quickly through the pulley, Donal's weight taking the net toward the forest floor. It happened very fast. One moment, Kirstin was leaning over the tree branch, the next, her shoulder was on fire, and she was falling, following Donal down toward the ground.

She screamed. She heard herself, landing on her hurt shoulder with a sick thud, the wind knocked out of her completely. The world went gray. Everything was a blur. She heard Lord Eldred drawing his bow again and opened her eyes to see Donal cutting himself free of the net with his dirk, his face a mask of horror and concern at the sight of her with an arrow through her shoulder.

She heard the zing of the second arrow and prepared for it, knowing it was aimed at her.

Donal heard it, too, and he roared, turning to face it and covering her body with his.

She screamed again, but she couldn't hear herself. The scream was coming from the inside, from the sight of the tip of the arrow that had pierced Donal's left shoulder appearing just inches from her eye.

Then Donal was on his feet, charging at the man in the underbrush, drawing his claymore, one-handed, a Herculean feat. Eldred screamed. Like a woman, he screamed, high pitched and frightened. He managed to draw his longsword at the last minute to stop a rageful, deadly swing that would have split him from the top of his head to his heart—even one-handed.

She tried to call out, to warn him, but she couldn't seem to find her voice. She was still screaming. It was just all in her head. Both men had their longswords out—Donal had abandoned the heavy claymore. It had been an impossible feat the first time he'd lifted it one-handed, and she didn't think he could do it again.

Donal was tiring quickly. She could see that much from her forest floor vantage point. Her shoulder screamed too, when she tried to move, but that was also on the inside. Eldred drove him back toward her, toward the net. It was disarmed now, useless. Then she saw it, glinting silver in the early morning light. Donal's dirk, the one he'd used to cut his way out of the trap.

The sound of their swords clashing filled the air. It hurt her ears, made them ring. Kirstin reached her good arm out, groping in the dirt. The knife felt like it was ten feet away, although it was probably only inches from her hand.

Donal yelled in pain when Eldred knocked him into a tree, his hurt shoulder up against the bark. But he didn't stop swinging his sword. Now she could see Donal's face, as they circled, Lord Eldred's back to her. Kirstin's fingers touched the hilt of the knife. Just barely. Almost there.

Swords clashed again, the men grunting, breathing hard. Kirstin winced and rolled, her shoulder burning with pain, but she grasped the dirk in her good hand. She had it!

Now, what was she going to do with it?

"Is this bitch really worth it?" Lord Eldred panted, using both hands to block a one-handed blow from Donal. "You're The MacFalon. You deserve better than to lie with the dogs."

"I'm goin' t'take great pleasure in runnin' you through," Donal growled, driving the older man back another step. "And draggin' yer corpse behind m'horse back to the castle, jus' like m'grandfather used t'do wit' t'wulvers."

"You're not going to win this fight." Eldred grunted and ducked, blocking another blow. "Even if you kill me. The wulvers are already doing my bidding."

Was it true? Kirstin trembled at the thought. Had the enchantress found a way to compel them, without using Raife's blood?

Or had Raife's blood already been spilled?

"Ye lie." Donal brought the sword, one-handed straight at the man's side, but Eldred blocked it, taking another step back. "Yer the lyin' dog 'ere."

"You won't make it back to the castle to see for yourself." Eldred was breathing hard as he lifted his sword to strike a blow that Donal had to ward off one-handed. "More's the pity. They'll all be dead by the time I ride your horse back to Castle MacFalon, and my wulver army will be ready to march."

"Ye talk t'much." Donal jabbed his sword at the man, who side-stepped, but just barely.

"But first, I'm going to rape your little she-wolf." Eldred laughed in triumph as Donal charged him, and Kirstin knew, it was a mistake. Eldred was baiting him, and it had worked.

Kirstin screamed. This time on the outside. It hurt so much she thought she was going to pass out, but she managed to struggle to her feet, the knife in her hand. Her scream had alerted the huntsman and he turned far enough around to see her holding the dirk up high.

"Ye touch me, and I'll be the last dog ye e'er lie wit'." Kirstin brought the knife down sideways, overhand, into the soft flesh at the side of the man's throat.

Eldred gurgled. He didn't say anything, but blood filled his mouth as he sank to his knees, his sword falling to the forest floor. Donal didn't hesitate. He ran the man through. Eldred gave one last, strangled cry, and then fell, taking Donal's sword with him as he collapsed into the dirt.

"Are ye a'righ'?" Donal pulled her against him with his good arm and she cried out, feeling dizzy and nauseous for a moment.

"Aye," she agreed, mustering enough energy to smile at him. "Would ye look'a'that? I saved ye this time. Now it's ye who owes me yer life."

"Ye have m'life, lass." His arm tightened around her as he pressed his lips to hers, and murmured, "Ye've had it since the moment I met ye."

Donal called Kestrel so he could put her on the horse. But first, he broke off the fletched part of the arrow, and pulled it through the exit wound.

"'Tis gonna hurt," he warned before he did it.

Kirstin saw stars and thought the world had gone gray for a moment.

"I'm sorry, lass," he murmured, doing the same with the arrow that had found its way into his shoulder.

He mounted behind her, but only after he'd resheathed his sword and tied Eldred to the back of his saddle with a length of rope, like he'd promised.

She heard the man groan and she looked at Donal with wide eyes.

"He's not dead?"

"He will be," Donal said grimly as he took Kestrel's reins.

Kirstin didn't look back, but there was something quite satisfying, knowing the man who hated and wanted all wulvers dead was being dragged behind them through the dirt.

They didn't talk about it, but she knew Donal was thinking the same thing she was.

It wasn't until they arrived back at Castle MacFalon that they knew for sure.

Lorien met them on horseback, and Kirstin felt Donal's good hand move to his sword as the wulver rode up.

"'Tis the witch," Lorien told them, pointing to the center of the field, where a shapely woman had been lashed to a tall post. "And I see ye found Lord Eldred."

"What's left of 'im." Donal's jaw tightened as he looked at the woman struggling against her bindings. His hand wasn't on his sword hilt anymore. Lorien was clearly not enchanted. Nor were any of the other wulvers in the yard. "Not much of a threat anymore, is she?"

Donal rode toward the post, drawing close—but not too close.

Moraga looked up, fire and hatred in her eyes, and she screamed at them in Gaelic.

"What's t'matter?" Kirstin asked, narrowing her eyes at the woman who had once sent an enchanted blade after her. "N'blood fer yer magic, witch?"

Moraga snarled like an animal. Her dress was dirty and torn, face streaked with dirt.

"Mayhaps ye wanna use his?" Kirstin jerked her thumb behind her and the witch turned her head and saw him for the first time. Lord Eldred was still recognizable by his clothes, if nothing else.

"Nooooooooo!" The witch wailed, railing against the post, trying to escape her lashings, but whoever had tied her had done their job well. Besides, she had three MacFalons, two of which were Aiden and Angus, and four wulver warriors standing guard. The woman wasn't going anywhere—except the dungeons.

Moraga sobbed, real tears, screaming Eldred's name over and over.

"Donal, I'm feeling nauseous," Kirstin confessed, although she wasn't sure if it was her wound or the witch's display that had done it.

"Aye." He kissed the top of her head. "Let's get ye t'Laina and Sibyl, so they can patch ye'up."

He slid off his horse, glancing back at Lord Eldred's body, now bent and broken from being dragged behind the horse. It was a horrible sight and Kirstin turned her face into Donal's chest as she slid off the horse into his waiting arms.

"Send what's left of 'im t'King Henry." Donal tossed Kestrel's reins to Angus.

"Donal," Kirstin warned, shaking her head, feeling dizzy. "Do'na start a war."

"When he finds out what t'man was plannin', he'll give me an honorary knighthood," Donal scoffed, and Lorien laughed. Donal grinned back, then leaned in closer to whisper in her ear, "Or mayhaps m'choice of a bride."

She thrilled at his words, in spite of the pain in her shoulder, the nausea in her belly, and the dizziness in her head. She lifted her face to his, smiling, and let him kiss her. For a moment, she didn't feel anything but pure bliss. She didn't hear the witch screaming, she didn't feel the pain of her wound.

There was only Donal. The only man in the world. In her world. She felt dizzy with him, filled with him. She was his, and he was hers.

Finally, completely.

"Uhhhh, MacFalon…" Lorien interrupted, clearing his throat.

"What?" Donal snapped, annoyed at being interrupted. Kirstin clung to him, close. She was so dizzy she could hardly stand.

"Yer bride…" Lorien replied, glancing over at Angus. "She…"

"Aye?" Donal prompted, looking between the two of them.

And Kirstin knew. She just knew, by the way they looked at her, with that little bit of guilt in their eyes.

Aiden rocked back on his heels, clearing his throat. Then he pointed at the front of the castle, where a carriage was parked, led by four big horses.

Lorien sighed and announced, "Yer bride's arrived."

And with that, Kirsten fainted.

"I'm goin' to run ye through wit' an arrow e'ery month, jus' t'keep ye in bed wit' me." Kirstin snuggled down under the covers, resting her head against Donal's shoulder—his unbandaged one. Thankfully, their arrow wounds were mirror images of each other, so they fit together, as always, perfectly.

"Ye do'na hafta shoot me t'keep me in bed wit' ye, lass." Donal chuckled, kissing the top of her head.

"I'd usually say yer betrothed might object," Moira called, grinning over at Laina as she readied their breakfast on trays on the table. Laina had been called in to play nursemaid—because Moira was so shorthanded and Raife insisted Sibyl stay in bed and rest for the bairn's sake, even if there'd been no more bleeding—and she sat at their bedside, tearing cloth to make dressings. "But Lady Cecilia Witcombe's been spendin' s'much time wit' the handsome Lorien, I do'na think she'd care a bit."

The mention of Donal's intended still made Kirstin wince, no matter how much he reassured her that he was, never, under any circumstances, going to marry the woman. They'd both been laid up in bed for almost a week with their wounds. Donal's was healing quite nicely, but Kirstin had broken out into a fever on the second day and was just now, finally, starting to feel human again.

Which made her laugh to herself, because that's all she was now—human. Her wulver side had been banished by the mix of herbs Sibyl had prepared. Kirstin still felt a little bad about stealing it and secretly taking the mixture. Laina had been beyond angry when she found out, but now that they had two instances of proof that the "cure" was permanent—and Darrow had been informed of its effects—Laina had come to her senses and had decided to stay a wulver, in spite of her deep desire to control her change. At least, until Sibyl could develop something that wasn't so permanent.

"Too bad yer not a wulver anymore," Laina grumbled, pulling back the covers to check Kirstin's bandage, as if she'd read Kirstin's mind. "Ye'd mend faster."

"I'm glad I'm not a wulver anymore." Kirstin winced when she pulled the dressing away. She was going to have an ugly scar there, she knew. "How's Sibyl?"

"She's doin' well." Laina couldn't help the smile that spread over her face. She stood, holding her linked hands out in front of her middle. "Startin' t'show."

"And the cure?" Kirstin knew it was a sensitive subject, but she was too curious not to ask. "Has she recreated it yet?"

"She's workin' on it. Silvermoon's plenty in the first den, but now we have to travel for the huluppa." Laina helped Moira bring their breakfast tray over to the bed.

Moira was still shorthanded, but at least she didn't have all the wulvers to feed anymore. They'd all moved into the first den, and from what Laina said, they'd made a home there in a very short amount of time. The space was the perfect size, and The MacFalon had no problem instructing his men to fix up the old barn to house their horses or build a fence in the field to keep sheep.

"'Tis always somethin'." Kirstin sighed, cracking her hard-boiled egg and beginning to peel it.

"Sibyl a'ready sent somma t'wulver scouts back t'gather the huluppa fer her," Laina said, pouring water into a cup and putting it on Kirstin's bedside. "They also herded t'sheep to t'first den, so they would'na starve. I was glad they brought home some more of our things."

"Laina!" Darrow's voice echoed through the hallway, floating into their room. Kirstin wasn't surprised to hear him. The wulvers and the MacFalons had been going back and forth, between the first den and the MacFalon castle.

Darrow and Raife had been in to see them at least once a day, sometimes together, sometimes separately. They had a lot to discuss with The MacFalon, who was doing business from his bed, which Laina and Moira insisted he not leave. This made Kirstin happy, because the longer they kept the real world at bay, the better, as far as she was concerned. She liked having Donal all to herself in their own little world.

"Here!" Laina called back.

Darrow poked his head in and grinned at Kirstin and Donal sitting up in bed together. "There's t'love birds. Ready to go ridin' yet, MacFalon?"

"I'm quite happy wit' t'mount I've got righ 'ere," Donal replied, sliding an arm around Kirstin and pulling her close. She giggled and flushed, but didn't object. "I trust ye and Raife 'ave e'erythin' handled, Darrow?"

"Oh aye," Darrow agreed, grabbing his wife to him one handed and planting a kiss on her cheek as she passed. "E'erythin' except the witch."

Kirstin shivered at the mention of her. She couldn't get the memory out of her mind of the woman screaming, sobbing, cursing all of them in Gaelic at the sight of Eldred's mangled body being dragged behind the horse. When they had unlashed her from the pole and taken her to the dungeons, she had been put in a cell alone, away from Eldred's four men. When one of the servants had gone down to bring her bread and water the next morning, the cell had been empty. Neither the bars nor the lock had been tampered with. She had simply vanished.

“I told ye she was a witch.” Kirstin couldn’t help ribbing Darrow a little about that.

“Mayhaps.” Darrow shrugged. He was still reluctant to believe, even now. “Although I think it more likely someone who had access to the keys set ’er free.”

“But no sign of ’er?” Donal asked, frowning. “Ye haven’t found ’er?”

The missing witch had been the main reason Raife had decided to keep the wulver pack on MacFalon land, in the first den. With her on the loose, there was at least one person in the world who knew exactly where the mountain den was located, and that made it too dangerous to live there. At least, at the first den, they had the MacFalons at the ready to watch their backs. Mayhaps they would find another place, in time, but for now, it was a good solution.

And it made Kirstin so very happy, to have her family close, even if she was no longer a wulver.

“Ye sent Eldred’s body t’King Henry, along wit’ me message?” Donal asked, taking the egg Kirstin had just finished peeling and popping the whole thing into his mouth. He asked this question every time Darrow or Raife or any of his men came in, and they always gave the same answer.

“Aye,” Darrow agreed.

“Nex’time, I bite yer finger off,” Kirstin growled, nudging Donal with her elbow for stealing her food.

“Yer not a wulver anymore, luv,” he reminded her with a reciprocal nudge. “I’m not afeared a’ye. Bite away.”

She turned and nipped at his shoulder, feeling him jump, but he grinned down at her, a dark light in his eyes that made her feel warm from head to toe.

Another knock came on the open door and the two MacFalon brothers, Aiden and Angus, who seemed to go everywhere together, appeared. Kirstin saw that Lorien was behind them, a head taller than both of the big men. He smiled over their heads at her and she smiled back. She wondered if it was true, what the women were saying about him and Lady Cecilia Witcombe.

Donal's intended had arrived, terrified of the Scots, afraid she was going to be raped and murdered the moment she stepped out of her carriage. It had taken her party a great deal of extra time to arrive, because according to castle rumors, Cecilia had sabotaged their trip on more than one occasion, including "accidentally" shooting the captain of her guard in the thigh with an arrow.

She had stepped out of her carriage to find a witch lashed to a pole in the yard, guarded by half-men, half-wolves and bare-kneed, bearded Scotsmen in kilts. She had screamed at the sight, attracting the attention of the wulvers. Lorien, who had forgotten he was in warrior form—half-wolf, half-man—had rushed to her aid, always the gentleman. She had taken one look at his face and screamed again.

And when he'd remembered, and changed back to a man?

She had simply fainted dead away

Kirstin's feelings for the woman had been nothing but venom at first, but the more she heard, the more she realized, Lady Cecilia Witcombe wasn't any more interested in marrying Donal MacFalon than he was in marrying her. But if the rumors were true, she had become quite enamored with the wulver who had caught her when she fainted and carried her into the castle. And Lorien had been spending a lot of time at Castle MacFalon, if Laina and Moira were to be believed…

"What's yer business?" Donal asked with a sigh as Aiden and Angus argued their way into the room, Lorien following close behind. "'Tis startin' to feel like a circus in 'ere."

"Ye were drunker than I was, man," Aiden protested. "Why d'ye think I won at dice?"

"Ye did'na win, ye cheated," Angus snorted. "An' I wan'me money back."

"Nuh, I would've known if he was cheatin'," Lorien replied. "A wulver can spot a cheater a mile away, at least."

"'Tis true," Darrow agreed, leaning against the door frame. "We're also vera good at cheatin', if we wanna be."

"T'was ye then!" Angus pointed a finger at Lorien. "Ye were cheatin' fer 'im! How much did he pay ye outta d'winnin's?"

"Do'na lookit me!" Lorien laughed, holding up his hands. "I do'na need yer worthless coins. I'm a wulver, remember?"

"Face it, Angus, ye're jus' not a winner." Darrow grinned at the man, who glowered at all of them. "Let's g'back out on the archery range, eh? I'd be happy t'beat ye again. This time we can wager on it…"

"I would'na lost if I was half-wolf either," Angus snorted over his shoulder at the wulver, pulling something from the pocket of his plaid, handing it to Donal. "This came fer ye."

"Yer half wild boar, but that does'na seem t'help ye." Darrow laughed.

"Sounds like wulver-human relations are improvin' a'ready," Kirstin giggled, looking over Donal's shoulder at the scroll.

Her heart stopped when she saw it had the king's seal. Moira glanced at it and saw too.

"Mayhaps ye should go along wit' King Henry and nullify t'wolf pact," Angus joked. "So I can drive these dogs back t'their kennels where they belong a'fore they give all the MacFalons fleas, eh?"

"The only flea-bitten dog 'ere is ye, Angus MacFalon," Moira said with a laugh, already shooing the two big, bearded men out the door. "Now, out wit' ye!"

Darrow snickered at that and Moira, who had no qualms about who ran the castle, smacked his bottom with a tray.

"Ye, too, dog! Out!" She threatened him with a tray over the head and he backed away through the door, still laughing. "I do'na care if yer a wulver or the Lord of the Wild Hunt 'imself, ye'all need to clear out. I've got patients t'heal before I'm called t'me own death, ye ken?"

"A'righ'!" Darrow agreed, pulling his wife into his arm. "But I'm takin' m'wife wit' me!"

"Take this one, too!" Moira waved Lorien out with her tray and he avoided being smacked by it—just barely—as he slipped out, all the men snickering at Moira's dramatic, but effective, display. She shut the door behind them with a sigh.

"That's that, then," she announced, fanning her red face with the tray. "I'll leave ye alone t'eat yer breakfast. Call if ye need me?"

"Aye, thank ye," Kirstin said, meeting the old woman's smiling eyes. Moira knew what was in the scroll, just as well as they did.

At least, she hoped.

When Moira had gone out Kirstin looked at Donal, feeling a lump in her throat that was hard to swallow past.

"From t'king?" she asked and he just nodded.

She noticed Donal's hand shook slightly as he broke the seal and she felt cold, in spite of the fire in the fireplace.

"Wait." She put her hand over his. "Donal… what if…?"

"I told ye, lass." His blue-grey eyes were clear, shining with love. "Yer mine, n'matter what. I'll fight for ye, I'll die fer ye, I'll—"

She kissed him, feeling the soft, full press of his lips against hers, a promise more powerful than any king's proclamation.

Kirstin covered her face with her hands as Donal opened it and began to read. She couldn't read the words anyway, and even if she could, they meant nothing.

Nothing except freedom or death. Nothing except peace or war. Nothing except her love or pain. Nothing. And everything.

"Kirstin…" he whispered her name, trying to peek through her fingers.

"Nuh. I can'na." Her voice was muffled, her tears—they seemed to come so easily lately, now that she had no wulver left in her—stinging her eyes.

"Kirstin, look a'me." She dropped her hands, feeling her mouth trembling as he cupped her face. "Yer mine. I do'na need any man's permission."

"He denied it again," she whispered, feeling a heavy weight tugging on her heart.

She had visions of war, King Henry's men marching to the borderlands, facing off against her whole family, all of them, the MacFalons and the wulvers, the green, velvet hills of her homeland running with blood. She could lose them all, in one horrible, bloody battle, simply because the English king was afraid a wulver might claim the right to his precious throne.

"Nuh, lass." Donal pressed his mouth to hers and a fat, salty tear slipped between their lips. "King Henry's granted the dispensation. As a thank ye fer exposin' Lord Eldred's treason, King Henry's given up all rights to the MacFalon lands."

"Ye do'na hafta marry an Englishwoman?"

"Accordin' t'this, James IV of Scotland's s'posed t'marry King Henry VII's daughter, Margaret Tudor some time this year."

"Looks like t'king's gettin' serious 'bout marryin' t'border." Kirstin's eyes widened. "What else does it say?"

"This says I'm free to choose me own bride."

"Free." She repeated the word softly, saying it out loud, hardly believing it could be true.

"Aye." He pressed his forehead to hers. "Free t'choose—and I choose ye, Kirstin MacFalon."

Kirstin MacFalon. Hearing him say it out loud gave her a little thrill of pleasure.

"Are ye sure?" She swallowed, feeling doubt now that there were suddenly no barriers at all between them. "Even if I'm… not quite a woman, and not quite a wulver?"

"Och! Ye've always been all woman, lass." He laughed, grabbing their tray of food and setting it aside on the bedside stand. He moved his body over hers, stretching her out beneath him, and she welcomed his delightful heat and weight, wrapping her arms around his neck.

"I told ye, nothin' could keep me from ye." His mouth claimed hers, hands roaming over her body, carefully avoiding her wound. They'd slept in the same bed for a week, but had been warned not to engage in any 'strenuous behavior' by Laina, their resident nursemaid, and Donal had taken her at her word, no matter how much Kirstin begged him to take her.

"E'en if ye were a star up in the heavens, I'd reach ye," he whispered against her throat, his big, calloused hand moving over her hip. "And make ye mine."

"I'm much closer than that." She took his hand and pressed it between her legs, rocking against it, moaning softly. "And I burn hotter, too…"

"Aye, ye do." He slipped two fingers into her heat and she gasped.

"But e'en if I was a star…" Her hand traced over the sloped hills and valleys of his belly, tracing that dark line of hair down from his navel to find him oh-so-hard and ready for her. "Ye could still reach me wit' this…"

He chuckled as he shifted his weight fully onto her.

"Yer a thousand times brighter and more beautiful than any star, m'love," he murmured. "And I'm t'luckiest man in the world, because I don't have to look up into t'sky to see ye."

"Nay, ye jus' have t'look in yer bed," she laughed, putting her arms around his neck. She would never,

ever tire of this. Making love with him was the deepest, best expression of who she was.

"Nay, lass." His breath was hot in her ear, and she realized with a little thrill that this was the first time they would make love as man and woman, free and unencumbered. "T'only place I'll e'er have t'look fer ye is in m'heart."

She met his gaze, smiling.

He was such an extraordinary man, who said such extraordinary things.

And he was hers.

Kirstin gave a little cry as his mouth laid claim to her first. She felt him, throbbing against her, seeking entrance, their hearts beating hard and fast together.

She knew she would burn for this man forever.

Kirstin parted her thighs to welcome him home.

The End

HIGHLAND WOLF PACT
Blood Reign

By Selena Kitt

Chapter One

Year of Our Lord 1525
Scotland
Outside the Wulver Den - MacFalon Land

Griff could smell them, not far behind.

Gaining.

He couldn't let that happen.

He signaled his men, using a low grunt and a soft growl. Rory MacFalon heard him and followed his hand signal, breaking right through the trees. The forest cover was thick and the horses didn't always find their footing, but the path they'd tracked through the woods—their own shortcut—was perfect for this purpose. Griff grinned—to an outsider, it would have looked like a snarl, his snout long, teeth drawn back—as he watched Rory slow in the underbrush, awaiting his next command.

They were going to make it. He could feel it, something instinctual.

He barked an order to Garaith, who gave a nod with his big, shaggy black head, giving Griff a grin that also looked much like a snarl, and he, too, broke off and joined Rory on the side of the path. The rest of his pack of wulver warriors—half-men, half-wolves, wearing full Scots armor and riding horses through the MacFalon forest—followed Griff's lead as he pulled his giant war horse aside, waving them past. They knew the shortcut as well as he did—they'd helped him create it.

"Cam!" Griff called to one of his teammates, who brought up the rear of the pack. Cam slowed his horse, surprised when Griff tossed him the giant rack of buck antlers he was carrying. "Take them to the safe area. Lead the team! Go!"

Horse hooves thundered through the forest. If the other two packs didn't know where the shortcut was, they would now. But it didn't matter, because Griff knew they were going to win.

He barked orders to Rory and Garaith to follow him. They needed more space than they had in the woods to end this thing properly. The two wulvers fell in behind him. Griff dug the heels of his boots into Uri's side, leaning over his powerful neck as the horse tore up the path and broke through the trees. His team, he noted with satisfaction, was already corralled in the "safe" area. There were wulver women gathered at the mouth of their den, watching with bright eyes as the warriors burst into the field.

Griff gave a war whoop, turning his mount to face the other two oncoming teams. He directed Rory and Garaith toward the first—both had already drawn their swords. They were wooden, just training swords, a fact that bothered Griff a great deal, but his father had insisted. His mother had protested as well—and he could understand a woman's protest, that someone might get hurt—but his father, Raife, was the pack's leader, and some day, Griff would take his place. Wasn't it about time they were allowed to use real swords? Even if it was just for this, the Great Hunt. It only happened once a year, after all.

Two dozen wulver warriors charged into the clearing, and Griff heard the women squeal and yelp as swords began to clash. Rory and Garaith were his best fighters by far, and they could hold their own against any of the rest. He saw them fighting off a dozen menacing pack members, while Griff himself took on the other dozen or so that had begun to circle.

Not that he let that stop him.

Griff swung his sword expertly. They all had wooden swords, so it was a fair fight. Not that twelve against one was fair, exactly, but it was what he'd planned. The antlers—their prize—and the rest of his men were safe. He had his two best fighters—who had already bested half the other pack—and he didn't doubt his own ability for a moment.

Even when he was surrounded. And he was. He'd bested three of them already, but there were more, and they circled him. Griff's horse pawed the ground, nervous, but he kept Uri under control, swinging his sword at all comers. And they came. Wulver after wulver, snarling and swinging, snapping their jaws and howling. Griff didn't hesitate. Three more wulvers had to fall back because his sword had slipped through and, wooden or not, dented their breast-plates—a "kill" shot.

He could hear the other wulvers, spectators, howling their approval. The women especially. They were all excited to watch the men compete. He knew his mother was among them, watching—with breath held, wringing her hands, no doubt. Sibyl might be married to the pack leader, but she'd never gotten used to or really understood the wulver warrior's constant training. She was human, and a woman. He could forgive her that.

Not that he was winning for her—or any of the wulver women he saw jumping up and down and clapping as he bested another of the rival team. Griff won because it was part of him. Winning was everything. To him, losing didn't mean just losing.

Losing meant death. He didn't care if it was a wooden sword to his breast plate or an actual arrow whizzing by his head. It was all death.

He didn't even realize it was over until he saw Rory and Garaith, who had taken down the last of the other team, dismounting and charging across the field toward him. Griff howled in triumph, sliding off his horse and clapping his teammates on the back. He shook his head, much like a dog who shakes off when it comes out of a lake, and heard all the girls sigh and exclaim as his features transformed from wolf to human once again. Many of the wulver women looked at him hungrily, giving him those appreciative, over-the-shoulder glances that meant they were open to... well, anything. He'd likely take one, or maybe two or three, of them up on that later. But for now, he was too interested in basking in the glory.

"We did it!" Garaith yelled, giving Griff a one-armed squeeze.

From the "safe" zone, Griff's teammates roared their approval. Rory threw back his dark head and howled, too, although Griff saw he was quick to change from wulver-warrior back to human as his mother rushed across the field to hug him. Kirstin was followed by her husband, Donal—The MacFalon. It was their land the wulvers' den resided on. They both congratulated their wulver-warrior son on a job well done, and Rory stood there grinning like a fool. Griff wondered if the grin plastered to his own face looked just as ridiculous.

Even Griff's bested pack-mates congratulated him, albeit a little grudgingly, on a good win. Griff saw his mother, her red hair starting to be streaked at the temples with a few gray strands, standing near the entrance of their den, watching. She was smiling, but it was a strained smile. She hated the fighting, he knew. He gave her a wink, grinning, and her smile brightened just a little.

Beside her, Garaith's mother, Laina, her white-blonde hair braided behind her like his mother's, waved to her son. There was no hesitation in Laina about her son's warrior ways. She was wulver through and through, and appreciated her son's prowess on the battlefield—training exercise or not. That made him think of his uncle, Darrow—Garaith's father—who had been overseeing the Great Hunt, along with Darrow's brother, Raife. Darrow was Raife's second in command. The last he'd seen them, Griff had been leading his pack, holding the antlers high, and riding hard to get back to the safe zone.

Then Griff couldn't see anyone because he was being surrounded again, this time by well-wishers who clapped him on the back and wulver women who kissed his cheek and rubbed up against him as close as they could get. Griff enjoyed the attention, although he didn't exactly bask in it. Winning had been a foregone conclusion as far as he was concerned.

"What in the gory hell did you think you were doing?" Raife's voice thundered through the clearing as he galloped up on his charger. Their pack leader could command anything, whether it was one man, a room full of people, or an entire army. Just the sound of his voice booming over the field got everyone's attention. Griff sighed inwardly, if not outwardly, glancing up to see his father's horse pulling up short of the crowd. Darrow was close behind. "Is that what you think leading looks like? You fall back to hold off the enemy, and sacrifice yourself?"

"I won, didn't I?" Griff shot back, feeling his cheeks go hot as he met his father's dark gaze. He heard some murmurs in the crowd, and knew what they were looking at. Any time Griff got angry, they told him his eyes would flash red. Literally. It had been that way since he was a baby, his mother said. There was something in the wulver lore about a prophecy, and a "red wulver,"—which he was, when he changed to wolf—a big, red wolf. He couldn't hide his coloring, but the red eyes he'd learned to control over the years. Somehow, though, his father always managed to bring out the worst in him.

"I beat them all!"

"Winning isn't everything!" Raife snapped. "A pack leader has more to think about than just winning! A stunt like that can cost a pack their leader. And a leaderless pack is a dead pack!"

Griff blinked at his father, feeling heat spreading to his chest. So mayhaps it had been a little reckless. Mayhaps his plan, while successful, had endangered not only him, but Rory and Garaith as well. He felt a little guilty about that. But they'd done all right, even by themselves, hadn't they?

"It's just a game," Griff grumbled, and knew he was attempting to deflect his own public shaming when he tossed his chipped, splintering wooden sword to the grass. "These aren't even real weapons!"

"It's never just a game!" Raife roared. "A pack leader—ANY wulver warrior—can never afford to think of training as a game. The pack we live in is the last of our kind. We are the last of the wulvers. Most humans would kill the last of us out of fear alone."

I should jus' take ye on right now, ol' man. Raife wasn't really old, not in human or wulver years. He could lead their pack for another thirty or forty, if he wanted to. More's the pity, because Griff felt ready to lead now. He felt it in every fiber of his being, all the way to his bones.

Griff glared at his father, seeing his jaw harden. Had he guessed what Griff was thinking?

"You want this?" Raife's voice lowered as he leaned into his horse, toward his son. So he had guessed. The heat filling Griff's face intensified and he tried to control it. His father's eyes weren't red, they were wulver blue—all wulvers had blue eyes—but they got dark as a bottomless ocean when he was angry. And he was angry now. "Come get it. By law, you can challenge me any time to take the lead."

Griff felt the urge to challenge him tingling in his limbs, pricking him like a thousand little needles all over his body. The hair on the back of his neck stood up and he felt a growl building in his throat. He wouldn't be able to control it in a minute and he wondered who would win if he challenged his father now. There were no guarantees, but he thought he just might win.

Then he glanced over at his uncle, sitting on a horse beside Raife, and he wondered why Darrow had never challenged for the pack leader position. Was he so afraid to lose? Or—mayhaps, he was afraid he'd win? Darrow met his eyes and he saw a warning there. Don't do it, not now, not yet. But Griff felt ready. His body sang with his desire to lead, to conquer, to win.

"Son, I'd love to turn my role over to you," Raife told him, dismounting and looking around at the crowd of wulvers that watched, tense, waiting. "Some day, I hope I will. But right now, I know my leadership is still what's best for this pack. And I would do anything to protect it. Would you?"

Griff did growl at that. How could his father believe he wouldn't do everything to protect the pack? It was what he was born, bred and trained for. The Great Hunt was practice for war—a war that just might come, one day. He would be ready to take anyone on, to protect all of them—his mother, his sisters, his aunts, uncles, and cousins. Just like he was ready, right now, to take on his father.

They faced each other, man to man, the same height, same build. No one would have questioned that they weren't father and son, with the same big, brawny shoulders, strong jaws, thick, long, dark hair—Griff had been born a redhead, like his mother, but his newborn hair had changed color. He was still the only red wolf in the pack, though. And his eyes, instead of the blue of his father's, were actually a strange amber color that went red when he was emotional or angry, if others were to be believed. He'd never seen his own eyes turn color himself.

Both men were in full gear, although Raife had an actual sword at his side, while Griff's wooden one lay between them on the grass. He felt both excitement and worry rising in the crowd. Would there be a challenge this day? Would father and son face off in a duel that could lead to the death of one of the two big men? Griff heard a soft cry from near the mouth of the den, and knew his mother's voice well. She didn't want this to happen—likely, ever. But a man had to become a man eventually, didn't he?

"Winners get served first at the feast!" Laina, Griff's still very beautiful, shapely blonde aunt announced, putting an arm around Garaith, her son. "But don't they have to muck out the stalls first?"

Garaith grumbled and rolled his eyes at that and Griff caught his best friend's glance. Garaith was Darrow's son, a few years older than Griff, but like his father, he had a tendency to go off half-cocked. Griff might do things that were risky—but he never made a decision without thinking it through thoroughly first. Even in that moment, when he felt his anger building and his desire to challenge their pack leader to a fight, he weighed all his options before reacting.

"Garaith and Rory, you were outstanding following your leader's direction." Raife praised both of the young men, clapping them each on the back with a smile. "Even if your leader made a risky move."

Griff let it slide, swallowing his anger, but Raife's words hit home. He would die for Garaith or Rory or any of his team or pack mates. But when his father gave him that knowing look, he understood, finally, what the old man had been so angry about. Griff's strategy had won them the competition, certainly. But it had also been very risky. Had they been using real swords, instead of wooden ones, he wondered if the outcome might have been different. And that's the doubt he saw when he looked into his father's eyes.

"Aye, take the horses to the barn and muck out the stalls," Raife ordered. "Remember, serving the pack is what will keep you humble. And you always have to keep the pack foremost in your mind."

He looked at Griff as he said this last, and Griff gave him a nod, grabbing the reins of both his own horse and Raife's big stallion. His father's hand slipped onto his shoulder, squeezing briefly, and Raife spoke the words, just for him, "I'm proud of you, Griff. You're a good wulver and a fine man."

"Hurry back!" Sibyl called over the crowd at Griff, his shoulders drooping less than they'd been just a few minutes before. "Dinner's waiting!"

"Congratulations to the winners!" Donal MacFalon called, smiling as he watched his son, Rory, taking the reins of the horses. "I'm proud of all of ye. Clan MacFalon has a surprise for all the winners when ye return, so do'na tarry long, boys!"

"Boys." Rory sighed, glancing over his shoulder at his father. "When are they going to start seeing us as men?"

"At least he didn't call you out in front of the whole pack," Griff grumbled as their team mates started gathering up the rest of the horses. "And ye're lucky—ye know ye'll be the laird of Clan MacFalon someday. Ye've got no one to challenge ye."

Griff gave Garaith a knowing look. As brothers, Darrow and Raife had worked side by side for years, Raife as alpha, Darrow his second. Griff didn't have any brothers, but he knew it was likely that someday, he would lead the pack, and Garaith would follow him, just like Darrow followed Raife.

"Ha, m'sister, Eilis, would have somethin' to say 'bout that." Rory laughed. He was so much like his father, good-humored, always smiling—even when he was facing his enemies. But he was deadly with a sword, and eerily accurate with his bow.

"Yer da would really let a woman lead yer clan?" Garaith asked, even though he knew as well as Griff did that the Scots had no qualms about letting a woman step into that role.

"Aye," Rory agreed with a nod. "But m'da wants t'marry Eilis off t'some English fop, last I heard, so she'll likely be givin' him heirs a'fore the year's through."

"Aye? Is that so?" Garaith bristled at this news.

Griff knew that Garaith had his eye on Eilis—since they were just pups, even though Rory's sister wasn't a wulver. It wasn't unheard of for wulvers and humans to mate. Griff's own mother was a human woman, as was Rory's father. His mother, Kirstin, had once been a wulver, but had taken a "cure" that Sibyl had developed for the wulver woman's curse of changing once a month due to estrus, or when she gave birth. The "cure" had worked all too well—Kirstin was now unable to change to wulver form at all.

Rory, Kirstin's first child with The MacFalon, had been quite a surprise to everyone, except maybe the midwife Beitrus, who had delivered Rory, when he came out as a wulver pup and not a human baby. Beitrus said Rory must have been conceived just at the cusp of Kirstin's change—completely out of her control—from human woman to wolf form.

"If ye want 'er, ye better tell m'father, or he's goin' t'send 'er to England and let King Henry pick t'richest match fer her," Rory warned his friend as they trudged up the hill.

"Aye," Garaith agreed, his eyes flashing. "I'll talk t'him."

Griff shook his head.

He liked women well enough, but he'd never mooned over them the way Garaith did over Eilis, or for that matter, the way Rory did over Griff's little sister, Maire. Griff could always have his pick of the litter—and he had picked, frankly, more than once—

but he'd never found a girl who could keep his attention for longer than it took him to catch them. There were some in the pack who still believed in the idea of "one true mate," but Griff didn't hold to such silliness.

"C'mon, let's go," he told his two best friends as they mounted their own horses and started rounding up the rest. "I'm starvin' and I can'na wait t'get served first tonight. We earned it."

Rory and Garaith both agreed, although they seemed less invested in the win than Griff. He supposed that was the difference between them, the reason he was destined to lead, and they to follow. His father might believe that winning wasn't everything, but he was wrong. Griff was willing to do whatever it took to win, at any cost.

❧

"Feast ready yet?" Griff asked as he came into the kitchen, seeing his mother standing at a fireplace taller than he was, basting a whole roasting pig on a spit. "I'm starvin'."

"You stink!" Sibyl wrinkled her freckled nose at her son as he bent to kiss the top of her head. "Go bathe in the stream with the rest of the men."

"Too cold," Griff complained. "Can I use yer spring?"

"Don't let your father catch you," Sibyl warned as Griff stole the apple from the pig's mouth, dodging his mother's swat.

"What?" He grinned, taking a big bite out of it. "I washed me hands!"

Griff grabbed an errant chair and pulled it up to the end of their long dining table. Beitrus, their old midwife, sat there kneading dough for bread. Moira, who ran the MacFalon castle almost singlehandedly, and had for years, sat with her, both of the old women chatting amiably. It had been poor old Beitrus who had offered to try Sibyl's "cure" for the wulver curse. She and Kirstin were the only two women who had ever taken the cure, and it had turned out to be quite permanent.

Sibyl had expressed her hope over the years that perhaps the effects would wear off and the women would be able to turn wolf again, but alas, that hadn't happened. Kirstin, who was married to The MacFalon now, didn't seem to mind. And old Beitrus said she was too old to turn wolf anymore anyway. She joked that the only thing turning wolf was good for at her age was better eyesight to sew by—and she didn't have hands to do that with in wulver form, so what use was it, after all? Besides, she often traveled back and forth between the MacFalon castle and the wulver den—she and Moira had become good friends and traded both recipes and herbal remedies—and while the Scots on MacFalon land had grown used to the wulvers over the past twenty years, it was still safer to remain human in their presence. Raife hadn't been joking, Griff knew, when he said they were the last of their kind, and most humans would kill them out of fear alone.

"I heard t'young girls talkin' 'bout yer sword skills in the Great Hunt today," Beitrus teased, pulling off a bit of dough and rolling it between her hands before putting it on a tray.

"They'd better not know anything about his sword skills," Sibyl called over her shoulder as she handed a young wulver girl—Colleen, a comely lass, Griff noted, who gave him a sly look—a stack full of wooden bowls so she could begin setting their places at the table. "Or they'll be scrubbing pots until their tails fall off."

Griff snickered, but he raised his eyebrows at Sibyl's sly smirk. "Aye? Is that so?"

"I heard ye got a scoldin' today, young pup." Moira stood, groaning softly as she put her hands at her lower back and arched. Griff just snorted at that, taking another noisy bite of apple. Moira gave him a sympathetic smile, leaning over to ruffle his hair. "He's hard on ye, but it's only a'cause he loves ye."

"Funny way of showin' it," Griff replied, mouth full.

"Ye'll understand why, some day," Beitrus told him, rolling another bit of dough in her hands. They were the very hands that had brought Griff into the world, which felt both comforting and strange at the same time as he watched her make biscuits. "Ye might even miss it."

"I doubt it." He rolled his eyes, ducking as his mother reached over to playfully smack him as she passed, finishing off his apple.

"You know, you're expected to lead them all, some day," Sibyl reminded him, stopping to press a soft kiss on his forehead instead of slapping him. She almost had to go on tiptoe to do it, even though she was standing and he was straddling a wooden chair.

"He'll ne'er let me lead," he growled, tossing the apple core into the fire—perfect aim. "Just like he doesn't even let us use real swords."

"Mayhaps yer destiny lies elsewhere," Moira mused, moving to help the younger wulver girls set the table on her end. Griff snorted at that, too. Talk of fate and destiny and prophecies bored him. He'd heard them his whole life, but they never really amounted to much. Just a lot of words in a book, written like code that they were supposed to translate.

"Moira..." Sibyl gave the old Scotswoman a dark glance, a clear warning. That caught Griff's attention.

"Aye, Mistress, aye," Moira muttered, eyes down as she set the table.

"Sibyl!" Laina poked her head in, glancing around at the crowded kitchen, wulver women bustling everywhere getting food ready for the feast. "Kirstin and Donal'd like t'see ye."

"Coming." Sibyl sighed, wiping her hands on her apron before untying it as she followed Laina out.

"What were ye sayin'?" Griff asked Moira as the woman came to take the tray, now filled with biscuits, from Beitrus. "'Bout m'destiny?"

"Oh ye've heard it all a'fore, lad." Moira gave him a half-smile as Maire, Griff's younger sister, took the tray from her hands, heading for the oven. "Y'know, t'prophecy of t'red wulver."

"Aye, t'red wulver, wit' t'red eyes." Griff rolled those same eyes as Maire came back carrying a tray laden with little pastries. "But what am I supposed to do? Whose savior am I again?"

"The future's uncertain." Moira sighed, leaning back and rubbing her tired eyes. "But there's somethin' to the prophecy, methinks. Even if it's the stuff of legend now."

"Ye're right t'question it, lad," Beitrus assured him with a pat of her hand on his arm. "The words're old and the translation isn't clear."

"Snitch!" Maire went to slap Griff's sneaky hand, but he was too quick for her. The pastries were juicy little bits filled with gravy and rabbit and he went to steal another one, but Maire gave him a dark look, sliding the tray down the table, out of his long reach.

"Brat." He scowled at his sister, wondering what in the world Rory saw in the girl. She was tall and dark-haired, like their father, and she had Sibyl's delicate features, but a wulver's blue eyes. She was comely enough, he supposed, but such a mouthy know-it-all, he didn't know how Rory could possibly stand being around her for more than five minutes.

"Jus' a'cause ye won at swordplay doesn'a mean ye get served a'fore e'eryone else." Maire wrinkled her freckled nose at him—she had her mother's pale skin and tendency to burn instead of turn brown like most of the wulver women.

"That's exactly what it means." Griff grinned.

"Not just ye, y'arrogant arse," his sister snapped. "Ye weren't t'only one out there swingin' a wooden sword."

"Aye, but I was t'best one," Griff called as his sister went to get more food for the table. She flipped her long, black braid over her shoulder in a huff and he laughed, tuning back into the conversation between Beitrus and Moira.

"We can'na tell 'em a'fore we know," Beitrus cautioned, glancing toward the entrance to the kitchen, as if worried Sibyl might reappear. "'Tis too dangerous, unless we know fer sure."

"What else could it be?" Moira scoffed. "It says the lost packs can be found in the Temple of Asher and Ardis—and legend says the temple's hidden on Skara Brae."

"Skara Brae, hm?" Griff's eyebrows went up at that. "What lost packs? You mean—more wulvers? I thought we were the last."

The two old women exchanged a look, and then looked up at him as he stood, staring down at them.

"Are there more of us, then?" Griff prompted.

"We do'na know..." Beitrus shrugged one frail shoulder. "Mayhaps. The text is unclear."

"Oh, I think it's clear enough." Moira snorted.

"Lost packs," Griff mused. A sharp zing of excitement went through his body at the thought. He hadn't put much stock in prophecies and ancient wulver texts, but the idea that there were, mayhaps, other wulvers out there—now, that was interesting.

"Do'na tell yer mother I said anythin'," Beitrus hissed. "Sibyl's still mad, twenty years later, that I stole t'cure and swallowed it, jus' to test it."

"Do'na worry. I'll keep yer secrets." Griff gave the old woman a wink as he headed toward the secret entrance to the spring that led to his parents' quarters. It was a cool spring, but not nearly as cold as the creek up top.

His mother had been right about one thing—he did stink. Griff stripped off his clothes and jumped in, the shock of the water hitting him like a wall, but he reveled in it.

It would serve two purposes—cleaning his body and clearing his head. The former wasn't all that important, except that he intended to find a little wolf tail later—but the latter was paramount. He needed a clear head to make the right decision. And he had a feeling that the decision he was contemplating would be the biggest decision he might ever make in his entire life.

Griff was up before first light. He had one candle lit to dress by. As the pack leader's son, he had the privilege of having his own room, even though the den was growing ever more crowded. In his bed, a young wulver woman—her name was Colleen, a shapely little lass who had offered her bottom up to him more than once the night before—rolled over and sighed in her sleep. She'd be surprised when she woke and found him gone. They both would—the other girl, Eryn, was curled up at the foot of the bed, in wolf form. Her white paws twitched in her sleep, like she was dreaming about running.

Griff thought of his mother as he rolled up the map of a route to Skara Brae he'd pinched from his father's room. Skara Brae was an island in the far north of Scotland, and it would be a long trip. Mayhaps even a treacherous one, given the number of reavers that roamed far beyond the borderlands now. But a necessary one. His decision had been made with a clear head. He would go to Skara Brae and find the lost packs. If there were other packs out there, mayhaps they were leaderless. Mayhaps he wouldn't have to challenge his father's position. Mayhaps that silly prophecy would serve a purpose after all.

Griff blew out the candle and slipped out of his room into the dark tunnel. His parents were likely still sleeping in the room beside his. The den was quiet, resting. Griff turned and headed toward the long staircase that would lead to the surface, where he would go to the barn and saddle his horse for travel. But before he reached the stairway, he stopped at the pack meeting hall, looking at the round table where his father always sat with the rest of the wulver council. His seat was to his father's left, Darrow's to his right. There was no head of the table, but everyone knew who was alpha.

Griff slipped his dirk out and stuck it into the wooden table in front of his seat. It was an old wulver way to mark your territory—it would let everyone know he'd be back, and that anyone who wanted his spot would be challenging him. Then he shouldered his pack and left the den of his childhood behind him.

Chapter Two

"I'm goin' t'win this time!" Bridget's sword glinted in the sun, and she had a brief hope that, just for a moment, it had distracted Alaric enough for her to triumph and turn her bold statement into truth.

But Alaric wasn't one to ever let her win, and while she was good—one of the best students he'd ever trained, as he often told her—she still had only bested him a few times.

His claymore was far bigger and heavier than her long sword, but he wielded it with frightening accuracy. Bridget went forward and back, her feminine form an advantage in the way she moved, with the grace of a dancer, but her footwork was wasted on a fighter like Alaric. He moved with the efficiency of a warrior, expending energy only when necessary, and despite his massive size, he was always ahead of her in some way. His claymore went left, and so did Bridget's long sword, but at the last moment, the big man's weapon changed direction, a feat which took a tremendous amount of strength.

She had always been vulnerable to fakes and feints, a fact Alaric used to his advantage.

"No!" Bridget brought her sword back just in time to block the blow. She panted with the effort it took to hold him at bay, but it didn't last long. Alaric saw her weakness and exploited it, unending her smaller form and sprawling her in the dirt. He pointed his claymore at her throat, although the tip stayed several feet away.

"Ye're dead." Alaric shook his head regretfully, as if he was truly sorry he'd "killed" her. "Ye lemme fake y'out again. Will ye e'er learn?"

"I did'na fall fer it t'first two times!" she reminded him, berating herself internally for falling for it the last time, or at all. Why did she always trust that someone was going to do what they looked like they were going to do?

"Ye know I've ne'er trained or fought a better student." He sheathed his claymore and held a hand out to help her up.

Bridget took it with a sigh, letting him pull her easily off the ground, even wearing mostly English armor, at least on her upper body. She brushed off her plaid. Her tailbone ached where she'd landed on it, but her pride was far more hurt. It wasn't losing that bothered her—losing was part of learning—it was making the same mistakes over and over that irked her.

"Yer doin' well, lass." Alaric's hand fell to her shoulder, as big as a ham, squeezing gently. "A fine guardian-in-trainin'. An' I know yer mother agrees wit' me, a fine handmaiden-in-training as well."

"Thank ye." She gave him an encouraged smile. Praise from Alaric wasn't earned easily, nor did she take it lightly.

"Jus' watch yer hips'n'torso. They ne'er lie." His left hand moved quickly, fingers snapping beside her ear, and her head turned left, instinctive. That's when he slapped her cheek lightly with his right. "D'ye see where me body was turned?"

He pointed to his chest and then left, dropping her a wink. "It gave me away, aye?"

"I'm too distractible." She sighed, sheathing her long sword, both cheeks burning, even though he'd only slapped one.

"Go t'yer mother by da pool, Miss Distractible." Alaric smiled. "It's time fer t'purification."

Bridget took off running—as fast as she could run with a sword sheathed at her side. Before she entered the temple proper, the sword came off, and she switched roles as quickly as she shed her armor. Alaric would yell at her for leaving it near the entrance, but she was already running late and her mother would be waiting.

She wore two temple hats, as both guardian-in-training and priestess-in-training, and learning both roles took most of her day. She didn't have a lot of free time, which seemed strange, given there were no other people in the temple, aside from Alaric and Aleesa. But it had always been that way, since she'd been abandoned at the temple entrance as an infant and the couple she knew as mother and father had taken her in. She really didn't know anything else.

Bridget stopped to quickly change from her plaid to her temple robe just outside the cave, taking the headpiece with the three-goddesses on it and placing it in the midst of her still-sweaty red hair.

"N'runnin', Bridget," her mother called with a sigh.

Aleesa was already kneeling at the pool when Bridget rushed in. She slowed almost immediately, still breathing hard. The pool was in the middle of a large cave with a tall, domed ceiling that had a central opening. It shone down into the pool below, and even at night, in the darkness, with almost no light in the sky, a beam of sun or moon focused in the pond. Alaric said it was due to some sort of reflective metal that had been embedded into the stone high above.

Bridget's heartbeat returned to some semblance of normal as she knelt opposite her mother, meeting Aleesa's soft, knowing eyes over the surface of the pool. Bridget's face flushed and she knew her mother understood exactly where she'd been, and why she was late. Could she help it that she liked training to be a guardian a little more than she liked training to be a temple priestess?

Not that she didn't love the sacred feel of the pool, how it calmed her soul. Just being amidst the stone monoliths that surrounded the little body of water in the cave helped ground and still her. Feeling the earth under her bare feet, looking at the beam of light shining into the center of the pool, gave her a sense of peace she didn't find anywhere else. She knew that the way the light fell, in relation to the stones, could be used to find and make many time and season calculations. She was in the process of learning the many ways these were related to both astronomy and astrology, starting to calculate these things as Aleesa taught her more and more.

But even if she hadn't been a priestess-in-training, she knew this place would feel like home to her.

"Are ye ready?" Aleesa cocked her head in question and Bridget took a deep breath, giving her a slow nod.

There was already a bowl in front of her filled with water and fragrant herbs and Bridget leaned over it, seeing a brief glimpse of her reflection—big eyes, mussed hair—as she picked the bowl up in both hands, breathing in the scent. The women worked together, perfectly in sync—they'd done this hundreds of times, since Bridget was very young—Alessa calling out the ancient words, Bridget responding in kind, as they dipped their fingers into the water, tracing patterns. Then, they took fingers full of the herbs, whispering the words in sync as they tossed them into the pool, kissing the side of the bowl before each pass. The whole cave smelled like silvermoon and heather. It was heady and made Bridget smile.

The bowls were then set aside, and each woman raised a ritual sword, incanting words together, the energy between them rising like a tide, their swords held out over the water. The ritual swords were far lighter than Bridget's practice one and were the only weapons allowed in the temple proper. Their voices melded together, almost a song, the rhythmic chant they spoke together, ancient Gaelic words, filling the cavern.

The prayer they spoke together was filled with power. Both women knew it, felt it. Bridget felt the hilt of the sword grow warm, as it always did, before the sword flared with flame. The first time it had happened, she'd nearly dropped it into the pool, even though Aleesa had warned her it would happen. She hadn't quite believed it, even though she'd lived in the temple her whole life and had seen the ritual performed.

As the prayer came to an end, the fire changed from a normal orange glow to silver. That was the time they slowly lowered their swords into the pool, extinguishing the flames with a low hissing sound. Steam rose up from the pool toward the domed roof of the cave. Bridget was always a little sad at the end of the ritual, but when she looked up and saw her mother's frown, her gaze fell immediately to the water.

"A single warrior approaches." Aleesa's eyes focused on the image reflected in the pool, widening in surprise. The pool served many purposes, and sometimes divination was one of them. "Ye mus' go out t'meet 'im, Bridget."

Bridget felt her mouth go dry. She'd only ever gone out to the crossroads once before to meet someone seeking entrance to the Temple of Asher and Ardis, and in that case, the man had not been worthy. Just someone seeking the riches of the temple—which were the stuff of legend, but not real. The only value within the temple was the magic it contained within its sacred walls, nothing payable in gold or silver, which is what most people seemed to want. Bridget hadn't even gotten to the point of challenging the old man—she'd simply sent him on his way. The entrance to the temple was hidden, and she was quite safe during the inquiry.

"Hurry! Go!" Aleesa urged her daughter, waving her away, and that got Bridget moving.

Her plaid was waiting, and she put that on instead of her temple robe, which she left on the floor as she rushed out to retrieve her armor. Aleesa would cluck and frown about her messiness, but under the circumstances, she knew she wouldn't be in too much trouble for not cleaning up after herself.

Alaric was standing at the temple entrance as she approached and she glanced guiltily down at her armor on the dirt floor. He frowned at it, then looked up at her, disappointment on his face, but that changed when their eyes met.

"Someone approaches?" he asked, eyes wide in surprise.

“Aye, a warrior.” She nodded, wondering if her fear showed. She hoped not. “Mother said I mus’ go out and meet ’im.”

Alaric gave a nod, already picking up her gear and helping her dress. Getting out of the stuff by herself was possible, but getting it on was much more difficult. They approached the secret entrance together. Alaric had been the one to do this before her, but he’d been training her over the years, and had deemed her ready. And if he thought she was ready, then it had to be so. Even if she was, at times, still susceptible to feints. Her challenger wouldn’t know that, would he? Alaric was one of the best fighters in the world, and he’d trained her—so if she could keep up with Alaric…

She’d have to trust that all would be as it should be.

That’s what she told herself as Alaric opened the underground passage that would lead her to the rock outcropping at the crossroads. She felt his hand on her shoulder, a sudden weight, and glanced back.

“Yer a fine guardian, lass,” he assured her. “It’ll all be as it should.”

Funny that she’d just spoken those words to herself. She gave him a nod, stepping out into the light of day. It was a glorious summer day and it made her wonder what normal maidens her age were doing. Picking flowers and making daisy chains, mayhaps? But not Bridget. She was walking out in full armor to meet a challenging warrior. Alaric and Alessa often said those words, “All will be as it should,” but sometimes, she wondered. Had she been meant to be abandoned at the temple? Meant to be trained as the priestess and guardian of the Temple of Ardis and Asher? It seemed a strange charge for a human girl who lived with and had been parented by wulvers, especially given that the legend of Ardis and Asher was a wulver legend and not a human one.

But she was doing it, standing behind the remote outcropping where she could disappear to safety inside the temple again, if she needed to. If the warrior sought healing and knew of the temple, the guardian had to yield and bring him inside. She had only glimpsed his image briefly in the pool, a big man on horseback wearing a Scots plaid and gear but no armor, not even chainmail or a helmet. Mayhaps he sought healing only?

Her armor was more English than Scottish, to be honest, made for a knight, with a breastplate and a full helmet and faceplate, although she had the freedom of her legs being bare—a Scot couldn't be tied down, that's what Alaric always said.

She was glad of the helmet, though, because it hid her face. She had learned, long ago, to disguise her voice, and had practiced throwing it beyond the outcropping into the crossroads, a booming reply to the inquiry of a seeker. There was a small, reflective piece of metal positioned so she could see the warrior's approach, although he could not see her or discern her position.

Bridget had a moment to just study him as he slowed his horse. She lifted her faceplate so she could do so more clearly. The war horse turned in easy, slow circles as the big man looked around, taking in his barren surroundings. The rocks were the only thing of interest, of course, as it was meant to be. The dark-haired warrior squinted at the rocks, brow lowered, mouth drawn down into a frown.

"Uri, this is ridiculous," the man muttered, patting his horse's neck. "'Ere goes nothin'."

The man sat back up, running a hand through his thick, dark hair. He was young, but not a boy. Mayhaps her age, she thought, cocking her head and staring at him. A considerable opponent to be sure. She really hoped he was here for healing, because she didn't want to have to fight him. She would, if she had to—but if she could just bid him enter, that would be better.

"I seek entrance t'the Temple of Asher'n'Ardis!" The man's voice carried to her easily. It was a pleasant sound, and she sensed no fear in it. No evil either. Just a little annoyance and impatience. This was a man who was used to gaining entry, wherever he went. That much was clear. Not royalty though. Not that kind of entitlement. She sensed more of a... confidence about him. Mayhaps a little arrogance?

Bridget swallowed, lubricating her throat, before lowering her voice and booming her own reply, "Who seeks entrance?"

The horse startled, giving a low whinny and pawing the dirt. The man handled the horse with ease, turning the animal toward the rocks.

"Now we're getting' somewhere," he muttered, calling back, "My name's Griffith."

Just Griffith? No surname? No title? She cocked her head, frowning at that. A simple man, then? But he did not look simple. The man was big, well-muscled. This man trained, and he trained hard.

"An' what d'ye seek, Griffith?" Bridget called, making sure she kept her voice an octave lower than usual. Funny, how his name felt in her mouth. Familiar, somehow, although she'd never heard it called.

"Knowledge."

Her heart sank. Not healing, then. A seeker who was true, who sought anything other than healing, would have to force the guardian to yield in combat if they wanted entrance. The guardian could, on rare occasion, choose to yield without a fight, but it hardly ever happened. Had never happened, in her lifetime, or Alaric's either, he'd told her.

"Are ye there?" Griff called. Impatient. She'd have to remember that.

She wasn't relishing fighting this man, who was twice her size at least. Were Alaric and Aleesa watching in the pool? They would be, of course. It would be her first real combat with an entrant, and she didn't want to disappoint her father. Especially after her loss to him that afternoon.

"Ye mus' prove yerself worthy, seeker," she called, managing to keep the tremble from her voice. It was both excitement, and, mayhaps, a little fear. "By bestin' me in combat."

"Then come out an' meet me, stranger." Griff straightened in his saddle, a slow smile spreading across his face.

"I'm t'guardian of t'temple." Bridget stepped toward the rocks, putting her face plate down, and her hand on the hilt of her sword. "And ye shall not pass 'til ye best me an'force me t'yield."

"I can'na best ye unless I can see ye." Griff stared at the rocks, blinking in surprise when Bridget appeared from behind them. She'd never used the secret entrance before, but it worked just like Alaric said it would.

"I can'na fight a boy." Griff snorted as he slid off his horse. She saw him searching the rocks with his eyes, wondering where in the world she'd come from. "T'would nuh be right."

"I'm not a boy." Bridget raised her sword, feeling anger burning in her chest at the man's words. A boy, indeed! Not only wasn't she a boy—and what a surprise he'd get when he was bested by a girl!—she was a warrior, trained by one of the best warriors in all of Scotland.

She might not have been quite good enough to beat Alaric, but she could beat this man—even if he was twice her size.

"I do'na wanna fight ye, lad." Griff sighed, shaking his head as he unsheathed his sword.

"Ye've no choice, seeker." Bridget straightened her spine to give herself full height, but the top of her head still barely reached his shoulder. "If ye wan' entry t'the temple, ye mus' force t'guardian t'yield."

"I do'na hafta kill ye?" Griff frowned. "I'd hate t'hafta kill ye."

"Tis not to the death." Bridget rolled her eyes behind her face plate. "But ye'll be lucky if I do'na kill *ye,* seeker."

"Let's get this over wit', lad." Griff stepped away from his horse with another deep sigh, moving quickly into fighting stance, sword up.

"I'm not a lad!" she snapped gruffly as she swung, their swords clashing with the ring of steel in the afternoon sunlight.

She was still a little tired, muscles sore, from her training with Alaric, but she wasn't going to let that stop her. The big man blocked her blow easily, taking a graceful step back and sighing again, like it was quite taxing to be forced to fight her. Bridget felt anger rising and tried to swallow it down. Her father had trained her to stay calm and cool-headed in a fight and normally, she didn't have any problem with that. But for some reason, seeing this giant, broad-shouldered man smirking, even chuckling as she advanced, made her furious.

Griff's sword blocked another one of her blows and Bridget swung again, more quickly this time, driving him backward. The horse pawed the ground a few feet away, as if objecting to his master's sudden predicament. It didn't take Bridget long to push the big man back toward the other side of the crossroads, going after him relentlessly, swing after swing of her heavy long sword.

"Well, lad, ye take yer job seriously, that much is clear." Griff panted as he rallied, getting his bearings and whirling on her, his sword blow coming so hard and fast, it actually knocked her off her feet.

Her pride was hurt more than her bottom as she struggled to stand.

"Ye'll right, lad?" Griff frowned, reaching down a hand to help her up, and that's when something inside Bridget snapped.

She was up in an instant, running at him like a bull, her helmet hitting him hard in the gut. She heard the air go out of him and he grunted. Her fast action had surprised him, caught him off guard, and he stumbled. Unfortunately, he didn't go down as she planned. It took him just two strides to regain his footing and he gave a low growl, whirling on her, sword at the ready.

"I'm endin' this now." Griff snarled, coming at her so fast and furious, she could barely see his sword flashing. She had to repel him only on instinct, which she managed, but it took her breath away. "Someone needs t'teach ye a lesson."

Bridget winced as the big man's sword slid against hers and she found herself pinned against the rock—

how they'd managed to get so far, she didn't know. He crushed her against the stone with his weight until she couldn't breathe at all, even in her armor. Her breastplate dug into her skin, compressing the air from her lungs. She tried to move, but there was no possible way. He covered her completely, his arm across her chest and shoulders, heavy as a log, his thigh between hers, so thick it felt like she was straddling a tree.

Bridget struggled, trying to lift her sword, but he had that trapped too, with the heavy weight of his boot. The anger rising in her blurred her vision. She could only see a slit of him through her face plate. His breath was hot and heavy, but not unpleasant. He ducked his head so he could see her eyes—his were the strangest color she'd ever seen, a sort of amber, and for a moment, she was transfixed. The man searched her eyes with his, far too much amusement in them at having bested her, but there was an empathy there too, that bothered her even more.

He let up just a little as he asked, voice soft, "D'ye yield?"

Bridget thought of Alaric, watching her in the clear surface of the scrying pool—or mayhaps he was standing even now on the other side of the rock wall, watching via the reflective metal she'd used to spy on the approaching warrior. She wouldn't yield—couldn't let him down.

She shook her head, glaring at him, and wheezed, "No."

"Yield, lad," he said gently. "I *will* best ye, and if ye yield now, t'will mean far less bruisin' fer ye—an' yer pride."

Bridget snarled, throwing all her weight at him—not that it made that much of a difference. How could

Alaric have handed over this task to her? How could he have believed she could best someone twice her size? But he had charged her with this task. He believed in her. He thought she could do this, had trained her to be better than this.

"Get off me, ye fat oaf," she snapped, hearing him chuckle, then sigh and shake his head as he eased back.

"So ye yield then?"

"No!" She grunted, bringing her knee up between his—it wasn't exactly fair, but she knew it would work. Luckily the man was a Scot, and like her, he wore a plaid to keep his legs free for running and climbing. She'd accidentally kneed Alaric this way on a few occasions and had completely incapacitated him for a while.

But the big man was too fast. He stepped back, just barely avoiding the knee to his crotch. That gave her the opportunity to go after him again, and she did, with everything she had. They danced and swung, metal clashing. It was exhausting, but Bridget didn't give up. This smug man wasn't going to enter her temple, not if she could prevent it. He wasn't worthy.

"Yield!" Bridget yelled, swinging her sword hard over her head at the dark-haired beast but he blocked her blow. She was satisfied to see the surprise in his eyes, though, at her onslaught.

It was that brief moment of patting herself on the back that was her undoing. That and the feint he made, untangling his sword from hers and jabbing at her. The sword went under her arm and Bridget took an instinctive step back, but it was too late.

He used his sword as a lever, pushing her forward, toward him. Their bodies jarred together and Bridget felt her teeth rattle in her head. Running into the man's chest was like running into a stone wall. She gasped, all her breath gone from her lungs as the man tripped her, hooking a foot around her calf and tipping her into the dirt.

"Yer finished, lad." Griff planted his sword in the dirt right beside her head and Bridget winced. "Now, take me t'the temple, a'fore I really hafta hurt ye."

"Aye." She swallowed her pride, along with a cloud full of dust, struggling to stand. She ignored the hand the man offered, making her way slowly to her feet and trying to find her balance. She leaned against the outcropping, ashamed that Alaric would be seeing this. "O'er there. See t'rock?"

Her voice was hoarse.

"Aye." Griff gave a brief nod, lifting a hand to shade his eyes in the afternoon sun.

"We'll meet ye by t'rock." She waved him on, limping toward the secret entrance.

"We?" The big man frowned. "Were d'ya think yer goin', lad? I did'na come all this way t—"

To lick my wounds.

A hand grabbed her elbow and she shook it off, snarling.

"Let go'a me!"

"Are ye hurt?" Griff asked, concerned. She bristled at his tone. It only made the hurt, real and imagined, worse.

"T'rock!" she snapped, pointing. "Go!"

"I'm n'accustomed t'taking orders from boys," the man snorted, and the arrogance in his voice broke her.

"I'm not a boy!" she snapped again, whirling toward him and flipping her faceplate up to glare at him. He stared at her for a moment, confused, as if trying to figure something out.

She could still scarce breathe and, in one swift motion, pulled her helmet off her head, letting her long, auburn hair spill like a rain of fire over the silver breastplate.

The look on his face was priceless.

His mouth dropped open, his strange-colored eyes going wide.

"Yer a lass?" he choked, blinking fast.

"Aye." She stared at him, drawing herself up as tall as she could, pointing again to the rock where Alaric would take the man and his horse into the temple. "Ye bested a woman. I hope yer proud o'yerself. Now, if ye wanna enter the temple, I suggest ye go t'the rock."

She didn't bother to stay and see what he would do. Bridget went straight to the secret entrance in the rock outcropping and slipped inside. She managed to walk upright, in a straight line, until she was out of his sight line.

Only then did she allow the tears that threatened to flow, and she went to her knees, sword and helmet forgotten in the grass, as she wept like she hadn't since she was a little girl.

Chapter Three

Griff stood at the rock face feeling like a complete fool. Not only had he just nearly killed a woman—what kind of temple used a woman dressed in armor as a guardian anyway?—but now he'd walked Uri down the road to yet another rock, and he stood waiting for someone to appear and allow him entrance to a place that, up until half an hour ago, he wasn't quite sure actually existed. Mayhaps it was all a ruse, he thought, glowering at the rock. It was almost as tall as he was and he saw no door, no way in or out of any temple.

Of course, the guardian—*the woman*, his mind corrected, and he felt another twinge of guilt at what he'd done—had appeared out of nowhere, or so it seemed. Mayhaps this rock was the same. Or mayhaps they were all just bandits, a ring of reavers working together with the pirates who had given him passage and had told him where to go, how to find his way to this strange island, to this particular crossroads and rock outcropping. Mayhaps the woman was just a distraction, and even now, there were men hidden somewhere with arrows pointed at his head.

Although if they were hidden somewhere, he didn't know where.

There were no trees on these rolling green hills, nothing from here until the sea.

Griff lifted his nose and sniffed the air, but caught nothing except the scent of his horse, the salt of the sea, and the green of the grass mixed with a carpet of heather. And the woman. He scented her still, something he'd noticed during their encounter, but had dismissed. He'd thought it was just the smell of a youngster, a pup. He'd realized the smaller figure in armor was just a lad right off, but why hadn't he realized she was a woman? He chastised himself again, squinting at the sun overhead, remembering the way she'd pulled off her helmet, the fire that flashed in her grey-green eyes.

He'd been more than surprised, truth be told. The lad—the figure in armor he was sure was just a young boy—had put up a good fight. He... er, *she*... had been taught well. If she'd been comparable in size, mayhaps she would have stood a chance. He'd started to feel a little bad for her, before he found out she was actually a girl. Now... he wasn't sure what he felt. Whatever it was, it was strange. He'd felt something when he first met her eyes, just peering into the slit in her faceplate.

But when she'd yanked off her helmet and glared at him, and he watched a cascade of red fire roll over her shoulders, it hit him with the force of a herd of horses. It had literally taken his breath away. At first, he thought it was just the fact that she was a woman, that he had spilled a woman into the dirt and threatened her bodily harm. But it wasn't just that. There was something else, something about her. He wondered if she'd felt it, too.

Then he remembered the way she'd glared at him, how her spine had straightened, her pride clearly bruised, maybe even more than her body, and chuckled to himself.

He was so lost in thought, he almost didn't see it happen.

Griff frowned, seeing the rock move out of the corner of his eye, an effect that startled his horse. Uri whinnied and stepped sideways, shaking his head, and

Griff grabbed hold of his reins to keep the big animal from bolting.

"Ye've bested our guardian, and so've earned entrance t'the Temple of Asher'n'Ardis." The voice made Griff whirl around and he stared at the man who stood at the cave entrance. It had been quite hidden by the rock, and Griff frowned, wondering how the man had moved the giant thing. "Follow me."

"M'horse," Griff said, but the man was already moving back underground, into the cave.

"Bring 'im," the man called over his shoulder.

Griff urged Uri forward, but the horse fought him. The animal didn't like the idea of going underground, not knowing what was down there in the dark, and Griff didn't blame him. But he hadn't traveled all this way to stop now. He tugged the horse's reins, making a gruff noise in his throat, and Uri reluctantly followed.

"Is the... uh..." Griff realized he didn't know the woman's name. "The lass... the guardian... is she hurt?"

The man snorted. "Only 'er pride."

Griff grinned at that. "I did'na know she was a lass."

"She'll be glad t'hear it." The man stopped, pressing something on the wall, and behind them, the rock moved again, blocking out the light.

Griff glanced back, checking to make sure his sword was still in his sheath, just in case. The other man lit a fire in a bowl, mumbling something, a prayer perhaps. Griff sighed with impatience. He'd traveled a long way to find this place, and he had a lot of questions he hoped someone here had the answers to.

The fire bowl lit the underground cavern. This place would provide protection, Griff realized, from both the weather and the sea. And, of course, enemies.

Much like their den at home, he thought, studying the big man who turned back toward him, the fire lighting his lined face.

The man was as tall as Griff, steel gray hair falling to his shoulders, a thick beard covering his face. It was only when he turned toward him and Griff caught his scent that they recognized each other—not as men who knew each other, but as wulvers.

"Yer like me." Griff blinked at the man, incredulous.

He'd never seen another wulver outside of his own den.

"Aye." The man wrinkled his nose, almost a snarl—it was a gesture Griff was used to. The man was scenting him. "Ye've come a long way, lad."

"Aye," he agreed. "I seek answers."

"C'mon, then."

The big man led him further into the cavern, and Griff pulled his horse along. They came to a turn, and the man led him left, showing him a place where he could tie Uri in a stall and leave him beside two other horses.

"D'ye 'ave anyone t'tend him?" Griff asked, glancing around the cavern.

"I'm 'fraid not." The old man shook his head. "There're jus' a few of us."

"Can ye wait fer me t'do so?"

"Aye."

Griff took the time to rub the horse down. The animal hadn't liked traveling on the ship he'd taken to the island. It had been quite an adventure so far, for both of them. There were two other horses in the stalls, fine looking animals, and Griff admired them. He gave Uri a feed bag and tossed straw down for him before following the other man through the tunnels of the cavern.

"Where'd ye hear 'bout our temple?" The man held the fire bowl aloft as he walked, far too slow for Griff, but he accommodated the man's pace. The other wulver was an older man, but by no means ancient. Griff guessed that he was mayhaps twenty years older than Griff's own father.

"The healers in m'den." Griff followed the man around a corner, light coming from the end of the tunnel.

"Leave yer weapons 'ere." The older man unsheathed a sword, leaving it on a rack built into the cavern wall, glancing back at Griff, who did the same. "No weapons're allowed in t'sanctuary. Ye may 'ave it back when ye go."

"But weapons're required t'enter?" Griff's brows went up, and he smirked.

"Nuh, n'required." The man balanced the fire bowl in his hands as he walked. They were entering the main part of the temple, exiting the cavernous tunnels. "Those who seek healin' here, receive it wit'out challenge. But ye're not in need of such healin'. Ye're seekin' somethin' else."

That much was true. Griff didn't know how the man knew. But mayhaps it was just a guess, and he knew nothing. How could he? Griff himself had only a vague idea of what it was he sought here in the temple of his ancestors. The lost packs. Mayhaps there was something he was meant to do, some greater destiny out there in the world for him, but whatever it was, there were wulvers out there who needed a leader.

The lost packs that Beitrus and Moira had spoken of must be part of whatever destiny awaited him. He was almost certain of that fact. To his knowledge, there was no other place where he could find out about the lost packs except for this fabled temple. Now he knew it was not the stuff of legend, but it actually existed. That was, at least, a step in the right direction.

The older man led him into a large, cavernous room. It was warm and inviting and felt very much like back home in his den. He didn't wonder at it too much—they were, after all, underground, and that's where all wulver dens were located, and for good reason. He supposed it shouldn't have been a surprise that the Temple of Asher and Ardis, the first wulvers, was also underground.

"Ye've bested our Guardian, seeker," the older man told him, as they neared the light at the end of the tunnel. "Ye're welcome in the Temple of Ardis'n'Asher, the first wulvers, and as Guardian meself, I'll do what I can t'help ye find what ye seek. Our temple priestess, Aleesa, is also at yer disposal, seeker."

"Thank ye." Griff looked up as they stepped into the warm, inviting room. There was a fireplace on one wall, with a fire lit in it. The smell of roasting meat made his stomach rumble. It reminded him of their big kitchen back home, in miniscule version.

The older man put the fire bowl in the middle of a wooden table. Griff looked at the bowl closely for the first time. He could not see how or what was burning in it. It was too close to magic for his comfort.

"Is this our seeker, then?" A woman, older as well, with long, dark, plaited hair shot with streaks of gray, entered the room from the other side. She smiled at Griff in welcome, holding out her hands to him as she approached. She was still a stunningly beautiful woman, with full, red lips, a curvy, voluptuous figure under her priestess robe, and a smile that lit up the entire room. "I'm Aleesa, the high priestess of t'temple."

"M'name's Griff." He took both of her outstretched hands in his, raising one of them to his lips to kiss it. "And I'm, indeed, a seeker. I do hope that yer other temple guardian's doin' a'righ'?"

"Bridget?" Aleesa glanced over her shoulder at the entrance she had come through. "She's a tough 'un."

"I told 'im 'er pride's bruised more'n 'er body." The older man chuckled. Aleesa gave him a knowing smile.

"So ye're wulver as well?" Griff asked Aleesa as she bade him to sit down at the table where the fire bowl still burned.

"Aye, a'course." Aleesa waved the older man into a seat beside her. "What else did y'expect at the Temple of Asher'n'Ardis?"

"I s'pose." Griff gave a rueful laugh. "I've jus' ne'er known any other wulvers outside of m'own den. I did'na know any others existed."

"But ye clearly do'na believe that." The older man raised his craggy eyebrows. "Ye're here seekin' others."

"How d'ye know that?" Griff's own eyebrows rose in surprise. "I've n'spoken of that which I seek."

"We see much." Aleesa folded her hands in her lap and looked at Griff expectantly. "But we'd hear yer request. And as guardian and priestess of the temple, we'll do our best t'accommodate ye."

"I hafta tell ye, I do'na b'lieve in magic." Griff bristled at the smile the dark-haired woman gave him when he said this. To Griff, things beyond comprehension only seemed unexplainable. Like his uncle, Darrow, he was very much a skeptic when it came to magic spells and potions.

Granted, he knew his own mother, Sibyl, had concocted the "cure" for the wulver woman's monthly curse, and at least two wulver women, Beitrus and Kirstin, had taken that "cure," and both of them seemed unable to change to wolf form now, but Griff still had his doubts. Even as he looked into the flame of the bowl burning in front of him, he doubted.

Even seeing wasn't always believing.

He remembered the way the armored guardian had appeared from the rock outcropping, and wondered how such an illusion had been accomplished. But he still didn't believe it was magic. Tricks, certainly. Those were commonplace and could be explained. He had lived with healers his whole life, women many would call witches, but he knew their "magic" had far more to do with the natural world than anything beyond it.

Remembering the guardian, the woman who had revealed herself to him in one glorious unveiling, he glanced around the room, wondering why this pair of temple guardians would have allowed her to go out and meet him, instead of sending the bigger, older man out to fight.

Certainly, the man was no longer a young pup, but he was a man, and a wulver, which Griff was sure the young redhead was not. The man and woman at the table with him were wulvers—he could smell it on them. The man was, like Griff, a wulver warrior. He could transform into half-man, half-wolf, at his choosing.

Griff didn't know why it bothered him so much—mayhaps it was because the woman had nearly bested him, twice—but the thought of this man, old enough to be the young redhead's father, mayhaps even grandfather, waiting underground while she faced danger…

"It matters not what ye b'lieve." Aleesa glanced over Griff's shoulder, smiling in welcome. "Here's our Bridget now."

Griff could smell her.

She filled his senses, even before he turned his head to look at the woman who approached. Without her armor to hide her figure, Bridget was all woman. Her priestess robes, cinched at the waist, surprised him. They were just like the other woman, Aleesa's, made of some shiny, reflective white material that clung to her generous curves, a sight that made Griff salivate like a starving man who had just come upon a king's feast. Bridget nodded to the older couple, glancing briefly at Griff as she went about gathering cups and warming water over the fireplace.

"I hope ye're n'hurt, lass," Griff called to the redhead, seeing the way her back stiffened at his words. She continued to pour water, now warm, into four mugs. But she didn't reply. Griff looked at the man, whose name he still did not know, and felt a flash of anger. "What sorta man sends a young woman out t'do 'is work?"

"One who wants 'er t'learn," the old man replied simply. He met Griff's dark stare with his own. The older man's eyes were wulver blue, as were the woman's. He wondered where the red-haired, green-eyed creature bringing tea to them at the wooden table had come from. She was not a wulver, but she was like no human woman he had ever known. He certainly knew no women who donned armor and wielded swords, and then changed into silky priestess robes and murmured niceties as she sat beside him at the table.

"It is as it should be, father." Bridget sighed, lifting the mug toward her mouth, blowing on the hot liquid. Griff cocked his head, looking at her, at the pucker of her lips, the way her eyes lifted to meet his own. The way she looked at him filled him with heat. He shifted in his chair, looking up at Aleesa as she stood.

"I imagine ye're hungry, warrior." Aleesa nudged the younger woman and Bridget put down her mug, getting up to help set the table.

Griff offered to help, something he would never do at home, but the women waved him off, so he and the older man sat together at the table, face-to-face, while Griff wondered where to start.

As if reading his mind, the older man half-smiled, and asked, "What is't that ye seek, wulver warrior?"

Griff frowned into his mug of tea, a mug that seemed giant in the redhead's hands, but diminutive in his own. He supposed there was no better way than to just come out and say it.

"I need t'know where t'find the lost packs'o'wulvers."

Bridget, who had been reaching over his shoulder to place a wooden plate and spoon in front of him, stopped what she was doing to stare at him.

"And why d'ye seek this knowledge?" the gray-haired wulver asked.

"He's a wulver?" Bridget blurted, blinking at Griff in surprise. "Is e'eryone beyond these temple walls half-wolf'n'half-man? Am I t'only one who can'na change t'animal form?"

“A’course not.” Aleesa smiled, putting the roast meat and a pot of vegetables on the table. “In fact, t’opposite’s true. Most beasts who roam this world are either man or animal, not both.”

“Tis true,” Griff agreed, giving a laugh. The redhead glared at him as if finding out he was a wulver was the last insult she could possibly bear. “’Ave ye ne’er been beyond these temple walls?”

“A’course I have,” Bridget snapped, pulling back, away from the brush of Griff’s upper arm as if she had been burned. The silk of her robe brushing his skin was intoxicating. “Jus’ not… far.”

“’Bout as far as t’rocks ye met me at, I’d wager.” Griff grinned.

“Ye’d n’lose that wager, lad.” The older man chuckled and the redhead’s spine stiffened again, her lips pursing prettily.

The old man looked at his daughter—Griff still couldn’t quite comprehend how the young woman called the old wulver father, when clearly she was not their issue—smiling ruefully. “I can’na take ’er much further than I a’ready ’ave. She’s been a fine student, an obedient daughter, an’ her mother an’ I love ’er dearly. We’ve trained ’er all these years t’fill two roles—that of temple handmaiden and temple guardian. Tis a heavy burden fer one so young, but there’s no other. And ’er mother an’ I’ll n’live fore’er. Certainly, we’ll live longer than most in the safety of this sacred place, and t’will keep us ’ere t’tend it ’til there’s another.”

“Tis as it should be, Father,” Bridget reminded him, putting a pitcher of cool water in the middle of the table as she sat beside Griff.

"I wondered why ye'd send a woman out as temple guardian," Griff mused, accepting a delicious smelling leg of chicken with an empty plate as Aleesa carved. "But clearly ye've no other choice."

"I almos' bested ye—twice," Bridget reminded coolly. She plucked two errant feathers from the wing of a chicken on her plate with a vengeance.

"I mus' confess, I almos' let ye win." Griff grinned when she gave him a look, eyes narrowed to gray-green slits, like a cat. "But I've traveled a long way, seekin' knowledge at this temple. If I had t'kill ye, I s'pose I would've. A'fore I knew ye were a woman…"

"What's that hafta do wit' anythin'?" Bridget wrinkled her snub nose at him, reaching for her mug of tea. "I'm jus' as much a warrior as ye're. Me father was ona t'greatest wulver warriors in history. I've learned from t'best."

"But ye're not a wulver." Griff stated the obvious, in spite of the way she glowered at him. "And ye *are* a woman. Men, 'specially wulver men, have a physical advantage ye do'na. It's simple fact."

Griff gnawed on the leg of chicken, picking it cleanly of meat, before reaching for another, trying to ignore the holes the woman was trying to burn into him with her eyes. But she wasn't about it let it go.

Bridget's voice trembled just slightly as she leveled her gaze on him. "Ye're t'most arrogant… foolhardy…" Her eyes dropped to the chicken breast he held in his fingers. "Slob of a man I've *e'er* met."

Griff met her unwavering gaze. She was nearly smoldering, she was so angry. Out of the corner of his eye, he saw the older woman, Aleesa, frowning at her daughter's words.

"An' how many men've ye met?" Griff inquired politely, managing to keep most of the smirk off his face.

"What does't matter?" she asked, straightening her shoulders haughtily.

Griff shrugged one shoulder, reaching for his mug. "I need t'know yer frame'o'reference."

"He's insufferable!" Bridget exclaimed, looking across the table at her father. "I'm sorry I did'na best 'im fer ye. He does'na deserve whate'er knowledge he's 'ere t'seek. An' I do'na feel ye should give it t'him."

"How d'ye know anythin' about me?" Griff asked, still keeping his tone conversational. He wasn't going to take the girl's bait, no matter how she set the trap.

"I know enough." Bridget snapped a carrot between her teeth, chewing noisily. The vegetable clearly hadn't been fully cooked. "I know ye're full'o'pride. Ye're boastful, ye're rude, ye b'lieve ye're entitled. Not only t'whate'er 'tis ye wanna know 'bout t'lost packs'o'wulvers, but ye act as if ye're king of 'em a'ready."

"Bridget," Aleesa warned, shaking her head.

"Accordin' t'prophecy, I am." Griff smiled, a little smugly, he had to admit.

He heard Aleesa gasp, and she put her trembling mug back on the table to gape at him. Her blue eyes stared into his, her head cocked, and he knew she was seeing, maybe for the first time, the color of his eyes.

He wondered if they were their usual, strange, gold color, or if they had suddenly flared red. He sometimes could feel when it happened, especially when he was angry, but not always. The older man was watching too, a look on his face that had not been there previously. It wasn't frightened, like the dark-haired wulver woman, it was harder, more knowing, and resolute.

"Wha' prophecy?" Bridget looked between her parents, frowning, and then at Griff. "I know of no prophecy about t'king of wulvers. Ye're an arrogant, assumin' fool."

"Mayhaps ye do'na know as much as ye think ye do." Griff blinked at her and Bridget glared back, grinding her teeth. He could hear it.

"T'red wulver?" Aleesa's voice trembled almost as much as her mug had in its journey from hand to table. She glanced at her husband, meeting his eyes, and something passed between them.

The gray-haired wulver stood, towering at full height, looking down at Griff and snarling, "That's not a claim t'make lightly."

"It's mine t'make." Griff stood, too, and it happened so fast that both women at the table jumped back in shock when Griff shook his dark mane of hair and shifted instantly from man to wulver-warrior. His half-wolf form was formidable, twice his normal size, with a wolf's head but a man's body, his fur a dark russet color, his eyes blood red, flashing.

He didn't need to see himself to know.

He saw it in their eyes.

He saw it on Bridget's already pale face that went stark white at the sight of him.

Not to be outdone, the older man shifted, too. His mane of hair turned to gray fur and teeth, as the two wolf-men faced each other across the table, growling deep in their throats, threatening each other, dark lips pulled back from their canines in warning.

"Enough!" Aleesa cried, standing and holding a palm out to each wulver, as if she could keep them apart. "Violence's forbidden 'ere. If ye wanna 'ave a pissin' contest, go do it top side, d'ye hear me?"

Griff shifted back first, with a shake of his big, russet-colored wolf head, and the older man followed suit, but the tension hadn't eased in the slightest. Griff felt the hair still standing up on the back of his neck as he faced the gray-haired wulver.

"If he really *is* t'red wulver..." Aleesa murmured to her husband. The gray-haired man's lip curled, and Griff saw, he didn't know what to believe.

"I *am* t'red wulver," Griff insisted. He'd been called such in his own pack for so long, he wasn't used to being doubted. "Ye're addressin' yer future king."

"Ye're no one's king yet, pup." The other man leveled him with a long stare. "And ye're addressin' Alaric, t'Gray Ghost, swordmaster t'yer father, Raife, and 'is father a'fore 'im, and senior guardian of this temple. Ye'll stand down, or I'll be glad t'remind ye of yer place 'ere."

Griff had the impulse to fly across the table, to take him on here and now, but he saw the way Bridget glared at them, how Aleesa's eyes grew wide as she looked between the two men, and so he held back. They had information he wanted—needed. Mayhaps if he could convince them of the prophecy, and that he was the wulver who fulfilled it, they would be more forthcoming with that information.

"Alaric, t'Gray Ghost." Griff held his hand out to the other man, who took it, and they shook. "Yer reputation proceeds ye. M'father talked overmuch of yer swordsmanship and yer bravery. Now I know where t'lass learned it."

That broke the tension and they all sat down again to eat. He was surprised by the girl beside him, whose anger seemed to have ebbed away entirely. She just watched and listened as they talked around the table.

"So ye're really Raife's son?" Alaric asked, studying him. Both the wulvers looked at him quite differently now that they knew his parentage. That both pleased and annoyed him.

"Aye." Griff reached for the last leg of chicken at the same time as the woman beside him.

"Ye look like 'im." Aleesa nodded over her mug.

"More's the pity." Griff snorted, struggling with Bridget briefly over the leg of chicken. Another test of wills. He glanced at her, smiling, and she rolled her eyes and gave up, letting him have it.

"Except t'eyes," Alaric noted.

"How'd ye come t'be 'ere, in this temple?" Griff asked, leaning over and depositing the last chicken leg in his hand on Bridget's plate. "Story tells that yer wife went out t'gather herbs and ne'er returned?"

"Aye." Alaric nodded. "Aleesa had a dream 'bout this place. She was called 'ere, y'ken?"

"By... who?" Griff blinking, glancing around, as if another presence might suddenly appear and make themselves known, although he knew that was unlikely.

"I do'na know," Aleesa said softly, her gaze dropped to her plate. "T'was a voice from… far 'way, 'cross t'sea. I had t'follow."

"So ye left yer husband an' young pup?" Griff looked over at Bridget as she tossed the chicken leg back onto his plate.

"Pup?" Bridget asked, looking at her mother, clearly surprised.

"A daughter..." Aleesa did not lift her lowered eyes, and her voice dropped to something so soft it was hard to hear her. "Kirstin..."

"An' ye followed 'er?" Griff asked. He picked up the chicken leg, studying it. He no longer wanted it, would have let the girl have it, but she refused. That irked him.

"Aye," Alaric agreed, sliding a hand over his mate's on the table. "I followed, and I found 'er."

"How?" he asked. "How could ye know where she'd gone?"

"I did'na know," Alaric admitted, looking at his mate with the kind of love Griff was used to seeing pass between couples he knew—like his parents, like Laina and Darrow, Kirstin and Donal. He knew that kind of love when he saw it, even if it continued to baffle him. "I followed 'er trail at first. Then, later, I discovered a woman'd sought passage t'Skara Brae from t'place where her trail ended, and I knew't mus' be 'er. I challenged the guardian of this temple—an' I slew 'im."

"There was a guardian 'ere?" Griff stared at him in surprise as he quietly snuck the chicken leg onto Bridget's plate. The girl noticed and glanced at him, but she didn't say anything.

"Aye, but no priestess." Alaric patted his wife's hand. "Aleesa knew… t'was 'er callin'."

The dark-haired woman lifted her eyes to meet his and Griff saw tears there. It pained him. He knew the woman who was her daughter, who had been without her mother for years, who thought the woman was likely dead—and her father, as well.

"Ye know m'Kirstin?" Aleesa asked him softly. Her lower lip quivered. "She's well?"

"Aye," he replied, nodding. "Her son, Rory, is one of me truest friends."

"She has a son..." Aleesa looked over at her husband and something passed between them. How long had it been, Griff wondered, since the parents had seen their daughter? Forty years, mayhaps? The older wulver woman turned back to Griff, asking, "She found 'er one true mate, then?"

"Aye, The MacFalon." He had already told her he didn't believe in magic—he wasn't about to tell her he didn't believe in "one true mates" either.

"The... who?" Bridget looked blindsided. She'd forgotten the fought-over chicken leg. She'd probably even forgotten her loss to Griff at the crossroads, from the confused, surprised look on her face.

"Donal MacFalon," he explained. "Son of Lachlan. Brother of Alistair."

"My Kirstin's married t'The MacFalon?" Alaric's voice was as hard as granite.

"He's a fine man," Griff countered, shaking his head at the old man's alarm. He could understand it, of course. There was a time when The MacFalon—in fact, all of the MacFalon clan—had actively hunted and killed wulvers. But that wasn't the case anymore, not since the wolf pact. King Henry VII, who had an encounter with Griff's grandmother, from which his father, Raife, was born, had initiated the wolf pact. It had resulted in peaceable relations between the wulvers, Scots and English for years.

"He's a good husband an' father," Griff told them. "An' a trusted leader."

"He's still laird of the clan?" Aleesa asked, cocking her head in confusion.

"Aye. He was when I left." Griff chuckled. "They live in Castle MacFalon."

"How?" Aleesa frowned. "I know t'wolf pact was keepin' the peace b'tween 'em, but... I can'na imagine t'MacFalons allowin' wulvers t'live in t'castle."

"Heh. You'd be surprised." Griff grinned, remembering how often he was at Castle MacFalon, or Rory was visiting the den. They passed back and forth quite often with no incident. Just thinking about it made him a little homesick. "Besides, Kirstin's not a wulver anymore."

Alessa sat back, truly shocked, whispering, "What?"

"My mother, Sibyl—she's a human woman, not a wulver—she's a great healer," Griff explained. He tried to think of the best way to present things to her, but decided there wasn't really a good one. So he just told her. "She found a cure for t'wulver woman's curse. They found an old text buried in the first den, and she deciphered its meanin' enough to gather the herbs she needed to make a cure."

"The Book of the Moon Midwives?" Aleesa asked, her already wide eyes growing wider.

"Aye, how'd ye know?" Griff wondered aloud.

"I know of it," she breathed. Aleesa looked at her husband, then back at Griff, and finally, her gaze fell onto her daughter—the one who she had not borne, but raised. "No one knew where t'was. Tis where the prophecy's told."

"Aye, m'mother and the wulver women have been pouring over the thing for years." Griff snorted, sitting back in his chair. "M'mother could only read English. But she got help from Moira and Beitrus."

"Beitrus..." A smile flitted across Aleesa's face. "She's still alive, then?"

"Aye, old as t'hills, startin' t'go blind." Griff smiled back at her. "…and she's no longer a wulver either."

"What?" Aleesa exclaimed.

"She's the one who tested t'cure," Griff told her. "Insisted, as she was t'oldest, and had t'least t'lose, if it killed 'er."

"They let 'er just take it?" Alaric cried.

Griff chuckled. "No, but if ye knew Beitrus—she's stubborn."

"Aye, that she is." Aleesa laughed, patting her husband's hand. "Always was."

"Why'd ye never send word?" Griff asked, looking between the two older wulvers with a slow shake of his head. "At least tell us ye were 'ere?"

"I can'na leave." Tears sprang to Aleesa's eyes again and she blinked them quickly away when her daughter looked at her. "Once a priestess commits 'erself to this temple, she can'na go."

"Yer daughter would've liked to know ye were alive," Griff said softly. He saw his words hurt her, but he felt they had to be said. "Safe."

"All is as it should be." Alaric stood, leaning over to kiss the top of his wife's bent head.

"Yer 'ere now." Aleesa lifted her gaze to meet Griff's, such hope in her eyes. "Ye can carry word back to m'Kirstin, can't ye?"

Griff nodded. "Aye."

The woman stood, too, helping her husband and daughter clear the table. Griff moved to help them, but Aleesa insisted, as their guest, that he sit.

"The Book of the Moon Midwives." Aleesa shook her head in disbelief as she made them all more tea. "I'd like t'see it. Read it—what I could make out. Ye could read it t'me, Alaric."

Bridget sat beside him, holding her own cup of tea. She was quiet now, far more subdued. Clearly he had brought new and mayhaps not welcome information into this little, isolated family. He worried about the way her brow wrinkled as she blew gently on the hot liquid, looking into it as if it might hold some answers.

"All t'wulvers in m'den can read'n'write both Gaelic'n'English," Griff told Aleesa. "M'mother was English—but she learned Gaelic right alongside t'pups."

"They read'n'write?" Alaric's eyes widened.

"Aye. She's big on education." Griff laughed. "And had quite an influence over m'father."

"I guess so." Alaric laughed too, shaking his head.

"I don't see much point in knowin' how t'read'n'write." Griff shrugged. "If wulvers were meant t'be men, we wouldn't be half-wolf, eh?"

"So you've seen t'prophecy written?" Aleesa asked, looking at him in wonder.

"No, I've heard it told," Griff replied. He'd heard so much about it, his whole life, he really didn't care to actually read the words. "M'mother, m'aunts, all t'healers've poured over that book backwards'n'forwards, since t'day I was born."

"What's this prophecy?" Bridget spoke up, frowning between Griff and her parents.

"I thought, mayhaps, t'was just legend," Aleesa told her daughter. "But if they've found t'book... if The Book of the Moon Midwives exists..."

"Oh, aye, it exists," Griff assured her. "That's how I found out 'bout t'lost packs."

"There's a prophecy 'bout a red wulver who'll bring together t'lost packs," Aleesa explained to her daughter. "I did'na know it would e'er come to pass in m'lifetime…"

Bridget sighed, looking at Griff, narrowing her gaze at him. "Yer this red wulver?"

"So they say." He shrugged. If it served him to be the red wulver here, in this temple, then he would be that red wulver. If it got him what he wanted—the location of the lost, leaderless packs—then so be it.

"If he's t'red wulver this prophecy speaks of..." Bridget put her mug on the table, leaning in to look at the other priestess. "Mother, only t'dragon can tell us fer sure."

"Dragon?" Griff's hand went to his empty sheath. He hated being unarmed. It was like walking around naked.

"Come." Aleesa nodded, holding a hand out to Griff.

"Where're we goin'?" he asked as they all rose. He didn't like the sound of this.

"To t'sacred pool," Bridget told him, a small smile playing on her lips. "Mayhaps t'find t'very thing ye seek."

Griff hesitated at the edge of the so-called sacred pool, watching Alaric take up as guardian across from him, arms folded. The men stood, simply a witness as the women busied themselves with bowls of herbs and ceremonial swords.

He had sought this place out in hopes of finding information about the lost packs, but now that he was here, he wasn't quite so sure that he wanted to know, after all. He'd dismissed the idea of the prophecy his whole life. In part, because his mother had been doubtful of it herself. She didn't come from the wulver world, even if she now lived in it, and she'd never quite believed that it was her son's destiny to fulfill some wulver prophecy.

Mayhaps that was only because she had wished it wasn't so, he thought, watching as the two women faced each other across the pool, chanting softly. The light in the sky overhead had changed, and the slant that came in from above hinted that it was past supper time. They had talked long at the table as they feasted, he realized now.

Aleesa had been overcurious about her daughter, not that he could blame her. But he had little understanding of the woman. How could she leave her husband and infant daughter and set out for this place, when she hadn't even known it existed?

Aleesa said she had been called here to the Temple of Ardis and Asher. By what? By whom? Griff glanced around, his senses keen, sniffing the air, getting the scent of herbs, the heather and the silvermoon, a heady combination. He felt no other presence here, heard no voices. The dark-haired woman didn't seem consumed by madness or melancholy, aside from a natural longing in missing her offspring.

Mayhaps a temporary madness, then, when she made her way here to Skara Brae?

But what had kept her? He wondered. After Alaric found his wife, why had he not brought her home? They had a small child they'd both abandoned back at their den, and for what? To guard an empty temple, to chant over some quiet pool? Ridiculous.

It saddened him, watching the two women as they stood, facing each other, ceremonial swords held aloft. So many years wasted, the two of them alone—and now this young woman they were training to take their place. He watched her, the way her auburn hair brushed her cheek as she bent her head, how her eyelashes trembled when she closed them over those bright green eyes, and felt a longing he didn't quite understand.

Mayhaps it was just that the girl was trying very hard to live up to someone else's image of her. That much was clear—and he could definitely relate.

That's when the swords caught flame.

Griff reached for his own sword, then realized, again, that it was no longer at his side. Across the pool, Alaric stood watching, unalarmed. Another trick then? The light overhead, cast in a certain way? Griff cocked his head, this way and that, frowning as the women chanted, louder and louder, in a language that sounded familiar, and yet he couldn't quite make out full words. Then they began to repeat one word in Gaelic, over and over, one he did know—dragon.

Arach. Arach. Arach.

Something changed in the room. A shift, movement, mayhaps just the flutter of a breeze, but Griff felt it tickle his skin, like a coming storm. Something was rising. It hung there, like impending doom, expectant, waiting. He found himself holding his breath, his senses heightened. The hair stood up on his arms and the back of his neck. The red-haired woman, Bridget, stared into the pool, her sword still appearing to glow, but the fire had gone from a normal orange to something blueish silver.

Griff's gaze followed hers and, deep in the pool, he saw a face. Leaning closer, for a moment, he thought it was just his own reflection—*it must be*—but then it began to rise, higher and higher, as if it was diving up from the depths. His heart thumped hard in his ears, the way it always did before a good battle was about to begin, and again, his hand went for his sword, finding only an empty scabbard.

Then, the dragon appeared.

It was there—and not there. A dragon's head, all long neck and wide, flaring nostrils, its eyes looking straight at Griff. He saw the image of the dragon, and yet, he saw through it, too, could look right into and past it to see Alaric standing on the opposite side of the pool, Aleesa to his left, Bridget to his right. They were all there, staring at the image of the dragon, transfixed.

Griff shook his head, doing everything in his power to keep from going full-on wolf and attacking the image in front of him. He knew it wasn't real—*couldn't* be real. He would simply embarrass himself and jump straight into the water, and then have to drag himself out and shake off like a wet dog.

Griff held himself back, staring at the dragon, who stared right back at him.

He felt it happening, before he heard them gasp. His eyes were turning red, mirroring the dragon's own blood-red gaze. Usually, when his eyes turned, he was feeling something very strong—mostly anger. Although, to his chagrin, his mother used to like to tell people that every time she nursed him, his eyes would turn red. But now, in this moment, he wasn't feeling anger—an emotion he often associated with strength.

No, he was on edge, certainly, senses more alive than they might ever have been in his entire life, at least while he was in human form, but it wasn't anger that filled him now.

It was power.

Pure, raw, unadulterated power.

He felt as if he, like the image of the dragon before him, could simply spread wings and fly away. He could burn cities to the ground with a simple sneeze. Fry a man to a crisp with a cough. And if he wanted to? He could rule them all.

Griff struggled to contain this feeling, to make sense of it. Gory hell, even his cock was hard with excitement—he felt like he had another sword under his plaid!

Then the dragon turned its head. It had no body Griff could see—mayhaps the rest of it was buried in the pool. He knew this thought would drive him mad if he lingered on it, trying to find the rest of the dragon who couldn't really exist that appeared before him and filled him with such feeling.

But then the beast turned its scaly head and looked at Bridget.

Griff moved without thinking. He saw it happen—saw the beast's eyes flash silver, instead of red, saw Bridget's eyes, like an answering call, flash silver, too. That grey-green moved all the way to the other end of the spectrum, her eyes glowing, like someone gone blind.

"No!" Griff charged, leaping over the corner of the pool to cut the distance, nearly losing his footing on the slippery rock as he tackled the young woman, her ceremonial sword still flaming, aloft, pointing at the dragon's head rising up from the center of the water.

He heard the other woman, Aleesa, cry out, heard Alaric shout, but he paid neither of them any mind as he covered Bridget's body with his own, taking her down to the wet rocks with him.

Bridget’s sword dropped, hissing into the water behind them. She cried out as he covered her, mindful of his weight, not to crush her, just to keep her safe from harm. She stared up at him in wonder, their eyes locked, and for a moment he saw himself, the red heat of his own eyes reflected in the silver pools of hers.

“Griff,” she whispered, and he felt the way his cock hardened at the sound of his name in her mouth. His erection strained against the soft, silky material of her robe, and beyond that, against her incredible softness. He had never wanted a woman more than he wanted her in that moment, and if Alaric hadn’t called his name, too, he might have rolled her over and taken her without thinking—right then, right there.

“Are y’all right, lass?” Griff asked, his voice hoarse with emotion.

“I did’na need rescuing!” Bridget struggled under him, movements that didn’t make him any less hard for her. In fact, quite the opposite. She pushed against his chest with both hands—the woman had a surprising amount of strength for a human girl, even without armor and a sword. “Ye’re such an impetuous fool! The dragon’n’t’lady could’ve told ye what ye wanted t’know.”

“What?” Griff puzzled at her words. “What lady?”

“Did ye n’see ’er?” She wiggled out from under him and he saw that her robe was in disarray, parting slightly in the front, giving him a view of her pale, creamy thigh. Griff saw her noticing him looking at the gap in her robe and she pulled it closed, color rising to her cheeks. “If ye had’na interrupted, ye would’ve seen ’er. She was turning t’me. Did ye n’see ’er eyes go silver?”

“I only saw... t’dragon...” He frowned, moving to his feet, feeling a little lightheaded in the aftermath. He held a hand out to help her up and she made a face, ignoring it once again and standing on her own.

“Father?” Bridget frowned, glancing behind Griff, and he turned to see both Alaric and Aleesa approaching. The look on both their faces startled him, but what they did next left him truly speechless for the first time in his whole life.

“What’re ye doin’?” Bridget blinked as both of her parents took a knee before Griff, bowing their heads.

“Y’are t’one true king,” Alaric said, a slight quiver in his voice, gray head bowed. “How can we serve ye?”

What in the gory hell was he supposed to say to that? Griff stared at them, alarmed. Then he looked at Bridget. It was the fear in her eyes that forced words from his throat. He took the matter in hand as best he could.

“Firs’ of all, ye can get up.” Griff huffed, rolling his eyes. He gave them both a hand up, which they accepted, unlike their daughter, who still stood, tall and haughty and disbelieving, beside him. “And then ye can tell me where t’find t’lost packs. Tis all I wanna know.”

“Alas, we can’na tell ye.” Aleesa looked distraught, wringing her hands, looking at Alaric. “We do’na know.”

“But we can show ye where tis written,” Alaric replied.

“A’righ’,” Griff sighed with impatience. “I s’pose that’s t’next best thing.”

“Except...” Aleesa bit her lip.

"What?" Griff threw up his hands. "T'book's hidden? We have t'tunnel t'the center of the country mayhaps?"

"No, it has t'be high moon time," Alaric informed him. "That'll be jus' a few days from now."

"Aye, a'course." Griff ran a hand through his hair, wondering how in the world he was going to wait, even a few days in this place—for a full moon, of all things. "Do t'stars hafta be in alignment, too? Mayhaps I have t'strip naked an 'dance 'round a fire while ye chant?"

"Aye, tis exactly righ'." Bridget looked at him, unblinking, a little smile playing on her lips. "Ye hafta dance naked 'round a fire under t'full moon."

"Bridget, hush." Her mother sighed. "T'dragon will'na return now. We'll hafta wait for t'high moon."

"If I hafta wait…" Griff sighed, too. He hated waiting. "Can I trouble ye fer a bed, mayhaps?"

"A'course." Aleesa nodded. "I'll make up a bed fer ye."

"And, while I'm thinking on it... a bath?" he suggested hopefully. He hadn't bathed since the day of the Great Hunt, and the pool in front of him looked very inviting.

"Aye." Aleesa smiled at him, putting a soft hand on his forearm. "I'll start boilin' water, m'lord."

"M'lord?" Bridget snorted under her breath and Griff glanced at her, remembering the way she felt underneath him, all softness pressed between the stone and the rigid resistance of his body.

"Pardon?" He cocked an eyebrow at her.

"Who d'ye think y're, a king?" Bridget exclaimed, crossing her arms and glaring at him.

"Aye." He chuckled, glancing at Aleesa and seeing her frown. Clearly the wulvers were now on his side, even if the girl was not. He told Aleesa, "And I'd like 'er to tend me."

"I will not—" Bridget protested, her eyes widening.

"Aye, lass, ye will!" Aleesa's eyes flashed, not silver or red, but there were some things far worse than curses and prophecies, and clearly Aleesa's temper was one of them. Griff grinned as Aleesa took her daughter's arm, yanking her out of the room. "Now come wit' me."

Chapter Four

Bridget grumbled to herself the entire time as she carried buckets of hot water back and forth from the fire to fill the wooden tub. She had it halfway full, and the floor was wet where she'd splashed—not to mention the front of her robe, which clung to her like a damned second skin—when the big wulver-man, Griff, came into the room. He glanced at her as she put the last two full buckets on the floor beside the fireplace in his room. These were for rinsing, of course.

"Are ye ready fer yer bath, m'lord?" She couldn't keep the venom from dripping off her tongue.

First, this beast bests her as temple guardian. Then, he somehow bewitches her parents into thinking he's some sort of "red wulver" who's here to fulfill a prophecy. Then, just when the dragon and the lady were about to tell them the truth, he attacks her!

Rescue, my foot, she thought, glaring as the man began to undress. His sheath was empty—no swords, aside from the ceremonial ones, were allowed in the temple—and he tossed it onto the bed.

Alaric and Aleesa had given up their room, with the big bed and large fireplace, for their guest. And why? Because they thought this arrogant fool was some sort of wulver king? He was nothing but a bragging, boastful boy.

Bridget turned to watch him, leaning against the tub, arms crossed over her chest. Well, mayhaps not so much a boy, she corrected herself, as he pulled his tunic over his head, tossing it on the bed, too. At least, not physically. His shoulders were big and broad, tawny colored in the firelight. He was so muscled, the hills and valleys in his arms alone were breathtaking, like the scenery of Skara Brae. Rolling and rather delicious.

Bridget told herself it was the heat from the fire, and her own toil in carrying water back and forth from the kitchen, that made her face flush when the man divested himself of his plaid. He half-sat on the bed, pulling off hose and boots too, tossing them aside.

She knew Aleesa would want them washed, and so Bridget moved to retrieve them. She set them all by the door—his clothes, boots, sword sheath, belt—ignoring the fact that he was naked behind her.

She averted her eyes when he climbed into the tub, but she couldn't help seeing the bulge of the man's strong thighs, the hollows at the sides of his buttocks, before he sank into the water with a low, soft groan.

"What d'ye wan' me t'do?" Bridget had hissed at her mother as they warmed water over the fire.

"Jus' tend 'im, Bridget," Aleesa told her with a heavy sigh. "Wash t'man wit' soap'n'water. Ye act like ye do'na know what a bath is!"

Of course she knew what a bath was. She'd taken thousands. Okay, maybe hundreds. But she'd never had to wash anyone but herself before. She didn't know anything about man parts, aside from the fact that, if you brought a knee up between their legs, they had soft stones that puckered and shriveled and turned them into howling babies. She'd learned that lesson by accident, but her father had used it, as he used everything, to teach her a lesson. If she absolutely had to hurt a man, if he was besting her and she had to escape, honorably or no, that was the best way to do so.

"Ye can leave me, lass," Griff called softly as Bridget put his things in order. Mayhaps she was stalling, it was true. "I can bathe m'self."

She glanced over, seeing his head tipped back, eyes closed, his big arms resting on the sides of the tub, elbows cocked, hands floating in the water. When she didn't answer, he peeped one eye open to look at her. She stood near the door, undecided, worrying her lip between her teeth. Griff opened two eyes, then his gaze moved down her robe, all the way to her bare toes peeking out from underneath, then upwards until their eyes locked.

"D'ye 'ave any soap, lass?" he asked, running a hand through his thick, dark mass of hair. It curled even more when it was wet, she noticed.

"Aye," she said softly, moving to get it for him. She had made the soap herself. Aleesa taught her that, the same way she'd taught her how to chant and throw herbs into the scrying pool. Her own soap smelled of heather and silvermoon, but this was sage and cedar, a far more masculine scent they made for Alaric, who protested going around smelling like flowers—when they could get him to bathe, that was.

Griff lifted it to his nose, sniffing it lightly, giving her an appreciative look as he soaped up his hands and began rubbing them over his chest. She noticed the hairs that curled there, circling his nipples, small and pink, like miniatures of her own. Hers were hard—probably because she'd gotten herself soaked carrying all the water back and forth, she told herself, trying to ignore the soft pulse between her thighs.

He had told her to go, but she didn't. Instead, she knelt by the side of the tub, her eyes glued to the way his hands roamed his chest and shoulders and arms, wondering what it felt like to map that fleshy terrain. His hands dipped under the water with the soap, toward areas she didn't dare peek at.

Her mother had bid her to tend the man, and so Bridget reached for a washing cloth, dipping it into the water to wet it, and then holding her hand out to him silently for the soap.

Griff looked at her for a moment, a bemused smile playing on his lips, but he handed it over, watching as she rubbed soap into the cloth, making suds.

"How'd ye come t'be 'ere, Bridget?" Griff asked, leaning forward when she put a hand on his shoulder and pulled.

"Tis m'home," she said simply, standing and moving in behind him so she could scrub his back. His flesh was beautifully tanned, his shoulder blades jutting like wings as he let her scrub, up and down, back and forth. He gave a little groan when she rubbed the cloth hard over his shoulders.

"Ye like that?" She cocked her head, her fingers digging into the muscle, and he gave another soft moan.

"Aye." He rolled his head from side to side. "T'was a long journey."

"Where d'ye come from?" she asked, wondering about it, knowing now that his pack had been the same that her parents had left. They had once lived in the same den. "Where's yer home?"

"Scotland," he told her, glancing back in surprise at her question. He was wondering why her parents hadn't told her. And she was wondering the same thing. "Middle March. Right on t'border b'tween Scotland'n'England. We used t'have a mountain den, back a'fore I was born. M'mother says t'was lovely, wit' a valley contained in t'mountain range, an' a stream runnin' through it. Now we live in a den underground—on MacFalon land. Tis a beautiful place. Reminds me of this."

"I've ne'er known any other home but this," she admitted, her fingers digging into the hard, bunched muscle of his shoulders. He let out a sigh of relief at her touch, and another groan when she dug her thumbs into his flesh. "I'm not hurtin' ye?"

"No, lass." He chuckled. "Not likely."

She stiffened at his words, withdrawing, knowing he was referring to their first meeting.

"Do'na stop." He looked back at her in the firelight. "I did'na mean t'insult ye. It's jus'… I've ne'er met a woman like ye a'fore."

"What's that mean?" She frowned, but she put her hands back onto his shoulders, continuing to knead his flesh like bread dough. He moaned again, eyes closing. He really seemed to like it, and for some reason, that pleased her. "Griff?"

"Hmmm?" His head tilted forward as she dug her fingers into his shoulder blades.

"What d'ye mean, ye've ne'er met a woman like me?"

"Where I come from," he said, hissing when she scraped him lightly with her nails. "Women do'na fight. Wulver women… they're not warriors."

"Ye do'na think a woman should be a warrior?" She frowned, watched the water trickling down his skin in little rivers. There were no scars or marks on the man, and she wondered at it, but then she remembered—he was a wulver. A warrior, like Alaric.

She had once nicked her trainer with her long sword, a gash in his arm that would have taken her months to heal from—and would have left a very bad scar—but on Alaric, the wound had closed up in moments. Within a quarter of an hour, there was no sign it had even happened at all.

"Yer a fine swordma—swords*woman*." He corrected himself, smiling back at her. "He's trained ye vera well. Ye gave me quite a beatin' out there, lass. I was afeared I was'na gonna make't into t'temple after all."

"Now you're just humorin' me…" She rolled her eyes, poking him in the shoulder with her finger.

"Mayhaps a lil." His smile spread into a mischievous grin. "But tell me t'truth… d'ye wanna be a warrior?"

"What d'ye mean?" She wrinkled her nose at him, cocking her head. "I've been trained t'be t'temple guardian'n'priestess. Tis what I'm meant t'do."

"Hm." Griff's gaze moved to the fire. In this light, his eyes were almost gold. "Mayhaps."

"Ye came 'ere because of a prophecy," she reminded him. "Ye mus' b'lieve in destiny."

"Ye'd think so." He snorted. "Y'know, the Scots—they let women lead their clans. The MacFalon's trained 'is daughters right alongside 'is sons."

"The MacFalon..." Bridget frowned, remembering their conversation at dinner. It seemed a million years ago now, but the things that had been revealed at that meal had changed everything for her. She couldn't look at her parents now without feeling a sense of loss and betrayal. Why had they not told her where they'd come from, what they'd left behind?

"M'father's told me stories about the Scots—and The MacFalon," she told him. It was true, but only in a general sense. Alaric had told her about a pact between wulvers and men that had been drafted by the king of England himself.

"Different man, I promise ye." Griff assured her, seeing her expression as she moved the washing cloth over his shoulder, down his arm, as she came to kneel beside the tub. "Donal MacFalon would'na hurt a wulver. He married one."

"Kirstin..." It was the first time Bridget had said the girl's name aloud, and it pained her greatly. Her parents, the people who had loved and raised her from infancy, had another daughter. And she had never known. How could it be?

Griff's wet hand touched her face, tilting her chin up so she was forced to meet his eyes. She knew he would see the tears there, the ones she'd been trying to hide. Her breath caught, her throat closing up, and she felt her lip tremble as he searched her face with those strange-colored eyes of his.

"Ye did'na know they had a child, did ye?" he asked softly.

"No." She barely whispered the word. One of the tears that threatened trembled on her lashes and fell down her cheek.

"Yer not their own." He wiped her cheek with his wet thumb, frowning. The look on his face made her want to sob—everything she was feeling was reflected in his eyes. Her anger, her sadness, bewilderment, confusion.

"They took me in," she told him, reminding herself of this fact. They were the only parents she'd ever known, and they loved her. She knew that was true.

"How old were ye?" He leaned back as she soaped the cloth again, washing his shoulders, his collarbone.

He seemed to like it when she rubbed hard, so she did so.

"Jus' a bairn," she said, making him lift his arms so she could scrub underneath. "M'mother says someone left me at t'temple, near t'secret entrance."

"The one in t'rock?"

"Aye." She traced the cloth down the center of his chest, between his ribs.

"How'd they know t'was there?"

"I do'na know." She shrugged, grazing the cloth over the row of hills and valleys that made up the man's abdomen. It was hard as rock, so unlike her own softness. "M'father thinks t'was a mage who knew there were guardians at t' temple who'd care fer me—and train me t'be like them."

"Tis strange, leavin' a human child wit' two wulvers." Griff watched her move the washing cloth lower. His eyes were darker now, almost orange. "How'd they know you'd not be breakfast?"

"But they did'na eat me." She laughed. The man had a line of dark hair that ran from his navel down under the water and she traced that with the cloth, too, fascinated. "All is as it should be."

"Ye keep sayin' that." Griff tilted his head at her.

"Tis true." She shrugged, wetting her lips—her mouth felt suddenly dry—when she saw the appendage between his legs had grown in size, pointing directly at her. She knew enough about mating—animals, humans and wulvers—to know what it meant. But Bridget found herself fascinated by it. She wanted nothing more than to reach down and touch him.

"If ye do what yer thinkin' of, lass, ye'll n'leave this room a maiden," he told her, voice low, and she startled, blinking up at him in surprise. "Not that I'll stop ye…"

"Oh… I…" She cleared her throat, leaning back, gripping the edge of the tub, and saw the way his gaze dropped to her breasts. Her nipples were achingly hard and completely visible through the thin, wet material of her white robe. She glanced down at them, and saw they were like little pink pebbles. Ripe cherries, waiting to be plucked and devoured.

"Ye've ne'er been with a man," he remarked. His voice was low, matter-of-fact, and it moved over her like a caress.

"I'm t'be a temple priestess," she confessed, swallowing past some sort of obstruction in her throat. "As well as a guardian."

"So ye mus' retain yer maidenhood, then, aye?" Griff inquired, eyebrows going up just slightly, waiting for her response.

"I… no…" She shook her head, denying it, although why she was so quick to do so, she didn't understand. Just like she didn't understand her body's response to this man's closeness—and his nudity. "A priestess mus' be whole in herself. Aleesa is no maiden, nor was she when she came 'ere. But a priestess mus'na be subservient to anyone—man or woman."

"Aleesa isn't subservient to Alaric then?" Griff asked. "But they're mates, aren't they?'

"Aye," she agreed, frowning. "But their marriage is that of equals. Aleesa holds far more power here than Alaric."

"I do'na understand." The man puzzled this out, brow drawn. "A man is naturally more powerful than a woman."

"Physically mayhaps." A smile played on Bridget's lips at his assumptions. "But energetically, a woman'll always be more powerful than a man. She's t'ocean, t'weather, t'very air ye breathe. She's t'life giver. N'man can say that."

"Has any man e'er told ye how beautiful ye're, Bridget?" He reached a hand out to rub a thumb over the line of her jaw. He stopped at her chin, his thumb moving over her bottom lip, back and forth. He seemed fascinated with her mouth and she swallowed, trying to take in the man's words. Earlier, he had infuriated her with his arrogance and sense of entitlement. He had come here assuming he would best the temple guardian, gain entrance to their sacred space, and then find and exploit whatever information he could glean from them. She didn't feel him deserving of the knowledge contained here, even if he had bested her.

But in the end, that was her own failing—if Alaric had been the one to confront him, mayhaps things would have been different?

But now, here in this room, with the two of them alone, he didn't strike her as overconfident. He'd let his guard down, and she wondered at it. His words didn't matter to her—although when he told her she was beautiful, something ignited inside of her she didn't quite recognize or comprehend—as much as the soft look in his eyes when he told her.

"M'father's told me I'm beautiful." Bridget cleared her throat, using the soap in her hands to create suds. "Now close yer eyes, wulver. I'm gonna wash yer hair."

"Aye, mistress." Griff dutifully closed his eyes as she stood to run her hands through his hair. It was thick, even wet, and she used her fingernails to scrape his scalp, hearing him give a little growling noise in his throat in response. "So tell me, Bridget, d'ye really believe e'erythin' happens as it should?"

"Aye," she agreed, moving around the tub to retrieve a bucket of warm water to rinse him. "Tis all as it should be."

"How can ye say that?" Griff wondered, opening his eyes as she approached with the bucket—but his gaze was on her body in her robe, the way it clung to her skin. "I mean… yer parents abandoned ye…"

"Mayhaps." She lifted the bucket, looking pointedly at him. "Close yer eyes, wulver."

He did, reluctantly, and she poured the bucket over his head, washing the suds away. She took a bit too much pleasure in the way he sputtered and rubbed his face with his hands at the onslaught of water.

"Mayhaps they no longer live," Bridget mused. "Mayhaps they could'na care fer me. I do'na know. But Alaric'n'Aleesa've been t'best family I could've asked fer."

"But livin' here?" Griff rubbed his eyes with his thumbs and focused on her, frowning. "Ne'er leavin'?"

"Oh, I can leave," she told him, smiling. "Before I take m'vows as priestess, I can come'n'go as I please. I go hunting. I trap small game. I fish. I jus' do'na wander too far from t'temple."

"But they cannot leave?" Griff pondered this, glancing at the closed bedroom door.

"Aleesa can'na." She shook her head. "I do'na know what'd happen if she tried. And Alaric—he will ne'er leave her. The Temple of Ardis'n'Asher was meant always t'have both a guardian an' a priestess. They complement one another. Male an' female. Masculine an' feminine. He protects an' contains, and that allows 'er life force t'flow. He's t'riverbank, and she's t'water, ye ken?"

"Tis madness," Griff murmured, frowning as she leaned her hands against the side of the tub. She realized, then, that he was looking at her body in her robe, and her breasts were eye-level to him.

"Tis love," she countered softly. "An' devotion."

"I do'na understand. Help me understand," he lifted his gaze to hers, real confusion on his face. "How could she jus' leave?"

"Did ye n'leave?" Bridget asked, arching an eyebrow at him, seeing him startle a little. A flash of guilt crept into his eyes and she wondered who he was thinking about back home. Who had this man, this wulver, left behind? A mate? A child? The thought made her throat want to close up for some reason and she cleared it, standing and crossing her arms over her breasts to cover herself.

"Aye, I left," he admitted, running a hand through his dark, wet hair. "But I left no one behind."

"No one?" Bridget swallowed, waiting for his answer. She didn't know why it suddenly mattered to her so much, but it did.

"M'mother…" He shrugged a shoulder, and there was that flash of guilt again. Then his face hardened. "M'father."

She nodded, pursing her lips, eyes narrowed at him. "No one else?"

"Friends, kin…" He shrugged again, then a smile began at the corners of his mouth. "Why? What're ye askin', lass? Certainly no pups."

No pups. Something in her chest loosened. That must mean, then…

“No mate?” She just asked him directly, giving up on trying to hide what she wanted to know.

“No, lass.” That bright, knowing look in his eyes made her want to smack him—or kiss him. She wasn’t sure which.

“So,” she mused. “You haven’t found your true—”

“I do’na b’lieve in true mates,” Griff growled, holding up his palm in protest, as if he could hold back the phrase “one true mate” from even being uttered. “I do’na b’lieve in magic. An’ I do’na b’lieve in prophecies.”

Bridget couldn’t help smiling at this. “What *do* ye b’lieve in?”

“M’self.” He crossed his arms over his chest, mirroring her.

“Why’m I n’surprised?” She laughed, and then did so again, even harder, when he scowled at her.

“What d’*ye* b’lieve in, then?”

“Magic.” She said this first, not that it wasn’t true. It was. But she also liked the way this fact seemed to irk him. “The divine. Love.”

“Tomfoolery.” He rolled his eyes, dismissing it all with the wave of his hand. “Nonsense.”

“Ye came ’ere ’cause of a prophecy, wulver,” she reminded him, delighting in the way his jaw hardened and his eyes flashed. They weren’t red, like they had been when they mirrored the dragon’s in the pool, but they were close.

“I came ’ere t’find m’kin,” he said through lips that barely moved.

“Aye, an’ ye succeeded.” She nodded toward the door, meaning Aleesa and Alaric.

"I came 'ere t'find'n'reunite t'lost packs," he replied with a shake of his head. "If there're more wulvers in t'world, I wanna find 'em."

"Is that n'yer destiny?" she asked softly, remembering what her mother had said at dinner. "Is that n'what t'prophecy says t'red wulver'll do? Reunite t'lost packs?"

"I do'na care a rat's ass 'bout t'prophecy!" Griff's eyes were definitely red now. She stared at them, fascinated. It was as if a fire had been lit inside of him. Did he know, she wondered, when his eyes did that? "I wanna lead a pack of wulvers. If I was born t'do anythin', I was born t'do that."

"Tis all as it should be, then." She smiled at the way that stopped him—at least for the moment.

"Stop sayin' that," he finally snapped, asking, "D'ye 'ave any wine in this place?"

"Aye." She nodded, doing her best to hide the smile that irked him so much, making her way over to the table near the fireplace. Her mother had left a bottle of their best wine, thinking the wulver might want to indulge. She'd tasted the stuff, but only ceremonially.

She poured a glass, bringing it to him.

"Why d'ye n'wanna hear 'bout yer destiny?" she asked, handing him the mug. He drank from it, meeting her questioning gaze over the rim.

"'Cause tis jus' magical nonsense," he protested, then he looked at the cup. "This is good."

"More?" She glanced into the cup and brought the bottle back over, filling it again. "I'd think ye'd like knowin' yer destiny. That ye had a place in t'world."

"I'm bigger than m'destiny," Griff said simply, a statement that served to stop her. Bridget's breath caught as she looked at him, incredulous. Was he so arrogant, then, so full of himself?

"Ye think so?" She blinked at him.

"I know so." He glowered at the fire, that red color back in his eyes as he drank his wine.

Bridget went over and poured herself a glass of wine, taking a sip. He was right, it was good. It burned her throat a little and made her eyes water, but it was good. He glanced at her as she took a seat beside him on the stool they used to get in and out of the tub. The fire was warm and the wine made her feel even warmer.

"S'ye wanna be a leader," she mused, sipping her wine. "Like yer father?"

"Aye." His frown deepened. "M'father's a great leader. But I wanna lead m'own pack."

"What if t'lost packs a'ready 'ave a leader?" she asked, thinking aloud.

"Then they would'na be lost would they?" He sighed. "Can y'imagine what tis like t'be lost? Leaderless? T'have no pack?"

"Aye." She nodded, feeling the weight of his words. Alaric and Aleesa were her family, had always been, since she could remember. But this man, this wulver, reminded her quite painfully that they were not really her family. She didn't belong with them, to them. They weren't even her same kind.

They had a family. Another daughter.

Bridget finished her wine and poured herself more from the bottle.

"Aye, I s'pose, ye can."

She felt his wet fingertips brush her cheek, moving hair away from her face, and she glanced at him. His eyes weren't red anymore. They were back to that strange gold color, and his expression was thoughtful.

"I wanna bring t'lost packs home. We're a'ready outgrowin' our den. Mayhaps, when I return wit' t'lost packs, we can move back t'the mountain den. Tis bigger, more accommodatin', and there, mayhaps, I can lead our pack."

"But yer father… Raife?" She looked at him, questioning, and he nodded. "Is he n'the leader?"

"Aye, he is now." Griff gave a little nod. "But when I return home wit' t'lost packs, he'll know I'm ready t'lead. T'will be m'time."

For some reason, Bridget was thinking about taking her vows. It would be soon. And then… then she would be finally fulfilling her destiny. It was something she'd always believed, had always known. She'd grown up her whole life knowing it, understanding it, not even questioning it.

So why was she questioning it now?

"I hope ye find 'em," she said, putting a hand on his arm. Water beaded his skin, making it slippery to the touch. "I really hoped t'dragon an' the lady would help ye, but now…"

"Ye saw that, too?" Griff's voice dropped, shaking his head. The wine was loosening his tongue, she thought. Breaking down those barriers he had put up against things that couldn't be explained. Like magic. Like love. "I thought mayhaps I was dreamin'… or seein' things."

"Ye were seein' things," she said softly, finishing her wine. "Ye saw t'dragon."

"I saw *somethin'*," he admitted, holding his cup out, and she obliged, filling it. "I thought… I thought ye were in danger."

"Far less danger than when I faced ye at the crossroads," she teased, smiling when he looked at her. His gaze moved over her again, his eyes gone from gold to a rich, dark amber. His gaze moved to the V her robe made above her breasts and he frowned, reaching out to press a finger below her collarbone.

"Did I do this?" Griff touched the purple discoloration of the bruise there. Bridget saw it when she glanced down.

"Mayhaps." Bridget shrugged, setting her cup aside. The wine was making her head fuzzy. She was remembering the way he had pinned her against the rock, how thick and hard his thigh had been between her own. "I do'na remember. Tis nothin'."

"If there was such a thing as magic, I'd make it disappear." Griff stroked her bruise, frowning at it, as if it displeased him. It was an intimate gesture. Bridget felt very warm all of a sudden.

"There *is* magic, Griff."

He looked up when she said his name, his gaze moving slowly from her eyes to her mouth. She could almost feel his thumb there, the way he'd rubbed her lips. That made her feel even warmer.

"Can ye prove it?" A smile played on his lips.

"Magic's jus' nature doin' what it does naturally."

"So *e'erything* is magic?" he scoffed. His thumb moved over her collarbone, lightly stroking. Her nipples were so hard they hurt. He was looking at them, and that just made them ache even more.

"Aye." She bit her lip when his fingertips trailed down the V of her robe, but she didn't protest, didn't stop him. "When nature's left t'divine direction, instead of bein' controlled by men—or women—that's magic."

"Wha' happens when men—or women—try t'control it?" He didn't open her robe. He just traced that V, down between her breasts, then up again. Over and over.

"That's dark magic," she told him, shivering. "And that has its costs."

"The dragon?" Griff's gaze moved up again, to meet hers, questioning. "Was that dark magic?"

"No." She shook her head, vehement. "The Dragon's t'masculine. The lady's t'feminine. All of nature fits together this way—mated."

Fated.

She thought this, but didn't say it. She saw the way he looked at her, the desire in his eyes, and wondered if he saw hers too. There were things in the world that were just meant to fit together.

"Male'n'female," she went on. "Tis like t'guardian'n'handmaiden of this temple. Or Ardis'n'Asher. They were true mates."

Griff shook his head, like he was clearing it. "But I do'na b'lieve in—"

"True mates. Aye." She smiled. "But all matin's magical. Magic only helps nature. It can'na do anythin' that nature doesn't intend. That's why all truly *is* as it should be."

"If all is as it should be, then…" He looked at her, a sly smile spreading on his face. "Then I was meant t'best ye this afternoon in our swordplay."

He was trying to bait her, goad her.

"Aye, wulver." Bridget smiled, nodding. "I s'pose that's so."

"If all is as it should be, then I was meant t'come 'ere. An' ye—" He grinned. "Were meant to be kneelin' beside this tub, scrubbing m'back clean."

"A priestess lives t'serve." She wasn't going to let this man win, she decided. Not in this arena, anyway. "The handmaiden offers her gift t'those who're worthy. An' a guardian knows when t'fight… an' when t'yield."

He chuckled, handing her his empty cup. "Ye've a hard time yieldin', lass."

"I'm still learnin'." She smiled, getting up to put their cups and the bottle of wine on the table.

"Mayhaps ye need a new teacher?" Griff grinned when she whirled to glare at him.

"Alaric's been the best teacher'n'father I could've asked fer." She had told herself she wasn't going to let him get to her, but he did. He got under her skin in a way she'd never known before. She didn't understand it.

"I'm sure he has," Griff agreed, picking up the soap and sliding it over his skin. "But e'ery daughter mus' someday leave 'er home fer a mate."

"But I'll never leave this place." She sat on the stool again, watching as the big man stood in the tub, water sheeting off his body, running down his skin in rivulets. He washed himself with big, soapy hands. She tried to avert her eyes, but she was too transfixed by the man's body. She was surprised she had a voice at all when she murmured, "I've been trained to be the handmaiden'n'guardian, both. Tis m'destiny…"

A destiny she had never questioned before. She'd never had reason to question it. So why did this man, and his ideas, make her doubt?

But he did.

"Tis that what ye want, Bridget?" Griff's hands moved down between his legs, and her gaze went there, too. She flushed, feeling shame at her inability to turn her head, but she could not look away. He held his erection like a sword at the ready, soapy hand moving idly up and down the shaft. She found herself face-to-face with his stiff length. Something that had seemed so small and soft, like a coiled snake, had risen to more than twice that size.

She knew what men did with it—what men and women were meant to do, how they fit together. That thought made the pulse between her own legs throb, hot, insistent.

"I've ne'er questioned it," she breathed.

"Maybe ye should." His hand moved down to cup those sensitive stones men had, the sack underneath taut, soaping them up.

"Why?" She shook her head, heard the pain in her own voice. She didn't like the way he made her think about things. Before he'd come, life had been very simple. Why had he come to complicate things?

"Why not?" he called as she stood, feeling wobbly on her own legs, not sure if it was the wine or the discussion, heading to the fire to get the last rinse bucket.

"Because…" She gulped, lifting the bucket. "Tis all as it should be."

When she turned, seeing him standing in the tub, soap suds sliding down his skin into the bath water, he took her breath away. She didn't understand it. Why should the sight of a naked man make her feel so woozy and warm? Her insides felt soft and gooey, like she was melting. It was the strangest thing she'd ever felt.

Griff met her eyes as she approached, and she wondered if he saw the confusion on her face. He looked at her like he was wondering what she was feeling. She was wondering herself. Slowly, she climbed onto the stool, so they stood face to face, Bridget holding the rinse bucket.

"Tell me, Bridget…" His voice was soft, his gaze too. "If… if somethin', some circumstance, some person… made it impossible for ye to stay 'ere, in this temple…"

She could barely breathe, standing so close to him, and part of her hated him for making her think of these things. The thought of leaving the temple made her stomach clench and her eyes sting. She loved her parents, she loved her home. And this was home. It always would be.

So why was she suddenly filled with such longing?

"If tha' happened…" Griff said. "Then is that as it should be, as well?"

"Ye make m'head hurt." Bridget lifted the bucket and poured it over his head.

Griff sputtered, laughing, rubbing his face clear so he could look at her.

"Too much thinkin'?" he asked, grinning as she climbed down off the stool, setting the bucket aside.

"No, I enjoy thinkin'," she protested, going over to get one of the dry bath sheets warming by the fire. "I play chess wit' Alaric. But tis folly t'question what is. T'would be like askin' yerself why y'er a wulver… and I'm a woman."

"I'm askin' myself that," he said, his gaze skipping down once more to the wet front of her robe. "Righ' this very moment."

"Noticin' an' askin' why're two very different things." She smirked, shaking her head as she unfolded the bath sheet.

"Aye, they are." He agreed, waiting patiently as she untangled the sheet. "Yer wet."

"Pardon?" She blinked at him.

"Yer shift." He nodded, his gaze heavy-lidded. "It's wet. Are ye cold?"

"The fire's warm." It was—but so were her cheeks, and those weren't facing the flame.

"Yer goin' t'need a bath after me." He chuckled as she shook the sheet, holding it out for him.

"I'll be fine." But she wasn't fine. She felt quite strange. Her knees shook.

"Bridget?" Griff tilted his head, frowning, and her face flushed even more.

"I'm fine." She felt it happening, the room spinning, her balance gone.

Griff reached out to grab her by the elbows and she gave a little shriek as she slipped, the stool going out from under her as she fell forward into him, both of them splashing together into the tub. There was nothing else to do, nowhere else to go.

Griff didn't say anything, but he caught her, keeping her head from hitting the other edge of the tub, but unable to keep her from sinking into the water. With both of them in it, the water overflowed the tub's edge, spilling onto the floor in waves.

"Are ye'll righ', lass?" Griff asked, holding her to him as she sputtered and blinked at him in surprise. She found herself stretched out against his naked body in the tub, and when she looked down, she noticed her robe had come untied entirely. Like any Scot, she wore nothing under her plaid—and nothing under her temple robes either.

Griff's eyes flashed as he glimpsed her nude form. Bridget saw them, for just a moment, go from that strange amber to red, the hands gripping her shoulders sliding slowly down her arms as they rocked together in the sloshing water. She didn't need to look down to know what was rubbing up against her hip, hot and hard as steel.

She half expected him to grab her, force himself inside of her—she was a virgin, still, of course, just as she'd told him. There had never been a man, or wulver, here to take her maidenhead. That flash of red in his eyes, and the way his gaze raked her now nude body, his hands moving over her skin, sliding the thin, wet, completely see-through material of her robe down her shoulders, all told her what he wanted.

And she wanted it too.

Her thighs gripped him, hips rocking all on their own. Griff gasped when he felt her shift in his lap, the seam of her sex rubbing against his erection. Bridget gave a little cry, biting her lip, the feel of her breasts flattened hard into his chest reminding her of their sparring that afternoon. This was sparring too, of sorts, wasn't it?

She swiped a strand of wet hair out of her face, trying to regain her composure, which was simply impossible in this situation.

"Well, lass…" Griff's face spread into a grin, hands settling on her hips. "I s'pose all is as it should be now, eh?"

"Yer insufferable." She rolled her eyes, putting her hands against his chest and pushing hard. She would have been too fast for him, if the weight of her wet robe, and the bath sheet that had tangled around her legs, hadn't restrained her. Griff managed to wrap his big arms around her waist, trapping her against him.

"Y'were meant t'fall into m'arms like this, lass," he teased. "It's fate. Destiny, y'ken?"

"M'knee in yer stones is goin' t'be yer destiny in a moment," she snapped and he laughed. But he let her go, and Bridget climbed slowly out of the tub, taking her wet robe and the soaking wet bath sheet with her. The whole room was a mess, water all over the floor.

She shivered, digging another bath sheet out of the bureau and wrapping herself in it. It wasn't fire-warm, but it would do.

"D'ye 'ave another one of those, lass?" Griff called, climbing out of the tub too.

"'Ere…" She tossed it over her shoulder at him, not caring if it fell into all the water on the floor.

"Thank ye." He chuckled.

Bridget glanced back at Griff. He clearly had no qualms about being naked around her, even with an erection the size of Stonehenge. She watched him dry himself in the light of the fire, his back to her, to give her privacy. She found another robe tucked way in the back of the bureau, one of her mother's, and dropped the bath sheet to the floor, slipping the dry robe on and cinching it closed.

Watching Griff dry off—he was far less concerned about exposing himself, and water ran down his back and sides in rivulets as he toweled his long, dark hair—she found herself fascinated by his body. How different from her own. He was lean and muscled, a truly stunning sight. And the way he felt, pressed against her…

Finally, Griff wrapped the sheet around his waist, tucking the material into itself, and asked, "Are ye decent, lass?"

"Aye." She was shivering now, although she didn't feel cold at all. "I did'na mean t'fall in."

"No, I don't expect ye did." He chuckled, surveying the wet floor. "Yer a'righ'?"

"Aye. But I should go change." She sighed, looking at the mess. "I'll come back t'clean up."

"Do'na worry 'bout it, lass." He half-sat on the mattress.

"Are ye sure?" She frowned, nodding at the bed. "Aleesa left ye a tunic t'wear, and a plaid—one of Alaric's. I'll take yer clothes an' we'll wash 'em."

"Ye do'na hafta do that," he said, watching as she made her way through the water. It was already starting to dry in patches, from the heat of the fire. She reached down and picked up her robe, wringing it out over the tub.

"I hafta wash these, anyway," she said with a sigh, wringing out the wet bath sheets too.

"Well, thank ye." He glanced back at the mattress he was leaning against. "T'will be nice t'sleep in a bed tonight."

"Tis Alaric and Aleesa's," she told him, regretting it the moment she said so, seeing the startled look on his face. "They wanted ye t'have it. Because… yer t'red wulver."

He frowned. "But where'll they sleep?"

"We've a room for guests." She smiled as she passed him. "Do'na worry. Sleep well, red wulver."

Griff grabbed her elbow and Bridget gasped. Her feet were still wet and she nearly slipped on the stone floor. Once again, he caught her.

"Will ye stay wit' me, lass?" His eyes searched hers, his voice low and soft, gripping her upper arm. "Keep a man warm?"

"Yer not a man, yer a wulver. And… tis not m'job t'warm yer bed." She glanced down at where he held onto her arm. His whole hand could encircle it. "If I wanted t'share it, ye'd know."

"How would I know?" He let her go, their eyes still locked. He was smiling.

"'Cause I'd be in it." She turned and went to the door, picking up his clothes and boots before opening it and glancing over her shoulder at him. "See ye at breakfast, red wulver. Have a g'nite."

He gave a sigh as she started to close the door, calling out, "G'nite, Bridget."

She stood outside his room for a moment, trying to catch her breath.

She stood there and fought with herself, fought with her own urges.

He'd asked her to come to his bed, and she'd been right to refuse him. She knew that much. It was the right thing to do, for the temple, for her role as both future high priestess and guardian. She'd made the right decision, and she knew both Alaric and Aleesa, who were bedding down at the other end of the long tunnel, would be proud of her.

So why did she feel so empty?

Chapter Five

Griff spent the next three days, until the high moon, avoiding Bridget.

It wasn't that difficult. Aleesa monopolized him at breakfast, wanting to know everything about his den and his pack. She had so many questions about her daughter, Kirstin, and the wulvers Aleesa and Alaric had known. And all those who had come after, too, those she'd never had a chance to know.

After breakfast, Alaric took Bridget out on the horses for training, and while Griff had attempted avoiding that, too, he'd been roped into it both days. Uri needed the exercise, anyway. That's what he told himself, as he found himself facing Bridget in her English-Scottish hybrid armor. Alaric was hellbent on using Griff as a practice dummy for his daughter, and while he'd refused, more than once, Bridget had managed to goad him into fighting.

The first time, he was a gentleman and he let her win—which wasn't easy for him—and then she'd accused him of such. So the second time, he beat her soundly, and she'd accused him of cheating. Could he help it if the girl's body was like a gory damned magnet he found himself drawn to? He hadn't been cheating. He'd just been—distracted.

Before lunch, the women did their purification ritual at the sacred pool. Griff steered clear of that, and Alaric did, too. The older wulver took him out to set snares and check traps. They spent time talking about Griff's father, Raife, and Raife and Darrow's father, Garaith. Of course, they both knew that Garaith was only Raife's father by name only. King Henry VII was Raife's father by blood—the same blood that flowed through Griff's veins.

But while his pack knew the truth, few people outside of Scotland's borderlands, where the wulver den resided, knew that King Henry VII had once bed a wulver woman, let alone that his issue, a warrior who was half-man, half-wolf, led the last pack of wulvers.

But were they the last?

Alaric told him he wasn't sure if their den was the last. The guardian Alaric had slain when Aleesa had first come to the Temple of Ardis and Asher had been a wulver, not a man. But he was not a wulver Alaric knew, and he hadn't had a chance to ask the other warrior where he'd come from. And there was no priestess who resided here then. Aleesa had explained to her husband that she had been called to the temple by the dying high priestess—the wulver woman who had been the slain wulver's mate.

So if there had been two wulvers living here, two wulvers that Alaric and Aleesa did not know—mayhaps there were others, somewhere. There must be, Griff reasoned. They might all be descendants of the first wolf-human union—according to legend, Ardis was a woman, who turned into a wolf during the full moon, and Asher was the human man she loved—but the world was a big place.

He knew this from Rory MacFalon, who studied maps with his father, Donal. Were there wulvers in England? France? Were there wulvers in lands beyond, that they had yet to explore? There were humans in those places—why would there not be wulvers? The thought of traveling to find those lost packs, of joining those wulver forces, excited him beyond words.

He was impatient to find them. Impatient to be off. But he had to wait. According to Alaric and Aleesa, they had to wait for the high moon to read the location of the lost packs in the scrying pool. This annoyed him more than he could say, but he had no choice but to believe what Alaric and Aleesa said.

The truth was, Griff wasn't sure what to believe. He'd dreamed of the dragon both nights, alone in the big bed. The mattress was very comfortable, and while he'd offered to give it up to its rightful owners, the wulver couple had insisted he sleep in their bed. Sometimes he wondered if he'd really seen the dragon rising from the pool, the one he'd been sure was going to attack Bridget when it turned its scaly head, or if he'd dreamed that, too.

The temple had that surreal feel to it. Mayhaps he was really dead and dreaming all of this, he thought sometimes at night, staring up at the shadows on the ceiling, wondering if Bridget was as wide awake as he was at the other end of the cavernous tunnel. Bridget, though, was made of flesh. That he was certain. He had felt it pressed against him more than once. Her flesh seemed to call to him, every moment of the day, in spite of his efforts to avoid her.

It was the most difficult at dinner, when she sat right beside him. He couldn't seem to resist her bait. That little smirk when she saw she'd goaded him into verbally sparring with her drove him mad. He'd noticed Aleesa looking between them, a knowing look on her face. The older wulver woman sensed something. Knew something, mayhaps.

He wasn't sure of it, though, until he overheard them on that third day, talking after the purification ritual as they made rabbit stew for lunch. He had ridden Uri out to the edge of the island—to the sea—and back again. He wanted to make sure that the ship which had brought him into Skara Brae was still anchored there, getting assurance from the captain that yes, they were sailing to another small island that day, but would be there on Skara Brae on the morrow.

Alaric had let him back into the temple at the rock. Rain had soaked Griff to the skin and Alaric sent him in to the kitchen to get dry, telling him he'd rub Uri down and feed him. Griff had meant to announce his presence to the chatting woman—but he'd stopped just outside the kitchen when he heard his name spoken in relation to hers.

"Bridget, ye can'na go wit' Griff," Aleesa told her daughter. "E'en if t'man wanted ye… has he said so?"

Griff stopped, wincing at the way his feet squished in his boots. There was a storm coming in topside, he was sure. He heard Bridget sigh.

"Nay, he's n'said a word." Bridget's voice was small. "But… what if…"

"Bridget, we've spent our whole lives trainin' ye," Aleesa insisted. "I can'na b'lieve he's yer one true mate. Unless… mayhaps… he's meant to be t'guardian 'ere in the temple…?"

Bridget snorted a laugh at that and Griff frowned, stiffening at her laughter. Was it such a strange idea, that he be a protector of this place? Not that it was something he was interested in doing, he had to admit.

"Ye said he's t'red wulver," Bridget reminded her mother. "Even if t'dragon and t'lady did'na confirm it."

"Ye saw him change, as well as I did," Aleesa replied. "I've ne'er seen a red wulver warrior a'fore, and neither has Alaric. He's t'red wulver. And ye saw 'is eyes!"

"Aye," Bridget readily agreed. "But Mother, I... t'way I feel 'bout 'im..."

Griff leaned against the cavern wall, feeling his heart beating hard in his chest at her words. What way did she feel? He wondered. Because for all he could tell, the girl hated him. At least, that was the message she'd been sending since the first time they met. The incident in the tub notwithstanding—and that had been an accident.

The truth was, he wanted to bed her. Bridget was one of the most beautiful women he'd ever seen, with or without clothes, and he wanted her. He would've taken her to bed that first night if she'd agreed. But she'd turned him down. It wasn't a common occurrence for him, he had to admit, but he understood her desire to retain her maidenhood. She was intended to be a priestess here, no different than a nun called to be married to the Lord in a convent, he supposed.

He couldn't say he understood it, exactly, but he could respect it.

So he'd done his best to avoid her. Not that it was easy in such a confined space. And even when they weren't together, in the same room, he could feel her somehow. Her presence was far bigger than her slight form, that was certain. He seemed to carry it with him wherever he went.

"Oh Bridget," Aleesa cried. "I wouldna expect ye t'understand t'ways of men'n'women. Ye've been so sheltered 'ere."

Griff grinned to himself. That was true enough. The girl was definitely a virgin. He'd bedded a few of them, in his time, but he preferred a more experienced woman, given his choice.

"I know what matin' is, Mother." Bridget laughed. "That's… that's not it. I could've mated wit' him if I wanted t'do so. He made that clear enough."

"Bridget!" Aleesa gasped, sounding shocked.

"We've done nothin'," Bridget protested.

Griff heard the lie in her voice, the defensiveness. No, they'd done nothing. Technically, they'd done little more than rub up against one another. But there was something between them, regardless of what physical contact they'd had. He wouldn't have admitted it out loud, either, but he couldn't lie to himself.

"But, Mother, I… I've ne'er felt this way a'fore about someone," Bridget said, lowering her voice, as if someone might overhear. As if her own mind might hear what she was thinking, and her heart take note. He understood that kind of caution, even as he stood in the tunnel and eavesdropped. "I do'na understand it."

Aleesa didn't say anything, and Griff wondered at their silence. He considered making his presence known, glancing behind him into the tunnel, knowing Alaric would be along soon.

"Daughter, listen to me…" Aleesa's voice was low, so low he had to strain to hear it.

"I'm not yer daughter," Bridget whispered.

"Oh aye, ye're m'daughter," Aleesa assured her. "Yer mine, ye've been mine, since the first day I held ye in m'arms and rocked ye t'sleep. I love ye jus' as much as if ye'd come from m'own body, chile."

Griff heard Bridget sniff and he wondered if she was crying. The thought made his chest feel tight, as if something heavy had just sat on it.

"Listen t'me," Aleesa said again. "T'marriage of t'sun'n'moon is due vera soon, y'ken?"

"Aye," Bridget agreed, sniffing again and sighing. "T'marriage of Asher and Ardis. And I'm t'take m'vows as high priestess… which means I'll ne'er leave 'ere again."

The sadness in the young woman's voice broke him. He wanted to save her from it, from the fate of living the rest of her life chanting over pools and talking to invisible dragons. If she would say yes—and up until then, he'd been certain her answer would have been no—he would offer to take her with him. He'd never met a woman like Bridget before, a woman who wore armor, who could hold her own with a sword, who could run almost as fast, mayhaps faster, than he could. He'd never known another woman he thought could be his equal, in or out of bed.

But this one…

She didn't deserve this life. He wanted more for her.

He wanted her.

"Oh, lass, do'na cry… a guardian'll come," Aleesa told her daughter in an urgent, reassuring whisper. "Alaric came fer me. A guardian'll come fer ye, too, Bridget. He'll be called here, jus' as I was."

"Aye." Bridget sighed, long and deep, a sigh so full of regret and longing, he was glad he couldn't see her face. If he had seen her face streaked with tears, those big green eyes filled with them, he didn't know what he might do. He was the strongest man—or wulver—

he knew. But the girl's tears made him feel as weak as a bairn. "And Griff'll be leavin' on t'morrow."

Ask me t'stay, lass. He closed his eyes, leaning against the cavern wall, trying to shake the feeling. He wouldn't really stay, if she asked him, would he? Mayhaps not. But if she asked him to take her with him? What then? Would he do so?

He thought he would.

Then Aleesa's words came to him, startling him upright. What did she mean, a guardian would come? They expected some man to arrive here at the temple, to take Alaric's place, like Bridget would take Aleesa's? His lip withdrew from his teeth and he snarled silently at the thought. Just imagining another man showing up at the crossroads, Bridget going out to meet him, made his jaw hurt, he was clenching it so hard.

And the moment she took off her helmet, the moment the man saw her green eyes and that fiery red hair flowing over her shoulders…

"Aye, Griff mus' go fulfill 'is own destiny," Aleesa said. "And 'is destiny isn't yers, lass. I'm sorry fer it. I wish yer feelin's fer 'im lined up wit' yer fate 'ere in th' temple."

"I do'na know what I'm feelin' t'tell t'truth…" Bridget sniffed again.

"I think it's jus' the energy of Ardis'n'Asher yer feelin'—t'lady an' t'dragon. T'marriage time's so close. Ye can'na be blamed fer it. And… he *is* a fine-lookin' man…"

"Mother!" Now it was Bridget's turn to sound shocked, but she giggled.

"Jus' remember," Aleesa warned. "Ye mus' be sure. Tis a lifetime commitment, bein' t'high priestess."

"Aye," Bridget agreed, sounding like the weight of the world was on her shoulders.

Griff wanted nothing more than to lift it and carry it for her, if he could.

But he knew it was impossible.

Aleesa was right about one thing. Even if he didn't believe in destinies and prophecies and all of that, he knew she was right about this—he had his own path, and so did Bridget, and they would have to travel them, alone.

With a sigh and a heavy heart, he ran a hand through his wet hair, put a smile on his face, and went into the kitchen, asking, "What's t'eat? I'm starvin'!"

❧

He didn't know what he'd expected—mayhaps dragon heads again, or ladies with silver eyes—but it wasn't this. He hadn't expected actual writing to show up in the scrying pool, reflecting the moon's light from above. And he hadn't expected how it would be, between him and Bridget, as they stood facing each other across the dark, reflective surface.

Aleesa had fretted, afraid the storm would provide too much cloud cover and prevent the high moon from shining in from above, but the storm had come, as Griff thought it might, while they had spent the afternoon in front of the fire in the kitchen, and it had gone again after dinner.

Before that, Bridget helped Aleesa with some mending while Alaric and Griff sat at the table playing chess. They'd been at it for two days, moving the board to the sideboard when it was meal time, since Alaric had challenged Griff after lunch the first day. The old wulver took forever to make a decision before he moved. Griff was impatient with his strategy, wandering restlessly around the kitchen, snacking idly on boiled eggs and whatever else he could find in the larder before Aleesa chased him out again.

He couldn't avoid Bridget in so small a space. He tried. He skirted around her chair, where she sat sighing and darning socks, complaining about Alaric's tendency to get holes in them. He squatted by the fire to warm his hands, glancing back to see her scowling at him. He returned her scowl with one of his own, growling low in his throat, muttering about the storm forcing him to stay inside and the moon that was taking far too long to come to fruit.

"Are ye always in such a hurry?" Bridget snapped.

Griff raised his eyebrows at her, seeing Aleesa frown at her daughter.

"Yer move!" Alaric called.

Griff stood and went over to the board, taking in the old wulver's move in a glance. Two more moves, mayhaps, and he'd have him in checkmate. It would be all over. Griff moved his bishop, knocking out Alaric's rook.

"Gory hell!" Alaric growled.

"Check." Griff went back over to the fire, squatting down to warm his hands again.

"Do'na worry, Father," Bridget said over her shoulder to Alaric, who grumbled, staring at the board, chin in hand. "He's far too impatient. He's bound t'make a mistake."

"Yer so overconfident." Griff chuckled. "I've got 'im in check."

"*I'm* t'one who's overconfident?" Bridget sniffed, raising her eyebrows, but she smiled back at him. He liked making her smile, in spite of himself.

"Oh damn!" Bridget swore, dropping the needle and thread and holding her finger. A drop of blood appeared on her pale skin.

"Distractible," Alaric grumbled from the table, not looking over.

"Aye." Bridget sighed, agreeing.

"Lemme see." Griff took her hand, holding her finger up in the firelight, and without thinking, he put it into his mouth.

It was a normal, wulver thing to do—a wulver could lick his wounds well in minutes, even bad ones—but Bridget cried out in surprise.

Their eyes locked and she tried to pull away, but he held her fast, tasting her essence against his tongue, salty sweet, intoxicating. It was just a tiny pinprick, a miniscule wound, but he couldn't bear to see her hurt. Slowly, she withdrew her index finger from between his lips, her own slightly parted as she traced the line of his mouth, her gaze never leaving his.

He felt Aleesa watching them, breath held. He felt Alaric's gaze, too. And still, he couldn't look away, couldn't for a moment pretend he wasn't feeling it. He didn't care if her parents were in the room—the woman was his, and he wanted her. The urge to take her was almost uncontrollable. His hands actually shook with the effort it took to hold himself back. His cock was like an iron bar under his plaid, pointing at her like an arrow.

"Does it still hurt?" he asked as she slowly pulled her finger away, putting her hands in her lap. Her breath was shallow, face flushed. He wanted to see the rest of her in the firelight, like he had that first night. He wanted to watch her nipples turn rosy and get hard. He wanted to gaze at the fiery hair between her thighs, to bury his face in her soft wetness.

"I'm a'righ'," Bridget breathed, glancing over and seeing Aleesa's face. Her mother was wide-eyed, looking between them like she'd just seen something that really, truly frightened her. "I… I think I need t'lie down fer a while…"

Bridget stood, her mending falling to the floor, but she paid it no mind.

"Call me t'help wit' supper," Bridget said faintly over her shoulder to her mother, moving past him, heading out of the kitchen.

"Do'na toy wit' her," Aleesa managed after a moment, reaching down to pick up Bridget's mending. Her eyes burned into his. "If y'intend t'leave 'ere after tonight, if y'intend to find t'lost packs… please, Griff, do'na toy wit' her."

"Aye," Griff stood slowly, handing her the sock Bridget had been mending. "I'll be in m'room."

Aleesa gave him a stiff nod, and Griff then retired to his room—their room, really. He stretched out on the bed and thought of Bridget, resting just down the hall from him. He thought about her for what felt like hours, until Aleesa's voice called him for supper.

And Bridget sat silently beside him the whole meal, their hands brushing occasionally, sending sparks through him like lightning.

But Aleesa was right, and he knew it. He had to get through that night, when they could tell him the location of the lost packs, and then he'd be on his way again. He would take Uri and ride back to the ship waiting in the harbor. He would set sail and work his way to wherever he might find his kin, the wulver warriors he would take back to his own den, to show his father, to claim his rightful place as leader.

He'd lost sight of what he was here to do. He'd let himself get distracted by a woman. But he was focused again as he stood across the sacred pool from Bridget. Focused and determined. He kept hold of that focus well, until the moon hit its highest point, until she shone her silver face down into the pool, and Bridget reached her small, trembling hands out, palms up, to him, and whispered, "Mirror me."

He didn't respond, not at first. He wasn't even sure what she'd said, until she repeated it, louder this time, her voice shaking. "Griff… mirror me."

He glanced at Aleesa, at the other end of the pool, her palms up. Alaric stood across from her, doing the same.

"I need ye." Bridget lifted her eyes to his, glinting in the moonlight. "Please, Griff…"

Slowly, he lifted his hands, palms out. They weren't touching, couldn't of course, they were too far away, but he felt her just the same. He felt her skin, her palms small and trembling, touching his own. It wasn't possible, but it was so.

"Griff," she murmured again, giving a little cry. "Oh Griff…"

Oh hell. His mouth went dry. His cock swelled. He felt her little mouth against his, as if he were tasting her sweet lips right that moment. How was it possible? His heart hammered in his chest like he'd been running for miles.

"Y'know I do'na b'lieve in magic, lass," Griff said, his voice far more hoarse than he expected it to be.

"Ye do'na hafta b'lieve," she breathed. "Jus' look."

"What am I watchin' fer? Fey folk? Sprites?" He gave her a smile and saw a flicker of one on her lips. "Magical writin' on t'walls?"

"Aye." She nodded. She was breathing hard. So was he. What was happening? "Writin'… in t'pool…"

"Nothin's happenin'," Griff said. His hands were trembling and he tried to still them.

"Oh aye, tis happenin'," Bridget replied, glancing down into the pool, just briefly. "Look!"

He did, and he saw. There, in the pool, was writing. It rippled and moved with the water, but it was writing. He blinked, trying to clear his vision, but the writing stayed. Then he saw the same words, glowing on the monoliths that lined the walls of the cavern. It was backwards on stone, unreadable, but when it was reflected in the pool, it was quite clear.

If it weren't for those ripples breaking the surface…

"Look a'me, Griff. Look a'me..." Bridget urged. She smiled when he met her eyes, and he saw a hint of silver in them, like the moon. "Aye, that's it… concentrate… focus on me…"

He could only see it out of the corner of his eye, because he was staring at Bridget, but the more they focused on each other, the more still the pool became—and the clearer the writing.

"Aleesa, write it down," Alaric called.

"Aye," the wulver woman agreed. She had pad and ink and was recording the words by the light of a small lamp on her end of the pool.

Griff wanted to look, wanted to read the words for himself, but every time he tried, the pool would ripple again, blurring it all.

"Look t'me," Bridget urged, reaching her hands out, as if doing so would touch him, and somehow, it did. She was over there, all the way across the pool, and yet their hands were pressed, palm to palm. He felt her breath on his face, could smell her sweet scent. Heather and silvermoon. "Can ye feel it?"

He nodded. He could. And for a moment, it actually frightened him.

"Do'na look away!" Bridget insisted, calling for him across the water. Griff's gaze lifted again to hers, saw a flicker of a smile on her face as she caught his attention once more. "Aye, good… concentrate… hold steady…"

Every time he looked away from her, the writing would begin to fade, as if the two of them together were powering the light of the moon itself.

"Tis ridiculous," he muttered, squinting down at the water. "What's it say? Does it give ye t'location of t'lost packs?"

"Aye!" Aleesa assured him. "But I will'na b'able t'write it down if ye do'na concentrate!"

"Madness." Griff grumbled again, but listened to Bridget when she called out to him across the pool.

"Tis ye, Griff," Bridget called to him, her fingers spreading wider, as if she were matching her palms to his. "We've ne'er been able t'see it this clear. Yer t'reason. Yer t'red wulver. Tis yer destiny, Griff."

Her words shook him to the core. For all his talk of not believing in prophecies or destiny, her words moved him. Just an indication that leaving his home and kin to follow this path, to find the lost packs, was the right one for him, filled him with hope and pride. When he'd decided to come to Skara Brae to find this temple, he'd made the fastest, most impetuous decison of his life—at least, it had felt that way once he'd been on the ship. And when he was asking around, trying to find out anything about the temple on Skara Brae. And even when he was at the crossroads with Uri, feeling like an idiot, calling out to no one.

But Bridget had been there. The temple was here. The answers, too, were here. He wasn't ready to admit that prophecies and destiny were real or anything—but he couldn't discount them, either. Not now, not after this.

Griff wanted to look down, to read the words Bridget spoke of, but he didn't. Instead, he looked at her, feeling something he'd never experienced before in his life. He wouldn't have been able to describe it if he tried. Bridget had captured him, with her voice, her presence. She was everything, in that moment. The moon. The sun. The universe.

"Hold me, Griff," she murmured. She spoke with a voice so soft, he shouldn't have been able to hear her, but he did. "Do'na lemme go."

"I've got ye, lass," he whispered. His breath was coming fast, as if he was working hard.

"Oh Griff, I…" She gave another small cry and he felt a sudden surge of energy sing through his whole body. It actually made his knees feel weak, and he almost went to them. "Please, hold on, hold on..."

"Aye, lass." His whole body strained with the effort it took to stay focused. But he wasn't about to stop, to let her go. He wasn't sure if he was carrying her, or she was carrying him, or mayhaps they were carrying something together.

"I've almos' got it all," Aleesa called, sounding hurried, rushed. She was writing as fast as she could.

"Hurry, hurry," Bridget urged her mother. Her voice was breathy, panting, and he knew she was exhausting herself with this, whatever it was they were doing together. Griff's hands trembled, and he realized it wasn't his palms, but hers he was feeling. Her little hands trembling, pressed against his.

Impossible.

"Are ye a'righ', lass?" Griff asked, calling across the pool to her. The images on the water shimmered, as if his voice had shaken it.

"Aye, aye," she gasped, crying out again, as if in pain. "Oh! I can't… I…"

"That's it!" Aleesa announced, looking up in triumph. "I've got it all!"

At that, Bridget collapsed.

Griff had her in his arms, before either Alaric or Aleesa could reach her. She was breathing, but too shallow, eyes still closed, mouth moving as if she was speaking, but no words coming out.

"She's still in the trance," Aleesa murmured, putting a hand on her daughter's forehead. "Go put 'er in our bed. She'll come back t'ye…"

"She'd better," he growled at the wulver woman. Aleesa blinked at him in surprise, and he knew it was his fault this had happened. He'd been the one who wanted to know, who insisted they find out where the lost packs were located.

But how could he have known it would be like this? Of course, what had he expected? Some chanting, herbs being thrown like they did during the purification ritual, mayhaps a map to appear?

He hadn't realized he'd be such a part of things, that Bridget would rely on him so heavily during the ritual. Or that it would take so very much out of her.

Griff lifted Bridget in his arms—she weighed hardly anything—and carried her into the tunnel. He ignored Aleesa calling after him. It was full dark, but he followed the light at the end of it, where he passed through the kitchen, the fire burning low. Bridget moaned and her eyes fluttered open briefly as he carried her through.

"Griff?" She half-smiled, putting her arms around his neck, clinging to him. "Ye did'na leave me."

She made his heart break in half.

"Nuh, lass."

He put her down on the bed, head on a pillow. She gave a little cry, reaching for him again, and he let her put her arms around his neck, let her pull him close. He kicked his boots off, resting beside her, feeling her heart beating hard against his, like a little bird's.

"Ye'll be a'righ," he whispered, his lips brushing her hairline, smelling her sweetness. He didn't know if it was true—but he said it anyway. "I should ne'er've asked ye t'do this. I'm sorry, lass. I'm so sorry."

He swallowed, tracing her soft features with his finger. She was so small, like a doll. The most beautiful thing he'd ever seen in his life. He could have stayed there, watching her just breathing, forever.

"Has she spoken?" Aleesa came in, asking after her daughter.

"Aye, briefly." He frowned. "Will she be a'righ'?"

"Oh, aye." Aleesa nodded. "She's just exhausted. It takes a great deal of energy. She jus' needs rest. I'll have Alaric come fetch 'er…"

"No," he snapped, reaching for the coverlet and pulling it over Bridget's still form. "She'll stay 'ere."

"Griff…" Aleesa warned, her eyes widening. "Ye can'na..."

“I’ll sleep on t’floor,” he told her gruffly, putting a big, heavy arm across Bridget. “But we’ll not be movin ’er.”

“A’righ’.” She sighed. “Call me if ye need anythin’?”

“Aye,” he agreed, not taking his eyes off Bridget’s sleeping face.

Aleesa moved around the room, straightening, coming over to check on her again, a hand pressed to her forehead.

“She’s really gonna be a’righ’?” he asked, meeting Aleesa’s concerned gaze.

“Aye, she will, lad.” Aleesa gave him a small smile, pressing her hand to his forehead for a moment as well. It was small and cool. He felt warm. “And so will ye, *Righ*.”

“*Righ*.” He blinked at her, surprised at her use of the Gaelic word for *King*.

“T’once and future king.” Aleesa sat beside her daughter, looking at them both, thoughtful. “T’will take me a few hours to decipher all the text, but... d’ye wanna know what I saw in t’pool?”

He hesitated. Of course, he wanted to know—it was what he’d come here to discover. Based on whatever she’d seen, he would set out in the morning in search of his kin.

And he would leave Bridget behind.

That thought made his bones hurt and he looked down at her again, those russet colored lashes still against her pale cheeks, her lips pink, slightly parted, her breath still coming too fast.

Aleesa’s hand touched his, the one flat on the mattress beside Bridget, as if the arm over her could protect her from all harm.

“In the mornin’.” Griff didn’t lift his gaze from Bridget’s face. “I think we all need a good night’s rest.”

“Aye,” Aleesa agreed. She leaned over and kissed Bridget’s forehead, and then she kissed the back of Griff’s hand. “G’nite, lad.”

The wulver woman hesitated as she opened the door, glancing back at the couple on the bed. Bridget stirred, mumbling something, and Griff stroked her cheek, whispering to her.

“Griff...” Aleesa cleared her throat. “I... about what I said t’ye, earlier tonight…”

He glanced at her and saw her meaning clearly on her face. She didn’t have to worry. He’d never felt more connected to a woman—to anyone—than he did to Bridget in this moment. Did he want her? Aye, he did. More than he’d ever wanted anything. But his feelings for her went far beyond the physical. He would protect her with his own life, from now until the end of days.

“I will’na hurt ’er,” he said softly. “I give ye m’word.”

Aleesa gave him a nod, closing the door behind her.

Chapter Six

He was hers.

It was a dream, she knew it had to be, but they stood, palm to palm, long cords of rope being wrapped around their wrists—a handfasting. Griff's amber-colored eyes were shining with love, and Bridget felt more whole, complete, than she ever had in her entire life. She knew that feeling, as a temple priestess, of being filled by light, lacking nothing, but this was a different sort of wholeness. This was a mating, of two halves becoming one, a union of souls. Someone spoke in her dream, of dragons and ladies, the marriage of the opposites. She knew the prayers, had studied them her whole life, but they sounded different to her ears as she faced the man she loved, cleaving her life to his...

The man she loved.

Griff.

He was there, facing her across a shimmering pool filled with moonlight. He was there, always there. Protecting her from dragons. Catching her when she fell. Even when she'd pricked her finger, he'd been there to comfort her. She saw nothing but him now. It was as if the man had eclipsed everything else in her life just by his sudden existence in it. Her conscious mind, the one that told her that this was impossible, that their paths had meant to cross only for a moment and then diverge again, turned away from him. But something deeper in her knew the truth.

This man was hers, and she was his. It had been meant to be, since before time had begun its neverending countdown to nothingness again. If everything was as it should be, then her deeper self, the one that called for him in her sleep, the one that longed for his touch, the one that surrendered to her feelings, sought only that which was true.

She'd never realized she wanted something so much until she woke, sobbing, at the loss of it.

And he was there.

"Shhh, lass, ye're a'righ'," he soothed.

She opened her eyes, feeling him stretched out beside her, floating as if they were on a cloud.

And then she remembered. She remembered the ritual at the sacred pool, the way the moon had lit up the words on the reflective surface. She remembered her whole body shaking with the effort to stay still, to concentrate, to keep her mind steady and focused. She remembered Griff's eyes, glowing red, looking straight into and through her.

"Did we find 'em?" she mumbled, trying to sit, but her head felt thick and heavy on her neck. "T'lost packs? Yer kin?"

"Aye," he nodded, putting a big hand in the middle of her chest, pressing her to the bed. "I think so. Aleesa's transcribin' it all."

"Does she need m'help?" Bridget struggled again to rise, but Griff's big paw stayed planted in the middle of her chest.

"Bridget, ye need rest." He frowned down at her, those amber eyes searching her face. "I did'na know it would be so..."

"Tirin'?" She smiled, closing her eyes again for a moment. "Tis like anythin' worth doin' I s'pose... it's a worthy effort. Like makin' love or birthin', mayhaps..."

"Interestin' comparisons." Griff chuckled and she opened her eyes to see him smiling down at her, eyes dancing.

"Why'm I here?" She glanced around, realizing they were in Aleesa and Alaric's room, the one Griff had been staying in since he arrived.

"Because I brought ye here," he said simply. "Because yer mine, Bridget, and I will'na leave ye, ne'er again."

She swallowed, breath caught at his words. She had to still be dreaming. She'd fallen back into unconsciousness, where things like this were possible. But she most definitely wasn't looking up into Griff's concerned face, feeling his warm breath on her cheek, the long, hard stretch of his body against hers. Those things couldn't really be happening.

"But ye hafta find yer kin." She reached up to touch his cheek with trembling fingers, just to make sure she wasn't still dreaming. "What 'bout t'lost packs?"

"I'm meant to lead 'em, Bridget." His face was pained. "But I can'na deny m'feelin's fer ye any longer. I want ye as m'wife. My mate. I wanna take ye from this place, this life. Come wit' me. Be mine."

She stared at him, eyes wide now, fully awake. This was no dream.

Griff was here, holding her, and asking...

"What're y'askin' me?" She struggled to comprehend it. "Ye wan' me t'come wit' ye... to find t'lost packs?"

"Why not?" He smiled. "Ye can handle a sword as good as any man I know and yer a fine horsewoman."

"As good?" she snorted. "Better, I'd wager, than most men *or* wulvers ye know..."

"Aye, aye." He laughed. "I'm glad t'see ye've got yer spark back... I was worried 'bout ye..."

"How long've I been sleepin'?" she asked, frowning.

"Jus' a few hours."

She blinked at him. "And what've ye been doin'?"

"Watchin' ye..."

"If I go wit' ye..." She swallowed, trying to let the thought sink in. "I'll miss t'marriage of Ardis and Asher. The ritual of t'sun'n'moon. I won't become high priestess..."

"But is that what ye want?" Griff asked, lacing his fingers with hers. Just his touch made her melt, gave her so many doubts about the course her life had taken thus far. "I will'na stand in t'way if that's really what ye want, lass. I'll leave righ' now..."

Griff made the move to go, and that's when she knew.

"No!" she cried, grabbing his tunic and pulling him back.

He settled back onto the mattress, looking down at her, smiling.

"I think ye wan' more than this life," he murmured. "More than what ye'd 'ave 'ere in this temple."

"How d'ye know that?" She jutted her chin out, defiant.

"I jus' know." He touched her chin with one finger, still smiling that knowing, arrogant smile. "I know ye, Bridget."

"Ye do'na know me," she said with a shake of her head. "Y'only think ye know me. I'm t'woman ye can'na have. If I gave m'self t'ye, ye'd be gone in t'mornin' wit'out a second thought."

His look darkened, and she saw something in his eyes. They turned dark, from gold to the deepest amber.

"Not wit'out ye," he growled.

"Griff, I can'na leave t'temple," she whispered. And that was the crux of it, truly. Even if she wanted to go with him, how could she? "I can'na leave Aleesa'n'Alaric alone 'ere."

"Can'na...?" His finger moved from her chin, trailing down to the hollow of her throat, his touch melting her. "Or will'na?"

"Ye know, I was left 'ere by someone who wanted me t'be trained as priestess and guardian."

Griff made a face. "Ye do'na know that..."

"But I do," she protested. "Just like ye knew t'come 'ere t'Skara Brae, t'look fer t'lost packs. I know I'm meant t'be 'ere, fer the marriage of Asher'n'Ardis, when the eclipse comes... I can feel it in m'bones."

"Och!" Griff rolled his eyes toward the ceiling. "More magic and rituals?"

"I know ye do'na understand it, but..." Bridget touched his chin, bringing his face around so she could look into his eyes. "Did ye *feel* it?"

He frowned. "What d'ye mean?"

"When ye were looking a'me, across t'pool tonight..." she breathed, remembering, her whole body filled with the memory. "Did ye feel that?"

Griff shook his head, eyes clouded, but then, she saw something. Just a flicker.

And finally, he broke.

"Aye," he whispered. His mouth quivered with his confession. "I felt ye. Ye looked a'me, an' it cracked m'heart wide open, lass."

"Oh Griff..." She felt tears coming to her eyes, knowing how difficult it was for him to admit the truth. She'd felt it, too.

"How can I leave 'ere on t'morrow wit'out ye?" he croaked out, lowering his head to her breast. Bridget stroked his hair, feeling tears slipping down her temples at his words. "It'll be like leavin' m'heart behind."

"Mayhaps…" She swallowed, taking a deep breath. "Mayhaps we're only meant t'have this."

"This?" He lifted his face to look at her in the firelight.

"This moment." She touched his cheek, shifting against him, so they were belly to belly. "Tonight. Now."

"I wan' more," he admitted. "I want ye—I want ye *t'be mine*."

"Aye." She nodded. "I want ye, too..."

She bridged the gap between them, easily, lifting her face and pressing her lips to his. They were soft, warm. But she felt him hesitating, felt his body stiffen, holding back as she ran her hands over his chest, putting them up around his neck.

"Och, we can'na do this," he whispered as they parted, and Bridget slid her soft, bare thigh between his. "I promised yer mother..."

"There are no laws 'ere in this temple or among t'wulvers that say we can'na be joined this way," she reminded him as she rolled toward him on the mattress, pinning him beneath her.

"Nay, but..." Griff protested, moaning when she wiggled her way fully onto him, trapping his erection between them. "Och, lass, if we do this, are ye gonna accuse me of leavin' ye in t'morning...?"

"We hafta follow our destinies," she whispered, sitting up on him in a straddle. "Tis as it should be, always."

He gasped when she unpinned her plaid, pulling it away from her body and tossing it aside. His eyes went from that deep, dark, amber color to a rich, bright red when she pulled her tunic off over her head and threw that aside too.

"Always as it should be, eh?" he asked, as Bridget took his hands in hers, putting them at her waist. His hands moved over her skin and she shivered.

"Always," she agreed with a nod, moving her hips, feeling his shaft against the seam of her sex through his plaid.

"Then I should be doin' this...?" His hands moved up to cup her breasts. They were full and ripe, never touched, and he plucked at her nipples like little cherries.

"Oh, aye..." Bridget breathed, rocking faster.

"And this...?" One hand slipped up behind her head and pulled her down to him for a kiss. This was no soft, hesitant thing, but something hard, hot, demanding. His tongue stroked and tickled the roof of her mouth, caressed the velvet walls of her cheeks from the inside, and Bridget looked at him with glazed, lust filled eyes as they parted.

"Oh, aye, aye, definitely that..." She nodded eagerly, wanting more, aching for something, although she wasn't quite sure what.

"And this?" His mouth moved down to capture her nipple, suckling like a babe, and Bridget almost sobbed at the sensation.

"Aye, aye," she cried as Griff rolled her to her back.

She ran her hands over him, greedy, mapping his chest and belly with her palms, memorizing every glorious inch of him. She hadn't been able to get the image of his nude body out of her mind, and now she drank him in as he knelt up to divest himself of tunic and plaid, and she saw him again, stripped bare for her.

"Please, please," she begged him, reaching for the part of him she hadn't dared touch the other day. "I want ye inside me."

Griff hissed through his teeth when she squeezed him, a sound that filled Bridgit with an incredible, feminine power.

"Not yet, lass." He gave a low groan as he leaned over to kiss her and she felt the full weight of him crushing her against the mattress. She gasped and reveled in it, rocking up, wanting more.

"Please," she begged, but that would be just the start to her pleas.

Griff spent eons—it was at least that long, she was sure—kissing and touching her body. He explored every inch of her, from nose to navel, front and back, with fingers, then tongue. She felt like a newborn kitten being given a bath, and all the while, she begged him for more.

Please, Griff, please...

She didn't even know anymore what she wanted, what it was she was asking for.

Then his mouth went lower. He skipped her sex and went to her thighs, rubbing his whiskers there until she was red and raw. Then he turned her over and did the same to her bottom. Her cheeks—the ones on her face—were just as red when he finally rolled her to her back, pushing her knees to her chest, and burying his face in her sex.

"Griff!" Bridget nearly screamed. She bit her lip, remembering Alaric and Aleesa might hear, but soon she forgot all about them. She forgot everything as he pressed his tongue between her aching, swollen lips, flicking a spot at the top of her cleft that made her shake all over when he did.

And then, something happened.

One moment she was trembling all over, crying out as if in pain—because whatever he was doing with his mouth and tonguc down there was pure, blissful torture—and then, she flew, or jumped, or mayhaps was pushed, over a shuddering, delicious precipice.

Her hips bucked up off the mattress, her hands reached for something to hold onto, sure she was tumbling, falling, flying, and Griff let her grab his hands. Squeezing them hard, she felt her sex contracting, squeezing too, again and again, quivering waves crashing through her, an ocean of them, all at once.

"What was that?" she asked in wonder, and Griff came up to kiss her.

He tasted strange, musky, and she realized that was how she must taste.

"This may hurt, lass," he whispered, and she felt him at her entrance, pressing slowly.

Oh, it was big!

Bridget cried out as her sex opened to him, the first painful stretch, a slight burn. She put her arms around his neck, clinging to him, and he held her, holding still, waiting. He was inside her now, she felt him, completely filling her. He kissed her, soft, slow. His mouth was entrancing, drawing her out, drawing her against him.

She felt herself untensing, her body unfurling, opening to him.

Then, slowly, he began to move.

"Oh! Griff!" His movements were easy, practiced. She had a moment to wonder if he'd done this before—how many times, with how many other women—but when she looked up into his eyes and saw the light there, she didn't care anymore.

He was hers. In that moment, he was hers. That was all that mattered.

"Och, Bridget," he cried, hips moving faster, rocking into her pelvis, the two of them moving together, like water, flowing over one another.

"Aye," she breathed, meeting him. It was like a dance, a beautiful, perfect dance. "Aye, Griff, oh, aye! Do'na stop!"

He groaned at that, driving her into the mattress with such fury she could scarce draw a breath, not that she cared. Bridget felt it again, that delicious tickle building up to a glorious climax. His shaft created such heat, such friction, everything between them was on fire.

"Look a'me, lass," he whispered, holding himself above her as he thrust. His eyes were pure fire and she cried out as the feeling washed through her again, her sex clamping down on his length. "Och! Bridget!"

He gave one last, hard, thrust, burying himself deep in her womb, and she felt the first wave of his pleasure flowing into her. She clasped him to her, and they rolled, breathless, on the bed, until they were wrapped up together in the coverlet.

When he asked if she regretted what they'd done, she laughed.

"I won't e'er regret that," she murmured against his neck. "Not if I died t'morrow."

"Come wit' me," he asked her again.

But she knew she couldn't. They had this, now, and that was all.

"Ye can'na stay?" she asked him. Griff sighed, and she knew.

They had to follow their paths, each their own.

She didn't know how many times they made love. She lost count. And still, she clung to him, wanting more. If this was all they had, this one night, then she wanted it to last a lifetime in her memory.

But they didn't just make love. They talked. They laughed. They fed each other fruit and drank wine and told each other stories. Bridget told him about the time Alaric thought she'd drowned in the sacred pool—when she'd really been hiding among the rocks. Griff told her about the time his aunt, Laina—Darrow's mate—had turned into she-wolf form and had nearly eaten him when he crept up on her while she was sleeping.

"Surely she would n'have hurt ye?" Bridgit asked, shocked at the thought.

"Wulver women can'na control their cycles." Griff sighed. "E'en their own bairns aren't always safe 'round 'em during their moon time. T'other wulver women take the bairns, and they go somewhere during their moon blood, away from t'pack."

"That's… terrible." Bridgit shuddered. She knew her own mother and father locked themselves in their room—this very room, in fact—during Aleesa's moon cycle. Now she knew why. She couldn't imagine not being in control of your own body in that way. As a human woman, bleeding once a month was bad enough. But turning into a wolf, and not being able to turn back until your moon time was over? Not knowing if you might do something to someone you cared about?

"T'be fair, I should'na been where I was," Griff replied with a shrug. "T'would've been m'own fault if she'd torn m'throat out."

Bridget shook her head, sighing. Even so, she couldn't imagine. Poor Laina—what if such a thing had happened, and she came back knowing she'd done something so awful?

"So, d'ye still think e'erythin's always as it should be?" Griff asked, raising an eyebrow at her.

"I can'na explain t'terrible things that 'appen in t'world," she admitted. "I do'na know t'reason fer 'em. But sometimes ye jus' have t'accept what is."

Griff snorted. "Ye sound like m'father."

"He's a wise man."

Griff snorted at that, too, rolling her over to spank her bottom, just once, making her cry out and laugh at him.

"Ye can'na spank t'truth out," she teased.

"No?" His eyes flashed red as he leapt for her, pouncing, making her giggle and thrash underneath him. "Mayhaps I can do somethin' else t'ye 'til ye forget..."

His hand reached between them to cup her sex and she moaned. She was sore there, they'd been together so many times, but she rocked up against him anyway.

She realized, when he slid inside her again, that although they only had this one night to be together, she'd never get enough of him.

Even if they had a lifetime.

“I thought we might find ye ’ere.” Aleesa knelt down beside Bridget at the scrying pool.

“I jus’ wanted to watch him go...” Bridget kept the tremble from her voice and was proud of herself for doing it.

She didn’t want to tell them they’d already said goodbye. Watching Griff ride away to the south, she felt as if she was watching her future get smaller and smaller in the distance.

“He’s a mighty warrior.” Aleesa stroked her daughter’s hair. “I b’lieve he’ll lead t’packs, like t’prophecy says.”

Bridget said nothing, just hugged her knees to her chest and rocked, watching him disappear from her life. The scrying pool could only see up to the horizon, and Griff was almost out of sight.

“Aleesa...!” Alaric said his mate’s name with alarm, staring into the pool at the other end.

“What is it?” she asked, frowning.

“Riders from t’north.” The gray-haired wulver pointed into the pool, peering more closely. “Wulvers… I think… tis Raife.”

“Raife?” Bridget’s head came up at the sound of Griff’s father’s name. The man had come after his son? How had he known he would be there?

“I’ll saddle up an’ go meet ’em.” Alaric was already heading toward the exit.

“I wanna come!” Bridget called, jumping up, thinking of meeting Griff’s father.

Any way to stay connected with him…

Then a sudden motion in the pool at her feet caught her eye and she stopped, staring at the sight unfolding before her. Bridget cried out, dropping to her knees, peering into the pool, her nose so close, it almost touched the water.

"What is it?" Aleesa looked over the edge and saw, too, her eyes going wide with alarm.

"Griff!" Bridget cried, and then Alaric was there beside her, all three of them watching the events unfold in the scrying pool, unable to do anything but witness the scene.

Griff had been intercepted by a massive band of both men and wulvers.

Not the party approaching from the north, but another one coming in from the south. They were being led by a man—not a wulver, at least, not that Bridget could tell—who yelled orders to men and wulver alike as they surrounded Griff on his horse. They could hear no words, of course—they could only watch.

"No," Bridget whispered, her heart dropping to her toes as she saw how outnumbered he was. What in the world could they want of him?

Suddenly, Griff's horse bolted. He urged it forward, through the mass of wulvers and men, and just as suddenly as it had happened, it was over. They were out of sight of the scrying pool's reach. The water was clear again.

"I'll go after 'im." Alaric's voice was hoarse as he turned to go, but Bridget was up again in a flash, grabbing her father's arm.

"No, I'll go," she insisted. "You mus' ride out an' meet t'wulvers coming from t'north. They know who ye are, they'll trust ye an' follow ye. Ye must bring 'em t'help Griff."

"Aye." Alaric hesitated, brow knit, torn. "But I do'na wan' ye t' go anywhere, lass. Ye stay 'ere wit' yer mother."

“That’s not what ye trained me fer.” Bridgit drew herself up to her full height, eyes flashing. “I’ll follow an’ track ’em. I promise, I will’na get t’close.”

“Jus’ track ’em, lass,” he warned, shaking a finger at her. “Leave a trail fer us t’follow.”

“Aye, I will.” She nodded, her heart already beating hard in her throat.

Aleesa put her arms around her daughter and Bridget let herself take comfort, for just a moment.

“Mother...” she whispered, thinking of Griff, of him in danger, and couldn’t bear it.

“T’prophecy says days’ll be dark before t’Blood Reign of t’Red Wulver.” Aleesa kissed her daughter’s forehead softly. “Nothing’s certain. Fate’ll ’ave its way.”

“All is as it should be?” Bridget whispered.

Aleesa nodded, but her eyes were cloudy. “I hope so...”

Chapter Seven

If he hadn't been thinking so much about leaving Bridget, he might have seen them coming. He should have at least smelled them—a few hundred wulvers and men—but he was lost in thought. He cursed himself for it later, of course, being just as moony as Rory over Maire or Garaith over Eilis. He'd never been one to moon about over some female, but instead of tearing over the hills of Skara Brae to meet the ship that would take him to the mainland, he was plodding along, heart heavy. The further he got from the temple, the slower he seemed to go. Uri, impatient with his master's pace, had tried several times to pick it up, but Griff had reined him in.

It was as if there was an invisible string tied from him to the temple—nay, to the lass, Bridget—and it grew more and more taut as he distanced himself. He had to admit, he was daydreaming. He was remembering the press of her full body against his, the creamy expanse of her thighs, the soft press of her lips. Not to mention how quickly lightning flashed in those sea-green eyes. The memory of the way she'd fought him as the guardian, how she'd rallied and come back again and again, made him smile. Little spitfire.

He had left his den to find the lost packs, had traveled to the temple with only that goal in mind. He had been ready for talk of prophecy and magic—he'd lived with it his whole life—but what he hadn't expected was Bridget. All the hoopla about fate and destiny had always seemed silly to him. He didn't like to think of God like some puppet master pulling strings above their heads, making them dance to an old man's tune. Then Bridget's words, "It is all as it should be," kept echoing in his head.

Why had he left his den and come here? Had it been to find the lost packs? Or had the divine had a larger purpose in mind? Had he really traveled all this way just to find his one true mate? To find the red-haired, bright-eyed, saucy little Bridget?

I don't believe in true mates, he reminded himself, glancing back over his shoulder. He could barely see the crossroads and the outcropping where the temple lay. He'd come that far, too far. *I don't believe in true mates, or prophecies, or destiny.*

But how could he say that now, having seen everything Bridget had shown him behind the temple walls? Moonlight and magic, dragons and ladies, had any of it been real? Certainly the way she'd fallen into his arms that night in the tub had been real. And then, when they'd been together the night before... He imagined he could still taste her lips, feel her breath in his ear, smell the sweet, light scent of her skin.

He was lost in his own thoughts when he reached the top of the last hill as he neared the sea. He was distracted, consumed by his own fears and doubts, and they had surrounded him before he knew what was happening. There were a dozen, at least, not just humans, but wulvers as well—wulvers he'd never seen before. They were no kin he knew. The sight startled him even more than the attack itself—wulver warriors he didn't recognize circling him and his horse, mixed with human men wearing armor and carrying swords.

Griff assessed the situation, scanning the line of soldiers, finding its leader—a man wearing dark armor, face plate up, shouting orders to men and wulver alike—and finding its weakness. There was a small break in their line. It wasn't much, but it might be enough. If he was fast.

Years of training took over. Griff made a noise in his throat, digging the heels of his boots into Uri's side, and the horse practically sighed with relief, taking off from a standstill to a run so fast, Griff had to choke up on the reins to keep from being thrown. Uri fled, letting Griff guide him, just as he'd planned, through the small break in his attackers' line. The horse, who had been clearly annoyed with Griff's plodding pace, was relieved to be running again. He had a great deal of pent-up energy, after spending too much time down in the cavern, penned up, and Griff used that to his advantage.

If he'd been home, if it had been their forest, escape wouldn't have been a question. Griff would have easily avoided the attackers at home, but this was Skara Brae, and he didn't know enough about the land and the terrain to lose them. He realized this as he found himself on the rocky beach, the horse struggling in the sand and rocks. A dead end. They could go no further, and there was no ship here to meet them and likely wouldn't be for another hour, mayhaps two. He had left early because if he hadn't left, he knew he would have stayed.

But there was another ship here, and Griff narrowed his eyes at it, seeing the mark on the side, along with a dragon's head. Is this what had carried the men and horses who were after him?

Griff turned Uri so they were galloping along the shoreline, leaning over the neck of his horse, a plan formulating in his head. If he could double back, get to the temple, mayhaps...

Uri tripped. It wasn't the horse's fault. He was used to running in the forest, over the rolling, green hills of home, not on this craggy, rocky beach. His hoof sank into an unseen hole in the sand, and he went down with a shrill, horrible scream.

His leg, it's his leg. The thought of having to put Uri down made Griff far sicker to his stomach than the sound of the approaching horsemen.

They were surrounded again. Griff's side ached—he was wearing full gear again, but the horse had thrown him a good three feet, and his face had been scraped on the rock, along with the rest of him. He tasted blood in his throat as he rolled, reaching for his blade, but it was too late. Three wulver warriors, fully turned, were already off their horses, on him with a net and ropes. Griff shifted. With a shake of his dark head, he shifted, growling and snapping at his attackers. But they were wulvers. They knew exactly what to look out for. The first thing they did was snap on a muzzle, which just made Griff struggle and fight harder.

He almost freed himself, even though it was now six—three men, three wulvers—against one, but then they bound his arms behind his back and chained him.

The only good thing about the entire situation was that Uri's fall hadn't seemed to break anything. The big animal was back up, and one of the wulvers had corralled him, grabbing his reins to lead the horse over the rocks. Griff howled—still in wulver form—when they slung him over the saddle of his horse. His arms were still bound behind him as they lashed him to the saddle and pulled the horse along the beach. Griff struggled, but his kidnappers had tied him well.

They led the horse back up the hill, away from the sea. Griff turned his head, trying to identify any of his kind. He scanned each man, looking for their leader—he remembered the dark knight who had been screaming orders at his men, all of them involving capturing Griff. But why?

"So this is the one." A smooth voice spoke from near the front of the horse, followed by a low, amused chuckle. Griff felt Uri pull instinctively away, the horse giving a nervous whinny, and Griff knew how he felt. His hackles rose at the sound of the man's voice, and he knew, even without seeing him, that this was the man in charge of this little venture. This man, whoever he was, had a purpose in capturing Griff, and whatever it was, it wasn't good.

I won't lead them to the temple. It was the only thing he could imagine they might be searching for. Mayhaps they had already attempted entrance, but had been turned away as unworthy. Bridget had told him, it had happened before. Only certain seekers were even entertained for entrance. Some were judged too dangerous or just plain unworthy, and their cries for entrance went unanswered. Mayhaps these men and wulvers—he couldn't understand how or why his brothers, his kin, for they had to be, if they were his kind, could do this—had already been turned away from the temple, and they had captured him in the hopes he could lead them in.

"I'm not impressed." The man sneered and Griff lifted his wolf head to see the dark knight approaching. He wasn't a Scot. At least, he didn't speak as one. And his armor was definitely English. So what was this shasennach doing with wulvers Griff had never seen before? "Are you sure he's the one?"

"He's wulver," one of the other wulvers confirmed. "And he was comin' from the temple."

So it was the temple, then. Griff felt his limbs go cold at the thought of this band of assailants invading the Temple of Ardis and Asher. He might not believe in the divine and sacred in the same way as the guardians and priestesses who resided there, but he had respect for it. Besides, he would take the information to the grave, if it meant protecting Alaric, Aleesa, and especially Bridget.

Bridget... The young woman's face swam before his eyes. All the blood was rushing to his head at this angle and he lifted it, taking in great gulps of air, determined now to find a way out of this. Not even for himself, or his family, or the lost packs. He just wanted to make sure Bridget remained safe, now and forever.

"Take him down," the man in dark armor instructed. "Off the horse."

The wulvers turned Griff around to the knight, who had taken off his helmet and held it lightly under one arm, his sword in the other. The man was handsome, well-groomed, young—probably Griff's age—and from his accent, quite English. Griff tried to place him. Someone who had visited Castle MacFalon mayhaps? If he could figure out who the man was, he might be able to figure out why the man wanted him.

"You have no earthly idea who I am, do you?" The other man chuckled, flashing a brilliant smile. His blonde hair fell over one eye as he dipped his head to look at Griff, searching his eyes behind the muzzle. "Hm. Where are those fabled red eyes of yours, wulver? Show me."

So that was it, then. The man knew he was the red wulver. Griff just glared at him, working hard not to show him the color of his eyes, because anger rose in him like a coming storm. He shook his head, changing back to human form in an instant, knowing it would be easier to control his emotions this way.

"No?" The man frowned, angry at Griff's resistance, but curious now that he'd changed back into human form. "Mayhaps this will change your mind, then..."

The armored man brought his sword hilt up against the underside of Griff's chin. The blow knocked his head back and he groaned, feeling his teeth rattle in his head as he went to his knees. He gagged, feeling light headed and nauseous, knowing he'd be lucky if he could talk at all for a while after that hit—luckily, he was a wulver and could heal relatively quickly.

"How about now?" the man asked gently, squatting down beside him and lifting Griff's head by the hair.

He snarled at the man, but didn't speak. Griff wasn't about to tell him anything.

"I have a secret to tell you." The other man's eyes were blue—dancing, dazzling blue. "You're not who you think you are."

Griff didn't answer him. He didn't care who this man thought he was. All he could think of was how he could protect Bridget from these marauders. If that meant letting them take him, then that's what he'd have to do. The thought of killing all of them was certainly his first choice, though.

"Should I introduce myself, little doggie?" The man's cruel slice of a mouth spread into a grin. "My name is Uldred Lothienne. Does that sound familiar to you?"

It did, although at first, Griff couldn't think why. He could hardly think at all, the way his ears were still ringing. But then he remembered the story his mother and aunts had told him when he was a pup.

"Ah, I see you have heard of me. Or, at least, my father before me." Uldred laughed, an overloud sound that brought light, nervous chuckles from his men. "Can you guess who my mother is, little pup? I'll give you three."

Griff wasn't playing games. He focused on trying to breathe—and in the midst of basic bodily functions, to think. Eldred Lothienne's son. King Henry VII's royal huntsman had always hated wulvers, had made it his mission to kill them all—after his consort, the witch Moraga, had used her magic to enslave the wulver warriors to do his bidding. Which, of course, had involved usurping the English king's throne.

He'd heard the story a hundred times, from Donal MacFalon himself, who had slain Lord Lothienne and thwarted his plan to become king of all England. And he knew, too, that the witch Moraga was the reason that no wulver could ever go back to their mountain den. She'd gone missing after being captured—according to rumor, she'd been locked in a cell, but had simply disappeared.

Darrow, just as skeptical as Griff, believed someone had let the evil woman go, and he had a tendency to believe this, more than he believed the witch had said some magic words and spirited herself away. As far as he knew, the woman hadn't been heard from again—both his father, Raife, and Donal MacFalon, had sent many men out to find her over the years—and most assumed her dead.

Griff's mother, Sibyl, spoke of returning to their mountain den often, but Raife wouldn't allow it. Griff thought it was ridiculous to keep their growing pack confined to such small quarters, when a much bigger, ready-made home sat empty, but now he wondered if his father might have been right. Was this English knight really the issue of the bewitching Moraga and the devious wulver-hating Lord Eldred Lothienne?

Because, if he was a guessing sort of man, Griff definitely would have guessed that Uldred was their son.

"No guesses?" Uldred's brows drew together in consternation. "What kind of fun is it, if you don't guess?"

Griff managed not to pass out, but just barely, when the other man hit him upside the head with the hilt of his sword. The world went black for a moment, and he heard the man's voice, but not the words he was saying. It took him a moment to tune back in.

"...as stupid as you look! My mother is the witch Moraga. Look at me!" Uldred grabbed Griff by the top of the head again, jerking his face up so Uldred could yell into it. "I have spent my entire life waiting for the time I could avenge my father's death—but I intend to do far more than that."

Griff knew his pack was in danger. He'd left them alone, undefended, with this madman on the loose. He couldn't have known, but that didn't matter. His mother, his aunts, his sisters—and the entire MacFalon clan. Because it had been Donal MacFalon who had slain Lord Lothienne, who had tied the half-dead man to his horse and dragged him behind until he was all the way dead. It's what Lothienne and men like him had done to wulvers for centuries, a fitting end to a cruel, devious man's life.

But Griff didn't think his son would see it that way.

So what was the younger Lothienne doing here, on Skara Brae? Griff had clearly been followed. So they wanted him, mayhaps to draw the other wulvers out, mayhaps to use him to find the den.

If they didn't already know where it was.

If his family wasn't already dead.

Oh God, that couldn't be true. He wouldn't let that be true.

"You see, my poor, sad, misguided, little puppy..." Uldred's hand moved through Griff's hair like he was petting him, a smile stretching the man's thin lips even thinner. He moved close, and whispered in Griff's still ringing ear, so that his men did not hear. "You're not the red wulver... I am."

Griff jerked his head away from the man's touch, hearing him laugh, a low, grating sound. If this man was a wulver, then he was a pig—and while Griff had a hearty appetite and occasionally found himself rolling in the mud, he definitely didn't have a snout or say "oink."

"Oh, I'm not yet." Uldred tapped Griff's cheek lightly a few times with a gloved hand. "But I will be. My mother... you've heard of my mother, the witch Moraga, have you not? She's more powerful now than she was even then. And she wants me to take my rightful place, among men *and* wulvers."

Rightful place? Griff sneered. Did this fool really believe he could lead a pack of men, let alone wulvers? No wulvers he knew would follow him. Which made Griff look both left and right at the wulvers on either side, who held his chains. Who were these dogs? Where had they come from? They weren't part of his pack—and no wulver he'd ever known would serve a Lothienne, even for the promise of gold. Wulvers were loyal, honorable.

They're being compelled.

This thought flitted briefly across Griff's mind and he wondered if it was true. That had been part of the story, hadn't it? He tried to remember what he'd heard about the witch Moraga, and her plan to enslave the wulvers for her consort, Lord Eldred. At the time, it had seemed ridiculous, of course. The thought that some woman could compel an entire den of wulver warriors to fight for this man was insanity.

The stories he'd heard as a pup, back in his den, were that Eldred Lothienne and the witch Moraga had planned to enslave all of the wulver warriors to use them to take the throne—and then have them turn on one another until there were no more wulvers left on Earth. The witch claimed all she needed was the wulver leader's blood—Griff's father, Raife, had been the wulver leader at the time—and she'd almost gotten it, too. Griff didn't know if it was still Raife she needed. Mayhaps Raife's son, Griff, would do?

Was that why he was being taken?

Uldred leaned in close enough that Griff felt the man's hot breath on his cheek. "You see, I don't need to actually *be* the red wulver—I just need them to believe that I am. Then I can reunite all of the lost packs, and use them all to take the throne. And with your blood, I can enslave them—forever."

Griff's stomach dropped. He knew about the lost packs. Uldred was using the prophecy, using it against the wulvers. But how could he have convinced these wulvers that he was the red wulver? The man couldn't shift. His eyes did not glow red. Unless, some magic...?

Griff would have said he didn't believe in magic before entering the Temple of Ardis and Asher, but after what he'd gone through with Bridget at the sacred pool, he wasn't so sure. They'd only touched briefly on the idea of "dark magic," but he wondered at it, because that was the kind of magic Uldred and his mother, Moraga, would be entertaining. Something foul, and unnatural.

Is that what they had planned?

"And if the prophecy is real?" Uldred was still speaking just to him, his tone gleeful. "Oh, I do so hope the prophecy is real, as my mother believes. You see, we share an ancestor, you and I, one that you can trace back to Asher and Ardis, as you wulvers call them—but we knew him as Arthur. The king who pulled the sword from the stone? Thanks to Merlin, who decided it was wise to teach his pupil by turning him into animals, we may not share a mother and father, but we are blood brothers, after a fashion. And I need yours."

"For what?" Griff snarled. To turn his wulver brothers against him? To compel them to follow this man, whose ravings were just simply mad?

"If the prophecy is real, when I look into the pool at the Temple of Ardis and Asher during the eclipse, *I will become the red wulver*," Uldred told him, his blue eyes dancing wildly. "And if it's all nonsense—well, then, I'll have your blood, and my mother can use it to compel the wulvers anyway."

Griff's blood ran cold at the thought.

"The eclipse is coming. The prophecy is at hand." Uldred tilted Griff's head up toward the sky, searching his face. He knew the man was looking for a flash of red, some sign that he'd grabbed the right wulver. His voice rang out louder. The men were listening. "The red wulver will unite the lost packs and become far greater than any king of England. The red wulver will become the Dragon King of the Blood Reign. And I am that wulver!"

Did the man really believe the wulvers would think he was one of them? Griff couldn't believe it, but the three wulvers around him howled, and then took a knee, as if Uldred was their rightful king. He could smell this fakery from a mile away. Why could they not?

Before Griff could think more on it, Uldred leaned back in to tell him something only for his ears.

"I may still need Raife's blood, but your father's on his way right now to bring his pup home. Then I will be able to control all the wulvers. Even you, pet."

"Over m'dead body." Griff growled, throwing himself forward toward the man, yanking the chain taut as Uldred stood, laughing at Griff's impotent display.

"That's a possibility." Uldred shrugged, glancing to his men. "Any wulvers who do not follow me will certainly die. I'm getting to the end of my patience with this one."

Griff howled when Uldred nodded at his men and they brought forth a wulver whose face had been beaten bloody, almost beyond recognition. Not that Griff needed eyesight to know his friend, Rory MacFalon, also in chains.

"Let 'im go," Griff croaked. How had they captured Rory? What had they done to him? Of course they would capture The MacFalon's son.

And now Griff's father, Raife, and, he imagined, Darrow and the rest of the wulver warriors, were on their way to Skara Brae, and were about to walk right into Uldred's trap. Griff felt his rage rising, felt the heat in his eyes, and knew they were turning red. He couldn't stop it.

"They'll ne'er follow ye!" Griff snapped at Uldred as Rory lifted his head, giving a low moan.

Griff shook his head, his snout filling the muzzle they'd put on him as he howled, his eyes burning as he looked around at the wulvers. Not just the ones who held his chains, or the ones who held Rory's, but there were more, still, wulvers who had joined this man's ranks. Were these part of the lost packs? Had they believed Uldred when he told them he was the red wulver?

"They'll only e'er follow t'red wulver, t'one true king!" Griff roared, yanking to the ends of his chains, snapping at the dark knight, in spite of the muzzle, frothing at the mouth. His voice rose into a long, keening wail, and to his surprise, several other wulvers responded in kind, throwing their heads back and howling.

For one brief moment, Griff had hope. Did they recognize his voice? Did they see him as the red wulver? One of the wulver guards who held his chains saw Griff's eyes flash red. Griff saw some sort of reaction—surprise? Recognition? He wasn't sure.

"Shut up, dog!" Uldred roared, bringing the hilt of his sword back around again at Griff's head. "*I am the one true king!*"

That was the last thing Griff heard before he hit the ground and sank into darkness.

Griff woke in a cage. A wulver's worst nightmare.

His sword was gone. He'd been stripped down to tunic and plaid, and not only was the cage made of thick, iron bars, but he was chained to it, too. His first memory was seeing Rory MacFalon, bloody and beaten almost unrecognizable, and he looked around, hoping to find his friend. Mayhaps, together, they could form some sort of plan to escape.

But he was alone. Chained inside a cage, inside a tent. They'd had time to put up a tent? Mayhaps, then, they hadn't found the temple yet. He could only hope. He had to get back and warn them. The thought of Bridget in danger made him crazy with anger and he moved to the front of the cage, testing the bars. Solid. There was a padlock keeping the cage door closed. He saw this by the light of a small lamp lit in the corner on a low table.

Griff shook his head, changing to half-man, half-wolf form, and then cocked his head, listening. He could hear far more like this. There were wulvers and men, and not just a few. Dozens. Maybe even a hundred or more. His tent wasn't the only one that had been set up. One conversation was close. A human and a wulver, standing outside the tent. Guards. They were talking about a dice game, amiably arguing over winnings. Distractible. That was good.

He knew it was likely useless but he had to try. Griff grabbed a hold of the bars and pulled. They didn't budge. Uldred knew enough about wulvers to know how to contain them. Griff knew he would likely be able to snap the chain, but the cage, that was going to be a problem. He'd have to work on the lock.

"Stand in the presence of your once and future king!" Uldred's voice carried in to him, even though the flap of the tent was closed.

Griff felt a growl growing in his throat, unbidden. He worked hard to control it, holding onto the bars and leaning in to listen. The wulver and the man mumbled apologies. Anyone else would have heard nothing but contrition, but Griff knew wulvers. This one was acting contrite, but mayhaps wasn't feeling that way. He heard a resistance in the wulver's tone, and that was heartening.

"Ye heard 'im!" A woman's voice snapped, clearly Scottish. "Take a knee before yer king!"

His spine straightened at the sound. Moraga. He didn't know, not for sure, but who else?

"Don't tease the animals, Mother." Uldred chuckled as he opened the tent flap and stepped inside. Griff snarled at him, and at the woman who followed him into the tent.

"So this is t'red wulver." The blonde who approached the cage surprised him. He'd expected a witch—an old woman, wrinkled and bent. This woman was tall, voluptuous, her blonde hair thick and long down her back. She spoke like a Scotswoman but she dressed like a shasennach.

"Not so loud, Mother," Uldred hissed, glancing toward the tent entrance. "Don't tempt fate. The other wulvers are already doubting and restless."

"They won't be fer long." Moraga swung her hips, moving toward the cage. "I've ne'er seen one wit' red fur…"

"Guess that's why they call him the red wulver." Uldred crossed his arms, glowering at Griff. "Fools."

"An' ye saw 'is red eyes?" Moraga murmured, stopping just short of Griff's reach. The woman had clearly been around wulvers.

"Yes." Uldred shrugged his shoulder. "His eyes glowed red when he got angry."

"Ohhhh so I need t'tease the animal, then." Moraga chuckled. She turned and went to the corner of the tent, coming back with a long spear. Griff glanced into the corner, seeing his sword and belt were there. He watched her raise the spear, her eyes dancing with amusement. "Ye've been a vera bad doggie."

Griff growled at her, lips drawn back in a snarl.

"So can we use his blood?" Uldred asked, taking a seat on a cot at the other side of the tent as he watched his mother wielding her weapon, stalking toward the cage.

"Yer men did'na intercept t'wulvers?" Moraga sighed. "Raife an' t'rest of them rode in from t'coast—how'd ye manage t'miss 'em?"

"They followed them on the road," Uldred replied. "But then… they disappeared."

The woman snorted. "They did'na disappear into thin air!"

"No, but… mayhaps they found their way into the temple." Uldred glowered at Griff. "Mother, you said you could find it! You said your magic would be strong enough to open it!"

"Aye." She sighed, looking over at her son, soothing him. "All will be well. Ye've found six o'the lost packs a'ready! And they're all out there, followin' ye. They all b'lieve ye're t'red wulver of the prophecy, that ye're destined t'be t'Dragon King, the one who'll begin t'Blood Reign—"

"They only follow me because of your magic," he reminded her, pouting.

Griff stared between the two of them, stunned by this news. This Uldred had found *six* of the lost packs already? They were all camped out there, right now, following *him*? It was news that made Griff tremble with anger, and he worked hard to keep his eyes from flashing red with bloody rage.

"Aye. An' it will'na last fore'er!" she snapped. "I need t'wulver's blood!"

“Well we have his.” Uldred pointed at Griff in the cage. “Isn’t that good enough?”

“Mayhaps.” She cocked her head, eyes narrowing at Griff as she took another step toward him. “He’s a descendent. And they do say he’s t’red wulver. Let’s find out.”

Moraga jabbed at Griff with the spear, moving quickly. Griff roared when the tip pierced his shoulder, blood pouring from the wound, and he grabbed the weapon, yanking it out of the woman’s hands.

“Uldred!” Moraga cried for her son to rescue her as Griff pulled the spear and the witch along with it—she was still hanging on. It would be her undoing.

Griff howled, and outside, another wulver howled in response. Then another. And another. Uldred scowled, rushing toward the cage to save his mother from Griff, but it was too late.

Griff dropped the spear and circled the woman’s throat with his big hand. He only needed one. He could snap her neck with the flick of a finger at this angle. She gasped and struggled as he lifted her feet up off the floor, growling at Uldred.

“Get t’keys! Let me outta this cage!”

“Mother!” Uldred cried, taking a step back as Griff’s other hand shot out to grab him.

Uldred just managed to sidestep.

Outside, the howling continued, and Uldred’s face clouded with frustration and anger.

And, Griff noted, fear. He could smell it on the man.

“Uldred!” Moraga croaked, her long, red fingernails raking at Griff’s hand, scratches that healed almost as fast as she made them. She was choking, her face turning blue.

"Help!" Uldred screamed. Literally screamed, something high pitched, like a woman. "Help! Help! Help!"

"Milord?" A wulver stuck his big head into the tent flap.

Griff howled, a sound that filled the tent, carrying far beyond, and the wulver at the door went wide-eyed at the sight. Then he threw back his head and howled too.

They're joining me. They know I'm the one. I'm their leader. They know...

Griff's brief moment of hope and the excitement that took flight in his chest was short-lived, as Moraga lifted her fist in front of her face. He actually laughed at the thought of this woman punching him, but something crunched between her fingers, something that sounded like bones and dry wings being powdered into dust.

The witch used her last bit of breath to blow the residue in his face.

It smelled like ancient death.

Griff coughed, suddenly, overwhelmingly nauseous.

Then everything went blurry, and he collapsed.

Chapter Eight

Bridget couldn't understand why Alaric hadn't come.

She hid high up in a tree, watching men and wulvers walking past, talking, laughing. She watched them set up tents and light fires. She watched, breath held, hand over her mouth to keep from crying out, as they untied Griff from the back of his horse, letting his big body slide, lifeless, to the ground.

She wouldn't believe he was dead, refused to believe it. They set up a cage and chained him into it, so she knew he still breathed. Bridget almost cried with relief. The tent went up around the cage, so she couldn't see him anymore. Two men guarded the front of the tent, but no one stood at the back. She could sneak underneath it, she decided. When it was full dark, when the camp slept.

So many wulvers, so many men! She'd never seen so many on little Skara Brae before.

But none of them were Alaric.

She left a clear trail for him to follow. He was an extraordinary tracker. If he'd come looking for her, he would have easily been able to follow. Why hadn't he come? He'd left to meet Raife and the other wulvers, who had come after Griff. And then…

And then…

She didn't want to think about it.

Bridget nearly fell asleep hugging the trunk of the tree, straddling a branch. She waited until the moon, still big and full, was high. She waited for most of the noise to die down. She waited until the man with the dirty-blonde hair and dark armor, the one she'd heard screaming, and the curvy blonde woman, left the tent, saying they were retiring for the night. The man gave orders to his men, told them to trade off a watch.

But there was still no one manning—or wulvering—the back of the tent.

Bridget had hoped her father would find them, but mayhaps he felt it too dangerous to approach with so many other wulvers and men around. She would have to rescue Griff herself, and take him back to the temple with her. She was grateful for the wulver ability to heal so quickly. If she could get him out of the cage—she had the pins in her hair, she might be able to pick the lock—he would be fine to travel.

The only thing she didn't see was Uri—Griff's horse. She would have liked to take him. And she hated the thought of leaving the animal there with the people—and wulvers—who treated Griff so badly. She didn't know who they were, or why they wanted Griff, but she knew they were bad news.

Bridget climbed slowly, carefully, down from the tree. She heard someone laugh and hid behind the tree, in the shadows, but there were no other voices. No one moved toward her or the tent. Peeking around the trunk, she saw just the two men—one man, one wulver—sitting on stools near the entrance. They were awake, watchful, talking softly, but not looking her way.

She moved as quietly as she could, sneaking around the back of the tent. Shimmying underneath it, she stopped as she cleared the material, finding herself inside the tent. There was no light to see by, but she heard him breathing. He was breathing. She knew he must be, but her heart fluttered at the reassurance. She just prayed there was no one else in the tent as she rolled to hands and knees and got her bearings.

"There's a lamp in t'corner, Bridget." Griff spoke in a hoarse whisper. "Front, on t'left."

Bridget startled, eyes wide when he spoke. But of course—he'd smelled her.

"Are ye a'righ'?" she whispered back, feeling her way in the dark. "Do I dare light t'lamp?"

"Keep it low."

She found the lamp, using the striker to light the oil lamp's wick. Then she quickly turned the flame low, not wanting anyone, especially the guards, to see it through the tent walls.

"Och, Bridget." Griff held his arms out to her and she went to him, finding herself trembling in his embrace through the cage bars.

"Yer hurt." She ran her hands over him, the wound in his shoulder. It was healing, but hadn't been healed entirely. "Who did this? Who are they?"

"We do'na have time fer questions." He kissed the top of her head, holding her closer, the bars digging into her flesh. She noticed they'd taken the muzzle off him at least, but his face was marked with long scratches. They were healing, too. "D'ye have t'key?"

She shook her head. "But we can break t'lock."

"Twill alert t'guards," Griff warned.

Tugging on the padlock, it held fast, but Bridget thought it wouldn't be difficult to break with a weapon. She had drawn her sword before he could stop her, bringing it down hard, cleaving the lock.

Griff was right—the human guard came in first, sword drawn, and Bridget whirled to meet him. Steel clashed and she winced. So much for staying quiet. The wulver guard ducked into the tent, already shifted in wulver-warrior form, growling, crossbow raised—and aimed directly at Bridget. Griff shoved his way out of the cage, the door hanging on its hinges as he busted through, the padlock in his hand. His chain caught him up short, but he managed to knock the other wulver aside and bring the heavy cage lock down onto the human guard's skull.

He groaned and dropped to the dirt.

Wulver faced wulver in the dim light, both growling low in their throats. Griff's eyes flashed red in the dark, making Bridget gasp in surprise, even as used to it as she'd grown. The other wulver hesitated. He'd seen it, too.

Bridget stared, stunned, as the other wulver sank slowly to one knee, bowing his head.

"My king," the other wulver growled. "How can I serve ye?"

Griff met her gaze, both of them so shocked it was hard to know exactly what to say or do.

"D'ye have t'keys?" Griff yanked on the chain attached to the collar around his neck.

"Aye." The other wulver rose, pulling out a set of keys and unlocking the collar. The guard looked between the two of them as he took a step back while Griff pulled off the collar and threw it to the floor.

"Thank ye," Griff said.

"Go, m'king," the other wulver said, keeping his voice low, reaching down and handing Griff his belt, sword and sheath. "Before they discover ye gone and raise t'alarm."

"I will'na forget this." Griff strapped on his belt, clapping the other wulver on the shoulder before grabbing Bridget's hand and ducking out of the tent.

She followed him in the dark, both of them trying to be as quiet as they possibly could.

"Bridget," he whispered, pulling her behind the big tree she'd scaled and hid in. "M'father and 'is men came 'ere t'Skara Brae—are they at t'temple?"

"Alaric went ridin' out t'meet 'em," she told him, her brow knitting with worry. "We saw ye set upon by a band'o'men at t'same time. I said I'd follow ye, track ye, and leave a trail. But..."

Griff finished her sentence, "Alaric hasn't come after ye."

She shook her head, feeling tears stinging her eyes. Something must have happened, and from the look on Griff's face, he knew it, too.

"Listen, Bridget." He took her by the upper arms, talking low, close, looking into her face in the moonlight. "This man who took me, Uldred Lothienne—"

"Uldred Lothienne? *Lothienne*?" Her eyes widened. She knew the story of Eldred and Moraga—Griff had told her that story too. Had it been only last night that they were in each other's arms, talking and laughing? "Is it...? It can't be..."

"Aye, tis." His eyes flashed red in the dark. "Eldred and Moraga's son. He's mad—insane. He thinks he's t'red wulver—thinks he's t'one who'll bring together t'lost packs. These men—t'wulvers—they're all part of t'lost packs."

"But how..." Bridget had wondered at it, all of these wulvers out of their den, camped with an English leader, but now she knew, with a low, sinking feeling in her belly, not even waiting for Griff to answer. "Dark magic."

"Aye." Griff's eyes were blood red. "Moraga, his mother, is a witch. She's worked some magic on t'lost packs, but she needs m'blood—or m'father's—to enchant 'em further. T'compel 'em."

"Compel 'em t'do what?"

"T'go to war," Griff said flatly. "T'claim t'English throne from King Henry VIII. I imagine that's where Uldred'll start. Where 'is father left off."

"We hafta get back t'the temple." She swallowed, hoping, praying, that Alaric had met Raife and his men. That they were, even now, safe in the temple, thinking it too dangerous to travel with so many men and wulvers on the island.

But if they knew there were strange men and wulvers on the island—she couldn't imagine Alaric would let her stay out alone. Not this long. He would have come for her.

"Aye, but I need t'find Rory." Griff glanced around at the light of dying fires, tents set up all along the grass.

"Who?"

"Uldred has captured Rory MacFalon." Griff's voice was like steel. "More unfinished business, I imagine. Donal MacFalon killed Eldred Lothienne."

"Oh no…"

"We need t'find Rory and bring 'im to the temple. He's…" Griff sighed. "He's been tortured. Wulvers heal fast, and he looked… I can'na e'ven tell ye. Bad. Vera bad."

"Where would they keep 'im?" she whispered, knowing Rory was one of Griff's greatest friends.

"I do'na know." Griff looked around, swearing under his breath in at least two languages.

"We'll find 'im." Bridget took his hand, leading him this time in the darkness. "I was hidin' in this tree all day, watchin' them set up camp. I think I may know where he is…"

"Yer an angel," he breathed, stopping just for a moment to kiss her.

It was a hard, fast, breathless kiss and they were on their way again in an instant, but Bridget felt like she was flying. She was so relieved to have him with her, safe. No longer trapped, muzzled, chained in a cage.

"There's a tent near t'edge of their camp," she whispered as they crept closer to the rocky beach and the sea. "Isolated. I'd wager that's where they'd keep 'im…"

"Smart lass." Griff smiled at her when she looked back at him. The moon was still high, shining off the water, but the weather was changing, quickly. There was a low fog rolling in, hanging thick in the air.

"There." She pointed down at the beach, where a tent had been pitched, far away from anyone or anything else. She'd seen them setting it up from her vantage point in the tree and hadn't understood its purpose, but mayhaps now she knew.

"Ye stay 'ere," Griff whispered, wagging a finger at her.

"I do'na think so." She caught his finger in her hand, leaning in and gently biting the tip. "But I'll let ye go firs'…"

"Ye're impossible." He sighed, but cautioned her to be quiet as she followed him toward the tent.

There was very little cover out here in the open, but she was glad for the fog coming in. Besides, there seemed to be no one around. Except whoever was in the tent, of course. She hoped it would be lightly guarded, and they could free Rory and hurry back to the temple. Even without horses, they could make it back in under an hour.

Bridget stopped, hearing a low moan. She pulled on Griff's hand and he stopped, too. The walls of the tent were thin. Another moan, this one louder, carried toward them on the wind. Her belly clenched, wondering how badly hurt the wulver was. She hoped whatever horrible experiences he'd had were now at an end. The scrying pool had great healing properties. Even for wulvers.

She couldn't imagine how badly he had to have been tortured to be making the noises coming from the tent. Her eyes widened as she looked at Griff in the moonlight, and then saw his face change in an instant, the moment the sounds changed.

That wasn't a man moaning in pain, Bridget realized. It was a woman, moaning with pleasure. Bridget opened her mouth to say something, but Griff pulled her close, shaking his head and pressing his finger to his lips.

"Oh yes, yes, that's m'good boy, yesss!" A woman cried out, so loudly it made Bridget blush and she was glad for both the darkness and the fog, because she knew her face must match her hair. "Ohhh harder, harder!"

The feel of Griff's body against hers, arms encircling her waist, holding her close, made her want to melt against him. The sound of the two people making love in the tent brought thoughts and ideas into her head that she knew she shouldn't be thinking. But she was.

"Yes! Uldred! Yes! Ahhhhh!" The woman's voice rose to almost a scream, and Bridget realized now why the tent was pitched so far away from anyone else.

Obviously the wulver they were looking for wasn't here.

Unless…

That's when the alarm was raised. The high sound of a horn in the distance, coming from the camp. Bridget would have gasped out loud if Griff hadn't put a hand over her mouth.

"Bloody hell!" They heard Uldred swear. "Mother, stay here. Don't move! I'll be right back."

Mother? Bridget's wide eyes met Griff's as he swept her back behind the tent, hand still covering her mouth. They stood there, right out in the open, hearing Uldred storming out of the tent and heading up the beach. He passed right by them in the darkness, swearing and stomping his boots over the rocks as he climbed the embankment toward camp.

She relaxed against Griff for just a moment, relieved they hadn't been discovered.

Bridget would have screamed out loud—did scream, behind the press of Griff's big hand over her mouth—when he dove toward the sand, taking them both down to the ground in an instant, covering her body with his. She didn't feel it for a moment. Above, the moon was big, but hazy, far away. Stars appeared between dark, low-hanging clouds like glittering jewels. She took all of that in, hearing the sound of the waves crashing against the shoreline, the distant shouts of men, and something humming, singing, close by. All of that registered before the pain.

"Are ye cut?" Griff rolled slightly off her—his weight was crushing her, in spite of the care he'd taken—hands roaming her body and she saw one of them come up bloody, almost black in the moonlight. "Och, Bridget, yer bleedin'!"

"Where?" But she knew. She felt the sting of it on her upper arm, and a sudden, queasy feeling, a dizziness that left her mouth dry and her hands trembling.

She didn't understand what had happened, not at first. But when she glanced over Griff's shoulder, she saw the ripped bit of tent flapping in the rising wind, a straight line right through the back of the canvas, about two feet long. That, alone, wouldn't have been enough to clue her in, but that humming sound drew her attention the other way, and she saw a big, half-moon blade sunk into an old, giant piece of driftwood on the embankment.

The blade was singing.

Enchanted.

She knew it immediately, and she knew something else too, as her blood flowed hot through her veins, the first wave of poison hitting her. Her heart skittered and jumped in her chest as she watched the blade try to pull itself from where it was buried in the driftwood. It gave an angry buzz, the hilt waving back and forth, like a fish trying to propel itself through the water.

The blade had been meant to kill her. And it was coming for her still. Bridget knew it, just as she knew the thing had been poisoned, and that poison was now in her bloodstream. Griff had saved her once again—she knew not how, because she hadn't heard anything, hadn't known the knife was coming—by throwing her to the ground.

"The blade's enchanted," she gasped, the pain in her arm finally, fully, hitting her. It burned, even as

Griff put his hand over the wound, squeezing hard in an attempt to ebb the blood flow. "It'll keep comin' for me!"

"I'm more worried 'bout where't came *from*," he muttered, rolling again, taking them both to standing in an instant.

And of course, he was right to worry.

Bridget's reaction time was fast, but nowhere near as fast as his. Griff half-turned, keeping his hand on her upper arm, but still protecting her as much as he could with his own body as he drew his sword and the full force of the witch came at them from inside the tent.

She came through the tear in the fabric, like some sick, wrong thing birthing itself from the seam of hell, clawing her way through with long, red nails, her face appearing at the opening, sneering at them with a twisted snarl.

They weren't close enough for Griff to run her through—he'd initially rolled them far enough away from the tent in order to make their escape—but the witch saw his sword, his ready stance, and hesitated. Her gaze skipped from them to the blade that jerked and thrashed, trying to pry itself free from the piece of wood.

"She's callin' t'blade," Bridget whispered to Griff, hearing the woman speaking words low in her throat. "Tis enchanted!"

"There's n'such thing," he snapped, glancing at the witch, whose attempts at widening the tear in the fabric were increasing, and then down at Bridget. "I hafta get ye to safety, lass. We hafta stop yer bleedin'..."

"Aye..." She wasn't going to disagree. She didn't know if it was the poison she was sure had been on the blade, or the fact that she was losing so much lifeblood, but either way, she was growing faint. "Hurry..."

Griff was torn, she saw it on his face. He wanted to finish the witch, here and now, but he also needed to take Bridget to safety. He gave a low growl, lunging forward as the witch pushed her head through the opening, her chants louder, and Bridget saw the knife, the blade still dripping with Bridget's blood, had pulled another two inches out of the wood. It was nearly free. And when it was free, it would come for her again.

Griff brought his sword up one-handed, raising it high with a low growl, and then brought it down at the witch's neck. If it had been as fast and sharp as a scythe blade, it would have severed her head from her neck instantly. But the witch sensed it coming and pulled back, like a turtle into its shell.

"We need t'blade," Bridget murmured, feeling herself slipping toward blackness, fighting it, hard.

"Bridget..." Griff frowned, looking between her and the knife.

"Trust me, Griff, please," she pleaded. "We need that blade...."

He gave a frustrated growl, but he turned and brought his sword down at the knife. That just snapped the hilt, breaking it off, and they both heard a low cry come from inside the tent, as if the witch and the knife were one. But at least the blade stopped moving, stopped that incessant buzzing sound as it tried to free itself and fly again. The magic in it had been broken.

Griff swung his sword again, knocking the full curve of the blade free, and Bridget grabbed it before he could, using the edge of her plaid. Griff's head came up and Bridget heard it too. The sound of mounted men approaching, coming from the encampment.

"Hurry," she whispered, turning to hide her face against his chest as he lifted her in his arms, carrying her quickly away from the tent, heading down the rocky beach. The blade rested in her lap, its curved edge glinting in the moonlight. Looking back, she saw the men on the embankment, saw their horses heading down it toward the tent where they had just been. She saw the witch, too, her face appearing at the front of the tent flap as Griff made his way toward the shoreline, saw the blonde's lips moving, chanting, mayhaps still talking to her blade, but it sang no more.

"Where're we goin'?" Bridget leaned her head back against Griff's shoulder, thinking, *There's nowhere to go.* They were trapped, with a hundred armed horsemen and a witch at their back, and nothing but the endless sea in front of them.

Griff slid her into a boat, pushing it into the water as he did. He hopped in, already rowing, as Bridget struggled to sit up, looking behind them as the horseman reached the beach. There were boats, she saw, lining the shore, tied up together, attached to the ship with the dragon's head on the prow anchored further out. Uldred's ship, the one he'd clearly brought them all in on.

"Stem that bleedin'," Griff growled, pulling harder on the oars. "Hurry!"

Bridget winced, not wanting to look at her wound, but she grabbed the edge of her plaid, setting the blade aside, seeing its wicked edge still stained with her blood, and tore the edge of the material. She wrapped her upper arm tight, as best she could, tying it using her mouth on one end of the strip and her hand on the other.

"I can'na outrow 'em, lass..." Griff pulled hard on the oars, his big muscles working, but Bridget saw the men in boats, some with four, five, six of them oaring in one vessel. That much manpower would win out, even over one wulver.

"I'll help ye." She grabbed a set of oars, wincing at the pain in her arm, but she knew it was useless. As she rowed, bright red blood bloomed, darkening the plaid wrapped around her upper arm. Bridget saw Griff's wound now, a matching gash on his upper arm. It had broken open with his effort and was bleeding again.

"Griff, wait." Bridget glanced back, seeing two of the boats had gained much ground. They were only a boat-length away, maybe two, and gaining, although due to the fog coming in, she couldn't see the shore anymore. "Give me yer hands."

"I need t'row wit' m'hands!" he snapped.

"Trust me!" she urged, pulling her oars into the boat and reaching for him.

"More magic?" Griff glanced at the gaining rowboats, and then at her. He sighed, pulling the oars in, his big hands swallowing hers as he clasped them.

Bridget took a deep breath, closed her eyes, and began to incant the words she hoped, prayed, would work.

"I hope yer magic can make us disappear," he grumbled, distracting her. "They're still gainin' on us..."

"Shhh!" Bridget cocked an eye open. "Concentrate with me..."

"What am I concentratin' on?"

"Us." She squeezed his hands in hers. "Concentrate on us, Griff..."

When she said that, she instantly felt the energy shift. The tides rocking the boat shifted underneath them. And when Bridget opened her eyes a moment later, she saw the fog that had been slowly gathering had thickened. She could barely see Griff, just a foot from her in the boat. And they had a tail wind, pushing them further out to sea.

"Did ye do that?" Griff frowned, his hands tightening over hers.

"We did that." She gave a relieved sigh. She could hear the men in the boats calling to one another. They sounded far away, but that could have been a trick of the fog. "But you'd better keep rowin'..."

"Aye." He let go of her hands, grabbing the oars again.

In the rush of trying to escape, Bridget hadn't had a moment to think, but now that they were floating out on the water, sailing away from an island she'd never left in her life, it hit her. Alaric and Aleesa were on that island, and she had no idea if they were safe. Griff's father, Raife, and his men were there, too. And his friend, Rory MacFalon. They would have to go back, they would have to make their way to the temple, find a way to...

Bridget remembered the blade and realized her wound had stopped aching. It had gone numb.

The poison.

"Griff..." Her heart lurched in her chest when she realized what Moraga had done. But she had to be sure.

"What is't, lass?" Griff pulled hard on the oars, his breath coming in short pants. He was rowing as fast as he could. The fog was so thick, there was no way to tell which way they were going—but given the wind she'd called up, she hoped it was due south.

Bridget found the blade, holding it up in the darkness. There was little light there in the fog. It even dampened the bright light of the moon from above. But she didn't need to see it to know. She just needed to taste.

Bridget brought the tip of the blade to the end of her tongue. There was blood, coppery and bitter. The metallic taste of the blade itself. And a tinny sort of heat, something that burned the tip of her tongue before she spit it out.

Griff had stopped rowing, watching her with interest.

"What is't?" he asked again, this time his voice sounding much softer, concerned.

"Poison." Even as she said it, she felt it. She'd suspected it when the blade had cut her, but now she knew for sure. Aleesa had trained her in the ways of dark magic—not so she could ever use it, but so that she knew how to recognize it. And combat it, if need be. There were those who would come to the Temple of Asher and Ardis for healing, and much of that healing had to do with undoing the black magic attempted by others.

"Poison?" Griff's voice was barely a whisper. She'd never heard him scared before, but there was a hint of fear in his voice. "What can be done?"

"T'Witch's Kiss," she said bitterly. "Tis poison an' curse. If't penetrates, deep into t'body, it'll kill quickly, almos' instantly."

"But t'blade jus' scratched us."

Well, it had just scratched him, Bridget realized. Her wound was deeper. And, she wasn't a wulver, with the ability to heal herself so quickly. The poison would work faster in her.

"Aye," she agreed, trying to remember everything Aleesa had taught her about this particular poison and curse. "If it does'na penetrate righ' away, it'll kill slowly. Painfully."

"How slowly?"

"A week." She swallowed. She didn't know if it was real or her imagination, but she was beginning to feel faint. "Mayhaps a lil more'o'less..."

"Can Aleesa heal ye?" Griff reached for her and Bridget went to him, letting him fold her into his arms. His heart was beating hard and fast in his chest and she pressed her ear against the steady sound. "Bridget! Can Aleesa undo this?"

"Nay..." she whispered, shaking her head. There were some things she could do—pack the wound with seaweed, mayhaps, when they got to shore, to draw some of the poison. But it wouldn't stop the progression. She told him this as she trembled against him. She could almost feel the witch's poison working its way through her blood.

"Bridget!" Griff lifted her face so he could search her eyes. His were blood red, blazing. "There has t'be somethin' to stop't! Wha' can I do?"

The witch had chosen her weapon well, Bridget realized, finally remembering what Aleesa had told her about this particular poison, and its only remedy.

"The Isle of the Dragon." She sighed. It might as well have been the moon. They were in a rowboat. Even with a wulver rowing, they wouldn't reach it in time unless Griff could fly. "There's a temple on t'Isle of the Dragon. It's northwest of t'Isle of Man."

"The Isle of the Dragon?" Griff blinked in surprise. "Tis where t'largest of t'lost packs is supposed to be—accordin' to what Aleesa gave me..."

"Hmm..." She smiled, feeling her eyes beginning to close. She was so very tired. "But there's no such thing as fate..."

"If there is, then yer mine, lass." Griff pressed his lips to her forehead, holding her so close it was hard to breathe. Or mayhaps that, too, was the poison working its way through her. "If I b'lieved in true mates, ye'd be mine..."

"Ye do'na need t'b'lieve..." She felt his lips meet hers under the cover of the fog, and she kissed him back, using the last of her energy to wrap her arms around his thick neck and cling to him.

She whispered the truth against his mouth as they parted, "I a'ready know..."

And then she let the fog roll in and claim her completely.

❦

When she woke in Griff's arms, she thought she'd died and gone to heaven.

They rocked together in softness. There was no pain—well, only a little, when she moved her arm. She noticed it when she lifted her hand to touch his stubbly cheek in the morning light. Mayhaps they'd both died and gone to heaven, she thought, seeing the way his thick, sooty lashes touched his cheeks. But the big wulver lying beside her was breathing, soft and shallow. He was on guard, even in his sleep, she realized, tracing the line of his mouth, suddenly longing for the press of his lips.

When she lifted her gaze, she saw his eyes were open. They were clear, gold, and looking at her with so much concern it broke her heart. She took in her surroundings in an instant, realizing their slow rocking was the motion of a boat. Nay, a ship. They were in a small state room, and she could see the sun shining on the water through a porthole.

"Tis good t'see yer eyes, lass." His voice was hoarse. "They've been closed fer two days."

Two days gone. Two days wasted.

She glanced at her wound, seeing it had been rebandaged. Looking closer, she blinked at him in surprise.

"Did ye pack it wit' seaweed?" she asked.

"Jus' like ye tol' me." He smiled.

A knock sounded on the door. "Bryce!"

"Bryce?" She giggled. "Who's Bryce?"

"I'm Bryce and yer Busby." Griff grinned. "Oh an'—yer a boy."

"A boy?" she squeaked, suddenly offended. "I'm not a—"

"Shh!" He pulled the covers up to her neck, gathering her hair in a knot at the back of her head. He took another frowning look, rolling her hip so she was pointing sideways. "Hide those damnable curves!"

She giggled at that, pulling the covers up so only her eyes appeared.

"Aye?" Griff pulled the door open.

"More seaweed fer t'lad," the voice said. It was low and gruff.

"Thank ye, MacMoran," Griff said.

"How's he doin'?" the voice asked.

"A lil better. He woke up a few moments ago," Griff replied. "We'll need some food."

"Aye, I'll bring ye some."

"Thank ye," Griff called, closing the door again.

"Where're we?" Bridget sat, looking down and seeing that, aside from the bandage on her arm, she was wearing nothing at all.

Griff noticed, too. His eyes moved over her body before she pulled the sheet back up to her chin.

"T'Sea Wolf," he said, putting the seaweed pack aside on the bureau.

"Is that a ship?" she asked.

"Aye." Griff's hand fell to her hip, over the covers, tracing her curves through it. "Uldred would've expected us t'follow the coast southeast t'Wick... so I rowed southwest to Thurso an' that's where I found Cap'n Blackburn. He was headin' to the Isle of Man."

Her eyes widened. "Wit' what cargo?"

"Do'na ask." Griff chuckled. "Ye do'na wanna know."

"Tis a pirate ship," she whispered, his look confirming her suspicions.

"Aye." He nodded gravely. "That's why I disguised ye as a lad."

"I've really been out fer two whole days?" she lamented, capturing his hand in hers and lacing their fingers. She brought his hand to her mouth, kissing his knuckles. She didn't like to think of him being alone, worried about her, that whole time. She licked one of his fingers, meeting his glowing gaze. Then she sucked his fingertip into her mouth.

"Two and a half, aye," he agreed, groaning as he watched her. "But yer awake now."

"I jus' hafta keep pretendin' t'be a boy." She was rather offended by this predicament, spitting his finger out and half-sitting. She struggled, though. Her arm burned. She winced, knowing they'd have to keep the bandages changed. If they could make it to the island, if they could get the antidote…

“T’was t’bes’ way t’keep ye safe on this ship,” Griff said, helping steady her with a hand at her elbow as she sat. “Pirates aren’t known fer their morals, lass.”

“Neither are wulvers.” She felt dizzy, just sitting up, but she put her arms around his neck anyway, pressing herself fully against him. She heard him moan a little through their kiss, and she found, when she let her hand wander under his plaid, just how much he’d missed her while she was passed out.

“Besides, this way, we get t’share a cabin,” he murmured, nuzzling her hair. “Och, yer hair, m’love… I shoulda cut it, but I could’na bear to…”

“What’d ye promise ’em t’get ’em t’take ye t’the Isle o’t’Dragon?” she wondered aloud, squeezing his shaft, making him shift and groan. “Mos’ men think tis haunted”

“M’firs’ born,” he said, laughing when she jerked back to stare at him. “I’m kiddin’, lass. I would ne’er promise our bairns to anyone…”

“Our bairns.” Tears stung Bridget’s eyes. The thought of having children with this man delighted her. And at the same time, she knew, could feel the poison coursing through her blood. Mayhaps it would never happen, after all.

“Shh, m’love,” he whispered, stroking her hair. She rested her cheek on his chest, and then saw it—a thick, dark line along his bicep. Frowning she traced it with her finger. “What’s this? Griff? Were ye cut too? Wit’ the witch’s knife?”

“Aye.” He looked down at it. “Tis numb. I do’na think the poison got into me.”

“Och, you insufferable wulver!” Bridget grabbed for the seaweed. “It’s in yer blood, trust me! It may take longer, but it'll kill ye, just like it's gonna kill me!"

"It's not gonna kill ye." Griff grabbed her by the shoulders. Her wound ached when he did that, and he saw the pain on her face and let go a little. "We're goin' t'the isle—we'll find this mage. And he's goin t'cure ye. And then we'll get back in time for t'eclipse, like Alaric said we had to, before… whatever magical thing happens then. And I'll kill Uldred and that witch meself wit' m'bare hands."

"Before t'eclipse?" Bridget raised her eyebrows in surprise. Alaric had told Griff to come back before the eclipse? But why? "Did Alaric tell ye? That's when I'm supposed t'take m'vows as a priestess. Although now…"

She swallowed, looking down at her burning wound—there was something dark seeping through the bandage.

"We a'ready threw that plan out t'window." Griff smiled. "Yer mine, Bridget. I told ye I'd come back fer ya…"

"Instead, I came t'find ye…" She smiled. Then she looked at her wound, lamenting the way things had gone. "If we'd just gone straight t'the beach. If only that stupid knife hadn't…"

"Listen!" He shook her again. "We're gonna find a cure fer this. I do'na care, whate'er it is, whate'er works! Ye hear me, Bridgit? I will'na lose ye."

"Aye." A little smile played on her lips. "I hear ye. D'ye hear yerself?"

Griff stopped, then gave a little, sheepish smile. "T'isn't necessarily magic. Mayhaps it's some herbal cure. M'own mother knows herbs, and she—"

"B'lieve what ye want." Bridget pressed the seaweed against his upper arm. "But tis magic."

"No more than that is." Griff reached for a clean bandage, letting her tie it around his upper arm.

"It's all magic, ye silly wulver." Bridget slowly climbed into his lap.

She was still dizzy, feeling feverish, but she didn't care. She prayed that her mother had been right—that there was a mage named Raghnall on the Isle of the Dragon, and that he had some sort of antidote, or could at least concoct one, for the Witch's Kiss. She could do nothing but hope, as the poison made its way through her body, and trust, that what should be, would be.

In the meantime, she was going to make love to this man. While she was conscious, as long as she was breathing, she wanted him inside her and nowhere else. Griff kissed her back, his hands roaming over her hot, feverish flesh, and she felt how much he wanted her through his plaid and longed to feel him, skin to skin.

A knock on the door interrupted them again.

Griff groaned, shaking his head in denial.

"I'm starvin'!" she confessed, nibbling on his ear.

"Well, that mus' be a good sign." He slid her reluctantly off his lap.

"I'm goin' to eat e'erythin'," she told him, sliding the sheet ever so slowly up her thighs. She watched his gaze follow it. "Then Busby's gonna come back to bed and show Bryce the whole world."

Bridget parted her thighs and Griff gave a low growl, grabbing her knees and shoving his face between them. She had to bite her own lip to keep from screaming as he devoured her, front to back, up and down, like a starving man.

The knock came again, insistent.

"Ye better get that," she gasped as he lifted his face, covered with her juices, and wiped it with the back of his hand.

"A'righ', lass," he croaked. "I'll let ye eat somethin'—but then I'm gonna eat ye!"

Bridget pulled the covers up again, all the way up, as Griff went to get the door.

No matter what happened, they were going to make the most out of whatever time they had left.

Chapter Nine

Griff held a sleeping Bridget against him as he rode his borrowed horse the last half mile or so. She was weakening day by day, and he couldn't bear to watch it.

He'd never wanted to believe in magic more than when he stood at the door of the temple on the Isle of the Dragon, calling out, seeking entrance. He hoped there wasn't a guardian—someone he would have to fight—although considering the mood he was in, letting off a little steam chopping of someone's limbs wasn't exactly a bad idea.

He just didn't want to have to waste the time.

"Please! We seek entrance! She needs healin'!" Griff boomed, his voice carrying over the rolling, green hills of the island—and, he hoped, deep into the temple, where a healer waited.

The island itself was bigger than Skara Brae—it had only taken him twenty minutes to ride into the island, using Bridget's instructions to find the temple. At least this one wasn't hidden. He'd seen it a mile away, marked by an open-air stone circle out front that towered up toward the sky. The temple itself had tall, Greek-style columns and a giant door, but it was all in serious disrepair. The door was twice the size of Griff himself.

The door opened and an old man peered out through the smallest of cracks. Bridget had prepared him for this mage—a man, Aleesa had told her daughter, who was said to be a direct descendent of Merlin himself. He was the head of all of the temples of Asher and Ardis located around Scotland, England, Ireland and Wales, but as the wulvers had begun to be hunted and die out, the old man had become reclusive. Bridget said her mother and father had met him only once and that no one had seen him in over twenty years.

Griff was about to change that.

"You!" The heavy door creaked open a little further, revealing a face lined with age, a thick, bushy white beard, which was odd, considering the old man had almost no hair on his head at all. "Both of you! Oh this won't do at all. What are you doing here? You can't be here!"

The old man turned, mumbling to himself, leaving the door slightly ajar. Griff blinked, staring after him.

"Well come on then!" the old man called. "And mind you close and lock the door behind you!"

Griff was too surprised to do anything else. He pushed the door open and closed it behind him, stooping to turn the lock. In his arms, Bridget stirred. He leaned in, pressing his lips to her throat, taking her pulse and temperature at once. She was still warm. And her pulse was far too fast. She'd told him this would happen, the closer the poison got to her heart.

"Come, come, come!" The old man shuffled through the temple and Griff followed. They rounded a circle, marked by more Greek columns, and he saw an arena down below, lined with hundreds of seats. What happened down there? Griff wondered, as the old man took a turn and pushed his way through another door.

"She's been poisoned," Griff told the old man as they entered a room so filled with artifacts, scrolls, and books, Griff literally had to shuffle through them on the floor. "We need yer help."

"You can't be here." The old man sighed, pointing upward, and Griff looked, surprised to find a model of the solar system spinning above their heads. Griff had seen them in books his mother shared with him when he was a small boy, except in those books, all of the planets and the sun had moved around the little blue marble called Earth. In this model, the sun was its center.

"I need yer help, old man," Griff snapped, clearing off a table of books and scrolls and putting Bridget on it. "She's been poisoned and we need the antidote. I know ye have it!"

"You both need to be here, and soon!" The old man pointed at the model, shaking his nearly-bald head. "On Skara Brae. Not here, in my temple! You need to be there for the solar eclipse. You're entirely too far south—and west! The Dragon and the Lady will be there, not here. Oh, well, they will be here, too, because they are everywhere, but they won't be here, if you take my meaning. This won't do at all!"

Griff sighed in frustration. The old man was babbling in some strange accent—it was hard to place. Definitely not Scottish, but not exactly English either.

"Raghnall!" Griff called the old man's name—Bridget had shared it with him—and he startled, looking at him over a pair of rimless spectacles.

"Griff?" Bridget spoke his name, faint, from where he'd placed her on the wooden table. "Did ye say... are we here?"

She struggled to sit and he helped her. The old man frowned between the two of them, shaking his bald head.

“I’m a servant of t’sun an’ t’moon.” Bridget’s voice was low, almost too soft to be heard, as she spoke to Raghnall. “I await t’blade an’ chalice.”

“Yes, yes, I know who you are! Both of you.” Raghnall waved her formality away, lifting his nose and sniffing the air. He frowned, taking a step closer to Bridget, reaching out to lift the bandage on her arm. Griff didn’t like to look at it. It had gone black, ugly, thick threads of darkness reaching up toward her shoulder, across her collarbone, toward her heart. “The Witch’s Kiss! You’re going to die soon! Oh, that won’t do at all! Why didn’t you say something, son?”

“I tol’ ye before y’even answered t’door!” Griff roared, holding onto Bridget as she leaned against him, eyes closing once more. She was barely hanging on.

“Wise and skilled use of this Seatwist poultice,” the old man mused, studying the wound. “It’s saved your life, but it won’t keep the Witch’s Kiss from reaching your heart.”

“That’s why we’re ’ere.” Griff managed this through gritted teeth. He also managed to keep from putting the old man, head first, into his enormous shelves of books, but only because he hadn’t yet produced the antidote they needed. “She’s dyin’, and as ye say, *that can’na happen.* She told me t’bring ’er ’ere because ye’ve a cure fer this dark magic!”

“I do?” Raghnall looked at Griff, tilting his head in surprise. Then his face brightened. “Oh, yes, you know, I probably do! Come!”

Griff groaned in frustration as the old man pushed his way through yet another door. Griff picked Bridget up again, carrying her through the entryway, following the little man into another room, this one more laboratory than library. There were hundreds of bottles lining the shelves on the walls, all various colors and sizes. Griff looked for a place to set Bridget down, seeing a long table in the corner, but it was occupied. A red blanket covered what had to be a giant body underneath, at least twelve feet tall. As he watched, Griff thought he saw one end of the blanket flutter. The end near the head.

Griff found a chair instead, knocking several books to the floor, and sat in it, Bridget tucked into his lap, as the old man assembled things on a table in front of him. The little man hummed to himself as he worked while Griff watched, impatient. Bridget stirred again in his arms and he looked down at her. She opened her eyes, smiling up at him, dazed, but still there. Still his Bridget. She looked over at the table where Raghnall worked, watching.

"Could he move any slower?" Griff complained.

"Shhh." Bridget shook her head. "Let t'man work."

Raghnall made an owl sound and, out of seemingly nowhere, an owl swooped down from a higher shelf, landing beside Raghnall on the table. The old man leaned in to whisper something into the bird's ear, an action so ridiculous, Griff laughed out loud.

"You have to speak quietly to owls," the old man explained. "Their ears are very sensitive, you know."

Griff looked at Bridget and she shrugged, smiling. "Tis true."

"I'm goin' mad." Griff snorted, blinking as the old man made a rasping noise on the table and the biggest, blackest snake Griff had ever seen slithered out from underneath. His hand went for his sword, but Bridget stopped him.

"Don't ye dare!" she gasped. She had no strength left in her limbs, but her tone stopped him anyway.

The snake, its eyes almost as gold as Griff's, started making its way up one of the shelves behind the old man, while the owl, who had a bottle clutched in its talons, dropped it in front of him. Griff thought it would shatter and spill its contents everywhere, but Raghnall's reflexes were eerily fast, and he caught it in one hand without even looking up from the book he was consulting. Then the snake had returned, too, a box twisted in its coils that it deposited on the table for the old man.

"Could ye hurry't up?" Griff called as Bridget's head drooped again. He could see her bandaged arm, a thick, dark liquid beginning to seep from underneath. The smell of it was nauseating. Then he glanced at his own arm. His wound was still there—astounding, given his wulver healing abilities. It was a thick, dark line under his skin. He'd been poisoned too, but the effects were taking longer. He might have another week beyond Bridget. Not that it mattered. If she died, he would die too. He couldn't live without this woman, he knew that now.

The old man ignored Griff's protest and pleas to move faster. He mixed and hummed, hummed and mixed. The owl flew back up to its perch, tucking its head under a wing. The snake slithered back under the table, where Griff could see nothing but one yellow eye. Raghnall went to the fireplace to fetch a teapot.

"Do you have the blade that cut you?" Raghnall glanced up at Griff, looking at him over his glasses.

"Oh, aye." Griff reached into the pack over his shoulder, drawing out the curved, half-moon blade, now missing its hilt.

"Moraga." Raghnall shook his bald head, taking the blade from Griff's hands. "You're both lucky to be alive, son."

"Aye." Griff knew it was true. The witch had nearly killed them both. If he hadn't heard, a split second before the knife had ripped through the tent fabric, the witch's whispered incantation, it would have found its way through both of them, right into their hearts. They would have died together there on that beach. And, he'd thought, several times on this insane trip toward the Isle of the Dragon, that mayhaps that would have been preferable to watching Bridget fade slowly away from him. He couldn't bear to see her in pain—and knowing he had to do this, to save her, while his kin's fate on Skara Brae was completely unknown to him, was anathema. For a man whose patience was thin, it was pure torture.

The only comfort was, if this worked, if Raghnall could do what Bridget claimed, the largest of the lost packs was here on the Isle of the Dragon. Somewhere. He just had to find them.

"Come along!" Raghnall called, glancing over his shoulder at Griff as he went out the door once again. "Oh, and bring the teapot!"

"We do'na have time fer tea, ol' man," Griff growled, rising, with Bridget in his arms.

But he picked up the teapot and carried it anyway, following the old man down the hall, around the circle, into another room.

This place, he recognized. It was like the spring in his den at home. Or the scrying pool on Skara Brae. Except this room was far bigger, and definitely more architecturally complex.

"Come, come!" Raghnall waved him over. He took the teapot from Griff—it was quite hot—and put it aside on a rock. He had the knife on another, flat rock. The old man gathered water from the pool in his cupped hands, letting it fall over the blade.

Griff stared as the knife hissed, making a high-pitched noise, almost as if it were crying. Then it began to melt. It turned into a liquid metal, like quicksilver, that glistened and pooled in droplets on the rock's surface.

"Excellent." The old man nodded, producing a spoon from somewhere in his robe, scooping up some of the liquid and putting it into the teapot. Bandages appeared from somewhere in the old man's robes, too, and he poured some of the liquid from the teapot onto them. Then he poured the liquid into a clay chalice.

"Bring her here." Raghnall pointed to a large, flat rock, about waist-high.

Griff carried Bridget over to it, stretching her out on the rock. The hair he'd carefully hidden and tied back, tucking it under her cap before they left the ship so no one would know she was a woman, had come undone and spilled over the dark slab like fire. Her eyes remained closed, her face flushed with fever. He pulled her tunic down on one shoulder, revealing her wound, the fabric stained with darkness. Blood and pus and God only knew what else. Dark magic.

But I don't believe in magic.

He wasn't so sure anymore, as he watched the old man remove Bridget's dressing, tossing the pungent bandage aside. He applied the new bandage. It was thin, wet, hardly enough to soak up the awful liquid seeping from her arm, and Griff frowned at it, doubting as the old man plastered it over the wound. It stuck, as if magic, adhering to the gash.

"That'll do." Raghnall nodded, eyes narrowed, watching.

Griff watched, too, seeing the dark lines on her skin, the ones stretching like tree branches stretching toward her heart, starting to fade before his very eyes.

"It worked," Griff breathed, the relief flooding his chest so palpable it felt as if someone had just lifted the weight of his horse from it. "Oh thank God, tis workin'!"

"Of course it is." The old man rolled his eyes, shaking his head. Then, he turned to Griff and slapped one of the bandages on his upper arm, where the dark line appeared. That spot on his skin had gone oddly numb to the touch, and a few times, he'd felt strange, lightheaded, but other than that, he'd been uneffected. Not like Bridget.

"That should do for you, wulver." Raghnall winked. "The Witch's Kiss would have taken another month to kill you, I'd wager. Your species is quite strong."

Griff shrugged. He didn't care about his wound. All he cared about was that Bridget was opening her eyes. And this wasn't the sort of half-awake state of being she'd been in for the past day or so. Her gaze was clear, eyes bright, with that delightful, grey-green sparkle he had come to seek whenever they were in the same room.

"Now, drink." Raghnall lifted the chalice to Bridget's lips as she sat up on the rock. Griff gave her a hand—she was still acting slightly tipsy, but oh, so much better than before. Coming back, instead of fading away. He could tell already.

Bridget drank readily, gulping down the hot liquid. Griff, on the other hand, turned his nose up when she offered it to him.

"Yer not invincible, wulver," she snapped, and Griff had to grin at her tone. Oh yes, Bridget was back. "Now drink!"

Griff crinkled his nose in protest—the stuff smelled almost as bad as the bandage that had come off Bridget's arm—but he drank it anyway. It made him gag.

"Such a lil bairn." Bridget teased when he handed the now empty cup to Raghnall.

"That's awful." Griff shuddered.

"The bandage will dissolve over time." Raghnall made sure Bridget's was still affixed. It was like a second skin. "It will keep working until then against the poison."

"That's it?" Griff snorted, blinking as he looked between the two of them. "We sail all the way here for a new bandage and a tea party?"

Raghnall snickered. "Oh, I forgot to mention—you have to go outside and do a rain dance. Like the Mongols. Mayhaps you'd like to sacrifice a virgin? Or at least scare one, like the Norsemen?"

Bridget giggled, a sound that made Griff's heart soar. She poked Griff in the shoulder—his uninjured one.

"Don't mind 'im," she said, still laughing. "He does'na trust magic... yet."

"Doesn't trust magic?" Raghnall huffed. "That's like not believing you'll get wet if you piss into the bloody wind!"

Griff snorted and rolled his eyes but he didn't protest.

Mostly because Bridget was laughing, more bright-eyed and aware than she'd been in days. And the feeling had suddenly come back into his arm, where he could see that thick, dark line had begun to fade.

"Thank ye fer yer help," Griff said to the old man. He'd been ready to put him through a wall when they first arrived, but now he just wanted to kiss him. Or, at least hug him. "Can ye tell me... there's a lost wulver pack on this isle. D'ye know where tis?"

The man looked up from where he was gathering his things. Then he grinned, and Griff noted it was more toothless than not.

"Lost pack?" The old man chuckled. Then he laughed out loud. "Lost pack? Oh that's rich!"

Griff and Bridget exchanged confused glances. But Griff was getting used to being confused around the old man.

"Aye, a lost pack of wulvers," Griff explained slowly. "A den. They'd 'ave a den 'ere, somewhere on t'isle."

"There's no lost pack, son." Raghnall smiled, picking up his teapot. "They know exactly where they are, and if they want you to find them, they'll let you know. You being who you are, I'm sure they'll find you, soon enough."

Griff spread his fingers helplessly at Bridget. "This man talks in circles."

"The world moves in circles." The old man snorted, rotating his finger in the air near his temple. "Now, you two need to rest. That brew hasn't really hit you yet, and when it does, you'd both best be lying down."

"We need t'get back t'the ship." Griff frowned, but Bridget was up—she was up and walking, following the old man!—and so he went after them.

"In here." The old man nodded to a mattress. It looked big and soft compared to the one on the ship.

And suddenly, Griff was tired. Beyond. Exhausted.

"Come." Bridget pulled him toward the bed.

"You two will be fine in here." The old man gave a nod. "I'll rustle up some food for later."

"But..." Griff protested as Bridget pushed him onto the mattress. She was already pulling off his boots.

Raghnall licked his finger, holding it up, as if testing an invisible wind. "If we leave tomorrow, by noon, we'll get back in time."

"We? What?" Griff shook his head, confused, and the world tilted. Everything came unhinged. "What the hell?"

"Shhh." Bridget thanked Raghnall—he heard that much—before shutting the door and coming back to the bed.

The last thing he saw was her slipping out of her plaid and sliding into bed with him. Her body was warm—but not as warm as it had been—as she stretched out on top of him, pulling the covers over. He felt the urge to take her, felt his cock rising between her thighs, but something else was taking over his body. The blood in his veins felt thick with it, a hot pulse that made everything hazy, blurry. It was like being drunk—only far, far worse.

"Bridget," he whispered against her lips, so soft and plump. She was smiling.

"Shhhh," she urged, tucking her head under his chin, resting her cheek on his chest. "Sleep."

And he did.

When he woke, Bridget was gone. At first, he didn't know where he was, but then he saw a clean plaid and tunic beside him on the bureau. His sword was still there. He dressed quickly, sheathing his sword, and headed out to look for her.

He couldn't believe how good he felt. For days, since his altercation with Uldred on Skara Brae, he'd been worried sick about Bridget, and when he wasn't caring for and fretting over her, he'd been consumed with thoughts of his pack. He'd been so concerned with other things, he hadn't noticed his own declining health. He was a wulver, so he was from hearty stock. Even big wounds often wouldn't kill a wulver. His uncle, Darrow, had once been run through with a long sword and survived.

But the poison had clearly affected him more than he realized. The world looked brighter, clearer, as he stepped into the temple hallway and glanced around. The open-air stadium below was quiet. But he heard talking to his right. Bridget's laugh. The sound made him smile and he headed toward it.

"Yes, that's just right," Raghnall said, smiling over his cluttered table at Bridget. "You'd make a fine priestess."

"She'll make a fine wife," Griff growled, shuffling through the books and papers on the floor to put an arm around her from behind.

Bridget smiled back at him, and he couldn't believe the transformation in her. She was dressed like a queen, in a white and silver robe, with silver combs in her thick, red hair. It tumbled down her shoulders, washed and brushed, shining like fire in the light that came in from the high windows above. It made him want to take her straight back to bed. But he knew better. There was an incredible urgency in him, flowing through his blood, now that he was awake. More fully awake than he'd been in days, to be sure.

"Guardian, priestess, wife, mother, she is all of those things." Raghnall nodded. "Now that you're awake, warrior, it's time for us to break bread and be on our way."

"Our?" Griff frowned at the old mage. "You're coming with us?"

"Of course." The mage laughed. "Why do you think destiny sent you here, young prince who would be king?"

"Destiny again." Griff snorted, and when he did, he caught a whiff of roast meat. His stomach growled. "Destiny and prophecy and magic. You can counteract some witch's cursed blade but you can't tell me where the lost packs are on the isle?"

"They've already found you." Raghnall chuckled and Griff bristled in response.

"Where?" He glanced around, as if a pack of wulvers might be coming through the door.

"As Dragon King, you'll have to learn to read the energy of magic," the old man informed him. "You'll have to trust it. Like you read the weather. Or like learning to trust a woman."

"What do you know of women, old man?" Griff snorted.

"Enough to live alone," the old man retorted, and then cackled. Griff couldn't help grinning, even when Bridget elbowed him in the side.

"Everything around us, everything we can touch, taste, feel—it's all a woman." Raghnall dropped him a wink. "And it's all magic."

"It's flowin' around us all the time." Bridget turned in his arms. "Like the wind. Like love."

"But I do'na trust it..." Griff frowned.

"Ye trust me," she whispered, reaching up to cup his face in her hands, bringing him in to kiss her.

He nodded as they parted, confessing hoarsely, "Aye."

"You're learning, wulver..." Raghnall chuckled.

Bridget went to the chair, pulling out a new pair of soft, silver and white boots and putting them on. Clearly a gift from the mage. Then he watched her slip a silver dirk into them under her new robes.

"Do they all look like angels an' fight like devils?" Griff wondered aloud.

"No." Raghnall grinned. "Some look like devils and fight like angels."

Griff laughed at that.

"Now let's eat so we can start our journey," Raghnall said, getting up from the table.

"I do'na mind ye taggin' along," Griff said as they followed the old man out. "But... why're ye comin' wit' us?"

"Would you like me to talk more about destiny?" Raghnall asked, glancing over his shoulder.

"No." Griff snorted.

"Let's just say… I'll be stopping off on Skara Brae before I take a journey with some old friends."

Could the old man be any more cryptic? Griff wondered.

He caught Bridget around the waist before they followed Raghnall in toward the delicious smell of food. "You'll hafta change outta that before we reach t'ship… more's the pity."

"D'ye like it?" Bridget smiled, putting her arms around his neck. "I do'na think t'will be necessary."

Griff frowned. "But t'pirates think yer a lad—and I'd like to keep 'em thinkin' that, t'tell t'truth!"

"Trust the magic, son." Raghnall just grinned that toothless old grin when Griff scowled in his direction.

But he didn't think about it overlong, because the food smelled amazing—and he was starving.

The Sea Wolf was there waiting for them to return, but it was surrounded by more than a dozen massive warships. They were huge, Viking by the looks of them, with wolf heads on the prow.

"Slow up." Griff reined in the horse when they were a half-mile away, assessing the situation.

"Trust the magic," Raghnall said from the saddle of his mule. He was leading another behind him, loaded with a very full trunk. The old man chortled and winked, taking far too much pleasure in being cryptic, as far as Griff was concerned.

"I wish ye'd both stop sayin' that." Griff grimaced. "Ye want me t'just ride into a trap?"

"Tis not a trap." Bridget, still wearing her silver robe and riding sidesaddle in front of him, spoke up. "Those are wulver ships."

"There's no such thing as a—" Griff frowned as the wind shifted, and he lifted his nose in the air. Wulvers. She was right. He could smell them, even this far off.

"Wulvers are warriors, not sailors," Griff protested, but thoughts of the lost packs spurred him on.

He couldn't get to the shoreline fast enough—and the old man and his mules slowed them way down. By the time they reached the shoreline, Captain Blackburn was on the deck with a spyglass, awaiting their arrival. Clearly, he'd been in contact with the other ships. Whatever it meant, Griff didn't like it. He really didn't like it when a dozen men appeared from behind the rocks as they approached. Griff already had his sword drawn, but he knew, even though they weren't shifted, that they were all wulvers.

"No! Wait!" Griff called, but Raghnall had broken away, his mule moving faster than it had the whole trip as he rode forward to speak to the men. "Stupid ol' man."

Then the wulvers drew their swords. He had visions of the old man being slaughtered by a dozen wulvers as he leapt off his horse, leaving Bridget safely behind as he advanced, sword raised, ready to take them all on at once. He felt the heat in his own eyes, saw it reflected in the eyes of the men who looked at him as he approached.

"Easy, warrior." Raghnall gave him a toothless grin.

And then, one by one, each wulver sank to one knee, driving their swords into the sand, hands on the hilts as they bowed their heads before him.

Griff stared, looking first at the grinning Raghnall, then back at the kneeling wulvers.

"Do'na leave me again!" Bridget snapped as she rode up behind him, reining in the horse. Then she stopped, staring at the kneeling wulver men.

"What?" Raghnall chuckled. "You two have never seen wulvers offer their swords and fealty before?"

Griff looked at Bridget, feeling a lump growing in his throat, and then back at the men who knelt before him.

"You can't leave them down there all night, son," Raghnall whispered, nudging him.

Griff cleared his throat. "Rise."

He blinked as they all got to their feet. The biggest one, a wulver warrior with long, thick blonde hair—Griff knew he'd be a giant, white wolf when he shifted—stepped forward, holding out a gloved hand.

"Lars." The blonde said his name in a heavy, Scandanavian accent.

"Griff." He took the other wulver's hand and shook it, feeling the power in the man's grip.

"We are ready to sail and fight for you," Lars told him. "You are the red wulver. You are our king."

"Thank ye." Griff cleared his throat—it wasn't easy talking around the lump in it. "I'm proud t'have yer service. I'm grateful for all of ye who've come t'serve me."

He spoke this last to all of the wulvers gathered on the beach.

Bridget had slipped off the horse and came to stand beside Griff. He glanced down, seeing the part down the center of her red head as she looked out at all the wulvers who had come to serve him.

Then, one by one, they lined up to bow in front of Bridget, all of them reaching out to touch her hand or kiss it, murmuring the words, "My queen."

When Bridget looked up at him, her green eyes were round and sparkling with tears. She accepted each one of them with the grace of a queen. She was, already, as far as he was concerned. She had been, since the first time he'd met her. Even wearing armor.

"Griff," she whispered, turning her face up to him. "Is this one of t'lost packs?"

He nodded, sure of it, even though they hadn't said. One of the places Aleesa had given him was across the sea, and he was sure these wulvers were Vikings of some sort. He'd never seen them before, but they were all ready to lay down their lives for him.

And, he had a feeling, as they got ready to sail back to Skara Brae, he was going to need them.

"Trust the magic yet?" Bridget whispered, putting her arms around him.

"Aye, lass." He smiled into her hair, watching the men—*his men*—returning to their ships.

Did he have a choice anymore? He wondered. Had he ever?

They got into one of the wulver rowboats and headed toward the Sea Wolf where Captain Blackburn was waiting for them. The two wulver oarsmen helped them out of the boat and onto the ship.

"Next time yer sendin' a wulver welcome party, lemme know, eh?" Captain Blackburn called as Griff approached. The big sea captain was grinning from ear to ear.

"I did'na know," Griff confessed, shaking the captain's outstretched hand.

"If they'd been enemies, t'Sea Wolf woulda been at t'bottom of t'bay by now." Blackburn snorted, looking behind them at the big, wulver oarsmen as they boarded, but his gaze kept returning to Bridget.

"Aren't ye gonna ask who t'woman is?" Griff put an arm around Bridget, pulling her close.

"Ye think we've ne'er seen a woman disguised as a man for passage on a ship before?" The captain snorted. "She ne'er passed, e'en when ye carried her on wrapped in her plaid. That hair alone…"

"Aye." Griff looked down at her, smiling. "I could'na bear t'cut it."

"Would've been a terrible sacrifice," the captain agreed with a shake of his salt and pepper head. "Right *Bryce*—and *Busby*."

Griff laughed. "It's Griff."

The captain gave a knowing nod, looking at Bridget, while Griff made the introductions.

"Busby played by the beautiful Bridget. This old gentleman is Raghnall. And this…" Griff turned to the two Scandanavian wulvers with a questioning look.

"Thorvel," said one, and, "Skald," said the other.

"Yer takin' this rather well," Griff remarked to the captain.

"Well, we did 'ave a message of warnin' an' promise of payment." Blackburn laughed. Just then, Raghnall's owl flew down from the mast above, landing lightly on the old man's shoulder. "MacMoran almos' shot 'im fer dinner before we realized he was carryin' a message."

Griff caught the old man's eye—Raghnall's toothless grin gave him away.

"Will ye be boardin' yer ship, then?" Griff asked Thorvel and Skald, but the two wulvers insisted on staying with Griff, which meant more to him than he could possibly say.

The room he stayed in with Bridget as they sailed toward Skara Brae was far better than the one they'd occupied on the way to the Isle of the Dragon. Not that Griff and Bridget saw much of the room. Of course, they didn't see much more than the room, either.

Thorvel and Skald took turns standing guard outside, but the door only opened a few times to admit trays of food and drink to keep up their energy.

Which was just the way Griff intended it.

Because once he got Bridget out of that stunning silver and white robe, he knew he wasn't going to let her put it back on again—until he had to.

Chapter Ten

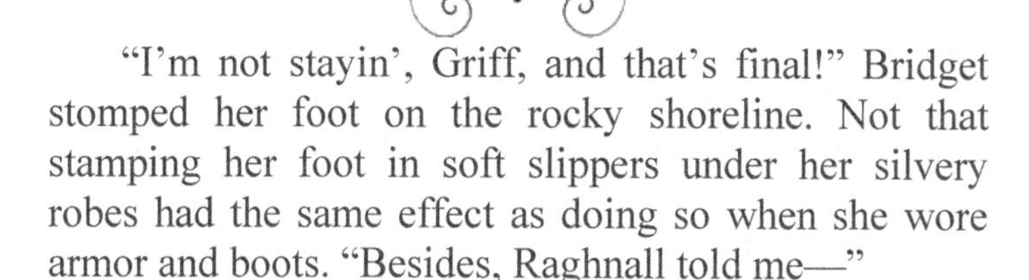

"I'm not stayin', Griff, and that's final!" Bridget stomped her foot on the rocky shoreline. Not that stamping her foot in soft slippers under her silvery robes had the same effect as doing so when she wore armor and boots. "Besides, Raghnall told me—"

"Bridget, this is war, not magic!" Griff roared. "You're stayin' here where ye'll be safe, and that's final!"

"Tis mos' certainly not final!" she snapped. "Tis m'kin, too, ye big oaf!"

"Bridget, I swear by all that is holy, if ye defy me..."

"Griff." Darrow rode up on his big war horse, reining it in when he saw Bridget. "T'men are ready, as y'ordered."

"Thank ye," Griff replied, surveying the encampment. Bridget could almost see his mind working.

They'd landed on the east side of the isle, hoping that Uldred was still camped on the west side, and their gamble had been correct. Bridget frowned up at Darrow. They'd been introduced, and she knew the man was Raife's brother. He'd been one of the few who hadn't been captured inside the temple.

The thought of that sick, twisted monster and his witch of a mother holding her family hostage made Bridget crazy with rage. She wanted to storm in there, sword drawn, but she knew that wasn't what needed to happen. Raghnall had been very clear on that point. They'd talked long, while Griff slept off the poison cure. The poor man had been through so much worrying about Bridget's wounds, he hadn't even realized how effected he'd been by the stuff. Until he passed out and slept for a good thirty hours!

"Griff, I wan' ye t'think this through," Darrow cautioned, leaning over the neck of his horse to talk to his nephew. "Remember what yer father taught ye—about doin' somethin' yerself that could get ye killed."

"Aye, I know." Griff waved this away, like he'd waved Bridget's protests away. "Like m'father send someone else into the temple, instead of goin' in 'imself?"

Darrow sighed, straightening in his saddle. "Alaric rode out t'meet 'im, I told ye. How were we t'know Uldred's men had entered the temple while Aleesa was alone."

Bridget cringed at this. The thought of Uldred's men storming into the temple while Aleesa was left, defenseless, made her stomach turn. When Raife and his men—and, it turned out, women, because Sibyl, Laina and Kirstin had insisted on coming with them—had been out meeting with Alaric, one of Uldred's men had feigned need of healing at the temple. Without Alaric there as guardian, Aleesa had unknowingly let him in. That was all the opening they needed. When Alaric returned with Raife and the rest of the wulver party, the temple had already been infiltrated.

Bridget couldn't believe the women had come too, but apparently, after Rory MacFalon had been captured—the same day Griff had left to go to Skara Brae, it turned out—Raife and Donal MacFalon had made plans to go find their sons. They'd assumed they'd run off together, some young pup's idea of sowing their wild oats perhaps, but the truth had been much darker than that.

Darrow said they'd pried it out of Moira and Beitrus, how they'd fed Griff information about the lost packs on Skara Brae, and they assumed he'd taken Rory with him. It was only after Raife and everyone had gone into the temple—and the scouts rode back to tell Darrow, who had stayed back on the beach with several of the men on Raife's orders, of the encampment on the other side of the island—that they knew Rory had been captured by Uldred's men.

Bridget still felt horribly guilty about leaving him behind. They'd intended to rescue him, but the witch's poison blade had put an end to that. Thankfully, Darrow and the few wulvers who had been left behind had raided Uldred's camp and rescued Rory MacFalon. He was, right then, recovering from his many wounds in a tent not too far from where they were talking.

"Do'na sacrifice yerself," Darrow said, trying one last time to convince his nephew not to follow through with this plan.

"I hafta." Griff shook his dark head. "It has t'be me. The prophecy..."

"T'hell wit' the prophecy!" Darrow roared, rolling his eyes. "This isn't magic, this is war!"

Bridget smirked, seeing the look of surprise on Griff's face. Hadn't he just yelled that at her, when she told him she had to accompany him to the temple?

"Bridget." Griff turned to her with a soft sigh. "Ye'll ride wit' me."

"Yer takin' a woman!" Darrow groaned.

But Bridget's heart soared. She knew, then, that he believed. At least to some degree. Enough to acknowledge that he needed her, not just because she knew where all the secret entrances to the temple were, but because she was part of this. They needed to go to the sacred pool together, during the eclipse, or everything would fall apart. Everything they'd done, everything they'd worked for, everything that had, so far, fallen in place, if not perfectly, then with some semblance of order and balance—all of that would disintegrate into nothing.

"I hafta." Griff sighed again, turning toward the tent. "Rory! Garaith! I need ye!"

And so their small little band was set. Rory, Garaith, Griff and Bridget would ride, alone, to the temple.

They would sneak in the back, secret entrance.

Griff, of course, thought they were going to simply surprise Uldred and his men, slay them, and free the wulver prisoners they'd taken.

Bridget knew better. The eclipse was coming, and with it, Griff's destiny. She caught Raghnall's eye across the beach, saw him watching, as always. He didn't always speak—and when he did, he often sounded mad, or addled—but he knew the truth, as well as she did. Things had fallen just the way they were supposed to. Everything, including her own near-death, had done nothing but propel them to this moment in time.

The thought made her tremble with both excitement and fear.

All is as it should be.

Mayhaps, if she kept repeating that to herself, it truly would be.

She hoped so.

Because she'd never been more terrified in her life.

She'd only known about the secret temple entrance for a few years. As a child, she thought it was magical when Alaric would appear during one of their rituals at the scrying pool. And it was, to some degree. The entrance was enchanted, made to appear as solid rock from one side, but a cavernous opening from the other. Alaric had shown it to her after the first time she'd bested him during training. It had been a wonderful reward, and Bridget enjoyed surprising Aleesa by showing up for rituals that way afterward. Until Aleesa got used to her using it, of course, and it became old hat.

Still, it always tended to be a shock, when someone appeared to walk through a solid rock wall.

"Yer sure they can'na hear us," Rory whispered. His words were slurred. His mouth was still healing. Uldred's men had made quite a sport of torturing the lad. Daily. Sometimes several times a day, since he had such enormous healing capacity. It was the cruelest thing she could imagine. If there'd been some score to settle that Uldred had been playing out with The MacFalon's only son, they were now more than even.

"Aye," Bridget replied, but she kept her voice down anyway. She'd tested it hundreds of times, yelling her mother's name—she could see Aleesa during these little sessions but Aleesa, of course, couldn't see her—and there'd never been any indication that she could see or hear anything until Bridget stepped across the threshold.

"Garaith, Rory." Griff unsheathed his sword. "Use the manacles I gave ye and chain Bridget over there."

"What?" Bridget gasped as Rory, looking quite guilty about it, and Garaith, who was nearly as tall and handsome as Griff, but not quite, took her, one at each elbow.

"I'm sorry." Griff sighed. "I needed ye to get us in 'ere, but Bridget... I can'na risk ye. Trust me."

"No!" she wailed, as Rory locked a manacle on one of her wrists, Garaith the other. It happened too fast, and she was too stunned to draw her sword and parry. "Griff, listen t'me! Ye do'na understand! Ye need me!"

"Aye." He sighed, surveying the gathering at the scrying pool. It was nearing noon. Nearing the eclipse.

Uldred and his witch-mother, Moraga, were talking by the edge of the pool. Across from them, all of the wulvers were chained, like an audience, to the stone monoliths. Seeing her mother and father chained was like a sharp stab to the heart. She didn't recognize any of the others, but she knew they were Griff's kin who had come to look for him.

"Griff!" Bridget cried, and he turned, coming over to her, shouldering Rory and Garaith out of the way. He pulled her to him one-armed—he held his sword in the other—and kissed her.

She knew he was kissing her goodbye. She knew, if he walked through that opening and left her behind, it would be a true goodbye. She'd never see him again. Things would fall apart, would succumb to the dark forces that had been working against them all along. And she couldn't let that happen.

"I need t'keep ye safe," Griff whispered against her ear as they parted. She was breathless with his desperate, aching kiss, heart racing in her chest. "Please, m'love, stay 'ere. I can'na bear t'lose ye."

"Look at me." She lifted her manacled hands, the chain that one of the other wulvers had locked to a ring in the wall, clinking loudly as she cupped his face in her palms. "Griff... I love ye."

She saw his face fall at her words, saw how they pierced his heart.

"An' I know ye love me."

"Aye," he agreed hoarsely. "I do love ye, lass. More than m'own life."

"Then trust me," she whispered, feeling tears stinging her eyes. She sensed Rory and Garaith watching this exchange. They hung back, waiting. "Trust t'magic. Can ye do that? Fer me? Please?"

"Bridget..." He croaked her name, shaking his head, the pain in his eyes breaking her heart. "Do'na ask this o'me..."

"I hafta." She kissed his lips, tasting the salt of her tears. "Ye mus' take me wit' ye. Ye mus'! If ye do'na, this ends 'ere. It all—e'erything—ends. Right 'ere."

Griff closed his eyes for a moment, sighing again. Then he took a long, slow, shuddering breath, and turned to go.

"Griff!" Bridget wailed, watching him walk toward the pool, toward the secret entrance. "Please! Trust me!"

He stopped, and she saw past him, into the cavern beyond. She saw Moraga pointing, whispering something to her son, whose eyes narrowed as he glanced toward the wall. It seemed as if he was looking straight at her and Bridget shrank back.

Griff looked over his shoulder, meeting her eyes. There was so much pain in them. And they were blood red.

"Unchain her," he whispered hoarsely, glancing at his friends.

"But... ye said—" Garaith frowned, looking at Rory.

"Unchain her!" Griff snapped.

Bridget fell to her knees, tears streaming down her face, holding her hands up to Rory as he came over with the key.

"Oh good, one of them's already chained up." Uldred's voice filled the cavern, but it was coming from the other side of the pool.

Bridget looked up, seeing the witch, her mouth moving, incanting, and she understood what had happened. She didn't know how, but the witch had discovered them, and had revealed their hiding place. She heard a woman scream, and saw a redhead across the way, one of the women chained to the rock. Griff's mother, she guessed. He'd told her they were both redheads. She called her son's name as his sword swung, clashing with Uldred's.

Rory and Garaith came out swinging, too, and Bridget reached for her own sword, realizing she didn't have one—Rory and Garaith had taken it—but she had her dirk. She slipped it out of her boot, ready to defend her family, when she heard Uldred yell at them all to, "Stop!"

Griff didn't. His sword came down again, steel clashing. There had never been weapons at the sacred pool before. Bridget saw her mother sobbing, Alaric doing his best to comfort her, both of them in chains.

"Stop, dog, or I'll kill them all!" Uldred snapped.

That stopped Griff. He faced the dark knight, both of them breathing hard, and saw that Uldred's men had blades at the throats of the women chained across the way. Bridget saw they were all collared and muzzled—

they'd been prepared, then, for the wulvers to shift, and had guarded against it.

"Chain them with the rest," Uldred ordered, giving Griff a sly smile as the men disengaged their swords.

"Trust," Bridget whispered to Griff as she passed by, glaring at Uldred.

Griff's eyes were already glowing red, Bridget saw, as one of Uldred's men dragged her around the pool to join the others. He howled as he saw her being chained to one of the high monoliths and Uldred laughed. The witch stood well out of the way of the wulvers, Bridget noted, but she was smiling, triumphant. She believed she and her son had already won.

Lifting her head to look up at the domed ceiling, Bridget wondered if mayhaps they had.

Trust.

That's what she'd told Griff, but that's what she had to do, as well.

Everything in her wanted to fight. But she had to watch, wait, and trust.

Above them the light was already changing. It was nearly full noon, but instead of a bright beam of light shining into the scrying pool, it was fading. The eclipse had already begun.

"Let them go!" Griff demanded. Uldred hadn't forced the big wulver to give up his sword and Bridget wondered at that.

"You're not in much of a position to make demands." Uldred smiled across the pool, and he looked right at Bridget. She felt his gaze on her, almost as if his eyes raking her body was actually the touch of his hands, and it made her shudder with disgust. "I think I'm going to enjoy your little redheaded whore later myself. I'll let my men have the other women. I prefer my cunts wetter than those old prunes."

Griff growled, giving a shake of his head, and shifted. Bridget gasped, watching him leap forward as a wulver-warrior, sword swinging, but Uldred turned just in time to stop the blow with his own sword.

"You want a fight, is that it?" Uldred pushed hard at the big wulver, although he didn't move Griff far. More of Uldred's men—there were at least a dozen in the temple, all human, Bridget counted—moved in, swords drawn. "A duel? If you win, you get your woman and family as a reward? Is that what you want, dog?"

Griff just snarled, his eyes so red they glowed, even in the fading light. He had four men behind him, holding him back, and Bridget cried out when she felt one of Uldred's men move in beside her, holding a knife to her throat. Griff heard, his gaze skipping across the pool to her.

"But what if I win?" Uldred actually smiled. "If I win… let's say, I get to use your blood. And all those wulvers out there…"

The dark knight waved his hand toward the wall, beyond which were hundreds of wulvers from the lost packs.

"Then they will follow me. Oh wait, once I look into the pool during the eclipse, I'll turn into the red wulver, and they'll follow me anyway, won't they?" Uldred gave a gleeful, mad laugh, and Bridget saw that the man was, in part, mad. He had to be. Given what Griff had told her about Uldred and Moraga's plans—had the witch made her own son mad with power? Like his father before him, he was obsessed with the wulvers, but he didn't want to kill them. No—*Uldred wanted to become one of them.* And his mother had convinced him it was possible. Had convinced him that they shared a bloodline.

Of course, that part was true. Raghnall had told her as much, while Griff was still sleeping off the poison, but she hadn't wanted to reveal that to him. She knew he wouldn't take it very well—and it didn't seem to serve much of a purpose. The fact was, Uldred was not and would never be a wulver, no matter whose blood ran through his veins. While Eldred, his father before him, had been sure he was part of Arthur's line, that the Tudors had stolen the throne and wrongly changed the bloodline of England's kings forever, Uldred seemed far more interested in gaining the wulvers' abilities and powers and using them to his advantage.

Eldred had wanted to use the wulvers and destroy them.

Uldred wanted to become a wulver—and enslave them.

"Let's fight, brother, as men!" Uldred laughed, swinging his sword around, and Griff managed to lift his to block the blow, even though four of Uldred's men held him back, and Uldred knocked his sword from his hands. Griff growled and went for it, but the men held him back. "And when I spill your blood into this pool, I will become the most powerful wulver—the most powerful king and leader—this world has ever known!"

Griff shifted back as Uldred reached down to grab Griff's sword, tossing it back to him, and when he did, Bridget saw it happen. She wasn't sure, not at first, but she saw a flash of silver in the dimming light coming in from the dome above. A blade? Griff gave a little howl and Uldred stepped back with a shrug, as if to ask, 'What did I do?'

But then the men were fighting, and there was no time to think.

Or even breathe.

Bridget covered her mouth with her hands, feeling an arm go around her. It was her mother, standing beside her, comforting her. Bridget let her arms slide around her mother's neck as she watched the two men fighting. Griff's eyes flashed red as their swords swung, chipping away at the stone walls when they missed, clashing angrily when they didn't.

Griff's eyes glowed a deep red but he stayed in human form, not shifting to his stronger, wulver one. Bridget saw Uldred's smile, the way he danced back and forth, avoiding Griff's heavy blows. And she saw his eyes glow red, too. A trick of the light, mayhaps? She was sure of it. A reflection of Griff's eyes in his own.

Griff was growing tired. She expected him to shift to wulver form, to take the man out in one mighty blow, but he didn't. He stumbled once, nearly falling into Uldred, and the other man pushed him back. Bridget clung to her mother, watching Griff losing the fight, sinking to her knees in horror as Griff reeled and swung, almost blindly.

They swung their way around the pool, drawing closer to the chained pack of wulvers—and humans—adorning the rock, Bridget among them. She sobbed into her mother's robes as Griff howled, the sound echoing through the whole chamber, shaking it to its foundation, while Uldred just laughed and danced away.

Bridget knew it was close. It was almost time. Moraga knew it too. The witch was on the other side of the pool, staring up at the hole in the ceiling and chanting something. Griff was fighting Uldred off now—bleeding from several wounds, deep gashes that would take a little time to heal. Uldred backed him up, swinging again and again, then took a step forward, swords sliding together, down to their hilts as they stood, face to face. Bridget was so close to them, she could have reached out and touched the wound bleeding on Griff's calf.

Then Uldred pushed Griff away, and the big man fell.

He fell to his knees, right in front of Bridget, and she reached out for him, unable to bear seeing him in so much pain. It made no sense, no sense at all. He was ten times the man, twenty times the warrior, of this man, and yet, Griff was flagging, failing.

"Trust…" Griff lifted his head to look into her eyes and Bridget saw how dilated his were.

"Ye monster!" she gasped, staring at Uldred. "Ye poisoned 'im!"

Just the flash of a blade, a small cut on his calf. Uldred had poisoned him, making sure he'd win this fight. Griff struggled to stand, but whatever it was Uldred had knicked him with was strong.

"Just a little help from *Natura Mater*, eh, Mother?" Uldred laughed, glancing across the pool at the witch.

"He's right." Bridget looked at Griff. "Mother Nature decides. That's 'er magic. We need t'trust 'er."

"Uldred!" Moraga snapped. "Stop playin' around! Tis time!"

Uldred practically skipped past them as the eclipse began to reach its peak. It wouldn't be long. Griff growled, turning to rise, to go after Uldred, but Bridget slipped her hand into his.

Trust.

"Trust," she whispered to him, squeezing. Holding him back, holding him to her.

"No!" Griff croaked, still on his knees.

Uldred was on his too, but he was on hands and knees, peering over the edge into the pool, as if waiting for something. Uldred's men murmured, uneasy. The light in the pool was strange, unlike anything Bridget had ever seen before.

"Noooo!" Griff cried again as the dragon's head began to rise.

Bridget cried out, grabbing his shoulders as Griff started forward. His body shook, wracked with the poison. Aleesa went to her knees, too, grabbing his arm, keeping him from confronting Uldred.

Uldred's men began to pray under their breath, some of them crossing themselves as the dragon's head filled the space above the pool. And turned its red eyes to Uldred.

"Look at his eyes!" one of Uldred's men cried. "Look!"

Uldred's eyes were blood red as he stared, transfixed, at the dragon. Across the pool, Moraga laughed, a high, delighted cackle. Bridget heard sobs, and glanced at the wulvers and women still chained to the rock. A dark-haired woman sobbed into the shoulder of a man. The redheaded woman Bridget assumed was Griff's mother, Sibyl, was looking, not at Uldred and the dragon, but at Griff and Bridget on their knees by the pool. She had tears in her eyes.

"It's happening!" Uldred called. "Oh, Mother, it's happening! I can feel it! I'm turning into the red wulver!"

Griff howled, the sound reverberating against the stone walls, and Bridget shivered at the sound, holding his hand so tight it hurt her own. She couldn't keep her eyes off Uldred, the way his eyes glowed red. Was it really true, then? The prophecy… could it be that either of these men could be the red wulver, able to bring together the lost packs, and heal the rift between man and wulver forever?

But it couldn't be—Raghnall had been so sure. Uldred couldn't be the one. His magic was dark, his purpose less than honorable. But if he was a descendent of Arthur—or Asher—then mayhaps it was possible for him to usurp that role. To become the once and future king of… everything.

"Look!" Sibyl gasped, pointing at Uldred. "He's on fire!"

Bridget stared as the red of the man's eyes spread. They were on fire, glowing, hot, and Uldred laughed, holding his arms out to the dragon as if in welcome. Didn't he feel it? It wasn't just his eyes—his whole body was outlined in flame!

Moraga screamed. "Uldred! Uldred! Noooo!"

"Mother!" The man screamed as he went to his knees, his body beginning to burn.

They all stared in horror as the witch threw herself at her son, sobbing, calling his name over and over—but that didn't last long.

Once the fire had begun, it burned hot and fast, consuming everything around it. Even one of Uldred's men, who tried to pull the two apart, was burned up in the flame. It was over in moments. The screaming stopped, and then the fire did, too. There was simply nothing left of either Uldred or Moraga.

But the dragon was still there, head raised.

And then, slowly, it turned to look at them.

"Unchain them," Bridget croaked to Uldred's man standing closest to her. She pulled her dirk from her boot and pointed it at him. "Do it now, and ye might live through this."

The man, white as a sheet and still staring as the dragon turned its red eyes in their direction, did as she bid him.

"Quickly." Aleesa bent to assist her daughter, once she was free. Bridget helped Griff toward the pool. He moved slowly, groggy. Whatever poison Uldred had used was very bad for wulvers, and Bridget worried that even the sacred pool wouldn't be able to heal him.

"Bridget," he murmured, on his knees, wavering.

"I'm 'ere." She slipped her hand into his, feeling tears sliding down her cheeks, realizing that this might be the last time they were ever together.

"I love ye," he whispered, and she felt him lean against her for support. He was fading fast. "Yer... m'one... true... mate..."

Bridget sobbed, clinging to him, feeling hands on her, holding her up, too, otherwise she would have collapsed as well. They were all around them, wulvers and humans, hands on their shoulders, under their elbows, holding them both, supporting them, and Bridget looked up, gasping at what faced her in the pool.

It wasn't just the dragon.

There was the most beautiful woman she'd ever seen, full figured and smiling, her eyes shining silver, staring straight at Bridget. She heard a collective gasp, heard one of Uldred's men moan, "Her eyes! Her eyes, too!" but she knew. She felt her own eyes flash silver in response, a cool, calm feeling of peace coming over her as the lady approached.

The woman carried a sword, blade high as she walked across the pool.

Beside her, the dragon, eyes glowing red, like blood though, not fire, opened its mouth.

For a moment, Bridget thought they were all going to burn.

But then the dragon's tongue uncoiled, and at the end of it was a chalice. It dipped first into the sacred pool, and then it was placed in Griff's hands. The big wulver was shaking so badly he could barely grasp it, but his mother and aunts were there, helping him drink.

Bridget looked up just in time to accept the sword. The lady held it aloft, hilt resting on one palm, blade the other. An offering. Bridget looked up into her face, into those strange, silver eyes, and saw her own. For one, brief moment, as she reached out to accept the sword, they merged.

Bridget gave a cry, her whole body shaking, the sword clattering to the stone where she knelt, and then, they were gone. The dragon and the lady disappeared. The peak of the eclipse had passed. The marriage of Asher and Ardis was over.

She lifted her eyes to the sun, to the strange light overhead. It was the middle of the day, but it felt as if the moon were shining down, and it filled her with an overwhelming urge. Bridget threw back her head and howled.

It was only then that she realized, she was a wolf. She had no hands to hold a sword. Only big, russet colored paws. Stunned, she turned to look at Griff, and saw he, too, had shifted. Not into a wulver warrior, but into full wolf form. Their eyes met—flashing red and silver for just a moment—before they rubbed noses together, and then Bridget tucked her head under his, a sign of surrender.

She was his, and always would be.

They were one, true mates, just as Ardis and Asher had been. In this form, she knew it in a way she'd never known it before. If she had been a wolf the moment they met, she wouldn't have ever questioned it. She was his. She belonged to this man.

Griff shook his head, giving a long, sustained howl, and she watched him change. Thick, red fur became long, dark hair. His eyes went from red to gold again. He stood there, naked, surrounded by his kin, holding a hand out to her. He saw her, he recognized her. He loved her. They gave him his plaid, and he wrapped it around himself, looking at her expectantly, smiling.

Bridget did what came naturally. She gave her big, russet colored wolf's head a shake, and transformed. Her mother was there, putting a robe around her shoulders, and she threw her shaking arms around Griff's neck, unable to fully comprehend what was happening. Had she really just changed into a wolf—and back again? What did it mean?

"M'love," Griff whispered against her ear, holding her close. He was so solid, so strong. Nothing about him wavered now. The sacred pool had healed him. And it had, somehow, changed her. "M'one true mate."

"Aye," she breathed, clinging to him. "Took ye long enough to b'lieve it, wulver."

He chuckled. "Look who's talkin'—*wulver.*"

That's when she heard it.

Whispered, murmured words, all around them.

She looked at Griff, disbelieving at first, and then, Griff took her hand, turning toward his subjects, turning her with him, to face them all. Even Uldred's own men. Mayhaps, sometimes seeing was believing, Bridget thought with her own sense of amazement.

"Righ."

"Banrighinn."

King.

Queen.

Bridget stared as, one by one, wulver and human took a knee and bowed their heads to the once and future king and queen.

Epilogue

Bridget had always thought of Skara Brae as home, but it wouldn't be for much longer.

Still, this room, the place where she'd first made love with her one true mate, would always hold great meaning for her. She crouched by the fireplace, warming her hands around the cup of milk she held. It had done a great deal lately to settle her stomach at night, especially nights like these, when she dreamed of the lady and couldn't sleep.

"Bridget." Griff called out, his hand searching her side of the bed for her and she smiled.

"I'm 'ere," she called softly.

"Come t'bed, lass."

She finished the last of her milk, leaving the cup on the table, before climbing in beside him.

"Up dreamin' of weddin' plans?" He chuckled, sliding his arm around her waist and pulling her near. She gave a happy sigh, snugging back against his warmth.

"Oh, I do'na need t'plan a thin'." She smiled. "Yer mother and m'mother are takin' care of't. All I need t'do is put on t'dress."

"And then I get t'take it off ye." His hand moved slowly over her hip, under the covers.

"Mmm, aye," she agreed, feeling him growing hard against her bottom. "Will it be a long trip back to Scotland?"

"Not overlong." His hand stroked her hip, a soothing motion. "Are y'afeared t'leave this place?"

"A lil," she admitted softly.

"If it's any consolation, t'mountain den'll be new t'me, too, lass." His lips brushed her temple. "But we've got s'many wulvers now that the lost packs have joined us, we need the room. And the witch who kept us from it is…"

"Aye." Her eyes narrowed as she looked into the fire. "Gone."

Besides, even if the witch hadn't burned up with Uldred in the fire, they now knew how to enchant the entrance to any den, the same way they did the temples, and they would simply disappear. No human would ever know they were there. Only wulver eyes would be able to see them, and only when they wanted to be seen.

They were quiet for a moment and then Bridget laughed. "Wolf packs. Raghnall loves his word play."

"Aye, t'old codger." Griff grunted, not sounding anywhere near as amused as she was.

Griff had talked overlong about the lost wolf packs, had set out to find them, had asked the old mage about them, when all along, it was wolf *pax*. It wasn't even wolf pact, if you traced the line far back enough. Raghnall had gleefully told them that there had been many translations of the prophecy over the years since the Latin translation that brought together the rest during the Roman reign of Constantine.

Raghnall had relayed that even the "wolf pact" they lived under was once known as the Wolf Pax, which translated to the Wolf Peace. Translation and time turned it from a time of peace to a treaty to prevent war. A subtle difference, mayhaps, but a big one.

The lost packs Griff had been looking for was really "the wolf pax." The peace the wulvers would live under, once the prophecy was fulfilled.

"D'ye wanna be more involved in plannin' t'wedding, then?" Griff asked. "Is that what keeps y'up a'nigh'?"

"Nay." Bridget snorted. "I'm more interested in trainin' than wearin' a dress. Besides, it brings all t'women together and gives 'em somethin' else t'do besides cook."

"Aleesa and Kirstin seem t'be gettin' along well," Griff said softly, treading carefully.

She knew it might seem like a sore spot, her adopted mother reuniting with her blood-born daughter, but Bridget didn't begrudge them any of the time they spent, the things they now shared together. She was happy for them both. And that Kirstin's son, Rory, was back to his old wulver self, all healed—at least, physically. And Aleesa was getting to know her grandson, and her son-in-law, The MacFalon, as well as her daughter.

"Aye, I'm glad," she said, truthfully. "Aleesa's been so busy teachin' Sibyl how t'be temple priestess, she's spreadin' herself thin. But I think she loves havin' everyone around, after being alone s'long."

"I'm still reelin' over that." Griff sighed.

Bridget put a hand over his on her hip. "I know y'are… but doesn't it seem fittin', somehow, that Raife and Sibyl will stay here in the temple as the new guardian and priestess?"

"I s'pose." Griff sounded doubtful.

"They were both called t'do it," she reminded him. Griff had come a long way when it came to believing in things like magic and prophecies and one true mates—but the idea of being "called" into service in the temple was still a stretch for him. "And we can come visit. We will, all t'time."

"Aye," he agreed. "And I'm ready t'lead the pack. I think it's one of the real reasons they decided t'stay here. So there'd be no conflict..."

"They love ye," she reminded him. "And they know tis time."

"When does Raghnall get back?" he wondered aloud, changing the subject.

"Before t'weddin', I hope." She smiled to herself. "He'll be the closest thing to a grandfather t'bairn'll have. At least on m'side."

She smiled, remembering that day when Raghnall had sat her down, while Griff slept off the poison, and told her how he'd found her, abandoned, at the door of the temple on the Isle of the Dragon. It had been the one time Aleesa and Alaric had met Raghnall—when he brought her to them to raise. He said he knew she was part of the prophecy, somehow. That she was fated to be trained as the temple guardian and priestess on Skara Brae.

Bridget still didn't know who her parents were—but Aleesa and Alaric were wulver, like she was now. They loved her, had raised her—and she didn't mind anymore that she didn't know her parentage. Besides, when she'd asked Raghnall about them before he left on his journey to meet up with the Dragon and the Lady, he'd smiled and said, cryptically, "There is always more to the story, m'dear."

So mayhaps, someday, she would know.

"The... what?" Griff sat up on his elbow, staring down at her. "What did y'say?"

"Hm?" Bridget turned her head to look at him, feeling warm and sleepy from her milk.

"Did ye say... bairn?"

Bridget stopped breathing. "Did I?"

"Are ye wit' chil', lass?" Griff's eyes glowed red in the firelight. She loved when they did that.

"Aye," she breathed, biting her lip. "I was goin' t'wait after t'wedding to announce it but…"

"When were ye gonna tell me?" he growled, turning her toward him and putting a hand over her lower belly. It was slightly swollen, but she'd made the excuse that she was getting fat on all the cooking the wulver women did, and Griff hadn't questioned her.

"Now." She grinned, watching him pull the covers back and dip his head so he could kiss her navel.

"Asher," he murmured, flicking his tongue over her skin. "Or Ardis, if tis a girl."

"We could call him Arthur," she suggested with a smile. "If tis a *human* boy."

"But yer wulver now," he reminded her. "T'will surely be a wulver."

"I do'na know." She shrugged. "Everythin' has changed—but ye got me pregnant before I was wulver, y'ken?"

He chuckled. "Well, I s'pose it makes life interestin'. Donal and Kirstin are human parents who have a wulver child. We could be wulver parents who raise a human one."

"But Kirstin can change again," she reminded him. "All t'wulver women can change as they wish now."

That had been the part of the prophecy no one had understood, or translated, or seen coming. The cure for the wulver woman's curse had always lain with the dragon and the lady, with Asher and Ardis and their marriage. Somehow, Bridgit's transformation from human to wulver had completed a circle that had changed every wulver woman's curse of having to change, without warning, during her moon time, or during birth.

No wulver woman was a slave to her cycles anymore.

Darrow's wife, Laina, whose cycles had long since stopped, but whose daughters' were just beginning them, had wept like a child in his arms when they'd discovered this fact.

"Thank God fer that," Griff agreed, resting his cheek on her belly and looking up at her, his eyes a soft, glowing red in the firelight. "I'm really goin' t'be a father?"

"Aye." Her fingers tangled in his long, dark hair. "Are ye happy 'bout it?"

"Ye make me t'happiest wulver alive, lass." His hand moved up to cup her breast. "I ne'er would've b'lieved I could be s'happy in this or a thousand lifetimes."

"So are ye ready to tell me ye b'lieve in magic?" she teased. "In destiny? In prophecies? In one true mates…?"

"Do'na rub it in." He laughed, rolling his eyes. "Ye know I b'lieve… in *us*."

"Aye." She opened her arms and he went to her. It seemed that everything had worked the way it was supposed to after all. The prophecy was large, and they had played their parts, but according to the wulver—and human—women who read the text, it was still unfolding. Mayhaps it always would be, as Raghnall said, because everything was a circle that came around again.

But for now, all was as it should be.

At least, Bridget thought with a smile as Griff kissed his way over the swollen mound of her belly where little Ardis or Asher slept, dreamless…

Until the story continued…

The End

GET FIVE FREE READS

Selena loves hearing from readers!
website: selenakitt.com
facebook: facebook.com/selenakittfanpage
twitter: twitter.com/selenakitt @selenakitt
blog: http://selenakitt.com/blog

Get ALL FIVE of Selena Kitt's FREE READS
by joining her mailing list!

MONTHLY contest winners!
BIG prizes awarded at the end of the year!

ABOUT SELENA KITT

Selena Kitt is a NEW YORK TIMES bestselling and award-winning author of erotica and erotic romance fiction. She is one of the highest selling erotic writers in the business with over a million books sold!

Her writing embodies everything from the spicy to the scandalous, but watch out-this kitty also has sharp claws and her stories often include intriguing edges and twists that take readers to new, thought-provoking depths.

When she's not pawing away at her keyboard, Selena runs an innovative publishing company (excessica.com) and book store (www.excitica.com).

Her books EcoErotica (2009), The Real Mother Goose (2010) and Heidi and the Kaiser (2011) were all Epic Award Finalists. Her only gay male romance, Second Chance, won the Epic Award in Erotica in 2011. Her story, Connections, was one of the runners-up for the 2006 Rauxa Prize, given annually to an erotic short story of "exceptional literary quality."

She can be reached on her website at
www.selenakitt.com

YOU'VE REACHED

"THE END!"

CPSIA information can be obtained
at www.ICGtesting.com
Printed in the USA
LVHW110100040422
715222LV00004B/175